AFTERGLOW

By Larry Felder

For Meg and Zoey, whose father loves them very much.

"The world is the best of all possible worlds, and everything in it is a necessary evil."

— attributed to Francis H. Bradley, (1846-1924), British Philosopher.

"The world has achieved brilliance without conscience. Ours is a world of nuclear giants and ethical infants."

— General Omar N. Bradley, (1893-1981)

"A clever person solves a problem. A wise person avoids it."

— Albert Einstein, (1879-1955)

"Genuine tragedies in the world are not conflicts between right and wrong. They are conflicts between two rights."

— Georg Wilhelm Friedrich Hegel, (1770-1831), German Philosopher

Monday, April 4

Prologue

John Raden sat outside the Oval Office just before eight a.m. with a cup and saucer in his hand, a quiet smile coming to his face. There's nothing quite like getting invited to brief a president who you know had gone out of his way to avoid you, and while waiting to be ushered in, being served coffee that would wilt a spoon. It wasn't much of a stretch to imagine that Elliot Hanford was unaware. The president left very little to chance.

A morning not quite awake had accompanied Raden to Washington. The nation's capital was still shaking off the fog-shrouded weekend, making the biting brew he was nursing a fitting compliment to the start of the day. And, the fifty-two-year-old analyst thought, to the meeting as well. This was Raden's ninth visit to brief a president, but he knew before it even began that it would be different from the others. For the first time entering this little corner of history, he wasn't welcome. His host didn't want him there, wasn't interested in what he would have to say and would do everything he could to trip him up once he left. Not that he expected Hanford to come out swinging, or even to show a hint of his intentions. It wasn't his style. The jousting would be subtle. Hanford would launch a charm offensive, extending every available consideration. And with so much on the line, probe for the slightest hint of weakness. To most others, it would make for a precarious situation, at best. To Raden, it made the assignment that would follow all the more intriguing.

Raden had arrived early. Most in his situation would have spent the few extra minutes looking over notes, or sweating out an imminent audience with a Chief Executive who was set upon getting them to fail. Instead, it gave him time to take in his surroundings. He patiently studied the art, the craftsmanship of the furniture. The aura of the White House, because it did have one. The history that surrounded him was the real enjoyment of this visit. The past was a passion, and its accouterments were oftentimes as fascinating as the people themselves. His knack for noticing details that others missed was what got him there in the first place, but it always amused him that what most considered an asset was to him nothing more than genuine curiosity, a discerning eye, and a little common sense. It was like his knack for not being surprised by much. He wasn't intimidated by this president. He had a hunch that none of that was lost on the person on the other side of the door.

Events had been moving swiftly. The president had been eager to spin a new narrative for the program begun on his watch. It wasn't public knowledge yet, but the most controversial federal undertaking in a generation was in danger of imploding, which threatened his re-election seven months from now. Right from the start, Raden's National Security Agency and the Administration had been at odds on the issue. There hadn't been anything from the White House in the way of an olive branch or new policy initiative, and Raden wasn't expecting one. But new data had surfaced just that weekend, and if confirmed, would cast the project in a whole new light. If Hanford was calling in one of the NSA's top analysts, even reluctantly, he had some new angle to work. It would be left to Raden to unravel, without letting himself be run over in the process.

The door opened at precisely eight a.m.

"All right Dr. Raden, the president will see you," Dillon Ridge barked with a scowl.

The bluster from the White House chief of staff wasn't unexpected. Ridge's arrogance was well-known. It usually got the desired effect; the retired colonel was among the most feared players in Washington. Raden eyed him for a moment. Then brushing it off to himself, he followed Ridge inside.

Thick gray light pressed through the three stately windows of the Oval Office. From behind his desk Elliot Hanford looked up. With a grin, he rose and extended his hand.

"Well, finally," he said. "Dr. Raden, it's a pleasure. I've been looking forward to this."

"It's nice to meet you, Mr. President."

"I see you've got your coffee. I usually have at least two, especially mornings like this." He went over to a very presidential-looking sideboard and poured himself a cup, no doubt from a different pot than the one from which Raden had been served, then sat on a couch while Ridge stood stiffly to the side.

Raden lightly swirled his coffee, and glanced at the presidential seal on the cup and saucer of the service-ware. It was a much more satisfying experience than the pungent beverage it contained. He wondered of the tales they could tell. They would no doubt be more than what the current and crafty occupant of the White House would allow.

"Have a seat," Hanford gestured. "It's Jack, isn't it?"

"Among other things."

Hanford laughed. "Are you okay with your coffee? Help yourself if you want another."

Raden thanked him, but he was enough of a morning person that even had it been worth suffering, the one cup would do just fine.

"I'm sure you know your reputation precedes you," Hanford said.

Raden thanked him again, recognizing that it was all part of being handled. His first impression of the current Chief Executive though had already set. It was based on a recollection from history, political boss Mark Hanna's observation of the 29th president a century ago; like Warren Harding, this guy *looked* like a president. An impeccable fifty-nine. A shade over six feet. Sandy brown hair peppered with gray. And that smile. He cut an imposing figure.

The president eyed Raden. "I understand you've been to the Oval Office before." Hanford liked asking questions to which he already knew answers.

"A few times."

"Okay," began the president, "so let's get started. About the scientist. I know you've been briefed on our plans, but events have been moving fast and opinions are all over the place. The colonel here thinks we should whack him in the head with a two-by-four. Most of my advisors agree. But I'm the lucky guy who has to decide. I know you have a sense of history. I don't have to tell you that the dirty little secret here is that this isn't a representative democracy. It's a benevolent dictatorship." As Raden laughed, Hanford added, "Lincoln once said something like that. You're one of the best soft sells in the business. This calls for finesse, a delicate touch."

"Dr. Raden," echoed Ridge, "whatever we do, there's a lot more at stake now. We could be looking at a different world a year from now, not to mention November."

"He's right," Hanford said, smiling. "There's something you figure out about insulting a person's intelligence. It's not whether you do it, but learning who you do it to that counts. I know not to question yours by saying I'm not thinking of the political implications of all this."

"Thank you," Raden replied dryly. Deceiving with the truth. Hanford's good cop to Ridge's bad was smooth, he thought, subtle enough to be almost imperceptible.

"I'll tone down the bull," added the president. "We just have to make it work. You know he hasn't had much to say, but we know what he thinks. That's why we never asked; we didn't want to deal with him turning it down. And up to now it really didn't matter. We've kept him hanging while we decided what to do, but I frankly haven't lost any sleep over it. The damn thing wouldn't even exist if it wasn't for him. But I'm sure you heard about the information we got this morning. It puts the issue in a whole new light. One way or another, whether he likes it or not, he's getting involved. So, what do you know about him?"

"Enough to know that he's still not going to go for it."

"Well," Ridge snapped, "that's not an issue anymore, is it?"

Hanford ignored him. "That's how we see it. Hasn't been interested from the start and won't be now, no matter what the new data says. People like that don't change their minds."

"I would agree with that as well," Raden said, nodding.

"That's where you come in." Hanford said. "So, what are you thinking?"

"That you're going to have your hands full. And I'm wondering what you want me to do about it."

"They said you were direct. So, what do you know about him?"

Raden's eyes widened. For an initial query it was modest. "He's brilliant," he said. "You'd have to say genius. A real one, not a fly-by-nighter who makes headlines a few weeks and is never heard from again. I've read his books, and several of his papers. Any one would be considered a life's work. When you look at the whole picture, it's staggering. And, he's thirty-eight. He's young."

"Some of my people would say green."

"I think it depends which side of the glass you're looking through, Mr. President."

"From my perspective it's more which side of the tent he's pissing out of." As Raden laughed, the president added, "And what else?" This was the money question, the kind that made Raden a repeat visitor to this most-influential piece of real estate on earth.

Raden studied his coffee cup again. "Okay," he said, "it's like this. If anyone told you when you took office you'd be dealing with this—well, you know what you would have said. No one saw it coming, least of all him, so I'm pretty sure he's shell-shocked." He looked up. "I wouldn't write him off. But I wouldn't be so quick to write him in either. He's more resilient than people think, and he's going to do what he wants. He may be MIA for now, but he's no pushover. Also know he's been poised for this. I don't mean for what you want or what was done with his work. I mean his success, the work itself."

"How much do you know about that?"

"There were three modest papers the year before you took office, and the two big ones a year later. Your science advisors could explain it better, but bottom line, they began to answer things that have kept physicists awake for years. Dark matter, dark energy. Spacetime. But the big one is quantum gravity."

"What's that?" Hanford sounded almost interested.

"It's the name they give to a workable theory of gravity. It unites gravity with the other forces. Now he didn't nail it, but he got closer than anyone before. It's revolutionary stuff."

"You did a good job describing it, Doctor."

"It's an interest, irrespective of this assignment. Unfortunately for him, it led to what's going on in the Pacific. So I can't blame him for not wanting to have anything to do with it. I'd probably feel the same way." Raden bored in on Hanford. Unlike those surrounding the president, he had no problem bearing bad news, even though they had never met. "You shouldn't be surprised he's avoiding it, especially after the Pentagon tried tinkering with it."

"That shouldn't bother him," Ridge said. "There's no way we could have known that."

"Oh, yes there is," Raden answered. Ridge frowned and looked away.

Raden eyed the chief of staff. His bald head glistened; the little hair he had, all gray, was so short as to be invisible. Severe glasses rimmed in the blackest of black. He could smell the birds that once decked that collar. Ridge was as tight as a kettle drum, but while Raden knew Ridge's place in the Washington food chain, he wondered if people would find the man so threatening if they took the time to see beyond the bravado.

"Then why hasn't he said anything?" Hanford barked. "What's he, a prima donna?"

"Have either of you ever dealt with scientists?" Raden smiled. "Particularly, physicists?"

The tiny scattered creases about Hanford's face merged into the smile that had become a media fixture four years ago. "Okay, Jack. Point taken."

"Read up on what Leslie Groves dealt with when he finagled the Manhattan Project."

Hanford nodded. He knew of the general and the seemingly impossible task he faced in 1941 of gathering the finest scientific minds of the time, bringing them to a built-from-scratch desert site in New Mexico and placating them enough to build the world's first atomic bomb. This current endeavor with the bomb had proved no different. He asked, "*You* ever deal with scientists?"

"Deal with them? It's more like I've had dealings with them. They're an interesting lot."

"I'll say. My God, climate change, bio-terrorism, NASA, you name it."

"What you mean, Mr. President, is you think they're a pain in the ass." As Hanford cracked up, Raden added, "I just think most physicists don't want to work on anything related to the bomb. During World War II, they knew the Nazis were working on uranium and it was still pulling teeth to get some of them on board. But you guys took it to a level they never dreamed of. You made it a spectator sport. I wouldn't expect any of them to want to be involved. And since it's based on his work, particularly him."

"Well," objected Ridge, "he'd be surprised how many of his peers are working with us."

"Perhaps. But I think his biggest problem is how popular the thing's become. It may be controversial, but it hasn't kept the crowds away. If you look at the history of science, it's a story of unintended consequences. You start with one thing and it leads to effects you never would have dreamed of. And nothing is more unintended than this. I'm sure it doesn't sit right."

"I don't really care," Hanford snapped. "He didn't see it coming? His crowd cooked it up, not me. No president *ever* had to deal with anything this nuts. So I don't care it doesn't sit right. Hit, shit; whether it grows bigger or folds, enough people want it to do one or the other that it's made my job hell, forget it's an election year. And with the new figures, it's moot; there's no way we can end it. We have to build on it. So I'll be damned I let the guy who started it all sit on his hands. I don't care he doesn't like that the Pentagon's involved. The project director wants him in. It's one of his fellow scientists, so he can't ignore it." He groaned. "Another prima donna, giving everyone a hard time who tries to get near the thing. Wants him to solve some technical thing. Only him."

"Just what is it exactly?"

"Don't ask me to explain it; I couldn't if I tried. Can't be much or she wouldn't mind sharing the credit. Point is, even though the Pentagon couldn't make it work, there are things he can help them with. They're on board, the director's on board—it'll all work out. Her husband heads up security on it. One of those incestuous power couples Washington loves. So it's time he stepped up. You sign him up, he solves their little whatever, we can move ahead. If not...."

"You're concerned it'll be a mess all around."

"Damn right. I will not allow any disruption of our plans. Frankly, I'm tired of science coming up with one newfangled this-or-that and then sitting back when the rest of us have to deal with fallout from their latest breakthrough. There's an opportunity to do something remarkable here. How often you think a chance like this comes around, once every thousand years? If you're lucky. But if we blow it, it'll be a disaster. Bottom line, he's getting involved. Period."

Raden focused on Hanford. "Okay, Mr. President. What is it you would like me to do?"

"Go up to Princeton. Work your magic. You talk his language. Make him go for it." Hanford buzzed his secretary, adding, "He was expecting this call later, but I want him on edge."

Raden's initial impression of the president was firming. The man was a consummate politician. It wasn't what Hanford was telling him, it was what he was holding back.

"I envy you," the president said, sniffing the air. "No meetings, no office, no asses to kiss. That's the big one. Hell of a job. I know you don't need it. Why do it?"

"I enjoy it." Raden noticed that while Ridge could have taken the comment personally, he didn't flinch.

"That's the best reason," Hanford said. "You remember I said I was impressed with your work? I'm even more impressed you get it done without attracting attention. I should be so lucky. I cut myself shaving and it's breaking news on cable. We were trying to figure out what to call you. "Roving Fixer-Upper of All Things Esoteric" is what we came up with." As Raden chuckled, the president added, "That's the kind of job I want when I retire."

The phone beeped. "I won't tell you what to say," Hanford said. "Just close the deal. And absolutely crucial, it has to be wrapped up by the weekend. We're announcing on Sunday. There's no way we'll be able to keep a lid on it past then. Just do what you do. What I will tell you is this, by the time you're done, I want him not only to have changed his mind but thinking it was his idea all along."

As the call went through to Kevin Herter, John Raden casually glanced at the clock on the president's desk. With all the talk of things going nuclear, he found himself staring, sure the meaning in the moment would not register with Elliot Hanford and Dillon Ridge. But it did with him. The clock read eight fifteen. It was the moment the first atomic bomb exploded over Hiroshima.

Six Hours Earlier

One

No one ever tells you how to wake up if you haven't yet fallen asleep.

Interstate 295 in western New Jersey stretched to a dark horizon as Kevin Herter neared the bend at 2:20 a.m. The exit off Route 1 had never been a favorite. An innocuous ramp slinking into a series of banks and curves that persisted further still, it never failed to wear out its welcome. You could never tell where the exit ended and the entrance to the interstate began.

A tired guardrail bordered the last curve before the highway. The night air hung damp as Kevin navigated the turn. Despite the car's heater blasting his hands felt clammy, and distracted, he fumbled his Bluetooth for the call he was itching to make. Then he looked up.

Hurtling toward him was the guardrail.

"Whoa!" he yelled, just missing the rusted hulk. "Damn!" he burst out as the car entered the highway, his heart pounding in a rush of what-ifs.

It had been twenty minutes since he had grabbed a sweatshirt off the floor and headed out into the night. With the dreaded phone call looming that morning at nine, he had mindlessly jumped into his car, fleeing the media, the buzz and another sleepless night. Left behind, the town of Princeton slept on.

He reached the posted speed limit of sixty-five, then edged a few miles over, just enough to avoid detection. The heat vent sent up a rush of warm air to balance the open windows.

He passed a Denny's and a Best Western Motel. He passed aromatic pine groves that recalled wreaths and a remaindered holiday season. In turn, he was passed by an eighteen-wheeler and the air churned with the aroma of diesel. And he passed a lone white car parked on the median grass, a triangular decal on its door, lights off, motionless.

With one eye on the speed trap in the rear-view mirror and the other on the darkness ahead, Kevin opened up his black Acura TSX. Mist hugged the ground. The car cut through it with a muffled roar, churning up pillows of dampness that buffeted its satiny contours. As the lights beyond the roadway thinned, he reached for his phone.

Three time zones away in Woodacre, a small town an hour north of San Francisco, Max and Jean Rosenkranz sat in their den. Their windows were open to the spice of bay trees lining the property. The news was ending when the phone rang. Even without Caller ID, they knew who it was.

"Sweetheart," Jean said to Kevin, "how are you holding up?"

"The usual. Did I wake you?" To the two night owls, the question was a formality.

"You know you didn't. I hear wind. Where are you?"

"Right now, on 295 heading south. Couldn't sleep."

"Well, you know what I would say. We love you and we'll see you soon."

A moment later, her husband got on. "I know I don't have to ask how you're doing."

"No, you don't. And guess what. I'm on an earpiece."

"So you joined the twenty-first century. I'm proud of you."

"Ah, it's a pain in the ass. Keeps me from getting pulled over though. And, I'd be doing better if I could stop by instead of having to call three thousand miles. When are you coming home?"

"Don't be a nudge. We'll be back in a few weeks."

The Yiddish banter from Max, a seventy-six-year-old Massachusetts Jew, had long endeared itself to the Midwestern WASP, tonight especially. "Who's being a pest?" said Kevin. "People go away for the winter to Florida. They don't buy a place in northern California to put up with cold rain and earthquakes. I still don't know why you moved out there."

"We didn't want you bothering us."

Kevin smiled. Max, a retired Nobel laureate physicist and his wife Jean, an acclaimed potter, were his two most favorite people in the world, the closest thing he had to parents. A winter's store of sadness welled up and his attention drifted. The eighty-mile-an-hour night coursed cooler through the car. He turned up the heat, not noticing the headlights to his rear.

"You should have called sooner," Max said after a few moments.

"I thought I could sleep. Two weeks now I'm dealing with this crap."

Max knew Kevin's dilemma, and his routine. "So," he asked, "what was it tonight?"

"*Forbidden Planet*," Kevin groaned.

"Ah, great movie."

"Not tonight." Kevin thought back to his bedroom. A bachelor's brew of laundry, forgotten cups of coffee and lust, it had begun to drone on like a frat-party hangover before finals. "Max," he sighed, "it's out of hand. I can't sleep, I got reporters driving me up a wall, and *they're* calling in the morning. I had to get out. Then I'm getting on 295 and almost hit a guardrail. That's where I am with this damn thing." He cupped his hand against the dense night. It coursed through his fingers like a stream of cool silk. He still hadn't noticed the car, closing the gap with him.

"You know you're going to have to tell them to shove it," Max said sympathetically.

"I don't want to deal with them."

"Well son, you're going to have to. You just can't let it get to you."

"Easier said than done. I've had it. They don't need me."

"Oh yes they do, more than you know. They need you on their let-terhead. I don't care how popular the damn thing is, it's always going to be controversial. But trust me, you don't want your name on that piece of drek."

"I know, I know." Kevin tinkered with the side mirror and noticed the car behind him. He eased up on the gas. "It's just that up 'til now I ignored it, and people got pissed. But if I get involved-guess what? People will still get pissed. Either way, I get hung out to dry. And it's government; they control the money. It all comes with a cost. How do you say no to that?"

"Simple. You just say *no*. Listen. You did some of the most incredible work in the field in a century. And what did they do with it? Let a bunch of idiots get off watching H-bombs. Only they would think up something like that. You don't need this. Washington doesn't like it, the hell with them. And believe me, money has a way of finding its way in." Max coughed lightly. "What does Sharon think?"

"She says the same thing you do." He was going to say something about his girlfriend of the past two years, and then stopped. "She's just fed up with the whole thing."

Ahead through the mist, he saw a dark patch in the road. He swerved, slicing through a scent trail of a dead skunk. As the pungent brew swirled about, he glanced again in the mirror. The car was still in the fast lane. He thought it would pass when it came up directly behind him.

"Max, I'm going to—oh hell." A blaring swirl of red filled Kevin's car.

"Max, I got a cop behind me. I'll call you back."

He groaned, hung up, and pulled over to a flood of adrenaline.

A tall man approached wearing a blue, black-strapped uniform. "State police," he announced. "License, insurance and registration." Kevin handed them over.

"So where are you headed?" the trooper asked, looking them over.

"Actually, nowhere. I couldn't sleep. I needed to unwind."

The trooper shined his flashlight at the license, then at Kevin, who winced. "You're that scientist," he declared. "I read about you. You're with that bomb thing in the Pacific."

"Don't get me started," Kevin said, glaring into the night.

"Yeah, I heard you weren't a big fan." The trooper stifled a laugh. Kevin repeated the comment. The trooper studied him. "I pulled you over because you swerved back there."

Kevin wavered. "Oh, yeah. I saw something in the road. I think someone hit a skunk."

The trooper studied Kevin's license again. "I caught a whiff of it myself." After a pause, he said, "Okay, I wanted to make sure you were all right. We're just trying to keep people alive." He handed Kevin back the documents. "Are you heading home now?"

"Oh yeah. Enough excitement for the night. Thanks, officer."

"The next exit has a U-turn. Watch yourself with the fog." He walked back to his car.

Kevin felt a wave of relief wash over him. He started his car and pulled out, followed by the trooper. As he took the U-turn and the trooper drove on, he remembered Max. He called back.

"What's going on?" Max asked.

"I swerved around a dead skunk, and for that they pull me over. Go figure."

"Spot check, I guess. Like you need that tonight."

Kevin smiled, but strained to hear the voice on the phone. "Max, you sound tired."

"We're about to hit the sack. Enough of that. What are you going to do tomorrow?"

"I guess I'll hear them out. After that, I'll find some way to get out of it."

"You want to be nice, more power to you. I wouldn't give them the satisfaction. At my age, I'll be damned if I have to suffer fools anymore, let alone gladly. But let me know how it goes."

"I'll give you a call when I—oh shit, I don't believe this." Kevin's car filled with flashing red and blue lights. "Max, I've got another cop behind me."

"Unbelievable. Go take care of it. I'll talk to you tomorrow." Max hung up.

For the second time, Kevin pulled over, this time with an edge. Behind him sat a marked state police cruiser. He had missed it, which annoyed him as much as the stop.

"Don't you guys have anything better to do tonight?" Kevin asked the trooper as he walked up.

"Excuse me?"

Kevin waved off his own remark and handed over his paperwork. As the trooper walked back to his cruiser Kevin watched another car pass, and caught the driver's eye. He thought back to times he'd done the same thing. It always reminded him of those nature programs on the Serengeti plains of Africa. Every time a wildebeest or zebra was pulled down by lions, the other animals would stand gazing at the carnage. You could almost hear the "Phew!"

When the trooper returned, he shined his flashlight at Kevin, asking, "Are you all right?"

"Yeah. It's just that I haven't been pulled over in over a year and tonight it's been twice within twenty minutes. I figured you guys were having fun with me."

The trooper eyed him hard. "Where was this?"

"Huh? You're kidding, right? The other side of 295."

"You say this was twenty minutes ago. Was it a state police car?"

"Yeah. I was on the phone talking to a friend in California. I figured it was a spot check."

The trooper eyed him. "May I see your phone?" Kevin handed it over. The last outgoing call listed under Dialed was posted eighteen minutes earlier. The trooper asked, "Where's 415?"

"That's Marin County, just north of San Francisco."

"Excuse me, sir. I'll be right back." After a few minutes, he returned. "Mr. Herter, there's no record of another traffic stop for you tonight. The last record we have was fourteen months ago. Can you describe the car and the individual to me?"

"Are you kidding me?" Kevin looked at him incredulously.

"No sir, I'm not. We don't do spot checks. I stopped you because the light on your license plate is out." The trooper shined his flashlight around Kevin's car. "I'd like to think there's an explanation for this. Did he identify himself as a state police officer?"

"Yeah. Same uniform and everything. The car wasn't marked though."

A second state trooper pulled up. The first walked back and began talking with him. Both then came over. "Excuse me sir," said the first. "Would you please step out of the car?"

As Kevin nervously got out, the just-arrived trooper said, "You're *thee* Kevin Herter?" Kevin shrugged. "He's that scientist with the bomb place," the trooper added. "Small world. My wife and I are going. I've been bugging her since it opened. I always wanted to see one."

"Tell her I said you're better off going to Disney World," Kevin said with a frown.

The trooper laughed, but with a puzzled look. Both officers stood unruffled by the traffic whizzing by. Kevin leaned into his door, arms folded like in a straightjacket, crimping his bottom lip. They walked away again and the first made a call. When it was over, both men walked back. "Okay," said the first, "we're going to have to look into this. Are you going home?"

"That's what the other whoever-the-hell-he-was asked."

"Did he happen to mention your light?"

"No."

The two troopers eyed each other. The first trooper then said, "Mr. Herter, you are heading home now, right?"

"Oh yeah," said a more nervous Kevin. "Now I'm going home."

"Okay then, an investigator will contact you. If you remember anything, give us a call. You should get that bulb replaced, but other than that you can go. Have a good night, sir."

"Thanks officer." The troopers walked off. Kevin got in his car, and glanced at the dashboard clock. It read 3:27. He then pulled away, slowly and deliberately.

Two minutes later, Max called. "We're about to pack it in. You okay?"

"Yeah, fine." As Kevin described what had happened, he could hear the phone crackling with Max's anxiety.

"Oh, brother," Max said. "Any other night you could brush it off, but tonight … listen, just get home, quick and careful. And remember what I said. Tell them to stick their offer with the next one of those damn things they set off."

"Yeah, yeah," Kevin sighed. "I should tell you," he added, knowing the reaction he'd get, "I still haven't forgiven you for moving out there. But don't worry, I'll get over it."

"Enough of that. Go home and get some rest. I'll talk to you tomorrow." Max hung up.

The drive home was a world away from any Kevin had taken since moving to Princeton. Though he could see stars the air was laden with moisture. It wasn't the mist though that begged a second look; every turned corner, every tree, every parked car, every passing truck, every drawn shade on every window somehow looked altered. It all looked the same. And it didn't.

By the time he entered the town, it was just past four a.m. As he turned onto Nassau Street, Kevin didn't remember getting there. Everything was a blur. The deserted street was shrouded in fog. Where the mist grazed the street lights, a radioactive green shone off the new growth of the trees. A lone patrol car crept through the Witherspoon Avenue intersection, moving like a cat stalking prey. As it passed, Kevin eyed it without turning his head, his raw angst boiling as he wondered whether the cop was watching him.

He pulled onto Park Place, locked his car, and ran into his house, bolting the front and side doors, checking them three times each. Like a cardiac monitor in ICU, a beep warned of a low battery on his phone as he left it on his kitchen table. It would wait.

He turned to his room, threw his sweatshirt back on the floor and embraced the mattress with a thud. The dark droned on. After a time he looked over to the space beside him. Sharon could sleep through anything. The TV, his occasional snoring, she could ignore it all. He stared in the blackness. He almost wished she was there, sleeping through this.

A diffused gray light had begun filtering through the blinds. He made for the window, stepping around the clutter he knew by heart. He parted a few of the slats. They crinkled their tinny melody while depositing a thin veneer of dust on the floor.

The mist had slipped past the dawn, recast as a dense gray mass. Down the street an arm appeared with regularity out of an SUV, emptying its supply of newspapers front porch by front porch. Another set of headlights went on, and as the car passed Kevin pulled back, his heart picking up.

After a while, he fell back onto the mattress, arms draped across his head. And for the first time since he got off the phone with Max he spoke, asking the darkness, "How the hell are you supposed to wake up if you haven't yet fallen asleep?"

Any reply Kevin Herter might have hoped for was cut off by the piercing scream of his alarm clock, still set to go off at six a.m.

Two

A raw echo pervaded the dark bedroom. The remains of the alarm clock lay still on the floor, a contortion of gears, polystyrene and vinyl-coated wires.

It was like one of those accidents where you trade awareness for control. As if trapped in a time warp, Kevin watched the clock's trail of blood-red digits arc across space and recollect itself in slow motion, the clock's shrieking barely beginning to Doppler down before it smashed itself into bits on the far wall, just missing a window. The final indignation from the malevolent device registered an instant after it left his hand, leaving him wanting to step in front of himself to grab the thing before it punched a hole in the wall.

Furious that the alarm had slipped his mind, Kevin felt no better after hurling the clock than before. It had roused him, but not how he'd wanted. He soon made for the shower.

A few minutes later, Kevin soaked under a rickety nozzle, trying to wake up. The old oil heat had yet to come on and the air was nippy but the shower would warm it up. He set it as hot as he could stand. It stung needle-like, yet felt strangely pleasing.

He was shaving when the phone rang. It was too early for the expected call, although not too early for some of the others he had been getting. Noting the Caller ID, he picked it up.

"I didn't think I'd wake you up," she began.

"You didn't."

Less than a mile away, Sharon Velazquez said, "I want you to get your stuff today."

"That's what you call for before seven in the morning?"

"Hey," she replied, righteously invested in the pause, "*you're* the one who's going to have all this free time after you talk to your friends. I need to clean out the clutter in my life."

"Sharon, cut the crap. They're not my friends and you know it, so don't start again."

"I'm not starting anything."

"You know damn well what you're doing and I don't need it, not after the night I had."

"You gonna get your things or you want me to leave them on the curb?"

"Fine! Do it!" He slammed the phone down. The answering machine blinked full, and he hit play. As a voice began, he hit the delete button, erasing the message without listening. Then with the zeal of a just-fired worker expunging company files he purged every last one, not listening to any. Mollified for the moment, he grabbed a stale pizza crust he had left on the kitchen counter a day ago and went to the living room window.

The Princeton spring day bore a familiar gray, ever more anesthetized with each new ray of light. The phone rang but he ignored it. He fell back in bed, zoning out to more of *Forbidden Planet*.

It had all seemed so *easy* back then. Later on, now, that's what struck him the most.

It was like going on the vacation of a lifetime, and hitting every green light on the way to the airport. After years of hard work it was coming together, like it was supposed to happen that way all along.

Then amid the warm breeze and sun a bit of turbulence made you notice that the plane was off-course, and before realizing it, you've landed and can't imagine how you got to a place so abhorrent that you can't stay one minute longer, before learning the flight you just watched take off was the last one out. It wasn't a case of *you don't know what you've got 'til it's gone*. He knew what he had. He knew how special it was. He just didn't know it would all prove to be so fleeting.

On the morning of January 1, 2000, people across the world awoke to newspaper headlines that welcomed them to the future. In Palo Alto, California, Kevin Herter was settling into graduate studies at Stanford. The previous night's revelry had come with a sense of promise, of possibilities. It wasn't naivety. Everyone knew the world's problems wouldn't be solved by the change of a date. And leading to that stroke of midnight, most would have granted that for every part cautious optimism there would have been another in the guise of fingers crossed or knuckles rapping on wood. But the dawn of the Third Millennium was cause for elation. And for a young physics student entering a field eager to embrace him, Man and Moment met in a spirit of expectation.

By the second decade of the new century it had been largely forgotten. The future was not the one imagined just a few short years earlier.

It was one of mutual mistrust. After 9/11, a decade of war, the Great Recession, and a series of natural disasters, Man and Moment were jaded. For Kevin, recent years were nothing if not surreal.

Even now, it was hard to imagine.

Three years at the Institute for Advanced Study, where Albert Einstein spent the last years of his life. Walking the halls Einstein walked; an office a few doors from his. Living just blocks from Einstein's house. Strolling sidewalks he'd once called home. And the work. Five groundbreaking papers; two best-selling books. Sharing thoughts with the most brilliant minds in the world, many now his friends. And on the horizon, a hint at that rarest of things in science, a paradigm shift, a new way of envisioning reality and all that went with it. Symposiums. Grants. Lectures. But most important, the freedom to follow his curiosity to wherever it would lead.

And where had it led? What did it get? A spiraling descent from world-renowned physicist before age forty to the guy who invented the World's Biggest Bang. Where people once watched enthralled as science revealed the mysteries of the universe, they now high-fived thermonuclear bombs going off. It wasn't supposed to be this way. And the only thing crazier than the idea was that they went ahead and did it. Max was right. That's all they'd remember. And all because of him.

He still wasn't sure how it happened. Caught in the complacency of hoping to be left alone, by the time he noticed what was going on, it was too late. While most saw in his work a sublime glimpse into the mind of the Creator, others saw something else; a little anti-matter here, a few isotopes there, one or two of his transcendent equations at just the right space and time and *voila*, clean thermonuclear detonations. No radioactive fallout when you set off a hydrogen bomb.

It worked. No radioactivity. No pollution; no half-lives. No trifles like strontium 90 or chromosome damage. No leukemia. No hair falling out. No radiation burns. Just a stupendous explosion.

And look what they did with it. Turned it into the world's greatest spectator sport, playing to customers who were booking years in advance for the spectacle of the ages.

Look at what you got for your money. A week in the South Pacific, palm trees, pinã coladas, a chance to get away from it all; and to round out your time in the sun a ringside seat at the grandest fireworks display in history. It was sublime cut from a different cloth. Hotels were full, deposits were being rushed and the swankiest cruise ships were making regular stops.

With all that, something had changed. The people who didn't need his help to get it up and running had now decided they couldn't keep it running without his help. People he fretted hearing from and agonized over calling. The ones he'd be damned answering to but couldn't bring himself to question. The ones he resisted saying yes to and hesitated turning down, for a project blamed on him that he'd had nothing to do with, wanted nothing to do with, and that he'd blamed on himself. It was a hit. It was vilified. It was revered. It was despised. It was every bit of drama swirled about the issue of the bomb, every ambiguity and contradiction rolled into one. Something was terribly wrong with the whole idea. And neither he nor anyone else could say just what it was or why.

Three

The Princeton Tea Room on Nassau Street was one of the town's more popular coffee establishments. With chessboards, couches, Internet access and incredible desserts, it sported an eclectic look, a business set that meshed seamlessly with an art and college crowd. The buzz was that owner Sharon Velazquez had an *in* with one of New York's finest pastry chefs. Few knew she did the baking herself, which suited her just fine.

None of that mattered to Kevin, nor that for two years he had been sleeping with the owner. He just liked the coffee. For three years the Tea Room had been a twenty-first century halfway house on the way to work, and after the previous night Kevin clutched his routines ever tighter.

Eyes darting about, he slipped into the sullen Monday at eight a.m. The five minute walk for his usual breakfast blend gave him enough time to get back for the call. A third of Princeton's residents walked to work, and they had long since become familiar. This morning, he ignored them all, and wrapped in his thoughts, he also missed the MSNBC van passing ahead.

Kevin held the door for a slight girl with mousy hair and an ample backpack. Several people noticed the handsome six-footer in the jeans and college chic brown corduroy coat. He had settled into a Princeton notoriety; people would recognize him and mostly go on their way. Steam from coffee glowed off a dozen laptop screens. Sharon was not yet in; most mornings she wouldn't arrive before ten thirty. Three of the regular staff, Derek, Laura and Stephanie, worked the counter. As they efficiently handled the line of patrons, Kevin fidgeted behind the girl.

"You're Kevin Herter, aren't you?"

Kevin turned to a frumpy guy in his thirties, clutching a raincoat.

"I've always been interested in physics and astronomy," he said. Kevin nodded.

"I don't know how you can say gravity can leak into other dimensions and at the same time say there's particles that are supposed to carry it," the guy began. "I would think particles in this universe would have to stay here instead of zipping out from one universe to another."

"It's not that simple," Kevin responded as a woman left with a tray.

"I mean, if you say gravity moves around like that, it would seem to me it would all leak out. Why only some? Why not all of it?" They both shifted to let a man clutching a coffee go by.

"So what do you do for a living?" Kevin said, tightening his arms.

"I'm an office manager for a computer distributor."

Kevin nodded, watching a man pay for a bagel and the girl with the backpack approach the counter.

"I took an astronomy course in college," the manager droned. "I love those pictures from the Hubble. And I keep up with all the new discoveries." Kevin grimaced.

The girl studied pastries. "Does that coffee cake have cinnamon?" Derek nodded yes.

"I don't know how you can make a living at it though," the manager persisted.

"Nuts?" the girl asked Derek.

"The cinnamon one has walnuts."

"Does the plain cake have nuts?" She continued perusing the display.

"No, just the cinnamon," Derek patiently responded as Kevin tried to catch Laura or Stephanie's eye.

"You came up with a great idea though," the manager offered. "Watching those bombs? I bet you're cleaning up!"

"You don't want to go there," Kevin said. "Not my idea. I don't make a dime off it."

"The cinnamon coffee cake," the girl asked, "does it have pecans too?"

"No," Derek answered, "only walnuts."

"You're kidding!" The manager shook his head. "Man, I'd be pissed."

"Normally I don't like nuts, but they look really good," the girl added. After a pregnant pause, she said, "I'll have a croissant, with a small cup of black tea." As Kevin groaned, the girl turned around. "Are you the scientist who started that bomb resort?"

"I didn't start it," Kevin said, austerely.

"But it's from his work," the manager said. "That's Dr. Kevin Herter. He's a genius."

"Well, thank you, but—"

"You should be ashamed of yourself," the girl snapped. "That's the most monstrous—"

"Hey!" piped the manager. "That ain't cool. You can't say—"

"You have to understand," Kevin implored, "I didn't—"

"I don't care! You're a criminal! The place should be shut down and you should be prosecuted!" Several heads turned.

"Excuse me," Laura broke in, "here's your order." The girl sneered and darted off.

"What a dickweed," the manager said. Kevin offered him his spot in line, saying, "You have to get to work." With a thank you, he patted his shoulder, causing Kevin to recoil.

As Derek took the guy's order for a banana-nut muffin and coffee, he sniped, "Jeez Kev, ya look like shit." Kevin frowned. It was lost on the smarmy junior English literature major. Kevin never understood why Derek had been hired but knew why he was kept—his knack for waiting at warp speed. The manager paid, telling Kevin, "It was nice meeting you!" and left.

Laura brought Kevin his coffee. "I'm sorry about that." As he shrugged, she added, "I didn't think you'd be in. Sharon said you guys were having trouble. You look it."

"What can I say," Kevin offered, handing over three dollars. "I like her coffee."

Laura flashed her infectious smile. Kevin liked the sophomore art history major's unaffected manner. She handed him back eighty-eight cents, which he plunked as usual into the tip jar. She smiled, and then beckoned him closer. "There was a reporter looking for you about ten minutes ago."

"Do me a favor," Kevin groaned. "If they come back, don't tell them anything."

"No problem. She was obnoxious anyway."

"Tell Sharon I'll see her later." Laura acknowledged Kevin's request with a smile, and moved to take the next customer's order.

It was now eight fifteen. Kevin was fitting a sleeve on his cup when the phone rang on the counter. It barely registered on him.

"Kevin, there's a call for you," Stephanie yelled.

"Are you sure?" She held out the phone. He sighed and walked over. "Who is it?"

"I don't know—some guy." She handed him the receiver. "Hello?"

"Dr. Herter, good morning. This is Elliot Hanford."

It was no joke. Kevin recognized the voice. "Mr. *President?*" he quavered as several patrons and Laura froze. "I, I—"

"I know this is a surprise," Hanford said.

"Yeah, well, I'll say. I—how did you know I was here?"

"We're all creatures of habit, Dr. Herter. I know you were expecting a call at home. But frankly, we have enough consultants."

"I have to be honest; I'm relieved. I wasn't interested, but I wasn't sure how to tell you."

"We had our suspicions. There is something you can help us with though. There's someone I'd like to put on." The president activated a speaker. "Dr. Herter, this is John Raden."

"Good morning, Dr. Herter," Raden said. Kevin hesitated, then greeted him in kind.

"John is a special assistant on loan from the Department of Energy," Hanford said. "I'd like to send him up to you this morning. He can be there by eleven. Does that work for you?"

"I suppose." He rubbed his eyes. "If you don't mind me asking, what do you want?"

"I'd rather have John discuss that with you in person."

"Dr. Herter," Raden said, "I'm looking forward to meeting you. I admire your work."

"Doctor," Hanford asked, "is there a place in Princeton where you and John could meet?"

"Where I am now works. I'll assume you can find it; you guys seem to be good at that."

"*Touché*, Doctor. Thank you for obliging us. It was nice to speak with you again."

"Well, you take care, Mr. President. Goodbye." Kevin hung up the phone and plowed his fingers through his thick brown hair, before vigorously rubbing his neck. He turned to see Derek and Stephanie craning their necks.

"Tell me that wasn't who I think it was." Stephanie stood with her mouth agape. During the time she'd worked at the coffee shop, famous people had stopped by. But none approached the thrill of talking with the president of the United States, even if she hadn't known it was him at the time.

"I hate to say, but that's who it was."

"Holy shit!"

"I heard you say you're meeting that dude here," Derek butted in. "Sharon's not going to be happy."

Crap, Kevin thought. He glared at Derek, annoyed that the guy was sticking his nose into something that was none of his business.

"I'll talk to her," he said. "Okay guys, later." He headed for the door.

Stephanie watched him go, then as the last person in line left, commented to Laura, "He kinda looks out of it."

"He's got a lot on his mind. And you saw what just happened."

"Well, it's his own fault. That's what he gets for thinking up all that bombs and shit."

"Hey, that's not his fault. He didn't know that would happen. Go easy on him."

"Well, he should have. I still think it's his fault." She then drew close. "He's cute though. I wouldn't mind doing him one time."

"You're a dog." Laura flashed the barest of a smile, and then picked up the phone.

It was eight thirty. A turn to the left began the walk home. Ahead was Nassau Street. Across lay the university. Just beyond was the Institute and between them were Springdale Road and Sharon.

To the right lay a walk away from those things.

Kevin lingered, an unaware obstruction to the stream of commuters. He took a gulp of coffee and on autopilot turned right. A moment later, a parking spot opened in front of the tea room, and the MSNBC van pulled in. Its occupants went into the shop, just missing their quarry.

One set of eyes though had not missed his departure. Their owner, a thirty-ish guy in a frumpy suit was across the street. As he was finishing a cup of coffee and a banana nut muffin, a girl with mousy hair walked up. She took a small package from her backpack and handed it to him. He unwrapped it. It was a receiving unit set to listen in through the tiny chip he had planted with a slap on Kevin's shoulder. He turned it on and reached for his phone, as the girl left, without them exchanging a word.

"Keep it short and sweet," Elliot Hanford instructed John Raden. "He'll still be thrown off when you get there, so just close the deal."

Raden rose, and reached out to shake hands with Herter. "It was nice to meet you, Mr. President. I'll be in touch." As he headed out of the Oval Office, he placed his cup and saucer on the sideboard. "Thank you," he said before leaving. "Good coffee."

Hanford narrowed his gaze as he left, then turned to Ridge. "We'll see if he buys it. It was subtle, even for a sharpie like him."

"Which one?"

"Does it matter? I don't trust either of them. Just because the NSA pushed hard to bring Raden in—" Hanford groaned. "At least he'll keep the Pentagon guessing. Who knows; maybe he's good. At least he's smart enough to know what he's doing here. He's also smart enough not to ask why. The problem with people like that is they can be an incredible asset or a fucking train wreck. Just keep after them. Raden's gotta make him buy it. I don't want a lick of a chance Herter figures out what's going on. My neck's out a mile on this."

Ridge's phone rang. He took the quick call from Princeton, and less than a minute later said, "Okay, it's in the works."

"That was fast," Hanford said with a condescending smile.

"We had things in place. We'll see what they do. I did have a thought though, Mr. President. Whoever leaked to the reporter got her all fired up. We've contained it, to get it out that we wanted Herter anyway, which of course we did for different reasons. She's been chasing him down, so it did get her to bite. She doesn't have to know why. Hopefully she'll be distracted enough to get us to Sunday. If he sees we're trying to win him over, it might help if he also sees there's others who feel differently about his task."

"I had the same thought myself. Just don't let it get too messy." Hanford snarled, "I swear, whoever fucked us with that—all right. What options does it give us?"

"Covers our backside in case things don't work out in the laboratory. No guarantee they will, even if Herter does get involved. He just may be a little more cooperative if he thinks others have it out for him. And it gives us flexibility should we need to pull his contract."

"Okay, do what you have to; I don't want to know about it. Dangle that atom smasher in Texas in front of him. If he hears his mentor knows—what's his name, Rosenkranz—maybe he'll fall on his sword. Just be thankful good cop bad cop hasn't gone out of style."

"Thankfully, not quite yet," Ridge said as he turned and left the office.

Four

The interlocking corners on the four lengths of wood were fit together and ready to be stapled into place. The stretcher bars, each 2½ inches wide by an inch thick had been mitered at the factory, but Sharon Velazquez wasn't happy. The outer edge had a lip over which the canvas would be stretched, and one of them was off by about a sixteenth-of-an-inch.

She knelt down in sweat pants and T-shirt, her thick honey-blushed hair draped over her shoulders, her elbows pressed in on her knees with her chin resting in her hands, staring down the dilemma confronting her.

Her studio, an airy addition to her home, was arrayed in canvas rolls and bins of stretcher bars, coffee cans with brushes and tubes of paint. Its south face caught light the entire day and was the envy of every artist who visited. Over the scent of turpentine and linseed oil, a dozen freshly-made fruit tarts hinted at six more minutes in the oven, while her marbled cat Chloe staked out a spot in the sun. For now, there was the issue of the frame.

Though the discrepancy on a 52 x 72 inch canvas was minor, it bothered her. Machined-cut wood shouldn't be off by that much. Most artists would never notice, and those that did wouldn't care. A select few would object because of the dollars—a painter commanding $40,000 a canvas might demand that those canvases be perfect. But the money didn't matter, the error did. She began pounding each suspect corner with a rubber mallet.

Between the beat of hard rubber against pine and the tingling harmony of the wind chimes outside she didn't hear the phone until the answering machine engaged.

"Laura, I'm here," she said, turning it off. "Morning. What's doing?"

"Morning, Sharon. Listen, Kevin just stopped by. He looked terrible."

"It's nice to know some things still bother him. Did he have anything to say?"

"Well, he asked for you, but that's not why I'm calling." She hesitated. "He got a call here. You're not going to believe it. It was from the president."

"Of the university?"

"No, the United States." As Sharon gasped, Laura added, "He wants someone to meet Kevin here. And these reporters have been in and out all morning. Kevin left kinda in a daze. He said he'd talk to you, but I thought you should know."

"Wow, thanks for the heads-up. I'll handle it." Sharon hung up and sat down, alternating sips of Earl Gray tea with biting the inside of her cheek. Chloe sat in her lap, purring like a motorboat. While the cat craned her head, Sharon scratched her neck. The cat closed its eyes and continued in its mindless bliss, while outside, the wind chimes danced away.

We're all authors of our life stories, but the prologues are penned by other hands. The out-of-wedlock daughter of a Venezuelan oil executive and a Jewish United States Consulate worker in Caracas, thirty-one year old Sharon Hannah Velazquez breezed through life attracting men, money and the machinations of power like iron filings to a magnet itching for a reversal of polarity. A stunning 5'7" tall and one hundred thirty pounds, she was blessed with a potent blend of looks, talent and an intellect to know she need not embellish her gifts with an undue sense of entitlement. The outside world saw a woman who radiated what appeared to be effortless success, someone with enough confidence and aptitude that she could be expected to make up the rules to suit her own station in life. But all Sharon Velazquez wanted was to be left alone to paint.

Raised in South Florida by her maternal grandmother, she displayed a need to create from the start. Shells, feathers, cycad fronds—anything from nature with a pattern made its way to her canvasses. Supported by a gushing trust fund set up by a father who specialized in buying love, mostly from afar, she built upon her wealth, creating a niche in the art world by focusing on subjects that bucked the political and social trends of what passed for important in the New York art scene and caring not a whit who was affronted in the process. This egged on curators and collectors, her looks and wit adding to the mystique.

By twenty-five, she'd parlayed her Bachelor in Fine Art degree from Princeton into a one-woman show at a 57th Street gallery in New York City. Her large oils—painstaking, layered images—were crafted with a finger-painting technique that blew everyone away. As one writer in *Art*

Forum magazine said, "It's so obvious that someone needed to paint pieces like this exactly the way they were painted that the amazing thing is that no one has bothered to do it before."

The show sold out opening night and brought her the kind of attention normally afforded sixty-year-old artists their first retrospective at the Whitney Museum. All thought Princeton a curious choice for the young painter. Many wondered why she hadn't attended a New York school, any of which would have seized the opportunity to add an exceptionally talented and attractive woman with a diverse cultural background to their student body. The reason was typically original and hiding in plain sight; though small, New Jersey had one of the most varied natural backdrops of any state, and the historic town was in its center. An hour ride could uncover fossil trilobites and corals from Stroudsburg, Pennsylvania, fossil shark teeth in Monmouth County, fossil fish and footprints from Roseland and North Bergen or horseshoe crabs and shells from Delaware Bay and the Atlantic. Ten minutes north was a quail farm in Griggstown. Its owner kindly supplied colorful feathers. The Nature Walk at the Institute for Advanced Study offered shed antlers, ferns and other objects. All were subject matter to be collected by hand, creating an unbroken line of creation, source, inspiration, acquisition, creation.

The Princeton Tea Room was a diversion, a fusion of concepts from here and there that came together in a style wholly Sharon Velazquez. It blossomed into that great idea hiding in plain sight. She had an uncanny knack for picking help such that petty theft and cash pilfering never were problems. The Tea Room was an excuse to share her much-envied baking, and the issue of who did the baking became a joke between Sharon and herself.

The main part of Princeton is six blocks or so of Nassau Street bordering the north face of Princeton University. It adds college town ambiance to a college town that despite world-class stature trends toward the understated. At the center is Palmer Square, an unassuming block partly taken up by the Nassau Inn, a fixture dating from the eighteenth century.

A tailwind propelled Kevin as he moved along in the cool spring. Ahead was Tiger Park, a spot of benches and inscribed cobblestones at the foot of Palmer Square. He reached for his cell phone. It was dead. "Son of a ..." he muttered, remembering the low battery ping last night. He had yet to put it back in his pocket when he saw the MSNBC van. He darted behind a tree, cut across Tiger Park and made for the Nassau

Inn. The courtly hotel had a pub and a phone. He could call Sharon from there.

"So what's with calling from the Nassau Inn?" she asked after noticing the Caller ID.

"Can I talk to you?" Kevin's voice rang with urgency.

"I hear you're getting calls from presidents now. I'm flattered you'd want to talk to me next."

"Sharon, it's too early, especially after the night I had. So you heard. Bad news travels fast."

"I've got my spies. And what are you complaining about? I'd thought you'd be happy to be dealing with the first team. I mean if you're gonna be spooked, might as well be by them."

"Sharon, enough."

"All right, all right. So what are you doing at the Nassau Inn? Get lucky last night?"

"Yeah, but not the way you think."

"So what happened?"

"I don't know. I mean I do, but I don't." Kevin rubbed his eyes, pausing just enough for Sharon to ask, "Listen, you wanna stop by?"

"Yeah, thanks. About ten minutes okay?"

"Make it fifteen. I've got a few tarts in the oven. And don't ever hang up on me again."

He got off the phone and rubbed his eyes again, wondering how long it would take to feel okay sleeping alone in bed.

Five

Kevin stood at Sharon's front door on Springdale Road, staring at the trees across the street. The swaybacked sentinels that separated the road from the golf course beyond were always worth a look. Their gnarly roots protruded like props from a Tim Burton movie.

He had a key but walking in didn't seem right. And ringing the bell just felt weird. He stared the better part of a minute, and then knocked, hesitantly.

"You could have come in," Sharon said as she appeared.

"I wasn't sure what you were okay with."

She frowned and turned for the studio.

The newly-conditioned stretcher frame lay against a wall. She laid a six-foot roll of canvas on the floor and unrolled a section. Chloe traipsed over to Kevin, rubbing herself against him.

"She still likes you," Sharon said softly.

Kevin scratched the cat's neck, then eyed the canvas. "What's this going to be?"

"I'm thinking of doing a mushroom cloud over downtown Princeton. Lot of art history there."

"I didn't come over to get into a pissing contest. And I'll get my stuff later."

She ignored him, positioned the frame on the canvas and began trimming the fabric. Halfway through, she stopped. "Kevin," she huffed, "what the hell is going on?"

"I don't know anymore," he said, collapsing into a chair. He began describing what had recently transpired.

"So let me get this straight," she said. "After the New Jersey state police pull you over to tell you that you didn't get pulled over, the president of the United States calls to say he won't be calling to offer you a job. Wonderful," she clacked as she finished trimming. "And?"

"They want to talk to me about something else." Chloe jumped in his lap.

"And you're still going to listen to them?" She got the stapler and a pair of canvas pliers.

"Let's not go through this again," Kevin glared at her.

"You're damn right we're not going through it again." She began stretching the canvas.

"You don't get it—you think I'm afraid to tell them off. You don't understand that I have to do business with them."

"Are you *kidding*?" She laughed. "You have no clue. You are so far out of your league, you don't even know what end is up. They are playing you for such an idiot that—I'm not going to say any more. So, what did Max have to say?"

"Well, you know what he thinks. He kind of said what you did, but—"

"No, he didn't. He'd tell them to stick it. I'd tell them to go fuck themselves. And I wouldn't lose a minute of sleep over it, never mind two weeks and my relationship." She pulled the canvas so tight it almost tore. "Listen, I love you but I can't watch this anymore. You keep thinking what should be, and don't want to see what is. I thought I could deal with you having one foot in and one out because I felt you were worth waiting for. But I will not watch them do the same thing to you. You won't admit it. Your head's so far up your rear end, but hey—your choice. You think you have a handle on this? Who do you think pulled you over last night?"

"I don't know," Kevin protested. "Max wasn't sure either. I will find out, but I'll be damned if I walk around thinking they're out to get me."

"They've *already* got you," Sharon rolled her eyes, "but you're too stubborn to admit it."

"Oh, bull."

"*Bull?* They take your work, *fuck* you over, turn it into that *thing*, and after all that tell you you'd *really be doing yourself a favor* if you help them out. So you tell me, who has who?"

"Fine. Then tell me what I should have done."

"Use your connections. Open your mouth." She shot more staples.

"And in the end they still build it. I don't want to argue. I just wanted to tell you—"

"Yeah, I heard. You afraid I'm gonna kick Hanford's lackey out? It's a public place. I toldja before, you're a big boy. Do what you want."

"It's I told you."

"Fuck you! I'll say toldja if I want. Toldja, *Toldja*, TOLDJA!"

"Fine! I'm not going to argue. I just didn't want to surprise you."

"Thanks." She stapled some more. "Who is he? And what do they want with you now?"

"I don't know. He's some whoever from the Department of Energy. But who knows."

"Great." The sound of more staples punctuated her words. "Now I feel a whole lot better."

"Sharon, I'm not promising them anything. I just wish you had a little more faith in me."

"That's what my father says every time he flies to Washington on business and expects me to drop everything and visit him—right before he flies home for another year. Listen, I gotta get ready," she said quietly. "Get out of here. I'll see you later."

Kevin rose. Chloe clung to his lap until the last possible moment. As he was about to leave, Sharon drew him close and kissed him, hiding the tear in her eye.

"This too shall pass." Her grandmother's grizzled adage hovered nearby, a reassuring divide to the bookends that were the past two weeks and two years. She held off sorting it out, instead fidgeting with a lock of hair. Every relationship unravels and does so in its own way, with no guidebook or precedent. The one with Kevin Herter was proving no different.

Six

John Raden settled in on the plane that would take him on the short trip to New Jersey. As the C-20D taxied down the Andrew's Air Force Base runway, he smiled to himself. The plane was the military version of the popular Gulfstream III. Only the bureaucracy could dampen the elegance of a Gulfstream into a watery C-20D.

Raden reached for his attaché case. The briefing papers furnished by the White House were voluminous, but he ignored them—he did his own research and knew his subject. Buried beneath was a CD, labeled Herter, *Dateline*. He wanted to watch it again, to see the style, the poise, the man behind the man. As the plane began to speed down the runway, he inserted the disc into the desktop DVD player.

The piece on Kevin Herter had run a year after the articles that started it all had appeared in *Nature*, *Science* and *Astrophysics*. Enough time for the theories they contained to have made a profound impact on physics and for the controversy their repercussions generated to spread. The opening became his working narrative:

"The question is deceptively simple. What lies five miles past the edge of the universe? It's been asked in various forms since people first lifted their gazes past the birds and the bees and the sun and the stars and towards the idea of the angels. Between tilling the soil and text messaging their flocks and the myriad other distractions imposed on living beings by the rigors of a material existence, Man has always found occasion to try to make sense of what is."

"The scientist has long occupied a place of reverent ambiguity in our relationship with the embers of creation. In trying to tap into the resonance of the universe we have made those at the forefront of that journey the repositories of our most fervent passions. We project onto them our highest hopes, that they may show us the way to surmount our technological shortcomings and enable us to lead more productive and fulfilled lives. And in the next breath we vilify them, for failing to impart the wisdom demanded by an enlightened mastery of their discoveries."

Raden watched intently. He was used to a certain bearing from scientists; they were typically comfortable discussing their material, less so themselves. Even Carl Sagan for all his media savvy had it.

Herter was different. At ease with himself, indifferent talking over his work. He came across not so much an esoteric genius lacking personality than a Michigan quarterback guarding Saturday's playbook. Photogenic, articulate, with just enough self-deprecation, the kid was a pleasure to watch.

And that was in itself interesting. The unassuming physicist had conceived one of the most creative and captivating theories ever devised in the history of science; quantum resonance. The idea that at its heart, gravity was less a force than a frequency. The simple, straightforward property of matter to attract itself that laymen took for granted and that vexed physicists for centuries was seen by Herter as a modulating presence ubiquitous to existence, flowing within, between and throughout universes, governing the production and decay of a myriad of universes. Underlying everything was something not unlike music. It was inspired.

As the C-20D descended to Princeton Airport Raden's initial hunch grew more certain; the physicist was not what he'd been told. He wondered if Herter knew what he was in for.

He also reflected on Hanford. At heart, the consummate politician was steeped in the language of power. To be able to keep power in the twenty-first century, you could only affect policies deemed controversial by going through the motions of having an honest debate. By having the right people in place before debate began you could achieve a preordained outcome and create the perception that it had been anything but. And nothing was more controversial than the bomb.

Raden understood why he was there. He also knew that had it been left to the White House, he wouldn't have been. He was acutely aware that to the Administration, his place in this issue was that of a necessary evil, someone whose presence was to be tolerated but never trusted. And someone whose position was to be undermined, and with a smile. He had been in the field long enough to know how much it involved skirting the line between the perception fed to the masses and the reality responsible for creating it, both working in the shadows. This assignment narrowed those margins to the thinnest degree possible, to the point where in the end, were it pulled off successfully, it would be next to impossible to tell one from the other.

More than anything, he was aware that in the scheme of things, he was little more than an aberration. To know you could be set up and that they knew you knew, while angling to best them at their own game without seeking material gain was something rare in Washington. It freed him to focus on the task at hand, and gave him a perspective that few in positions of power appreciated. The nation's capital was littered with careers of politicians, consultants and appointees who thought they had a handle on how things worked and who was working them. Raden though, unmindful of office, money or power, saw the challenge in what was to most a shark cage. What wasn't Hanford telling him? Dealing with what lay hidden and deciphering that puzzle would prove the most daunting challenge of all.

"What am I supposed to do with this?"

Sharon glared at the delivery supposedly containing ten thousand napkins, coffee cups, lids and stirrers. Though Laura had yet to finish unpacking, it was clear something was wrong. The restaurant suppliers had botched an order only a month ago, and here was another one. It was the last thing she wanted to deal with.

"Is this the only box that came?" She knew the answer, but had to ask.

"Yeah. I asked the driver if there was anything else on the truck. This was it." The small box before them held a thousand napkins and like number of straws. Sharon scrutinized the bill, along with her own computer receipt confirming the correct order.

"Dammit!" she snapped, hurling the papers at her desk. "I haven't got time for this shit!" She fell into her chair. Laura went to get her a mug of tea. Sharon thanked her softly as Laura brought it over. As Laura left the office, Sharon sat still, waiting for it to cool down.

Out front, Laura began brewing fresh coffee for the ten a.m. crowd. As Derek was leaving, his shift done, the MSNBC crew reappeared. He turned to Laura, and said, "I smell trouble."

A stunning, impeccably-dressed woman in her late twenties walked up, followed by two men, one holding a camcorder.

"Hi," she began. "We were in earlier. Jessica Enright; MSNBC. We've been trying to locate Dr. Kevin Herter. Have you seen him?"

"Well …" Laura began when Derek piped in, "You just missed him earlier. He's supposed to meet someone—"

"I'll take care of this." Sharon bolted over from the office. "He was supposed to meet someone but the plans got changed."

"You're the owner, aren't you," Enright offered, as the cameraman lifted the camcorder. "His girlfriend."

"Turn that off in my place!" Sharon snapped.

Enright motioned to lower the unit, and then said, "Listen, do you know—"

"No."

"We don't want to bother you; we just have a few—"

"He doesn't want to answer them. And neither do I."

"Okaay…." Enright took out a card. "Could you please tell him I had a few questions and he can reach me at this number?" They turned and left. Sharon ripped the card up and threw the pieces at the trash.

"You think you might have come down on her too hard?" Laura asked.

"She didn't introduce herself to me in my place of business or bother asking my name. She assumed I'm Kevin's girlfriend and expected me to play receptionist. At the least, she could have bought a cup of coffee. This place is becoming a circus, and I won't have it."

"Fuck her," Derek declared as he headed out.

"What do you think she's up to?" Laura asked Sharon.

Sharon eyed her employee. Her anger now had stiff competition from the satisfaction that came from validating it. She poured Laura a cup of coffee. "Sit," she said as she got one herself.

Laura took a guarded sip. "Are you okay?"

Sharon wistfully gazed up. "When Kevin and I began dating, we'd talk about our experience with reporters. He'd always find time to talk to them, or maybe it just seemed that way 'cause I had no patience for them at all. They were interested in fitting me into their little subplots—Velazquez the feminist entrepreneur, Velazquez the Latino Jew, Velazquez the tortured woman artist in a man's world. I didn't bite, and they didn't like it. And they'd always get something wrong. I'd call to correct them, but they weren't interested. They wanted their story, and it didn't matter if it wasn't the right story. Kevin brushed it off, but it always irked me. It didn't seem to bother him though I knew it had to. You think society's changed. Some things have, but a lot hasn't. When you're a woman who's accomplished things, you learn that going through those motions puts a target on your back. They go after it right from the start 'cause they're the ones who put it there in the first place. Always keep 'em guessing."

"Wow. I hope you're not getting too jaded in your old age."

"Never say old age to the person who cuts your paycheck." She winked and took a sip from her cup. "Good coffee."

Laura thanked her, and then Sharon frowned. "Honestly, I hate what Kevin's doing. At this point, I've given up on anything working out with us. But I hate what they do to him even more."

Seven

John Raden plopped his tired suitcase on the bed. The tie loosened after leaving the White House was thankfully off his neck, his suit on a hanger. A splash of water on his face and the khakis, sport coat and polo shirt would soon take their place.

Some things weren't worth the bother. For instance, the directive to come off to Kevin Herter as authoritatively as possible. Raden was far too seasoned to fret over things like that. For most of his life, he'd cared little for rules and regulations certifying the inanities of life. Best to smile, ignore and move on.

A stint as an inconspicuous but influential Wall Street broker had burgeoned into a $147 million dollar nest egg before he turned thirty-five. But fleeing boredom, he wound up in Fort Meade, Maryland, at an obscure though influential subdivision of the National Security Agency. The position was created especially for him, at the NSA's Defensive Information Operations and Security Evaluations departments, in a gray area suited to his skills. Both divisions let him use his knowledge of information-system technologies, cyber-defense, national security issues and the finances underlying each. He wasn't so much assigned projects as allowed to analyze concerns and trends, then probe and consult.

An untitled analyst with no real authority, desk, salary or boss, his intellect and foresight routinely immersed him in the most sensitive and far-reaching endeavors in which the United States was involved. Never fancying himself a James Bond or even a Jack Ryan, despite the similarities in names, he wasn't interested in hanging out of planes, aiding defecting Soviet sub commanders or running for president. That was for more adventurous souls. The world was a riddle to be solved, and he would solve them.

Riddles such as history. As much as it was a passion, the past was a puzzle. But there was history and there were history-makers, and while he had an insatiable curiosity for the one, suffering some of the others could take a bit off the luster. Like presidents. While all were interesting in their own right most were too often enamored with themselves and the sound of their own voice, often and sadly at the expense of wisdom. He was now at a place where he could pick and choose assignments. It was why meeting a Kevin Herter was to be looked forward to.

Raden's interest in the physicist went back farther than two years. As the program based on his theories developed, he called on the gleaning from his curiosity. His reputation brought a steady stream of secret information from those wanting it to surface as prudently as possible. A briefing to the right people on the bomb project was enough to get things going with the powers that be, who took a closer look at events in the Pacific. A word dropped in the right ear could wend its way to those you wished to attract. Like a news director whose eager young reporter could indulge a twenty-year sense of unfinished business. Or a president eager to forge a legacy.

Raden entered the Princeton Tea Room just after ten thirty. Tucked under his arm was the morning's *New York Times* crossword puzzle.

"Looks like its getting nice out," Laura smiled at him as she propped open the door. He smiled back, looked around, ordered coffee and sat down.

A few minutes later Sharon approached Laura.

"Listen, Kevin's supposed to meet someone here at eleven. Just keep an eye out for him."

"I thought you told—"

"Yeah, well, if I'm in the back, just let me know."

John Raden looked up for a moment, took a sip of coffee, and then went back to his puzzle.

The black MSNBC van crawled north on Witherspoon Avenue like a shopper stalking parking spots on Black Friday. Jessica Enright alternated between scanning the sidewalks and punching redial on her phone, neither of which was successful.

"What do you want to do?" asked intern Jim Leffert from behind the wheel.

"Drive around." The van made the next right as 10:55 a.m. flashed on the phone. An instant later a Text Message appeared. "Head back to the coffee shop," she said.

Kevin had just arrived at the Princeton Tea Room. Seated about was a woman in a business suit absorbed in a laptop, a young man lost in a calculus textbook and two college-age girls trying to conceal their clasped hands beneath their table. And a middle-aged guy with a newspaper and pencil tapping his I Phone. The man looked up, then went back to his paper.

Kevin sat by the window. It was warm and he removed his coat. Laura brought him a coffee, a frothy nebula revolving on the surface. "I'll tell Sharon you're here," she said.

Sharon walked up to find him lost in the image on his cup.

"You look more tired," she said sitting down. "Where did you go?"

"Walked around." He stared at a sunbeam behind her then met her gaze. "Just walked."

"Did you find out who's meeting you?" she asked, crossing her arms.

"Some guy Raden." He half listened, thinking how you could lose yourself in the formality of breaking up. It was so much easier to just walk away.

"You haven't seen him yet, have you?" he asked as the hands on the elegant wall clock moved to eleven o'clock.

"No, but that Enright broad from MSNBC was looking for you. I told her to take a hike. Did you know they were looking for you?"

"Yeah." As she groaned, he pleaded, "Sharon, what do you want me to do?"

"I really don't care, but I'm not going to let this place turn into a circus."

"That's why I asked if you minded if I met him here."

"No, you asked if I mind if you met *him* here, not a bunch of reporters."

"Listen, Sharon, what do you want me to say?" He shook his head in disgust.

"Well, she said she wanted to talk to you, so you tell her. I told her you didn't want to."

A moment later, two men in suits entered. They casually glanced around, and then walked up to the counter.

"False alarm," she sneered, glaring at Kevin. He refused to meet her stare, and she shot up. "I can't believe you!" she erupted. "You still say you can deal with this? You don't even want to admit what it's doing to you! Where is he?"

"Sharon, how do I know? I don't even know what he wants."

"What difference does it make? I swear, he'd better get here soon or I'm gonna *lose it*!"

"This was a mistake," Kevin said, rising. "I shouldn't have said I'd meet him here."

"No, you shouldn't have said you would meet him *period*."

"All right, that's it," Kevin fumed, taking his coat. "Listen. I'm sorry. I'm leaving."

"And where the hell are you going? You told the president of the United States you'd meet his flunkey here! What do I do when he gets here? And just what am I supposed to tell the *president of the United States* when he calls again looking for you? Invite him over for a latte` and wait for your ass to show up? Unbelievable!"

"Sharon, enough. Maybe he got held up in traffic. Maybe the plane got delayed."

"Maybe they just came up with a new way to fuck you over again!"

"Maybe it's not what you think."

The voice from behind startled them. The man with the newspaper was sitting back with his arms folded, watching them intently. "Son of a bitch," said a shocked Kevin.

John Raden walked up to them. "You're allowed one bop," he said to Sharon. He turned to Kevin. "You, you're just going to have to deal with it."

"All right," Sharon snapped, "that's it." She threw her hands up and began walking to the back. Raden followed her and upon reaching the counter, asked, "Miss Velazquez, could you please be so kind as to get me a small coffee? And a large light breakfast blend for Kevin?"

She paused. *The shit does his homework*, she thought as she painstakingly filled his order. "I'm trying to get your number," she said.

"No doubt." He pulled out some bills to pay, but she waved him off. He thanked her and put the money in the tip jar. Before turning for her office she saw Alexander Hamilton gazing up.

"You look like this won't be enough," Raden said, placing the cup before Kevin.

"Okay," Kevin folded his arms, "I'm here."

John Raden smiled and politely extended his hand. "Jack Raden."

Kevin hesitated, and then shook. "Sure it's not Jack Ryan?"

"I'm sure," Raden smiled, sitting down. "You know, you're not the first."

"You always sneak up on people like that?" Kevin asked.

"Not always. Then again, like your girlfriend says, always keep 'em guessing."

"How would you know? Anyway, she's not my girlfriend anymore."

"She's still invested," Raden said, shaking his head. "Don't be so quick to write it off. And she makes a good cup of Joe. Kinda hard to find all that in one package."

"Is that what you came here for? If she had her way, you wouldn't even be sitting here."

"I know." Raden removed his coat and rolled up his sleeves. "Why are you here then?"

Kevin shrugged.

"Okay," Raden said, "so let me ask you then. What's bothering you?"

"Oh, come on—what, do I *know you*? I can't believe you're even asking me that."

"Fair enough. And you're right. I was curious as to why."

"It's asinine! Of all the things to do with physics. For crying out loud, with the Manhattan Project they had an excuse—there was a war. And even then it bothered them. But Einstein never had to deal with crap like this; Fermi, Szilard. No one blamed them for the bomb. And you ask me why? Two years I steered clear of this damn thing. I never minded reporters. But now I know what Sharon means. Go see what my answering machine at home looks like."

"I thought it might be that you felt bad for discovering the theory behind the thing."

"I think most people know what's going on. I don't think they blame me."

"Maybe, but you've been on the receiving end of some bad press. And a few threats."

"Well, mostly Internet crap, but I never read that. I get some from the left, no matter that I never even imagined what it's been turned into. And there's the religious right with, 'Science is what God says it is'. God forbid you suggest God keeps popping out universes. Every so often, I get a nutcase who comes up with some kind of whackadoodle this or that. I had a couple this morning. Does it bother me? I suppose. But what you guys did bothers me more." Raden nodded.

"You know what I want?" Kevin leaned forward. "I want to be left alone."

"That I can understand, too."

Kevin was on a roll. "I want to spend my time on what I'm interested in. I want to spend more time on quantum gravity. I want to spend more time on inflation; that's cosmic inflation, not the economic one. I want to spend more time on unification theories. I don't need to come home and see my answering machine full. I don't want to have to duck into an alley every time a van goes by. I want to get a decent night's sleep for a change. I don't want be remembered for this. I couldn't care less if I'm remembered at all, but damn if it's for this. And," he groaned, "I don't need to be turning down the president of the United States because he and a bunch of pinheads can't run a resort setting off H-bombs without me telling them what brand of toilet paper to hang in the bathrooms. They don't need me, so just go back and tell them."

Raden lightly laughed, and Kevin snapped, "It's not funny."

"Well, it is, in a way."

"All right," Kevin frowned. "You know, during the Middle Ages, people decided they didn't have to bathe. It was beneath them. So they stunk. And lo and behold the perfume industry appears so they could cover up the smell. When they land in the New World the Indians, who bathed every day, took a whiff. Some people know when things stink."

"I know."

"You know. Then you know it still took them centuries to decide to start taking a damn bath. All that time they didn't want to deal with it. They thought piling on toilet water was the answer. You had a whole industry show up because people thought the smarter thing to do was cover up the smell. Point is, some things can't be sanitized. No matter how you gift wrap 'em or clean them up with a happy face, it's still H-bombs. And it still stinks." He sighed. "All right, Hanford told me you didn't need me consulting. So what the hell you want?" He knocked his coffee container against the table, then tilted his head back to wring out the last few drops.

"We want you to run it."

Eight

"Are you *nuts?*" Kevin shot up. "No way! Forget it! Wasted trip." As he turned, Raden saw the bug. For now, he needed to bide his time, but everything had changed.

"Are you listening?" Kevin demanded.

"Sure. You're thinking about it."

Kevin froze. "Are you trying to be funny?"

"You're thinking about it," Raden pressed in. As Kevin sat bewildered, Raden intoned, "I've been asked to convey a request by the president of the United States that you entertain directorship of the program known colloquially as Club Afterglow at the site designated Tuvalu Alofa. Now, I know you're thinking about it." He looked about him. "Up for walking? It's been years since I wandered around Princeton."

Kevin stared. "Is that it?"

"For now."

Kevin shrugged. "Let me tell Sharon I'm leaving." Just then she appeared. "We're gonna walk around," he said.

"Fine," she glared. "So what's it gonna be now? Are you—" She stopped. Jessica Enright and her crew were making a beeline for the door. "All right, enough!" She stormed out.

"I've had it with you idiots!" she yelled as Kevin followed. "Learning not sinking in? How many times you have to be told to stay the hell away from here?" Cameraman Cliff Abreau lifted his unit and she lunged at it, almost knocking him back.

Kevin grabbed her by the waist. "Kevin, let me the fuck go!" she yelled.

"Sharon, calm down!"

"Don't you tell me to calm down! Get your hands off of me!"

Abreau was struggling not to fall while his unit swung about, still recording.

"Miss Velazquez," Enright glowered, "don't *ever* go after me or my crew again."

"I told you to keep away from me and my place of business. Understand?"

"I'm not interested in—"

"PERIOD! STAY AWAY! END OF DISCUSSION!"

"Just come inside," Kevin tugged at Sharon. "Please." She sneered, then went in.

"I'll give you a minute, but back off," Kevin told Enright before following Sharon inside where she stood hyperventilating, her nails gouging deep pits into her arms, mounds of angry flesh pillowing up about her fingers.

"This isn't helping anything." Kevin implored while Laura stood by awkwardly.

"Oh," Sharon said, her eyes welling up, "just—go." She sat down, and turned away.

"I'll be outside," Raden said softly to Kevin. He quietly bought two more coffees, then left, passing the film crew who took no note of him. Kevin wavered, then turned and went out.

Outside, Kevin glared at Enright. "I'll give you a minute, on one condition. *Never* bother her again. And no camera." Enright nodded. Abreau lowered the unit. "Minute's counting."

"Dr. Herter, Jessica Enright, MSNBC. You're a difficult person to track down."

"I'm easy, as long as I want to be found."

"Come on Dr. Herter," Enright said, flashing her killer smile, "work with me. I only have a few questions. Someone from CNN is angling to stop by tomorrow, and I'm sure you'll like them a lot less."

Kevin whirled his finger in the air.

"Dr. Herter, there's a lot of buzz of late about the bomb resort. One report says you're being tapped as a consultant. In light of your views about the program and considering it's a direct outgrowth of your work, could you give us some insight as to your plans in that regard?"

"I can tell you no one has offered me any consulting position with the program, and if they did, I wouldn't be interested. Even if they didn't, I wouldn't be interested. Fifteen seconds."

"Do you have any other comments about the program as it has developed? It's very popular, but we're beginning to hear concerns."

"Nope. You're asking the wrong person. Okay, time's up." For the first time, he felt anger towards a reporter. "I'm serious about what I said. This is not a negotiation. Tell your pals as well. You want to talk to me, fine. You leave Sharon alone, got it?" He walked off.

Kevin trudged up to the waiting Raden. "I'm sorry about that," he said.

"No need. She does have her passions. Is she going to be all right?"

Kevin looked away. "I don't think so. Not for a while."

"They do what they do." Raden held out a coffee. Kevin thanked him, then grew silent as they walked. His thoughts though were deafening.

To someone coveting life in the shadows, it was hard knowing how to insulate yourself from them. And it was getting harder. As his stature grew, he forged an uneasy truce with himself, baring just enough to rub elbows with the ruling class without getting dirt on his sleeve. More than a learning experience, it became a survival technique, a defense mechanism that grew to second nature. You learned how to talk to people, and remain above the fray. You learned to pick your battles, the skirmishes disguised as policy reviews, the dinner parties and conferences that doubled as turf wars. You learned that not saying no and not saying yes were different from straddling the fence, which meant a sore ass no matter which side you fell down on.

And you learned that science and politics didn't mix. Look what happened to Robert Oppenheimer, who ran the Manhattan Project that developed the atomic bomb and was then stripped of his security clearance for being on the wrong side of a policy dispute. Look what happened to the biologists who studied evolution. Politicos who made judgments about science too often preferred to see it as they wished instead of how it was. And scientists who courted bureaucracy sooner or later had to pay the piper, accommodating polls and fashions of the day, subjugating this work or that find into a sound bite or agenda. In between was a no-man's land, a maze one could get mired in and spend a lifetime never getting out of. As he walked, he realized that what he had long dreaded had come to pass. That's exactly where he was.

Nine

As they walked along, Jack Raden mulled his course of action. With all the notoriety at the NSA in recent years, it was the first time he'd been spied on. Was it Hanford? Those around him? Others? In time, it would come out. For now, he needed to speak with Kevin. More unsettling than having to watch how he dealt with Kevin because of the bug was that there was a bug at all. With the politics involved, it was a given that someone would take issue with his assignment. This time, they were put off enough to listen in on what was being said.

He felt for the scientist but what followed would involve walking a fine line, winning him over while not letting on to those listening that he knew, placating them without revealing anything of substance. He needed to play it out, but knowing was an advantage. And maybe Herter needed to talk. A few tense moments later, he said, "It's been a while since I was here."

"It's a lot different from where I grew up," Kevin answered.

"Michigan, right?" He already knew the answer.

"Yeah. How long's it been for you?"

"Twenty-some years. It's a great town. They have an interesting walking tour."

"I took it when I first came here. Kind of an initiation rite for the physics crowd; you know, finding Einstein's house. It's our version of channeling."

Raden smiled. "You been living here long?" Again, he knew the answer, but it was a way of getting Kevin to relax.

"Three years. You hear talk about New Jersey, but it's nice. Too much traffic though."

"Heh, try living around Washington."

Kevin felt his guard drop a hair. It was too much. "Listen," he said, "I don't know what you expect at this point." The previous night was taking its toll. He wanted to cut this guy off and go home.

They approached an intersection. An awkward silence ruled while they awaited the light.

"What happens now with you and Sharon?" Raden asked.

"I don't know. I think that's about it." He caught himself again. "You're going to have to stop with the questions," he said curtly.

Raden pretended he didn't hear. As the light changed and they crossed Nassau Street, he said, "How 'bout turning right. I want to see if I remember that walk." He was betting he could get Kevin to open up. People liked to tell their stories. Give them an opening and they would. When they had gone about twenty feet, he asked, "Isn't the Institute this way?" Kevin nodded. It was his daily walk to work. Raden asked, "Isn't Mercer Street that way? Where Einstein lived?"

"After twenty years I'm impressed." Kevin took a sip of coffee. "So who do you work for? And why can't I get a straight answer out of any-one about this damn thing?"

"A straight answer? All the times you worked with Washington, you still ask that question?" He downed his coffee, stepped to a trash can and threw away the cup. "I do a little consulting."

"That's it? After everything that's happened the past two weeks, this is it? I would think that if the White House wanted to make an impres-sion they'd send red carpets and brass bands, not Jack Ryan with a Mr. Coffee. No offense." As Raden laughed, Kevin said, "You still didn't answer my question."

"Well, not to sound cryptic, everyone and no one. A little for this one, little for that."

"In between stops in the Oval Office."

"Now and then. In the end, I work for myself. And as for style, well, we all have our own."

Raden could see that Kevin was stressed. But he was enjoying him-self. College towns had their own special feel. The comings and goings of life were there, but they came with a refined hum. He took in the rarified rush and said, "You really should learn to relax."

Kevin glared at him. "Oh, you so don't want to go there."

"Okay, but me, I have a soft spot for college towns, especially ones with history. I was here in 1991. It was the build-up to the first Gulf War. There was tension then too, but my mind wasn't on it. All I thought of were people who walked these sidewalks. F. Scott Fitzgerald, John F. Kennedy, Woodrow Wilson. Even seventy years ago Einstein, Oppenheimer, Von Neumann." He eyed Kevin. "Max Rosenkranz. They walked this very pavement, coming to town, talking with friends, living their lives. I was in my twenties, decent job, making money. Still doing twenties stuff. Still thinking about getting laid even though I was married with a family." He smiled. "Didn't do it. But even then I was awed by the time line involved. You're in the same physical space as people who've contributed. Only difference is time. They still cast shadows. It's inspiring. It stays with you. I had a professor who was an undergrad here. He told a story that he was once on Nassau Street and saw Einstein, Oppenheimer and Thomas Mann waiting for a bus. *That's* a bus I would have liked to have taken." They reached Mercer Street. "If I remember, Einstein's house is not too far. It's not that big, I recall."

"No, it's not," said Kevin, thinking Raden wasn't what he expected. "A lot of us get a kick out of that. Einstein was eccentric, but he was accessible. There's stories he would help students with their math, their physics. When I moved here, I wanted to get a feel for the town. That's the first time I saw his house, Oppenheimer's too. You can't help noticing the difference. Oppenheimer lived in Olden Manor. It's a three-hundred-year-old mansion that's reserved for Institute directors. Oppenheimer was this patrician kind-of-guy, and even though the house is for directors it's like it was made for him. Aloof; set back from the road. Then you see Einstein's house out in the open. Accessible. You can go right past it, even when you're looking for it."

"I got something of the same impression myself. I remember thinking, *this is it?*"

"Sharon noticed too. She'd notice everything. The Institute has a popular nature walk. She could tell you the trees, the rocks, the plants, everything. That's what she paints. She's big into fractals. Not like Jackson Pollack. Different. For being an artist, she's a math whiz. She's got as good a mathematical mind as any of my peers. She just expresses it differently. She can see patterns no one can. She's great with anything in nature that shows a pattern and goes back."

"Time-wise, you mean," said Raden, intrigued.

"Yeah. I have a paleontologist friend. He was telling us about the trees around here. A lot of them have exotic fruits and seeds; weird stuff. Kentucky coffee trees, with long twisted seed pods. Osage oranges. Ever see an Osage orange?" Raden smiled no. "Look like breadfruit. They mess up streets, walks. Look like they don't belong. Anyway, he said that things growing today that look out of place to us make sense when you think about what was walking around ten-thousand years ago. Mammoths, mastodons, big mammals. That's what they ate. The trees evolved seeds with the animals around. Each influenced the other. Animals get a meal, disperse the seeds, everyone's happy. They're gone now, but the plants remain. She was really interested. After hearing that, those things started making their way into her work. Critics got all worked up interpreting it. None of them got it. She likes things about time. Things that linger."

"That's interesting. Makes you wonder what it was like back then." They continued walking. "There's a sign down the street, if I remember. Something about a song."

"Now I'm impressed. You'll see it." They passed the Princeton Theological Seminary and soon stood before a modest dwelling, a Greek Revival with white posts and the number 112.

Raden gazed on it. "He was quite a character, I heard."

"Oh yeah. In 1919, astronomers verified part of his General Theory of Relativity. During a solar eclipse, they photographed stars behind the sun whose light had been bent by the sun's gravity. When he found out, he said he knew the theory was correct. And when they asked him what would have happened if the observations had contradicted the theory, he said, 'Then I would have been sorry for the dear Lord. The theory is correct.' " Raden laughed.

"I wonder about his life here," Kevin mused. "With the war and gas rationing, you couldn't drive much. There were fewer cars. You could probably hear yourself think. Look at it now. It reminds me of those historical markers they put on streets. You can only read them when you're stuck in traffic. If you're driving, you miss them. The only time you really get the chance to appreciate this house is doing this—walking past it. Not many people do that anymore. It's like a language that dies out. One day, people just stop speaking it." He thought what it would have been like to have met the great scientist, whose life had not overlapped with his own. The every day walk past 112 Mercer wasn't force of habit. It was reverie.

Kevin sighed. "Go figure. All this talk about things that go bang, I guess they really do end with a whimper."

"Something like that." The two men continued down the walk.

Ten

Jessica Enright leaned on the open front door of the MSNBC van, her leg propped up. Though her phone conversation faced in, passers-by had no trouble hearing it.

"I don't care what my source said. It was a waste of time—"

"You saw the feed. His girlfriend threw the fit, not him—"

"I spent the whole morning tracking him down and got nothing. He's not worth it—"

"I'm telling you, I don't care who the source is. A whole morning and all I got was 'no comment'—"

"Fine—"

"Well, you run with the footage then." She hung up and told the crew to get in the van.

Jim Leffert pulled away. Cliff Abreau asked, "What do you want to do?"

"Head back." Jim turned the van towards Route 1 and New York. As he drove Enright fidgeted with the phone.

Abreau leaned up from the rear seat. "What?"

"I don't know," she replied. "Something."

The modest marker read, "Here in the year 1859, Karl Langlotz composed the music for *Old Nassau*, the prize song of Harlan Page Peck '62. May it be sacred to the Sons of Princeton Forever." John Raden beamed. "Heh, it's still here. I love snippets of history like this, even if I never heard of Karl Langlotz or Harlan Page Peck '62. I gotta admit I've heard *Old Nassau*. I'm just glad there are still places where you can see things like this, and enough people that care so you can."

Kevin listened intently. He was tired, he had a headache, and aside from a stale pizza crust he hadn't eaten and was still trying to gauge where things were headed, but amidst the roller-coaster ride he had an unexpected realization: he was enjoying talking with John Raden. "Oppenheimer's house is on the next block." He motioned in the general direction. "He's the only director anyone ever heard of. Then again, most people never even heard of the Institute."

"That's a shame. Why do you think that's so?"

"I'm not sure. Most people there would be perfectly happy to be left alone to work. It's more this state. New Jersey's nice, but I'm still trying to get a handle on it. A lot slips under the radar. It's the richest state, but the most middle class. It's the most crowded, but no city's got more than a quarter-million people. It's like a study in contrasts where you can't square one side with the other. As if mixed feelings are a state trait. The Midwest's got stoicism; New England's got stubbornness. I know. I've lived in both. Here it's ambivalence. Ever see the end of that movie where Robert Redford is elected senator and wonders what to do next?"

As Raden nodded, Kevin said, "Kinda like that here. You work hard, get to be number one, and don't know what to do with it. Princeton University is ranked top in the nation, but you'd never know it living here. The Giants and the Jets have been here since the '70s, but they're still called the New *York* Giants, the New *York* Jets. Try that anywhere else, they'd laugh in your face. Here, they just shrug. I don't get it. One guy wrote a paper saying that they should combine the team's names. He suggested taking the New from New York and the Jersey from New Jersey—" Raden laughed. "Of course it went nowhere. And that's all there was. They have this radio station that advertises, "*Not* New York, *Not* Philadelphia. Our *own* radio station." Can you imagine a New York station saying "*Not* Connecticut, *Not* New Jersey. Our *own* radio station?" It's the same with the Institute. One of the world's leading think tanks in a town with a world class university in the richest state in the nation and most people don't even know it's here, what it is, what it does, let alone care. You'd think they'd promote it, but no. It's just kind of there, hiding in plain sight. It's as if half the time they need to remind the country they're not second class and the other half to stop telling themselves they are. But go figure; I still like it here. So did Einstein."

"And here you are," Raden said, eyeing Kevin.

J. Robert Oppenheimer's house was at the end of a sinuous driveway. "He was director almost twenty years," Kevin said, nodding at the house. "It was just after the war and Einstein was here, so I guess he felt sort of at home. But he got caught up—"

"I'm familiar with it. He had his security clearance stripped in the '50s."

"Yeah. It was front page news. Think about it—the guy who runs the atom bomb program for the government gets told publicly that they don't trust him anymore. It had its effect. You learn his history, you see the house and you can't help but think it was built just for him, especially after seeing where Einstein lived." He paused. "I have to admit, you're not what I expected for a Hanford honcho. To people like them, history began the year they were born."

Raden laughed. After a few moments he asked, "So, what do you know about the thing?"

"Funny how it's called the *thing*. During World War II people didn't want to call the bomb the *bomb*. They called it the *gadget*. And this; it's the *thing*." Kevin pointed to a nearby tree. Suspended from a branch like a gun-metal beach ball was a large hornet nest. "You see *that* thing? Let me tell you a story. This one's true. I had recently moved here. I'm walking through the university. I was working through a problem and walking helps me focus. It had to do with galactic clusters. Know what they are?"

"Large assemblages of galaxies."

"That's right." He glanced at Raden. "Some things in physics are straightforward. Anyway, it was eating at me. So I'm walking, it's spring-time, breezy, and I hear this flittering sound. I turn and I see this wrapper from a Milky Way bar scooting down the pavement."

"Wasn't Snickers or Three Musketeers?"

"Nope," Kevin laughed. "Milky Way. Try to get the number on that and they'd laugh in your face. But it happened. Every scientist has a story like that." He motioned to the nest. "You know how long that thing's been there? At least three years. So you ask me what I know about the *thing* at the moment we're approaching a hornet nest, well, you tell me what to say."

"Remind me to tell you what they think of irony out in the Pacific. You may think you were minding your own business until now but good or bad, things get noticed. I'm surprised it's taken this long. The work has, but the person behind it lagged a bit. History's full of people who make a difference but escape notice. I mentioned John F. Kennedy before. Ever hear of a guy named William Greer?"

Kevin shook his head no.

"He was the Secret Service agent driving Kennedy's limo when he was shot in Dallas in 1963. Right after the second shot, instead of flooring it he turned around to see what was going on. It gave Oswald just enough time to line up the fatal shot. It wasn't Greer's fault, but he couldn't have timed it better if he tried. Yet he slipped under the radar of history. I think that up until now, you've had kind of the same thing go on. No one bothered you, and you were able to get some good work done. And maybe it was easier in a place where hiding in plain sight is the water. But it wasn't going to go on like that forever."

Kevin stopped, shaking his head.

"When the Russians built their bomb," Raden added, "it was going to happen regardless how much spying Klaus Fuchs did. Or anyone else for that matter. Edward Teller said the same thing after he thought up the H-bomb. It was physics. Sooner or later, someone was going to come up with clean fusion detonations. It just happened to be you."

"But that's what they were trying to do. That's not what I worked on. I didn't plan it."

"And so? Life's full of unintended consequences; especially in science. Teflon, Post-it-notes. Penicillin."

They continued down Olden Lane, coats slung over their shoulders like two fraternity buddies. Off to the right, at the end of a long stretch of grass, there was a solitary redbrick structure with a white tower.

"Is that the Institute?" Raden asked.

"Yeah. It's a nice walk. Einstein walked it all the time." He smiled. "It's not like we do everything he did. I do drive it. But there's a stretch in spring and fall when it's great." He rubbed his eyes. "I really need to get home and get some sleep."

"Come on. We'll head back."

Eleven

After a pause, Raden said, "Earlier, I asked what bothered you about this. You know during the '50s, these things were big-ticket items. People knew they were radioactive, that they could be raining down on them any minute. Didn't matter. They had to watch. Whenever they tested, they lined up. Now, they don't have to worry about radiation."

"Listen," Kevin waved his hand, "I'll admit you're not what I expected. You know your stuff. I appreciate that. But I don't care if they're clean. It just rubs me the wrong way."

Raden nodded. "I recall an arch up ahead."

"Yeah, there's an arch. Good memory."

"Talk about arches; you ever been to Rome?"

"About fifteen years ago."

"See the Coliseum?" Kevin nodded. Raden added, "Pretty impressive, isn't it?"

"Yeah, I guess so." He was getting frustrated. "What's the point?"

"This. Two thousand years and what's survived? A few arches, temples, some columns and this huge circular structure. Know why it lasted so long? Because it started out so much bigger than the rest. Societies erect structures proportional to their value. During the Middle Ages, churches and cathedrals towered over everything because of the meaning God had then. Today, it's office buildings. God's taken a back seat to commerce. Two thousand years ago God, well, Gods were important as well but right up there was entertainment. Like today. If we go the way of the Romans, two-thousand years from now, what do you think will be left? Provided no one knocks them down, the Sears Tower and the Rose Bowl. Remember why people went to the Coliseum?"

"Yeah. Chariot races, sword fights, things like that. I saw *Gladiator*."

"Of course. *Ben Hur*. History's gotta be a movie to be real." Kevin smiled and Raden added, "What else? Come on, you know, blood and gore and guts and veins in my teeth. Just like today, though we like to think we're more civilized. Back then, you could fill the Coliseum with thousands of people who came to see things we'd consider barbaric, but they found it entertaining. Not only the Romans. Think about what the Mayans and Aztecs were doing. People need that, especially when times are bad."

"Oh, come on," Kevin protested. "This is different."

"It's only different because it comes from your work." He paused. "Okay, think about this. Throughout history, societies have held matches with opposing teams. People had fun watching their locals beat up the visitors. That's been going on since history began."

"That's not what I'm talking about." The men reached a road and turned right.

"I know. And that's one category of entertainment. But there's another. When Rome ruled the world, yes, people watched slaves get ripped up by lions, and yes, it was barbaric. But it had a certain rationale. It's what their values allowed, but it was also what the technology allowed. They had their chariot races and their sword fights, but the rest was left to wild animals because they hadn't progressed much past the wheel. During the Middle Ages, you had jousting, matching strength and deftness, knowing your horse and balancing those qualities in a way that kept you from having your insides gored out. But they had little else as well. It's only recently that technology started growing exponentially, and what happened? Entertainment grew with it. That's why instead of guys on horses with lances seeing how close they can get without getting clipped, we have guys in jets at air shows seeing how close *they* can get without getting clipped."

"Fine. None of that has anything to do with what I'm being dragged into."

"Actually it does. Let me ask you a simple question. Why do you think it's so popular?"

"Because people are stupid."

Raden laughed lightly. "Maybe so, but they like what they like."

"Listen," Kevin groaned, "my head's spinning from all of this."

"Okay, but there's a little more you need to hear. Have you ever *been* to an air show?"

"A couple."

"Ever been to one where a plane crashed?"

Kevin stared. "That's not the same thing."

"Well, actually it is. You like to drive fast?"

"What's that got to do with it?" He was now flustered.

"Ever get a ticket?"

"Yeah," he grunted.

"Didn't stop you from driving fast, did it? But you didn't take up NASCAR."

"So what?" he huffed.

"That air show; you got a thrill watching it, but you didn't take up flying afterwards, did you?"

"No!"

"That's why people like watching bombs going off." Kevin waved him off, but Raden added, "You don't have to like it, but it is what it is. It's why people take their kids to fireworks on July fourth. It's why building implosions are headline news. People like controlled excitement. They don't have to worry about getting hurt. Controlled explosions are fun. People like watching things blow up, the bigger the better. Think how you scientists sat with your mouths watering when those comets hit Jupiter." Kevin groaned in response.

They now turned onto College Road, another entrance to the University. The narrow road with its expertly manicured shrubs and trees but no sidewalks to encourage pedestrians could be dismissed as an afterthought were it not for the massive stone arch guarding it. It always made Kevin think of London Bridge in Arizona, a wholly incongruous relic that someone must have regarded with some affection. Christened the Luther P. Eisenhart Gateway, it was the type of structure that would sorely stick out were it to be found anywhere else, but in this neighborhood it oddly fit in.

"Remember when the Nazis entered Paris in World War II?" Raden gestured.

"Funny."

"I'll be honest with you. When I first read your work, I didn't see this thing coming. But I should have. Stranger things have happened. When they confirmed part of your theory with that first detonation a few years ago, I had a feeling something was going on. In a way, it was predictable. I think the things that scare us, we avoid. The things that terrify us we surround with seats and charge admission to see."

They entered the university in silence, Kevin mindful of the frown he was holding back while Raden was just as focused on the bug relaying their conversation to ears unknown.

Twelve

They walked on. Raden was content to await a response. He could tell Kevin was frustrated, but he was opening up. Raden needed to build a little more trust before letting the other shoe drop. He had been expansive without discussing anything sensitive. He had an idea as to who was listening but didn't want to tip his hand. Someone had presumed that he would never catch on, a critical mistake. It gave Raden time to keep surreptitious watch on their surroundings.

As for Kevin, he was letting things sink in. When they passed a trash can sporting a Hanford-Stephanson sticker, he motioned at it. "So, what's he like?"

"Hanford? This morning was the first time I ever met him."

"Really? I thought you went way back." He laughed. "I've met him twice. That means I know him twice as well as you do." As Raden smiled, Kevin grew serious. "Going with my gut, I don't trust him. He expects me to grab my ankles and be an Oppenheimer. Forget it."

"No one expects you to be an Oppenheimer. But there's no one else with the name recognition and the knowledge." He paused. "Listen, for someone who spends so much time figuring out how the universe works, you need to spend some learning how the world works. You think this is a philosophical discussion but it's reality, a lot more real than some things you physicists study. You need to understand how things are done in Washington, and everywhere else for that matter. And you need to think about what you should do. There are people who won't let you avoid that decision."

"Are you threatening me?" Kevin felt his defenses rise.

"Not at all. I'm trying to help you by telling you that you have choices. But elemental to that reality is that sooner or later, you will have to choose."

"Oh, come on. Is that how you guys talk in real life? You don't get it—I don't want to deal with this. Now just go back there and tell them." He was exasperated.

"There's something you need to hear." Raden looked squarely at Kevin. "It's about to make headlines. Remember the talk about the Romans? There's another reason they built the Coliseum. There's another reason we have competitions and professional sports teams, though you'd never get anyone to admit it back then or now."

"And what's that?"

"It blows off steam for the masses." Kevin huffed in disgust. "Again, you don't have to like it but it is what it is. Even two thousand years ago, they knew that letting people watch things inside the stadium would keep some of them from doing those same things outside."

"And today?"

"Pretty much the same. We all have primal energies. Part of controlled excitement and sports is channeling some of that into a form that society can live with. It's respectable. People compete, follow rules, learn to work with others. All those things that looked good on report cards. Builds character. A lot of positive has come out of that one negative."

"Fine. What's that got to do with the *thing?*"

"We've compiled data on terror-related events for years now. It didn't stop because we got Bin Laden. Since the program began, we've seen a trend. International incidents have dropped twenty-three percent. And regional crime is down nineteen percent. And it's spreading. We're projecting a drop of thirty-six percent in bombings and other events worldwide over the next two years, and more after that. That's significant. Intelligence can't explain it other than to say people coming to see these things go home and aren't doing the things they used to."

"Well that's fine," Kevin said. "And what happens if Al Qaeda finally manages to sneak in a bomb? What if they take out Seattle? What happens then to your little tourist trap?"

"People'll get hot and bothered and a year later the hotels will be full again."

Kevin waved him off. "Stop being so damn glib."

"The difference between being glib and being realistic is a week of sound bites on cable. People are who they are. You know what they'd do if it did happen? They'd watch. Until people decide watching these things is repugnant they'll keep watching, the same way they still go to air shows and watched *24* after 9/11. You know what people did during World War II for entertainment? They went to see John Wayne in war movies. It happens with every war. It's time you started smelling that coffee you drink so much of."

The men had reached a green between buildings, near Nassau Street.

Kevin said, "So let me get this straight. This entire thing is on me. The future of terrorism, crime in the Pacific. What else? Re-election of the president of the United States? Is that all?"

"No. Would things be easier for him if you got on board? Sure. But in the end, you have to do what's best for you." He took out an envelope. "You look like you could use a few days off. There's an event this Thursday evening. I'd like you to fly out and see it."

"Are you *kidding?*" Kevin stood stunned.

"No. All this talk and you've never seen one. You need to see what we're discussing. You've seen them on TV, but it's nothing like seeing it live. Go out to the South Pacific for a week. Get drunk, get laid. Get a tan. They've got a hell of a resort there. I'll show you the ropes. It'll give you a better idea what to do. I will say this, whatever you decide, it will leave an impression. You don't want to get on the plane, that's fine as well. I can't force you."

Kevin stared at the ticket. He couldn't think of a reason not to go, but wasn't able to say that yet. Raden held it up. Kevin took a deep breath, and then took it.

"Good," Raden smiled. "Then I'll see you there Thursday."

Before Kevin could reply, Raden shifted, quickly looking around. He knew instinctively that he had a window for what he was about to do but that it could close at any moment. He grabbed Kevin's coat, removed the bug, clenched his fist around it and tucked it under his arm.

Kevin stood for a moment in shock. "What the hell was that?" he snapped.

"Okay," Raden spoke, now with urgency, "here's the deal. We don't have much time."

"What the hell was that?" Kevin repeated.

"Someone planted a bug on you. I noticed it at the coffee shop." Kevin's mouth dropped open. "Listen, we don't have much time. Bad news first."

"Whoa! Hold it! Are you shitting me? What the hell do you mean?"

"Just calm down—"

"You calm down! I don't need this crap!"

"Dr. Herter, I'm serious. Take a deep breath."

"And I'm serious! Last night I got pulled over by the state police *twice*. The second time I was told they had no record of the first stop. Don't tell me I need to calm down!"

"I didn't know, but I'm not surprised. Now hear me out. Everything we discussed is legit, and for now, forget it. Other things are happening.

You can pretend they're not or you can get real and deal with it. I can help you, but you need to listen. Like it or not you've been drafted."

Though ready to bolt, Kevin caught himself. "If you're in on this you might as well tell me now, because if I find out—wait, if you were, you wouldn't have told me—my head is spinning."

"I might have told you," Raden said calmly, "but no, I'm not involved. For now, just call me a softie for hard luck cases. I'm here because the president wants you as the high-profile face of the program. Ostensibly. The program head needs you to solve some kind of technical issue. They say it's not serious but want it dealt with quickly. Then they trumpet those terror figures."

"Oh, for Christ's sakes. Why do that?"

"What do you think it would mean to a president if he could find a way to suppress terrorism worldwide by a third in two years? And during an election year? The man's got religion. He thinks it's once in a lifetime where mankind gets a chance to curb its violent streak. Until now, the program was all recreation and money, but this is about to become the rationale for the thing. This is legacy material. And, they're looking to expand it."

"I don't believe what I'm hearing," Kevin said, dumbfounded.

"There are bids from half-a-dozen Pacific nations, and Hawaii. Now what do you want to do? You've had strong opinions on this from the start, ones you've kept to yourself. The result is you've been followed and bugged. You can't sit on your hands any more."

"And what does that mean? You tell me to relax, then you hit me with this. And right after I agree to go out there. Soften the guy up then whack him?"

"I'm sorry. I had to get you to think about its merits. But you'd only appreciate them hearing it from the start. And frankly, I needed time. You want to learn who's behind this and what they're up to? You have to get involved. There's no other way."

Kevin was at a loss for words. The enormity of his predicament was sinking in. "Okay," he said, rubbing his face, "what are you suggesting?"

Raden looked about. It was still clear. "We can't talk now. You have to go on a leap of faith. Nothing's occurring by accident. First, you need to see one of these things. You fly out in the morning with a layover in San Francisco. The flight to Tuvalu leaves tomorrow night. It puts you there Thursday. Time there is a day ahead. The event is that evening. There'll be people to help you along the way, but a big part of this will be you learning to trust your intuition."

"Okay." Kevin looked at the ticket. "I can't believe I'm doing this. And why San Francisco?"

"I thought you might want to spend a little time with Max Rosenkranz first."

Kevin paused. "Hanford doesn't know you're doing this, does he?" As Raden shrugged, Kevin asked, "What's your angle? It's not just God and Country."

"Nothing like that," Raden smiled. "I'm just doing what I need to do."

"That's another one I'll have to take on faith. So, what did they learn over the past hour?"

"Time will tell. I think they wanted to know your thoughts. And mine. I talked a lot without saying too much. They need to think you're interested, and then they'll plan accordingly. What they don't know is that we know, and right now, that's the only thing we've got going for us."

"Who's behind this?"

"I'm not sure yet. Now, I'm going to be blatantly honest. The reason they've given you to come on board is valid, but it's not the real one. Something else is going on."

"And what's that?"

"You know someone wants you in. Be smart enough to realize that others don't. Now understand something—I was brought in for a reason too. We all have our talents. They expect me to soft-sell you. You being involved keeps plausible deniability for them. But remember, adversaries define struggles by how they quantify them. Someone upped the ante, for both of us. I've been doing this for some time now. This is the first time anyone's eavesdropped on *me*, and I'd know. Appreciate how they think. They'd expect this to insult my intelligence. Actually, it doesn't. But it does insult my sensibilities. For that, I'll go out on a limb."

"And what does that mean?"

"The Administration's making an announcement on Sunday, that grand vision I told you about. The idea was that by then you'd have figured out on your own what was happening."

Kevin felt his heart pick up. "And what's that?"

"That they're covering. For what exactly, we still have to figure out. We don't have much time."

"What could be so wrong they have to drag me in to cover for it?"

Raden took a deep breath. "I was interested in this long before I was called in. I had hunches and began to look into them. It's what I do. It opened me up to hearing certain things." Kevin still looked perplexed.

"Understand, little of consequence in circles of power is on the surface. Most things occur behind the scenes; leaking, muddying the waters. That's the beauty of what they're doing. It's the perfect cover. It does have merit. By the time Sunday came around, whatever you learned wasn't supposed to matter. You'd be so taken with what they're doing that you couldn't be against it. You want to be the only voice arguing against world peace, even if it comes from setting off clean H-bombs? And being it's from your work, they'll accuse you of being more concerned with your ego than bettering mankind. You're about to be set up."

"Why?" Kevin stepped back. "What the hell's going on?"

"There's more going on with the devices than they're admitting. And the policy. They didn't insult my intelligence telling me up front. They let it slip as an aside. They knew I'd see it and I wouldn't tell you." He smiled. "Some people just aren't the best judge of character."

A gleam came to Raden. "Why do you think rules and ruling class come from the same word? The playing field's different for you and me. Play ball with them, fix their little problem, you're a hero. Hanford gets his Coliseum. But it also gets him off the hook for something. They'll never let on why they want you, but it's gotta be mighty important to come up with something this elaborate. You don't play ball, you're screwed. Which means between now and Sunday, you're going to find yourself with a dilemma the likes of which you can't imagine."

Stunned, Kevin tried to soak in everything he was hearing. "I really don't need this."

"No, but I need you. They need your help working the cover-up. I need your help figuring it out. Someone's hiding something. You're gonna help me learn what it is and why."

"Me?"

"Yeah, you. We're going to work it together, you and me."

"Just like that?"

"Just like that. It involves you, and you're going to help me. I have sources that are as high as things go, but they haven't let on what it is. They have their reasons, but they seem as intent on bringing you in as Hanford. I think they need you onboard before he has time to close the deal. It's going to be a race to see who can get to you first. This is going to unfold very fast. By Sunday, if we haven't found out, it's going to be too late. It's got to be something that has to do with you, with what you do as a physicist. You know something, something you may not even be aware of yet. But by Sunday, you will, if you can keep it together being a pawn that long."

"You're making it real easy not to get on that plane," Kevin said, looking ashen.

"I know. But it'll be harder for you if you don't. A lot of interests have a great deal riding on you doing one or the other. You need to play it out."

Kevin froze. "One of those whackos I mentioned earlier tapped my shoulder. Son of a bitch." He took a deep breath. "Okay ... okay. I'll go." He took the ticket.

"All right. I wrote a briefing for you about the program. I'll have it at the airport. Now I won't lie to you. You have to go into this with a clear head. It might get ugly."

"What does that mean?"

"I don't know. I don't know what I don't know. You just need to be prepared for anything."

"Great. I can't believe I'm doing this. All right. What time is my flight tomorrow?"

"Seven a.m."

"Ouch."

Raden laughed. "It arrives at ten a.m. It gives you most of the day with Max and Jean. If you want, I can have you picked up this afternoon and put up at the airport hotel, say five?"

"Yeah, maybe." He nodded. "Yeah, I'll do that. Thanks." Raden extended his hand, and Kevin shook in kind. "Well, it's been—interesting, to say the least."

"Dr. Herter, it's been a pleasure. You have a few hours. Go get some rest. Set your alarm."

"You don't want to go there. Before you go—really, who's behind all this?"

"I think it's better I hold off for now. By the time you get back, I'm sure we'll know. Just play it out. Well, Dr. Herter, again it's been a pleasure."

"Thanks. Just call me Kevin."

"I'll see you Thursday," Raden smiled. "Enjoy your time with Max and Jean. I know they're important to you. And if you don't get on the plane, so be it. You should, but I can't control that. You do what you have to. In the meantime, don't be paranoid. But keep your guard up."

"That's easier said than done, but thanks."

"You may appreciate this. My wife collects pottery. She has one of Jean's pieces. It's a vase. It comes in on itself. I'm not describing it well. It's very elegant."

"I'll tell her. I'm sure she'll appreciate that. Where do you go from here?"

"Back to the hotel to relax. I'm heading into the city later. My son is following in his old man's footsteps—he's a broker on Wall Street. Personally, I think he could aim higher. We're having dinner tonight. Back to Washington in the morning, then I head out."

"Well, enjoy yourself."

"Thanks. I'll see you Thursday. Now, I need you to think about something. I left things out of the briefing. Things in the shadows. For one, why the urgency now? And, you know the Pentagon wants you in. You curious about why they haven't added these things to their arsenal?"

Kevin shrugged. "I heard they ran into problems."

"That's right. They were never able to make it work. But why? In the process, they realized people liked watching the things go off. I know what you think of that, but what would you have said had they actually weaponized the thing?" Kevin's eyes widened. "Okay," Raden added, "you get it. I need you to start thinking like that. Outside the box."

"Are you saying that's what they want me for?"

"I'm not saying anything. I want you to begin thinking differently. Creatively."

"Wow," Kevin groaned. "You don't make it easy."

"No, I don't."

"Okay. That's enough for now. I'm going home and starting on a really serious hangover."

"Well, then, I'll add to it. It's the most important thing to keep in mind. Hanford's one of the best at reading people. Knowing why people do what they do and getting them to do it is power. They're expecting something from you. Know what it is?"

Kevin shook his head no.

"For you to be you. They know you. When you're unsettled, you tend to sit with things, stuck. Like most people. He's counting on it. It buys him time till Sunday. You stick to form and you don't have time to figure out what's going on. He wants you on edge. It's like the resort. It's what the times call for. Ambivalence incarnate. People are simultaneously scared and awed. So what do they do? Sit and watch. That's why you need to be aware of it and fight it. Why do you think they came to you precisely now? A month ago would have been too soon; next week too late. Okay. I'll see you in a few days. Kevin, have a good flight."

Kevin stood with his mouth half open, then recovered and said goodbye. Just before leaving, he pointed to the bug Raden had taken from his armpit and now held in his hand. "What are you going to do with that?" he asked.

Raden placed it back on Kevin's coat and with his hand still over it said, "Have this cleaned."

With a wry chuckle Kevin put his coat back on and the men parted.

Thirteen

The noontime rush was in full swing when Sharon returned to the Princeton Tea Room after slipping out to clear her head. She sidestepped the counter, gathered some receipts from the office and exited.

Ten minutes later, a dazed Kevin stood in the entrance of the coffee shop. He had walked in, unsure about why he'd come, clutching an airline ticket he wasn't sure he would use, knowing something important had just happened though he didn't know exactly what. The notion that everything he'd said over the past few hours had been listened to still had him unsettled. On his way back to his place, he'd been about to pass by, but felt himself being drawn in. He went past the line of people waiting to place their orders to the counter and caught Laura's eye. When she told him Sharon had stepped out, he decided to wait for her in the office.

Lumbering about, he looked around the familiar place that somehow felt different. The TV was tuned to MSNBC.

Sharon returned just in time to catch him intently peeling off a freshly-dried coat of Elmer's Glue from his palm. "Will you stop that!" she snapped. "God, I *hate* when you do that."

He frowned and muted the TV. "Where'd you go?" he asked, trying to be friendly.

"The bank." She felt her edge returning. "What are you doing here?"

"I was heading home. I wanted to see how you were."

"I'm fine. I went home for a while." As she filed the bank receipt, she added impatiently, "You look funny. What happened? What did he want?"

Kevin rubbed off a few remaining shreds of glue. He remembered the bug, but he surprised himself by not caring about what he would say. "He's an interesting guy," he answered. "The rest—I don't even know where to begin."

"At this point, you can tell me. It doesn't matter anymore."

Kevin paused. "They want me to run it."

She broke into an anxious laugh. "It doesn't surprise me. Naturally, you said yes." She threw down her bag and began sorting through some papers.

"Thanks. Actually, I said no. Sharon, I have to play this thing out, okay? And there's something else."

"Fine. It doesn't matter," she said, stuffing papers into the file cabinet near the desk. One page ran across her finger. She jerked her hand out. "Fuck!" she yelled, looking at a thin line of blood swelling from the paper cut.

"I felt that," Kevin said. "You okay?"

"Kevin," she snapped past the bloody finger in her mouth, "I don't have time for this anymore. If you said no you wouldn't be here. What do you want?"

"I—" He was about to answer when he glanced at the TV. The muted report from Jessica Enright panned to a tussle on a familiar-looking sidewalk. Amidst the blurry footage were a few clear seconds of Sharon Velazquez shouting out, then scuffling with Enright and her crew.

"What?" Sharon asked. She eyed Kevin, then the TV, which had gone to commercial. He buried his head in his hand and rubbed his face, shaking his head in feigned indifference, even as he felt his innards racing to his throat. He was at a complete loss for words.

"So?" Sharon prodded.

He stumbled. "He asked and I told him no—"

"But that's not it, is it."

"He wants me to fly out to the Pacific to see one of the things."

Sharon's rage was complete, with nowhere to go. "And of course you're going," she seethed. "You need me to decide for you? Give you permission? That all the balls you have left?"

"Oh, enough already. I came to tell you that before I make any kind of decision, I'm flying to San Francisco tomorrow to see Max."

"Fine. Maybe he can talk some sense into you. Or he can hold your hand while you see how far you want to bend over and grab your ankles!"

"Dammit, that's enough! You just decided for me!" Kevin broke for the door, fleeing the place that had long been a haven but that now had the feel of a courtroom, and heading to a house that had lost the feel of a home. Sharon continued to nurse her cut, stinging from tears that had nothing to do with her injury.

Tuesday, April 5

Fourteen

The night view of Diamond Head from the eighth-floor condo on Kalakaua Avenue was stunning. Lights danced off the water while a breeze teased with the scent of hibiscus. It might as well have been a basement flat for all the time Lisa Whiteman took to enjoy it.

Although it was one a.m., it was just another workday for the thirty-eight year old physicist. She sat as usual in sweats, attended by the glare of a computer. There were figures to view and emails to dispose of while she awaited Glen Daniels' arrival on-line. Instant messaging was her preferred form of contact with her assistant in New Mexico, who was as much an early-bird as she was a night-owl. Their overlapping lifestyles suited both of them just fine.

While waiting she thought she heard something above the background whir. At last glance, her husband was asleep in front of the living room TV. Impelled by her anxiety, which had been growing of late, she tiptoed toward the door, past the bed still made from that morning.

Although the TV was on, Tom wasn't on the couch. She thought she could hear him on the balcony. Concerned with the off-chance he might come back in and catch a word or phrase across her computer screen, she eased the door closed, then angled the laptop to the window. With the door closed, the cross breeze died and with it the fragrance on the night.

As project head of the government's thermonuclear resort program, Lisa had met Major Tom Whiteman at the beginning. She had immediately been pursued by the reserved and determined security coordinator for the program, who'd set his sights on the shapely blond with the alluring green eyes. To the surprise of her friends, they'd married within a year. Serious, matter-of-fact, and in Lisa's view not the greatest communicator, she had once described him as the kind of man who could sit at a meeting for a half-an-hour before anyone knew he was there. Though dealing mostly with physicists and bureaucrats, his chain of command extended to the Pentagon.

Three months earlier, Lisa had transferred to Hawaii from Sandia National Laboratories in Albuquerque to oversee the next stage of the program. Sandia was a division of the US Department of Energy (DOE), and was the government's main nuclear weapons laboratory.

The move capped what was regarded as a singular accomplishment. In an era of ballooning deficits and maligned bureaucracies she had taken a conception mired in controversy and had it poised on new heights. The program had become Exhibit A for those who argued government could run efficiently, and could even turn a profit. She juggled roles effortlessly; physicist, politician, diplomat, academician, administrator. And wife. At the beginning, she had run the program without drawing much attention to herself, as she preferred. It was easy. As with many new things, you could make it up as you went along. It was natural to think things would continue to work out, and as far as her staff knew, they had for some time.

Lisa engendered considerable respect at Sandia, and not a little fear. A consummate control freak renowned for shepherding bothersome and unrelated matters, she was a stern taskmaster. She could admonish an underling with a simple inflection or raised eyebrow. However, most of them tolerated it because it wasn't malicious. They knew it was just Lisa being Lisa. They knew how devoted she was to her work. And she didn't go for the jugular; she got her point across and moved on. Eccentricities aside, she was an excellent physicist. Her talent lay in a specific realm. The Kevin Herters of the world were the ones to delve into the deepest reaches for the most pioneering, creative work. It would be the Lisa Whitemans who applied what they found. And the science needed them both.

Now, as she stared at the screen, there was much to weigh. She was too disciplined to descend into a morass. But it was hard to ignore just how badly things had gotten out of hand. While the program was part of the DOE it was administered jointly with the Department of Defense (DOD). One bureaucracy overlapping another meant both were subject to power games, as each maneuvered to gain the upper hand. Owing to Lisa's skill, the relationship was at first amicable. The DOE and DOD had well-delineated responsibilities. But success breeds jealousy. As it grew, so did the infighting. Lisa Whiteman's DOE sought control and funding for new sites. Tom Whiteman's DOD wanted the same. Each trying to best the other, and at the confluence the departmental heads were married to each other. If she allowed, the irony would engulf her. One more thing to control. Something else to handle.

Until now, the Administration was content to let her have her way, tolerating her control issues because she produced results. However, as the spoils grew, an increasing number of hands sought to get in on the take. Keeping the balls in the air was growing harder. And at the heart of it was something she alone knew, something she had manipulated from the start to insure no one found out. And with everything changing now, keeping that hidden until the right people learned it was proving the hardest thing of all.

Hi Lisa. It was 1:03 a.m. when the instant message flashed.

You're early, she began before jumping into matters in typical fashion. *I went over what you sent yesterday. When can I expect the revised figures?*

Lis, Glen Daniels replied, *I'm still home. I didn't want to discuss this at the lab.*

Okay. What's going on?

I got an email this morning from the Pentagon. They're pushing for the data. I wasn't sure how to answer it.

Lisa knew about the growing military presence in the Albuquerque offices. There had been a change in tone and solicitations coming from Washington. While she expected a request for the program's raw data, she had not received the formal query. She was shocked that it had gone to her assistant. *I anticipated that*, she recovered.

There was a pause. *I'm not sure you understand. They're looking for all the data, even the preliminary numbers, not just last week's. And there's something else. Normally, what I get is cc'd to you. This wasn't. And Lisa, it has a request not to share it with you.*

As Daniels awaited a response, his cell phone rang. "All right, Glen," Lisa began, opting to continue the conversation by phone. "What's going on there?" Hiding her apprehension, she hoped no one was listening.

"Lis, we're all creeped-out. The email's from the Secretary of Defense. It requests all program data be compiled and sent to his office."

"Fine." She wanted to raise her voice, but held back. "Just keep putting them off until the weekend. I know what they're doing. They have no authority over it. What else?"

"It's just different. Before, anytime the DOD came by, it was like a visit from the folks. You felt they wanted to tell you what to do, but they knew it was your house. This feels like a company that was bought out and the new owners barge in like they own the place."

"Okay," she said assuredly. No way she was letting on they were looking to hand her her hat. "I expected this. I'd heard, but I've been too busy to deal with it."

"We figured. But maybe we've been putting them off so long they decided to do an end run and move in."

"Well, it won't work. What they want isn't important anyway."

"We don't think so either, but what's the deal with preliminary figures? They've been fine with the revised ones—"

"Let me worry about it. Just hold them off."

"There's something else." He paused. "There's been a lot of buzz. Talk is that operations here are being transferred out."

"Glen," she whispered, "that won't happen. I don't answer to them."

"Okay. We're just not sure what to think. And, I'm not sure how to say it, but some of us are worried about, well ... about Tom. We know he's your husband but none of us are happy about military calling the shots."

"That won't happen. It's important to stay focused. Just hold them off until the weekend."

"Okay." He paused. "Does any of this have to do with bringing Kevin Herter on?"

"A lot. And if it happens, none of this will matter."

"Okay. I just can't see him involved if he knows Defense has the upper hand."

"Let me worry about that. If he's in, those other things take care of themselves. Your only worry is to find an excuse to stall them. Blame it on me; say I need to sign off on it."

"Well, I hope it works. What about Thursday? The Pentagon is sending out another monitoring team. They want to coordinate with the DOD liaison."

"I didn't hear about that," said Lisa irately, upset she didn't catch herself in time to hide her surprise. "Hold on." She went to the door. "Tom," she snapped in the dark. When he didn't answer she came back to the phone. "Let me run. I'll call. Just don't let them strong-arm you. Don't send anything out." She hung up.

Fifteen

Unlike his wife, Tom Whiteman had made time to take in the balcony view. Now, he had his back to it, cell phone closed, eyes furtively scanning inside. He'd unceremoniously hung up on his caller when he'd heard Lisa call him. After waiting out the tense silence, he called back.

"Okay," he muttered, "let's hear it."

"Sir," Captain Christian Deloy replied, "the subject left his house at oh two hundred. I made contact at approximately oh two forty."

"Why did you pull him over? Your orders were specific—conduct surveillance, make him think he was being tailed, and report back."

"Sir, my understanding was that operational parameters made allowances for targeted contact if the opportunity presented itself. I made a split-second decision that it did."

"Only at times of minimal risk. Pulling someone over on a federal interstate opened you up to blowing your cover, understand?" Whiteman spoke tersely. "Okay, explain."

"I followed the subject when he left his house. He'd been showing signs of increased stress. We thought he might be running. I was just to his rear when he swerved around something on the road. It presented a legitimate opportunity to pull him over. I had just passed a speed trap, and the patrol car didn't move. It was a judgment call."

"You were supposed to keep him on edge," Whiteman groaned, "not act overtly and give him something concrete to worry about. I want him feeling paranoid, not persecuted. Okay," he huffed, "what's done is done. You dodged a bullet. But don't take a risk like that again." He was still angry. "It better not fuck things up. How did he react?"

"I'm sorry sir." Deloy sounded less than contrite. "I didn't think that violated the directive. He reacted as would be expected."

"All right, you keep me updated." Whiteman ended the call. He then warily went back to the couch and began channel surfing.

Five minutes later Lisa came out of the bedroom. "I thought I heard you on the phone," she asked, determined not to let on about the conversation she had just finished.

"Uh huh," Whiteman grunted, not breaking his gaze from the TV.

"I got an email about the second team for Thursday. When were you going to tell—"

"I'll handle it."

Lisa frowned. "Yeah."

Still slumped into the couch, Tom Whiteman remained glued to the screen, the cell phone in his pocket pressed into the leather. She stood a moment, then bit her lip before disappearing. By the same time tomorrow, the phone would be on the bottom of nearby Mamala Bay. But he had one more call to make, and as he snuck back to the balcony he thought to himself how much he hated talking to Dillon Ridge.

Sixteen

United Airlines Flight 448 departed Newark Liberty Airport at 7:38 a.m. bound for San Francisco. The five-hour flight was expected to be smooth, an announcement Kevin paid particular attention to as flying had never been a favorite. Or so he told everyone. Deep down, he hated to fly. He knew why; not being in control, not trusting people he never met with his life. He knew the coping mechanisms. He recognized the irony—one of the most rational people on Earth yielding to unreason. No matter; he hated it, but he did it anyway.

This was his first flight on a Boeing 787 Dreamliner. So far it had lived up to its billing—quiet, comfortable, and with a soothing interior even Sharon would have liked. An hour aloft, he had yet to finish his second Bloody Mary. It made flying almost worth the bother. Or maybe it was just traveling first class. Six miles up and he even allowed himself a look out the window. For a moment, he ignored his anxiety and had a thought. Maybe Jack Raden had missed his true calling. The guy should have been a concierge.

Every step had been a carefully scripted success. The limo, the Airport Marriot suite, dinner. The charge at boarding who delivered the packet marked *Confidential* couldn't have been nicer. Even the flight had a feel of forethought. The seat beside him remained empty despite most others being filled.

If he could only relax. He never slept well before flying, and nodding off in the air would never happen. There was too much to sort out; mainly, who could be trusted. The answer was no one. He found himself looking behind, about, at everyone he met. Strangers looked different. Food looked different. And yesterday tugged like a lead weight. Hanford, Sharon, John Raden, the bomb, the bug, any one would have been a handful. Taken together, maybe clenching his arm rest at 35,000 feet was bearable. And it was going to be good to see Max and Jean.

He thought of Sharon. They had been growing apart. Now with an additional mile every ten seconds, the distance between them was never greater. He picked at his three-cheese omelet, then settled on a few slices of orange. It was enough to complement the buzz from the vodka.

As the plane hit a pocket of turbulence, Kevin clenched the arm rest, took a swig of Bloody Mary and reached for the packet. Inside a sealed folder addressed to him lay a map of the South Pacific with a full-color brochure that read DiFusion-The Ultimate Spectator Sport. It had the look of a typical resort pamphlet, but contained photos of scantily-clad people enraptured at the sight of an enormous mushroom cloud in the distance. Several technical reports were beneath the brochure. On top was a short note:

04/04

Kevin,

Hope you got some sleep and you're enjoying your flight. It was a pleasure meeting you yesterday.

I think you'll find this interesting. I sense there's a lot you've steered clear of over the past few years so I decided to include most of it and lay it out chronologically. Some you may already know but a lot will turn out to be new. You'll get an idea how things developed with the project, and where it currently stands. You may notice the speed with which this occurred. Compared to most things run by government, this was given a fast track.

There'll be a representative to collect the outline and technical portion of this report when you land. Enjoy your visit with the Rosenkranz's. I'll see you tomorrow. We have a lot to discuss and very little time.

Best,

Jack

There was a typewritten brief that ran to almost a dozen pages. He adjusted his seat back, finished off the Bloody Mary and began to read.

Seventeen

CONFIDENTIAL

A Brief History of *Operation Frontier* and the Development of the
Thermonuclear Resort Program in Tuvalu

Report prepared for Dr. Kevin Herter by Dr. John Raden

The entertainment and resort facilities in the South Pacific island nation
of Tuvalu have attracted global attention since opening twenty months
ago. The site is the world's first showcase for the recreational use of
thermonuclear detonations. This paper will outline the development of
the resort, provide an administrative overview and identify trends with
emphasis on integration of regional and international security concerns.

The site is an unanticipated outgrowth of Dr. Kevin Herter's landmark work in physics and cosmology. A paper in *Nature* four years ago
entitled "Spacial Distortion and Gravitational Displacement at Event
Horizons" proved noteworthy in this regard. It explored the extreme
effects of black holes on spacetime, described conditions approaching
and transiting the singularity of black holes and delved into interactions
of dark energy and gravity on the fabric of spacetime, theorized in-
ter-dimensional realms and correlations to the afterglow left from the
Big Bang.

The widely-read paper drew the attention of Department of Defense
(DOD) physicists. Soon after, the Pentagon commissioned a study by
Sandia National Laboratories, Sandia being the nation's main nuclear
weapon development and weapons technology research site. The lab
insures the stability of the nation's nuclear arsenal. Site physicists were
intrigued by the analysis of the fabric of space in extreme conditions,
though research proceeded without specific developmental goals.

Almost simultaneously in an unrelated development, Japanese physicists unveiled a process to create hitherto unrealized amounts of anti-

matter, and to store it indefinitely, unlike previous breakthroughs that allowed only fifteen minutes at most to study the substance. Labs worldwide now had first-time experimental access to the rare and exotic material.

Mindful of the Japanese breakthrough, Sandia physicists began evaluating antimatter as a possible trigger to induce thermonuclear detonations. Pure matter/antimatter explosions were deemed unfeasible due to the limited amounts the new process could create, but enough can now be produced to initiate detonation, insofar as the extreme pressures and temperatures that occur when matter and antimatter unite and annihilate each other could propagate nuclear fusion in conventional hydrogen fuel.

Formulations from Herter's paper applied to the trigger issue led to an unforeseen development. Projections indicated matter/antimatter blasts sequenced through Herter's findings would generate a complex detonation wave shunting off lethal gamma and other high-spectral emissions, resulting in an event expressed in infrared and visible light. This process is still not fully understood and remains an area of intense research and considerable skepticism. Nonetheless the plausibility of radioactive-free thermonuclear detonations was established. Advisements from Sandia officials were to proceed beyond computerized simulations.

Sandia's findings set off fierce debate on dual tracks in the Administration. One line related to whether the developmental process was practical, while the other concerned itself with the diplomatic, environmental, political and societal implications of the technology. Even testing clean devices was controversial, though adding fallout-free weapons to the nation's nuclear arsenal was deemed highly desirable. The Administration tasked the NSA to coordinate a study between the DOD with respect to weaponization and the Department of Energy (DOE) to testing.

The Joint Task Force presented its findings a month later. Indications were that an actualized expression of the technology would follow as predicted. The task force advocated further research and proposed an atmospheric test to evaluate the system and integrate it into the policy debate.

The following week, the Administration briefed Congressional leadership, broaching the possibility of a one-time test. As a consensus emerged that restricting information would prove futile, the president addressed the nation ten days later, revealing the existence of a technological breakthrough that could allow clean thermonuclear detonations.

The president also raised the discovery as a potential source of clean fusion energy, though this has lagged significantly behind the weapon component.

The Hanford address took on the tone of a homily. Following World War II, nuclear weapon use was deemed unworthy of serious consideration, the chief constraint being radiological consequences. Before Hiroshima the effect was underappreciated, but subsequently emerged as the most significant deterrent to their use, also seen in the Al Qaeda Baja California incident and the limited nuclear exchange four years ago in the Middle East. For decades, the threat was such that despite massive nuclear arsenals in the United States and former Soviet Union, neither nation wielded them. Treaties restricted testing, which in time was outlawed wholly. With radiation no longer consequential to detonations the threat of use increased. The United States would seek to forestall a new arms race, insuring that the first use of the new technology would be the last.

The address set off a firestorm equaling the 1983 Reagan Strategic Defense Initiative, known as Star Wars. Despite a small though vociferous opposition, Congress voted approval. Operationally designated Frontier, the test commenced under province of the DOE with extensive support from the DOD. Sensitive to environmental effects of a megaton-range blast, even a non-radiological one, an intensive effort was taken to secure a test site affording minimal impact. A remote swath of the North Pacific was selected.

On November 29, the United States announced a three-month withdrawal from the Limited Test-Ban Treaty, which prohibits nuclear tests in the atmosphere, outer space and under water, and the Threshold Test-Ban Treaty, which limits underground tests to yields of 150 kilotons. The test was set for the week of December 11, north of Hawaii. The exact target date and site were deemed Classified, owing to expected interference from Greenpeace and like groups.

Frontier detonated at 11:38 a.m. Hawaii-Aleutian Standard Time on December 17, seven hundred twenty miles northeast of the island of Laysan, eighteen months after the *Nature* paper. The test was conducted in clear conditions without incident and was extensively photographed in all spectral wavelengths. Major media outlets were allotted restricted live coverage.

Preliminary readings indicated a yield of 12.53 megatons, revised up to 12.89. The cloud reached a height of 127,000 feet, with maximum width of one hundred nine miles atop a stem of twenty-seven miles.

Extensive monitoring during and up to three weeks after detonation showed no gamma, X-ray or neutron emissions, confirming a radiological-clean detonation. The test was deemed an unqualified success, and the Administration tasked Sandia to continue research.

At this point an unanticipated consequence emerged. Developmental findings foreshadowed a technology unsuitable as a deliverable weapon. Frontier required a weighty and elaborate device not unlike a miniature atom smasher to detonate its thermonuclear core. The Pentagon held this would prove conclusive, unlike what had transpired with the original hydrogen bomb in 1952. The first thermonuclear device, code-named, Mike weighed 62 tons, a fusion experiment completely unusable as a weapon. However, much smaller designs deliverable by plane and missile soon emerged. Frontier was different. It was felt that practical weapon research would soon terminate.

Meanwhile, events accelerated in media and social networks. Test footage broadcast virtually nonstop created nostalgia for bomb-related memorabilia. Amid talk of a new arms race, of fighting terror through wholesale destruction sparing radiological effects, and expressions of anger at scientists dumping yet another mess into humanity's grasp before retreating into their test tubes, talk began of the human experience, the emotional response of watching a twelve-megaton explosion. It quickly moved to a desire to watch one again.

Kevin had to put the report down. The flight had three hours to go. He picked some more at his fruit, and ordered another Bloody Mary. Thirty minutes later, he had enough of a buzz to keep reading:

The program began as an afterthought, a series of measured phrases and dropped words on late night talk shows and blogs. But the underlying idea swiftly attained respectability, a trend noticed just as quickly by the White House, owing to the president's keen political ear. Within weeks of Frontier, the Administration began fielding queries from business, entertainment and international sources desiring to know whether other explosions were planned and how seats could be had. It was likened to politicians expressing interest in flying the space shuttle when the program began in 1981. Once broached, the floodgates opened. Much was made about how popular tests were in the '40s and '50s, when civilians and servicemen watched them.

A month after Frontier the Administration quietly commissioned a study. Coordinating data with potential sites as well as input from the tour, cruise and resort industries and intelligence services the study concluded that a pilot program was feasible. The Administration issued guidelines in early February, inviting bids to design and run a site integrating recreational use of clean thermonuclear detonations. It opened dialogue with the Pacific island nations regarded the best locations for the resort. Remote tropical settings were deemed ideal, from both administrative and security standpoints. Several nations tendered proposals touting logistical access, labor, facilities and efficacy integrating existing infrastructure into proposed construction; interestingly, these criteria were not unlike those adopted during the earlier testing phase in the 1950s. The irony has not been lost that the new bomb program has been located in the same region as the old. A prime consideration for those applying was fiscal, particularly relevant due to the issue of climate change. Most potential sites lie less than twenty feet above sea level. As they may vanish by century's end, theirs have been some of the loudest voices on the subject. They responded with well-considered proposals.

After review the primary site was awarded to Tuvalu. The resort is located on Vaitupu, largest of its nine islands and most suited to observe the events, which are optimally viewed at sunset. The site opened eighteen months ago. A second phase of construction ended last month. Named Tuvalu Alofa after a local word, it is colloquially known as Club Afterglow.

The program blends the amenities and ambiance of a four-star resort with the most dramatic visual experience on Earth. Guests enjoy the pampering and scenery that have made the region a draw for decades. Visits culminate in the explosions, which are essentially carefully managed and choreographed events. Where many resorts offer fireworks as send-offs, Tuvalu Alofa features the ultimate pyrotechnic display. Coordinators integrate factors including temperature, humidity, cloud cover, wind and other atmospheric and seasonal conditions into explosions to maximize the entertainment experience.

The explosions are harmonized with an extensive database of music. Surprisingly, New Age and Contemporary Jazz have proved most popular, with New Age heading the list. The ethereal quality of the genre lends itself to the awe felt while viewing the ascending cloud. Coordinators integrate every aspect of detonation into the musical and multimedia repertoire, from the fireball and its ascent to the shock wave, expansion and dispersion. The goal is to impart a feel of transcendence, which has resulted in numerous repeat visitors.

An especially popular facet of the event occurs at nightfall. The clouds reach the stratosphere within five minutes and further expand more slowly over the next several hours. This height allows them to pick up on the afterglow of the setting sun well after darkness sets in, a spectacular sight creating the resort's nickname. Detonations range between sixteen and twenty-one megatons. By comparison, the largest explosion the United States conducted during the initial stage of thermonuclear testing, Castle Bravo in 1954, detonated at fifteen megatons.

The site employs a fleet of more than eight hundred boats arrayed with enormous high-power LED spotlights. As the afterglow fades they situate within and behind the cloud, lighting and backlighting it. When engaged the light display is among the most awe-inspiring imaginable. Visitors have likened it to a bigger-than-life live viewing of the Eagle Nebula, the most stunning picture ever taken by the Hubble Space Telescope. Many guests remark that while they visited because they wanted to see a detonation, they were completely taken aback by the staggering beauty of the finale. In many ways it has proved more popular than the explosion itself. Owing to the events as displays of nuclear fusion each explosion is given the name of a star. Memorable events have their designations retired, much as is done with catastrophic hurricanes.

With this in mind and an eye on the future, planners have revisited the designation of the program itself. As terror-related events and regional crime levels were analyzed and weighed with the program's rationale, they have resulted in a decision to promote the site's effect on international tensions, however unintended they might have been. A final decision awaits Administration guidelines but planners have affirmed the redesignation DiFusion, a derivation based on the program's original parameters. What began as a recreational use of fusion detonations morphed into a vehicle assisting in the struggle to diffuse global tensions.

As the program is set to enter its third season it is at a crossroads. Wildly popular, it is in ways a victim of its own success. The facility can accommodate eighteen hundred guests at a time. It has never operated with an empty hotel room and its current waiting list of twenty months is growing. Presently, three cruise lines offer regular stops at events, in addition to the private boats which routinely park themselves in surrounding waters each week. Coupled with support personnel, upwards of twenty thousand people see each event, a number expected to grow by 50 percent in the next two years. The government claims a territorial economic zone of two hundred miles but as a practical matter cannot police such an area. Logistical support from the United States has helped but intrusions have proved problematic. While initially a pilot program Tuvalu Alofa has become a lucrative, self-sustaining entity, amply demonstrating the program's feasibility. With the subsequent focus on suppressing tensions, and having already strained the island's infrastructure the government of Tuvalu has not objected to expansion, as it is not expected to affect their revenue stream.

In this regard the Administration entered into negotiations with several Pacific nations last year as well as the state of Hawaii. Preliminary proposals have been made by Kiribati, the Federated States of Micronesia, Vanuatu and Honolulu, with a proposal soon to be offered by Samoa. The strongest bids so far have been tendered by Vanuatu and Kiribati. Hawaii's bid is problematic. The state's only practical site is on the island of Kauai, home to extensive wildlife habitat and unique biozones. Though a long shot, Hawaii no doubt will continue in the process.

The terror-related data compiled this week have put the entire course in flux. It is impossible to predict how the Administration plans to integrate this reality, but it seems certain that the existing goals will be fast-tracked and augmented.

With the rainy season about to end, the site is beginning a new cycle of events. Whether the program can sustain itself and grow in measured fashion as opposed to falling victim to bureaucratic infighting or unsustained expansion remains to be seen. While enormously popular, it remains the most controversial entertainment venture ever conceived or built.

Pressure both for and against the program and its underlying conception is deep-seated and has grown more polarized. With the added complication of integrating the Administration's new vision during a time of election year politicking, the next few months will determine in just what direction this most unique of attractions will proceed.

Kevin put down the report and rubbed his eyes. With two hours left before landing, more than ever, he was looking forward to talking with Max.

The enormity of his concept's evolution was something he hadn't even remotely envisioned. Now, Raden's clinical analysis was laid out in stark reality. It left him numb. He wasn't sure what felt worse, grasping the cynical arrogance of what had been created or knowing that it was built on his spark of insight. Head pounding, he called over a flight attendant for another Bloody Mary. She smiled, and before getting it told him that a phone call had just come in for him.

A hesitant Kevin picked up the in-flight phone. "Hello?"

"Dr. Kevin Herter? This is Captain Joseph Scardano of the New Jersey state police."

"Oh, I'm sorry. I completely forgot to call you guys. I'm surprised you got me. You know where I am?"

"Yes, Dr. Herter. We felt it couldn't wait. One of our detectives tried calling you yesterday but kept getting your voicemail. We sent someone by."

"This trip came up fast. What did you find out?"

"Our investigation is ongoing. It's what we discovered when we stopped by your home that prompted this call. What time did you leave your house this morning?"

"I left yesterday, about five, and spent the night at the airport. Why? What's wrong?"

"That explains it sir. We'll check it out. Doctor, when the detective stopped by last evening, he found something on your front step."

Kevin paused. "What do you mean?"

"First, there was a FedEx delivery at 5:43 p.m., from Cambridge University Press."

"Yeah, those were some books I ordered."

"Yes, we confirmed that. But next to it was a coffee cup from the Princeton Tea Room."

"Oh, for crying out loud. That's Sharon, Sharon Velazquez. She's my girlfriend, actually now my ex-girlfriend. Why are you calling me—"

"Dr. Herter, the cup was filled with blood."

"*What?* Oh my God!" Several people turned to look. "Is she *okay?*"

"We spoke with her. She's okay. We don't believe she had anything to do with—"

"She doesn't. She would never do anything like that."

"That's what we think. She seemed preoccupied with another matter, a televised interview."

"Yeah, I know," said a dejected Kevin. A wave of guilt hit him. "How is she?"

"She's rather agitated. And this I'm sorry to say didn't help."

"Oh, God." A moment later the flight attendant brought over his Bloody Mary. He recoiled and gave it back. "Please make sure she's safe," he said. "My God, I can't believe this."

Scardano paused. "Dr. Herter, can you think of anyone who might want to do this? When we add it to what happened Sunday night, it's something we obviously can't ignore."

"I honest-to-God don't know," Kevin huffed. "I don't know what's going on anymore."

"Dr. Herter, we had someone contact us from Washington, a Dr. John Raden. Does he—"

"You think he's involved?"

"We don't believe so. He had information that correlated with what we learned."

"Okay. Maybe he can come up with some names. Captain, what do you need from me?"

"We wanted to let you know. Dr. Raden was particularly concerned with your safety."

Kevin sighed. "Well, thank you, I guess. And please, please keep an eye on Sharon. She should never have been involved with any of this."

"We've spoken with her and with the Princeton police. They'll look in on her."

Kevin took a deep breath. "Okay. What do I do when I land?"

"For now Doctor, you can stick to your routine. We'll continue our investigation. Someone's obviously sending you a message. We'd like you to keep in touch. Dr. Raden gave us the names of the folks you're visiting. We've notified the local police, and the California Highway Patrol. If you have any problems, you can contact them."

"Okay, Captain. Thank you very much." The call ended. Kevin called over the flight attendant and ordered a gin and tonic. As she left he reached in his coat pocket for a tissue. Instead he felt a piece of paper he hadn't noticed before. Written across it was a terse note: "Herter. You're warned. Go back home." A deep red stain was brushed across the bottom.

He was beside himself, wanting to bolt from the plane. A few people nearby noticed his agitation but passed it off as in-flight jitters.

One set of eyes though observed him differently. Their owner, a tall blonde man in his early thirties had been watching from the second row in coach since they'd boarded in Newark. Captain Christian Deloy quietly reached for a magazine, his current task accomplished.

A minute later the flight attendant brought over Kevin's drink. As she turned he downed it in one gulp.

Eighteen

The girl at the Princeton Tea Room told the caller Miss Velazquez wasn't in. John Raden thanked her and hung up. As he walked up the path, a package under his arm, a warm morning breeze brushed by. Spring had decided to appear. A front door placard read, "No Solicitations," while a handwritten sign warned, "No Media!" He rang.

A stomp of footprints issued inside. "God-dammit, I told you bastards," burst from Sharon as she flung open the door. "I don't believe this," she said. "What the hell you want?"

"I called the shop," Raden wavered, "but I was sure you weren't in."

"Really," she snarled, itching to slam the door in his face. "And why's that?"

"Well, I saw the news. And, I know about the thing on Kevin's stoop."

"If you know that, you wouldn't be here."

"Uh, do you have a few? I'd like to speak to you." She glared, looked around, then motioned him in. The living room was spacious, but the spectacular art work made it feel almost modest. A TV in another room appeared to be tuned to the news.

"Okay," she snapped, "what do you want?"

"After seeing Kevin yesterday I went back to the hotel. I was channel surfing—"

"And I bet you're happy."

Raden shook his head. "Not at all. I wanted to tell you I was sorry. I also wanted to say I'm more familiar with that kind of thing than most people. It'll blow over—"

"Yeah, that's easy for you to say." She visibly stiffened.

Raden looked around. "Do you mind if I sit?" he asked. Sharon stared him down, but motioned to a couch. She had a look of a trapped animal, resigned but scared. Still, he couldn't help being taken by her. Though obviously more stressed than yesterday, she was incredibly attractive. She was the kind of woman who was beautiful because she looked average. Practically every one of her features was "typical," at the midline of perfectly normal. Aside from elegantly arched brows, her eyes, nose and mouth were in the mean. But taken together, there was no way to think of them as other than stunning.

Her eyes were red from a night spent scrutinizing the TV. Fox, CNN, MSNBC; it was on their revolving feed of breaking news: "Well-known artist Sharon Velazquez, reputed love interest of physicist Kevin Herter, got into an altercation with an MSNBC news crew that had stopped by her Princeton coffee shop yesterday to speak with the renowned scientist. While reporter Jessica Enright was unhurt in the melee, a cameraman narrowly avoided injury when an angry Velazquez confronted the crew. Herter was unavailable for comment, both on the incident and on his reported involvement with the Pacific bomb program his theories …" She persisted in revisiting the pain, watching until it no longer aired. So far it had yet to stop.

"What do you want?" she barked.

"Well, I wanted to know how you were feeling."

"Oh, come on!" she rolled her eyes.

"Miss Velazquez, I spoke with the state and Princeton police. They think your involvement is incidental. I agree. They're going to keep an eye out for you."

"Yeah a cop stopped by an hour ago. This is my life now, this and the damn reporters."

"I know. I checked on a few things. There's a lot happening with Kevin but as far as your own safety, nothing you need to worry about."

"Oh, you think I'm not going to worry? I warned him about this shit for two years. I knew this would happen." As Raden nodded politely, she groaned, "What else?"

"I met my son for dinner in the city last night. He lives near the Museum of Natural History. Kevin had talked about what you paint. I was curious. I wanted to see some fossils."

"What did he say?"

"He talked about your work; your approach, your subject matter. I had an interest in those things but after listening to him, it made me want to take a closer look."

Sharon crimped her lip. "What else?"

"We talked about the obvious. But he also talked about the two of you. I'm not sure I should say this but he's bothered by what happened. I like him. There's a good person in there."

Sharon wasn't sure how to answer. There was a decency about Raden she hadn't figured on. She had invested so much time nurturing her anger that it was unsettling. But because she had so much time in it she couldn't let it go just yet. "Yeah, well I know, but listen, I'm not going into this with you. It's too personal. So, all right, you still didn't say what you want."

Raden lifted the package. "I saw this in the gift shop, and thought you might enjoy it."

Sharon waved him off. "I can't. You didn't have to, but I can't."

"Kevin told me you have a thing for works connected with time. I got the sense you like to collect the subjects you paint yourself, but I thought it could give you some inspiration."

"Okay," Sharon skewed her head, "I have to be honest. I said yesterday I was trying to get your number. You're not what I expected. I still want to know what you want."

"I need your help on something, but nothing to do with this. I must say, you look like Kevin did yesterday. Did you manage to get any sleep?" She would never believe it, but as he had felt with Kevin yesterday, he had looked forward to meeting the noted artist.

"I can't believe this. I argued with him about this yesterday. I always had a problem with the media. For years they tried to bullshit their way into doing pieces on me that were full of crap. And now this. That's who I thought was at the door." She teared up but tried to hide it. "I'm not sure why I'm telling you this. I'm sorry I bit your head off. I guess I should thank you for making sure I was okay. But this is just too much. And yesterday, after making a life for myself, a business, a career, in two minutes they make me look like an out-of-control moron. He complained they filled up his answering machine. He gets annoyed when I tell him 'toldja'."

"Toldja?"

She smiled sadly. "Toldja. Told ya. Told you so. I'm always good for that. Day's not over, same thing happens to me. I had to turn off my phones because of those shits. And then last night the cops showed up. I can't believe it. So, yeah, I didn't sleep last night."

Raden listened sympathetically. What he said was the absolute truth- the storm she was in would be old news before she even got over feeling bad about it. But she was raw, not ready to accept that just yet. He smiled. "I seem to be getting the two of you on your best days."

"Okay," she motioned at the package he held, "let's see." It was the size of a gift-wrapped shirt but heavy. She approached it like a haz-mat tech nearing an unattended box in a mall. Delicately peeling away cotton padding revealed a large gray rock, upon which were brownish-black impressions of two fossil trilobites, each about five inches long. They were stunning. A hesitant smile came over her. "Thank you; they're beautiful, but I can't take them."

"Before saying no it's not a peace offering. I have my reasons. They're personal as well."

She ran her fingers across their alien-looking forms. Trilobites are among the most coveted of natural history items, owing to their bizarre shapes and often exquisite preservation. These were the most spectacular she had seen in some time. And she had painted them before.

"Tell you what," he said, "sit with it. If you decide to pass, send it back, no questions asked. There's a stand with a label if you want to display it. It lists the scientific name and the locale. Other people might not be interested, but I think you would." She slowly nodded. Raden said, "My pleasure. You probably don't believe me, but the honor's mine. I admire your work."

"I don't think I have to tell you what I think of this whole thing."

"I know. Even if Kevin hadn't said anything, it's pretty obvious."

"So what the hell do they want with him? You have to know, this thing broke us up."

Raden lightly nodded, though he was sure there was more to it.

"So," Sharon sneered, "you're not going to say anything. You two, you're like cousins."

"There's a lot I can't say, but just the same I can't speak for him. Some think he's a natural for the program, but he's going to have to decide what's best for himself." He walked over to a large canvas. A subtly beautiful piece in white gold and ocher with teases of thin black-outlined cerulean patterns that looked like shells danced across the surface. "Is this yours?" She nodded, and he added, "I wasn't sure because it wasn't signed, but it looks like your style."

"Yeah, well, I don't sign works that don't leave the house. I know I did them."

Raden stared at it. "It's stunning. Kind of lyrical, but understated."

She eased in, taken not with the flattery but the critique, which was surprisingly astute. It was seldom that she heard a layman express a comment about art so well. The piece was a favorite, an image of ammonites, ancient ancestors of the present-day Pacific nautilus. His description was what she'd tried to evoke when she painted it three years ago. She had yet to finish the piece when she knew she wasn't going to sell it, and had once turned down $90,000 for the canvas.

Raden smiled. His instincts were on target. She was fiery, bright, complex and a thorough pain-in-the-rear. And hurting. And worth getting to know and helping, and getting help from.

"Miss Velazquez," he said, getting ready to leave, "again, it was a pleasure. And trust me, the best way to deal with this incident is to smile and ignore. The media may seem to have a lot of sway, but the thing is they're like children. Distract them and they lose interest. All of this will blow over before you know it." He went for the door.

"Kevin's headed out to watch one of the things," she said. "Is that where you're going?"

He nodded. "I suggested that he see one before deciding how much to get involved."

"Yeah, well tell him I said to have fun, or whatever you guys say at those things."

"People really don't say much of anything. Mostly it's things you can't repeat." In that he thought Sharon would fit right in, but knew not to press his luck.

"Yeah, well," she snarled, "if you're talking things you can't repeat, you can tell him I'll remember he took off without any kind of call or anything. He had to have seen the news."

"Well, it seems like you guys parted pretty final. Maybe he didn't see it. But even if he did, I'm not sure what I would say either."

"Yeah, when you don't have any balls."

"Well, I'll tell you. My wife knows I have them, but we both know she's got 'em nailed to the living room wall. Knowing that, I don't have to worry about fighting over where they are. It's not if you have 'em, it's where you hang 'em. You pick and choose. At least that way I don't have to worry about having them chopped off wherever I go." As Sharon tried to keep from laughing Raden said, "Take care Miss Velazquez. I'll be in touch." He smiled, and walked out.

Nineteen

The White House receptionist put the call from John Raden through to the Oval Office. "So Jack," Elliot Hanford asked as Dillon Ridge listened, "where do we stand?"

"Mr. President, he's on a plane right now. I got him to think about watching a detonation." He was packing, preparing to check out of the Nassau Inn.

"That's good work."

"Well," Raden lightly laughed, "it will be if he shows up. But I think we're in good shape. I'll keep you posted. Have you ever seen one?"

"No." Hanford paused. "Know something? I'm going to Hawaii this weekend. I think I'll fly out and watch the thing with him."

Raden smiled quietly. His subtle cue had worked. He zipped up his bag and said, "That's a good idea Mr. President. I'll look forward to seeing you."

"Keep me updated. Make sure he's there."

Raden said good-bye. After checking out, there would be a cab to Princeton Airport, then the hop back to Washington. The flight from there would have him in Tuvalu by late tomorrow.

Hanford turned to Ridge. "That may work. I hadn't thought of it, but it's a good idea."

Ridge was more circumspect. "If he sticks to script. We can issue a release; play it up."

"That's the problem with mavericks. That's why we keep tabs on them both. This flying Herter out on his own, that going to cause problems?"

"Too early to tell. Maybe."

"Okay. His itinerary square with your people?"

"Yes, Mr. President. We have it covered. He's flying into San Francisco. Rosenkranz lives there."

"Good. You going to have him met at the airport?"

"No, but definitely before he leaves."

"Who do you have on that? The security head, what's her name's husband?"

"Whiteman. Yeah, he's been of help."

"Good then. I don't want a chance it could be traced back to us. I want the press talking about the merits; nothing else. I don't want to hear even a hint of negative coverage on this."

"We can arrange that, Mr. President," Ridge said, both knowing it was impossible.

On the way to the airport Raden mulled over his accomplishments, and Elliot Hanford's words. By day's end, his subtle hint would be co-opted by the White House and turned into a decision of far-reaching insight. "That's good work" was politico-speak for "I wish we had thought of that and we'll never admit we didn't." A familiar refrain in Washington, it came couched in a compliment, though little in the nation's capital was face-value. Everything was below the surface; the higher the position, the deeper the intrigue and muddier the waters.

In the space of a day he met two of the most accomplished if imperfect people he had come across in some time. A challenge, but inspiring. Now he felt something different. If there was a downside to his work, it was the drop-off that came from meeting a Kevin Herter or a Sharon Velazquez and dealing with the powers-that-be. No one at the White House would have thought to fly Herter out to actually see what they wanted him to get involved with. It wouldn't have been considered or would have been lost in bureaucratic review.

Hanford had a sharp mind but he excelled as a political animal. It got him elected and kept his ratings over 50 percent, despite the ongoing weak economy and having made a spectacle out of the bomb. He didn't bother with small things. He was smart enough to know what he didn't know, and how to get it done. Getting people to do things was key to gaining power and keeping it. Neither Hanford nor those around him would ever be accused of three-dimensional thought. Where they excelled was thinking in two-dimensions. It was what the times called for and Raden knew it. He also knew the intrigue Hanford had initiated was well along. The media was addressing the issue. And he was being watched. He could deal with it, but his plan to fly Herter out with a stop in San Francisco was paying off.

Raden had leeway to accomplish his task. Hanford would be told just enough. He had his short-term politics and Raden had his long-term puzzles. Each suited both men fine. But for a quick refueling stop in Hawaii, the next eighteen hours would be spent in the air. Time to sleep, read, relax. Unlike his subject, he loved to fly.

After Raden left, Sharon was in a daze. She was agonizingly aware both of the quiet and the contradiction she faced. She barely knew the guy who'd just left, but he had made an impression. She tried to hate him, but couldn't. The guy who precipitated the visit she knew too well. He too had made an impression. He was someone she didn't want to hate, but was finding she could. And that someone had taken a coffee cup from her shop, filled it with blood and left it on his step was beyond horrific. She felt violated. She tried to block it out.

She looked in the box that the fossil had come in. Inside was a bronze placard, a stand, and a card documenting where it had been found. Sharon knew something of the fossil trade. Oftentimes, spectacular forms come from remote and unstable corners of the world, trilobites among the most coveted. This one was from Morocco, known for stunning specimens. And it was barely restored. Many are extensively reconstructed to make them more saleable but this one was 95 percent natural. Raden had spent some money on this.

She turned on her laptop. A quick search revealed that the guy who had turned up unannounced, who had brought such turmoil to her life in such a short time had spent almost a thousand dollars on a gift for her. She stared for several minutes until the screen saver appeared, then decided to put the piece in her breakfront for now, with the other fossils, shells and large bird eggs she owned. Its intricate form made a beautiful addition. The stand had a space for the placard.

It was when she was attaching it that she began to wonder whether there had been another reason for Raden's visit. She reflected on his manner, thinking about whether he was trying to tell her something. The placard bore the Latin name given to the 550 million-year-old species years earlier. It was one she had seen before and thought nothing of. Now she couldn't help but wonder whether *Paradoxides* carried more meaning than just the name of an extinct arthropod.

Twenty

"Jean?" an excited Kevin spoke into his cell phone at the car rental agency.

"Oh, it's so good to hear you! How are you feeling?" Jean's beaming smile was obvious in her voice.

"Hanging in." He couldn't wait to see her and Max.

"Oh, that's so good. We've been worried about you."

"Thanks. Actually, that's part of why I called. I have a surprise. I'm at the airport."

"Which airport? San Francisco?"

"Yeah. I know this is last minute, but I have a day in town. There was too much going on to call earlier. I'd love to see you. I could be there in an hour."

"Yes, but—"

"If you're busy, I'll understand. I have to leave by the evening, but I wanted to see you."

"It's not that, but—"

Kevin paused. "Jean, is everything okay?"

"I'm okay—"

"You sure? Is Max all right? Can you put him on?"

"Sweetheart, he can't come to the phone right now."

In the warm sunshine of the parking lot Kevin felt a chill. "Is he okay?"

"It's hard to go into right now. Please come up. Max would love to see you too."

"Jean, I gotta say, after the last few days you're giving me a funny feeling."

"Sweetheart, it'll work out. Enjoy the drive. It's a beautiful day. We'll see you soon."

Kevin loaded his bag into the car, a task complicated by the knot in his stomach. He tried ignoring it by focusing on the drive ahead. Not knowing what to look for that was suspicious, he looked around nonetheless. Not seeing anything of worry, he exited the lot. Five minutes later, windows down and shirt sleeves rolled up he was headed north on US 101. He didn't notice the car that pulled out a short distance behind him.

Return to a place you knew by heart and something happens. It can be unsettling to think things don't grind to a halt when you leave. It's still there, but deep down you nurture the illusion that it froze in place the day you left and only resumed moving the instant you returned. And when you see that it kept up without you, you feel cheated. It was a pure self-absorbed fiction, Kevin knew, but he thought that someone should have hit Pause on Central California three years ago. No one did and part of him was taking it personally.

The route was coming back to him as if it had never left, 101 North to 380 West to 280 North to Route 1 North toward 19th Avenue and the Golden Gate Bridge, back on 101. Drive a road enough, he realized, and it's about less names and numbers and more about feelings and familiarities. Highways have a presence, like articles of clothes. Some hang easy like old sweatshirts, others unforgiving like funeral suits. Each bend and mile-marker reflects part of you back to yourself. But now he set those thoughts aside, to think about Max, and what he would tell him.

The gruff easterner had already been a presence in physics when he'd accepted a Berkeley professorship early in 2001. His Nobel Prize was for a series of discoveries on plasma physics but was as much a recognition of a life's work as any single contribution. He was a driving force behind the Superconducting Supercollider, the immense particle accelerator in Texas that had been cancelled by Congress in 1993 due to budgetary problems.

Soon after he'd arrived at Stanford, Kevin attended a seminar on string theory. He was about to enter the lecture hall when he held the door for a middle-aged guy who looked like the actor Richard Kiley with a paunch.

"Thanks," the man said, juggling a briefcase and several long plastic tubes, the kind made for posters and charts.

"No problem," Kevin replied.

"Yeah, it is. Three times today I had some kid slam a door on me they could have held. It's nice to know at least some young people haven't lost their manners."

Kevin smiled. As they were both headed in the same direction. Kevin held the auditorium door. When the man thanked him again Kevin shrugged, "Something to fall back on if physics doesn't work." It was partly what he said, partly the way he said it, but Max eyed him with a look that said this wasn't just another kid in the crowd.

"You here for the seminar?" he asked. When Kevin nodded yes, the man put down his briefcase and extended his hand. "Max Rosenkranz."

"Oh," Kevin blushed, "I'm sorry." He had been too close to the noted scientist and guest lecturer to recognize him. "It's a pleasure."

"You sticking around after the program?" Kevin shrugged, to which Max replied, "Stop up afterwards," as he walked down to the stage. A five-hour cup of coffee after the question and answer session followed. Though separated by different schools and thirty years, the two became fast friends. Kevin soon met Max's wife Jean, and by year's end was crashing on their couch. The couple, who had but their work and each other took to the single only-child as if he were their son. For Kevin, whose parents were gone before he was twelve, Max and Jean became more of a Mom and Dad than his biological ones ever were.

There was another side to Max and Kevin's relationship as unexpected as it was congenial, their affection for the automobile. In Kevin's case it was positive, with Max, negative. As much as Kevin loved being behind the wheel, Max hated it, and in no time, Kevin became designated driver for the two. It suited both hand-in-glove. Whether running up to Berkeley for dinner or heading to Marin County on weekends or running Max down to the airport or picking him up or driving north to a winery in Calistoga or south to Big Sur and Carmel, the two men bonded as much in the car as anywhere. Where Kevin once drove alone with his thoughts he now had a sounding board who to his delight relished the same. The four years when they both lived in the state had given them barely enough time to keep pace with each other's minds. For Jean, it got Max out of the house so she could work. She would often accompany them on trips to more picturesque country, but would fall asleep in the back while Max and Kevin rambled on up front. Though influenced by other factors, both knew deep down that some of the seeds that led to Max's Nobel Prize and Kevin's conception of quantum resonance were sown on the highways of central California.

Eventually, Max accepted a position at Princeton, but Kevin stayed on at Berkeley. For the rest of the decade he and the Rosenkranz's saw each other regularly. Upon Max's retirement, Kevin began thinking of moving on. Max's Nobel Prize, and its focus on the whole of Max's life's work, nurtured his unrest. Kevin published for the first time soon after, and a few years later joined the Institute for Advanced Study. The chance to live and work in the same town was something all three looked forward to. It wasn't to be. Kevin was barely able to catch his breath before the unintended consequences of his work erupted. And later that year, Max and Jean were quietly looking to move.

It happened rather suddenly. Years earlier, Jean had lived in Sausalito, just over the Golden Gate Bridge in Marin County. While Max was at Berkeley, they lived a short drive over the Bay Bridge in San Anselmo, just to the north. In a way it made sense that they might wish to return, but still the move seemed to come out of nowhere. Kevin was never able to get an answer as to why they chose to go. The money from the Nobel Prize enabled them to keep their house in Princeton, but they began spending more time out west. Less than a year after Kevin arrived in Princeton, Max and Jean bought a house in Woodacre, a small town up the road from San Anselmo. With little fanfare and no explanation, they had essentially changed coasts. Kevin missed them.

He was now less than a half-an-hour away, turning from 101 north and west onto Sir Francis Drake Boulevard, past Marin General Hospital towards Woodacre. The last time he had visited Max and Jean was six months after they moved. Kevin's comment to Max about finally beginning to lose his gut was rewarded by the Nobel laureate with a "go schtupp yourself." Although they would return to Princeton twice after that, something had changed. Kevin couldn't shake how odd it felt. It wasn't like visiting your parents in their snowbird escape in Florida or saying goodbye after they dropped you off at college. Something was different.

Twenty-one

Kevin arrived at twelve fifteen. The appropriately named Woodacre is a small and forested community. Sun-drenched bay trees gave the neighborhood a flavor like a setting for a Food Network program.

Max and Jean's house sat on a tight, curvy road. Kevin had to squeeze around two deer and a gray panel van parked across the street. A long brown fence in front of the house barely hinted at the structure behind. Jean scrambled out of the front gate to greet him.

"Oh, I am so glad to see you!" she said, tearing up and holding Kevin tightly.

"Jean! What's the matter?"

"I'm so glad you're here," she continued, wiping her eyes with a neatly-folded tissue. "Come, come inside."

Kevin wanted to ask about Max, but held back. The rattle of the suitcase wheels broke the quiet of the cloistered neighborhood. The gate opened to a large house partially supported by posts, sitting on a hill leading down a ravine to a small stream.

The living room was spacious and comfortable, with almost as much greenery inside as out. One of Sharon's paintings hung amid colorful weavings that covered most of the walls.

"You changed a few things," Kevin commented.

"I wanted new furniture. You know Max; he could do with card tables and folding chairs. Sometimes you have to put your foot down. Come, sit." Jean's long gray hair was tied in a ponytail. It made a striking contrast to her eyebrows, which remained dark. Kevin thought the gray did nothing to detract from her looks, still winsome at sixty-seven.

"Are you hungry?" she asked as they sat on a sofa. "You should be ready for lunch."

Kevin leaned back into the cushions. A wizened smile came to him. "Okay, where's Max?"

Jean folded and refolded the tissue in her lap and wet her lips. "He's in the hospital."

"I knew something was up. What happened?"

"Well, he fractured his arm yesterday. He was lifting a carton of milk and felt a snap. It's the smaller bone, the radius. They brought him into Marin General."

"Oh, for Christ sakes," Kevin huffed. "I had a feeling. Come on, let's go."

He started to get up, but Jean stopped him. "Wait," she said, "there's something I have to tell you." She took his arm and gently sat him down. The sinking feeling roared back. "There's a reason why he broke his arm." Kevin's brow furrowed, as Jean bit her lip.

"I don't follow," he said. She repeated herself, quietly. Kevin pressed, "What's wrong?"

She hesitated. "He's in the last stages of prostate cancer."

"What!" Kevin bolted up and began pacing about. "*WHAT?*"

Jean gazed at him with a plaintive cast. "Sweetheart, he's in his final stages. When the disease metastasizes it can settle in the long bones and they can weaken."

Kevin spun in place, flailing his arms left and right. Jean rose, holding him firmly. "Why didn't you tell me?" he bleated. "Why didn't he? How long has this been going on?" She sat him down again. "Oh, shit," he moaned.

Jean pulled him close and he crumpled into her. "Oh sweetheart, I'm so sorry. I'm sorry this is how you had to find out." She patted and stroked his head, repeating everything was going to be okay. And for the first time since they'd met, amidst the anguish a pretense was gone, and a mother comforted her son.

Kevin kept shaking his head. "Why didn't anyone *tell* me?"

Jean began rocking him. In the simple act, she found herself engulfed by a lifetime of pent-up maternal instincts. Three miscarriages years earlier were wounds long suppressed. The comforting was cathartic, on a wound that could only heal if the scar masking it was ripped off.

All Kevin heard within the circle of her arms was Jean repeating it would be all right. And in the simple act of being rocked, he found himself engulfed by a lifetime of pent-up hurt of a child longing to be held. In the eleven years spent brooking his presence before she passed on, his mother had never allowed such a gesture. For him, it also was cathartic. They sat a full ten minutes, not moving.

In time, he said, "I don't understand."

"This was his decision. You're the one person who drove it. He was afraid to tell you." Again and again Kevin asked why, and over and over she replied, "Honey, he was afraid. This man could tell anyone anything, and he couldn't tell you this one thing."

"*Why?* Afraid of what? That I'd see him die?"

She nodded yes. As Kevin let loose a spasmodic sigh, she added, "We found out about it seven years ago. They did the usual—radiation, chemo. These days it can be a chronic condition. A lot of men with it wind up dying of other things. But it recently began to metastasize."

"I don't understand. What was he afraid of then?"

Jean began to pace. "Oh, who *knows*. Everything and anything. Of being honest with himself. Of dying. Everything. He couldn't have been more proud of you if you were his own. By not saying anything he could protect you, and in a way himself."

"Why didn't he go for more aggressive treatment at that point?"

She shook her head. "He just didn't want to. But again, I think he was afraid."

"And look at him now." Kevin stared at the ceiling in exasperation.

"And look at him now." Jean stroked his hair. "You don't know what you've meant to us. Max and I think of you as our own. He always looked at you like the son he never had. And, he's stubborn. Were you ever able to tell him anything?"

"Why didn't you say anything? I would have been there for both of you."

"You can't imagine the arguments. When he first found out, I could understand. But when it metastasized, I said it was time. He couldn't. Why do you think we moved out here?"

"Are you *kidding me*? I don't believe it."

"God's-honest truth. He just couldn't bring himself to tell you, so he began talking about moving. This area was the only place we could agree on. It was easy for him to rationalize since we'd lived here before."

"I can't believe it," Kevin slumped back. "Unbelievable."

"Sweetheart, I feel horrible. I'm his wife. I had to respect his decision but I hated it. It's been eating me up. I don't know what to say. I am so sorry, for him too. He missed out on so much. I think he just began to realize that." As Kevin hugged her, she cried through a smile. "You don't know how much I wanted to do this."

He continued to gently rock her. She softly beamed.

"We were coming back in a few weeks," Jean said. "The doctors said the disease was beginning its last stages. We got home and something changed. I'd like to say I did it, but it came from him. I think he finally wanted some sense of family."

"On Sunday, I thought he sounded tired. I mean, Max tired before midnight? I had too much going on to put much into it, but I should have been able to tell something was up."

"Oh, you couldn't have known. There's nothing you could have done."

He rubbed her shoulder. "How have you been dealing with all this?"

"I've met some wonderful people out here," She smiled. "We joined a temple—"

"Wait," Kevin said mordantly, "Max Rosenkranz in temple? God."

"Like we Jews don't have enough trouble," Jean laughed between tears. "We started going to services. Of course, Max being Max, he gets into discussions, how God works through science, how people spend too much time arguing about what He wants. The two fleas arguing about who owns the dog they're on. They love him. The token Nobel laureate curmudgeon." Kevin laughed. Jean added, "I was never religious but it's meant something. They're wonderful people. I started going to a support group, a healing circle. Max wouldn't let me say anything so I put my foot down about finding something to help me. They're very special people."

"I can't believe he was so afraid," Kevin sighed.

"You'd be surprised. In a way, deep down he was always a scared kid."

"As are we all." He sighed. "Ah, shit. So, what now?"

"Oh, honey," she said haltingly. "I think we're not going to be coming back east."

Kevin bit his lip and nodded softly. "I think I'd like to go see him now."

Twenty-two

They drove down the hill to Sir Francis Drake Boulevard. Behind them, the car that had been tailing Kevin was gone. A tow truck that neither of them noticed had taken its place.

Jean thought about giving Kevin a hard time about driving but was glad she didn't. Just having him do a simple thing like driving her to see her dying husband had more vitality than anything she'd experienced in some time. She thanked him, saying that for the first time in her life, she felt like a Mom. He understood, saying though he had spent twenty years thinking of her and Max as parents, for the first time, he felt like a son as well.

Jean sat folding a tissue until it couldn't be doubled over any longer, unfolded it and patted her eyes. Kevin had seen her engage in the habit when she was upset, never thinking much of it. Now she seemed as fragile as the tissue. He wished he could comfort her.

"Max does love you," she said. "As do I. He may surprise you and say something."

"I may surprise him and bop him one."

"I know," she chuckled. She then said, "Please don't be bitter. Don't be mad."

"Oh, I know. I know, but—"

"Sweetheart, you have to promise me."

"I know. It's not that. It's just—I'm numb."

"I know. I wake up and look at him, and I have to hold it in." She caught herself and no longer able to control it, purged herself in a fit of wailing. She held Kevin's hand until she was spent. When she calmed down, she said, "I'm sorry sweetheart. I'm so glad you're here. I needed to do that for a long time. Thank you."

He squeezed her hand, his eyes tearing up. "Don't ever think you're burdening me. My life wouldn't have been the same without you two in it." He changed the subject. "Did Max like living here again?" he asked as he looked past the twisting road to the chaparral-looking country.

"Yeah. We liked going to the shore at Point Reyes. It's chilly but so beautiful. The hills near the coast really look purple." She was delighting in finally being able to talk. "We'd stop for a cup of tea. It was so nice. Sometimes the fog would come in and he'd say he wished he could paint. Those times he'd say he envied Sharon."

"She always liked you two. I don't know anyone she's ever given a painting to."

"I wish we could have spent more time with her. How is she?" Kevin inhaled deeply. "Don't tell me," Jean pleaded. "Okay, let's hear it."

Kevin sighed. "It's the whole bomb fiasco. It was too much for her."

"I didn't even get a chance to ask you about that."

"Jean, you don't even want to know. All I know is, if I come out of this week alive with my sanity intact ..."

Ahead, the hospital came into view. The day had warmed. Kevin parked in back under a tree. "I hate hospitals," Kevin said as Jean took his arm and they entered. Still unnoticed, the tow truck crept up to Kevin's Prius, blocking it from view.

"How's he look?" Kevin asked as they awaited an elevator.

"Considering, all right. He lost weight, but he's a normal weight for someone his height, go figure. It took terminal cancer for him to lose that belly of his. Of course, he hit up the doctors, asking if they wanted to be co-writers on a cancer diet book."

They walked down the hall to Max's room. Jean entered first, and yelped. Kevin rushed in to see Max's bed empty and Jean's hands covering her mouth in anguish. An instant later a nurse ran in.

"Mrs. Rosenkranz! We moved your husband to his own room a half-hour ago. We called, but no one answered. He's three doors down."

"I didn't need that," Jean said, cutting her a look. She grabbed Kevin, and they went out, passing an older man asleep in the other bed, his white hair striking against his dark brown skin.

Max was napping, his right arm in a light cast. He woke when Jean entered, and smiled warmly as he saw Kevin. Jean glowed as Kevin gave him a kiss.

"So, good news travels fast." Max rustled his hair and reached for Kevin's hand. Kevin shook his fist affectionately before he took it. There was a weariness to Max. Gray stubble poked through his face and his gray-streaked brown hair pillowed about unkempt.

"Look who called from the airport today," Jean smiled.

Max's lunch tray sat in front of him. He asked Kevin, "You hungry?"

"What's this with Jews, pushing food every time you visit?"

"Helps with the guilt. We have lots of guilt."

Kevin looked away and Jean pulled up a chair. "We had a start when we didn't see you in the other room."

"Wasn't getting any sleep there." Max looked at Kevin. "The guy next to me."

"What's the problem? Does he talk a lot?"

"No, he's in a coma." Kevin snickered. "Old guy," Max scowled. "Completely out of it. It's his wife. All she does is sing to him from the Good Book; Jesus this, Jesus that, Saint the other thing. Hosannas up the wazzu. No god-damn rest. Had to get out." As Kevin and Jean smiled, Max frowned, "Whole big hospital, and they put a Yiddlich *alta cocker* who wants quiet in with an *alta schvartzeh* whose wife wants to hold a revival meeting."

"Enough with that," said Jean as she took a brush from her bag and combed Max's hair.

"Yeah, yeah," he whined as she admonished him to sit still. He looked at Kevin. "See the crap I gotta deal with?"

"I told her that you're lucky I didn't bop you one."

Jean was set to cut him off but stopped. Max bit his lip. "I'd been trying to think about what to say. I get as far as, 'Son,' and it stops. I keep waiting for the rest to come. It just never did." Kevin reached over, stroked Max's hair and gave him a kiss on the forehead. Max looked up, his eyes moistened. "I'm scared," he quivered.

"You know I hardly knew my father. I just want you to know I never had to." As Max teared up, Kevin added, "I want you to know I love you very much." He looked at Jean. "Both of you."

Jean looked away, tears streaming down her face. She walked over and kissed Kevin on his head. "You see," Max blurted out, "this is the kind of crap I didn't want you to deal with."

"Shut up … *Dad*," Kevin smiled. He winked at Max. "You taught me well." Max teared up and he pulled Kevin over and kissed him again. Jean rubbed Kevin's cheek. He looked up with a smile and said, "That okay with you, being a Mom?" She embraced him, and began to cry.

Twenty-three

Kevin, Jean and Max were immersed in the kind of small talk families use to veil what can't be discussed: How is the food; who are the doctors. They avoided the Great Unspoken, that one of them would not be there for long, but this time avoidance itself was no longer an issue. And there was something to be said for reveling in meaningless nothing. It's what families do.

Max picked at a dish of green gelatin. "Why do they always give you lime?" he complained. As Kevin eyed him wryly, they began to hear the sound of chanting from down the hall. Max motioned towards it, and then asked, "So what brings you out here?"

"God, I'd forgotten. I've got a story for you. They want me to run it."

Max coughed a few times, and then recovering, said, "You're kidding." Jean was incredulous, eyeing Max with concern.

"Believe it," Kevin went on. "And there's more." He described the past two days, the police stops Max knew about, and the things he didn't. He talked of the call from the White House at Sharon's coffee shop, John Raden, their conversation, and about being bugged. How Hanford hoped to sign him up. He spoke of the news crew that tracked him down and their altercation with Sharon, and how it got on the air. He described his deteriorating relationship, the phone call on the plane, and showed them the note that he found in his pocket. And he told them about Hanford's grand vision of using hydrogen bombs to tamp down global tensions, flying out to see one of the things and how Raden thought and he agreed that it was probably a setup.

Max and Jean listened long and hard. Max was tired but his mind was sharp, and he asked the question that was on both their minds, "So who's this Raden?"

"I don't know. I'll tell you though—I had a hell of a conversation with him. He's the most ruthlessly up-front person I ever met in government."

"Deceive with the truth. I don't know why they chose him but I do know a fish stinks from the head down. Hanford's one of the cagiest people to come down the pike in a long time. So you watch yourself. If you shook his hand and noticed a finger missing, he'd say you miscounted. And he'd do it in a way that half the people would think he was right."

"Raden told me his wife collects pottery," Kevin told Jean, "and she has one of your pieces."

"Really? Did he tell you what it was?"

"Some kind of a vase that came in on itself."

"I did pieces like that twenty-five years ago," she said to Max. "Remember, honey? Maybe he's on the level."

"He seemed sincere," Kevin said. "Normally with those guys the hair on the back of my neck stands up. Didn't happen."

A doctor walked in, nodding at them as he picked up and read Max's chart.

"How are you feeling Dr. Rosenkranz?"

"Today's a good day. Dr. Spencer, I want you to meet my son, Kevin."

The doctor warmly shook Kevin's hand. He checked Max's IV drip, and then listened to his chest. "I noticed you've had a small cough since yesterday. Do you have any heaviness or discomfort when you breathe?" Max nodded, and the doctor said, "There's a little fluid on your right side. I'd like to get an X-ray." The chanting down the hall picked up as the doctor said goodbye and walked out.

"I want to check on that," Kevin said, walking out. Once outside, he caught up with the doctor. "Dr. Spencer, thank you. I want to ask you something. I hadn't seen him in several months. I know what's going on, but frankly, I expected worse." Kevin had to raise his voice a bit over the chanting coming from Max's old room.

"I've treated your Dad the past year," Dr. Spencer said, raising his voice as well. "I'm not trying to give you any false hope. He's in a terminal phase. It's important to make sure he's comfortable. According to the book I'd say don't expect much, but I'd have said that four months ago. You get patients who surprise you. The disease is particularly onerous once it gets beyond the pelvic cavity, but he's been kicking it in the teeth every step of the way. That's why I want to make sure his lungs are okay. I like him. He's always cracking us up. Everyone feels honored to treat him."

Kevin thanked him, and nodded towards the chanting, "You guys okay with that?"

"Not really, but we try to be respectful. It's a hospital, but people have rights. Personally, she reminds me of my grandmother. You couldn't tell her anything. So I tread lightly. We've kept the rooms around her empty. Now, your father was something else. We had to move him."

Kevin thanked him again and went back to the room. Max winked, "What did he say?"

"He wants you to go back to the old room. Says you're a good influence on the guy there."

Jean laughed and as if on cue, changed the subject. "You didn't say what they want with you. They know you're not an administrator. What do you think Raden was trying to tell you?"

"I asked him point blank. He wasn't sure. Maybe he expects me to figure it out for him. And with what Hanford wants to do now—"

Just then the chanting grew louder. Kevin asked, "That's what it's been like?"

"Yup. The nurses told her to keep it down, but one of her kids raised a stink so they backed off. If you weren't sick before you got here, that drek will do it to you by the time you leave. So, getting back to the first point, what are you going to do?"

"Well, that's what brought me here," Kevin said. "He paid for me to fly out to watch one of the things go off, and arranged for me to stop by and see you first."

"Hold it," Max declared. "He specifically suggested that you stop by here on the way?"

"I was going to surprise you." He waved his finger around. "I didn't count on all this."

"I wonder if he knew." Jean looked studiously at Max.

"They didn't know nothing," Max said. He looked to Kevin. "They don't know."

"I wouldn't put anything past this guy." Kevin was about to say something when a sound in the hall caught their attention. Five men walked in. Four ranged in age between the mid-fifties and sixties and were dressed casually while one, slightly younger, wore a suit and hat.

"Rabbi!" Jean greeted them. "Nat, Ted …" She gave each a kiss, and then turned to Kevin. "Sweetheart, this is Rabbi Yellin."

"Oh my, yes," the Rabbi said warmly. "It's a pleasure to meet you." Kevin beamed.

Jean introduced everyone. The names Nat, Jack, Lenny and Ted went by Kevin. All were Temple members. They were gracious, and obviously held genuine affection for Jean and Max. For Kevin, it was a different side to Max and Jean. They never showed they had any interest in their faith.

Max was characteristically cantankerous, but in an easygoing way. "So," he asked, "just happened to be in the neighborhood?"

"What, you're in the hospital and we can't stop by?" joshed temple president Jack Aboff, a lanky gentleman with silver hair and a yellow Polo shirt. "All this guy does is eat my kishkas out," he told a smiling Kevin. "'Bout time he got a little in return."

"And," said Ted Gechtman, a trustee, "the rabbi thought we'd do a small service."

Max waved him off but Jack said, "No one asked you. Pesach's coming. It's a mitzvah."

"A mitzvah's a good deed," Ted told Kevin. "And Pesach's Passover."

"Thanks," said Kevin warmly, "I know." He asked Max, "If your neighbor's wife can do what she's doing, why can't they do a little something for you?"

"What do you mean?" asked Nat Josloff, a retired United pilot.

Jean gestured outside. The woman had lit into a stream of hosannas. "You believe that? Max's old roommate, the wife. He's in a coma. Maybe she thinks she can bring him out of it."

The rabbi peeked out the door. "She sounds—focused."

"Such a diplomat," said Max. "You try sleeping with it."

"Well, then they won't mind a little davening."

Jean looked at Kevin. "Praying." Kevin nodded.

Rabbi Yellin opened a large black valise and passed out yarmulkes and prayer books. The service lasted fifteen minutes, and notwithstanding his protests, Max enjoyed it. Kevin held the book for him. He had been to Jewish services only a few times, but the sense of belonging he got from Jean and Max was appealing. This side of Max, who'd always put a rational understanding of the universe above everything, was curious. Maybe it was basking in the afterglow of his newfound connection with the most important people in his life, but it didn't matter. It had meaning to them, and that was enough. Born to a Methodist mother who would have hardly been able to explain the workings of her own faith let alone another he had grown up with the security that came from the Plan, learning how it worked without much interest in who or what got it going. There wasn't Jesus or Jehovah or Allah or even God but an amorphous Creator who ruled through Natural Law. While he was sure that would never change, for the first time he experienced something that didn't detract from it as add to it a new dimension.

When they finished, Nat told Max, "I got a surprise. I've gotten better with the shofar." He went to the Rabbi's valise, and from a felt-lined case took out a horn. It was about sixteen inches in length, spiral, in shades of dark brown and ocher.

"It's a ram's horn," the rabbi explained. "It's blown on some of the High Holidays."

"I think I've seen it," Kevin smiled. *"Ten Commandments*, right?"

Nat laughed, and said, "I figured I'd give you a preview."

"Oh, no, no, no, no, no," Max said, appreciative but adamant. "This time I gotta say no."

"You sure, Nat?" Jean wavered.

"I won't do a whole schpiel. Just a note."

"Come on," Max implored. "You can't do that here! Christ, it's a hospital."

"And besides," Ted said, "Sister what's-her-name down the hall is louder,"

"Ah, it'll be over before they know it," Jack said. As Max frowned, the rabbi closed the door. Nat took the shofar to the window and blew a single drawn-out note.

A scream rose from the hall. Ted, closest to the door, ran to investigate.

"Oh, for crying out loud!" Max said.

"What was that?" the rabbi exclaimed.

A nurse ran into the room. "What was *that?*"

"Oh my God, I'm sorry," Nat said, holding up the horn. "It was the shofar, a ram's horn. We did a service for Dr. Rosenkranz. We blew it when we finished."

Just then, Ted walked back, barely containing himself.

"What the matter?" Jean asked.

"That woman next door? She ran down the hall yelling something about 'Gabriel coming to get her and it ain't yet her time'."

Twenty-four

As seen from Secaucus, New Jersey, where the MSNBC studios once resided, the New York City skyline was illuminated in late afternoon gold. The new studios at Rockefeller Center always felt like a techno club to Jessica Enright, and with the light that Tuesday afternoon, it was like being on the set of *CSI Miami*.

Enright had been at MSNBC three years, long enough to watch the transformation of the perennial laggard in the cable news world into a player. A shift in corporate policy had the left-leaning network on a decidedly centrist path, and the year broke with it approaching longtime leader FOX for the top spot in ratings and revenue. Up to now, Enright had been regarded a promising and attractive journalistic prospect, but had otherwise done little to distinguish herself. She was reviewing notes for a meeting with her editor when her cell phone rang. It read Private.

"Miss Enright," the caller began, "you'd make a good sparring partner."

John Raden wasn't ready to reveal himself as Enright's source secret.

"Thanks. I'm assuming you're referring to my go-round with Herter's girlfriend."

"That's right." He knew her brush with Sharon Velazquez had brought some notoriety to her fledgling career. What he wouldn't say was that she'd done a good job egging Sharon on. "But next time," he added, "don't use a camera man trained in Zapruder-vision."

"Excuse me?"

"Google Abraham Zapruder. Z-A-P-R-U-"

"Oh, I think I know who you're talking about."

"Perhaps. You'll learn."

"Yeah well, I'll see what I can do." As she spoke, she typed Abraham Zapruder on her laptop. Links to the Dallas, Texas women's clothing manufacturer popped up and of the shaky home movie footage he took on November 22, 1963, that captured the assassination of President John F. Kennedy. "I have a meeting in five minutes," she added. "I'm not expecting you to tell me your name, but at least you can say how it is you know what you've told me."

"You shouldn't have much trouble vetting what I've said," the voice advised.

"I'll ignore the wild goose chase. Just tell me what yesterday was all about."

"Well, you can tell yourself. What did you hope to accomplish?"

"I wanted to get a statement from Herter."

"And that's what you got, correct? So what's got you puzzled?"

"I didn't learn anything is what's got me puzzled. It was one big 'No comment'. I don't know any more today than I did yesterday."

"Sure you do. You learned he's willing to talk provided you respect his boundaries. You learned the artist isn't. You learned that's enough to get you notoriety. And when he walked away, you learned that he hadn't any more interest in the program than he had before you chased him down."

"I guess," Enright responded tersely, looking at her watch.

"Okay. Now you can share something. What happened after you left Princeton?"

"Nothing. We tried to follow up, but got nowhere. And Velazquez has been—"

"Forget her. They appear to have gone their separate ways." He wasn't about to fill her in on what happened after she left. He said, "Which brings us to today."

"Right." Enright was tapping her fingers. "I need to run. So what's so important that I dig up that 1993 Op/Ed from the *San Francisco Chronicle*?"

"Miss Enright, I'm not connecting the dots for you. I'm just laying some of them out. Think of it as one big jigsaw puzzle." She huffed, and he added, "You should be getting a little present about now."

An email entitled "Link" appeared. Enright opened the article. "Thanks," she said. "I'll look into this."

"Go to your meeting," the voice concluded.

"You going to call back, or is this it?"

"You'll hear from me. One more thing. The person or persons I speak for have an interest in informing you the scientist landed in San Francisco this morning."

"You're kidding. That's very interesting." She ran through the article. "Okay, I see this now. Thank you."

"My pleasure. I'll speak with you soon." As Enright hung up and ran down the hall, Raden prepared to board his flight.

He had just taken his seat when his phone rang. As he had been to Jessica

Enright, the person on the other end was an unknown source. They had been communicating for over a year.

"Dr. Raden," the female voice began, "do you have a few minutes?"

"Absolutely." His attitude was markedly different from Enright's. "I'm glad you called. I have some information you may find interesting."

"So do I. The situation at Sandia has deteriorated. My back's against it." She sounded grim.

"I gathered that. It appears they're looking to change the dynamics of the program. There's a lot coming out over the next few days."

"You can tell something's going on. You may know the politics, but I see how it's affecting things on the ground."

Raden agreed. "I suspect it involves wholesale administrative changes. Is that what—"

"That's part of it. For now, I'll leave it at that."

"Okay." Raden gave a deliberate sigh. "Before we go on, there's a possibility this line may now be compromised, even considering my background. For certain reasons, I'm willing to take a chance."

"That wouldn't surprise me." The caller groaned. "But too much is happening now. I'll have to take my chances as well. Now, do you have any news?"

"Yes. It looks like the focus of your interest may go for it."

"Really!" She sounded genuinely excited.

"He's scheduled to take in one of the things this week—"

"Then I have to move. I'll take a chance that he goes through with it. I think that's enough for now. Thanks, I'll be in touch."

Raden said goodbye, and leaned back in his seat. In her bedroom Lisa Whiteman jumped up from her desk, got a suitcase from her closet and began to pack, taking care to keep it quiet.

Twenty-five

Jean was all smiles as the temple group said goodbye. She turned to Nat. "And you! That's one that's going to make the rounds!"

"I'm just not sure how to put it on my resume." They all laughed.

"If that doesn't make me an honorary Jew," Kevin wryly told Max, "I don't know what will."

Max smiled weakly. Although thankful, he felt drained. Like a testimonial where the honoree cherishes the effort but wants to crawl under the table, he had a place in his heart for the people who visited but was ready to see them go. The shofar episode had put the right mark on cutting things short. They promised to visit again, minus the shofar, and the rabbi said he would say a prayer for Max at Saturday services. As they left, to a person they told Kevin that his presence was the best thing that could have happened to Jean and Max, for they had never seen the Rosenkranz's so at peace.

"So sport," Max asked Kevin wearily, "what time do you have to leave?"

"I would have to be at the airport by seven, but I'm not leaving now."

"The hell you're not. You don't stop what you're doing because of us."

"Sweetheart," Jean smiled, "we appreciate it, but we'll work everything out. You do what you have to. We'll be here when you get back. So, tell us what you're thinking."

"I have very mixed feelings. But if there's any good that came from this, it was coming here." Max nodded, but Jean saw how tired he was. "Honey, I'm going to take Kevin down for a cup of coffee," she said as he closed his eyes.

"This meant more to him than you could know," Jean tenderly told Kevin as she nursed a cup of tea five minutes later. "You know how good he is saying anything but what really matters. Maybe it took something like this for him to realize that."

"Still can't believe it," Kevin glowered at his coffee.

"I wake up every morning and still can't." She paused, and then asked with a sigh, "Okay, tell me about Sharon."

Kevin talked how they had been drifting apart, and how Sharon had reacted to the government's effort to muscle in. Jean listened intently, then smiled. "You two are the most evenly-matched couple I've ever seen not work out."

Kevin laughed. "I know."

"I guess it's okay to say this now. She called me last year, when you two began having problems. I think she was looking for a woman's perspective. I won't betray any confidence for either of you. But I told her what I'm going to tell you." She sighed. "I once had an art teacher who'd look at work, and even when it was very good he would just shake his head and say, "Haven't suffered enough." As one woman artist looking at another, there's a dimension most people can't relate to, even other women. She and I have had success, but the one thing that comes through when I look at her work is how much hurt she keeps under wraps. She may paint leaves and shells, but beneath it, believe me there's pain. She's suffered. Think about why she paints so much of what's old. She may be passionate, but there's more that she keeps a lid on. I'm not sure she realizes it herself. Just keep that in mind when you see her."

"Okay ... *Mom*." As Jean laughed between tears, Kevin said, "I never thought of that. But why do you think she's so mad about the bomb issue?"

Jean took a sip of tea. "I think," she said, choosing her words carefully, "it reminds her of what she's been going through with you. Maybe she's so anti nuclear, she can never get past it. You should hear people around here. But a woman in a relationship feels, then she thinks. If I had to bet, she wants to see you passionate, not like you're just going through the motions. You have to remember, those things have been around three generations. Who knows what effect they've had on people. No one knows what to do with them; no one decides anything. Just as you are with a lot of things. Maybe she's less mad at the program than she is with you, that you're sitting on your hands." She paused. "I was never a marcher. It's not like I ever liked the things, but I never got up every morning hating them like some people I know. I never thought about it much. But they've been hanging over people's heads so long it must have consequence, maybe in ways we aren't even aware of. You don't see them, but you know they're there. Maybe that *is* the consequence. Maybe it's spilling over into how she sees the two of you."

Kevin could only listen. A moment later Jean's phone rang. "Oh, it's

our neighbor." She answered, "Hi Mike." After several seconds, she added, "Oh yes, please, that would be nice. Can you hold on?" She turned
to Kevin. "I'm thinking if he visits, I can get a ride back with him. That
way you don't have to rush going back to the airport."

"That's fine with me, but my suitcase is at your house," Kevin answered.

"That's okay. Mike can get it." She returned to Mike. "Oh, thanks so
much. You'll get to meet Kevin. Can you pick up Kevin's suitcase at our
house? We'll see you in a little while." She hung up. "That'll work out
nice. He and his wife Barbara live right behind us. Our backyards share
that stream. They're two of our closest friends. He's an interesting guy.
He's a retired FBI agent I think, but you wouldn't know it. He doesn't fit
the part. Of course we told him about you. I'm sure he's as interested in
meeting you as seeing Max."

"You've met some really nice people here."

"Such gifts. Just like you. Having you in our lives has meant the world
to us. I don't know how much longer he's going to be able to fight this
thing but whatever time he's got, well, he can spend it like a father. I
know what it's meant to him. Telling him you've always felt he's been
like a father is—" She clasped her hands together, almost choking up.
"Me too. Having you here even this short time; I don't know. It makes
whatever's going to come somehow bearable."

Kevin gestured to Jean, and he stood up. He hugged her and cradled
her head as she patted him on the chest. "Come on," she said, "let's go
see our old man."

Twenty-six

"Joshua, I want to explore this Herter thing further," said a winded Jessica Enright as she arrived at her boss's office. "There's something going on with him and the program."

Deputy News Editor Joshua Emerson removed his reading glasses and looked up. "Before you go on, the White House just issued a release. The president's going out there on Wednesday. They've requested time for an announcement on Sunday. They're lining up the talk show circuit this weekend. But nothing's leaking, and that just doesn't happen." He folded his arms. "So let's hear what you've got."

"Josh, this story, it has the strangest feel. I can't seem to get a handle on it."

"Sometimes in this business, you have to go on that."

Enright described what her research had uncovered. Emerson had let her pursue the story when she first approached him, intrigued with the information she'd gotten from her source. But he had been taken aback by her run-in with Sharon Velazquez, dramatic as it was, and was seriously considering assigning her another story.

"It's a lot of loose ends," he noted. "All that's tying it together is that source."

"The guy's a pain in the rear."

He laughed. "Some are."

"He sends me off on wild goose chases. He's like a professor assigning reading material. I wouldn't mind if he was more open, but it's like a tutorial. He just texted me a link; not something from today but decades ago. It's an editorial that scientist Max Rosenkranz wrote in the *San Francisco Chronicle*, about the cancellation of that atom smasher in Texas."

Emerson perked up. "The SSC. I had a front-row seat for it. I was a reporter there back then. He made a big stink. I tried following up with him but he avoided me like the plague; in fact, he avoided most media. He held us responsible for killing the thing."

"How so?"

"There were huge cost overruns. The scientists grudgingly agreed, including Rosenkranz, but it didn't keep them from being angry. Scientists are a lot like us. We're not supposed to take things personally, but everyone does. What do you think it has to do with Herter?"

"Well, Rosenkranz was his mentor. If it meant something to Rosenkranz, maybe it means something to him. My sources are hinting that there's talk about bringing back the collider, and Herter left for San Francisco this morning."

"What's in San Francisco?" She shrugged. "Okay, what do you have in mind?"

"I don't think we should ignore it." Emerson nodded and she added, "I'd like to track him down. He's been very tight-lipped. I want to see what made him up and run. I asked him—"

"I know what you asked, but he left himself enough wiggle room to drive a truckload of plausible deniability through." He caught her reaction, then smiled. "You'll learn."

"Well, he's gotten a pass the last few years. I wonder if maybe that wasn't a mistake."

"The girlfriend might beg to differ. But I agree. The feeling's been that while it's true his work got the thing going he hasn't had any role with it, so no one saw a need to look at him. But if there's a different angle maybe it's time. No one knows what the White House is doing. Maybe it all ties together. They've managed to keep the thing off the front pages, which is interesting. Okay, go with it. When do you want to leave?"

"As soon as I can. You'd think with the election, they'd be trumpeting the thing. But without a primary challenge, maybe they're keeping their powder dry."

"Could be. Or Hanford's up to something." Emerson clasped his hands behind his head. "You're young, so just listen. You remember this. You're living through journalistic history. You'd think something this controversial would be an issue, but neither side wants to touch it. Either they're so clever they manipulated us into keeping it off the front page or this is one of those rare things no one wants to visit. I've never seen anything like it. When it first came out both parties backed it, but neither wanted to be seen taking the credit. Each wants brownie points for getting it going, then blames the other for letting it happen. They're all sleepwalking. It's like entitlements. They know it's unsustainable, neither side wants to fix it and all the public wants is keeping costs low enough so they can go. And both sides have their fringe groups in check. Environmentalists push the issue but have lost credibility because no one sees detrimental effects. The left wants the funds spent on other things but they forget it makes a profit. All the right cares about is security, keeping Al Qaeda and the Chinese out. But so many of them love the mushroom clouds, they keep their mouths shut. They've all made their own deal with the Devil. This issue is going to be taught in journalism schools as a course in political and journalistic cognitive dissonance for years to come."

"Well, that by itself makes for an interesting story, especially during an election year."

"That's it," Emerson's eyes widened. "Run with it and see where it goes. Where do you want to start?"

"Max Rosenkranz."

"All right." Emerson froze. "Wait a minute—"

"That's why he went out there!"

"Okay. Follow up Rosenkranz and you'll find Herter. Did you get a sense he's an active player with Hanford, or—"

"No. Not even close. Like the girlfriend. She really doesn't like us."

Emerson smiled. "You mean she really doesn't like *you*."

"She's got a bug up her ass about me big time," she laughed. "She doesn't seem to like any of us. But yeah, she particularly doesn't like me."

"That was Rosenkranz years ago. Let it go. But Rosenkranz is a different matter. He's a Nobel laureate. He should carry some weight. But even if you don't see Herter, stop by the *Chronicle*. Some who were around then might want to bend your ear. I'd put our people in San Francisco on it with you, but I'll let you run with it." Enright's heart fluttered at thought of having to share the story, but Emerson's last words left her relieved. "All right," he finished, "keep me posted. And I'll be interested hearing if you come up with any connection between Rosenkranz and Herter and the SSC."

As Enright left, Emerson began to wonder if her source knew his own interest in getting closure on the story. He then weighed whether having that come to mind was a hint he was beginning to get old. Either way, he wanted to know.

Twenty-seven

Max awoke just past four p.m. Jean and Kevin had been sitting quietly, having come back ten minutes earlier. Jean was flipping through an old *People* magazine while Kevin surfed the TV. A fine-spun calm imbued the room.

"Morning," Kevin said. "Good nap?"

Max coughed. "Not bad, sport."

"I think we scared off your neighbors."

"That's why I was able to sleep. So, sport, Jean take you to the choke and puke downstairs?"

"Yeah. We ran into the rabbi. He was finishing a pork roll. Nat blew the shofar again and all the rats left."

Jean laughed and Max rocked his head. "Yeah, yeah, yeah," he cackled.

"Don't be such a big shot," Jean admonished him. She winked at Kevin, adding, "He's been hanging around you long enough. You think it doesn't rub off?"

Max smiled smugly, thoroughly satisfied. "I missed this," he sighed.

With a smile and a sneer, Kevin said, "It's your own damn fault, you—"

"Yeah, yeah. You see," he upbraided Jean, "this is the kind of crap kids these days say."

"What do you expect?" she shot back.

Max broke into a smile. "So sport, what are you going to do?"

Kevin took a deep breath. "I think I'll go."

"Are you sure that's what you want to do?" Jean said.

"Let the boy go," Max snapped.

"I'm not telling him not to go," she protested. "I'm just asking him if he's sure that's what he wants."

"Oh listen to the two of you," quipped Kevin. "You're such …*parents.*" Jean and Max beamed, relishing the moment, and knew he was right. "I've given it lots of thought," Kevin added. "I've been avoiding it. I've been followed, and there's other stuff as well. I can't live like that. I'll go, I'll see, I'll decide. Maybe I'll be in a position to do something about it. And hey, it's a beach. I'll get a tan. What the hell, maybe I'll meet a girl. So, what do you think?"

Jean and Max eyed each other. "Just be careful," Jean counseled. Max agreed.

"Oh, I will," Kevin said. "Who knows, maybe they'll regret it more than me."

"Honey," Jean told Max, "Mike called. He's going to pick up Kevin's suitcase."

"Good." He turned to Kevin. "You'll like this guy."

"So, former FBI agent?"

"Well, I think he was FBI." Max looked at Jean. "He might have been an agent."

"He never talked about it fully and we never pushed," she said. "Maybe you can talk to him. You get the idea that he doesn't miss what he used to do. He and Barbara have taken us up to Napa Valley many times. We've spent a lot of weekends at the bed and breakfasts there."

"They sound like good people," Kevin smiled. Much like he felt with the temple group, he already respected the couple he had never met for their loyalty and devotion to the two most important people in his life. "Promise me when I come back, we'll go up there."

"Oh yes!" Jean glowed. "That's a great idea! They'll love it. That okay with you, honey?"

"Okay, sport," Max nodded, "you go. Look, listen, learn, and don't promise anything. Let them sweat for a change. Okay?"

"That's perfect. Thanks."

"When you get back, we'll talk. I don't have to ask if you'll be able to sack out on the plane."

"I guess I'll crash when I get there. Sorry, poor choice of words. Anyway, Raden will be there. The event—that's what they call them—is that evening." He shook his head incredulously. The one thing he had studiously avoided was talk of what the police had found at his door. He had a lot to tell Raden. "Well, Thursday looks like a busy day."

Jean said, "Just take care of yourself." The words had barely left her when footsteps were heard in the hallway.

A lanky fellow in his early sixties, wearing black jeans and a black button-down shirt with sweptback gray hair and a thick gray mustache, trod in. He looked like he belonged more in El Paso Texas than Marin County California.

"Mike!" Jean exclaimed.

"Mike Yahr," the gentleman offered. "Kevin, it's a pleasure to meet you."

Kevin smiled warmly as they shook hands. Though outwardly craggy, Mike had a refinement. Beneath it lay a footing of steel.

"Thanks for bringing my bag," Kevin said.

"Couldn't pass up seeing this guy." Mike grabbed Max's hand. "Hey, Rosenkranz!"

"Up yours, you old fart. Mikey, thanks for coming."

Mike eyed Kevin. "Is he as charitable to you?" As Kevin smiled, he said, "Stands to reason. Miss Manners aside, these are two of the finest folks we know." He sat down. "Barb said she'd stop by later."

"Have her sneak me in a piece of pie," Max said. He turned to Kevin. "You should see what this woman comes up with in the kitchen."

Mike leaned back. "I saw something interesting when I stopped by the house. There's a van parked across the street. It's been a while, but I know a surveillance op when I see one."

The others immediately lost their smiles.

"You're kidding," Kevin said.

"I'm not trying to get you rattled, but we need to talk."

"Crap." Kevin felt a chill. He remembered seeing the van. "Are you sure?"

"You park a few houses away, just enough to avoid attention. Most times, no one would notice, except an old SOB like me. If I were checking you out, that's exactly where I'd set up. And, I spoke to some friends. There are eyes on the ground." He reached in his pocket. "Then there's this. It was on your car." He handed a piece of paper to Kevin. Written across it was a short note punctuated by a dark red stain. "You are being watched. If you're smart, you'll go home. Forget the program or there will be consequences."

Kevin reached into his own pocket. "I found this in my coat pocket, on the plane."

Mike compared the two. "The writing's the same," he said. "So's the paper."

Max and Jean sat dumbfounded.

"Great," Kevin said. "How do—how'd you know my car? And who are your friends?"

"Let's just say some pensioners from the office. Point is, you're not here in a vacuum. It's common knowledge in some circles. So, all aside for now, what were your plans?"

"I was going to fly out to watch an explosion."

"And knowing what you know now, would you change anything?"

"Wow. I want to, but something tells me I shouldn't."

"Good. That's what I hoped you would say."

"Why is that?" Jean asked.

"Because turning tail would cause him more trouble than if he went," Max said. "Correct?"

Mike nodded. "And, not letting on gives you options that hightailing it back home doesn't."

"So he pretends he doesn't know anything?" Jean said. Mike nodded yes, and she added, "Sweetheart, now I'm the one with the bad feeling. You don't have to do this."

"No, he doesn't," Max said. "But I think we should listen to Mike."

"I'm not saying not to. But I have a queasy feeling now, and I didn't before."

"You're not necessarily wrong," Mike agreed. "I mean, who do you go to when the cops are bent? Oh, and by the way, you're going to have company when you get there. It was just announced that Hanford's flying out. You know what that means."

"It means now they're not letting me back out." As Max and Jean blanched, Kevin rubbed his face. "Mike, maybe I should tell you what's going on."

"I know what's going on." They grew silent. "But put aside what I know. There's different ways you can read this. You can be too clever by half and draw wrong conclusions. So. The other night, if you hadn't been pulled over again and learned that something was fishy about the first stop you wouldn't have thought twice about it."

"Probably true, but the second time was random." He froze. "How'd you know that?"

"Possibly random. On the one hand you've got people posing as cops, covertly watching you. On the other, people are going out of their way to let you know they're watching you." Mike smiled. "Either someone's careless, or underestimates you, or both, or—"

"Or what?"

"Or you ask 'Who?' " Kevin threw up his hands. "Okay. But by now you're thinking the people looking to hire you are the ones watching you, right? What do they want? I admit, it's convoluted. But ask who and you learn why, and the more you know the better you deal with it." He paused. "You'll like this. I'm always asking your friend here about his work, right?" Max smiled. "You see a picture from Hubble or hear about a discovery. I was always interested, so I'd ask. And the answers I got—I still roll my eyes on entanglement. Two particles fly off in opposite directions, something happens to one and the other knows about it? And you expect people not to look at you like you got a screw loose?"

They all laughed. Jean said, "Now you know what it's been like with these two."

"Well, dealing with this is just as bizarre. But remember, in your field you deal with crazy particles disappearing here and reappearing there. In mine, you're dealing with people. Just remember this about people: They're oftentimes as predictable as those particles of yours. So know this—you're caught in the middle of a pissing contest."

Max sat up. "Now that makes sense."

"Look who's involved," Mike said. "The NSC, Defense, Energy, a dozen Pacific nations. The White House in an election year. And you in the middle. Don't think any of them wouldn't throw you under the bus in an instant. When it comes to money and power, there's no such things as friends."

Kevin looked at Max. "Shows you how much a couple of smart scientists know."

"I told you you should talk to him."

Kevin eyed Mike. "I have to ask—what did you do, and for who?"

"I was a janitor." Kevin groaned. "Yeah," added Mike, "I … cleaned things up."

Kevin's eyes widened. He felt skittish, but it came with a tinge of familiarity. "You know, it's funny. Talking to you is like talking to a guy I just met back east, Jack Raden."

Mike smiled. "He was my closest friend in the agency."

"Son of a bitch."

"We waited for the right time," Mike smiled. "When I said we had to talk, I meant it."

Jean looked perplexed. "Mike, what's all this? What's going on? And just who is Jack?"

"My friend Jack Raden came from Wall Street. He made a fortune, behind the scenes. That's how he works. He didn't knock on our door. It's more they knocked on his. We hit it off from the start and kept in touch after I left. Great guy."

"What did they want him for?" Max asked.

"Figuring things out. There aren't any better. What's going on isn't his doing. But he knows the system. Kevin, what did you think of him?"

"Interesting guy. It struck me how up front he was. Do I trust him?"

"Absolutely. It's ironic that he and I know each other, you know Max and Jean and we're neighbors. Odds are nothing would have come of it if not for what's happening. We realize this isn't your world." He eyed Max and Jean. "You too. You know what Barb and I think of you. That's why I went into all I did. I don't do lectures. I like retirement. We've been discussing this for weeks. We felt Kevin needed to come out here. And, Dr. Rosenkranz—" Mike shot Max an all-too-knowing gaze, "—it was time Kevin knew."

Jean smiled sadly. "I'll speak for my husband for once." She stood and planted a kiss on Mike, eyes watering as she sat down again.

"Yeah, Mikey," Max conceded softly. "Thanks." Kevin thanked him as well.

"My pleasure, but don't thank me yet. One objective was precisely what happened." He held up the notes. "They bit. What's happening now has us concerned."

"I don't understand," Kevin pulled back. "And who's 'us'?"

"Certain people."

"Oh, come on," Kevin said, annoyed. "Don't do that to me."

"I get it," Mike smiled. "But for now, it's for your well-being. Just trust me. And listen, I know what learning about Max meant to you. But it was also a distraction. It slowed you down, enough for interested parties to show their hand. Did you use a GPS or your cell phone here?" Kevin nodded. Mike smiled, "They're easy to compromise. And that episode in Princeton. I would have liked to check your car and your home phone. Someone knows a lot about you and your friends." Kevin blanched, knowing he was referring to Sharon. "And more than just from your coat collar. You learn a lot inside."

Kevin huffed. "I have to ask now. Where—"

"The NSA. National Security Agency."

"Oh, boy," Max grunted.

"Yeah. It's more than just listening in on phone calls. You've heard some of what goes on, I'm sure, but you can't possibly imagine what can be done today. I had enough of that life. But you learn. You see things for what they are, how they work. People want you, they get to your friends. And with power, things need balance. Like the White House; they didn't want Jack in. But others did. There's give and take. This bomb business for instance. Hanford's got this vision, selling this little project of his."

"Mikey, what do you think about that?"

"Perverse thing is, on paper it could work. But Jack and I agree, depends who's running it. Odds are, with this crowd it won't. Whatever happened, they're up against it. Leaks are popping up. Something's going on. They're nervous. That's why Kevin's getting the bum's rush."

"Jack asked me to start thinking outside the box," said Kevin. "Is that what you mean?"

"Partly." Mike smiled. "Barb and I saw the run-in you and your girl-friend had with the reporter. Damn shame. But interesting, how she happened to fixate on you." Mike looked at Max. "Remember that collider in Texas?"

"The SSC. How can I forget?"

Jean said, "Remember how worked up you got when they cancelled it, honey?"

"There was a reporter then," Mike said, "Joshua Emerson, who tried to—"

"I remember him," Max said. "Pain in the ass. Tried his damnedest to get me to sit down."

"Well, he remembered too. He's a news editor at MSNBC, where he has a junior reporter Jessica—"

"Enright," Kevin snapped. "Son of a bitch."

"I can't believe this crap," Max said.

"It's not that complicated," Mike said. "Why do you think I got out? I got tired of it."

"Now you know why I said tell them to shove it."

"Yeah, but you shove it, you don't find out what you need to know. Enright's a pain but she's uncovering things. You don't know what she'll turn up. On her own she found her way to Kevin here. But remember what happened. Media may be annoying, but usually they don't cross into the other things Kevin's experienced. The stakes have been raised, higher than even she's accustomed. She may need a reality check if she gets out of hand again but let her play it out. I know it seems confusing with all these parties involved. But if you have to keep them all in per-spective, it means others do as well. The danger is that if they keep too much in the air at once, it's liable to come crashing down on them. It's like those particles of yours. They do what they do. Being aware of that gives you leverage. The White House for instance. You may not appreci-ate it, but they're walking a very fine line with you. They want something from you, but they have to push you just right. Be aware of that. I know they brought up your solving some supposedly minor technical problem they have."

"Yeah," Kevin said, "Jack talked about that as well."

"Hanford raised it with him and dismissed it in the same breath. Which means—"

"That it's important."

"We concur. We don't know what it is or how important, but we're sure it's up there. He felt they're looking to cover their ass on something. I agree. They know not to hit you like gangbusters, but they also won't sit on their hands waiting for you to come around the way they did the past two years. There's reasons for all this. So let the reporter do her thing."

Jean, busily folding a tissue up and down, said, "Mike, I'm very nervous with all this. How can you help Kevin? What can you tell us?"

Mike eyed Kevin. "It's as much what he can tell us as what we can tell him. You have your universe. Welcome to mine."

"What can Kevin tell them?" Max asked. "They expect him to take a crash course in hotel management? They just want a schmuck. All goes right they get the credit. Something happens, they have a patsy."

Kevin agreed. "I told Jack they're looking for another Oppenheimer, and to forget it. But regardless, I don't know what I can help them with."

"Doesn't matter," Mike smiled. "Everyone thinks you're the only one who can fix this. It's perception. That, my friend, puts you in an advantageous position. Someone in the program's been leaking. Bomb problems, DOD and DOE directives, how it's trickled down to the contractors. It has us concerned but the data we're getting is contradictory. This thing's supposed to have been humming along. But it's not, and no one can read between the lines. They're covering their backsides. People inside are very tight-lipped, but the source has been begging to get you involved. We need you to look at the data. We think it has to do with the physics. No one knows that better than you. Since we don't know what's going on, we're unsure how it affects policy. But we're very sure it has little to do with what Hanford wants. His vision is a red herring but it's a viable red herring. That makes it especially dangerous because it diverts attention legitimately. Whatever it is, it's likely something they try to set you up for. But they may hope you'll be a good soldier who falls on his sword. Hopefully, you'll hang around long enough to learn what's going on and get out before there's trouble. So, there it is."

Kevin was aghast. "Unbelievable."

"Maxie, you're a physicist," Mike said. "What do you think they want Kevin for?"

"I don't know. I'm not privy to how it works, so I can't say. I wish I was; I'd go on TV and trash the god-damn thing. But I'd start with the fuel mix."

"Mike," Jean interjected, "what can you tell Kevin?"

"Play dumb. Act like you're not onto anything."

"Well then," Max said, "wouldn't they assume he'd be on to them?

Those notes?"

"Maybe. But you don't tip your hand, they'll never know for sure and they'll have to keep to script. That gives you flexibility. Scientists can be thick, but don't lose sight of the fact that they know you're an intelligent adversary who doesn't miss much. They just don't know how much. They'll probe, test for weakness. To them, weakness is being ordinary, letting on you're onto them. So act like them; be deceptive. Keep your eyes open and your guard up, which can be hard in a tropical paradise. You can act ordinary, but don't be ordinary. Don't be common."

"You said adversary." Max looked serious.

"Don't ever forget it. There's a lot of money at stake. Follow it; you'll get answers. There's something to remember though. I hear you're like me, a movie buff."

"Oh, yeah," Kevin smiled. "Especially old ones, black and white."

Mike nodded. "I've been getting this guy into some of my favorites. Last week we watched *The Mask of Dimitrios.*"

Max smiled. "Peter Lorre, Sydney Greenstreet."

"Great film, watch it sometime. It's about a guy who slinks around Europe. Wherever he goes he causes trouble. In the end, it catches up with him, but not because Interpol typed his name into a database and ran his credit card transactions. That's what technology has done. The old mysteries where people hide in shadows and vanish in thin air—it's not like that anymore. Today you're a mouse click or cell call away from everything. Max and I, we're the generation that remembers that world. We know how much has changed. I miss it. Nowadays, intrigue, secrets, they're buried in keyboards. I saw it inside. And it's moving so fast that even Jack and I can't keep up with all of it. All the phone tapping and everything connected to it that you hear about; Jack and I are on the tail end of that. There's a breed of younger analyst that's so tech-savy that it put us to shame. I know this isn't your world, and what can be done is amazing. But high-tech or no-tech—you can still think outside the box. It still gives you options. In this case, it's the laptop box. They may not have even have thought up that contrast. They may not even think it worthwhile, but trust me, creativity always is. And, this isn't nuclear war, but it's not rocket science either. It's interests. Everyone has them. The resort's become the most spectacular thing around, but the rules they're using are timeless. Money and power. And lucky you, you're the center of it all. You keep your eyes, ears and most of all your mind open."

Jean shook her head. "Is there anyone Kevin can trust?"

"For now, yourself and Jack. See who's calling the shots, if you want to play ball with them. It may not be Hanford. Presidents come and go but bureaucracies endure. What's the expression, it's like marriage. A president's like a husband, the head of the family or government but the bureaucracy's the wife. She's the neck. She turns the head. And remember, you're an interest too. You have things you want. Assert them, they'll respect you."

"He's right," Max said to Kevin. "Okay, so you fly out and see one of the things."

"I suppose that's going to be something," Jean said.

"Yeah," Kevin replied, "that's the prevailing opinion." Jean's perfectly reasonable comment was the opening to a reality he'd been avoiding. Deep down, although laying the groundwork for this was inadvertent, he had never shaken the idea that he had done something wrong. He had a sneaking, secret thrill every time one went off on TV or in a movie. That he might actually enjoy it though in real life was too much.

Mike looked at Max, who was visibly getting tired. It was nearing time for Kevin to leave. He said, "So Maxie, what do you think about what Kevin should do?"

Max took a deep breath. "Thinking morons will stop blowing things up because they watch bombs go off, who knows. At one time, I would've said he's as crazy as the idiots he's protecting us from." He paused. "There's nothing I can tell you that you need to hear. It's keeping you up at night. You have a conscience. We trust you to do what's right. If that's how you deal with this, you'll be fine. That's what I think."

"That's it, sweetheart," Jean beamed. "That's how I feel."

Max's voice got softer. "There was a time I'd say tell them to go schtupp themselves. But go watch the thing. See what they're not telling you. If they want to set you up, it won't matter whether you go or not. Just trust yourself. Come back, and we'll talk."

"I know you have to head out," Mike said. "Have you decided to get involved?"

"Not really."

"You're undecided? Or just not ready to bring it up yet?"

"I'm undecided as to whether to bring it up yet."

He laughed. "You're learning."

"Maybe," Kevin paused. "Or maybe it's time we call Nat back here with the shofar."

Late afternoon light filtered through the curtains, further bleaching out the whitened walls of the hospital room.

"I know you have to head out," Mike told Kevin. "Give me your keys. I'll run your bag down." Kevin thanked him and he left.

"I better get the show on the road," Kevin said. He slowly rose and went to Max's bedside.

"Sport," Max said, fighting back tears as Kevin took his hand, "you be careful."

"Coming in I kept thinking just what to tell you, how I thought you'd react."

Max squeezed his hand. "I know sport."

"No. What I want to say is that despite everything I'm happier that I came out here than with anything else I've ever done in my life."

"Sweetheart," Jean said, "I can't say enough what having you here means to us."

Max brought Kevin's hand to his chest. A tear ran down his cheek, disappearing into his pillow. "Son, you come back and let us know what happened."

"You know I will," Kevin said, rising. "Get on home and we'll head up to Napa."

"If anything comes up," Jean said warmly, "call, okay? Doesn't matter what time."

"Okay, sport," Max nodded. "Have a good flight. And be careful."

"Yeah, yeah. Don't give everyone a hard time, all right?"

Max beckoned Kevin closer. "Son, we love you very much." Kevin teared up and kissed him. "I love you too, Pop." Max ruffled Kevin's hair. He began to cry. "Take care," Kevin said, "and get out of here. I'll keep you posted." He got up and gave Jean a hug.

"We'll see you next week, okay?" she said.

Kevin kissed her. "Next week."

"Have a safe flight, sport," Max smiled. Jean said the same.

"Bye, guys," said Kevin. "I love you both very much." He had all he could do to turn and leave.

Jean lay her head on Max and began to softly rock.

Twenty-eight

Mike walked across the parking lot with a curiosity tempered by unease born of experience. He wanted to check Kevin's Prius again. From a distance it looked okay, but the feeling he used to get in the field when something wasn't right gnawed at him. Enough in tune with his intuition to pay it heed, he looked around, and found himself eyeing a distant tow truck.

Keeping one eye on it, he approached Kevin's car. He gingerly walked the perimeter, checking every visible surface, then bent down and scrutinized the shadows. He got in, sat still a few moments, and then looked about. Nothing seemed out of order, but instead of locking up, he popped the hood. As he got out, he heard tires screeching and looked up to see the tow truck barreling out the exit and disappearing into the afternoon.

Under the hood, his seasoned eyes looked past the engine and zeroed in on the device. Squinting in the sun, he disengaged the wires from the putty-like material. Then he closed the hood, locked up and trod to his own car. He put Kevin's suitcase in the trunk, took out his phone and made a call.

"I'm at the hospital," he said. "He had a little something wired to his engine. I'll have it towed, and keep you posted." He walked back to the lobby.

A minute later, the elevator opened and Kevin walked up to Mike.

"I want to thank you again," Kevin told Mike. "You've been an incredible help, but I really want to thank you for being there for Max and Jean."

"No thanks necessary. You meet people and just click. Now come on, we have to talk." Mike's tone was now serious as he led Kevin out of the hospital and to an empty part of the lot.

"Things have changed." He took out his car keys. "My Explorer's behind you, the dark green one. Your luggage is in the back. Take it to the airport. I'll return your car."

Kevin looked at him confused. "Why?"

"There's a nice chunk of C4 wired to a piece under your hood."

"*WHAT?*" Kevin felt the blood drain from his head. "Mike, that's IT! I'm *out* of here! I don't *need* this shit!"

"Get a grip," Mike said, trying to sound reassuring. "I can't have you falling apart."

Kevin was ashen, speechless for the moment. "All right," he finally said. "But Max and Jean don't hear about this."

"That's a given. Now, I just spoke to Jack. He'd say exactly what I'm saying now. I know you want to run but you can't."

"Whoa!" Kevin snapped. "You're saying I ignore even this?"

"No, you can't ignore it. But this isn't the kind of thing where you can call the cops."

"What are you saying?"

"The notes were meant to scare you off. This piece is different. I'm going to have it analyzed but 'til then, you're going to have to live on edge. The best thing is still to go out there. I know you feel completely out of your league—"

"You think?"

"They're expecting a deer in the headlights. If you charge, it may knock them off their game. And showing up will surprise them the most."

Kevin breathed in deeply. "I want to know how you found that thing."

"Kevin, with these things you have to go on your gut. It told me to look."

"Well, thank you. You saved my life."

"My pleasure. Now you can do something for me. In Princeton when they listened in on you, they were listening to Jack as well. He's a good person, and he's got a lot of respect for you. We both do. Someone clearly doesn't. Whatever they're hiding is big, big enough to warrant all this trouble. So go out there and look under the hood."

"Okay, I'll try. How do you deal with all this, being so laid back?"

"I'm not laid back. To me, they're not as scary as they used to be. I'm more pissed."

"I still don't know how you deal with them."

"Like this," Mike smiled, extending his hand. As Kevin shook, Mike grabbed hard. For an instant Kevin was thrown off but quickly recovered, holding firm in kind. Mike looked him steady in the eye. "See what you did? It's in you. People smell fear, they'll treat you a certain way. But they see you hold your own it'll throw them off. You'll know you've got a handle on it when they become less intimidating and more obnoxious. It's that first ten seconds. Get through it, you'd be surprised how emboldened you can get." He loosened his grip. "And learn to listen to your intuition. It's there for a reason."

"To be honest," Kevin laughed, rubbing his hand, "that's what I've done. I haven't wanted to deal with it."

"And a great many other things, I'd bet." As Kevin grinned, Mike added, "I'm not belittling you. It's human nature. And with fight or flight, flight usually wins. The point is not to make it a lifestyle. Look at Max. He built this whole alternate reality. I tried talking to him. Wouldn't go there. Don't get me wrong, if he had, they wouldn't have moved out here and we wouldn't have met, so in a way your loss has been our gain. But at what cost." He sighed. "I really have a soft spot for that ornery SOB. I saw how much you meant to them. Jean talks about it to Barbara. They're like sisters. Both pretty New Age."

"Yeah," Kevin smiled, "Max and I got a kick out of it. Crystals, incense—"

"Bet it's big in scientific circles. Not my thing. Anyway, I know there isn't much time left, but whatever he's got is going to be better now. You need to know that."

"I really want to thank you," Kevin sighed. "This has been one hell of a day. I'm heading out now to be on a plane for twelve hours. And I hate to fly. But I'm almost looking forward to it, just to down a bottle of wine and zonk out."

"Well, if you like wine, we'll treat you to a week up in Napa. I'll be designated driver."

"Okay," Kevin laughed. "Deal. That was my function with Max."

"Oh, I know. He *hates* to drive. Me—I love it. Barb and Jean yack it up in back the whole time. You'll fit in well. Leave my car in the lot, and lock the keys inside. They may want to try again but with people around it won't be easy, especially if one of them is a president. But I think they're getting arrogant. That breeds complacency. Don't forget—you've got more power in this than you realize. I'll let you know what we learn about the piece, and we'll talk. In the meantime, have a blast out there."

"Oh, yeah," Kevin rolled his eyes, "it's going to be fun hitting wineries with you."

"And tell Jack I said hi," Mike laughed. He held out his hand. "I promise to shake normal."

Kevin smiled and shook in kind. "Mike, thanks again. I'll see you next week."

As Mike turned to head back, Kevin walked to his car and hesitantly started the engine.

Even though he knew it wouldn't explode, he drove off feeling relieved nonetheless.

Twenty-nine

Kevin sat strapped into his seat on a United 777. The last sun of the day was streaming through the left side of the plane, filling the cabin with a golden fire, and making it difficult to see. The muffled hum of the engines pulsed as the huge jetliner crept up in line.

He'd arrived at the airport expecting a standby seat on a FedEx flight, like Tom Hanks in *Cast Away*. But again, Jack Raden had left nothing to chance. Kevin sat in a window seat in first class, the seat beside him empty. Once again, a representative had delivered an envelope. And once more, a bottle of Reserve Syrah had been set aside, compliments of Mr. Raden.

Even before boarding, Kevin had known this flight would be different than the one from Newark. Billboards along the approach to the airport showcased airlines flying to the resort. Inside, ads and corporate endorsements bombarded travelers. Stores in the terminal were stocked with all kinds of merchandise featuring mushroom clouds.

The plane from Newark had been a routine cross-country flight. This was one of the scheduled excursions to the resort. A flight where newlyweds and couples, families and friends, first-timers and veterans flew across the planet's largest ocean to experience firsthand what had begun in the mind of the man who fidgeted in seat 3L. To be on a flight bound for a destination neither of which would exist but for you was surreal. He was recognized the minute he reached the terminal. The five guys from Boston on spring break. The retired couple from Omaha who asked to have their picture taken with him. He was unsure how to react. Were they admirers? People with agendas? He eyed the two stunning women in their twenties across the aisle. The blond, was she eyeing him back? The sunlight backlit her with a radiance like a nuclear furnace. The afterimage persisted as he looked away.

Kevin inspected the cabin's interior. It was busy work, a diversion, for the moment he paused, the events of the day revved up with an intensity that drowned out the engines outside. He had to juggle the disparate elements in the air, for if he stopped gravity would kick in and they would come crashing to earth, like one of Jean's pottery pieces not yet shattered but set to slip from reach.

It wasn't long after he'd left the hospital that he began to realize what happened. The ride back to Princeton two nights ago had begun the turn and now waiting for the plane to take off, it had come full circle. It wasn't that he could barely remember a day like this. It was that he had no frame of reference for what had happened. Universal laws had broken down. There was no relativity, nothing from which to relate. Nothing resonated. All was different.

Barely eight hours earlier, he had landed in San Francisco. In the space of an average day at work, life as he had come to know it had been upended, wrenched from experience, turned inside out until every corner, every crevice, every remaining vestige of familiarity had been excised with surgical precision. What was left, he did not know. It came with no sense of proportion. And no matter the encouragement he'd received, he had no idea how to handle it.

The plane reached its point of departure. As it revved its engines and began to roar down the runway, Kevin glanced out his window onto the ascending twilight. The runway lights had taken over from the setting sun and were casting a glow on the surrounding grass. He did not know that at that very moment, eyes on board were watching him. He could not know that in barely two hours, Jessica Enright and her crew would be landing on that very same ground, hot on his trail.

Wednesday, April 6

Thirty

The word Private lit across the phone was the only thing visible in the darkened motel room. "Miss Enright," the caller began, "it's seven a.m. I'm probably waking you up."

"Got that right." Though working on four hours sleep, she was alert, if annoyed.

"My apologies, but you've got a busy day ahead."

"Now hold it. I flew cross country last night following your leads. I appreciate the information, but don't go planning my schedule for me."

"Come on. MSNBC didn't fly you guys out there to rack up your frequent flyer miles."

"Okay, okay." She rubbed her eyes. "What can I do for you?"

"It's what you can do for yourself. Got a paper and pencil?"

She turned on a light and went for the desk. There was a chill in the room, more so as she always slept nude, and she hurried back to bed. She took down several names and addresses and some notes, then asked, "And what about Herter?"

"First things first, Miss Enright."

"He's the reason I flew out here."

"In good time, Miss Enright. Meantime, you've got enough to get started."

"You're a real pain. You won't tell me your name or what I can call you but you expect me to rearrange my whole schedule for you."

"Not for me, for you. You're not the first reporter who's had to get up early for a source."

"No, but most of them don't fly cross country to do it and then have the source give them a hard time once they get there."

"Well there's a first for everything."

"You are *such* a pain. I don't need a tutorial."

"Well, then consider it independent study."

"Oh, you are SUCH a pain! You called me, remember? And maybe you can tell me how you find out about people coming and going the way you do."

"The same way you do, following up sources and expending a little elbow grease."

"Okay." Though pissed, she knew he was right. But what she'd said to Joshua Emerson was right as well; the guy was maddening. It's what she got from professors at Columbia, where she'd gotten her Master's in Journalism. This guy delighted in parceling out information he deemed necessary and no more, just enough to whet her appetite. She held some doubt about whether it was worth it. The calls always left her wanting. But the leads were on target and the information as high-grade as anything she had encountered in her three years at MSNBC, so she stuck it out, in spite of his marked comments and erudite manner, which gnawed at her. Again, she wondered whether he was an educator.

"Miss Enright, your higher-ups wouldn't have ponied up airline tickets and hotel fare if they didn't think this worth following up. So why don't you follow it up?"

"Fair enough. You caught me waking up."

"You're forgiven. I'll let you go. But I'm serious—you have enough to keep you busy. I'll touch base later, agreed?"

"I suppose. I guess I should thank you."

"Then why don't you?"

"Okay," she sneered. "Thanks. I'll give you a complete book report, fair enough?"

"That's fine. And don't bother with a nice plastic cover. I grade to content, not presentation. Goodbye." John Raden hung up.

Morning in Mill Valley broke cool with a threat of showers, which was sweatshirt and shorts weather for the town across the Golden Gate Bridge from San Francisco. She had arrived at the Travel Lodge just before midnight. The call had been expected, though not at the hour, but once up, there was no going back to sleep. She used the room's small coffee maker to brew a cup while she dressed, fired up her laptop, and began looking over her notes.

The calls had begun austerely, inquiring whether she was interested in exploring a story about the government's nuclear bomb resort in Tuvalu. When pressed, the source would only promise to call back, but left a seemingly mundane question about the detonations, whether she had any knowledge as to how the explosives yield in megatons compared to predicted values.

The call came late on a Friday. Over the weekend she'd spent a little time online, analyzing the blasts. To her surprise, all had exploded slightly more powerfully than anticipated.

On Monday, the source phoned again, and brought up a subject that seemed unrelated—the State of Hawaii's investment in pleasure craft and small boats. She coordinated reports across the islands. Sure enough, the state had begun to stockpile surplus craft.

The next day, a report broke that the Administration was planning an expansion of the program. Despite it being an election year, the Administration sought to increase its stake in the controversial project and open new sites. This wasn't news to Enright; her source had tipped her off a few hours earlier. And later that day he called again, asking if she was familiar with the Nobel laureate Max Rosenkranz.

The calls were creating a pattern. At first the image was hazy, and the leads were so cryptic that she couldn't decide whether to be amused, annoyed or affected. It was only after she'd checked them out that she began to take him seriously. Raden knew this. He'd been diligent in laying out the pieces, all part of the puzzle he created.

Every call left her peeved. The nameless source had treated her more like an itinerant pupil than an established journalist, and she resented it. But what irritated her intrigued Joshua Emerson. He knew she was inexperienced. He also knew she had potential, and that she hadn't been approached by chance. Like it or not, she was back at school. With this morning's call, what had become a rough draft was now a dissertation, requiring footnotes, documentation and a summary. She reached for the phone and called her crew.

Thirty-one

Jean had been out of the shower about fifteen minutes and was headed downstairs when the phone rang. "Hey, I hope I'm not calling too early."

"No Barb. Good morning."

"How are you?"

"It's a good morning. It was a good day yesterday. Thanks so much again. Max loved the apple pie. You see how fast he finished it?"

"Please! You're family. I just took some blueberry muffins out of the oven and have a fresh pot of coffee going. Come over."

"Oh, that sounds like just the thing! I was just about to put on a pot. I'll be right there." She hung up. A lifelong casual dresser, she donned a sweater and pair of jeans. While heading downstairs, she glanced out the window in the stairwell. The van was still there. After Kevin left, Barbara had come to the hospital, and Mike had filled the two in on some of what was going on. It left her at ease but still made her wince. She took a hooded sweatshirt and left through the back door, locking it securely. She went down the hill, stepping over the narrow stream and ferns growing on the banks and came up to Mike and Barbara's open screen door.

"Oh, they smell *wonderful!*" Jean said from the doorway as she removed her wet shoes and sweatshirt. The back of the house was a large den with a fireplace, connected to the kitchen. Barbara gave her a hug. A stunning woman in her late fifties, she reminded people of the actress Lee Remick.

"You look so different," she beamed. Jean softly smiled.

"That coffee smells great," she said. "I was going to the hospital and hadn't eaten yet." She poured a cup, took a muffin and sat down.

Barbara got a cup and joined her on the couch. "Yesterday meant a lot, huh?"

Jean fought back tears. "You have no idea. I'm afraid for them both but it's different now."

"We'll have a good time next week. But you, look at you! Even Max looked different."

"I know. When Kevin left I didn't want to say 'I told you so', but he surprised me by saying it himself. Can you imagine my husband admitting he was wrong?" As Barbara laughed, Jean added, "Maybe things happen for a reason. All I know is, God-knowing, when He finally comes for Max, it can be without regrets. A lot of closure occurred yesterday. I think he knows that."

"And you too," Barbara said as Jean picked at her muffin. "You're glowing."

The sound of a door opening and closing broke their conversation. Mike walked in from the front door, sporting a dampened gray sweatshirt, running shoes and shorts.

"Hi doll," he greeted Jean.

"Hi Rocky."

He plopped himself down in his recliner. "My wife stunk up the whole neighborhood."

"If you think my muffins stink," Barbara sneered, "don't have any."

"Guess again, Rachael Ray." Jean laughed as Mike undid his laces.

"Will you *please* do that on the mat!" Barbara snarled. "God, every time he comes back from running I spend half the day cleaning. And today's wet outside."

"Nag, nag, nag," Mike complied, looking at Jean. "My wife's just lucky I'm afraid of her."

"Mike," Jean said, "the van's still there."

"I know. I ran past it." He hadn't wanted to be the one to bring it up.

"What do you think?" Barbara asked.

"Not sure. If they're on the ball, they know Kevin left last night." He had made several calls and had an idea the van was reporting back to the Pentagon. He wasn't about to let on but he also had a team discretely analyzing the car bomb, and was awaiting word on its origins. None of this was he about to let onto his wife, Max or Jean, nor what happened to Kevin.

"Well, I'm sure at this point, they know you know," she added. "Should we be worried?"

Mike picked up a still-warm muffin, and took a bite. "Kind of defeats the purpose of running, you know," he cracked with a full mouth.

"But that's how you're able to eat them, right?" Jean smiled. She awaited a response, but Mike didn't seem to notice; instead, he was staring at his muffin with a hint of a smile.

"Oh, no," Barbara broke in, glaring at her husband.

"What's the matter?" Jean asked.

"He's up to something." Barbara scowled at Mike. "You being a smart-ass again?"

Still smiling, Mike said, "Just rustling the grass to startle the snakes." He walked over to the kitchen, and got two disposable coffee cups, lids and a brown paper bag. He wrapped two muffins in napkins, and filled the cups with coffee and a little milk. He then covered them, added a few extra napkins and packets of sugar, put everything in the bag and put his shoes back on.

"You're not going to waste those, are you?" Barbara asked.

"Waste, no. Someone needs a smack in the face. Funny; I was in the business thirty years, but it takes until I'm out to pull a stunt that I once saw in a movie." He went out back and scampered down the hill. He walked around the side of Max and Jean's house, past the wrap-around fence that blocked the view into the first floor. He opened the gate, approached the van and knocked on the door. When no response came, he banged harder.

"Come on guys," he hectored. "Don't make me rock this thing. I'm too old for that crap."

A moment later, a man poked his head out. "Sir, I'm going to have to ask you to stop."

"And who are you parked here on my street?"

"Sir, you're interfering with—"

"Don't give me the party line. I said it often enough to know it by heart, and every time it was a crock of shit. We just figured since you're watching the house, you might like some breakfast."

"Huh?"

Mike uncovered a cup. Steam rose from the top. "My wife just took these muffins out of the oven. So have a decent breakfast instead of the crap you got in there."

The man looked to the back of the van, fumbling for words. "Before you say anything," Mike said, "I did this for thirty years and plenty of times I wished someone would drop off something like this, even if it came from the people I was watching." The man went back in and returned a minute later.

"Okay," he said. Mike smiled and handed him the bag.

"Enjoy. Oh and by the way, Max is still in the hospital, and Jean will be there all day. Kevin Herter left and I'm headed home, so this place will be quiet as a graveyard. Might want to pass it on. You also might want to pass on that I said to back off."

"Sir, we're not author—"

"Yeah, yeah, I know. 'You're not authorized to reveal blah, blah, blah'. When I leave, call in and report there's nothing to report. But if that's not enough, tell them Mike Yahr of Woodacre, formerly of Central Security in Fort Meade said that tomorrow his wife is baking corn muffins, so you should get your orders in early." Eminently satisfied, he turned and left.

The man scratched his head and disappeared into the van as Mike reached the gate. He was just about to open it when an SUV pulled up to the house.

Thirty-two

A stunning young woman emerged from the vehicle with two men, one holding a large camera unit. Mike didn't need to hear her introduction to recognize her.

"Hello," she said. "I'm Jessica Enright, MSNBC. You wouldn't happen to be Dr. Rosenkranz, would you?"

Still feeling feisty, Mike smiled. "Can I help you?"

"It's nice to meet you. I was wondering if we could speak with you."

"What about?"

"Your relationship with Dr. Kevin Herter—"

"Great kid, great scientist." Mike was already enjoying this.

Enright smiled. "… and also about the Pacific bomb program."

"Biggest pile of horseshit ever." Mike leered at the cameraman. "You're not live, are you?" Cliff Abreau shook no. "Good," Mike said smugly.

"One thing I can say about you, Dr. Rosenkranz. Your reputation for speaking your mind is well-deserved."

"Fuckin' A."

As the crew eyed each other Enright said, "Come on, Dr. Rosenkranz, we're trying to expand our audience with younger people."

"You're right. Gee, you guys are almost kids yourselves."

"Uh, yeah. Uh, do you have some time?"

"I think so, but let me go inside and call my wife."

"Is there a problem? We can reschedule."

"No problem. But my wife is over at the neighbor's. Let's see if we can squeeze you in."

"Maybe fifteen minutes, if that works for you."

"That's okay. I know how important your work is. Give me a minute; I'll be right back." Mike disappeared through the gate, scooting to the backyard like a kid running downstairs on Christmas morning. When he reached the porch, he took out his phone.

"Hi hon," Barbara answered.

"Put me on speaker, quick," he said in a loud whisper.

A moment later Jean asked, "Mike, is everything okay?"

"I dropped off the coffee to the clowns in the van and when I was walking away, a car drove up with a news crew. Jean, it's that Jessica Enright."

"Oh God, *her?* At our house?"

"In the flesh. Now, here's the thing—she thinks I'm Max."

"*What?*" both women exclaimed.

"She started talking to me like I was Max. I just didn't bother correcting her."

"Oh, for God's sake," Jean exclaimed as Barbara chortled.

"Now try this out," Mike added. "How 'bout we do a number on them?"

"Oh, you *bastard!*" said Barbara, syrupy. "What are you thinking?"

"They want to interview me, I mean Max, about Kevin, the bomb. You up for it?"

"Would serve her right," Jean said. She looked at Barbara.

"Let's do it."

"Okay. Jean, I told her you were at our neighbor's house. I'll invite them over to our place. I'll be Max, Jean, you'll be yourself, and Barb will be our friendly neighbor. For crying out loud, Max and I are close enough to be brothers anyway. This may work out good. It'll throw them off balance and off of Kevin until he gets out there. That okay?"

"You know how I feel about that," Jean said.

"Okay," Barbara replied, "invite them over. She needs to know her place. And she needs to do her homework. If she had, she would have known Mike wasn't Max."

"See you in two minutes," Mike said as he hung up.

Jean nodded, biting her lip. Barbara saw she was uncomfortable, and said, "You and I are sisters, and I would say this to any sister of mine. You know how upset you were when this broad did that number on Sharon. And if anyone can pull this off, it's Mike. Just watch."

Mike went around to the front of the house. "Our neighbor Barbara invited everyone over for coffee and muffins."

"Great!" Enright said. She held Mike's arm as they navigated the hill, a trip made slower by her heels. She lost her footing several times, yelling "Whoa!" as she went.

Barbara was at the door. Enright introduced herself and the crew, and thanked her.

"Did you have breakfast?" Barbara asked.

"At the motel, but all that smells so good I think we could go for a second one. Those muffins look like heaven!"

Mike introduced Barbara, then said, "And this is my wife, Jean."

Mike, Barbara and Jean grinned at each other, feeling a flutter of excitement.

Thirty-three

"I can't believe how good this is." Jessica Enright dabbed butter on her muffin and polished it off with coffee. Cliff Abreau and Jim Leffert were equally effusive. As Abreau readied his camera, she asked Mike if he wanted to change clothes but he brushed her off, saying it was his usual uniform.

"Is that right?" Enright asked Jean.

"We had all we could do when he got his Nobel Prize to have him wear a suit."

"But I got back at them at the ceremony," Mike countered. "I didn't wear underwear." As Enright laughed nervously, he said, "So, what can I do you for?"

"There's a lot of controversy swirling around the bomb program," Enright began. "I was wondering whether you wouldn't mind answering questions about that."

"First of all," Mike jumped in, "it's not my project. I have nothing to do with it."

"Yes, but you can see—"

"I see diddly-squat. It's a perversion of science, and they know it. You agree, honey?"

"Absolutely," Jean smiled.

"That sounds like something Kevin Herter would say."

"Kevin agrees with everything I say. That's why I have such high regard for him." Mike's response had Jean and Barbara fighting giggles.

"Come on now, Doctor. Are you saying you only respect people who agree with you?"

"Of course not," he said, feigning earnestness. "But it makes it easier."

"Honey," Jean interjected, trying to suppress a laugh, "stop being difficult."

"Kevin's a wonderful person, with his own opinions. Just so happens, on this we share broad agreement. I feel his discoveries have been hijacked for a waste of money and resources that will ultimately prove a source of regret."

"When you say waste of money and resources, you mean—"

"I mean it could have been spent more wisely elsewhere."

"Are you talking about the super collider you worked on?"

"No. But the point's valid. The money spent letting a bunch of losers watch those damn things would be better spent on pure science." Mike well knew of the SSC. Jean and Barbara sat in stunned amazement. Max could have been mouthing those very same words.

"Then considering how you feel, do you think it's influenced your relationship with Dr. Herter to where you would counsel him to adversely influence the program one way or another?"

"Could you repeat that a little slower?" Mike asked as Barbara and Jean suppressed grins.

"Considering how you feel, Doctor, do you think your feelings have influenced Dr. Herter to a point where you have counseled him to actively oppose the program?"

"Oh, I understand. No, not at all."

"I see. When was the last time you saw Dr. Herter?"

Mike looked at Barbara and Jean. "Last night."

Enright sat up. "You mean you've seen Kevin Herter within the past twenty-four hours?"

"He flew out yesterday. He just broke up with his girlfriend and was looking for a little action. We set him up with a friend." He looked at Jean. "I think he got lucky, didn't he?"

Jean folded her hands properly and glanced at Barbara. "I wouldn't know."

"Wait a sec," Mike said. "Aren't you the one who interviewed his ex the other day?"

Enright fidgeted. "We wanted to speak with Dr. Herter, and she took offense."

"Bitch. No wonder he dumped her." Abreau and Leffert exchanged uncomfortable glances, while Enright turned demure.

"Well, Dr. Rosenkranz, she seemed under a lot of stress. I'm sure she'll be all right."

"You think Kevin's up to no good? Is that what you're interested in finding out?"

"No, not at all. We're trying to learn more about the program's direction and his participation in it. We've also heard more controversy about it, though it's still very popular."

"So are dog fights."

"That's true. But we were wondering if you could elaborate on your participation with—"

"Again, I have no participation. My only involvement is I get Kevin laid when he visits. You should get to know him. He's great to hang with. You're hot, he's a stud; maybe something'll happen. You'd be surprised how passionate scientists can be." Enright was non-plussed. "Understand," Mike added, "I'm retired. I'm more his Dutch uncle than advisor." He was enjoying himself, every squirm from his guests adding to his pleasure. Barbara and Jean had all they could do to keep their composure, so Barbara offered them more coffee.

"Okay, Dr. Rosenkranz." Enright softly laughed. "There've been rumors for months the government is considering bringing back the collider—"

"About fucking time." Barbara suppressed a laugh, coughing instead. "Sorry. I should watch my language. My wife tells me I have a mouth like a truck driver. But I'm serious."

"Is that something you would publicly support?"

"Sure. Never should have been cancelled. They blew a billion bucks. Whatever the cost overruns, that's a lot of money wasted. Meantime, the Europeans jump ahead of us and we lose leverage. Just like the manned space program. Now all these years later, we're playing catch up. How much will it cost this time? Damn thing could have been running all along. Instead, it's more important we let a bunch of bozos watch bombs go off. They diddle around again, it'll cost a hundred billion. So, yeah, it's a good idea for a number of reasons."

Barbara and Jean sat spellbound. Barbara knew her husband's talents but it had been a while since she had seen him in action, and Jean had never seen it. Her first thought was that Max would have loved to have been a fly on the wall for this.

"And you guys in the media are just as responsible," Mike added. He hadn't realized until he heard himself say it, but now he had a new weapon at his disposal. Chastisement.

"How so, Doctor?" Enright said, stung.

"Simple. You have a responsibility to take the long view and educate people about what you cover instead of looking for quick sound bites. I bet there's loads you miss cause you don't do your homework and walk around thinking the world began the year you were born. People rely on you to give them accurate information, and too many of you are falling down on the job. Don't be surprised if things wind up biting you in the ass." Mike sat back, arms crossed.

"Well, Doctor, you're right to an extent, but that's what we're trying to do now."

"If you say so. I'll reserve judgement." Mike sipped his coffee. "Talk about the SSC; you're too young, but I saw how coverage was slanted. So now you got a chance to right some wrongs."

Enright had lost her edge, but still had an opinion. "I'm not sure that's our job, but if the story develops, a lot of good reporters will approach it the way it should be covered."

"We'll see."

"Okay, Dr. Rosenkranz. Do you have any idea about Dr. Herter's plans?"

"I told him to throw a monkey wrench into it."

Barbara rubbed her face while Jean said, "Now sweetheart, don't go making trouble."

"Yes dear. My wife tells me I'm retired and should keep my mouth shut. But sometimes, I have to say what needs to be said. Kevin's a big boy. What he does is his business. But were it me, I'd make their lives miserable."

"You're kidding, Dr. Rosenkranz. Could you be specific?"

"We love Kevin like a son, but he's too nice. That's why I said I could fix you two up."

"Well, thanks. But getting back to Dr. Herter. What do you think his response will be to what's going on? What do you think he'll do?"

"Well, again, he's too nice. But I'm not."

"Does that mean you're going to—"

"I won't do anything. Remember, I'm retired. The only thing I do is get him girls."

"Oh honey, stop." Jean laughed nervously, as Barbara hid her face into her hands.

"My wife thinks I make trouble. But I'd have him fly you guys out there and hold a news conference denouncing the thing. And then I'd buzz the beach with a plane trailing a banner that said, "Fuck the bomb!" It's about time people ended their love affair with that damn thing."

"Well Dr. Rosenkranz, thank you."

"Of course you know it releases more radiation than they've let on."

Enright perked up. "Do you know that for a fact?"

"I know enough to know they haven't let on what's really going on out there," Mike said.

Enright smelled blood. "Are you saying you know there's a problem?"

"No. What I am saying is I know government. When they're involved there's always something that doesn't get reported."

"Dr. Rosenkranz, you should know that as a Nobel Prize winner, your word carries considerable weight. If you say something like that, it'll attract notice."

"Ah, that's a crock of horseshit too. People don't care. They don't remember who lost the last Super Bowl. They'll care diddly-squat what I say."

"I don't care what he says half the time," Jean offered. Everyone laughed.

"See what I mean?" Mike winked. "All I know is they cooked this up. Any government that warns of the dangers of smoking and in the same breath—excuse the pun—subsidizes tobacco farmers is one I'm going to question. You fill in the blanks. You gotta admit, they put a lot of food on your table."

"Dr. Rosenkranz, thank you for your time. You've been very candid." Enright told Cliff to stop recording, just as Mike spoke again.

"Remember what I said. I'm small potatoes. Honestly, I enjoy being a trouble maker. You'll see. Either way, that's not the story. But neither is Kevin. He may not be as involved as he should be, but if you investigate him, you're barking up the wrong tree. You wanna waste time talking to me, that's time I can spare. But I'm not the story either. Check out the program. Follow the money, the people involved. That should be your focus."

Enright stood up. "Dr. Rosenkranz, thank you again for your time. You've given us a lot to think about." She thanked Barbara for her hospitality. "It's a lovely home you have. How long have you ..." She glanced behind Barbara. A photo hung of her with Mike on a cruise ship balcony. "Uh," she said haltingly, "I just have to ask ..."

"Barbara's also my ex-wife," Mike said.

"Wow," Enright tried to hide her shock. "I must say, that's quite—"

"Oh, don't feel bad," Barbara replied. "It's a good arrangement for us and the kids, right honey?"

"Oh, yeah," Jean smirked back at her. "Barbara and I get along great. Just one of those things that works. It's not for everyone, right sweetheart?"

"Oh, for damn sure!" Mike laughed. "We're very adult about the whole situation."

"I can relate," Enright shrugged. "My ex lives in the same building I do in New York."

"See, you and Kevin are near each other. Let me know if you want to get hooked up."

"Leave the girl alone," Jean said. "I'm sure she knows how to meet men."

Enright thanked them again, and as she and the crew left with Mike, Jean grabbed Barbara and the two women burst out laughing, hoping they weren't heard.

"Well, Dr. Rosenkranz, it's been quite an interview," Enright said as they reached their vehicle.

"I'll bet," Mike answered, noticing that the surveillance van was gone. "I'm sorry you didn't get me at my best." At their confused looks, he added, "Usually I'm in jeans and a clean sweatshirt."

"Well, we'll be sure to put that in our background piece. Thank you." Enright and the crew said goodbye and got into their vehicle and drove off.

"You believe this guy?" Leffert said as they exchanged incredulous looks.

"I wonder if every Nobel laureate is a fucking whack-o," Enright said, shaking her head.

Jean went up to Mike as he walked back into the den, wearing a broad grin.

"You were *amazing!*"

"You should have seen their faces. They thought I had a screw loose."

"I told you what he was like," Barbara said to Jean. "But this time honey, you outdid yourself."

Mike sat back in the recliner and put up his feet. "Speaking of screws, I was going to ask if she knew 'news crew' and 'new screw' were spelled the same, but I felt it might be too much."

"Oh, you *think*?"

Jean sat down, shaking her head. "I wish Max had seen this. He would have lost it."

"I feel a little bad, but five minutes of research, this wouldn't have happened."

"I wonder what repercussions it's going to cause."

"Trust me, girls," Mike said, "there's a lot going on with this that needs stirring up. As for her, she'll have to deal with it. The same way Sharon's dealing with it." The women agreed, and he added, "By the way, the van's gone."

"What do you think happened?" Jean's eyes widened in relief.

"Don't know. They got either what they needed or realized they were never going to get what they needed. Or they hated the muffins. Meanwhile, I'll wrap one up for Max."

Jean began to put on her shoes. She was slipping on her sweatshirt when her cell phone rang. The display showed the number of the hospital.

"Mrs. Rosenkranz? This is Nurse Janet Palmer at Marin General Hospital."

Jean's heart was racing. "Is my husband all right?"

"Yes. We just wanted to tell you we moved him to Intensive Care."

"I thought you said he was all right."

"He has a little fluid in his lung. The doctor wanted to monitor it. We can do that better in ICU. Right now, he's resting comfortably."

"I'll be there soon," she said, a little relieved.

"Is everything okay?" Barbara asked, concerned.

"They moved him to ICU. They want to watch that fluid on his lung."

"Come on," Barbara turned to Mike, "let's get dressed."

Jean turned to her. "I'll meet you at the hospital, okay?"

"Oh, no," Mike said. "We'll be ready in ten minutes. You come with us."

Max was hooked up to a saline drip and a cardiac monitor when Jean and Barbara walked into the ICU. He looked weak, but smiled when they entered.

"How do you feel honey?" Jean kissed him.

Max twirled his hand in a so-so motion. "They want to keep an eye on the chest. Hey, good-looking," he said to Barbara. She bent over and gave him a kiss.

"Is it bothering you?" Jean asked.

"Feels a little heavy, but hey." He cleared his throat. "The cough kept me up."

"Were you able to get any sleep?"

"Ach, hospitals suck."

"Well, this should make you feel a little better." Jean took out the blueberry muffin.

"Now, we're cooking!" Max said in a graveled voice. Jean pulled over a tray and he broke off pieces with his left hand. "That is good," he kept repeating as he ate. "Too bad I can't get a cup of your coffee to wash it down with, but look at this fa-cocktah place. Promise me you'll put a pot up when I get home. So, Mike home?"

"No," Jean answered. "He's in the lobby. It's ICU. They only let in two at a time."

"The hell with that! Go get him! They give you a hard time, tell them to go *schtupp* themselves." Jean looked at Barbara and shrugged, and a minute later Barbara walked in with Mike.

"I'm having trouble keeping track of you and all your new address-es," Mike said.

"Up yours, Yahr." Mike took Max's hand and looked at the women. "You tell him yet?"

"Tell me what?" Max asked.

Barbara grinned, and pulled over a chair. "You should have been there," she said. They regaled Max with the story of their visitors. Max began laughing, which turned to a cough. Jean and Mike would frequent-ly threaten to leave, but he insisted they continue.

"You mean none of them caught on?" he asked.

"Nope," Mike said.

"Serves her right," Max said before another fit of coughing. He qui-eted down, and then added, "I wonder if they'll cause trouble for Kevin. He doesn't need that crap." He paused. "Mikey, I was thinking about what Kevin said, running the thing through my head. I have an idea what kind of problem they have. If I'm right, they're headed for trouble."

As they all exchanged looks a nurse walked in and broke up the visit, promising that they could all stop by later but for now needed to leave so Dr. Rosenkranz could rest and not further aggravate his cough.

Thirty-four

In New York, Joshua Emerson was reviewing the video footage that Jessica Enright had transmitted from California. Emerson had just returned from having a cavity filled on his lunch break. The video he was previewing added markedly to his distress. He picked up his phone.

"I just saw the footage you sent," he began curtly. "What happened?"

"What do you mean?" Enright asked hesitantly. The brusque tone from her editor had her perplexed.

"I need you to explain what happened."

"Josh, I don't understand the question."

Emerson's face was an annoying cascade of pins and needles. "Maybe I'm not making myself clear or you're totally missing this. I need you to tell me how you think that interview went."

Enright tried to keep her wits. "We picked up some interesting information, but he's a train wreck. His personal life is a circus. His ex lives next door, his wife is clueless, and he's a whack-job. It was a farce."

"Okay," Emerson exhaled noticeably. "Are Cliff and Jim there?" She answered yes. "Okay, put me on speaker. Can you guys hear me?" Both answered yes. "I'm trying to figure out what went wrong here and I realized something. Your laptop on?" When Abreau said yes, he growled, "See if we can follow this exercise. Go on line and type in three Ws and the word Google, then dot com," he exclaimed irately. "Got that?"

Abreau complied, muttering, "What, he thinks we don't know how to Google?"

"Good!" Emerson responded, "glad you got that." Enright and Leffert eyed each other, unsure of the reason for the sarcasm. "Now see if you can follow the next step. See the word Images in the upper left-hand corner?"

Enright cut in. "What's going on, Joshua?"

"Don't interrupt. I don't want to give you more than you can handle. You got it?" They contritely answered yes. "Goood! Okay, now comes a tricky part. Click the word Images with your cursor. That's the little thing you move around the screen."

"Okay, Joshua." Enright was irritated by his attitude, but growing flustered.

"Another white screen popped up that says 'Google Image Search', right?" Leffert mumbled yes. Emerson said, "Hey, we're moving now. Okay, now's a really tricky part. See the little vertical line flashing on and off, inside a white horizontal bar? Now slowly, carefully, I want you to type in the name Max Rosenkranz, got that? M-A-X, new word, R-O-S-E-N-K-R-A-N-Z. Type it in then hit the little bar that says 'Search Images'. Now, do it!"

The first of more than three thousand images had scarcely come up when muffled groans came from all three. A searing torrent of icy shock tore through Enright.

Row upon row of photos, some formal, some just snapshots, showing a particular gentleman appeared. Some showed him in front of a chalkboard, others with personalities and political figures. Several showed him beside one of the women seen at the house earlier. And not one was of the person they interviewed.

"Oh, *fuck!*" Enright moaned, burying her face in her hands.

"Oh, *YEAH!*" Emerson roared. "Look at it! People are already calling you Wrong Way Enright. I told them not to waste their time cause Wrong Way Corrigan would be lost on you as well."

"Josh, I'm sorry—"

"Wait a minute. You even know who that was?" She fumbled for a snappy answer, but a flood of embarrassment overtook her. "Precisely the problem. A Nobel Prize-winning scientist, and no one thinks it a good idea to research him before you talk to him. I have to ask; any of you ever hear of Wrong Way Corrigan?" The silence was palpable. "Okay, we have a big problem."

"Josh, I—"

"No. Just hold it. I'm astounded by the lack of curiosity here. And I'm embarrassed that I sent you out. If you think you can just show up, stick a camera in someone's face and congratulate yourself for a hard day's work, you'd better start looking for another line of work, all of you. For whatever it's worth, Douglas Corrigan was a flyer who took off from Floyd Bennett Field in Brooklyn in 1938 on his way to California and a day later landed in Ireland. It made worldwide headlines. Papers even printed the headline in reverse." Emerson was fuming. It never used to be like this. Back then, people cared. If they didn't know something, it ruffled them.

"Now, that I have to explain this to three professionals in the NEWS business speaks volumes about the three of you and what you think is important. The public has very little good to say about our profession. We rank lower than politicians. Hell, we rank lower than lawyers. Now you know why. You will either become more intellectually involved with what you are doing, or you don't belong here. It's as simple as that. Now, I want to tell you one more thing. You go back and study that footage. He may have fucked you over but he sure as hell was trying to tell you something."

"Josh—" Enright was close to tears.

"Just hold it. Maybe they're neighbors or friends, maybe they just decided to have some fun at your expense, but they couldn't have done it without your help. I'm sure they got your number the minute they met you. You could have avoided all this—"

"Josh, I know."

"I don't want to hear I 'know'!"

"What do I do?" Enright was crying. "What am I supposed to do? Am I being fired?"

"No. But you damn well better change. Jet fuel is too expensive to fly the three of you three thousand miles to interview the wrong person. I'll be honest. People here want you gone, all of you. But unfortunately, that's not my view. I'm crazy enough to still think you have enough potential that you can learn from this. But you're on probation. We're going to try to keep a wrap on this, but if it gets out, it gets out. You want this career, you'll have to live it down. No more easy rides or passes. You think that's unfair, too fucking bad. Get over it."

Abreau and Leffert were slumped in their chairs. Jessica lay in a near-fetal position on the bed. Her humiliation was complete; never had she been so thoroughly brought to task.

Emerson sensed it. He needed to knock her down, enough to cause her to brutally confront her reality as a journalist. He believed she had potential, but truly needed to take stock. He had long felt his profession had grown too enamored of white teeth and empty suits, and if any weeding out needed to be done, he was more than willing to do his part. But if she could stand at the abyss and not fall in, he would afford her an opening. Having knocked her down, he would give her the chance to get back up. But first, there were dues to be paid.

"Okay, you three," Emerson asked after some silence. "You feel like shit?"

Abreau and Leffert mumbled, "Yeah." Enright was mute, consumed in humiliation.

"Jessica, what about you?"

"You want to know if I feel beat up enough?"

Emerson groaned. Enright was still stuck on playing the victim. "Do I feel I beat you up enough? One day you'll be able to answer that yourself. But for now, it was sufficient."

"Thanks," she dripped sarcasm. Leffert looked at her. "That's not what he's saying."

"Easy for you, you're behind the camera."

"Don't even go there. I've just as much of a reputation to carry as you, right, Joshua?"

"He's right," Emerson said. "Even more, because he could be doing it a hell-of-a-lot longer than someone in front. I'll ask again. The three of you feel like shit enough?"

Over the "yeahs" from Leffert and Abreau, Enright snapped, "Yeah, okay?"

"Goooood!" Emerson replied.

"That's how you want us to feel?" Enright asked.

"Jessica," Abreau said, "shut up. For once just sit and don't talk back." She glared at him, then looked to Leffert for sympathy. When it wasn't forthcoming, she sat stewing.

It wasn't all Emerson wanted, but for now, it was enough. "Okay," he announced, "this is how we'll proceed. I want you to follow up contacts and leads that will give us a better idea how this is playing out. That means you stop by the *Chronicle*. You research their archives, talk to people there who were around then. That means people older than you, people who've been around the block and have experience and wisdom that come from a time when things didn't happen just because someone clicked a mouse. You take the time to listen. And if you don't hear what you want, you thank them anyway. You don't roll your eyes if information isn't forthcoming. And you get Max Rosenkranz's phone number and call his house. You get his wife. You talk to her. You apologize for intruding and stopping by unannounced. If Rosenkranz isn't there, find out where he is. Ask graciously if she can help and thank her for any assistance she offers. You're an investigative reporter. You investigate. You report. Those are verbs, action words. And the one thing you don't do is go back to the house with a bug up your ass demanding to know who lives there and why they fucked you the way they did. They did because they could. Leave them alone. If your source calls, kindly thank him as well. You don't rip him a new one either. You remain professional. And you find out where Herter is. You got that? Now get back on the road pronto, and send me what you get." He hung up.

The three sat chastened and subdued. They all knew Emerson was right. His reputation for treating those under him fairly and his reserved wit were renowned. He wasn't known for sarcasm or losing his temper. It was why they were now dazed by the level of his indignation. For Enright, the sting would burn as long as the memory of the mistake.

"Fuck," uttered by Jim Leffert, broke the silence. It opened up a rapid-fire free-for-all, a self-serving litany of denigration directed toward the news editor, he who had no right to pass judgment on those in the trenches when he'd sent them out with no preparation or information and who damn well knew that kind of crap would happen, most probably the result of some nefarious scheme or deal that only he would be in a position to take advantage of or orchestrate.

And almost as quickly, it blew itself out.

They sat spent and silent, as if it were enough that it heard itself and no more. Cliff Abreau broke the tension by announcing he was heading back to his room to change. Jim Leffert left with him, and fifteen minutes later they met in the lobby and walked toward their car.

Thirty-five

Across the strait that bridged city and suburb, the sky opened into a pelting perturbation. Enright decided they would first drive into the city and stop by the *San Francisco Chronicle*. They were quiet as they crossed the Golden Gate Bridge. The threatening skies had delivered and with the radio off they traveled to the cadence of wipers.

Even in the rain, San Francisco is a beautiful city. The image of low clouds shrouding the bridge and the Transamerica building has long fired the imaginations of artists and writers, but on this gray afternoon it was lost to Enright and her crew. For them it was an afternoon of bleached donuts and gray coins thrown at toll buckets, an afternoon of going through the motions, especially for Enright. In their dressed down state, Leffert behind the wheel and Abreau in the back seat, even the mournful city itself, had the feel of adjuncts, window dressing to her own torment.

The people at the *Chronicle* were helpful, letting Abreau search archives while Enright spoke with some of the older staff. She began to get a sense of the kind of thing Joshua Emerson had berated her about. They talked of things not too long ago that she would have once shrugged off. Of a time when paste-ups were state-of-the-art and memory held no thought of an Internet. When a new Administration brought a sense of a fresh start, and not a jaded changing of the guard.

They reminisced about the largest peacetime science project in history, of a noted scientist, his Nobel Prize years in the future, who had given them grief over its cancellation. As they regaled her with a past no longer there, she began to feel barely there herself. It was like an out-of-body experience. She couldn't shake the notion that it was all a facade, that what unfolded was but a shadow world to the real one behind the curtains, where editors, anchors, the news desk, the guy at the newsstand downstairs, the college-aged kids at the coffee place across the street were also going through the motions, and were all onto her.

Gradually, as she first spent an hour there and then two, and the pelting heavens didn't crash down and the ground beneath didn't swallow them up, she began to realize that her private hell was truly that, her own. She sat with it, and still breathed. She asked about Max Rosenkranz, what he was like, whether anyone had ever spoken to or had any personal dealings with him. If anyone could tell her anything about him that had happened more recently.

It was when she met Features Editor Linda Driscoll that her rebirth as a successful reporter began. The woman's sister was a nurse working oncology at Marin General Hospital, who had remarked just the other night that a Nobel Prize-winning scientist had been admitted, and that he had been a patient at the hospital numerous times over the past two years. And with a quick call Jessica Enright learned that this same Dr. Max Rosenkranz was still at the hospital and was dying of prostate cancer.

Thirty-six

Christian Deloy was at San Francisco International awaiting the airport shuttle when his phone rang.

"I don't need you riding my ass every two minutes," he snapped into the prepaid unit, in no mood to explain anything. His caller was in no mood for excuses.

"If you weren't such a fuck-up," Ron Sanderson, the lieutenant governor of Hawaii barked, "I wouldn't have to keep after you. I just heard about the piece in Herter's car. I have enough trouble dealing with everything on this end and making sure *you're* getting your money on time. I can't believe you let that happen."

"I let nothing happen." Deloy walked away from the people around him and in a low voice seethed, "I've had it with all of you. None of you are on the ground so you don't see shit. You want to whack him, Whiteman wants to wet-nurse him, and none of that gets him to back off and not draw attention to yourselves. If any of you were here—"

"Well, you fucking better—"

"Don't want to hear it. I told you to go easy but you had to do it your way and blow it out of proportion. Putting that under his hood is killing a fly with a Howitzer and calling the news."

"We had nothing to do—"

"Cut the bull. I said I don't want to hear it. You know the trouble Yahr can cause? If I handled it, we wouldn't be having this conversation. It would've been done. So, congratulations. Now everyone you wanted to keep it from knows. You tell me how smart that is."

Sanderson was bristling. He pulled into an IHOP parking lot to avoid rear-ending anyone, then took a spot in a far corner. The lieutenant governor didn't need his constituents to see him vent, even through his tinted windows.

"You're not hearing me, dipshit," he snapped. "I said we had nothing to do with it. And keep him the fuck away from there! He shows up we're all screwed. We don't care what you have to do—"

"Now you don't care. Well, I don't care. I'll be damned this gets back to me and that's just where it's headed if you idiots keep going the way you are. You think that fool Ridge knew what was up? Or Hanford? But you upped the ante. Now that bitch Enright has a hard on. You went so far out of the way to scare Herter off he's in whether he wants to be or not. You fucked it up. Deal with it." Deloy snapped the phone shut. Like all he used it would soon be discarded.

Sanderson sneered into the phone. He needed to cool off.

Christian Deloy had been the perfect mole, with ties to Integrated Microphysics, and an inside track to the Oval Office. As Tom Whiteman's aide he had access to data few knew even existed. Whiteman reported to Dillon Ridge, giving Deloy an unimpeded stream into Hanford's frame of mind. Despite Lisa Whiteman's best efforts her husband had gleaned much from her, even though he wasn't a physicist. Deloy learned more about the Whitemans by heeding what they didn't say than listening to the little they did discuss. And as a college buddy to Ron Sanderson's chief of staff, it gave him access to Honolulu. He seemed the perfect money runner and enforcer.

But now, he too had become a liability. What was supposed to be a simple operation now loomed as a public relations nightmare. And where did he get off accusing anyone of trying to knock off the scientist? Another cluster fuck to deal with.

For two years, the setup couldn't have been better. Integrated Microphysics, known as IM, was an established weapons development firm with a branch in Honolulu. Their expertise perfecting the anti-matter firing mechanism that allowed the explosion to occur without producing radiation was inspired. And the guy in charge was a friend. IM had contributed mightily to the Hawaiian economy, and to many a political campaign as well.

Who knew there was another way to design the things?

When word began trickling out from Sandia of clouds on the horizon, it didn't take IM long to realize its dilemma. Lisa Whiteman had been such a hard-ass about sharing information that no one at first knew anything was up. The design was based on her specs. But four months on, there was no hiding it: The devices were exploding more powerfully than forecast. The DOD, eager to solve the problem, also had another issue in mind. Ever since Frontier, they had sought to weaponize the supposedly impractical technology. They refused to take no for an answer, to accept that the devices were too big to put on a missile or in the belly of a bomber. An arsenal of fallout-free bombs would give the US unassailable nuclear supremacy for a decade or more. Based on the data they had, they began demanding design changes in hopes of hitting on ways of reducing their size.

As it happened their hunch was correct, only they didn't know it. At IM, Sandia's findings were known. It could be done. Just make the firing mechanism smaller. The blasts evened out to predicted levels. The whole device became smaller as well. With Sandia withholding test data though no one at IM knew just why it worked. But it did, which led to an equally ominous reality—anyone could build the things. The monopoly on a supposedly unique design was gone. In its place was a simpler design any contractor could fabricate. So IM placated the DOD, trotting out meaningless modifications while sitting on the fix. The issue would remain a nonissue. The devices would remain big and cumbersome, unsuitable as weapons. And incredibly profitable.

However, the question persisted: why wasn't Sandia letting on? No one knew, and with Lisa Whiteman tightlipped, things would remain that way. IM wasn't interested in why she wasn't sharing, just that she wasn't. They were more interested in keeping their billions.

On those occasions when trouble surfaced, CEO Mark Rivers would take out his checkbook, or more precisely, his briefcase. The money was a pittance compared to what he would stand to lose were anything to leak. Rivers wasn't happy but it was a business expense. The arrangement suited everyone involved. A few colonels and a general at the DOD who could blow things open. Two division heads at the DOE who ensured that the issue remained stalled in bureaucracy. And the lieutenant governor of Hawaii, who had cut his teeth in politics while in college and was the only one who knew them all.

Maybe it was wishful thinking that it could have gone on. But it was unraveling. To the DOD, it had dragged on too long. They had nothing to show for their efforts. And now the White House was involved, mucking things up with politics. Moreover, by trying to do an end run around the design impasse word had trickled up to Hanford of a situation that threatened everything. Seven months before an election he learned that the program he had gained so much political capital from by managing so adroitly had been window dressing to test bomb designs. It hadn't begun that way, but there was no doubt that when looked at with more than a casual glance, it's what it had become. Guests had been unwitting participants at a proving ground, guinea pigs in a controlled experiment no one knew even existed. No president could survive that.

Instead, Hanford had concocted a harebrained scheme to make himself look good, trumpeting the program as a heaven-sent way to get the idiots of the world to stop blowing themselves up and inadvertently showing that if it came to pass, no one needed Integrated Microphysics and their expensive system anymore. And in the middle, clueless about everything, was Kevin Herter. Each side wanted him to do their bidding. Still stewing, Sanderson paused for a moment, then flipped open his phone again and dialed.

Thirty-seven

The phone rang in Jean's kitchen just after five p.m.

"Mrs. Rosenkranz?"

"Yes?"

"Mrs. Rosenkranz, this is Jessica Enright."

"Yes, what can I do for you?" Jean asked, feeling a run of apprehension.

"Well, Mrs. Rosenkranz, you can let me apologize to you."

Jean was unsure how to respond. Her unease was tempered with an equal measure of annoyance. She was bothered by what happened earlier, but the sense that the girl received a well-deserved comeuppance had made up for it. "I guess you've become enlightened since you left us," she said.

"Oh, and then some, believe me." She sank into the large chair in her suite. "I was wondering if I could meet with you and your husband for a bit."

"Miss Enright, I'm not sure what you know, but we're not up for any more interviews."

"Mrs. Rosenkranz, I completely understand. I'm not looking to interview you. I'd just like an opportunity to meet you alone. I'd also like to meet your husband. I know you don't have any reason to trust me and I'm asking a lot, but it would mean a great deal to me."

"I don't know how much you know of our situation."

"I know your husband is ill. And I don't want to intrude. A lot has happened since this morning. I feel as if I aged ten years. I just hoped you could spare me a little time."

Jean listened quietly. The girl sounded sincere. Of the three collaborators in the hoax that morning, she was the least enthusiastic about the deception they ran. "Okay," she said. "I'm going to the hospital in a little while. You can meet me there at six thirty. My husband's in Intensive Care. I'll talk to him but if he isn't up for it, then that's that. I'm not going to try to change his mind, and you'll have to accept that. Is that okay?"

"That's fine, Mrs. Rosenkranz. Thank you very much. I really appreciate it."

Enright pulled her knees to her chest. She had spent the afternoon at the *Chronicle* in a blur, not knowing what to feel or who to be mad at except herself, and in that regard not knowing how angry to get or how long to keep it going. She had been hurt, humiliated and reproached and with all that it was raining. She was numb. And then she met Linda Driscoll and learned of the real Max Rosenkranz.

The stark reality of his circumstance brought the entire episode into perspective in a way she never anticipated, prepared for or remotely envisioned. The fiasco at the Rosenkranz's house, the rebuke from Joshua, her humiliation, everything that day paled in comparison to the reality that Max Rosenkranz faced. It had the force of a tipping point. It was too much to take in at the *Chronicle*. She realized her visit to the paper, the first thing she did that day would be the last. By the time they pulled up to the motel she knew she would be giving Cliff and Jim the rest of the day off.

Jean got to the hospital a few minutes before six. Max was alert but tired. His dinner had just been served. As she helped him with the tray, she brought up Jessica Enright.

"Sounds like some shit hit the fan with her," Max observed.

"I think so. I don't know what she found out or from whom, but she sounded different."

"Well, maybe she'll learn something from it."

"I hope. She didn't seem like a bad kid, just immature." Jean cut up the roast chicken on Max's plate and handed him the fork. He began to eat slowly. "Not bad," he remarked.

"That means it's good." She tried a piece of chicken. "It's very good." She broke off a piece of a roll as Max continued eating. "So what does she want?" he said between mouthfuls.

"To stop by and talk. I didn't say one way or another, just that it would depend on what you wanted and how you felt."

"So," Max said as he swirled off a dab of potato, "what do you think?"

"That's a switch. I expected you to say tell her to go you-know-what herself."

"Well, maybe I will."

Jean bent over and kissed her husband. "I'm trying to eat here," he grumbled. He then asked, "Why did you tell her you would talk to me first? Why didn't you just say take a hike?"

"Honestly, I felt a little funny with what we did. Don't get me wrong. I'd probably still do it; I saw what happened with Sharon, and they get too pushy. It's just easier when someone else takes them to task than if it comes from you."

"So what are you going to say to her?"

"I don't know," she sighed.

ABC World News Tonight was starting when a nurse came in to tell them that a young woman had arrived. They looked at each other, and within a minute Jessica Enright was standing in the doorway.

Jean immediately noticed a difference in the young woman. Her thick blond hair, so elegantly draped over her shoulders earlier, was tied up in a ponytail. The mauve dress had been replaced by jeans and an earthy green sweatshirt. She held a handbag, shoulders slumped, the barest hint of makeup on her face.

Jean smiled briefly, but stayed seated. Max said nothing. Jean stared for a moment, and then invited her in.

"I'm sorry I interrupted your dinner," Enright said as she entered. "I can come back."

"No," Max replied, sounding hoarse, "I was finishing up."

"Do you want to sit down?" Jean asked.

Enright eased over to a chair. She clutched her handbag as if it contained all her worldly possessions. "I really appreciate you seeing me," she said demurely.

Max didn't know what to say, but began with, "You look different from on TV."

"Well, you're not getting me at my best."

"It's not only the clothes and the hair," Jean nodded.

"You look like you've been through the wringer," Max said. "I expected fireworks."

"I would have thought that myself," Jean added. Seeing the wounded Enright, despite the morning's events, she felt sympathy for her.

"I would have two days ago." Enright clasped her hands together.

Max cleared his throat. "Two days ago you wouldn't be sitting here."

As Jean smiled, Enright said, "I half-expected that when I called."

Max eyed Jean, and then asked Enright, "What can we do for you?"

"I'm not completely sure. I wanted to meet you, but I'm not sure what to say."

"So," Jean said, eying her empathetically. "What kind of trouble did we cause for you?"

"Oh, wow!" Enright laughed.

"You know, that wasn't our intention."

"Oh, yes it was," Max said. Jean was surprised, so he qualified his remark. "A little. My wife wouldn't hurt you intentionally, but our friends—maybe they felt you had it coming."

"I gathered that. I suppose I can't blame anyone."

"Well, you can," Jean answered.

"You're right. I could still be pissed. I was earlier, like you wouldn't believe."

"So what happened?"

"Honestly, I don't know." She looked bewildered. "I really don't know."

"An honest reporter," Max said, breaking off a piece of roll.

"Be nice, honey," Jean admonished her husband.

"No, it's okay," Enright offered. "We sometimes deserve that. And I have to admit, it was a great practical joke."

"So what happened when you left?" Jean smiled.

"I'll tell you, but first I have to ask—who were those people?"

"Our neighbors, Mike and Barbara. They're family. Anyone knows my husband, it's Mike."

"Tell them I said, *touché*. They were devastatingly good, especially him."

"He'll appreciate that. But what happened to you?"

"I had my head handed to me." Jean apologized, but Enright said, "No. Maybe it was for the best. So there you go, I hate to be criticized. I don't know why I'm telling you this. I was told not to come in with a head of steam. I wouldn't, but I'm pretty persistent. Until now, I've usually gotten what I want."

"And what do you want now?" Max asked between bites.

"I'm not sure anymore. Maybe if I were in your place, I would've done the same thing. And I have to admit, if we … if *I* had done my homework, it wouldn't have happened. But when you're mad you don't want to hear it's your fault. Anyway, I was all set to rip you all a new one." She looked at Max. "Then, I found out about you."

Max leaned back and looked at his wife. "Why should that matter?" Jean asked.

"I don't know. I was doing some research, finally. I went to the *Chronicle* to talk about their recollections of you and the SSC. I met a woman whose sister is a nurse here. She told me. I just was struck, knowing you were ill, that everyone would go through with something that would cause me that much embarrassment. It hit me—that kind of effort must have meant something when you had so much more on your mind. I was all ready to march in. I know, a lot of me, me, me. And then it didn't matter anymore. I guess something happens when you feel the need to apologize to people who embarrass you. I just have to ask—was it the interview I did with Kevin Herter?"

"No," Jean said firmly. "We know what you do. Kevin is a big boy. It's what happened with Sharon Velazquez. Understand, we're very protective of Kevin, but he's been around the block enough with reporters to hold his own. But you made Sharon look like a raving lunatic and that's not her at all. You people need to respect boundaries. If you feel all's fair and you violate them for a story, you have to be prepared for anything. She's a remarkable woman. What happened to her wasn't fair. I hope you can appreciate that."

"My wife is right," Max said in a raspy voice. "I don't care about anything anymore, except for Kevin." He looked at Jean. "And my wife."

"And Sharon," Jean added, "we were hoping they would wind up together. That's over now. They were in a rough spot and what happened couldn't have come at a worse time. Our hearts went out to her when we saw it; Kevin as well, because we know what it did to him. And honestly our hearts go out to you, too. I'm sorry this ran away from everyone."

"I couldn't have said it better," Max declared.

Enright sat with her hand over her mouth. The episode earlier was a monumental embarrassment. This was different, the purest pain she had felt in a long time. It wasn't something they prepared you for in journalism school. She hadn't done anything that could be considered unethical yet felt a weight on her conscience she had never experienced as a reporter. It was the first time she'd seen the residuals of her work after the cameras had gone off.

"I'm so sorry about this. You have no idea." She stood. "I should go."

"Please sit," Jean said.

"I guess I'm old and sick enough that I can be a mensch," Max said, pointing to the chair. "Sit back down. Don't worry; we don't bite."

Enright broke a smile and slowly sat. Jean studied her. "Where do you go from here?"

"I don't know," Enright said. "Back to square one. My boss told me that earlier, but I didn't want to hear then. Funny, my source has been saying the same thing. Best I start to listen."

"I'm going to be a mother now," Jean said, smiling. "You seem very nice. We're not telling you how to do you job. I just think you're selling yourself short. It took a lot of courage to come and talk to us. Not everyone would do that, especially someone so young."

As Max agreed, Enright lightly smiled. "I have to be honest. I was petrified."

"I always tell Kevin how sorry I feel for your generation," Jean added. "Things move so fast, you don't sit with them and see how they feel. I get that impression from you. Maybe it's the sculptor in me, but it's like looking at the world with a hand over one eye. You do the same thing with your cameras. You see but miss the depth. You point, walk away, and miss the subtleties, the things that make getting to know something in three dimensions worth it. And you never miss what you're not seeing because you're so quick to move on. It's sad."

"This is what happens when you get old or sick," Max said. "You get philosophical."

"I could use a dose now and then," Enright said. "I took a class. Not the same as living it."

"I hope you got what you came for," Jean said, noticing Max's fatigue. "I am sorry, but I think this happened for a reason. You get older, you'll look at things a little differently. You said you feel like you aged ten years today. We just had our own epiphany of sorts. I've come to realize something about them—you expect a smack in the face, but it can also be a tap on the shoulder. I hope next time it doesn't take something so dramatic to see what you need to see."

"I want to thank you," Enright said as she rose and smiled. "You've given me a lot to think about."

"We wish you luck. Are you going back to New York?"

"I'm not sure. My gut still says there's a story here."

"There is," said an energized Max. "Just stop going for a cheap gotcha."

Jean agreed. "I know Mike had quite a go at you but if you're smart you'll think about what he said. It just as easily could have been coming from my husband."

"That's my Mikey," Max added. "What part?"

"He said the real story isn't us or Kevin but what's going on out there."

"My editor said the same thing," Enright added.

Max jabbed his finger at an absent Joshua Emerson. "Yeah," he told Enright in his stead. "You remember something. For the most part I've had no use for any of you. But you're not without purpose. We learned a lot yesterday. Something's going on out there. If you're a good reporter, go and look into it. Look at the money, the people. And see what makes the thing tick; how they fire the things, the fuel. There's too much going on for something not to be going on."

"You may not know this," Jean said, "but your editor sent you here because of my husband. Joshua Emerson was the reporter who followed him twenty-five years ago after a big science project he was working on in Texas was cancelled."

"Oh, wow," Enright said.

"My husband's right; a lot of this is connected. We're very concerned about Kevin. They're dragging him in for a reason. Maybe you can help him, and yourself."

"Do you know where Kevin is now?"

Jean and Max eyed each other. "They asked him to go out and watch an explosion," Jean said.

"Now," Max jumped in, "you can run after him and do the kind of number you used to do. But maybe you'll do things differently. Whatever you do …"

Max looked at Jean, who completed the sentence, "… do it like a good reporter would do it, not like a—"

"Sleeze," Enright intoned.

"I wasn't going to say it," Jean smiled.

"I was," Max declared.

As Enright blushed, Jean added, "It's your choice. You seem intelligent. Everything comes with consequences. You do what you feel is right for you."

"Dr. and Mrs. Rosenkranz," Enright smiled warmly, "it's been a pleasure. It's not what I expected, but—" she laughed, "—nothing today was. You've been very kind. Thank you."

"That's how we are most of the time," Jean remarked.

"When we're not screwing around with pain-in-the-ass reporters," Max added.

Enright burst out laughing. "Please take care," she said, "and Dr. Rosenkranz, I hope—"

"You don't have to hope anything. Whatever will happen will happen. But thanks." Enright smiled and left. It was a little after seven p.m. Max had missed the news.

Thirty-eight

Jessica Enright left the ICU with a smile. It was the best she'd felt since that morning. Night had fallen and she was thinking of dinner. She turned toward the waiting area on her way to the parking lot, and jumped in shock. Seated near the exit was Mike Yahr.

She bit her lip and walked up. "I didn't expect to see you again."

"I figured." He clutched a large yellow envelope. "Have a nice chat with Max and Jean?"

She warily nodded. "They were very kind. Truth to tell, I told them you were very good earlier. Please tell them I said thank you again."

"Thanks, I will. But I came to see you. Can I buy you a cup of coffee?" Enright gave a confused shrug, and five minutes later sat nursing a cup of tea at the cafeteria. "I know we had some fun at your expense," Mike began. "I'm sorry it caused you trouble, Miss Enright, but if I had it to do over again I probably wouldn't change a thing."

"Please, call me Jessica. I guess I had it coming. I don't know why I'm not pissed, but I suppose it's for the same reason I wasn't angry at them." She chuckled. "You should have been an actor."

"Thanks," Mike smiled, "but then I wouldn't be able to help you. We need to talk. I know you feel like something the cat dragged in, but you were actually a lot closer to the truth than you know. I've spoken to several people about you. We'd like to help you get back in the game."

Enright grew perplexed. "What do you mean? And after this morning, why?"

"I won't say how I know what I know and for now I'll hold off on my reasons, but I'm proposing a working deal with you. I'm offering myself as a source. A lot's happened since our coffee and muffins. You'll learn that what I'm giving you is dead on. Something here needs flushing out. If you're open to that, sit back and listen. It's a hell of a story."

Over the next hour, Mike methodically presented information about the bomb program, from the bureaucratic layout to the players involved. He held off mentioning him by name but he described Jack Raden's findings and their implications. He spoke of Max Rosenkranz and his history with Joshua Emerson. He recounted how Kevin Herter had been stalked, bugged and almost blown up. He told her about the notes Kevin had been given and the blood-filled cup on his steps. He talked about the president's grand vision for using the bomb to curb the world's violent streak, and how in an ultimate expression of cynicism, that it was all probably a ruse. And he spoke of indications of a dark secret that was frantically being kept hidden in a cascade of good intentions.

Enright sat spellbound. From a human standpoint, the story captivated her. From a reporter's outlook, she was hooked. She peppered Mike with questions, and he saw that despite the earlier incident, she did have talent. Once unshackled from her inclination towards immaturity, her probing questions and inquisitiveness grew, and with it grew his respect for her.

An hour later, she checked her phone, which had been on vibrate. Ten voicemails and eight text messages were in. "Busy night," she said, not listening to or reading them. "They're probably wondering where I disappeared to. I can't believe all this. I had an idea something was up, but not this."

"Now I have to ask you something, Jessica," Mike said. "What are you going to do?"

"My God," she sighed. "I know what I have to do. I just need to sit for a few minutes."

"Not a bad plan. I meant something different though. There's a reason why I told you all of this, and it's not because I felt I owed you. You've stepped in it, in ways you don't know."

"What do you mean? And why get me involved?"

"You'll find out soon. It's true that Kevin Herter's the focus of this. He was set up. But so were you. The Administration was hell-bent on getting you to take the bait."

"Explain. I take it you're not only talking about my editor's interest."

"They consider you the embodiment of today's media," he nodded, "a photogenic lightweight. They were hoping you'd crowd out more serious reporters. How does that make you feel?"

Enright turned a flaming shade of red and looked down, but within moments Mike saw it turn to fire. "So tell me then," he inquired, "is that the reputation you want?"

"The question answers itself." She glared at him. "Is that why you did what you did earlier?"

"No. But I want to take advantage of it, and if you're smart you'll do the same. I know that Kevin was just told something, something that you need to hear as well. There are people expecting him to act a certain way, which is to be how he's always been. My guess is, they'd expect the same from you. It's time to do things differently, to stop being ordinary, both of you. Maybe now you can appreciate the position he's in. So let me ask you, how pissed are you?"

"It's up there," Enright nodded resolutely.

"Good. You want this to work for you?" Mike hectored. "Then you're ready. Channel your anger into correct action. Throw them off."

"What's your angle in all this? Why are you so interested in having me involved?"

"Good question. The short answer is that decisions are being made that will cause trouble, and the people behind them don't belong making them. A lot more's going on than you know. Kevin Herter's involved whether he wants to be or not. He knows he's over his head. We're trying to keep him in one piece and give him a hand but there are things he can't do, which is where you come in. We need someone to dig and to bring it out in the open. And fast. By this weekend it's going to be too late. So, you in?"

"Damn right I'm in," she smiled.

"Good. First, you know you took a hit today. Like I said, it's not my job to rehabilitate you. You'll have to do that on your own. But not being taken seriously lets you slip into places easier. You're less of a threat. This is a chance to make people forget it quickly. And they can. But it'll get messy, maybe worse than what Kevin's dealing with. You have to be prepared. Your sources have directed you a certain way, but that's gonna change as well." Mike well knew Jack would be identifying himself to her soon.

Enright pulled back. "How did you know about my sources?"

"It's my business, just as I know that when you leave here, it's better than even you'll be tailed." Enright grew still. He added, "That's the world I came from. You've been given good information and it's taken you this far but the situation has radically changed. A day ago, no one was thinking about planting bugs and cars blowing up. So don't go in with any false illusions. Whatever's going on has people concerned, enough that they're pushing someone retired like me back in the game. Now I'm pushing you. I'm sorry, but we're putting both of you in a tight spot. Remember, for now this is a story without an ending. Maybe you can help with that."

Enright took a deep breath and let out a long sigh. "You're just a load of surprises."

"That's what my wife tells me every week."

"I can see her saying that," she laughed. "Okay, where do we go from here?"

"Well, tell me what you're thinking."

Enright sat a few moments. "The obvious would be to follow Kevin Herter out to Tuvalu. But my gut tells me that Honolulu is the place to start."

"I think you'll go far in this business. But for my own edification, I want to hear why."

Enright flashed her formidable smile. "Here's how I see it. The project head and her husband moved there months ago. The state has been stockpiling used boats for months now, presumably as launches for the bombs. They're counting on getting a site. But I think they're a long-shot, which means someone's peddling some kind of influence. A lot of contractors connected to the program have offices in Hawaii. And Max Rosenkranz mentioned looking into the bomb device itself. He specified the fuel. I think something's up with the Pentagon and the people who build the things, and it's connected to the election. And I just have to ask—what's in that envelope?"

"It's a list of the main contractors connected to the program," Mike smiled, "along with names and addresses. I've included a flash drive with the same information." He handed over the envelope.

"There seems to be a great deal that a lot of people are going out of their way to hide," she said.

Mike leaned back and folded his arms. "I think you're going to go far in this business."

Thirty-nine

Jessica Enright approached the Mill Valley Travel Lodge just before eight thirty. On the drive from the hospital, she'd been weighing her situation and the turn of events. Mike had been ruthlessly honest. While devastating, his words were ones she needed to hear. The only way to lessen the sting would be to do what he'd asked. And as she drove, she realized more and more that she cared little for showing *them*, which surprised her. She knew what she was capable of, and increasingly, she was eager to show herself.

Another part wanted to hold back. Before leaving him, Mike inspected her car as he had done Kevin's. Though not finding anything, that he'd had to do it left its mark. The weight of her situation hit home. His parting words were to take extra care, words that had given her a chill. She'd held off calling her crew, wishing to fill them in personally. But as she came up on the motel, all that was forgotten.

In the dark and drizzle, the flashing red and blue of ambulances and police cars lit up the motel like a rain-streaked fun house. She neared the entrance where an officer challenged her. Upon identifying herself, they ushered her in. Police bustled through the lobby carrying boxes and rolls of yellow crime scene tape. Employees fumbled about in a futile stab at business as usual.

Her eyes fell on a dazed Cliff Abreau on a couch surrounded by paramedics, and a flash of gauze and blood. She tried running up but was restrained by two officers.

"You can't talk to him, Miss Enright," said an officer, who instead led her to a meeting room, where they were joined by two detectives.

"What happened?" Enright demanded. "I want to know what's going on!"

"Miss Enright, could you tell us where you've been the past three hours?" Detective Steve Chapman stood with a notepad, intimidating in his black leather jacket.

"I was meeting with some people at Marin General Hospital. I'm working a story, and that's all I'm prepared to reveal. Why? What's going on?"

"Can you verify that?"

"The hospital can, but I won't reveal who I spoke with. I want to know what happened."

"Miss Enright, your co-worker Jim Leffert was stabbed to death tonight."

"*What?* What happened?" she kept repeating.

"We're thinking it was a robbery gone bad. Mr. Leffert and Mr. Abreau walked in on two men ransacking the room. There was a struggle and both of them were knifed. Mr. Abreau's wounds were superficial, but Mr. Leffert bled out before an ambulance arrived. I'm sorry."

"Oh, my God!" she agonized, working to keep her wits. "Jim! I can't believe it!"

"Can you tell us about what they might have been after?" Chapman asked. "Their video equipment is gone, which could fetch some dollars. But why would they have—"

"I can't believe this," she muttered. A flood of thoughts raced by, the first being there was no way this was a robbery. She had stowed the envelope under her car seat but clutched her handbag which contained the USB stick. "Listen," she began, praying she wouldn't be searched, "I don't know what they were after, but none of us carried valuables. We just flew out from New York. We had our equipment, but nothing else."

"Miss Enright, we spoke to your editor in New York, Joshua Emerson. He gave us some information, but we need more from you about your visit here."

She sat down, her fears drowned out by the determination across the rest of her face. Though she hadn't known him well, she'd liked Jim. But more than anything was the realization that in one fell swoop, she was now in the Big Leagues. There was no going back.

A moment later, an officer walked in to say that Joshua Emerson was on the phone. The call was patched in. "Joshua," Enright murmured, "I can't believe this."

"Are you okay?" he answered. "Is there anything we can do for you?"

"No. I mean, I don't know." She paused. "Can I have a few minutes alone?" There was no other entrance to the room, so Chapman nodded yes and they left.

"Joshua, Jim was killed because of this story. I'm convinced of it," she said in a low but frantic voice.

"Hold it. You don't know that yet, but why do you think it?"

"I'm hanging up now, and calling you on your cell." She dialed up his phone. "Okay," she continued, breathlessly, "what did they tell you?"

"Jessica, first of all, are you okay? Were you hurt?" He seemed sincere.

"I'm okay. I got here after it happened. I know Cliff was hurt, but I think he's all right. They didn't let me talk to him." She was almost hyperventilating.

"Okay, good. Just hold it together. Why do you think—"

"Josh, I need to know what they told you."

"They weren't too forthcoming. I don't think they know much. They just said Jim and Cliff surprised two guys. They asked me what the three of you were doing there. I didn't go into detail. They requested that I consent to the two of you remaining local until the investigation—"

"That's it!" Enright cried. She was in a frenzy, then caught herself, cupping the phone with her hand. "Josh, that's why they killed him. They weren't looking for shit. I have a list of leads. Killing one or both of them keeps me from checking them out. If they succeed, whatever it is happens without anyone catching on." She eyed the closed door. "Oh, my God," she yelped.

"Jessica, I have to tell you, word about that interview this morning is out. I don't think anyone would be concerned with you investigating anything—"

"Josh, I'm telling you that's what's happening! You don't know the half of it. I've learned a shitload since this morning. My God! This morning's a lifetime ago. I'm telling you, someone knows I'm onto this and they're trying to slow me down. Killing me draws attention to it. Killing Jim doesn't. But it makes me hang around like a moron while… Josh, these people aren't stupid. They know what they're doing. You gotta get me out of here!"

"I won't dismiss what you saying", Emerson said, "but you have to give me something to work with." He was torn between the memory of her monumental incompetence twelve hours earlier and his well-honed instincts as a reporter. He wasn't sure which to follow but let her talk. Enright feverishly searched for some scrap to convince Emerson she wasn't the fool he surely thought she was.

"Josh, I have to be honest about something," she finally conceded, hesitant about taking the risk. "I met Max and Jean Rosenkranz earlier tonight."

"God dammit!" he intoned. "What the hell did you bother them for?"

"Joshua, please! I didn't go there with an attitude!"

"I don't care! I've had it covering your ass—"

"Josh, please! Just hear me out! I had a very nice conversation with them. They were very kind. I only went to apologize to them."

"I don't care—"

"Will you just listen? When I was leaving, I met the guy who did the number on me earlier. He approached me. He wants to be a source. He told me something about Max Rosenkranz that I'm supposed to tell you if anything came up that needed to be investigated. I'm going to say something. If you still want to fire me after that, I'll accept that, okay?"

"All right," Emerson groaned, almost ready to hang up on her. "What is it?"

Enright paused. "It's a boy."

"Oh, my God," gasped Emerson. Enright heard what sounded like a glass being knocked over, then a long huff. "Okay," he said, sounding out of breath, "do what you need. I'll fix it so you can leave there. Where are you headed?"

"I need to get to Honolulu as quickly as possible."

"Okay, go. This stays between us. Do you need a crew?"

"I don't know. Maybe." She felt lightheaded.

"You let me know. One more thing—are you going to be all right?"

"I'm not sure." She paused, still a little dizzy. "I'll keep in touch, okay?"

"You do that, with everything. Just be very, very careful."

"For sure." She paused. "Josh. I just have to ask. What does it mean?"

"I can't tell you. Maybe someday I will. Just be careful." He hung up. Enright closed her phone and slowly got up.

Back in New York Joshua Emerson slowly sat down, feeling every breath. God, he thought, it's a hell of a business. What had passed with Max Rosenkranz a generation earlier had remained the one truly unresolved episode in his career. The physicist had been stubborn and abrasive, and try as he might he couldn't get him to open up. As Rosenkranz grew in stature, in time receiving a Nobel Prize, it had burgeoned into a sore spot for the up-and-coming reporter, even as he went on to success himself. The last response he'd received from the scientist had rankled him the most. Rosenkranz steadfastly refused to speak to any media, seeming to revel in his role as a curmudgeon. But in a tersely worded send-off, Rosenkranz remarked that should he ever choose to open up, he would do so with a code. While Emerson didn't know at the time, it was the code that physicist Edward Teller, the father of the hydrogen bomb, had devised to inform a colleague that the first test of the weapon had been a success. Teller had been unhappy with the government's commitment to the bomb's development. His impatience led him to form his own weapons laboratory. He failed, and his obstinance cost him the chance to witness the test. He had instead holed up beside a seismograph in California, awaiting the detonation shock wave from halfway across the Pacific. When it reached the detector at the predicted time, the needle moved, indicating it was successful. Teller relayed the news to a friend with the simple message, "It's a boy."

Emerson hadn't known that the phrase had any meaning until years later when he watched Teller relate the story in an interview. Now, he understood that Rosenkranz recognized his own stubbornness but hadn't yet reached a place where he could move past it. The communication from Enright wasn't Rosenkranz letting on about the Superconducting Supercollider, nor was he commenting about the new program in the South Pacific. But it was his way of opening up to Joshua Emerson in a way that said, "It's okay now. And you were right."

It was worth waiting for. Maybe obstinacy and impertinence do share a potentiality for redemption, he realized, as much as impatience and frustration. For scientists as well as reporters, male and female, young and old. Even if it sometimes takes a generation.

Forty

"Goddammit!" Dillon Ridge blazed into the phone. "What the hell's going on out there?"

Tom Whiteman was equally irate. "If you weren't so hell-bent on following him for no-good reason—"

"That's not for you to decide. You were to keep him on edge. The president is fit to be tied. What's with that other crap?"

"No one here had anything to do with it. Who's running things back there? If you had kept a lid on things, he'd still be home and we wouldn't be in this mess. *Edge?* You've got enough *edge* now—"

"All right, hold it," Ridge fumed, not used to people calling his bluster. "If you hadn't—"

"I hadn't done shit! You had to park that damn van right where that fucking genius could see it. If you hadn't, that bitch wouldn't have had that run-in with him. Now she's hightailing it out here with a bug up her ass. Who knows what she'll find. And who the hell put that thing in his car? So don't tell me about other crap. I'm up to my ears in other crap!"

"Fine," Ridge huffed, knowing he wouldn't win this on points. "I have to brief the president. You better get on your horse and find out who the hell's running around—"

"Like hell I will! I don't have the time or resources to investigate your loose cannons. You want damage control, run it yourself. It's enough dealing with your messes without figuring out which one of you fuck-ups made them."

"If you'd kept your wife in check—"

"Fuck you!" Whiteman slammed down the phone. He was tired of Ridge, and the White House as well. It may have seemed that they were on the same page with how they wanted to deal with Herter. But no one else knew how things really were except for him. He no longer cared what Ridge was hiding from the president. The situation was out of hand and threatening to get worse. That was Ridge's problem now. They'd have to figure it out themselves. He was done giving them updates. In the meantime, he would do what he had to. He went back to packing, knowing that Lisa had a twelve-hour head start on him.

An hour later, Elliot Hanford received a call over the Pacific. He was not known for late nights and was getting ready to retire. He had just been briefed by Dillon Ridge. Despite the resources at his command, Ridge's people had yet to get a hand on who was behind the occurrences. Hanford was eager to listen to what John Raden had to say.

"Jack," Hanford said to Raden in his hotel room in Tuvalu, "are you settled in?"

"Yes, Mr. President."

"So where are we?"

"He'll be landing early this morning. We have a full day set with him. I'm not expecting too much right away—he doesn't fly well."

"Just as well. What's that trouble he had in California? And Princeton?"

"The investigation is still ongoing." The events in Mill Valley had yet to reach any of them and Raden wasn't about to tip Hanford off to anything he hadn't brought up himself. But the president's low-key re-action to what happened to Herter was conspicuous. It meant Hanford was behind it, knew about it or was being inscrutable by design. Raden knew to ignore it for the moment. "Just be aware that the incident at the hospital was a close call," he added instead. "You don't need me saying it, but your people may want to beef up security."

"It's already in the works." Both knew the Secret Service had factored in the events. "I heard about the reporter and her snafu in California," Hanford laughed.

"I just heard about that myself." Mike had phoned him. He got a kick out of the story and agreed it could help but wouldn't let on how he knew. Raden had also been told of the car bomb and the surveillance van. A lot seemed to be fraying around the edges. People were losing focus or falling back on their own agendas. Either way, the situation was growing more precarious. Mike had also told him about briefing Jessica Enright. Raden appreciated that she now knew a lot more than Hanford realized. More than ever, he would play his cards close to the vest. He could only say of her mishap, "I'll tell you, it was a hell of a subplot."

"I'll say. It won't cause us trouble, will it?"

"No. Just the opposite—might be something we can use."

"Okay, good. You think she'll be able to live it down?"

"In time. Short term, she may have a problem. That might be an asset for us."

"I was thinking the same thing. Is she on her way out there?" Again, he knew the answer.

"No. She's headed for Hawaii."

"How'd she find out about that?"

"It's not too hard. There's enough out there to put two and two together, even for a rookie."

Raden had just maligned Hanford's strategy to opportunistically take advantage of Enright. It gave him a sense of quiet satisfaction. Joshua Emerson's history with the matter had lent itself to exploitation, which meant using Enright, and Raden was astute enough to know the White House recognized that connection and would expect him to know it himself. Their error was they had no misgivings about throwing her under the bus. By dismissing her, they missed the flexibility she offered. They saw her as little more than a means, instead of realizing she could be a potential asset—another error. With Hanford's penchant for cloak and dagger, the White House had worked her without letting Raden in on the scheme. The president couldn't call him on criticizing it, as he wasn't supposed to know, and Raden knew he wasn't supposed to know. It was a hell of business, he thought.

Hanford grumbled, "You think it's worth sending her down the wrong road?"

"No, not at all." Raden ignored his disquiet. "Let her do what she's doing. Just keep in mind our long-term goals, and let everything fall into place. It will."

"Okay John, keep me posted. Too much is getting fucked up now."

"Will do, Mr. President. You have a good evening now."

Raden hung up, and readied himself for a late dinner. He would be long asleep by the time Kevin Herter landed. Tomorrow would be an eventful day.

Thursday, April 7

Forty-one

The sun teasing through the shuttered doors and draped windows awakened Kevin at seven thirty. Though coming off five hours sleep, he felt surprisingly rested.

The plane had landed at one forty a.m. Except for a spell of thunderstorms south of Hawaii that kept him white-knuckling for an hour the flight had been smooth. He'd managed a few fits of sleep, but like with every flight he ever took he was more tired upon landing than before taking off. Once again he was whisked through deplaning. In his room a bare half hour later, shoes and pants on the floor, he was sound asleep within ten minutes.

He hadn't noticed anything before falling off, but the morning light let him appreciate his surroundings. In the spacious coral and sea green suite, he was greeted by a large fruit basket decorated with fresh-cut flowers and a ribbon proclaiming, *Welcome to Tuvalu Alofa*. With accompanying palms and shells it all said Polynesian. Clipped to the basket was a note from John Raden:

Good Morning. Hope the flight was bearable and you slept well. When you're dressed, ring my room and we'll have breakfast. Jack.

Kevin drew the curtains and opened the balcony doors. Like a travel brochure bursting out in a multitude of dimensions, the equatorial beauty that was the island nation of Tuvalu spread out before him. In the bright sunshine, he gazed out over a palm-studded expanse of pools, thatched huts and a riot of flowering greenery. Beyond it a pristine beach opened to a turquoise sea, met in the distance by a sky of limitless blue. His third floor suite was near the apex of a wide V-shaped complex. A mall area below held an outdoor buffet, and numerous sunbathers idled about. Guests on their own balconies leisurely enjoyed breakfast. A few smiled and he waved back. A contemporary jazz mix over the creamy scent of jasmine completed the picture. The scene was seductive, every bit as exotic as Tahiti or Fiji, and with all the events the past few days, all he could think was, "I could get used to this place."

"Look at Joe tourist," Kevin clucked to the smiling Raden in his floral shirt and khaki shorts as he opened his door to Kevin at eight fifteen.

"Good to see you!" Raden answered. "How was your flight?"

"The usual. Hate flying but love having flown. It's been a hell of a forty-eight hours."

"I heard some, but you'll fill me in. Hungry?" They headed out for the elevator.

"I just have to ask," Kevin quipped as they rode down to the first floor, "is that sanctioned attire for the president's official Tuvaluan representative?"

Raden laughed. "It's kind of a national uniform. Most of the time it's super casual. I see you'll fit right in," he added, nodding at Kevin's tan shorts and light turquoise shirt.

The elevator reached the main floor. A sumptuous buffet beckoned, but Raden said, "There's much to discuss, but first I want to show you something."

To the right was a gift shop, a sign by the entrance reading, *Welcome to Tuvalu Alofa.* Inside was a large assortment of souvenir items: T shirts, sweatshirts, mugs, postcards. Tropical butterflies. Many featured the resort's theme, nuclear detonations. There were posters of explosions with bikini-clad women, postcard booklets and videos of the site and its history. Several items proclaimed *Having a Blast in Tuvalu* while others said *Positively Aglow.* Some simply read *Club Afterglow.*

Raden brought Kevin over to a table. Stacked for sale was an assortment of pale rocks. They looked like pieces of concrete with bits and pieces of shells and coral glued to them. A sign on the table read Herterite.

Kevin stood with his mouth agape. "What the hell is this?"

"Congratulations for having a rock named after you."

"Oh, God. I know what it is. But I need to hear you say it."

"It's created by the bombs. It's the sea bed and coral that's melted and lifted into the fireball. The stuff rains down and eventually gets washed on shore. It's pretty popular. People spend hours beachcombing for it."

"Oh Christ, Jack, you had to show me this before breakfast? Come on, let's go eat before I get sick." Kevin grabbed him by the arm and escorted him out. "How come no one told me?"

"Things get overlooked," Raden shrugged. "They had to name it something. You just need to deal with the fact that around here you will attract attention."

Forty-two

Over palm-nestled grounds where tropical butterflies danced, a security presence was evident. Kevin knew there had to be more, less obvious, like federal marshals on planes, and with Elliot Hanford arriving, it would increase.

Several long tables held every breakfast food imaginable, along with carving stations and chefs preparing omelets. The servers wore a smart number of beige shorts and light green and mauve shirts sporting the resort logo, a design combining its name with the image of an atom.

"I don't know what will come from this," Kevin said as they got on line, "but I could do a serious staycation here, if they'd just ditch the Herterite."

Two young women got on line behind them. Kevin recognized them as the ones on the plane. One wore a long white T-shirt and shorts while the other, the blonde who kept eyeing him, wore a flower skirt and bikini top. Both were even more attractive in the morning light.

"Excuse me," asked the blonde. "Are you Dr. Herter?"

Kevin nodded. "You guys were on my flight, right?"

"We thought we recognized you," she smiled. "It's nice to meet you."

Her friend, a shapely brunette asked, "Have you been here before?"

"First time. And you guys?"

"The same," said the blonde. "How long are you here?"

"Probably till Sunday," Kevin said. He and Raden began serving themselves.

"Excellent! Us too. I'm Robin, and this is Gina. Can we look you up?"

"Sure. Call me Kevin." The women beamed and walked on.

Raden took some pancakes and syrup. "Hey 'Call me Kevin'. Go for it."

"If I knew it was that easy I'd have come here last year." He squinted, "You didn't hear that." He added a few pineapple slices to his Western omelet. As they sat a server rushed over with coffee.

"Before we go into anything else," Kevin began, "thanks for having the cops watch Sharon. She didn't need to be dragged into this. And thanks for what you did with Max and Jean."

"We felt it was time," Raden smiled. "I'm sorry. I know what they mean to you."

"You have no idea. It puts a whole different perspective on this. Your parents alive?"

"My mother."

"They're the only ones I ever really knew. Jack, thanks. It means a lot to me." He shook his head. "I can't get over how you knew when they managed to keep it from me for years."

"You'd be surprised how easy that is. There's so much information out there, you just have to know where to look. And hey, at the NSA we're supposed to be famous for that, though we're just the tip of the iceberg. It's funny; people get pissed at others for holding back things they won't say themselves. Most people, the closer they are to someone, the less they tell them. Ever see families triangulate? They talk nonsense, but something important to say, forget it. They tell complete strangers things they won't say to those closest to them. On sitcoms, it's hysterical."

"I know. Living it's different. So again, thanks."

Just then, three college-age girls approached. Unlike the previous two, these had a look just one beer short of roles in *Girls Gone Wild* and it was only eight thirty a.m.

"My friend Sonia thinks you're cute," a picturesque blonde told him.

Kevin eyed them. "Which one of you is Sonia?"

A demure yet stunning girl with flowing honey-toned hair stepped up.

"We saw you on TV," the third girl said, nudging her forward. "She thinks you're hot."

"Well, Hi," Kevin smiled.

"He's cute," the first one giggled, as Sonia smiled in silence. The third girl grinned. "I can't believe you thought this whole place up yourself. All that atoms and stuff."

"It wasn't really my idea," he said, hoping to avoid talking with the budding physicists.

"It's still cool. We came out here 'cause we heard you guys got the best parties."

Kevin felt at a loss for words. "Where you from?" he finally managed.

"San Diego," said the first. "You just gotta come. We'll take you to La Jolla. We can get you into the best clubs."

The first girl took out a black Sharpie. "Could you sign my shirt?"

He looked over her pure white T-shirt, which covered an ample figure despite being two sizes too big. "And just where do I, uh, sign?" She giggled and stuck out her chest while the others covered their mouths and tittered away. Raden raised his gaze skyward. "All right, let's have the pen. What's your name?"

"Candi with an i."

"Why doesn't that surprise me? Anything special you want me to write?" Kevin added.

With a sex-kittenish shimmy she squeaked, "Nope!"

Kevin arched his arm well away from her breasts and wrote across the upper end of her chest, "Candi, Have a Boom-Boom time in Tuvalu. Kevin Herter."

The two others squealed, "I love it!" and "That is *hot!*" Candi stretched her shirt down and twisted her head to see. It had the effect of revealing her braless figure and pert nipples. Kevin stole enough of a look for her to nail the response she desired. She screamed and planted a big kiss on him. "Oh, that is the best!"

"That's a first," he sheepishly responded. He felt awkward but wasn't kidding himself; he could imagine a hop in the sack with her.

"You are so cool," she purred. "Meet us later and we'll party!"

As they departed, Raden grinned. "I usually see that stuff only on TV."

"Six hours here and already I'm doing better than I could do in six months at home," Kevin laughed.

"Like I said go, for it. You just gotta decide how important it is to carry on a two-sentence conversation when you're getting laid."

Kevin cracked up. He slouched into his chair, clasped his hands on his belly and gazed lazily at the sea. "Okay," he sighed, "give me the bad news first."

Forty-three

"So, that's it." Jack Raden leaned back and in the warm morning sipped some water.

Kevin sat numb. "I don't know how to even begin to respond," he finally stammered. "Jack, what the hell did I get myself into?"

"Well, that's a good question."

"Jesus, you gotta do better than that. What do I do, get whacked or get laid? You guys want me to be eyes and ears, but you can't tell me this kind of shit would happen."

"No," Raden frowned, "you're right. We expected something, but not this fast. Someone's got a lot at stake. We know the pressure's on."

"And you have no idea what happened to Jim Leffert?"

"No. The police are still—"

"Investigating, I know. He didn't deserve that. I agree with Enright; that wasn't any accident. She may be a pain, but maybe she's onto something."

"That's how we see it. But you need to keep it together. I know about California, but—"

"Oh, cut me some slack.

"I am. Just focus on today. This place will get crazy enough. Hanford's flying in about noon. The event is set for 5:47, just before sunset. There's several people eager to meet you. We don't see anything happening today, but expect to be hit up for things. So, what is it?"

Kevin was staring off. "I keep thinking about that car bomb. And Jim Leffert."

"Listen. We'll deal." Raden changed the subject. "So, what did you think of Mike?"

"Him I like. I can see why you two are friends. I also like he's good to Max and Jean."

"Some coincidence, huh?"

"Yeah, it is. Now, Jack, what the hell's going on? Who had it out for me?"

"We don't know yet. I dropped a casual comment to Hanford, whether he had ever seen one of these things, and he bit. People are consistent. He's coming out here to show he's a visionary, and to close the deal with you. He'll sweet talk and strong arm you at the same time, and trust me, he's good at both. Now, fair warning; you were probably followed. Someone will make a move. We're not sure who or what. Just play it out."

"Great. Any more car bombs to look forward to? What did you learn about that?"

"Mike's people are looking at it. They kept the locals away. Usually, you can tell handiwork and trace it back, even after it goes off. These guys have their signatures. This is different, a patchwork. Clever. Even the material itself. C 4, like any explosive, leaves manufacturing traces. This seems to be an amalgam. They meant to cover their tracks. On the other hand, had it gone off it would have received a lot more attention than they bargained for, so they might not have thought it out so well. Depends on what they were really after. That'll show how clever they really are, whether a lot or just too much by half. We'll get it."

"Before they get me?" Kevin shook his head. "Just where does that leave me?"

"Still asking questions. Seriously, keep asking. Hanford's leaving tomorrow and coming back on Sunday to make his announcement. They're planning another event for that evening."

"Another explosion?"

"Normally, they fire them off every week or so. This will be the first time they fire two this close together. It's a sendoff for his grand vision. And something else. All this crap, Hanford knows about it. Don't be surprised if he uses it to win you over. And trust me, it won't be easy turning him down."

Kevin leaned back and huffed.

"Consider yourself warned." As Kevin rolled his eyes, he noticed a cruise ship. Raden said, "That's *Star Princess*. They get two to four ships an event."

"It had to be *Star Princess*, huh?" Kevin chuckled.

"I told you to prepare yourself for the irony here."

"Speaking of irony, I wish I could've been there for that thing with Enright."

"That's what Max said. I know why Mike did it. I would have done the same thing."

"But at what cost. Look at Jim."

"You can't think like that. That wasn't anyone's fault except those who did it. And it may have happened anyway. Enright's headed to Hawaii now. A lot of contractors are there. The governor's pushing hard for one of the new sites. That's the last-minute politicking I mentioned. It may get intense. And the program head is flying out here as well. She's been angling to get you on board from the start. Expect to meet her, too."

"She's the last person I want to talk to. She's responsible for all this. I don't need to be meeting with her." He sighed. "What's her name?"

"Lisa Whiteman." Raden looked at his watch. "It's almost nine. Expect company in a few. The prime minister wants to meet you. Also, the chief resort administrator."

"I get to meet the prime minister?"

"He's been looking forward to it. Remember. It's a nation of nine islands, maybe 12,000 people. You're talking a quarter of Princeton. But the people here are proud."

A moment later two men and a woman appeared at their table. A jovial gentleman extended his hand. "Dr. Herter!" he said, his island accent evident, "I am Lionel Latasi. I am so pleased to make your acquaintance! Welcome to our islands!"

"Kevin," Raden said, "this is the prime minister of Tuvalu."

"It's a pleasure to meet you, Mr. Prime Minister," smiled Kevin, standing and reaching out to clasp Latasi's outstretched hand.

"Oh, please, Dr. Herter. The pleasure is all ours." Latasi, a rather rotund chap with a bronze tone and infectious smile, energetically shook Kevin's hand. "We're indebted to you and your wonderful work. It has completely changed our nation and our future."

"Well, thank you, Mr. Prime Minister. I came in last night and already love it here."

"Dr. Herter, may I also introduce Greg Huntington. Greg is our resort's Chief Administrator. And this is Stephanie Lange, Deputy Coordinator for the Department of Energy and Tuvalu government."

"It's nice to meet both of you," Kevin said.

"It's a pleasure, Dr. Herter," Lange replied.

"We've been looking forward to your visit," Huntington said. "Our Coordination Director Tim Cain is looking forward to meeting you as well. You'll meet him this afternoon."

Huntington and Lange were casual in their shorts, while the prime minister was the most formally dressed of the group, in dark gray slacks and a short sleeve blue dress shirt with no tie. Intent on the introductions, no one noticed the man watching them from across the mall.

"Dr. Herter, we would be most honored if you and Dr. Raden would join us for dinner," Latasi added. "Your president will be there as well."

"Thank you very much, Mr. Prime Minister."

"Dr. Raden has become a very dear friend. He'll show you around. Dr. Herter, anything we can do to make your stay more enjoyable, please let us know." Latasi took Kevin by the shoulder. Beads of sweat glistened off his forehead like golden glitter. "Dr. Herter, I would appreciate an opportunity to discuss some concerns with you." He seemed sincere and Kevin agreed. "We'll see you at five p.m.," Latasi smiled.

Raden patted Latasi on the back. "I told you you'd like him. We'll see you later."

"By the way, Mr. Prime Minister," Kevin then asked. "What does 'Alofa' mean?"

Latasi offered a gleeful grin. "Love!" The group said goodbye and left.

"It begins," Raden said. "The politicking. But Latasi's a straight shooter, so give him a fair hearing. I was thinking. You might be up for a nice afternoon on the water. How about going out with the crew to set up the device?"

"That might be interesting."

"We leave at eleven thirty. It's about two hours out and back. They have lunch on the way."

"Okay." Kevin paused. "Alofa, huh? Love the bomb? Kinda like *Dr. Strangelove*."

"I told you, they love their irony out here."

At that moment, the man watching them got a text message. He rose and disappeared behind a row of bushes.

Forty-four

Christian Deloy arrived on the same flight with Kevin. From his seat back in coach, he could avoid any contact with him.

California had been a mixed bag. Like his boss Tom Whiteman, he thought things never should have reached this point, but for different reasons. Herter should have been dealt with in Princeton. The trooper charade was just a blip, and after listening to the surveillance recording, he was convinced more than ever that bringing Raden in was a mistake. The man was a train wreck, so overboard with analyzing that anyone would be left paranoid. A few well-placed words to Herter would have sufficed to back him off a project he didn't want to be involved with in the first place. Raden didn't need to raise the stakes and fill his head with garbage. And Whiteman needed to cut the surveillance, especially if it wasn't going any further. The bug wasn't necessary. Never should have come to that. It created needless anxiety, leaving him open to Raden's hectoring. By ratcheting up the heat, Herter was now on a mission. Whiteman's whacko wife was on her own bend, Sanderson and the idiots in Hawaii were set to lose it, and Enright was off to Honolulu. It was a pisser how people could go to such efforts and still get the very result they tried to avoid. With the other interests he was balancing the added complications threatened to blow it wide open. It was why Enright and her co-workers needed to be dealt with expediently. And sooner or later, Herter himself.

Deloy opened the large yellow mailer with his gloved hands and went through the photos and printouts. Satisfied that all was in order, he sealed it and reached for the phone. He had sent the text two minutes earlier. The call was placed at exactly nine fifteen a.m. The room guests were at breakfast and housekeeping had left, which was the plan. The phone rang two quick times, and was answered with a prearranged code.

"Is this Mr. Retreh?"

"I'm sorry, but you have the wrong number."

The call to Mr. Herter in reverse over, twenty seconds later a still-gloved Deloy knocked three times slowly and twice fast. The man inside echoed the knock, and Deloy slipped the envelope under the door. In the few seconds it took the man inside to open the door and leave, Christian Deloy was gone.

Forty-five

"What did you think of the prime minister?" Jack asked Kevin.

"He's a character. Reminds me of a Polynesian Jack Nicholson."

"Okay," Raden laughed. "Let's meet in the gift shop at ten. I'll give you a tour and we'll head down to the pier. See you then."

As Kevin awaited an elevator, a man walked up. He was tall, about his age. The door opened. Kevin pressed 3 and asked the man his floor. "The same, thanks."

As the elevator passed the second floor, the man pushed the Stop button.

"Dr. Herter," he said, "I need to speak to you."

Though startled, Kevin was beginning to appreciate what Mike Yahr meant when he said you'd know things were different when situations got less scary and began to get obnoxious.

"There are better ways to do it," he said, annoyed.

"There's an envelope under your door. It'll explain everything." The man restarted the elevator.

When the door opened, Kevin blocked him.

"You want to talk to me, next time walk up like a normal person," he said.

The man remained unsmiling. In his cargo shorts and T-shirt he could be a guest, but beneath his sandy hair and sunglasses was a regimented rancor. "Look at the envelope," he directed before disappearing down a staircase.

Kevin tried to keep his cool but walked quickly to his room, all the while looking behind him. Sure enough, a large yellow envelope lay on the floor inside his door. He turned the lock, then checked inside the closet, behind the shower curtain and the balcony. There was no way he was meeting Jack until he'd looked over the package.

Inside were a number of photos and a map of the Hawaiian Islands. The photos showed beaches, forests, and images of birds, seals and nests. On the back of each was the name of the particular animal or site, along with data about its ecological status. The map highlighted the military bases on the larger islands, in particular those closest to the island of Kauai where the resort was to be located. There was also a short note:

Dr. Herter,

You will hear this week about how Hawaii would make a great location for a new Bomb resort. You should be as well informed as possible before deciding to support this.

The resort would have a devastating environmental effect on pristine beaches and natural refuges. But more importantly, it would be the first on United States territory. This will give the military access to the site and make it easier to reach their ultimate goal—unrestricted authority over this terrifying technology. We are sure when you investigate further, you will agree and do everything you can to oppose this insanity.

We will be in touch.

The note was left unsigned. Kevin threw the photos into his suitcase, stuffed the note in his pocket and lay back on the bed. He crossed his hands over his forehead and the headache coming on.

Forty-six

Kevin found Jack Raden in a Tiki bar milking an ice tea. Jack took one look and asked, "What's wrong?"

"The vultures are beginning to circle." Kevin handed him the note.

Raden read, and listened to the story. "Forget it," he replied.

"You told me I needed to relax. You tell me how with something like this."

"Well ... how do you propose we handle it?"

"That's what you say? Next, you'll tell me to start humming *Don't Worry, Be Happy.*" Kevin grabbed back the note. "I expected something more realistic," he said.

"You want realistic? Look up one of those girls." Raden finished his drink and rose. "I'm serious. There are other things to worry about. Vultures only circle if they think you're dead. Move around, and they ignore you."

Kevin rolled his eyes. He crumbled up the note, tossed it in a trash can and walked off. Raden brushed past the can and followed.

As they walked Kevin worked on staying angry but it was proving to be an effort. Above a brilliant almost cloudless blue met the most indescribable turquoise at the horizon. In the distance another cruise ship appeared. Near the pool, he saw Candi laying on her stomach, her top undone. The area beyond opened to a series of palm-shaded booths with souvenirs, artists and jewelry makers. "Okay," he allowed, "have it your way—for now. But if I start having problems, you're going to hear it."

"Fair enough." They stopped at a booth featuring local jewelry. Raden picked up a twenty-dollar pendant. "My wife would like this," he stated.

The attendant smiled and came over. Her bronze skin was perfectly set off by a sky blue dress with white flowers. Kevin found her genuinely pleasant, a far cry from the arm-twister an hour ago. She began working the deal, but Raden wasn't biting.

"Describe the guy," he asked Kevin instead.

"Tall, about my age. Kinda light complexion. If I see him, I'll point him out. I normally wouldn't notice, but with all of them here, he could pass for military. Same look."

"That was my hunch. The note was meant to sound like Greenpeace, but it's the wrong tone. Oh, the thing in your car—they think some element of those people." He said to the girl, "Twenty?"

"Yes, sir!" She began wrapping it up.

"What, the Pentagon has it in for me?" Kevin asked.

"Officially, no. Possibly some elements there."

"So aren't you worried about him then?"

"Yeah, I'm worried. But where's he going? You want to notify the authorities?" Kevin rolled his eyes, and Raden said, "Okay. You just did."

"Okaayyy ..." Kevin paused, and gave a nervous laugh. "I'm curious. You look around, you see people haggling. All except you. You pay retail. I know you have the money, but—"

"Houses I haggle. Pendants I don't. These are good people. They work hard. I'll bust chops about more important things." As they left, Kevin felt himself smile.

The beach stretched ahead as they ambled past the huts. The second cruise ship had anchored, and in the distance a third appeared. Ahead, people were waxing and polishing surfboards. "I never heard of Tuvalu as a surfing destination," Kevin said.

"Follow me." They walked over to them. "Excuse me," Raden asked the people there. "My friend's new here. He didn't know this place was known for its waves."

A young deeply-tanned guy sat with his board propped up, cloth in his hand. He didn't appear satisfied with the finish he was getting. "Ever surf?" he asked Kevin.

"A little. In California."

A young woman walked over. "You look familiar," she said.

"I get that a lot. I'm curious. I never heard any raves about this beach."

"Oh, man!" The seated surfer broke into a smile. "There are now!"

Two others walked over. "It's the waves the bombs make," said one.

As the others grinned in agreement, Kevin stared, incredulous. "You're kidding," he said.

"No way, man. I've surfed Hawaii, California, Australia. Never got a high like this."

"I didn't know this." Kevin stood shocked.

The girl stepped forward, still eyeing him. "It's not the height—"

"Yeah," said the guy polishing the board. "They'll run twenty feet. I've ridden forty foot waves. It's not the height. It's the high you get from that thing behind you."

"Absolutely nothing like it," she said. Everyone emphatically agreed. "This place is—" She stopped, and began stabbing her finger repetitively. "You're him! Kevin Harter, Harter, Herter, that's it. Holy shit! The scientist. He's the guy who invented this place!" She burst into a smile as the others gushed out a litany of 'Oh my God!', 'Dude!', and 'Way to go'!

"How does it work?" Kevin asked. He was beginning to get used to the attention.

"We head out about half an hour before the explosion," said the first surfer.

"And you're okay out there?"

"They make us sign all kinds of stuff," another guy said.

"It's a pain," the girl said, "but it's worth it." She paused. "Gets warm."

The group nodded. "You do get a lot of heat out there," said one guy.

"No more than the cruise ships," said the first surfer. "But all they do is pitch." He motioned a wave with his hand. "We rock and roll!"

Kevin stood, disbelieving. He had not given it any thought. While loathe to admit it, he actually entertained the thought of riding a wave backed by a twenty-megaton explosion.

"Don't you miss seeing it as a spectator?" he asked.

"Nah," said the first. "We see plenty. We see the fireball. Being out there is something else. First there's the shock wave. About five minutes later the waves come."

"It's not scary?"

"Not really. It don't bother us. No time for it, man. Too juiced." They all agreed.

"And we get back in plenty of time to party!" said another.

"Guys," he said, laughing, "thanks. You've been a big help." He shook everyone's hand, and as the other women had done, the girl gave him a hug and kiss.

"Never thought about that, huh?"

Raden's comment had for the moment fallen on deaf ears. Kevin was in an equatorial haze. A warm trade wind was blowing. Overhead, frigate birds wheeled about like streamers in a ticker-tape parade. The Pacific was lapping on the sand, whispering up froth. The scent of sea spray lingered with every wave. It was like a dream, a blue and turquoise dream. A dream with surfers hanging ten to the tune of twenty megatons.

"It's easy to lose yourself here, huh?" Raden added.

"My head's a blur. Surfers, girls. Herterite." He wiped sweat off his forehead. "And waivers. So much for paradise, huh? Any more surprises?"

"Well, since you asked." Kevin rolled his eyes, and Raden laughed. "Think about it. They try to work entertainment into every part of the detonation. They're getting creative. They've begun glider flights around the clouds. And the partying."

"You want to party, check out the Jersey shore in summer." They were a quarter mile from the pier when they neared a solid rack-like stand, with ledges and what looked like cup holders. "What's this?" Kevin asked.

"One of those surprises. They're called Shot Stations. After the first few detonations, they noticed that people at certain parts of the beach were getting knocked down by the shock wave."

"What's so unusual about a shock wave with these things?"

"By itself, nothing. But the idea's for people to enjoy themselves safely. They thought the shots were far enough away. But they found parts of the island act as natural—"

"I get it. Amplification channels."

"That's it. The shock wave gets focused in spots. As word got out people began gathering, hoping to get knocked down. Didn't take long to work it in. The lawyers went batty but there was no keeping people away. They put up pads and netting to keep them from getting hurt. And these. They do shots before the wave hits."

"Unbelievable," Kevin muttered, shaking his head.

About a hundred yards from the pier, Kevin saw a security fence and a small hut. As he and Raden approached they were challenged. "This is a restricted area," said a guard. Raden took out two cards and he and Kevin handed over their room keys. The guard ran them through a scanner and went inside. After a few moments he came out. "Just wait here, gentlemen."

"I take it we're expected," Kevin said, turning to Raden.

"Yeah. This is where security kicks in. Can't blame them, with the device on the boat."

Ahead, two boats sat docked. One was a sleek thirty-footer. The other was larger, plainly older. Numerous armed men and technicians stood by. Several small sleek craft lolled about. Kevin instinctively knew that the device was on the larger, older boat. It was disconcerting to be so close to the thing.

The hut door opened and a man came out. Though sporting shorts and sunglasses, he had an air of authority. "Jack," he smiled, "great seeing you again." As he and Raden shook hands, the man turned to Kevin. "Dr. Herter, this is a real delight."

"This is Don Frazier," Raden said. "Don heads the support team on event days."

"It's nice to meet you," Kevin smiled.

"Are you ready for us?" Raden joked.

"Absolutely! We'll just be a moment. Tim's finishing up with the Control Center. Tim Cain's Coordination Director. He runs technical support between the Tuvalu Interior Ministry and the DOE. Dr. Herter, when we learned you were coming, we suggested to Jack that you go out with us to deploy the device. It's not often you meet the person responsible for your career."

"Okay," Kevin objected with an awkward grin, "make you a deal. You want me on board, you gotta cool the 'special guy' treatment. No more Dr. Herter. It's Kevin."

"Deal! Then we'll get you on board and open up some beers or wine."

"Now you're talking!" Frazier smiled and went back in.

"I spoke to Mike," Raden said. "Enright's starting to uncover some interesting information in Hawaii. I think she'll have a lot to tell us tomorrow."

"Like what?"

"Like I said. Follow the money. People are starting to talk. So don't be surprised if—"

A moment later the hut door opened again. "I was just telling them about you," Frazier said to the man following him. Kevin's smile vanished. He needed no introduction to Tim Cain. He was the man on the elevator.

Forty-seven

The small flotilla was making nineteen knots, which would put them at ground zero in about two hours, at one forty p.m. From the decks, Vaitupu shimmered like a postcard shot.

The two main boats were attended by six smaller Tuvalu naval patrol boats. Kevin and Raden were in the older boat with Don Frazier, Tim Cain and a dozen technicians. And the device. The security detail remained unobtrusive, though they could make themselves known in an instant. The resplendent day was delivering everything the South Seas were known for and Raden and Frazier were completely at ease, a state yet to kick in for Kevin as he wasn't sure what to make of Cain.

A feeling Kevin had never before experienced hit the instant he saw Cain, almost a sinister chill. The two exchanged glances and forced handshakes. Though they hadn't spoken, Kevin knew it was just a matter of time, as much a ticking bomb as the device they carried.

A physicist himself, forty-two year old Don Frazier had come to Tuvalu as a support agent, but soon ascended to team leader on the strength of his organizational skills, scientific knowledge and temperament. An inner-city success story, he had made it out of Philadelphia by channeling his innate curiosity about the universe to a place that included everything and everywhere except the streets where he'd grown up.

He was eager to show Kevin the device and discuss his theories, but Kevin seemed reluctant. Kevin actually liked the affable Frazier, but with Cain in the picture he was hedging his bets.

Raden sensed it, but had no such compunctions. As the waters drifted from turquoise to blue, he turned to the group. "Anybody have to feed the fishes?"

"Oh, no," Frazier laughed, like Raden, relaxing on a railing. "I love this."

"Same here," Kevin answered. He was itching to speak with Raden.

Frazier turned to Kevin, "I have a little prep work to do down in the hold. When I'm done, come down."

"Don, thanks. Give a holler." As Frazier left, Kevin looked around. Tim Cain was nowhere to be seen. He asked Raden, "Do you like sci-fi?"

"Good sci-fi."

"There's a movie called *Journey to the Far Side of the Sun*. One of my favorites; kind of a cult film. There's this sublime dream sequence. Anyway, the Europeans find a new planet—"

"Now I remember. It's hidden."

"Yeah. It's in the same orbit as Earth but on the opposite side of the sun, so we've never seen it. Roy Thinnes and Ian Hendry fly there and crash, but turns out they crashed back on Earth. So everyone's pissed at them. They think they turned around and came back early. No one believes they landed on the new planet. But then things get weird. Everything's the same, but slightly different. People write backwards, drive on the wrong side of the road—"

"Shake hands with the wrong hand."

"Yeah. And it turns out they actually did land on the new planet, but it's a duplicate of Earth, only in reverse. Everyone has a double who's a mirror image of themselves. Everything's the same, but opposite."

"I remember." Raden shot Kevin a knowing gaze. "And why are you telling me this?"

"Because when I tell you things aren't what they seem, don't think I'm nuts, that's why."

Raden nodded. "You can give me a 'Toldja'."

"You've been talking to my ex," Kevin laughed.

From behind, Frazier reappeared. "Okay, we're all set."

Kevin and Raden descended a few steps to a large deck hidden from view by curtains.

"Wow," Kevin murmured.

Before them was the device. It filled the deck. A spherical unit held the core while dozens of arrays rimmed its margins. The requisite flashing lights and illuminated panels ticking off numbers were there, but the Hollywood techno-bling was absent. In its stead was a professional normalcy, an almost bureaucratic routine. These people had done this before. Tim Cain stood at the far end. He tacitly acknowledged Kevin, then went back to work.

"What do you think?" Don Frazier beamed like a new father.

"Impressive." Kevin wasn't versed in nuclear bomb technology, but Jack Raden was right—this was no weapon. The scientist in him held a genuine curiosity about the thing. Even Max would have been intrigued. Pissed, but intrigued.

But he was torn. There was more that he didn't know and he was certain that they hadn't figured it out either. While they had solved the radiation issue, seeing it up close left him uneasy. Seeing Cain left him uneasy. Though the security detachment stood watch, Cain was right beside the thing. Suppose he was on a suicidal jag, bent on going out in some apocalyptic form? He didn't know him, trusted him less, and was sure others didn't know about him either. He didn't know how to broach the subject without coming off as a paranoid lunatic. Or whether he should.

"Let me give you the nickel tour," Frazier said to Kevin, eager to engage him. "The device is complex in design, but somewhat counter-intuitive in operation. Think of quantum theory."

"How does that factor in with this?" Kevin asked.

"First, we use antimatter initiators. They're the surface arrays. They begin the explosion. We sequence detonation along the lines of your equations to create a resonant shock wave. It's like a musical note, but very complex in its propagation. It results in fusion of the deuterium fuel core in a way that shunts gamma emissions off to a minimum." He turned to Raden. "In laymen's terms, gamma radiation's the bad stuff. Quantum theory describes motion of atoms and other particles. But it's not logical. It's not like you predict an event and it happens. It's weird."

"So it's not as if you don't produce any radiation?" Kevin asked.

"No. But it barely registers and dissipates very quickly. We advertise that guests get more radiation flying to the island than when they land."

"Matter/anti-matter annihilations should flood the vicinity with gamma emissions."

"I know, but these don't." Frazier could see Kevin was skeptical. "Trust me. We monitor constantly. We get nothing."

"I don't understand that."

"Quite frankly, neither do we. It's all too new." Kevin looked at him askew. "Seriously, we hope you can look at it. We have a very good working knowledge for controlling it, but its dynamics are an enigma. We could spend a lifetime studying its nuances."

"I'd hardly call twenty megatons nuanced."

"Actually, it is very subtle."

"Let me get this straight. Are you hinting that it's inherently unstable?"

"No, quite the contrary. It's extremely stable, where we keep it. We detonate within a narrow range of yields. We've yet to push that envelope."

"Do you mean yields you're getting from the explosions?"

"I mean its applicability as an energy source, explosive and otherwise. There's a considerable amount that we've yet to learn. And honestly, I'm looking forward to picking your brain on it."

"Okay. I'm actually glad to hear that. I was hoping you guys weren't getting cocky."

"Oh my, no. Far from it. But it's a fascinating area of physics to work in."

Deep down, Kevin had to agree. It was fascinating. He just wished he could study it without the annoying distraction of his own contributions. He scrutinized the mechanism. "You said the design was counter-intuitive in its operation. Explain."

"We use a fixed amount of fuel. But depending on conditions, we get different yields."

"Okay, back up. I can understand how atmospherics can affect things to a degree. But you need to explain that. I mean we're talking megatons, not a few sticks of dynamite."

"It's the proximity of the antimatter firing sequence to the fuel. It has to do with your physics. The sequencing of detonations, coupled with how closely they occur to the hydrogen core, affects the wave they generate and with it, the yield."

"That I can't accept."

"We couldn't either, but it's what happens." Frazier turned to Raden. "You've heard of dark matter, dark energy? They make up ninety percent of the Universe. We still don't know what they are. We just accept that they have their place and hope to one day figure it out. We think the same thing's going on here. We don't completely understand these explosions. But we know they work. We accept that and work with it. And every day we learn more. We'll get it. It's analogous to focusing sunlight through a magnifying glass on paper. By varying the focus of the blast wave, depending on how near or far away you hold it, you'll get a different result. We're not sure why it works, but we accept that it does. And we use it."

"Define different," Kevin said.

"We project yields from about sixteen to twenty-two megatons."

Kevin shook his head. "I'm astounded. I would have never thought that possible."

"In a way, it's happened before. The biggest US test before this was a fifteen-megaton blast in 1954, Castle Bravo. They were expecting five. It ran away to three times what they predicted. It knocked them for a loop. What we have here is a lot more manageable. Since we anticipate it, it's not a surprise."

Kevin nodded. "So where do you guys get these boats?"

"Good question!" Frazier remarked as everyone laughed. "No one ever asked before. They're hand-me-downs, donated by guests. We have boats lined up for the next two years."

"And they don't get anything?"

"We comp them a room with a balcony and ocean view."

Kevin turned to Raden. "Wanna get rid of your boat, Jack?" As they all laughed, Frazier was handed a notepad. "The weather specs," he said. "Now we program distance and yield."

"Who makes the final decisions?" Kevin asked, genuinely curious.

"Actually, they make themselves. We just decide to concur. The weather dictates the yield. We detonate closer with smaller yields and farther away with larger ones. Overall, the look is about the same." He called to a station across the deck. "Is that verified?" The young woman at the screen nodded yes. "Okay," Frazier smiled, "we'll be sailing out forty-two miles."

A chorus of "Wows!" ran through the deck. Kevin said, "What?"

"That's the farthest we've ever detonated. We usually go out thirty-seven, thirty-eight miles. At forty-two we're at our limit. Anything more, the curvature of the earth affects the view. Turns out you've come on quite a day. We'll be detonating at twenty-one and a half megatons, twenty-one point seven to be exact."

"That's the largest yield they've ever had," Raden said. Kevin's eyes widened. Raden added, "Don, do you have an operational designation yet?" He looked at Kevin. "The names they give to the events."

Frazier returned, "Tonight's shot has been designated Eta Carinae."

Kevin's expression grew sober. Raden asked, "You know it?"

"It's a giant star in the southern sky. It flared up in brightness in the 1800s. Hubble took a great picture showing two enormous discharges of gas blowing off the star like huge bubbles. Each is much bigger than the star itself. It's really spectacular. Google or Bing it, you'll see."

"Incredible image," Frazier said, nodding in agreement. "Stellar evolution is a hot topic in cosmology these days, excuse the pun. Really interesting stuff."

Raden looked back at a still-subdued Kevin. "And what else?"

"We expect it to go supernova in the near future."

Forty-eight

The convoy arrived at the detonation area and the tired vessel dropped anchor for the last time. The staff took final atmospheric readings, and made some adjustments. After transferring over everyone and everything not nailed down, the two-hour trip back to Vaitupu began. The detonation prep had taken less than an hour.

Kevin watched the detonation boat recede from view with a disconcerted eye. By sunset, the gently rolling boat and placid waters beneath would vaporize in a seething maelstrom. The more distance put between himself and the thing, the better. Jack Raden and Don Frazier kicked back in folding chairs. Kevin joined them, while the others took benches ringing the deck. Tim Cain sat looking annoyingly innocent. All along he had been quiet. The security personnel were quiet too, but theirs was of a different sort.

Frazier opened a cooler, and everyone helped themselves. The staff went mostly for soda or beer, some for wine. The security contingent chose water. Kevin poured himself a glass of Riesling. The scent of sea spray and suntan balm drifted above an ocean too relaxed to come down between green and blue and too lazy to care. A few cirrus clouds traced out a wispy arrow, guiding the way back to shore. There were no thoughts of car bombs and listening devices.

Frazier opened another cooler holding sandwiches and wraps, containers of salads, salsa and fruit. Bags of pretzels and chips sat nearby.

"I noticed you went for the alcohol first," Kevin said. "Nice to see you guys have your priorities straight." Everyone laughed.

"We don't often have celebrities on board," Frazier said. "But being on the water gets you hungry too." The food went in short order. He was polishing off a bag of potato chips when one of the technicians spoke.

"Dr. Herter," said Cindy Russell, a very attractive woman in her early thirties with thick honey-colored hair and a tattoo peaking out from beneath her shirt, "we're curious. What do you think of this whole experience? Are you enjoying yourself?"

Kevin slouched back, in a relaxed pose but not quite feeling it. "All due respect to the kids here, if someone told me a week ago that I'd be out in the South Pacific today catching rays on a boat with a gourmet chicken and mango wrap in one hand and glass of Riesling in the other, right after having set up a twenty-megaton hydrogen bomb, I would have told them they were out of their friggin *minds*." The group erupted in laughter.

"Yeah, but aren't you interested in how this project has made use of your findings?" Cindy was known for speaking her mind, and as everyone was curious, they let her have the floor.

"How do you mean?"

"We were all looking forward to your visit. Your work, well, the result of it anyways, is what we do here. But, this is the first practical application of your findings."

Kevin feigned earnestness. "Practical?" Everyone chortled.

"Oh, well ..." she laughed, making a so-so wave with her hand, "*practical*. It's the first use of your theories in any physical form. I can't help but think you'd be curious. We'd love to share with you what we've learned from working with your findings."

Kevin wiped a bead of sweat from his lip. "Captive audience, huh?" he quipped, prompting a laugh. "Okay," he said, feeling a bit trapped but buzzed and emboldened, "the ground rules. First, no one talks to me unless they cut out the Dr. Herters. It's Kevin, deal?" They nodded and smiled. "Second, I never talk to anyone sober when I deploy hydrogen bombs. Give here the wine." More laughs broke out as Frazier passed the bottle.

"And third?" Cindy asked.

"Third. You guys have to answer things for me as well." His bantering tone was gone.

"What can we help you with?" asked an animated Cindy as the group leaned in.

"Things will come up the next few days I can't go into now. You gotta be as willing to talk with me as you want me to be with you." Everyone settled a bit. "Don't worry," he assured them, "I don't bite. But you can help me. Deal?"

"Deal!" She smiled. The others including Tim Cain nodded their heads.

Kevin took a slow sip of his wine. Cain or no Cain things were gnawing at him. "Do you guys have any vibes about what's going on here?"

"We hear things," Cindy added. "We all enjoy what we do, but it's a job. Being able to do something you like isn't easy, and in physics it's especially hard to find jobs that pay." Most in the group nodded in agreement.

"I can understand that," Kevin said.

"We have a pension plan, health care," another technician added. "It's like geologists who wind up working for oil companies. You have to go where the work is."

"What we do," Cindy said, "it's a unique way to make a living. But it's still a living."

"It's just that the politics make for an unsettled work situation," Jack Raden said.

"That I understand as well," Kevin said. He swirled the Riesling around. "How do you guys feel about this? I know it's controversial. How do you deal with it?"

It was the question that weighed most heavily, and that no one wanted to discuss. Tim Cain then looked squarely at Kevin and said, "We deal with it the same way you do, I guess."

Everyone cringed. Kevin broke the tension. "I did say captive audience."

They all politely laughed. Cindy added, "We're kind of used to it. We really don't think about it much. Or I guess we don't talk about it much." Again, everyone nodded.

Kevin had wondered when Cain would speak up. For now, he decided not to press. "I can accept that. Have you guys heard anything about what's coming from Washington?"

"We hear rumors." Most still played their cards close to the vest.

"What do you mean?" Frazier asked.

"Well," Kevin rephrased the question, "what are they like to work for?"

"It's been very nice." Frazier leaned back. "How is everyone about that?" He looked around, seeming pleased with himself.

"Oh, don't put people on the spot," Kevin laughed. Frazier shrugged a self-effacing smile. Everyone relaxed, but Kevin again became serious. "I can understand people being hesitant." He looked up. "Like Tim. Something on your mind?"

Cain shifted uncomfortably, just what Kevin wanted. "I'm just listening," he said.

"That's a switch," Cindy said, with a playful smile. He blushed and looked away.

"Guys," Kevin said, "anyone wants to talk while I'm here, please feel free. Jack and Don are professional enough to know where I'm coming from. Or even Tim." Cain smiled weakly. "I know people can be reluctant to say things, okay?"

Everyone agreed. Kevin finished his wine. In the bright sunshine and with a nice buzz, he was finally relaxed. He said, "All this reminds me of that atomic bomb movie—"

"*Trinity and Beyond,*" Cindy jumped in. "It's required viewing here."

"I figured you knew. I thought of it when you were setting up the bomb. They had servicemen in the '50s on the beach barbecuing and watching them go off. It's interesting how all that foreshadowed what's here."

"I told Kevin they were hot ticket items back then," Raden added. "Just like now."

"If this is your first time here," Cindy smiled, "you're in for quite the experience. Peter Kuran had a ball when he was here. He made the film. So did William Shatner. He narrated it."

"I *love* him!" Kevin lit up. "What's he like?"

"He's a riot! Great guy! In his eighties, and we had more fun with him—" She paused. "It's funny. They did the film that brought these things to public awareness, and even they had to see one to appreciate them. They were beside themselves. Two great guys. There's just something about seeing these. You'll never forget it."

Kevin turned to the security personnel. He had just begun to relax. "I hope you guys don't feel we're ignoring you. I'm curious. Are you connected to this directly through the government here, or on special assignment?"

One of the officers stood up, an earnest-looking chap of about forty. He had been on his cell phone. He walked over to another guard. They both then approached Kevin. "Excuse me, Dr. Herter," he said. "We need to speak with you."

Forty-nine

Jack Raden hovered over Kevin. Three guards surrounded them, wearing grave expressions. The others had moved away to far corners of the boat.

"Where was the body found?" Raden asked.

"Face down on the bed. Her hands were tied behind her and her throat was slashed." Captain Peter Natano of the Tuvalu Integrated Home Force stood with one hand on his phone, the other on his hip. The island's chief of security, he had kept a low profile during the trip. The phone call changed that instantly.

Kevin remained glued to his seat, numb from the news. He was just starting to relax, he thought, just letting down his guard. The feeling of terror was as complete as the guilt. Someone had died a horrible death in his room. "I can't believe it," he lamented. He paused. "You know I didn't do that."

"Right now, Dr. Herter, you can best help by answering questions. What time did you leave your room?"

Kevin looked at Raden. "When did we meet, ten o'clock?"

"That's about right," Raden confirmed to Natano. "What else have you come up with? Was there a sexual assault?"

"We think so, but forensics is only beginning to analyze the evidence. The time of death appears close to that. The scene was very bloody. Her name was Consuelo Vacca, from housekeeping. We'll discuss this further on shore."

"My God, that poor girl," Kevin said. "Wait … are you arresting me?"

"You are, as you say in your country a person of interest. We prefer suspect."

"You must have something else to lead you to that," Raden said, crossing his arms.

"Dr. Raden is right. We searched the victim's room and found an envelope with photos and diagrams on some beach area in Hawaii—"

"Holy shit!" Kevin snapped. He shot a look at Raden. "Tell them what I told you."

"First of all," Natano interjected, "there was information attached to them that led us to Dr. Herter here. We've already lifted his fingerprints from the photos."

"Son of a bitch!" Kevin yelled. "I saw those things the first time this morning. I left them in my room. How'd they get there?" He shot up. "Cain! Where's that piece of shit! He's the one who gave them to me." Kevin looked across the deck and saw Tim Cain had just walked up from below deck. Kevin tried to rush him but was restrained by two guards.

"Hold it, Doctor! No one's going off on anyone." Natano went over to Cain. When he came back, he said to Raden, "He claims Dr. Herter tried to peddle the photos to him and he blew him off. And he doesn't know how they got in the victim's room."

"We have a lot to discuss," Raden told Natano.

Still restrained by the guards, a seething Kevin agreed. A moment later he added, "Damn, I threw out the note that piece of shit left me."

Fifty

"It's beautiful. Now I know why so many people come here."

At the moment Kevin was conferring with Jack Raden and Peter Natano, Jessica Enright sat in a beachfront Waikiki steakhouse parking lot with Michelle Sapena, gazing out to the water. The sunset took the edge off the stop but even with the car doors locked, it wasn't enough.

"I can't believe this," Enright said. "And you, you're taking a big risk. I appreciate it. Are you sure he'll show up?"

"He'll be here," Sapena said, a diminutive thirty-year old brunette. "It's been bothering me, but I didn't know who to talk to. When you stopped by I had to go for it."

Enright looked around. The happy hour crowd was filtering out and the lot was filling with dinner patrons. In the waning light she watched each intently. A moment later Sapena received a text.

"Okay," she said, "let's walk."

Enright hid her apprehension. It could have described her entire day in Honolulu. She had flown in that morning, alone. She'd traveled inconspicuously, dressing down in a modest shirt and jeans, braiding her hair, trading contacts for glasses. Seemingly, she hadn't been recognized. In the twenty-four hours since her now infamous interview, her reporting skills had risen as her capacity for trust had declined. Cliff was still recovering, and when Joshua had offered her a crew, she'd passed.

He'd been eager to hear about her progress. As she learned and shared, he'd realized that letting her go it alone was the right choice, as was his decision not to fire her. She'd also consulted with Mike Yahr, who was becoming a mentor. By afternoon, she was reconnecting to something that she had forgotten was lost. But it came at a price. She became adept at checking the engine as well as beneath her car. While not wanting to feel paranoid, she couldn't get Jim and Kevin Herter out of her mind.

She'd made reservations under her maiden name, Jessica Alexandra Wilson, still on her driver's license. Upon landing, she'd become Alex

Wilson, an unobtrusive reporter from an NBC affiliate in Hartford, Connecticut. It gave her anonymity that Jessica Enright from MSNBC may not have been able to pull off, and let her focus on research. It also let her avoid undue attention following her disastrous episode in California. As the day wore on, her confidence had grown.

Mike's list had been a godsend. She'd begun with businesses near the airport, widening her circle. Previously unnoticed, resentment toward the program was considerable, and was growing. To her surprise, she was the first reporter to show an interest in something besides the mushroom clouds and the money they brought in. People were eager to talk.

A picture emerged of a bewildering, almost schizophrenic bureaucracy and huge, inexplicable cost overruns. One exec likened the program to a home in the Hollywood Hills, a weighty house on stilts just waiting for a little shake to topple it over. It was a wake-up call. While she had had doubts about the program, she'd never thought to question its success.

It took four hours to change that. By midday, Enright had spoken to enough people to alter her itinerary. She had planned to drop by Integrated Microphysics later that afternoon, but the name had come up enough to make it her next stop.

It was two thirty when she walked into the branch office on Ala Moana Boulevard, a mile from the Capital District. Until then, the reception from the four other firms she'd visited had been similar—accessible but businesslike. Though none of the executives she'd spoken with had anything overtly derogatory to say about IM, there was a sense that its presence had the effect, as one of the CFO's put it, of "sucking all the oxygen out of the room."

At IM, she was ushered into the plush offices of Mark Rivers. She'd presented a plausible cover, investigating how the bomb program was affecting the election. It wasn't entirely untruthful and gave her a legitimacy that lifted her confidence.

The silver-haired CEO with the golf player's tan had been unusually helpful. She'd been given a tour, and had been shown a short film explaining the principle behind the bomb and IM's contribution to its development. It didn't quite sit right. She couldn't shake the feeling that she had been expected.

It was when she raised issues that had been brought up during her other meetings that Rivers grew evasive. He'd begun to couch replies in vagaries, citing shareholder obligation and security concerns. It had come with enough of a smile and reasonable air that Enright had felt herself being won over, almost. But she'd stuck to her instincts and when she mentioned names, Rivers's defenses rose. The one he'd reacted to the most was Ron Sanderson. It wasn't that he'd thrown her out or feigned ignorance over the lieutenant governor's efforts to develop a site in Hawaii. It was how he'd done it, the subtle shift in expression. She'd immediately known that he was lying, and that he was aware she had picked up on his deception. She had ended the interview though politely.

As she'd been leaving River's office, his administrative assistant Michelle Sapena bumped into her. Sapena was all apologies, helping to gather the items that fell out of Enright's bag. While handing them over, Sapena, heart racing, had slipped her a note. Unaware, Enright had stuffed it inside with the other items and Sapena wasn't sure she had noticed. But a woman-to-woman exchange that both instinctively knew Rivers had missed left her heartened.

Once outside, Enright had again looked under the hood and beneath the car. Not seeing anything, she'd exited the lot. After a few blocks, intuition raging, she pulled over. She went through her bag and found the note.

I need to speak with you. I'll be leaving the office at five o'clock. Please call me at five thirty. Below Michelle Sapena's signature was a phone number.

Enright had headed back to her motel room to wait. Even though there were more names on Mike's list, there would be no more stops that day. What she was unaware of was the device that had been placed underneath her rear bumper while she was at IM, one she had missed. Someone was now tracking her every move.

Fifty-one

Still apprehensive, Enright walked the beach with Sapena for about a hundred yards. It was getting dark, and recognizing people was becoming difficult. Enright hoped the same held true for them as well.

Sapena began filling her in on recent events at Integrated Microphysics. As Mark Rivers's buffer, she knew everyone who visited. Although unversed in technological intricacies, she knew people. For some time, there had been repeat visitors, people like the lieutenant governor of Hawaii, visits that involved clandestine looks and whispers. As her anxiety grew, she began talking of quitting. Rivers had smooth talked her into staying. But when she began delivering briefcases and packages that supposedly held paperwork to places like parking decks, her anxiety went off the chart. She was considering calling a newspaper when Enright appeared.

Enright saw how she was affected. She realized however the story unfolded, Michelle Sapena's role would prove pivotal.

"Michelle," she said, "I have to be up front with you as well. You're putting a lot on the line for me." She told Michelle her real identity.

Sapena was startled. She had thought that there was something familiar about the reporter, but had brushed it off as jitters. She paused, then said, "Let's get the fucks."

A dimly lit stand of palm trees with benches lay ahead. Just past that was a tiki bar. They stopped at a bench, and Sapena lit a cigarette.

A good-looking guy in his thirties approached from the bar. "Hi hon," he said. He and Sapena kissed.

"Jessica," Sapena said, "this is my boyfriend. Glen, this is Jessica Enright."

"Glen Daniels," he smiled. "Nice to meet you." When Sapena had called and told him she'd made contact with a reporter, he was more than willing to meet her. Enright was heartened when he said he hadn't recognized her.

Sapena said, "Glen is Lisa Whiteman's assistant—"

"Lisa Whiteman?" Enright interrupted. "Isn't she the—"

"Yeah," Daniels nodded. "The program director. Michelle and I met when this began two years ago. We keep it quiet 'cause they may not like the idea."

"Yeah," complained Sapena, "but it didn't stop Lisa from marrying Tom Whiteman."

"True," Enright said. Daniels had more the appearance of a Malibu beach bum than a physicist. She thought he and the equally attractive Sapena made a cute couple.

"Kinda long distance for you guys," she added.

As Sapena sighed, Daniels said, "We're working on it."

"Yeah, I've been there. Are you here visiting?"

"No. Lisa left yesterday in a rush. I'm sure she's headed to Tuvalu to catch up with Kevin Herter. She's trying to get him involved." Upon hearing the name, Enright felt herself blush.

"And I was worried about Michelle," Daniels added. "There's a lot going on I don't like. It's coming to a head. Michelle and I have been communicating about it for months. They're trying to drag her into some pretty heavy shit. I needed to make sure she was okay."

Sapena squeezed his hand and held it to her face.

"What has you so spooked?" Enright asked.

"The Pentagon's muscling in. That's trouble, but not enough to get Lisa on a plane."

"Before you go on, I need to know, what's her deal? I've heard all kinds of things."

"A lot's been said about her. But she has a good heart. It's her husband I don't trust."

"Really? He's the security chief, isn't he?"

"Yeah. People think she's a control freak and she is, but in a good way. I'd put her instincts above anyone's. He's greasing the skids for the Pentagon. None of us like that. If she's trying to control something, must be something worth controlling, huh? I think I know what it is."

"Wow," Enright said. "So who or what do you think she's trying to protect?"

"For weeks the Defense Department's been pressuring us to send them our data, all of it. We've never had that before. And somehow, it involves IM. Lisa's been fighting it. And believe me, no one knows this material like her. After she left, I went into her files—"

"Glen!" Sapena exclaimed.

"I know. I think she wanted me to. She left her encryption codes in a way only I could see. I never knew what she was doing. She could be such a pain. But she was always professional, so I gave her the benefit of the doubt. Seeing what she left, *I'd* be a control freak. She's been running the tables on the DOE and DOD. Each knew just enough to do their job, but not what the other was doing. I don't know how she pulled it off. But it's catching up with her. I think that's why she's so desperate to get to Herter, and why Michelle's been running payoffs."

"I suspected that," Enright said, "but you beat me saying it."

"Yeah," Sapena said. "And I'm not doing it anymore."

"But what had her so worried that she felt it necessary to fly halfway around the world?"

By now it was dark, the western sky ebbing the last blue-green vestige of dusk. Daniels reached into his pocket and removed a USB stick. "This. I downloaded it before I left. It's re-coded, which should buy us a little time. I wanted to hide it here, then Michelle told me she had met you." As he went to hand it over, a bright red dot appeared on Sapena's shirt.

Instantly, Enright pushed Sapena down. As they toppled over, bullets whizzed by. A burning sensation stabbed her lower right cheek. Daniels was startled for a moment, then collapsed onto the sand.

"Don't move!" Enright hissed. In the dark, she couldn't see if Sapena was hurt. "Michelle, you all right?" she scratched out, frantically patting her down for wounds.

"Uh, what?"

Enright covered her mouth. "Nod if you're okay," she whispered, and felt Sapena's head bob. She then whispered wildly to Daniels, "Glen, you okay?"

He didn't answer. She thought he was hit, but he grunted, "Uh, huh." He muttered, "What the—" when a more bullets whizzed by. One tore a hole through his shirt.

Sapena screamed and Enright hissed, "Ssshhhhh!" Her eyes darted about to see if the shooter had reacquired them. "We gotta get out of here!"

The music from the bar drowned out the shots. The crowd was unaware that bullets had been fired.

"We gotta get out of here!" Enright repeated. "Make for those tables and chairs," she pleaded, "but don't move straight. And don't follow me. GO!" She began feverishly moving toward the water where it was pitch dark and she wouldn't be seen. She watched Sapena and Daniels head right.

She had gone thirty feet when she saw Daniels, mindlessly shadowing Sapena, targeted by the scope. "Glen, *ROLL!*" she yelled. Like a fish on a skillet he flipped over as three shots flew by. One grazed his arm and coincided with a lull in the music. The bar crowd now hearing the shots, screamed and scattered. Enright yelled, "Dammit, *RUN!*"

His arm wincing in pain, Daniels grabbed Sapena and they ran with several of the crowd toward a deserted stretch of beach. Several more shots followed. One splintered a bench, sending wood slivers into a girl who was taking cover. She screamed and grabbed her leg. Enright then bolted.

The three met up a hundred yards past the bar. Several more shots sounded, then no more were heard. Distant lights sent out a soft glow that barely let them see.

"You guys okay?" she panted.

"My God!" Sapena responded, trying to catch her breath. "What—"

"No time to talk," Enright remonstrated. "We can't stay here. Don't go back to your place," she told Sapena. "And forget cars. I learned a whole lot in one day."

"How did you know to push us out of the way like that?" Daniels said.

"I did a piece on snipers picking off Taliban in Afghanistan," Enright panted, trying to catch her breath. "You see the red, you just act. Take time to think about it and it's too late. I guess you do learn something being a reporter after all. We can't stay here though."

They set off. As they slogged through the sand, she asked, "Where can we go?"

"I have an idea," Sapena said.

Fifty-two

"I can't believe here," Daniels whispered. "Of all places."

"It's already nine. We don't have time to find anyplace else," said Enright.

"What if they find out?"

"We'll have to take our chances," Sapena frowned. "We just have to get in."

It had taken half an hour to reach the offices of Integrated Microphysics. They moved swiftly, darting in alleys and hiding behind bushes amid a wail of sirens racing to the beach. Enright noted whoever targeted them did themselves no good by rousting up witnesses. It was now a major story sure to hit the eleven o'clock news.

The idea had been to make copies of the USB stick, but Daniels had dropped it when the first shots rang out. He was beside himself but hoped someone would grind it into the sand, or wouldn't attach importance to it were it found. The data was accessible if he could get on line.

As they passed under a street light, Daniels noticed blood on Enright's cheek. "My God, Jessica," he said, "you got hit too."

She felt her face. It was warm and wet. Sapena gave her some tissues. She held them against the stinging wound. "God," she winced, "I remember now, a bullet zipped by me."

"You were lucky," Daniels said. He poked a finger through the hole in his shirt.

"We all were. If it had just been a little lighter out."

"Who was after us?"

"I don't know. Any of us could have been the target. Maybe it's all of us." Enright panted, "I'm sorry I got you guys into this."

"We were involved way before you showed up. But thanks."

The IM parking lot was empty except for a white van.

"Good," Sapena said. "The cleaning service. I hope Maria's there. She's good people."

Their hearts beat up a storm as they surreptitiously approached. A

Honolulu police cruiser raced by, and they froze, praying it wouldn't stop. It kept going. She gasped in relief, looked around, then tapped on the glass.

A fifty-ish woman poked her head out from the inner office.

"Oh, there is a God," Sapena said. "Maria, thank heaven." Maria Sanchez walked up, smiling. As she unlocked the door, Sapena held a finger to her mouth. "Maria, is anyone here?"

"Oh, no, Michelle, no one here." She saw the blood. "Oh my, you okay?"

"We'll be all right. These are my friends. We have a little work to do. Please don't tell anyone we were here, okay?"

"Oh, that okay Michelle. No one tell."

Sapena hugged her, and then asked, "How is Felipe?"

"Oh, still bother him. Doctor say at least a week."

"Her husband," Sapena told the others. "Threw his back out at work." She took fifty dollars from her wallet. "You make sure you buy groceries this week." Sanchez was all smiles and brought them paper towels and bandages. The wounds were minor, but painful. "Don't let us keep you," Sapena added. "We won't be long." Enright and Daniels each added a fifty from their wallets for Sanchez, now beside herself in tears as she went back to dusting.

Sapena's desk guarded Mark River's rear office. The decor was a motif of mauve and grey with art several steps above the usual corporate work-up, as Rivers always strove to impress.

"Aren't you afraid they'll know you logged on?" Daniels asked.

"Not this place. Secretaries are on different servers than the big shots."

"That was very nice of you, by the way," Enright said.

"You think Rivers would ever slip her a twenty?" Sapena said. "You know how many times he's been here late at night?"

"Then we need to hurry up," Daniels said, giving his girlfriend a kiss. She smiled and moved the mouse. The screen lit up. "Half the time I never bother to shut it down." She dug around in her desk drawer, pulling out USB sticks as Daniels logged onto the site. He started making copies, one for each of them

Enright's curiosity reared its head. "Glen, what's on here?"

Sapena wasn't ready to listen. "Hon," she pleaded, "we have to get out of here!" The process didn't take long but felt like an eternity. Her heart raced the whole time.

As Daniels watched the scan bar move he explained, "It's a history of the explosions. There are answers there if you know what to look at." He tapped his finger. "Almost done." Sanchez kept nervously working, Enright and Sapena darting between the screen and the front door. Daniels felt his heart race as well. "Almost," he said as the last one finished. "All done."

He had just logged off when they heard a car outside. "Shit," Sapena whispered.

Sanchez had been in the lobby setting up a vacuum cleaner. She ran to the back. "Michelle, you boss, Mr. River, he outside."

"Okay, Maria, don't say anything. Make believe we're not here." Sanchez nodded.

"What do we do?" Daniels said.

"Get behind the desks and keep quiet," Sapena said. They all dove for separate desks, as Rivers was unlocking the door. He walked in, followed by Ron Sanderson. Enright could see Sapena and Daniels, though they couldn't see each other. She froze, as she remembered the mirror on the nearby wall. If someone passed just right, they would plainly see her reflection.

Crouching down, her heart pounding, she prayed that she wouldn't be seen. Just then, she remembered that her phone was still on. She realized the others probably had theirs on as well, and none of them could turn them off. She beseeched every saint she knew to keep them from ringing, agonizing through every second it took Rivers and Sanderson to walk past through the office. Her stomach itched to growl and she covered her belly, pleading for it to pass.

Rivers smiled to Sanchez. Sanderson ignored her. Rivers missed seeing anyone in the mirror, but he did notice the screen saver was running on Sapena's computer.

"Maria," he yelled, "why is the computer on?" Enright felt her blood run icy-hot.

"Oh, Mr. River," Sanchez said, flustered, "I bump into desk. It go on." She had done it before.

"Okay," Rivers said. Enright sighed silently in relief. Rivers turned to Sanderson. "Damn Michelle. I gotta tell her to turn things off. Costs money."

"Which we need to discuss." He motioned Rivers into his office. As the door was closing behind them, Sanderson said, "What the fuck happened on the beach tonight?"

"How the hell should I know?"

"Check into it, then. There's enough attention on us without having to worry about that kind of shit."

"This is your state," Rivers glared, "you fix it. My worry is my little corner. Now hurry up and get this over with. I don't know what the hell else you're talking about." Rivers slammed the door closed.

Back in the main office, the three were paralyzed with fear. None wanted to be the first to move. After a few unbearable moments, Sapena eased her head up. Sanchez was pacing, unsure whether to keep working or not. "Maria," Sapena whispered, "is anyone in the car?" Sanchez checked and shook her head no. "Gracias!" Sapena mouthed.

Sapena motioned to Enright and Daniels. They could still hear Rivers and Sanderson. The conversation appeared to be heated. Sapena inched up, followed by the others. They tiptoed past the desks and were headed toward the lobby when Rivers's door opened. Sanderson was still yelling. Though in the open, they froze, then the door closed again. Sapena grimaced, signaled Sanchez, and then motioned toward the vacuum cleaner. Sanchez turned it on, and they made a run for it, racing out the door. Sanchez locked it behind them, moments before Rivers and Sanderson came out of the office, Sanderson clutching a briefcase. By the time they reached the door, Sanchez was vacuuming, Sapena, Enright and Daniels having already disappeared into the night.

Fifty-three

The boat docked just after four p.m. During the last half-hour of the trip Kevin remained seated, minded by guards, while Jack Raden conferred with Captain Natano, in between Natano's phone calls. Upon docking, the staff and support personnel, except for Cindy Russell, scattered in the bright sunlight. Don Frazier left to arrange last minute details for the event. Tim Cain was escorted off by police. They continued questioning him on the beach.

"Your president's arrived," Natano explained, commenting on the noticeable increase in security. He cleared his throat and motioned the guards away. One asked to speak to Cindy and the two walked to the pier, leaving Kevin, Raden and Natano alone on the boat.

"I've been conferring with the Mill Valley police," Natano said. He brushed back his dark hair and rubbed his forehead. "Dr. Raden filled in some of the gaps. Dr. Herter, for now we're keeping up appearances. I still need to hear more, but after speaking with Mill Valley, I'm inclined to exclude you as being responsible for this incident."

"Okay, thank you," Kevin said with a loud sigh.

"Don't thank me yet."

"The captain has something to ask you," Raden said.

"This is the first murder we've had since we opened," Natano said, "and it comes on the day of our first presidential visit. Naturally we're concerned, and your Secret Service is beside themselves. I don't believe in coincidence. After listening to Dr. Raden describe the turn of events in your life over the past few days, I find myself needing your help." Natano reached in his pocket and took out a plastic bag marked Evidence. Inside was the note from Tim Cain that Kevin had tossed away.

"I thought it might come in handy," Raden said with a wry smile. Kevin shook his head.

"You should thank Dr. Raden," Natano said. "We'll examine it, what we found in Miss Vacca's room, and the photos you said you received from Mr. Cain. Our investigation is already taking some interesting turns.

You seem to be the focus of this. Now it's one thing to throw suspicion on someone for something minor. But knifings, murders, car bombs; someone's throwing a lot of attention your way. It must be important to raise the stakes that high. And it's been brought to our shores. And I don't like that on my watch."

"Those had been my thoughts," Raden said.

"I'm aware of your reluctance to get involved. But it should be plain to you you're involved whether you want to be or not."

"If I didn't know better," Kevin frowned, "I'd say you'd been talking to Jack here."

"Kevin," Raden smiled, "it didn't take much to get the captain interested."

"Quite true," Natano said. "I know you have your concerns. But we have our own, and they're on an altogether different level."

"Security concerns," Raden explained. "They don't have the civil libertarian issues out here we have in the states. They take security very seriously. If they make a mistake, that mistake will take their country out in one flash. I won't argue with them. They actually receive more training from the Israelis than from our people."

"They're a small country too. Those people don't take anything for granted."

"And, the talk about instability with the devices has been building."

Natano looked squarely at Kevin. "Dr. Herter, if there is even the remotest possibility anything is wrong with these things, I need to know about it."

"Okay," Kevin sighed. "What do you want me to do?"

"We'll continue investigating. That means looking into Mr. Cain and everyone else here. We'll look at who came in with you and at those arriving tomorrow. We will get to the bottom of it. We would like to continue to treat you as a suspect without arresting you. If others think that the pressure is on you, they may drop their guard, get sloppy or show themselves other ways. It may not work, but we can legitimately watch anyone who approaches you. What I ask of you then is simple—just keep doing what you've been doing. Find out what you need to learn about these things. What you learn for yourself will help us. And this stays among the three of us."

Kevin summoned a weak laugh. "Jack already has me doing things I never did before. Why not add government informant to the list?"

"We don't choose to look at it like that, Dr. Herter. But thank you anyway. And if there's something I need to know, I want to hear it fast. Deal?"

"That goes two ways. Okay?"

"We will most definitely talk," Natano said with a nod.

Kevin sighed and rose. The buzz from the Riesling wearing off, he felt a palpable sense of going through the motions.

"Don't think they haven't picked up on Cain," Raden said, trying to be reassuring. "That kind of thing doesn't go unnoticed. Let it play itself out."

"You know, for someone so rational, there's an awful lot of Zen in you."

"Yeah, six parts Zen, half a dozen Ben Franklin," Raden laughed as they disembarked.

There was a flurry of activity on shore. Cindy was still with the guards, and thirty feet away Cain continued to be questioned. He kept glancing over to her. Natano walked away for a few moments, then returned. "A Dr. Whiteman stopped by looking for you after we left," he told Kevin. "Do you know her?"

"Never met. I know she heads the program in the states. I have nothing to say to her."

"I'd appreciate if you made the time. She arrived today. If we need to worry about her, I want to know. Or, if she can shed light on our situation here, I want to hear it. Our prime minister is getting concerned as well." Raden strongly agreed. He had his own motives for getting Kevin to meet with her. He had a sense that Lisa Whiteman was his Sandia source.

"Okay, but I need to get into my room," Kevin said as he watched Cindy approach.

"Doctor, it's a crime scene," Natano said, as if Kevin should know better. "We can furnish what you need; clothes, anything. But the room is off limits."

Kevin shrugged. "Come to think of it, I wouldn't want to go back there," he said. "But where am I supposed to stay?"

"With Hanford here," Raden said, "there isn't an empty room."

"Some VIP treatment."

Cindy leaned in. "I have a couch."

"You sure? I don't want to put you out." He tried to smile. "You know, you might not want to be seen with me."

"We live in apartments. It's no problem." She looked at him wryly. "As far as that other thing goes, I'll take my chances."

Raden saw the interest she was showing in Kevin. He asked him, "Does that work for you?" Kevin nodded yes, and thanked her.

"Dr. Herter, we have a problem," said Natano, loud enough for all to hear, including Cain. "Our investigation is ongoing. We need you to keep yourself available."

"Don't leave town, huh?" Kevin frowned. "Where would I go?"

"There are ways to get off this island. You'll need to surrender your passport. Were it up to me we'd detain you, but your president wants you to present yourself this evening at the Terrace. That doesn't hold much weight with me, but our prime minister wants you there as well. He's someone for whom I have more respect." He caught a smirk on Cain.

"Please send our compliments," Raden said. "We'll see you in about an hour."

"That's fine. Dr. Herter, expect your Secret Service to contact you. The police in Mill Valley, California are eager to question you as well." His trap baited, Natano approached Cain and the police questioning him, and escorted them away. Cain's gaze fixed on Cindy again, then he sneered at Kevin before leaving. She didn't notice, but Kevin did. He tried to ignore it, asking, "What's the Terrace?"

"That's *the* place for guests and muckety-mucks to watch the events," answered Raden. "Like an upscale reviewing area, but it's also a first-class restaurant."

"And you know the dress code tonight, don't you?" Cindy said.

"He wasn't given the briefing the guests get," Raden said. "Business casual is the best description, but it needs to be light."

"You mean lightweight?"

"No," said Cindy. "Light color. Because—"

"Oh, I get it," Kevin said.

"In the beginning, people wearing dark colors got mild burns from the fireballs," Raden said. "Light colors were quickly mandated. Something we learned from Hiroshima."

Cindy walked back to one of the guards.

"Eager ears are now properly warned," Raden told Kevin. "Just hang in. And watch whom you share things with," he added, glancing at Cindy.

"What's the deal on her?"

"An up-and-coming talent here. She's okay, but be careful."

"I'll be all right. Nice kid. She seems on the ball. And she's cute, too."

"She is. She'll go far. Just watch out; Cain's got a thing for her."

"Ah, nothing's gonna happen," Kevin shrugged.

Cindy returned, and said, "Jude's one of the pier guards. He says they don't have enough on Tim Cain for an arrest, but they're very suspicious."

"What do you know about him?" Kevin was concerned. "I could tell you a story."

"I don't know him, really. He's odd. He once asked me out but all I could get through was a cup of coffee, just to be nice." She smiled. "I guess I have to clean up my place now."

"You should see my place. Don't bother; I'll feel right at home." She looked back in a way that said there was more substance there than she had let on. He paused, and then asked, "Would you be up for being my date tonight?" She flashed a winning smile, nodding yes.

"When you get a chance, check out the Atomic Channel on TV," Raden suggested.

"The *WHAT?*"

"It's my favorite," Cindy gushed.

"It's a station devoted to the atom," Raden said. "It's mostly sci-fi from the '50s, but it also has things like *Dr. Strangelove*, *The Atomic Café*. You'll love it."

"Unbelievable," Kevin said with a nervous laugh. As they left, he looked back at the police still at the pier and muttered to himself, "That poor girl."

Fifty-four

There was a marked difference in the grounds as Kevin and Cindy walked toward the mall. The souvenir huts were gone. The pool was deserted. Offshore, three cruise ships sat anchored, while numerous small craft lolled about. The increase in security was palpable.

"I must seem out of it," Kevin explained, thanking her for putting him up. "I'm sorry; there's a lot going on I can't tell you. You seem very nice. I don't want anything to happen to you." She looked at him funny. "I'm serious," he added.

"I can understand. What happened earlier—I can't imagine how I'd feel."

"You have to know I had nothing to do with that."

"I know. I saw how you reacted." She smiled. "I know a good bet when I see one."

He shrugged. "Still a lot going on. Maybe next week I'll have figured it out."

"Well, if you need an ear," she said, taking his arm, "I'll be in the next room. I know you're close with Max Rosenkranz. Having a Nobel Prize winner who wants to be in your life says something."

"He's the father I never had." He told her about Max and Jean, feeling himself sag.

Cindy's heart went out to him. "I feel so bad for you," she said.

"Thanks. It's still sinking in. I'll tell you. I have a new mission in life; kicking the rear ends of people who don't open their mouths." He looked away, biting at the inside of his cheek.

Cindy took his hand, her feelings mixed. She was genuinely sickened by the killing. And she saw Kevin's state. But she was drawn to him. She could talk to him, taken by how down-to-earth he was. And he was attractive. She had wondered if he felt anything for her but had dismissed it as wishful thinking. As they talked though, she found herself imagining it again. If something could come of it, she didn't want to lose the chance.

By the time they arrived at her apartment, Kevin's head and heart were all over the place. The sense of going through the motions had set. He knew what had happened, but had no real idea of what it meant. And once a compartmentalized abstract image, the event now loomed real. He knew what was to come, but had no clue of what to expect. And hovering over everything was that Jim Leffert was dead, a woman had been murdered in his room and both were connected to him. Though he hadn't wanted to inconvenience Cindy, the thought of a night spent in his hotel room made him cringe. He was glad she made the offer. The most he had expected in the way of a relationship from his time in the South Seas was a casual fling. The last thing on his mind was getting involved, and with the murder he was acutely aware of even mildly enjoying himself. But as they'd walked he realized she wasn't someone he would take lightly. She had made an impression.

They had just entered when she eyed him momentarily, then wrapped her arms around his neck and brought his mouth to hers.

"I'm sorry, but I just had to do that," she said after the warm, wet kiss. "I told you. I know a good bet when I see one." He was taken aback, but made no attempt to break it off. She smiled, half embarrassed but wholly unapologetic. "I'm gonna take a shower," she said. "Make yourself homely." He grinned and she vanished into the bath.

Feeling a newfound rush, he looked about. Her taste in film, music, even the informality of the décor all had the feel of home. He checked out the Atomic Channel and was instantly hooked.

When she walked into the living room, he had trouble keeping his eyes off her. "You look *great!*" he said to a welcome smile. Her long white dress accentuated her hourglass figure, her flowing hair and her tan. Though hiding it well, she was stunning.

After showering, Kevin donned khakis and a light violet shirt, courtesy of the gift shop. They left for the Terrace.

"Thanks for inviting me," she said, taking his arm. "I never met a president."

"That's me, Kevin, the meal ticket. Oh, I hope you don't mind but I checked out that channel. I could seriously get used to it. It was in the middle of *The Giant Behemoth*. Must see."

"I could spend a whole day watching that station," she grinned as they walked. "No kidding."

"I thought I was the only one. People still make fun of me for watching that *crap*." She gave him a peck on the lips. He smiled. "Can I ask you something? There's a lot you're about to see. Hanford's looking to sell me on this. How do you feel about this place?"

"How do I feel?" She bit her lip. "Mixed. I've been here a while, and most of the time I've enjoyed it. I've seen several dozen of these. They're really something. You'll see. I do think of the environmental impact, even without radiation, but there's something else. They've been talking about you for a while; nothing bad, but they definitely expect a lot. I hadn't thought of it, but then I met you. It bothers me now when I think about them discussing you. I feel bad saying it considering what happened, but I like you. I don't often meet guys I can talk to. That doesn't happen much, especially here. There's that 'people not opening their mouths' thing."

Kevin turned to her. "I—"

"No, you don't have to say anything," she said, smiling sadly. "I understand—"

"No," he cut in, "it's not what you think. I thought about this at your place. I already like you." She blushed. "Trust me though; you don't want to get involved with me right now."

"And why is that?" she leaned forward, still with a hint of a smile.

"Where to begin? First, I just ended something I was in for more than two years."

"Okay," Cindy said sympathetically, "you're on the rebound."

"Rebound? I'm in a different arena." He fumbled about for another pretext. She put her hand to his mouth. "How bout this. We make it up as we go along." As she leaned forward, it had the affect of accentuating her cleavage.

"Know what?" He smiled. "That may be the best offer I've had all week." As she beamed, he teasingly asked, "But what about Tim Cain?"

"Oh, he's a creep," she snarled. "I mention one thing about environmental concerns and he became Mr. Sierra Club. Would not leave me alone, like he really gave a shit. I didn't want to say it earlier, but my God."

They were just approaching The Terrace when from behind them came a voice. "Dr. Herter?"

Fifty-five

Kevin and Cindy turned. "Dr. Herter," the woman behind them said. "My name is—"

"Lisa Whiteman. I figured I'd run into you sooner or later."

She managed a smile, but it quickly vanished. She was attractive, in her thirties with dirty blonde hair, though her winsome green eyes darted about as if watching for something. Her white dress imparted a ghostly impression.

Kevin introduced Cindy. They traded awkward greetings.

"Well," he added, not sure what to say, "I suppose—"

"Please, Dr. Herter. I don't have much time."

"I heard you were looking for me," he said brusquely.

"I got in this morning and I was trying to find you. I heard you were going out on the water. I ran up to the pier, but I missed you by fifteen minutes. I could see the boats in the distance. I've been trying to meet you for months now. If you knew the trouble I went through."

"Dr. Whiteman—"

"Lisa, please."

"Lisa. I had been asked to speak to you—"

"Good, I'm glad."

"But this whole thing's left a bad taste in my mouth. I know you're the person most responsible for this place—"

"What? *That's* what you heard?"

"That was my understanding, too," Cindy said.

"Then please, we need to speak," Lisa said. "Tonight, tomorrow, as soon as you can. You don't know the half of it."

"I don't know what I can tell you. I'm not in the loop here. Everyone mentions you as the person who got this up and running, so you haven't exactly been my favorite person." He caught himself. "All right; you have to know I really didn't want to get involved in this. I'm only here as a favor to the White House. What are you saying?"

"I can't go into it now. Please, give me twenty minutes and you'll understand. Believe me, you want to hear this. And Cindy Russell, I want you there, too." As Cindy and Kevin eyed each other, Lisa added, "I know you're watching the detonation with Hanford—"

"How do you know that?"

"Dr. Herter, I just know. I won't be there. No one knows I'm here, officially."

"Well, someone knows."

"Oh, believe me, I'm aware. It's just like everything else with this." Her eyes darted around again. The low profile she had long cultivated was now a liability. None of the people who might have been in a position to help her knew that she was coming. The only ones who would recognize her were the ones she had reason most to fear. "Dr. Herter, I came here just to meet you. I had to get to you first, before Hanford and his people. I know what they're doing."

"I know, too—"

"Oh, no you don't. You don't know the half of it."

"I was only asked to help you with some problem," Kevin said. "So it's big, right?"

"It's big, all right," Lisa said, "but not what you think. Trust me, there's a lot they didn't tell you. Please, don't mention any of this tonight. But I do need to speak with you, and soon."

"I've really had it with cloak and dagger. You have no idea what I've been through the past few weeks. Put yourself in my position. How am I supposed to take this seriously? I don't even know you." Cindy squeezed his arm.

"I know. But after we talk you'll know a hell of a lot more than you bargained for." She looked around. "That's all I'll say for now. Please, let's meet as soon as possible. You have no idea how important this is. And please, don't commit to anything. Just tell them you'll sleep on it." Her eyes darted around again. "Go. I'll find you. But in the meantime, hold onto this."

"What's this?" Kevin snapped as he was handed a USB stick.

"I can't answer now. Just hold onto it, in case anything happens to me."

"What is it?"

"I can't talk now. You'll find out soon." With that she turned and blended into the crowd.

Kevin turned to Cindy. "Well. What do you make of that?"

"I don't know. We all thought she was behind this. We knew issues needed to be addressed, but it didn't seem to be anything to get all worked up about. But she looked sincere; I mean, her nervousness didn't look fake. If that's the case—I don't know."

"That was my impression, too. Maybe we should meet with her." As she agreed, he added, "I'm sorry you're involved with this, but I am glad you're here." She smiled, and he looked at the stick in his hand. "Maybe we shouldn't say anything about this."

She patted his arm. "You seem like you have a lot more on your mind."

"You're very perceptive. You'll see when you meet Hanford. Just watch him. He's been trying in the worst way to get me involved."

"It's an incredible project; at least I thought it was. And I'd be lying if I said I didn't want to work with you." She paused. "I have to admit, it's a little intimidating meeting a president."

"Trust me. It passes. Like when you realize there's a lot he's not telling you. I need to know things before I can decide what to do. I don't trust him to tell me."

"What are they planning to do here."

"You'll see. Things have happened I wouldn't wish on anyone. What happened in my room earlier was the tip of the iceberg." He described the events that week. Cindy was aghast.

"My God. Maybe Lisa Whiteman is onto something."

"I know I didn't have patience for her," Kevin nodded, "but I won't dismiss her. But it all goes back to Hanford. Now do you know why I was so reluctant to get you involved?"

She squeezed his hand. "Listen, Dr. Kevin Herter. I know you said you don't know me and I don't know you yet either. I'd like to. But putting aside what I want, I couldn't in good conscience keep working here if I knew something was wrong."

"This is where I need your help," he smiled. "My head's all over the place and my stomach's in knots. You know this place. Watch him, what he says, how he operates. But be careful. He's smooth. You might not know what hit you until it's too late. You said you had some issues here. I want to pick your brain about what they are. Cin, I really need your help."

She smiled. "That's the first time you called me Cin. You got it."

He eyed the stick. "Maybe we should take a look at this before we meet up with her."

"Yeah, maybe." She thought for a moment, then said, "Let's go kick ass."

Fifty-six

Christian Deloy stood near the portico in the shadow of a slouching palm. In his chintzy pink and yellow shirt and tan shorts, he had the tourist thing nailed. Passing security personnel were treated to stares at his watch and scowls at the elevator. The eager reveler awaiting friends. All pretense, and at 5:09 p.m. unnecessary. The impatience and irritation were real. Dillon Ridge was four minutes late.

Elliot Hanford was habitually tardy, meaning Ridge was as well. Deloy knew the retired colonel had no patience for his boss's issue, but he didn't care. Ridge had called the meeting and he wasn't about to indulge him. When he appeared at 5:12, Deloy snapped, "You're late."

"You try working with him and being on time. Come on." They slipped into an empty men's room. Ridge wasted no time. "You hear about Honolulu?"

Deloy turned on a faucet. "Who didn't? You better have something. This is a risk."

Over the running water, Ridge said, "People get shot up, media's in an uproar, and not a word from Whiteman. He wouldn't notice sand at the beach. What the hell's he doing?"

"He doesn't confide in me. He has his priorities and I have mine."

"Well somebody better get back to me. I'm trying to hold this thing together and everyone's running around half-cocked. Now it's the mayor with the hard on. Snipers don't play well in cities that cater to tourists. The police moved in before our people knew what happened."

"Like everything else in this cluster fuck." Deloy sneered, a gesture made easier by the sixty-year-old Ridge's appearance. Some military needed to learn when not to be military. In a place where blending in should be requisite while flirting with covert activities, this guy was clueless. With everyone hanging loose, he was his uptight best as a drill sergeant on a three-day pass denying himself a light beer. Black slacks, a collared blue shirt. Polished black shoes, posture tight as a drum. Clearly, he hadn't received the dress memo. Then again, maybe he had.

Ridge didn't give an inch. "We know it wasn't you, since you were here."

"If you say so."

"Cut the shit." Deloy ignored him and asked what he learned. "Whoever pulled the trigger was rusty," Ridge replied. "No bullet hit its mark. And the gun's from your people."

"My people? The Deloys?"

"Don't fuck with me. One of your pals."

"Hey, they're just as much yours … *Colonel.*"

"Right. And there's a stick. We think it's Daniels's. We can't get to it so we're trying his files, but he's walled himself off well. This will get out of hand and we don't need it."

"It's already out of hand. And right up there is Rivers and his idiots. Or maybe that's your doing. All you guys went to Fuck-Up U, so it wouldn't surprise me. Not my problem."

"*Make* it your problem. Whose ever bright idea that was, it didn't work. The police have Daniels and Sapena under wraps. But Enright's a different matter. She'll look to make her way here. We can't find her. She's not using her phone and her name isn't on any flight manifest."

"Well, that's fine," Deloy said with a malevolent laugh. "Someone else coming out here. Why don't we all do lunch. I guess you want me to ask her out or something."

"You do what you were hired to. It hasn't broken yet that she was a target. Discredit her. She becomes a victim or lets on what she's learned, we're all screwed."

"Then step aside and let me do my job. You guys are a piece of work. Why not hire CNN to follow your boss around? Whose bright idea was it to haul his ass out here and bring half the press corps with him? You know how much attention you're attracting?"

Ridge contorted his face. "I'm not going—"

"I don't want to hear it. It's fucking Times Square. And after he gets all starry-eyed when he watches that thing tonight, you tell me how I'm supposed to work what you expect from me. Why the hell did you let him come?"

"You know what he's doing," Ridge groaned. "He thinks it'll all work out."

"Well, that's just great. Keep working it like that, you'll guarantee it doesn't. And in the meantime—aw, hell, I'm done talking. I'll have to handle it myself."

"I don't have to explain myself to you, *Captain.* Coming out here solves problems for us and none of that's your concern. You want to worry about something, worry no one can find your boss and his wife is coming out here—"

"It's already taken care of."

"What's that mean? This wasn't supposed to go down this way. I'll be damned any of this gets back to the White House, understand? Stop worrying about my boss and start worrying about your own. Your job is to find ways to keep things from happening, regardless. Deal with it. And speaking of drawing attention to yourself, what about that incident up in Herter's room?"

"What about it? You think that was my doing?"

"Wasn't it?"

"Maybe. But you don't know—"

"All I know is bodies keep piling up. I don't need it and neither does the White House. It's bad enough we have that damn thing in his car to deal with—"

"Another thing not my doing."

"Great. No one knows nothing. Just like his damn hotel room; no one knows nothing."

"Fine. But if you don't know, maybe that's not a problem. Word is they're looking at Herter. Couldn't have happened to a nicer guy."

"No one will buy that he was involved."

"Does it matter? Maybe that's what's called for. You get my drift, Colonel? Which brings us to the purpose of this get-together. I take it you didn't take my last message seriously."

"I took it seriously all right. So did the people writing the checks. They don't like it one bit."

"I don't give a rat's ass they do or not," Deloy smiled contemptuously. "All your fuck-ups have seriously jeopardized this task. My ass is now on the line. If they expect me to do all this now, they can pony up the extra half million or find themselves another errand boy."

"You know we don't have the time—"

"Oh, you're so right. You have even less than you realize. I don't know if you caught the weather report. There's a front moving in. Expect your boss to move everything up."

"Oh, shit."

"Oh, yeah. You idiots don't notice things like that. At least someone in this fiasco does. This is now a rush job. So make sure they come through. It's a business expense. Costs have escalated, and your mismanagement does not constitute an emergency on my part. If it does for them, I expect the funds to be deposited by midnight; otherwise I consider the contract null and void." He leaned into Ridge. "And don't even think of invoking a 'kill' fee."

Ridge was silent for a few seconds. "I'll convey your request. This meeting is over." He turned and left.

Deloy smiled. "Dillon my boy, didn't your mother ever tell you not to waste water?" He shut off the faucet then left, following the route past the gift shop a few beats behind Ridge.

Lisa Whiteman looked up. She had stopped by the gift shop after speaking with Kevin and Cindy, and saw Dillon Ridge scurry by. She didn't think anything of it until she saw a more leisurely Christian Deloy tracing his footsteps. Her blood ran cold. She instinctively hunched down behind a display rack, hoping she hadn't been noticed. Someone she didn't recognize approached Deloy. She listened as best she could. She knew Deloy's voice and heard what she thought was a room number. From the other man, she heard what sounded like, "I'll take care of it." Deloy handed Tim Cain a piece of paper, and they parted ways.

Ridge, then Deloy, one after the other, both headed in the same direction. A hundred scenarios raced through her head, none of them good. She didn't know the second man, but knew Deloy all too well. It was now all the more important that she meet up with Kevin Herter. She waited until Deloy passed, then inched her way to the front of the store. Not seeing him, she warily fell in behind the people headed to the mall.

Fifty-seven

Security was exceptionally tight as Kevin and Cindy passed through screening just after five. Kevin was thinking that had they kept her out, he would have opted out himself. With the underlying drama he was enjoying the company of the woman beside him in ways he hadn't expected.

Jack Raden was waiting. "We decided to be fashionably late," Kevin quipped.

"No such thing in the South Seas. Hanford's not even here yet. But he's always late."

"And, we have to talk."

"We do. Meantime, nice place, huh?"

It was more than nice. The Terrace was an aptly named trattoria. The outdoor restaurant jutting from the hotel's north wing exuded money and good design. The tile floor commanded as much attention as the troughs of flowering foliage, while tropical jazz cut a relaxed beat. They went to an upper level, near a small fountain framed by blooming vines and security agents.

Seated at a large table was Don Frazier. "Great to see you!" he beamed.

"Hey, Don!" Raden said.

"Hi," Kevin said, as they sat. "Where's my good friend Tim?" he added, wryly.

"Oh, he'll be around," Frazier replied innocently.

Kevin tried to relax. Despite his anxiety, it was beautiful. The hotel's coral hue reflected the late afternoon, glowing with a radiance no photo could ever capture. Birdwing butterflies diligently visited flowers in the calm breeze. He noticed that the paint on the walls and trim was blistered. The heat of the fireballs. Forget about relaxing. His tension was off the chart.

"Lots to discuss," Raden whispered, noticing. Kevin nodded vigorously back.

A moment later Frazier's phone beeped. He apologized, and excused himself.

The moment he left, Kevin said, "We just ran into Lisa Whiteman. Something's not right here." As Cindy nodded, he said, "She wants to talk to us in the worst way. She didn't say why but she slipped me this." He held out the USB stick.

"Okay," Raden said. "For now, hear Hanford out. Don't commit to anything. And meet with her. I'll see what I can learn in the meantime. Mind if I take a look at that?"

"Be my guest," Kevin said, handing it over.

"I'll let you know. What do you know about Hanford's chief of staff, Ridge?"

Kevin's gaze tightened. "I'm supposed to say nothing, but you're being cagey again, right?"

Just then Frazier returned. "We have a weather front moving in. It wasn't supposed to affect us until Monday, but looks like we'll start seeing it Sunday."

"It means Sunday night's shot is likely to be moved up," Raden said.

"The president has been briefed. It's on Saturday night now."

"Oh, wow," Cindy said. "We've never staged events this close together."

"That means this place will be crazy over the next two days," Frazier nodded.

"They need a backdrop for that announcement," Raden told Kevin. "It means pressure for you, too." Kevin groaned. "But," he said changing the subject with a rare exuberance, "speaking of weather, you lucked out! What a glorious evening! You couldn't have planned it any better!"

"He's right," Cindy agreed. "You nailed it." Frazier's big grin said he agreed.

Off to the west, the sun was going out in resplendence. The brilliant azure sky had quieted to a silvery blue, with flecks of pink and salmon near the horizon. Not a cloud floated by.

"I always thought scenes like this were a little too perfect," Kevin conceded. "Must be those movies from the '50s I grew up with. Every time the ocean was calm like this, something happened."

The Terrace seated several hundred people and every table was occupied. At each setting was a pair of futuristic blue and violet goggles, like virtual reality scopes. The parasol at each table made it difficult to see, and as Kevin was about to comment, a clicking noise began and they began folding up. Once folded, they withdrew into the table, and a cover snapped into place.

"Very efficient," Kevin said. He could now see to the horizon. Hundreds of people milled about, spilling out past the pool. On the beach, Shot Stations had been stocked. Surfers headed toward open water.

"I take it these are for the detonation," Kevin said, examining the goggles. As Raden nodded, he chortled. "I caught that channel of yours. I wish I got it back home."

"I told you," Raden smiled. "What was on?"

"*The Giant Behemoth.*" As Raden cut him a look, Kevin explained, "A dinosaur gets resurrected by atomic tests and runs amok. Of course, that describes half the movies from the '50s. This one takes out London."

Cindy laughed. "Remember *The Beast from 20,000 Fathoms?*"

"Ray Harryhausen! How about *Beginning of the End?*"

"Yeah, yeah! Peter Graves!"

"Which one was that?" Raden asked.

"Grasshoppers get mutated by radiation into giants and attack Chicago."

"Yeah!!!" Cindy said. "And *It Came from Beneath the Sea?*"

"God," Raden lamented. "She's one of you."

Kevin exclaimed, "Tonight they have *The Monolith Monsters, Them!, Kronos* and *The Monster That Challenged the World.*" He saw Raden's skewed look. "You don't get it," he said. "Give me a bag of Chips Ahoy! and a gallon of milk and you won't see me for two days. You guys are just lucky there's something like a hydrogen bomb around to get me away from that."

"That's how I spend days off," Cindy added. "Except for me it's pretzels, Doritos and Diet Peach Snapple." Kevin eyed her with added interest. She pressed her leg up against his thigh. He smiled and felt a flush.

Raden shook his head. "Maybe I'll just—" He was cut off by a growing commotion and clapping. A moment later, amid his entourage, Elliot Hanford was walking their way.

Fifty-eight

"There he is!" Elliot Hanford approached with a big grin. "I'm glad you made it, Dr. Herter," he said. "I was looking forward to this."

"It's good to see you again, too, Mr. President. I'm glad you made it as well."

Hanford flashed an affected smile and patted his shoulder, then greeted Jack Raden. Kevin introduced Cindy, who despite his earlier admonitions was plainly taken with meeting her first president. Hanford also greeted an obviously thrilled Don Frazier. Despite his own misgivings, Kevin felt genuinely happy for them. The president took a seat next to Kevin, while the Secret Service agents stationed themselves nearby.

"Colonel Ridge should be here shortly," Hanford said. Kevin and Raden eyed each other.

Anxiety aside, Kevin was struck by the president. His beige khakis and light yellow shirt may have been what was called for, but they were a perfect complement to his backslapping manner. The inescapable reality that this guy, so effortlessly smooth, was a sitting American president filled him with wariness, and a touch of envy. He couldn't remember meeting anyone so comfortable in his own skin. Still, the unease was palpable, the tension high.

"I want to thank you for coming out here," Hanford told Kevin. "I'm happy you'll be working with us. My back's against the wall with this, but if it's handled right, none of that will matter. There's a chance we can make history with what we do here."

Kevin shot a glance at Raden. He hadn't agreed to anything and Hanford damn well knew it. He wasn't about to make a scene now, but Mike Yahr's forewarning rang louder by the minute.

Just then came the silky voice of a woman who sounded as if she could do GPS voice-overs:

"Welcome to Tuvalu Alofa. It is now thirty minutes before tonight's event, Eta Carinae. If you have not yet done so, please take the time to change into light-colored clothing before viewing the spectacle. Also, make sure that your safety glasses are at hand.

"Tuvalu Alofa is pleased to extend greetings to US President Elliot Hanford, who has traveled all the way from Washington to be with us. President Hanford is the first American president to visit our island nation. And among this evening's guests, we also recognize Dr. Kevin Herter. Dr. Herter's landmark work provided the basis for the DiFusion program, and we extend to him a warm Alofa welcome."

A hearty round of clapping broke out.

"I'll never get used to that," Kevin confided to Cindy.

"I think you might have to," she said, drawing close to him.

"Trust me," Hanford advised, "you find a way." Kevin laughed lightly and the president told Cindy, "Our friend here will attract his share of attention." She smiled and he added, "Kevin, if I may. I'll hold off comment until we see this. But let's meet tomorrow after breakfast. There's a lot we have to discuss. I need your help."

"Okay, but what did you mean your back was against the wall?"

"We had an important announcement to make on Sunday, but I just learned they're expecting rain. We need to move it up." He leaned in. "I know you think this represents science gone haywire, and you resent having to be here."

Kevin felt himself blush. "Well... I—"

"Come on, Doctor," Hanford laughed. "I've seen faces on senators who hate my guts that are more collected than yours. A day doesn't go by where someone doesn't rip me a new one over this. I have ideas about where I want to take this but nothing's decided. That's one of the reasons I'm here, to see how the talk from the geniuses jibes with seeing one of these things. None of us realized it, but I'm the first president to see one. Presidents have tried figuring out what to do with the bomb for seventy years. But none of them bothered to take the time to watch one until now."

"Mr. President," Kevin responded to the president's unexpected words, "I'm pleasantly surprised to hear you say that." Just then, he wondered how sincere Elliot Hanford was. He remembered Jack Raden's cautions about the president, and how he would come at him so subtly he wouldn't know what hit him until it was too late. Was this one of those times? He shifted in his seat, catching Raden's eye, and watched him nod slightly. A warm breeze rustled by. He felt the hair on his neck rise, and he knew it wasn't only from the breeze.

"Don't think I take you for granted," Elliot Hanford told Kevin. "I've given this a lot of thought, more than people give me credit for."

"I appreciate that Mr. President. So, Jack said you had some problem you need fixed."

"It's nothing big they tell me, but we do need your help. Don't ask me to describe it; I couldn't. We'll go over it more tomorrow. It's too bad the project head couldn't be here."

"Mr. President," Raden said, "Dr. Whiteman arrived today."

"Excellent! You two put your heads together, I'm sure you'll solve it." He leaned back. "They tell me seeing these are an experience."

"Oh, yes, Mr. President," Cindy nodded.

He nodded, then squarely eyed Kevin. "I hear you had some trouble." Everyone grew quiet.

"If that's what you want to call it," Kevin forced a laugh, which eased the tension a little.

"Damn stupid. I'm sorry you had to deal with that. We will get to the bottom of it."

Kevin thanked him. He wasn't sure what to make of Hanford, but for now would take him at his word and move on. He barely had time to think about it when Lionel Latasi arrived.

"Ah, Mr. President!" Latasi said. "Good to see you! I hope you're enjoying yourself!"

Hanford rose. "Mr. Prime Minister. Thank you for your warm welcome!"

"It has been our pleasure! And Dr. Herter, it's good to see you again too!" As he sat, he grew serious. "Mr. President, Dr. Herter. We are extremely sorry your visit coincided with the tragic events earlier. We are working hard to deal with it, I assure you."

"Have you learned anything?" Raden asked, not expecting an answer.

"The police tell me they've made substantial progress with their investigation." Latasi reached out to take Hanford's outstretched hand and then they shook. So that's how it's done, thought Kevin; surnames and titles, a little brown-nosing, and that would be the end of it as far as the two leaders were concerned. It didn't make him feel any better.

"My friends," Latasi smiled, "you are about to see something you will never forget. We thank Dr. Herter for his wonderful work and the president for allowing us to share its good fortune. We look forward to our friends in the region sharing its rewards."

"Thank you Mr. Prime Minister," Hanford said, unwilling to engage Latasi on the issue of new sites. Just then Dillon Ridge arrived. He seized on the moment, jumping up to introduce his chief of staff.

Ridge took a seat, and glared at Raden. "What are you doing here?"

he asked brusquely.

"Oh, I just heard they put out a nice spread," Raden said casually. He and Kevin shared a quick glance. Kevin turned his gaze to Ridge, taking an instant dislike to him.

"So, how does this work?" Kevin asked Raden.

Raden deferred to Cindy. "There'll be a few announcements before the detonation," she said, grinning at Kevin. "None of them have to do with you." Everyone laughed, even Kevin, who whacked his knee into hers. She was growing on him.

"These things really necessary?" Hanford asked, examining the goggles.

"Oh, yes," Cindy said. "In the 1950s, Mr. President, they used simple sunglasses. These explosions are considerably more powerful. You definitely need filtering."

"Besides," Raden added, "remember, the lawyers run this place."

"They're that powerful?" Kevin asked.

"Which," Hanford said, "the bombs or the lawyers?" Everyone howled.

"Yeah," Raden said, "they're that powerful. The lawyers don't want anyone going blind."

"And yeah," Frazier nodded, "they're that bright. The bombs, not the lawyers."

They laughed again. A moment later Greg Huntington and Stephanie Lange walked up. After greeting the two leaders, Lange handed Raden a tablet.

"Okay," Raden said, "we're set for a 5:47 p.m. explosion, seventeen minutes from now. We're looking at a twenty-one point six-seven-five megaton yield, at a distance of forty-one point eight miles. We anticipate a fireball four-and-a-half miles in diameter. Waves offshore will run nineteen to twenty-two feet."

"That sounds impressive," said the president.

Raden turned a wily eye to Kevin. "The detonation is set to a piece called *Papillon.*"

"Okay," Kevin shrugged.

"That's the French word for butterfly," Lange said.

"It's from a CD by David Arkenstone," Raden told Kevin. "*In the Wake of the Wind.*" As Kevin rolled his eyes, he added, "And the finale piece? Brian Eno's *An Ascent.*"

"Welcome to Club Afterglow," Cindy added as everyone laughed.

Fifty-nine

An announcement broke in at 5:32 p.m.: "It is now fifteen minutes before the event. If you have not yet done so, please change into white or light colored clothes.

"The Imaging Center will open at 5:50 p.m. Those interested in photos with the event are encouraged to proceed there shortly after the all clear has sounded. You can take advantage of this opportunity until 7:40 p.m. All guests will be provided with a video of this evening's spectacle before you check out.

"The yield for this evening's event Eta Carinae is estimated at twenty-one point six megatons. This is the largest in the history of the program. Please check that your safety glasses are secure before the two-minute warning. Thank you."

Shouts erupted. The Shot Station crowds pumped fists, high-fived, and downed more beer and liquor.

For Kevin, the announcement was a punctuation mark. His heart beat faster, and his breathing picked up.

"First time jitters," Cindy whispered, noticing. "Happens to us all."

Despite himself, Kevin was excited. "Jack," he asked, trying to deflect it, "Imaging Center?"

"I love doing this to him," Raden answered to laughs. "You can get photographed with the cloud." As Kevin groaned, Raden added, "Ever see pictures they take on cruises of people with the ship? Same thing."

"People go for that?" asked the president. "Amazing! This is an incredible place." A mischievous grin came to him. He turned to Raden. "Jack, how is it you seem to know everyone? It's like you're everybody's best friend."

"Oh, my yes," Lionel Latasi said. "We all know Jack here."

"Mr. President," Don Frazier explained, "Jack's like the guy in that joke. He's in Rome standing next to the pope and someone in the crowd doesn't recognize the pope but knows the guy. We've wondered about Jack for some time."

Raden folded his arms, a smug smile across his face. "Up yours too, Don," he said to howls. "I've seen your security dossier. They bought a new file cabinet just to store it all." To continued laughter, he said, "Okay, we're getting close. Let me tell you what to expect. You've seen footage of these, but it's nothing like what you're about to experience. The fireball will be intensely bright. When the all clear sounds, you'll be able to remove your glasses. You'll be stunned. With an explosion this size the cloud will be immense. Now, it's not like an atomic bomb. These things rise slowly. It's hard to tell it's even expanding. It'll reach the stratosphere in about five minutes. It begins to crest then and will get bigger still."

"It's really that big?" Hanford asked.

"They're impressive," Dillon Ridge said. "I was here a year ago."

Lange turned to Cindy. "Remember that women's studies lecturer?"

"Oh, my," Cindy blushed. "I'm not sure I should repeat it."

"Oh, Cindy, let's hear it," Hanford laughed, his encouragement adding to Cindy's fluster.

"Well, don't say I didn't warn you," she said, feeling herself blush. "It was last year. A lecturer from Brown did a paper on why these things are so popular with women. You wouldn't think so, but it's true. Her theory was that the detonations are comparable to the female orgasm."

The president and Latasi began howling.

"Tell them what she wrote," Lange pushed, vigorously nodding. She glanced at the men. "You'll love this."

Cindy was thoroughly embarrassed. Giggling, she said, "She wrote that they subliminally remind women of their own orgasms because they build slowly, gain strength and size and aren't over in an instant but linger long after the explosion is over. I can't believe I'm telling this to a president," she said, losing herself in convulsive laughter, the rest of the table joining in.

"Three years in this job," Hanford howled, "no one's ever briefed me like that."

Kevin looked around. "Okayyy ..." he said to hysterics. He turned to Hanford. "Uh, Mr. President, one atomic bomb to another." Everyone lost it and he added, "This is what you want me to sign onto? You can't give people openings like that."

Hanford chortled out a good-natured laugh. Cindy squeezed Kevin's hand and felt herself turning redder, though in the late afternoon glow, no one noticed. A moment later, the smooth jazz that had been playing eased into an ethereal number.

"That's the event piece," Raden said. "All of you ready?"

"No," Kevin said, feeling his heart rate increase. "But don't stop on my account."

"Damn!" Hanford said, "I haven't been this worked up since election night!" He looked at the Secret Service. "You guys all right?" They fumbled with their goggles and awkwardly smiled.

The announcer broke in again: "It is now two minutes to the event. Please secure all beverage glasses and bottles. Please also check that your safety glasses are at hand. Remember, looking at the fireball with the unshielded eye is dangerous. Keep your eyes closed and glasses on until the all clear has sounded."

Everyone in the group sat up. Hanford fidgeted with his goggles. His agitated Secret Service stood at the ready, uneasy about having to shut and shield their eyes and with no real notion as to what they would do if something went wrong. Shutters over the hotel windows began closing automatically, while doors were shut and bolted. Anticipation rippled through the crowd. Kevin clutched his glasses and waited. Nearby, two large butterflies crossed paths.

The music was building. The announcer proclaimed: "It is now thirty seconds to the event. Please put your safety glasses on. Remember, viewing the fireball with the unshielded eye is dangerous. Keep your eyes closed and glasses on until the all clear has sounded. We invite you to sit back and relax, and enjoy this unparalleled event."

Everyone put on their glasses and shut their eyes tight. The music had been like an overture. As it approached a crescendo, Kevin felt an indescribable chill ripple through him.

"Jack," he haltingly told Raden, as his heart pounded, "there's another old joke about a guy who sticks his head in a guillotine. They ask him if he has any last words. He says, 'Yeah'."

He covered his eyes just as Raden said, " 'Yeah, I don't think this damn thing is safe!' But in the meantime, Mr. President, Dr. Herter, get ready to confront a whole different scale of what you define as entertainment." As Kevin anxiously smiled and his heart raced, Raden said, "Okay, heeeeere … weeeee … *go!*"

Sixty

A brilliant flash of light burst out from the east.

In an instant it reached out toward the island and beyond. Ten thousand square miles flooded with a whitish-purple luminosity like an immense magnesium flash. Kevin felt an immediate rush of heat. A hushed moan rippled out from everyone, including Elliot Hanford. The main movement of the music began, timed to an instant.

Despite his shut eyes and hands and goggles covering his face, Kevin sensed the light. "My God, John," he whispered, "I can see it."

"You feel that heat?" Raden asked.

"God, it's like a broiler!" Hanford exclaimed.

"And that's over forty miles away, Mr. President."

The detonation was eerily silent. The only sound was the building music. A few pounds of his heart later, Kevin felt the intensity of the light begin to taper. As if on cue with the music, a loud, extended beep sounded, and the announcer said:

"All clear. It is now safe to remove your glasses." Kevin haltingly peeled off his goggles and opened his eyes.

Out toward the horizon as if arising from the very innards of Hades, the fireball of Eta Carinae had just broken free from the ocean surface, a blazing five-mile wide hell-storm slowly beginning its ascent to the heavens above. A vapor cloud twenty miles wide towered over it, itself slowly rising.

"Oh, my *God!*" Hanford smiled, his head shaking.

"My God," Kevin echoed. He felt his jaw drop. Every one he had ever seen, in books, on film, TV, in magazines, posters and art, every one big and small, none had prepared him for this. Immense could not begin to describe it. It took up the entire horizon and was growing. And the heat! As hot as a barbecue pit and not letting up. It was every color in the rainbow and changing, roiling, churning, writhing, with a life of its own, a mindless, enormous entity unto itself.

From the crowd rose whistles, whoops, claps and a rush of celebration. It was mortifying, especially when the president of the United States joined in. Even Lionel Latasi shouted, "Way to go, Dr. Herter!" Kevin's eyes darted back and forth between the sight in the distance and the reactions of the people nearby. He wanted to crawl under the table, but he just had to watch the explosion. He was stunned. But he had to watch.

"Are you okay?" Raden asked. Kevin could just shake his head. He tried to quash a nervous grin. The music was timed precisely to the event, and to his embarrassment, he felt another chill. "Just hang in," Raden counseled. "Things are going to happen."

Slowly, inexorably, Eta Carinae began to take on the characteristic mushroom cloud shape. Within minutes, it spread ten miles in diameter, on a stem a mile wide. From the heat he could only imagine the inconceivable temperature inside the cloud. The vapor clouds had elongated in a series of bowl-shaped strata over the fireball. They began dissipating as the cloud expanded. The setting sun illuminated it in a brilliant yellow-gold, a striking contrast to the silvery sky.

At the Shot Station, people had locked arms in groups of three, five, and six.

"What are they doing?" Hanford asked Raden.

"Just watch, Mr. President. They live for this. Oh," he motioned to Hanford and Kevin, "you gentlemen might want to hold onto something."

They turned back to the sight. A white line had appeared parallel to the horizon, quickly growing larger. Though expecting it, Kevin instinctively gripped the armrests of his chair as if suffering a turbulent flight. The Shot Station crowd waited until the line was just upon them, and then gulped their drinks, while the Secret Service agents crowded around the president. Kevin gripped tighter and in the last instant winced as the shock wave of Eta Carinae rolled over the island, a sudden blast of near-hurricane force and speed. It bent trees and bushes, whipped up dust and toppled chairs. People at Shot Stations were blown back, some into nets, some onto the sand, in some cases, a dozen feet. Their whoops of ecstasy couldn't be missed.

While Hanford heartily clapped and shooed away the guards, Kevin let loose a string of "No! no! no! no! no! no! no!" His skittish laugh was lost in the hoots and hollers.

The shock wave heralded the detonation sound, a deep rumble that competed with the music and the heat. A slight movement on the ground caught Kevin's attention. It was one of the butterflies, flailing helplessly.

The other was nowhere to be seen.

The moment the shock wave passed, staff swarmed over the grounds. Some collected goggles; others wiped tables, swept up, and made quick work of tidying anything blown down. One picked up the stricken butterfly and disappeared inside. Greg Huntington pointed out the many small boats heading to open water, preparing to illuminate the cloud later that evening.

By the time Eta Carinae was five minutes old, it had reached over fifteen miles in height. The mushroom cap had expanded forty miles, on a stem five miles wide. The roiling eddies in the cloud were growing more slowly, but with the sun now lower, they were reflecting yellows and oranges and pinks with a radiance that stopped onlookers in their tracks. The rumble and heat were dissipating. The initial excitement was shifting to awe.

The music had meshed seamlessly with the blast. Its final moments coincided with the arrival of the waves. In the distance surfers rode twenty foot swells. The cruise ships handled them well but smaller craft visibly pitched. As the sea calmed, the liners began turning parallel to the cloud. All had been pointing toward it. Kevin knew the smaller profile they showed the blast had kept them from capsizing, and the shift would now give everyone on board a better view. The music, the detonation, the shock wave, the surfers; it had all gone off without a hitch.

A relaxed air seemed to come over everyone, as if the cloud had reached a milestone and was settling in for the next stage of its life. *Papillon*, the New Age piece that served so fittingly as the opening number concluded, and Buster Poindexter began pounding out *Hot! Hot! Hot!*

"Nice," Kevin cracked.

"I told you they love their irony here," Raden grinned.

"We go by that saying, strike while the irony is hot," Cindy said.

The staff who'd wiped down tables were followed by others laying out place settings. "Wow," noted the president. "They're like army ants. I wish Washington worked that fast."

One enthusiastic young fellow came up. "Mr. President, Dr. Herter," he asked in an engaging tone. "May I get you a latte? Or perhaps a nice piña colada before dinner?"

Elliot Hanford smiled and shook his head, gazing instead on the ascendant thermonuclear cloud, stunned. "That is the most amazing thing I have ever seen! I knew what to expect, but—my God!"

"Isn't it something?" Lionel Latasi beamed.

The president didn't answer, still enthralled by the scene. Finally, he asked, "What happens now?"

"Now," Greg Huntington smiled, "we party!" Everyone laughed.

Kevin though remained transfixed. As had happened to Hanford the blast had left its mark, but unlike the president, he had yet to reconcile its implications. He sat, painfully still.

"You okay? What are you thinking?" Cindy asked, seeming to sense his plight.

"That the waiter was right. A pinã colada would do it now."

Laughing, she called him back.

All around like a glow-in-the-dark trinket that soaks up light and surrenders it in the dark, the masses that had been in hushed awe at the spectacle were now releasing their pent-up energy as the initial intensity of the blast began to wane. Tables which five minutes before had been swept clean by a hydrogen bomb-induced shock wave now sported napkins and bread sticks. Revelers at Shot Stations blown down by the concussion now refilled their cups and high-fived the billowing entity. Partyers on ships sent rocking to twenty-foot waves now rocked to music and toasted the astounding display. At the world's most incomparable resort where a thermonuclear fireball played host, rows of serving tables now offered filled chafing dishes and carving stations.

Off to the west, the sun had just set. In the east, Eta Carinae reached sixty miles wide and twenty miles high, on a seven mile wide stem. It had taken on classic mushroom cloud shape but its immense structure now spouted eddies and new columns. The blue sky had deepened.

Though at sea level the sun had set, at three, five and seven miles up it still shone, and the cloud picked up every last bit of radiance. Near its base, a dusky violet haze spread out for miles. The stem emerging from it became a dull reddish-purple and salmon further up. As it entered the massive main cloud it turned pink, then gold, and finally a rich yellow near its upper limits in the stratosphere, reflecting sunlight unfettered by dense sea level air. It cast a golden glow on the island, and Kevin remarked the resort couldn't have been given a better nickname.

Those still watching could see the cloud tops slowly churning and spreading, and to his surprise, Kevin couldn't stop watching, nor turn away. It was hypnotizing, every special effect from every spectacular film times ten all rolled into one real-life extravaganza. And as much as he loathed admitting it, it was beautiful. God, it was so incredibly beautiful.

Raden, small-talking with Hanford, noticed Kevin's staring at the sky. "I had a feeling you'd be taken by this," he said quietly.

Cindy had the same thought. "Now you know why we detonate at sunset," she offered.

"I didn't want to think about it," Kevin conceded. "I know what you mean now—you have to experience this. It really is astounding. And it bothers me to say that. My ex is an artist. I know she'd say the same thing. She'd hate it and still not be able to stop looking."

"People aren't supposed to think of them as beautiful. But they are. Mr. President," Cindy said, "I have to ask. What do you think?"

"Astounding is the word for it," Elliot Hanford said, gazing out with a most curious expression, a beneficent ruler pridefully surveying his realm. "I can't get over that no president ever bothered to see one before. I think the head of every piss-ass country who wants these things should come here and see for themselves what they're really like." He turned to Kevin. "I know what needs to be done now. You find Dr. Whiteman and we'll meet tomorrow. I need her to hear this." Only Raden noticed Ridge's barely perceptible frown.

"My friend," Latasi told Kevin, "you may appreciate this. We often have artists visit. Many are anti-nuclear, all set to give us a piece of their mind, but when they see this they react the way you did. Many integrate it into their work. We're hosting an exhibit later this year, work by artists who've visited and done pieces based on their experience."

"It's one of the things so striking about this place," Don Frazier said. "You can't help but get caught up in it. The prime minister said creative people try to integrate it into their work. Well, they also try to integrate it into their beliefs. They come here with preconceived notions, but they leave ambivalent. Kevin, it's not you, it's the thing itself. It's exceptionally powerful, but it's a power that has two sides. It's like a coin with one side beauty, one side destruction. Which side do you look at? That's your choice, but the catch is there's no such thing as a one-sided coin. Even though it's out of view, the other side's always there. Mr. President, all of us understand the dilemma it leaves you with. We see it every day." Hanford quietly nodded.

"Mr. President, you know it's been on my mind," Kevin added. "But I'm not the first. Back in the '50s, a physicist named Marshall Rosenbluth watched a big explosion. He was stunned too. But he said something that stuck in people's minds years later. He said it looked like a diseased brain in the sky, like what the brain of a madman would look like, with these turbulent rolls going in and out. Hell of an analogy. I thought of that when it was rising. You feel powerless when you see all that energy. But look at it. The thing's unbelievable. I don't see how you can't get philosophical when you see this."

"That's why, in Princeton, I told you that you really had to see it," Raden added.

Hanford listened, then said, "This is a big help to me, people. I have to let it sit, but I'm very glad I came out here. I don't think there's any way to make this decision without seeing this. I don't know how a person in my position honestly could."

Dillon Ridge had remained silent, which surprised Hanford as Ridge had seen one before. Ridge finally said, "The president's correct. It makes what we do that much more important. We've a lot to go over, people." Ridge's all-business air was a red herring, and he was betting no one would notice. He was beginning to think it may indeed have been a mistake for Hanford to come out here. The president was already starry-eyed, just as Deloy had forewarned.

Hanford turned to him. "Relax for a night."

"No, sir, it's not that—"

"I know. You've seen it already. But it does confirm what we were thinking, doesn't it?" Ridge gave him a disingenuous nod.

Raden sat back, still observing. Without knowing what they had discussed, he had already begun to give more thought to Ridge, especially after his conversation with Mike.

A moment later, a server opened an Australian Shiraz that Raden had ordered and poured glasses all around. Without waiting for it to breathe, Kevin took a sip. It was a relief as it hit his system, though he said, "I suppose this needs to sit as well." He eyed the cloud. "I know I asked before, but I was serious. What happens from here? Do people settle down to—I can't believe I'm about to say it—do they just settle down to party with that cloud hanging over their heads?"

"That's another one I needed to hear," joked the president as the table roared.

"But, yeah," Frazier granted, "they love it."

Kevin shook his head, and took another sip of wine, which had begun to even out and was quite good. Baskets of bread with olive oil and more wine had been served. While the others ordered Kevin passed, zoning out to the scene in the distance. He was finishing his wine when his piña colada arrived. He decided he couldn't care less if he got buzzed in the presence of a president. "Okay," he shrugged to Cindy, "when in Rome... could you please pass a menu?"

She was handing it over when Captain Peter Natano approached. After introductions, he said, "Excuse me, Mr. Prime Minister, Mr. President. I need to speak with Dr. Raden."

Sixty-one

"I just took a call for you," Peter Natano informed Jack Raden as they left the Terrace.

Raden checked his phone and saw several missed calls and a text from Mike Yahr.

"He couldn't get you," Natano added. "That happens a lot here when the bombs go off. So he called us. We had a nice chat. I was impressed. He has some interesting information."

"He wouldn't call if it wasn't important," Raden said as he called Mike. They spoke for a bit, then he said, "Thanks for the update; I know it's late there."

"Past late, before early. You remember. I thought you'd want to know. You want to tell him, or have me fill him in?"

"Let me. He's still with you-know-who. I'll bring it up and watch what happens."

"Those were my thoughts. And just so you know, I briefed the captain. He's a good guy."

"He thinks the same of you."

Mike sighed. "I'm not sure you want to tell Kevin right now, but Max isn't doing so hot."

"Ah, damn," Raden lamented. "I'll hold off. I'll have him call tomorrow. Thanks again for the info. Interesting how it's playing out, huh?"

"That's an understatement. Just watch yourself."

"Is there any other way? Talk to you soon." Raden hung up. "Lots happening," he said to Natano.

"Too much for my sensibilities. We're not used to this. But I think we took the right track with your scientist. Are you going to brief him?"

"I think over dinner. Some of the others need to hear it as well."

"We think alike. And you think they'll respond—how?"

"I'm not sure. The other players aren't there yet. But you plant seeds, you never know."

"Okay, Jack. We'll talk soon." They shook hands, then Natano faded into the twilight.

Raden paused. It was a fine line he was walking. Not unlike what Kevin was living, though Kevin was unaware. He wouldn't appreciate the benefit of dealing with a guy like Peter Natano. The Tuvalu cops could have been a problem, but the captain got the bigger picture. Having him in the know would prove wise. Raden gazed up, wishing he had more time to indulge in the iconic image in the distance. A perfect backdrop to the night, as much as this entire story and the news Mike just conveyed. That was sure to make some at the table stop and give pause, especially those involved up to their armpits. He was sure that at least one of them was there. It was simply a matter of dropping a word or two, sitting back and letting events take their course.

Raden was heading back to the table when his phone beeped. He expected to see another message from Mike. Instead a text flashed from a private sender: *Dr. Raden. It's time we met.*

He had an idea as to who'd sent it. He tapped out, *Depends*.

He had just hit Send when his phone rang. "I can't blame you," said the familiar caller.

"I didn't think so. What do you have in mind?"

"Turn around."

She stood twenty feet away, leaning against a post near a row of jasmine-infused planters.

Raden walked up to her. "Dr. Whiteman, I presume."

Lisa Whiteman tried to smile, but the concern draping her eclipsed her haunting eyes and winning shape.

"I was pretty sure you had it by now," she said, extending her hand. "You don't miss much. That's why I chose you in the first place."

"I figured you'd make yourself known when you were ready."

"It was time." Her eyes darted around. "I saw you with the officer. Is anything wrong?"

Raden shrugged. "Actually, lots."

"Do you trust him?" He nodded and she added, "I'm not sure whether I should talk to them."

"Dr. Whiteman—"

"Lisa, please."

Raden smiled. "Okay. Lisa. That was Captain Peter Natano. He's the equivalent of the chief of police here. You can talk to him. He does know you're here—"

"Oh, God." She grimaced.

"You stopped at the pier looking for Kevin Herter." He smiled.

"Don't be discouraged."

"Jack, it's too late for that. You probably know that I spoke to Kevin earlier."

"He told me. He's with the president right now. What I don't understand is what has you so worked up that you had to follow him out here, even considering what you told me."

"I can't tell you. I will, but I have to talk to him first. There are things going on here that only I know. He'll know what I mean when we meet."

"Okay …"

"And something else. I just saw someone who scares the living daylights out of me. I'm not going to have a good night."

"Lisa, I'm sure Natano can protect you. Something happened this morning that has him more concerned than Hanford being here. He'd want to know."

"What happened?"

"A chambermaid was killed in Kevin Herter's room—"

"Oh, my God!" She began pacing like a wound-up spring. "I could have told you something like that was possible."

"Lisa, calm down. This is not how you avoid detection." She hesitated, and he said, "You have to tell me." As she made no move to speak, he added, "Lisa, this is what happens when you freelance things like this."

She took a deep breath. "My husband's aide. Christian Deloy. Even with police protection, if he's responsible for what happened to the maid, I'm fifty-fifty making it through the week. Tom swears by him but I never trusted him. I had no idea he'd be here. I came out here for one reason, but now I have to deal with this."

"You're serious." She nodded and he said, "Tell me."

"Things aren't good at home. We're on opposite sides of this. I can't go into it right now. You don't know this guy, though. If he's here, it means something."

"What can you tell me about him?"

She looked around. "He comes out of Special Forces. Don't ask me what he did; I don't know. But even in Sandia he would make my blood curl." She folded her arms. "Jack, tell Kevin he has to watch himself. I can't stress that enough. Deloy was relaxed; he looked like he was headed to a ball game. If he killed a maid without breaking a sweat, none of us are safe."

"Lisa, are you sure it's him?"

"Positive." She looked around again. "I've stayed too long. Please, tell Kevin he's got to meet me, okay? The sooner, the better."

"He'll be there. But are you going to be okay tonight?" She shrugged, not knowing. "Okay," he said, "I have to head back. There's something you should know. Your assistant flew out to Hawaii. There was an incident in Honolulu with him, a friend of his, Michelle—"

"Sapena. They're an item. And I know why Glen went there. He must have seen what I left." She smiled. "He got the hint." She looked around, and though nervous, described her history with the program, not going into her deepest fears but enough to fill in some blanks. When she was done, Raden told her about the beach incident.

"Oh, my God!" She became even more obviously agitated, attracting attention from people nearby.

"Lisa, calm down. I'll tell you what I told Kevin; you have to keep it together. That reporter Jessica Enright will be here tomorrow. I'm sure she'll find you. Talk to her. She's quickly putting things together. But know this. The Pentagon just had the FBI issue arrest warrants for Glen and Michelle. I'm not sure how that will go down; the Honolulu police have them in protective custody. I expect they'll put Enright on that list. We'll see if the captain here will honor it. So talk to her before anyone gets to her."

"Or me. And I know what they're after."

"What you gave to Kevin, right?" She nodded, and he added, "Lisa, I'll fill the captain in on what you told me. He had wanted us to speak anyway. Will you be okay?"

She bit her lip. "I can take care of myself. I don't think he knows I'm here. I'll keep out of sight until tomorrow." Her eyes darted around again.

"Lisa," Raden said, now concerned, "are you sure about Deloy?"

She nodded her head nervously. "Okay Jack, go. I hope to see you soon. And please, please, tell Kevin not to commit to anything until we meet." With that she turned and quickly disappeared.

Raden first texted Natano: *Meet me after dinner.* He then texted Mike, asking, *Find out what you can about a Captain Christian Deloy.* As he headed back to the Terrace, wondering if he should bring up the captain's name at the dinner table, he veered off to make a quick stop.

Three minutes later at the resort's Internet café he sat before a computer, loading the documents from the USB stick. A blizzard of graphs and figures appeared. On a whim, he took out his phone. It was 7:40 p.m. He knew it would be much later where he was calling.

The caller ID came up Private at 2:40 a.m., but Sharon answered it nonetheless.

"Miss Velazquez?" the person began.

"Oh, boy." She immediately recognized the voice. "Only two people have called me that in the past six months and one of them is dead. I guess you must be the other."

"I certainly hope so," Raden said. "Something told me you might be up." In her bedroom lit only by a muted TV, Sharon Velazquez managed to crack a smile.

"And nobody dead or alive would even think to call at this ungodly hour. How are you, Jack?" she asked, friendly but reserved.

"I'm holding my own."

"Tsk," she muttered. "We have to get you a girl."

He laughed. "I'll run it past my wife. How have you been?"

"Oh, just peachy. You know, decorating the east wing, writing my memoirs, flying to Gstaad for some late winter skiing." She sounded tired of talking, but interested in being heard.

Raden let the witticisms pass. "Miss Velazquez, I'm calling because I find myself in need of your special talent."

"I'm sorry. I'm not dating right now."

He laughed lightly. "Well, how about platonically?"

"Oh, wow, I don't know. Last time I had so much fun." She paused, expecting something cutting. When all she got was a slight chuckle, she said, "Okay, I guess. You've been on my mind. I have it sitting in my breakfront. Thanks again."

"Please, it's my pleasure."

"Considering what it cost, it's my pleasure too." He laughed. "So what can I do you for?"

"Well, Miss Velaz -"

"No one calls me Miss Velazquez at three in the morning."

"Okay, Sharon. I was wondering if you could do me a favor. I'd like to email you a file. Somehow, I have a feeling you may be able to tell me something about it."

"What are you looking for?"

"Any kind of pattern. And yeah, it's about you-know-what. I know how you feel about it, but you're the only person I know who may be able to think outside the box. Let your mind wander. Maybe you can see something. You up for that?"

"Well, I'm up. I guess that's a start."

"Okay, good," Raden laughed. "Could you get back to me?"

"I guess. I'm not sleeping right now, so I'll give it a whirl."

Raden thanked her and left his number with an invitation to call whenever she wanted. He got off the phone, took a moment to log into his email account, sent Sharon the file, then logged off and within five minutes was approaching the dinner table.

Sixty-two

The sun and wine had gone down further by the time the servers brought the appetizers. Between the stuffed mushrooms and prawns, Kevin kept looking toward the east.

Eta Carinae had taken on a luminous pinkish-orange glow. Flashes of lighting danced amidst the ruddy purplish cloud base. The three cruise ships stood out as bejeweled floating cities in miniature, numerous small craft between them flitting about like fireflies on a warm evening. Set against the deepening sky, it was all breathtakingly beautiful.

"You just want to stare," Cindy said, sitting with a glass of wine and a glowing countenance. "In the beginning, we often didn't get work done on event days. It's addicting." Kevin agreed.

Lionel Latasi had excused himself to meet with some staff, just before Jack Raden returned. On the Mall the buffet opened, and people were settling into dinner. Others kicked back, watching the cloud. A snappy piece of Latin jazz played, while on the beach the Shot Station crowd was deep into third and fourth rounds. Several girls were now topless.

"This is so bizarre," Kevin noted.

"I had somewhat the same reaction myself," Hanford smiled.

Don Frazier produced a pair of binoculars. Hanford took them and began peering. He spotted small planes flying around the cloud margins and asked Frazier about them.

"We call them Cloud Surfers," Frazier explained. "Gliders with retractable engines. They fly out, glide round and fly back. They're popular."

"Sounds like fun," Kevin said.

"Damn right it looks like fun!" Hanford roared.

A moment later, an aide approached with a notepad. Greg Huntington reviewed the data and said, "We have a preliminary readout on the event. Radiation levels are nominal."

"How do you define nominal?" Kevin asked.

"No measurable levels above normal background amounts."

Kevin looked at the data, and subtly frowned. "And this number's the yield?"

"Correct. Twenty-two point three three five. Almost twenty-two and a half megatons."

"That's something we've been looking at for a while now," Cindy said.

"Is there a problem?" Hanford asked.

"We seem to be spiking over predicted yields," Huntington added.

"I wouldn't call it spiking," Kevin said. "You've got almost three-quarters of a megaton more than you were expecting. That's significant."

"I agree," Cindy said. "We're not sure why. But it's been consistent."

The president leaned forward. "Is that the small problem you were hinting at?"

"It appears so," Kevin said.

"We'd like you to look at the figures, "Frazier said. "Maybe you'll see something."

"Is that something you're worried about?" Hanford asked.

"Well, sir," Huntington said, "it hasn't caused any problems. It just shouldn't be there."

As the president nodded, Raden told Kevin, "Tomorrow, okay?"

"Sure as hell not tonight. I punched out at six."

As everyone laughed, servers began delivering entrees, just as Latasi returned. Kevin ordered cedar-planked salmon, with scented jasmine rice, fresh asparagus and mango and cilantro salsa. He had a hard time remembering enjoying a meal so much.

The prime minister had chosen a curried chicken dish. Raden was savoring a rack of New Zealand lamb with a mint reduction, while Cindy was content with a pasta dish with fresh scallops and shrimp. The president had opted for blackened yellow snapper with roasted potatoes. Everyone was hungry and the conversation quieted down as they ate. With the darkening sky, candles lit and Eta Carinae's afterglow, a tranquil mood prevailed.

"This is excellent," Raden said, as everyone agreed. "H-bombs sure whet the appetite."

"My goodness, yes," Hanford echoed, laughing.

"I am very happy everyone is enjoying themselves," Latasi beamed.

Raden looked at Ridge, who had been methodically devouring a swordfish steak. "And colonel," he began, "You must be enjoying that. You're so quiet."

"Dillon always keeps us guessing," Hanford quipped, to laughter.

Raden was between sips of wine. "I hate to upset his dinner so I'll wait till he's done. But I have some information about the earlier incidents that we should discuss."

In the waning light, Raden noticed Ridge's reaction to his words. Raden would wait until dinner was over. He was fairly sure what would follow.

Sixty-three

"That was a hell of a meal," Elliot Hanford said as they settled back and awaited dessert. "So, Jack. You had some news."

Raden nodded, his earlier comment a trial balloon. He'd wanted to see who would react and how. He didn't have long to wait.

"Well, Mr. President," he began, "we're getting a better picture of what happened in California." He eyed Kevin. "This should be of some interest to Dr. Herter."

Dillon Ridge leaned forward. "Frankly, Dr. Raden, I'm not interested in what happened there or what you found out. Mr. President, there are more important things to discuss."

At once everyone grew quiet. Raden had no illusions of what Ridge thought of both him and Kevin and had expected some kind of response from Ridge, but wasn't sure what approach he would take. Now he knew: Guns fully blazing. A glance at Kevin told him that Kevin had picked up on it as well.

Cindy also noticed. Without waiting to be asked, she said, "If no one minds, Don, Greg, Steph, let's hit the bar." She got up, patted Kevin's shoulders, smiled at the president and said, "Adult swim." Hanford winked back. Kevin said he would see her later. She left with the others.

Kevin turned back to Raden. "Jack, I'd still like to hear—"

"Dr. Herter," Ridge interrupted, "first things first. Mr. President, there's been an incident directly bearing on what is to happen here. There's been a security breech at Sandia." Hanford's eyes widened. "We're still piecing it together," Ridge added, "but we're looking at a catastrophic intelligence leak. So Doctor, I'm not concerned with your little episode back in California."

"Whoa, now just—" Kevin shot back.

"I said I'm not interested. You've been acting like a fucking prima donna. There's a hell-of-a-lot you could have helped us with that might have prevented this, but it's been like pulling teeth to get you to step up to the plate."

"Now, hold it," Raden jumped in.

"No, you hold it. We know all about Mill Valley and what happened in Herter's room earlier today. And none of it would have happened had you been on board from the start. You snivel around feeling sorry for yourself, and half of this shit you brought on yourself."

Kevin was incredulous. "That is such a load of—"

"I told you I don't want to hear it," Ridge snarled. "You know what we had to deal with because of you? Sandia's assistant director, some pinhead named Daniels, downloaded an entire data stream, flew to Honolulu, met up with some contractor's secretary and hooked up with a reporter. That's just for starters. Then last night, they're involved in a shooting on some beach. You think we need that? And now the director herself is traipsing around here doing God knows what. Suppose they're shopping around for the highest bidder? Ever think of that? And with all that, you can't be bothered. I'm sorry Mr. President, but none of this had to happen."

Latasi sat watching, unsure of what was happening while Raden knew all too well. Kevin was fighting back his rising anger. "And that's my fault? Where the hell do you—"

"Doctor," the president cut in, "Colonel Ridge can be passionate, but I do want to hear all opinions. Dillon," he entreated, "I still want—"

"I'm sorry, Mr. President, but I can't sit back and watch this and not hold my tongue." He scowled at Kevin. "You know what you've cost us? This technology gets out, we've had it. And all you care about is giving us attitude!"

"Okay, Dillon," Hanford said, giving Kevin a sympathetic eye, "go easy. What do we know?"

"Daniels and his squeeze are being detained," Ridge replied, "but that reporter, Enright, no one knows. My understanding is the FBI's putting out an APB on her, which will mean diddly-squat if she makes it out here. So watch her show up looking to nail a Pulitzer, unless after screwing up her career in Princeton she's in on the take as well. Damned media; I'm convinced they have a hand in this. So if she comes out here, well, Mr. Prime Minister, don't say we didn't warn you. But you do what you want."

"I'm not sure what you people think we should do," Latasi shifted uncomfortably.

"Mr. Prime Minister, this is as much a security issue for you as for us. And Dr. Herter, we already know you met up with her. So I don't want to hear any more from you about—"

"Then you can hear it from me," said Raden. Ridge's indelicate bad cop to put Kevin on the defense was obvious. Unfortunately for the scientist, a neophyte in political maneuverings, it was working.

"We've learned more about the device in California that nearly took out Kevin," Raden told Hanford. "Very sophisticated. Someone put in a lot of effort to throw off investigators. We were lucky though. We were able to lift a partial print from an inside panel. I'm sure that had it gone off, it would have been obliterated. It was traced to a former Special Forces operative—"

"And even that's a load of bull," Ridge charged, heading Raden off before the name was divulged. "I don't buy it. Mr. President, none of our people were able to take a look at that so-called piece. We've tried every channel, and all we get is the runaround. The local police don't even know about it."

"Is that true?" Hanford asked Raden.

"That's not true and the colonel knows it. Mr. President, the incident was handled by the retired NSA operative who discovered the device. We kept it out of the papers for this—"

"That's another load of bull," Ridge bellowed. "Surprise; he's a friend of yours."

"Hey, pal," Kevin snapped, "I was there." He glared at the president. "What the hell is this?"

"I don't give a damn you were there," Ridge barked. "You have no training with that sort of thing. You could have been looking at Silly Putty for all you know. I don't even believe there was a bomb. I don't trust that crowd as far as I can throw them. Ever stop to think the people who were so hot to kiss your ass tried to make it look like someone wanted to shoot it off?"

Kevin sat back, not knowing what to say. It was the same argument Raden and Mike had used to win him over. He felt a tinge of doubt. He eyed Raden for an answer.

"Mr. President," Raden said, "there's more going on than what Ridge is alluding to."

"Damn right there is," Ridge said. "Mr. President, what happened is no coincidence. I have problems with the doctor here but in fairness to him, he's being set up as some kind of useful idiot. There've been interests against this from the start, and now it's come to a head. This goes right back to them, with a convenient little stopover at the media. Talk about idiots; how bout that clueless pain-in-the-ass Enright! They couldn't have done any better! Interviewing the wrong person? No one will take her seriously now. Problem is, she's just stupid enough to do some really serious damage. But if she's trying to rehabilitate herself and she can get enough people to buy into it, or if she's involved with hackers in some kind of espionage—"

"Oh, come on!" Kevin yelled. "That's enough!"

"It may be enough for you Doctor, but we take these things seriously. If it turns out she's on some bend to jump start her career and got in bed with a crowd looking to do harm to national security, inadvertent or not, you'll find yourself in just as much trouble. She made a big splash with you in Princeton, but who knows what you talked about when the cameras were off. I'm warning you; if it so much as brushes past anything you have said or done, so help me—"

"That's it!" Kevin shot up. "Mr. President, you're going to have to excuse me. I've had about all of this I can stand."

"Dr. Herter, Kevin," Hanford said. "Just sit down—"

"Sorry; I'm done with this fool. Mr. President, Mr. Prime Minister, you have a good night. I'll see you in the morning and we'll talk. Without this moron." As Ridge sat sneering at him, Kevin grabbed his glass of wine and bolted. Raden excused himself and followed. Latasi then quickly said his goodbyes and left as well.

Hanford gave Ridge a subtle smile. Ridge then said, "Mr. President, that wasn't only just for show. We may actually have a containment issue in New Mexico."

Hanford's smile quickly disappeared. "What are you saying?"

Sixty-four

"Jack, I was just going to look for you."

"Likewise, Captain." Jack Raden had just crossed paths with Peter Natano outside the Terrace. Raden hoped to catch up to Kevin, but was glad he ran into Natano first.

"What do you have for me?" Natano began. "And by the way, it's Pete. I have a feeling that by the time you leave, formalities will have worn out their welcome."

Raden smiled. "I think that's true. You know by now you're not going to get anything from the Administration except a run-around, so it's going to come down to us."

"I just caught sight of Dr. Herter from a distance," Natano nodded. "Looks like he worked up a head of steam. I wouldn't have expected either of you to have left dinner so soon. Something happen?"

"We had some fireworks. Hanford's chief of staff went off on him. Mostly bluster. Man's a moron, but he achieved his desired effect."

"I hope your scientist will learn to see these things for what they are. He's an interesting fellow. You get a feel for good people."

"I've been trying to educate him. Takes time. But I was struck by the timing. Ridge chose just now to unleash a broadside. The questions are why, and why now. I'd also be interested in hearing anything you learn about a Captain Christian Deloy. He's the aide to the program's head of security in New Mexico. I believe he came out here yesterday, which is in itself intriguing."

"I recall seeing the name on the hotel manifest. Military always raises an eye. I'll take a look." Natano grimaced. "Whatever's happening here is picking up. I don't like it."

"Any second thoughts about making Herter a moving target?"

"No. But I have been surprised at how he's attracted attention. I just can't put it together yet. There are things that don't make sense. A lot of it seems contradictory."

"That's been my impression. Everyone's doing the opposite of what they want and hoping nobody notices. I don't have to tell you; in this business you get used to people hiding intentions. But people here seemed more concerned with unintended consequences than with getting caught. Something has them spooked. They're all hung up but I get the sense they expect it to work out."

"I know. So far, it hasn't. Okay. We've had some movement on our murder investigation. The chambermaid had been dating a maintenance worker for several months. It was a troubled relationship with talk of abuse. Her co-workers had been after her to make a formal complaint. He was a jealous individual and had been exhibiting a significant degree of controlling behavior. We don't take kindly to that sort of thing here, but we hadn't any tip-off that anything was wrong." He sighed. "So often with those things, the first hint, unfortunately, is a body. My guess is, she had been preparing to end the relationship, which is what set him off. Now, I'm almost certain he's the individual who did the killing, but it brings up a problem."

"The Herter connection."

"That's it. Too much coincidence for my sensibilities. We've been questioning him and we're close to filing charges, right after we square away certain physical evidence. But it does leave us with the whys—why there and why now."

"And who would know this guy was a loaded spring."

"That's it. Perhaps they dropped the scientist's name to the boyfriend as the person she was interested in. He's reluctant to talk. Something's holding him back, more than just the obvious. People that angry and jealous are deep down usually scared and insecure, but it's been a while since I've interrogated someone who exhibited such fear. I wonder who on this island could create that much intimidation in so short a time."

Just then Raden eyed his vibrating phone. "Pete, I need to get this." He answered the call. "Sharon. I didn't expect you to call so soon. It's been barely twenty minutes."

"Hey, Jack. I didn't expect to be calling this soon."

"Wow. What do you have?"

"Well, there's something I need to speak to you about. I opened the file—"

The call was interrupted by a chirping noise. A staid female voice broke in: "This call has been terminated for reasons of national security." The phone then went dead.

"Holy *crap!*" Raden stammered, glaring at his phone. "I got cut off!"

"What?"

"This call has been terminated for reasons of national security." In all my years with the NSA, I never had that. Son of a bitch!"

"So, who is Sharon?"

"Sharon Velazquez, Kevin Herter's ex. I had her look over data from the blasts. She's quite the abstract thinker. I thought she could tell us something. Okay; they've upped the ante."

Natano took out his phone. "Here, get her back. I'll take a chance this isn't compromised. I'll be damned if I sit on my hands with that kind of garbage on my watch."

Raden dialed up, and within half a minute was speaking with a dispatcher at the Princeton police department. He identified himself and asked for an officer to be sent to Sharon's house. A patrol car happened to be three blocks away. The department had already been watching out for her, and a minute later an officer was ringing her bell. She answered through the bolted door, but when the officer explained he was conveying a message from a Dr. Jack Raden, she swung it open. The call was patched through the patrol car, and less than four minutes after being cut off they were speaking again.

"Jack, what the fuck just happened? National security?"

"We were being monitored and they cut us off. Listen, we can't talk long. I hope now you see how serious this is. You tell me what you found some other time. I have an entirely different question I need to ask and please be honest. It's been three days since you and Kevin split up. If you could get back with him, would you?"

"Holy shit, Jack, you sure know how to knock someone for a loop. In the middle of the night, with the spooks eavesdropping, you call ten thousand miles for that? Why do you ask?"

"I have a reason."

She gave up a nervous laugh. "Okay. To answer you, I'm not sure. I mean, I do miss him, but honestly, I don't miss the drama. It's like I'm spent. I love him and always will but—you know—yeah, I think we ran our course. Does that help?"

"A great deal. One more. Do you see a possibility the two of you could be friends?"

This time she didn't equivocate. "Yeah, that I'd like. We shared a lot. But the past few days have given me a lot of time to think about him and what we were doing to each other. I really do love him. But I'm not sure I was really *in* love with him. I was so in love with what I wanted him to be, I don't know if I ever got around to falling *in* love with him. You know what I mean? We were so close and spent so much time together and always hit it off in the sack, but half the time we were dealing with each other's bullshit. And we were both guilty of it. I couldn't deal with it anymore. And I don't miss it."

"I can imagine."

"Honestly, I'm no better. I have to fix things. I spent two years trying to make him into what I wanted instead of just accepting who he was. I can't do that the rest of my life. Shitty combination—someone who needs to fix things and hates doing it and someone who need things fixed and hates having it done. The only good thing with this breakup, he's not six blocks away. We can't get together and have make-up sex." As Raden laughed, she added, "I know I was a pain in the rear too. Maybe it's better we move on."

"Thank you. That's very honest."

"Does that answer your question?"

"Yes, it does."

"Okay, Jack, then why ask? What kind of trouble is he in? I told him not to go out there. Bloody cups; phone taps? Cut off phone calls? In a million years I couldn't come up with that. I wish I could do something to get his head out of his ass. If I could, I'd go out there and kick it so hard he wouldn't be able to sit for a week. And believe me, I'm good at it."

Raden said nothing. She waited a few moments, then it hit her. "That's what you want, isn't it? That's what you want, right?"

"I had my hopes. A lot's changed and I need your help. So does he."

She sighed. "You knew I would do that, even though we split up, right?"

"Sharon, that's why I asked if you wanted to get back with him. I saw you two in Princeton. If you had answered yes, I wouldn't have."

"In a weird way, I can understand that. What do you expect me to do out there?"

"We can't talk now. I'm going to have someone pick you up at your house very soon and take you to Newark. There'll be a flight for you to San Francisco. I'll be there in the morning. We have to put this together fast. Pack light and fast, and have the officer stay there till you leave. I'll see you early tomorrow." He hung up.

"Jack, what's going on?" Natano asked.

"A lot more than I figured on. I need to head out and meet her. I'm running out of time. I'll take any help I can get. She's sharp. If she saw something, there's something worth seeing."

"Evidently someone thought so."

Raden shook his head. "My thought as well. There's something there that someone doesn't want us to see. No one breaks off conversations between an analyst and an artist unless it's damn important. I never had a call terminated before. I don't like it one bit. And I don't have time to find an analyst to do an exhaustive study on the thing. I trust her."

Natano anxiously puffed up his cheeks. "Jack, you keep me posted while you're away."

"Pete, you too. We'll be back by Saturday. And keep an eye on Kevin. He's out of his league." He shrugged. "Guess it frees up my room. Maybe he can relax a bit." He shook his head. "I don't like this. There's something else going on, more than we figured on. I have to check it out while there's still time. In the meantime let me use your phone again. I have to put this together, and quick."

Sixty-five

Armed with a glass of red wine and flushed with anger, Kevin strode the mall. It was shortly after nine, but felt later. Balmy trade winds and a warm tropical mix danced in the air. They were a welcome distraction, as was the wine. The equatorial night blazed with stars, the Milky Way arcing across the heavens. It recalled growing up in Michigan, where clear nights revealed satellites moving across the sky. Though its afterglow had waned, Eta Carinae had billowed out to stupendous size, filling the entire eastern sky.

From a distance he saw the women. Half a world away and oh-so familiar. The Marina District of San Francisco, the Columns and the Beachcomber on the Jersey Shore. Names and faces melding to a state of mind. It was every club he'd ever partied in—the stench of barley and hops, the amber glow of flesh for the taking. The throttled fury of countless Saturday nights. None though were ever framed by a twenty-megaton hydrogen bomb.

Cindy was leaning on the wooden deck wall rimming the courtyard. Beside her were Robin and Gina, the women who'd been on his flight, and another woman he didn't recognize.

"Hey, you made it," Robin said, like the others, nursing an island concoction.

"We saw Cindy sitting with you and the president," Gina smiled. "When she came down we introduced ourselves."

The women were stunning. A palpable sexual tension hung in the air, but in his state Kevin missed it. Gina introduced Shelley, the other woman. Her flowing dark hair draped a jet black dress she had wasted no time changing into after the detonation. Though it was dark, it wasn't hard to tell it hid a multitude of sin. He asked her where she was from.

"Highland Park," she said with a hint of a Texas twang. "It's near Dallas." Kevin knew it, an island of money encircled by a sea of a city. Shelley wasn't in Tuvalu just to see an explosion.

He rubbed his eyes and turned to Cindy. "You missed the fireworks."

"I had a feeling something was about to happen. How bad was it?"

"What a piece of garbage. He tried tearing me a new one. I don't know what the hell his game was. I had to get away."

"Political drama," Cindy explained to the women. She asked Kevin, "Are you okay?"

"I'll live." He tried to smile, but was still fuming. "Later," he mouthed. He turned to the others. "Sorry, long day."

"We'll live," Gina said.

"I would've done the same thing," Shelley said.

"I might have," Cindy said wryly. She flashed a grin, a lock of hair falling across her face.

Kevin smiled and leaned up next to her. "So," he said to Robin and Gina, "I guess you guys are from my old stomping grounds."

"You used to live in California?" Robin asked.

"Portola Valley. And my closest friends, more my adoptive parents, live in Woodacre."

"Oh, wow," Robin said. "We're right next door, in Petaluma. Been there recently?"

"I was visiting them before I flew out here. When I leave, I'm heading back." As he listened to himself, he thought of Max and stared off for a moment.

"Well," Robin said, "you *have* to look us up. Where do you live now?"

"Princeton."

"Any plans on moving back?"

"Oh, I don't know. Only if the Institute for Advanced Study relocates, I guess."

"It was worth a shot," Gina said, elbowing her friend. Robin shrugged.

"It's my favorite part of the country," sighed Kevin.

"So Stanford boy," Gina asked, "why not move back?"

"Ah," he shrugged, "you stay in one place a while and it gets complicated. In my twenties, it was easier to pick up and go. Now, you think about it a little more."

"Oh, listen to the old man," Gina said. Had they been written, her words would have read as sarcasm, but spoken as they were they landed empathetically.

"Be nice," Robin admonished.

"I am. I just think life is as easy or hard as you make it."

"What are you doing here?" Shelley asked Kevin.

"I'm sorta on a job interview. They want me to run the program, though God knows why."

Robin cut in. "We told her who you are."

"It's a pleasure to meet you," Shelley said. She shook his hand, holding on longer than a casual greeting called for. "I can't believe what we just saw! And to think it's all because of you!"

"You're a popular guy," Robin said.

Kevin waved her off. "Trust me, after this week I'd settle for anonymity."

A moment later Don Frazier appeared, accompanied by Greg Huntington. "Hey, Dr. H," Frazier said, "I heard what happened. Don't listen to that idiot."

Kevin shrugged, as if to say I'll get over it.

"Just as well we left," Frazier added. "I checked on the boats for the finale. We had to add two hundred more because of the cloud's size. But it's all on schedule. We'll be starting in ten minutes. You'll love this!"

"It really is something," Cindy added, introducing everyone.

"So how does this whole thing come off?" Kevin asked.

Frazier turned serious, enjoying his role as expert. "Each cloud is different. As it cools we image it. We scan it from all angles, even from space. By plotting density, how it's growing, we form a digital diagram. We have an extensive database of stellar nebula images. We compare them with the particular cloud that evening. They help color and lighting angles. We then plot out the best placement and how many boats we need. The lights we use are the most powerful LED lamps in existence, thousands of times more powerful than anything in industry. They're one of the most expensive items here. We essentially create an enormous three-dimensional light sculpture."

The anger at Ridge was waning. Kevin felt a buzz. "This is like the swankiest club I've ever been in," he said. "You have music, dancing, a light show, great women." He motioned to them, getting smiles in return, and added, "I wonder what else to expect."

A moment later, Tim Cain slipped out of the shadows. He nodded to everyone, pausing to greet Cindy, a hint of hops following him. He glared at Kevin, standing beside her, but in the dark, no one noticed. He carried a tablet, which he gave to Don Frazier.

"Are these the final figures?" Frazier asked. As Cain nodded, Kevin watched intently. Since that morning he had tried to work a balance towards Cain, growing contemptuous of him yet not wanting to provoke a meaningless encounter. The incident on the boat though was fresh in his mind. After the episode with Ridge, loosened up by wine, he felt no inhibitions and glared back. No one as yet picked up on the tension between the two.

Cain stared at Cindy, enough for her to catch his eye in kind. "Tim," she said politely, "this is Robin, Shelley and Gina." As they said hello, she asked, "What's doing at the Center?"

"Uh, it's okay." A quizzical look came to her and he added, "Um, you know, it's just hectic. The preparations for tomorrow."

"What's happening tomorrow?" asked Robin.

"We have people coming in from Hawaii," Cindy explained. "The governor, legislators, a whole crowd from the Defense Department in Washington."

"Yeah," Cain grumbled, "and we don't need them." He glared back at Kevin, and this time, it was noticed. Kevin was fed up.

"You've had a bug up your ass ever since I got here," he pointedly told Cain. "What the hell's your problem?"

The group fell quiet. Frazier, caught off guard by the animosity between the two, tried to get his bearings. Cindy clenched the railing.

"You're the problem," Cain sneered. "All this is your doing."

"You know, after that bullshit you pulled on the boat, I don't need to hear from you."

Cindy broke in. "Tim—"

"No. None of this would be going on if he hadn't shown up."

"Tim, that's enough," Frazier said.

"No," Kevin interrupted. "I've been dealing with this since this morning. You got something to say? Say it or shut up. I'm tired of you and your attitude."

Instantly, Cain lunged, pushing Kevin away from Cindy. Kevin grabbed the railing, preventing himself from toppling over but yanking his shoulder in the process. A surge of pain erupted and his glass flew off and shattered, spraying wine over Frazier's pants and Gina's foot. The tablet went flying too, and although it remained intact, it would never function again. Robin and Shelley yelled, while Cindy and Frazier went for Cain, trying to restrain him. They had barely reached him when three security guards swooped in, subdued the still yelling Cain and hustled him away.

Frazier and Cindy helped Kevin right himself as Robin held Gina. Shelley ran off to get something to wipe off the wine.

"God, I'm sorry," Frazier said sheepishly. "I don't know what that was all about."

"Bouncers. I forgot about bouncers," Kevin said as Shelley reappeared with paper towels.

Frazier looked puzzled. The women began laughing nervously.

"I got it," said Gina.

"The only thing you forgot to mention about clubs," seconded Robin. "Bouncers."

"So," Kevin asked Cindy as he righted himself, "I look okay for the press?"

She forced a smile while brushing his shirt. "I don't know what to say," she confessed.

"Why? That wasn't your fault."

"I feel like it is." Kevin wasn't sure what she meant.

"I don't know what happened," Frazier kept saying.

"I smelled beer," said Robin. "But I don't think he was sloshed."

"He wasn't," Gina added. She looked at Cindy. "So what happened between you two?"

"Nothing, I swear," she said, mortified.

"You never hooked up?"

"Never. I had a cup of coffee with him, that's all." Robin and Gina eyed each other knowingly.

"I have to find my roommate before she forgets I'm here," Shelley said after a moment. "It was nice meeting all of you." She then vanished into the night.

"I guess that scared her off," Gina remarked to the considerably smaller group.

"Well, I have that effect on women," Kevin grinned.

"You should be so lucky," Robin said.

Just then, the music tailed off. Lights began to dim.

"We're getting ready to start. You sure you're okay?" Frazier asked Kevin, who nodded and followed the women as they scouted out some empty chairs.

The announcer came on: "We are about to begin our finale. There is no safety warning associated with this segment of the evening. We invite you to find a comfortable seat, sit back and relax. You are about to witness one of the most spectacular events ever staged by man. The staff and associates of Tuvalu Alofa wish you an enjoyable viewing experience."

"I need to check on what just happened," Frazier said, excusing himself. "I'll see you in the morning. In the meantime, just sit back and enjoy. I'll send over a server, if you want anything." As they thanked him, he said goodbye and left.

Cindy felt an irrepressible urge to comfort Kevin. "Are you okay?" she inquired.

"Little banged up in the shoulder, but I'm okay. Been a while since I was in one of those."

"I'll get you an ice pack." Before Kevin could even stop her, she dashed to a bar.

"By the way," Robin said, "that happened because you're stealing his thunder."

"You're a threat," Gina agreed. "He's got it for her. She's got it for you. And he knows."

Kevin shook his head and a server arrived with a tray of wine and piña coladas.

"Listen," Kevin told them, "you don't have to hang. Don't let me cramp your style."

Robin smiled. "We're big girls. If we get bored, believe me, we'll leave."

"You're interesting," Gina added. "Besides, one of us might get lucky."

"Oh, Christ," Kevin said, blushing. "I don't even know how to handle that stuff anymore."

"You handle it like you always did," Gina said.

"Well, I *never* handled it well, even when things were normal, whatever that was." The words had barely left his lips when the lights dimmed further. A background piece began with an ethereal feel. Kevin said, "I was told this is called *An Ascent*. I don't mind a touch of irony. For once it has nothing to do with me."

"Brian Eno," Gina smiled. "Great piece. One of my exes was an Eno fanatic."

"Among other things," Robin quipped, finally getting the chance to elbow Gina back.

Cindy returned holding ice cubes wrapped in a towel. She pressed it against Kevin's shoulder. The chill was a shock but felt soothing. He smiled softly and she sat leaning into him, holding it in place.

"Just watch this," she said.

The Eno piece was a departure from the smooth jazz and island beat of the evening. As the volume increased, the lights on the distant myriad of boats went on. A thousand enormous LED lamps began to glow.

The illuminated cloud slipped softly into view.

Kevin slumped back in his seat. "Oh, my *God*," he whispered, joining in the surrounding hushed chorus of Oh my God's ascending into the music.

It was as if an arc of celestial energy had burst forth from another dimension for the singular goal of granting earthly viewers a glimpse of what the Creator envisioned when summoning the universe. Spread over dozens of miles, the lights were imbedded in and behind the cloud, causing it to glow with a light that seemed supernatural. Vast pillars of gas glowed yellow and green, blue and purple, maroon and pink with the majesty of untold eons, not the entities that had materialized hours ago. Some of the lights backlit towers of gas against the sky. Jack was right; as much as the blast was a sight, by any stretch this was more astounding. It was incomparable, the most beautiful thing he had ever seen.

"I can't believe this," Kevin said. They leaned back in their seats, lost in the spectacle radiating in the heavens above.

Sixty-six

In 1995, NASA released pictures of the Eagle Nebula taken by the Hubble Space Telescope. The immense towers of gas glowing with a primordial light fired the public's imagination like few outworldly images before or since. Calls flooded the TV stations that broadcast the images from people wanting to know more about them and how to get copies of the pictures. And as much as Kevin too had been taken with them, what he beheld now was on an entirely different order.

Eta Carinae had ascended to a celestial event. It broke through the stratosphere, extending from one end of the horizon to another. Ever more slowly, it continued to expand, spawning huge new columns of gas. Whispers of bluish-purple and pinkish-orange and a symphony of every color between accorded the island a glow he never could have imagined. The rowdiness, the raw unfocused sexuality of a typical night-club that had been present just minutes ago was gone in a simple flick of a switch. The resort had cut all ties with the club scene and had gone off in an incomparable direction.

Cindy had just repositioned the ice pack on Kevin's shoulder when he lifted it off. "Getting cold," he said warmly, thanking her.

"Are you okay?"

"I'm fine, thanks. It helped."

"No," she whispered, still leaning against him. "I mean, are you *okay*?"

"Just thinking," he said, gazing off at the display.

"For us here, after you've seen a few, you get off watching the reaction of first-timers as much as watching the thing itself. Really amazing, isn't it? But I have a sense that after what you've been through, you have something different on your mind."

"With everything else that's going on with this thing," Kevin said softly, "I didn't think it would affect me. I hoped it wouldn't. And it bothers me to say it, but I needed this." His ambivalence had roared back.

Robin and Gina listened intently.

"What do you guys want people to walk away with?" Gina asked Cindy.

"A sense of awe," she responded. "We discuss it a lot. I think it's missing in this day and age. People are jaded about so much. Maybe it's why they're so taken with the images from Hubble. It lets them connect with something bigger than themselves. This is the closest they can get to being in space and seeing live what's in those pictures. In some of the bigger explosions, the mushroom cloud shape alters. It doesn't look like a nuclear blast anymore. It really looks like an interstellar nebula."

Kevin agreed. It was strikingly similar to images the space telescope had captured. Added to the majesty was the Milky Way, perfectly complementing the cloud like a brilliant nebula against its host galaxy.

Scientific musings aside, something else was occurring. Whether conscious of it or not, every person there held an undeniable awareness of a presence larger than themselves. It wasn't religious. And it was above the actuality of pure knowledge that the best of science imparted. Spiritual didn't quite do it justice either. It was a pure essence of transcendence. The music, the warm breeze, the exotic scents, the alcohol, the cloud; there was nothing like it. The sense of wonderment so often shunted to the back burner by the inanities of modern life was reawakened in a stirring incontestable event. And it was then that Kevin had an ominous realization. Elliot Hanford was probably having the same reaction. It meant he was already planning out the next phase of that damn vision of his, and for Kevin, arguing against it just became that much harder.

Even in the dim light, the two men drew attention. The purpose in their step as they approached clashed with the mood in the compound.

"Dr. Herter," said one as they walked up. "Security. We wanted to see if you were all right."

Kevin sat up. "I'm okay. Shoulder's a little bruised, that's it. Thanks for asking."

"Dr. Herter," the second one asked, "are you interested pressing charges?"

He frowned into a shrug. "Ah, just as soon forget it. But keep him away from me."

"Okay, sir," said the first guard. "We would like to get a statement from you. We don't want to bother you now, but could you stop by the Security Office sometime tomorrow?"

"I think I can fit that in. Morning, afternoon?"

"Whatever fits your schedule, sir," he said sympathetically. "It'll only take a few minutes." As Kevin nodded back, the man turned to Cindy. "Miss Russell, would you please follow us?"

"Is everything okay?" Kevin asked.

She looked at the guard. "Tim Cain?" He nodded. She turned back to Kevin. "Sorry, but I have to deal with this." Although he'd already said that he'd be staying with her, walking away now when she felt a connection growing was a letdown. "I'll see you later, huh?" she said as she left with the two guards.

"Well, that kind of sucks," Gina said.

Kevin leaned back with a mischievous grin. "Are all women troublemakers like you guys?"

"Oh, no. Most are a lot worse."

"You better believe it," Robin laughed.

"Well," Kevin shrugged, "I don't know she's that pissed. Trouble seems to follow me. Anyway, she's putting me up, so I'll see her later. My room's off limits with what happened earlier, so I didn't have a place to stay."

"You should have said something," Robin said. "We could have put you up. If she snores or something, look us up. We have loads of experience with troubled guys." Kevin laughed.

"Just know," Gina said, "you will be hit on." As he brushed her off with a wave of his hand, she added, "Do you really believe for a moment she's not going there? Robin, kick him in the ass or something. He needs it."

Kevin took a long sip of his wine and smiled, almost sorry he hadn't spoken to them earlier.

Sixty-seven

Jack Raden appeared out of the darkness. "I had a little trouble finding you."

Kevin gazed up, hands on his belly, embracing his empty glass. "I don't know why," he snorted. "I've just been sitting here minding my own business."

"Yeah, I heard about your little run-in."

"Good news travels fast here. I told you, might want to keep an eye on him."

"They did, just not with him going off on you. He's being questioned, but since you didn't press charges they're letting him go. The captain's okay with it. We'll see who he talks to. If he's smart he'll behave himself, though I don't think it's in him." Raden greeted Gina and Robin, and then said to Kevin, "We need to talk."

"Every time you say that," Kevin said, rubbing his shoulder, "things happen." He motioned to the sky. "I thought at least you'd want to know what I thought of that."

"I was getting around to it." Raden pulled up a seat. "So, what do you think?"

"What do I think?" He eyed Gina and Robin. "What I think is you don't make it easy." He slouched down. "When I was growing up in Michigan," he added, "we'd have these autumn afternoons when the weather was just great. We had acres of tall grass and goldenrod with these gently rolling hills and stands of silver maples. After school, we'd ride our bikes out and lie in the fields. The sun would dart in and out and you'd just lose yourself. Then the breeze would pick up and the grass and goldenrod would ripple and the underside of the maple leaves would shimmer. They really look silver. It was just perfect, like floating in a sea of white gold."

"When you're a kid," he sighed wistfully, "it's funny how your mind works. It would be a lazy fall afternoon and I'd think of Christmas. Ever see a Christmas tree lit by the late afternoon sun, gold light reflecting off the tinsel? I'd see the fields, the leaves, the sun, and I'd imagine I was in the middle of a thousand Christmas trees. Time would just stop. And you'd just know that somewhere there was that one perfect tree all lit up waiting, and lying under it somehow everything would be all right …" He tailed off, losing himself in the scene.

Robin and Gina sat entranced by the scene he painted. Even Raden, familiar with Kevin's early years and thinking he knew what to expect from him, was waylaid into silence.

Kevin caught himself. "I'm a poet and I don't know it," he allowed to quiet laughter. "I'm sorry. I haven't thought of that in twenty years. That thing out there; my God, look at it. It's like the most perfect Christmas tree."

After a minute, the music shifted to another ethereal piece, one with more of a beat.

Gina fixated on Kevin. "I hate to see it end," she said.

"People would be here until the sun came up," Raden said. "The lights can't take it that long." He smiled. "Overhead. Gotta watch the bottom line. There's a few more hours though."

"Speaking of overhead," Kevin said, "what the hell was that upstairs? For weeks they kiss up, tell me how they can't make do without my help, then that asswipe goes off on me? And Hanford sits and says nothing? What the hell's their problem? First those two, then that idiot Cain. You may not make things easy, but they sure do. *Real* easy."

Raden paused. "Take a walk." He and Kevin excused themselves. They had gone about twenty feet, when Raden said, "Good cop, bad cop; presidential style."

"Oh, for crying out loud."

"I keep telling you, learn. Nothing's happening by accident. Did Ridge piss you off? Make you feel a little guilty? Maybe more open to hearing Hanford out? Then they accomplished what they wanted." Kevin groaned and Raden said, "Hey, it worked. You had things to talk about. They didn't want to hear. And they certainly didn't want to hear about what happened in California. So Ridge blustered up a diversion. Hanford sat back and watched. And tomorrow, he'll be your best friend."

"Son of a bitch," Kevin sneered. "I've had it. Was the thing in my car his doing too?"

"Probably not. They're just taking advantage of it."

"So why the bullshit now?"

"I don't know. But right now, I can't talk about it. Something's come up. I need to go pack."

"Huh? What do you mean?"

"I have to take a little trip. I'm leaving within the hour. I'll be back before Sunday."

Kevin's eyes widened. A feeling of vulnerability flew through him. "That's a bolt out of nowhere. Jeez, Jack. I kind of got used to having you around."

"Pete Natano knows what's going on. Keep in touch with him. He's the person here you can trust the most. Just hang loose and remember—you're still in the driver seat. Don't take any of this personally." He reached into his pocket. "It does free up a room. Here's the key. It's a suite that's similar to yours, a floor down, without the you-know-what that happened."

"I'll have to find Cindy then," Kevin said as he took the card. "Wow, Jack. Kinda feels like we met years ago."

"I know. I spent more time with you the past few days than with my kids the past few months." He held out his hand. As Kevin shook, he felt the USB stick. "Just pocket it, quiet-like," Raden said. "As soon as possible, look it over. I think there's more on it than we realized. Now I'm especially curious about what Lisa Whiteman has to say. By the time I get back, maybe we'll know." He glanced about. "Lot more here than we bargained for. That whole episode with Ridge might have something to do with it, so just keep cool. When Hanford talks, hear him out, but don't commit to anything. Get into their heads for a change. Don't let on any more that Ridge got to you. Just say you had a long day. And put him off until I get back."

"Oh, jeez. What's their game?"

"I don't know, but they're forcing it. You're not used to this, so just watch your back."

Kevin bit his lip and surreptitiously slipped the stick in his pocket. "I guess I should say have a good flight. I hope whatever you have to do goes well."

Raden thanked him and warmly shook Kevin's hand again. "Tell the girls I said goodbye and to keep you honest. I'll see you on Saturday." He turned and disappeared into the night.

Sixty-eight

Christian Deloy sat in a corner of the mall, scrutinizing the Tuvalu security offices a hundred yards away. The big cup of fresh fruit was almost gone when he saw Tim Cain leaving. Cain didn't see him in the dark and was about to pass by but turned to the low whistle skittering through the crowd.

"Community service or litter patrol?" Deloy quipped as Cain approached. He polished off a chunk of pineapple. Juice dripped down the fork onto his hand.

"Huh?"

"Never mind," Deloy frowned, knowing he shouldn't have tried. He stabbed the last piece of fruit, a chunk of mango. "Are you hungry?" Cain mumbled no. Deloy finished the fruit, wiped his hand on his shorts, then said, "Let's head to the beach. It's darker."

On the way, he eyed his hapless lackey. An Indiana native who thought a sense of belonging might come by way of the Marines, Cain never quite fit in, arriving in Tuvalu through an affinity for high tech and managerial capacity. He came to Deloy's attention after a furtive search of the resort's personnel records. Essentially friendless, socially inept, his short fuse and hots for Cindy Russell made him the ideal patsy. Deloy had groomed him for months.

"Man," Deloy began, "maybe lighting into him wasn't the best idea, but I can't blame you. I would've done the same thing."

Cain turned. "Yeah?"

"Took balls. It's a matter of respect."

"I'm glad somebody sees it for what it is," Cain said, nodding vigorously.

"And don't worry about trouble. If they had anything they would've charged you. Sometimes a guy's gotta say enough! And if that don't sink into that fuckhead Herter—"

"I been trying to get him to back off since this morning."

"You think he'd take the hint. Even that thing in his room today didn't make an impression. Man's got a problem."

"I know. He had enough chances. Whatever happens now, least he was warned."

"That's how we see it. But I want you to know, I can appreciate what you did. You got every right to feel the way you did."

"Thanks, man. He's fucking lucky he didn't press charges." As Deloy grunted in agreement, Cain added, "He had no fucking right to move in on her."

"See, that's the respect. Anyone could see you two were getting tight. She was starting to open up—"

"You think so?"

"Definitely. Word on the boat is she was loosening up. Things take time. I'd be pissed too if I spent time getting a woman to warm up and a dickweed like that muscled in."

"Thanks, man. I knew you'd see it. I thought it was me."

"No way, man. You got nothing to feel bad about."

They were nearing the beach. Ahead several fires had been lit, warming the people there with an orange glow. Deloy motioned to a darkened area. "Okay, Tim," he said, "something's come up. It's serious. First, I gotta say I appreciate everything you've done. I know it's a risk for you, but now you see the shit going on and what they're trying to do." Cain nodded, and Deloy said, "So, here's the thing: We think he may be using her as some kind of easy mark."

"Huh?"

"Yeah. I knew you'd feel bad. But all the evidence points that way. There's a memory stick that was taken from Sandia; real important data. We think there are buyers for it here. The thinking is Herter's somehow involved peddling it."

"I didn't like that fuck from the minute I saw him. Even before he hit on Cindy."

"That's the situation. Now, we think he pressured your higher-ups to have her put him up. Believe that shit? *She* has to put *him* up." As Cain began fuming, Deloy added, "I wanted to tell you because we don't think Cindy knows what she's being set up for—"

"That piece of shit," Cain snarled. "You know, I can see him doing that."

"Yeah. It's nasty business. If he hides it at her place, she won't even know what hit her when they show up. And I don't want anything to happen to her. She seems like a very nice person."

"She sure is."

"That's my impression. Nice enough not to know she's being used. Now, I know you. You and I are forgiving people and wouldn't believe she was involved in any kind of espionage business, but the feds or the cops here, well, you know them—"

"Better than you do." He paused. "So, what do I do?"

"You know her apartment. Our guess is Herter hid the thing there, in either the place itself or his luggage. It's a simple USB stick. If we can get it back without her knowing, she'll be in the clear. I'd like to involve her as little as possible. We'll arrest him later."

"Thanks," Cain said, sighing in appreciation.

"Yeah, she don't deserve this. She's good people. He's strutting around here like he owns the place. I know she's still at the station. You have some time. Go through her place and find the thing. Anyone messes with you, deal with it how you want. You don't take any more shit." He slipped Cain a key. "This should get you in. And wear gloves."

Cain grunted. "Just keep her out of it."

"Absolutely. This is important work you're doing. She don't need to be dragged into it. And if she didn't notice you before, she sure as hell will now."

Cain gave a self-righteous nod then headed toward the apartments. Deloy stood momentarily then strolled toward the mall, thinking to himself that the time spent cultivating this fool had been well worth the effort.

Sixty-nine

Lisa Whiteman gnawed at her thumb like she was back in Catholic school hiding it from the nuns. The dress she had worn earlier was now hanging in the closet; the jeans and a black T-shirt she changed into were more suited to her current activities. Although the explosion and the light show that followed were impressive, as she knew they would be, she allowed herself but a moment of enjoyment. Too much whirled about.

From her secluded perch in the mall she watched Kevin Herter. She saw him bolt from the president's side. She watched him meet up with several attractive women. She witnessed the altercation, recognizing the man who jumped him as the one Christian Deloy had met earlier. Curiosity aroused, she continued observing from the shadows, unsure about which side he would eventually come down on.

It was when Jack Raden approached him that her interest rose. As the men parted, her anxiety grew, and she made a beeline for Raden, meeting up with him at the end of a row of serving tables.

"Jack," she observed, "you look determined. I noticed Kevin earlier. Did something happen?"

"You could say that." He forced a smile. "It's a good thing I ran into you before I left."

"Left?"

"I'm heading out for a day or so. There are a few things I have to check out. That stick of yours is starting to attract attention."

"I figured it would. I was hoping you would share it."

Raden smiled. "You know. I like you." She flashed a grin. "Yeah, I showed it around. So far, no one's been able to tell me what it is. Of course, you know, but you're not ready. I gave it back to Kevin and told him to piece it together."

"I have to hold back until he sees me. He'll know what's there. When he sees it, he'll want to talk to you real bad. Does he intend to meet me?"

"Yeah. I want him to look at it first. I know you're afraid we'll give away the store but a lot's happened since we spoke. Ridge went off on him like a rabid dog, and someone who works here did a number on him right after. I wouldn't expect too much from him tonight."

"Yeah, I saw. Okay. I suppose I'll hang tough until tomorrow." She sighed. "I'll have to."

"He's staying in my room, suite 227, if you want to talk to him. You might also want to meet up with Cindy again. She's in the apartments, Building B, number 236."

"Thanks. I know you have to go. But first, a couple of things. The guy who attacked Kevin is the same guy I saw talking to my husband's aide."

Raden's eyes widened. "That's Tim Cain. That's interesting. Thanks."

"And one more thing. Kevin's smart enough to piece together what's on that stick. But so you know, there's a small file on it. It'll get a lot of people very nervous, both the ones who see it and the ones watching them." She looked around then said, "Jack, take very special care. I'll see you Saturday." With that she walked off.

Lisa walked about twenty feet before stopping. For the first time since arriving, the frenzied energy that had kept one step ahead of her tangled emotions had chance to pause and she caught up with herself. She froze, unsure what to do.

Eta Carinae still blazed away, but she could not look on it for long. The more she watched, the more pressing was the realization that while it may have begun in the mind of Kevin Herter, its actuality was something she had created. Exhibit One in the Law of Unintended Consequences. By going out of her way to deter it from happening, it happened anyway, creating what she feared most. The terrible beauty of the thing became unbearable. Her thoughts cascaded in a torrent of second-guessing.

After reaching out to Kevin Herter, would he even look at the stick and see the data he now held? Would he think her a Hanford pawn? What was the president's game? Knowing what he knew, how could he do what he was doing? Where was Tom? How could they have lived and worked so long together and wound up so far apart? What was Deloy up to? Why did she fear him so?

So much could be traced to her doorstep. The disparate elements removed from each other, that came together in a maelstrom of horrific beauty. So real as to be unreal, so intimate as to be unrecognizable. It made her want to separate herself from herself.

It was then that she glimpsed Tim Cain beating a line through the Mall. Her anxiety had renewed purpose. She followed, staying a discreet distance behind, not too difficult in the crowd.

He passed the gift shop, walked beneath the portico, then headed toward a group of buildings about a half mile away. The stream of people faded to a trickle. She darted in and out, hiding behind palm trees and bushes, glad now that she wore a black shirt and dark jeans.

Halfway down the path, he looked like he was about to turn around. Heart pounding, she scooted behind a large palm, scrunching up against the trunk. Her mouth turned instantly dry. After several moments, she peeked out. He was gone. She cursed to herself, not sure what to do. Behind her was a young couple hand in hand. She asked them where she could find the staff apartments. They pointed to where she had been headed.

The apartments were nicely maintained three-story buildings. They could have been any apartment complex in Florida or Hawaii. The grounds were quiet, and Lisa realized most staff were still working. She entered Building B, then went to the second floor. The hall light was low, the floor empty. She passed rooms where music played, and a door marked Utility.

Apartment 236 was up on the left. A dim light shone from under the door. Though sure Cindy would have no problem seeing her, it was late and she was hesitant about knocking. A low shuffling noise, the sound of items being moved came from inside. She wavered, then knocked.

The sounds inside ceased. She paused once more, and then knocked again. "Cindy," she said spoke softly, "it's me, Lisa. If you're not up for company, I can come back." Again silence, then steps and a noise like a patio door sliding open. She instinctively felt the steps were from a man. Something wasn't right. She backed up. Her heart beat faster and she hastened to the stairway.

The attack came without warning. As she passed the door, the figure bolted from the Utility room. In an instant he had his hand around her mouth. Arm locked about her waist he pulled her inside and shut the door. A muffled shriek was all she could manage in the dark. The hand was so tight she couldn't breathe. It reeked of soured fruit, the most vile scent she would ever suffer again.

"Move or scream," the familiar voice said, "and I'll snap your neck so fast that by the time your feet know it, your brain'll be dead. And you know I can."

"Mmmm!" she mustered, trying to squirm, heart pounding.

His hand gripped tighter, covering her nostrils so she couldn't exhale, as his arm locked her waist firmer. "Again, Cool Hand Lisa. What we have here is a failure to communicate. Want me to keep the hand on until you stop moving?"

She shuddered no, managing a moaning "mmmm" to Deloy. She could never forget his voice.

"Okay. We're gonna have ourselves a little chat. First, I'll flip on the light." His elbow hit the wall and a dim bulb lit. The closet held cleaning supplies and mops. She still couldn't see him. "Good. So, we feeling a little nervous?" He tightened his grip and she moaned again.

"Good. Feel the adrenaline? Interesting sensation for those unaccustomed. See, you're getting an introduction to hormones you never knew anything about." He loosened the grip on her nostrils, and she quaked in her breath deeply amid another "mmmm."

"Good. Let's continue. You've become quite the investigative reporter in a short time. I'll tell you though, you really should stick to your area of expertise. I mean, that thing out there? Amazing! The Spy vs. Spy thing you're not cut out for. So I'll do you a favor, okay?"

She didn't say anything, and he tightened his grip on her mouth. She let out a strangled "Ummmm." Her heart pounded so hard it felt like it would erupt from her chest.

"That's better. Now, I'm going to loosen my grip and let you stand. Here are the ground rules. No turning around. No screaming or loud talking. No pounding. Any of those happen, you get to find out whether there's a God or not. Understood?" She hesitated, then shuddered her head up and down. "Good!" He released her and she staggered to her feet, still facing away from him.

"We won't even pretend you don't know who I am. Frankly, it don't matter. So here's how we'll proceed. Tomorrow you wake up, have a nice breakfast, get on a plane, fly back to Hawaii and forget all about your excursion into Investigative Journalism 101. I needn't lecture you on the areas you're butting into that are none of your business, so let's just say this: you're so far out of your league, it's laughable. In a week when you calm down, you can have a laugh and think about how close you came to becoming part of your story."

She was breathing hard, her arms folded tightly in on herself. "Christian—"

"Very good."

She paused. "I don't know how you think you're going to—"

"Before you go on, I want you to know I feel very appreciative tonight. That thing outside? You should be proud! I enjoyed it! So let's not go anywhere we might regret."

She took a deep breath. "Then you tell me what Tom will say—"

"He'll say 'Job well done' or something like that. You're so sure of yourself, you never stopped to think I might be doing advance work for him."

"I don't believe that."

"There's a lot you don't know about your better half," he laughed. "So I don't know how sympathetic he's going to be about this misunderstanding."

"Misunderstanding?"

Deloy breathed deep and cleared his throat. "You've been a very good girl, so I'll allow you to turn around."

The words had barely left him when Lisa realized that the fear now coursing through her would skyrocket by confronting him. She slowly turned around, knowing that Deloy instantly read it, his steely eyes staring down from his six-foot three frame without the slightest shade of emotion.

"Misunderstanding," he said with a malevolent grin. "It so often happens; one person thinks one thing and the other doesn't get what they're saying." His gaze narrowed, milking every drop of fright from her precisely on target. "Now there's another misunderstanding we need to correct, a little matter of a memory stick. See, someone copied some very sensitive data from a computer in New Mexico. It seems they misunderstood they weren't supposed to do that. So, if you let me know where it is…"

"I don't know." She began to tremble, and tried her best to control it.

"That's so disappointing. I know you don't have it, because you would have given it to me. Right?" She stared, and felt her lip quiver. "So, it must mean someone you spoke to has it. Now I know you wouldn't want to get yourself involved in anything—"

"I don't know where it is," she said softly, horrified that it sounded like a plea.

"I suggest you find out before you leave. It would be a shame getting on your flight not having helped us. Then again," he chuckled, "it would be a shame not getting on your flight."

She stared, feeling every terror-stricken drop of blood freezing in the warm closet.

"Okay, I think we're done with our little chat. So here's how we'll proceed. You'll turn around and I'll turn off the light." She began to shake, convinced she was not long for this world. "No words or sounds. When the door closes, you wait five minutes. Then I suggest you head back to your room. You look like you could use a good night sleep. Room 168, I believe, right? Now turn around."

Five minutes later, her heart ready to burst, she bolted from the dark closet, tears of terror spraying in the night.

Seventy

The lights were dim and the sounds were hushed in the Intensive Care Unit at Marin General Hospital in the wee hours of the night. Max Rosenkranz was in a deep sleep. He had been slipping in and out of consciousness throughout the day, and his condition had been downgraded to critical. With tears and sadness, accompanied by Mike and Barbara Yahr, Jean had signed a DNR order for her beloved husband before going home for a semblance of a good night's sleep before beginning what she knew would be her vigil.

At the other end of the unit Cliff Abreau was asleep as well, as were the eight people between them. Abreau had rested comfortably since the attack, and while still listed in serious condition, he was scheduled to be transferred to the general population in the morning. His wounds, though extensive, had stabilized. Their dressings needed to be changed regularly, but the blood he had lost had been replaced. Almost five hundred stitches were keeping Abreau from bleeding out, and with pain killers he was managing to sleep the night. He had been able to make a preliminary statement to the police, and was set for a more extensive interview that afternoon.

The lights flickered as they had done several times that evening, not only in ICU, but on several other floors. The electrical glitches that had originally been passed off as a wiring issue were now being examined as a software problem in the electric grid. Staff on nursing stations on several floors had begun checking patient monitors as a precautionary measure, since there was some indication that backup systems were affected as well. Everything was set, precisely as planned.

The hackers flipped the switch a minute later. At 2:48, lights and monitors next to Max and five patients nearby went out. They also went out in what appeared to be random fashion on several other floors. The ICU nurses immediately headed to the darkened rooms, using the ambient light from the rest of the unit to make their way and check on the patients.

The woman timed her entry into Abreau's room at precisely the same moment. In her nursing uniform she slipped through unnoticed, the syringe held surreptitiously at her side. With her gloved hands, she injected the anticoagulant into the saline drip, and left silently without attracting attention.

Abreau would sleep for another thirty minutes before the hemorrhaging began affecting him. The massive dose of Coumadin would prove fatal before anyone in Intensive Care knew what was causing the uncontrolled bleeding. By then the woman would be long gone. Security cameras would later pick up on an unidentified female in her thirties, but as she had no record and was extensively made up, no facial recognition program would identify her.

Seventy-one

On Vaitupu it was approaching eleven p.m. While the mall was still crowded, people had begun heading to their rooms. A lone jet could be seen ascending, its lights a compliment to the illuminated cloud in the distance.

"Guys," Kevin sighed, "I think I'll call it a night. It's been a long day."

"Will you be all right?" Robin asked.

"I suppose," Kevin shrugged. "The Atomic Channel has a great line-up tonight." He paused. "I gotta say, it's been great meeting you. As far as spending a first day with people goes, I don't remember another quite like it."

Robin drew him close and warmly kissed his cheek. "Thanks," he smiled. "I needed that."

"Hold on," protested Gina. "Give here." He grinned and she gave him a hug and a kiss on his forehead. "It's been great meeting you too," she said. "We're leaving Saturday. Do we get to see you the rest of the week?"

"Oh, yeah. Just get in line. Loads of people fighting to see me."

"Fuck you," Gina said, pretending to knee him in the groin. "Just remember, we've been turned down by better guys than you, so don't be a smart-ass."

"Damn right," Robin seconded.

Kevin gave up a sad smile. "I don't know why." As he heard himself say the words he knew he meant them, but he realized how his feelings had changed from scant hours earlier. Thoughts of sex, of relaxing, of giving the place a chance, all were gone, replaced by something like a dead zone, a numbness. Both women smiled though, and he added, "You guys have been great. I can't think of anyone I'd rather have around when things blow up in my face."

Gina laughed. "We had a great time."

"We're packing it in soon ourselves," Robin said. "I'm an early riser."

"But I'm not," Gina said.

The line was lost on Kevin. "How do you work that out?" he asked. "Separate rooms," she added, with a touch of melancholy.

He nodded, still missing the moment. "Well, have a good early and a good late night sleep. I guess I'll see you tomorrow." He said goodbye and slouched off into the night.

As he walked, Kevin fiddled with his third room key of the day. More than tired, he was drained. He wanted to speak with Cindy but didn't know how to reach her, so he decided to go to Jack's room and try to send her a message.

When he arrived, he saw his belongings on the bed. Jack had come through again. Within minutes, wearing just his shorts, he stared out from his balcony on the night. The crowds had thinned. The Terrace was nearly empty. Eta Carinae still glowed, still gracing the heavens with grandeur. It had expanded further, lighting the entire eastern sky.

As he gazed out, his thoughts drifted to the subplot embraced by so many there. How ironic. How he detested what this had become. And yet, so beautiful. How unsettling it all was. Fate, too, it seemed, was not without a sense of irony, but it was its sense of proportion that so often went unappreciated. He stood, zoning out.

A knock at the door broke the moment.

He lumbered around the bed in the dimly-lit room to the anteroom, and opened the door to see Cindy. He smiled, tired but pleased to see her.

"I didn't know how to reach you," he said. "I'm glad you found me."

For a moment, she paused. She then walked in, kicked the door closed, took his face and brought his mouth to hers. She explored its recesses, caressing the sides of his head, his ears, his hair. Her kiss was soft and warm, and moist. She soon moved her hands down and drew at his bare chest, teasing his hairs.

Without a word, she stood back and slipped off her dress, her bra, and her panties.

A rush of earthiness pulsed through him at the unexpected encounter. Amidst the countless conceptions vying for supremacy, the simple sensuousness of flesh and sweat would be the night's culmination. How ironic. And fitting.

She quickly cast his shorts aside, pushed him to the bed and mounted herself on top. He ran his hands across her face, her breasts, and the nape of her neck. An echo of perfume drifted above the track of lust, while stealing through the rafters the iridescence from the nuclear eruption undulated across her pounding form like a strobe, shaking along with the bed. Her long thick hair swirled about his chest and neck. As they reached their moment together his mind emptied in a flood of clarity.

In time, he returned and tried to speak. She once more covered his mouth, a motion tendered with the timeless compassion of an all-too-knowing smile.

Friday, April 8

Seventy-two

Marin County Airport in Novato, California was enveloped in fog as the Learjet bearing the logo of Braddock Industries made its approach at dawn. Across the International Date Line in Tuvalu it was Friday morning. For Sharon it was still Thursday. Losing a day, gaining one, she was too tired to tell and too unsettled to care. She had managed to sleep fitfully during the five-hour flight, but as the only passenger on board, the sleep held a heightened awareness bordering on surreal. It was like sitting in a snug chair with a cup of tea watching the Weather Channel announce that a hurricane would be bearing down on your home. Too tired to sleep for long, she would periodically awaken with the realization that she could have scarcely imagined her situation just days ago, even more so when she crawled into bed earlier that night.

Much as he had done for Kevin, Jack Raden's hastily arranged series of moves led to the flight. What he'd lacked in time was made up for by the flexibility of his nimble mind, and in the fifteen minutes Sharon had taken to go inside and pack, a limo had pulled up to her house.

Right before she left Raden called again and told her to sit back and relax, that everything would be taken care of. Torn between fluster and fatigue, she agreed to give it a chance.

With the police escorting her limo to the township border, she felt a momentary sense of relief. And when she got to the airport and saw others there to help her, she felt a little better still. But as she boarded the plane in the dark, the entirety of the night took over. Over the hum of the engines and the vinyl scent airplanes always seem to have, she took her seat, taken with just one thought—what the hell did I get myself into?

Raden as yet knew nothing of what she had seen in the file he'd sent. But he knew the alarm it created. She was now a target. The problem was that the people interested in her were in a completely different league than anything she had ever experienced. In the time it would have taken him to convince her to what degree, they would have already dealt with the problem.

He needed to get her out of Princeton as quickly as possible, without her giving him a hard time. At one point, she would have dismissed any concerns about her safety and done little to protect herself. He knew that had changed, but wasn't sure just how much. The trick would be putting her to work. He wanted to meet her face to face, to learn what she had seen, and it was important that Mike Yahr be there as well.

Roger Braddock was another retired NSA analyst who like Mike and Raden had done very well as an investor. The trio had formed a close association during their agency years, one that continued after Mike and Roger had retired. Braddock owned a townhome in Sausalito and had an office in San Rafael, a few miles from Mike's home in Woodacre. And while a resident of Maui, he happened to be in California that week. Raden had scarcely needed to detail the situation to him when he had a limo appear at Sharon's house. A quick ride up Route 1 and the New Jersey Turnpike, and less than an hour later she was strapped into one of his jets awaiting departure from Newark Airport.

Sharon had been told that a Mike would be meeting her, but the lanky guy on the tarmac wasn't what she expected. Aside from his dreadful chauffeur's cap, his black sweatshirt, black jeans and boots made it look as if he'd stepped out of a cowboy bar. The fog was so heavy that just twenty feet away, he seemed to be an apparition. She paused; no one else was around.

Then he held up the sign. Had it been a major airport, a limo driver holding a piece of paper bearing her name would have been routine. But seeing this lone character in a sleepy regional airfield holding a paper that read "Hey Sharon" was just enough of a non sequitur to tease out a weary nod. She stepped onto the runway.

The man held out his hand. "Mike Yahr," he said sincerely. "It's nice to meet you."

She shook in return. "Jack told me to expect you but I wasn't sure, with that hokey hat." She sighed in fatigue. "I've had one fucked-up night."

"I heard." He removed the cap. "One-time joke. It served its purpose. My wife will like what you said. She said the same thing." In the misty air Sharon managed a smile. She was struck by his mane of sweptback silver hair.

The pilot exited and handed Sharon her bag, then headed toward the small terminal.

Mike took the bag. She thanked him, adding, "I guess that goes with the chauffeur's job, too. But what's the union going to say if you don't wear your hat?"

"In my union hats are optional," he smiled. "Mike's Local, 103." She laughed and he said, "My wife's president and CFO. I'm just the designated driver. But the perks aren't bad. You'll see. Come on, I'm nearby." Sharon zipped up her red hooded Princeton sweatshirt against the cool damp air, and they began walking.

She followed him to a dark-green Ford Explorer that materialized out of the mist.

"I've heard a lot about you," Mike said as they got in.

"I promise not to hold that against you," she yawned.

He smiled, and pointed to two large coffees in the car's cup holders. "Help yourself."

"Hard Lemonade?" As he chuckled no, Sharon took the cup beside her. Alongside was an aromatic bag.

"Fresh-baked peach muffins. My wife made them," Mike said. "One of the perks. I know about your place in Princeton so this may not be up to your standards, but—"

"No, I appreciate it. Thanks." She broke off a piece of muffin. "Oh, that is *good*," she said as she ate. "So's the coffee. I needed that. Thanks."

"My wife's other job," he smiled. As they drove off, a gray sedan entered the road about a quarter-mile behind them. Though it blended in with the fog, Mike noticed it directly, having seen it earlier. He said nothing, but kept an eye on the rear-view mirror.

"Tell her I said they're excellent," Sharon said, "and I know about those things. I think I just found a new supplier."

As he thanked her, they turned south on the Redwood Highway. "Oh," she noted as the traffic picked up, "the 101. And we're in?"

"Novato, about an hour-and-a-half north of San Francisco. We're heading down to San Rafael and Woodacre, where I live. Have you been to this area before?"

"A few times with Kevin. I guess you've met him." As Mike nodded she asked, "What's with this fog?"

"You get used to it," he said, sipping his coffee. He was glad it hadn't lifted.

"Okay, so now that we're buds you can tell me what I'm doing here. Where are we going?"

"Jack said you were subtle," Mike smiled. "First, we're stopping at my house. You can meet my wife. Then I'll fill you in. There's a lot I could go into that I've already told Kevin, but I'll explain it this way: I saw the clip of your altercation on TV."

"Oh, fucking great," Sharon groaned. "I just started putting that behind me."

"Sharon, it wasn't your fault; just the same this isn't, nor Kevin's. But like it or not, the two of you are being dragged into this, and you have to deal with it. Whatever you saw on the file has people pretty riled. Before going out to help Kevin, we need to know what it was. And trust me, you don't need to be in Princeton."

"And, why's that?"

"It's just better you're not in Princeton right now," Mike said, sniffing the cool air.

She glanced at him. "I'm too tired to ask," she said, stifling a yawn. "So, did Jack tell you one reason I came out here was to take Kevin's head out of his ass?"

"Yeah, something like that," Mike laughed. "I can see him needing it. And you doing it."

She smiled. "So what's your deal with Jack? You guys army buddies or something?"

He took a deep breath, glancing in the mirror at the car tailing them. "It's a bit more complicated than that."

As they passed through San Rafael, Mike spoke of his years in the NSA, of meeting Jack Raden and Roger Braddock, and how Raden had involved Mike with Kevin.

Sharon listened, incredulous. "How do you deal with this bullshit?" she asked.

"That it most certainly is," he nodded, eyes on the rear-view mirror.

"Then maybe you can tell me what the hell's going on?" she grunted in frustration.

"I promise. As it unfolds." He took a sip of coffee.

His words were measured, echoing something he hadn't experienced in some time. The vehicle shadowing them was six cars back. To a casual observer it would have escaped notice but he had seen this before, the subtle shifts in motion, the lane changes at just the right moment. Though he didn't miss the bureaucratic bull, he did have a passion for field work. There was an exquisite sense of expectancy to it, like driving to a first date. He was certain that his car, parked in a secluded spot at the airfield and concealed by fog, had been bugged. It left him initially wary, a feeling quickly supplanted by a healthy dose of resolve. He would use it. He began to sort out what might lie next.

"Okay," he said, hiding any concern, "my house is ten minutes away. Jack should be landing in an hour. He'll meet us at Roger's office in San Rafael. By the way, he flew you out here."

"I don't know whether to thank him or give him a knee." Mike laughed. Unaware of his concerns, Sharon groaned, "I told Kevin this shit would happen."

"Sharon, there was no way for either of you to know. Even with our contacts, we don't know what they're after. We just know the reaction that file is getting. That alone, I don't like."

Sharon forced a smile. "You're going to like it even less."

"That's what we figured. Whatever you saw may be something you don't fully appreciate. But thing is, you did see it. There are people who don't like that. If you show us what's there, we'll be better able to tell what's going on." He turned to her with a wry look. "I'm assuming you brought a copy."

She nodded.

"If you don't mind me asking," he added, "what really made you come out here?"

She frowned, which curled to a sneer. "I hate this whole thing, everything connected to it. Always did. And even though we split up I hate what they're doing to Kevin. I hate hypocrites."

"Fair enough. I'm not sure if Jack told you, but Jean and Max are my neighbors—"

"Oh, wow! So *that's* your connection. I really like them. I've missed them."

"They've spoken about you too. I like the painting you did for them."

"Thanks. I have one of Jean's pieces as well. It's one of my most prized possessions." She rubbed her eyes. "I know they must hate this shit, Max especially. He'd run their asses up a flagpole. We always had that in common, our mutual disgust for bullshit. I know he's dealt with it, and how frustrated he got."

"Oh, yeah," Mike sighed. "That's Maxie."

"I get it in my field as well." She finished her muffin with a gulp of coffee. "I always get asked why I don't work in the City. Every art school has these painters. They take out their tubes of *cadmium* yellow, *cobalt* violet, *titanium* white, *manganese* blue, and they sit for hours mixing up a huge gob of paint trying to get *juuuusssst* the right color. Then they dip in their triple zero brush with the three hairs on it, make one dot on the canvas, tear off the sheet of palette paper with the paint and throw it out. And the painting's to raise awareness about toxic metals leaching into ground water from landfills. And the critics get wet between the knees." Mike snickered, and she added, "I just didn't want to deal with it any more."

"I can see that." Mike turned on Sir Francis Drake Boulevard toward Woodacre. He glanced again in the rear-view mirror. The car following them turned discreetly, keeping pace.

Without missing a beat he said, "Excuse me a minute." He picked up his phone. "Hey, *paisan*," he began. "We left the airport. We still on at your office? Eight thirty? Okay, I'll tell her. Yeah, we'll bring the file. Ciao." He turned to Sharon. "That was Roger. He's looking forward to meeting you. And trust me, you'll want to meet him as well."

"Okay. What's with the *paisan*?"

"Both of our mothers were Italian."

Sharon finished her coffee. "What's he got to do with seeing the thing?"

"You'll see."

"All right. So, you live near Max and Jean?"

"Right behind them."

"I'd really like to see them. I think I'll stop over."

Mike sighed, and turned to her. "Sharon, there's something I have to tell you. Max is very ill. Prostate cancer. It probably won't be long."

She looked stricken. "Oh my God, no! Kevin never said a word!"

"He just found out himself."

"Are you *kidding*? Why on earth—"

"Max didn't want to tell him."

"Oh, for crying out loud," she gasped, visibly shaken.

"Yeah. I feel for him; all of them. That's why he and Jean moved out here. Max didn't want Kevin to see it. I know you're fond of them, and them of you. I thought you'd like to know."

Sharon turned to Mike with a pained look. "How did Kevin take it?"

"It knocked the stuffing out of him. It's one of the reasons why I wanted you to stop at my place first. I'm sure Jean is already there."

"Oh, I can't believe it," Sharon said, rubbing her wet eyes.

Seventy-three

It was still early, just after seven a.m. when Mike opened his front door. Barbara and Jean were having coffee in the den. Jean looked up with a sad smile. "Hi, Mike," she said. "Good morning."

"Hiya, doll," he greeted her. "I have a surprise for you. Someone wants to say hello." With that, Sharon poked her head through the door.

"Oh, my *God!*" Jean shrieked. She leapt up and arms outstretched, ran over. Sharon came in with a tear-filled smile and they embraced.

"It is so good to see you!" Jean cried. "I can't believe you're here!"

Between smiles and tears, Sharon tried to keep her composure. But when she said, "Jean, I just heard," she began to cry. Jean pulled her close and stood rocking her.

Mike had walked over to Barbara and sat on the back of the couch. Fighting back tears herself, Barbara took his hand.

Sharon brought her hands to her tear-streaked face. "I'm supposed to be there for you, not the other way around," she blubbered out. "Jean, I'm heartbroken."

With a smile that glowed through her anguish, Jean said, "Oh, sweetheart, I'm just happy to see you. We've missed you the past few years."

"I missed you too, so much. I didn't realize how much until now." She turned to Barbara. "I'm sorry; I didn't even say hello. I come in your house like a stranger and start bawling away."

Barbara walked up to her with a warm smile. "Sharon, it's so nice to meet you. Please, sit down."

As she and Jean sat, Sharon wiped her eyes and smiled. "You make a great muffin," she said. "I want you to supply me. And I'm going to embarrass your husband, but we also have the same taste in chauffeur hats."

"I like her already," Barbara grinned. Mike let loose a stream of raspberries and flung the hat on a chair. While Jean warmly laughed and Barbara got Sharon a cup of coffee, Mike explained to Jean why Sharon had come, and that he'd been the one to tell her about Max.

"I am so sorry this is how you had to find out," Jean said, taking

Sharon's hands. "My husband, God bless him," she said, shaking her head, "I couldn't talk to him about this. He just wouldn't tell Kevin. That's why you didn't find out either."

"Jean," Sharon smiled sadly, "it's all right—"

"No, it's not—"

Sharon shook Jean's hands. "No, it is. It's okay."

Jean looked up at Mike. "All this craziness. Sharon and Kevin don't need ours as well."

"You don't have to worry about us," said Sharon. She asked about Max, and Jean sighed. "Oh, sweetheart, there's not much to say. He's sleeping a lot." Her voice cracked. "Right now they're just trying to keep him comfortable."

"Shit, Jean. I wish I could have been there to help."

"There's nothing you could have done. You have enough on your plate. Max would say the same thing. Just having you here now helps, more than you know; Kevin too." She paused. "I am so sad about you two."

Sharon bit her lip and shrugged. "Just wasn't meant to be." She slunk down into the couch.

"Listen to me," Jean implored, drawing Sharon close. "I know you don't have much time. There's plenty to say about that, but first things first. I'm not going to lecture you, but you need to hear something before you see him." She sighed. "In a way, we watched you both grow up. You were coming into your own when we first met. Look at you now," she glowed, "you're accomplished, famous. And though you may not be aware, you're wiser. You survived. So don't sell yourself short. You've paid your dues."

"Okay, I suppose."

"Not suppose." She sighed. "You know Max and I were hopeful you'd wind up together. But if it didn't work, don't let anger get the best of you. Do you know how mad I was at Max for what he did? What good did it do? Now especially, appreciate how short life is. It doesn't mean there aren't things to be angry about. Just don't make it about Kevin."

"I know what you're saying. It's hard; letting it go." Sharon sat back, trying to take it in.

"You know you'd be jumping down someone's throat by now," Jean smiled. As Sharon grinned, she added, "You know you have a good head on your shoulders. You've been right a lot more than you give yourself credit for. I've come to think that as much as being attracted to a person, we're attracted to their baggage. Dealing with their issues I think helps with our own. But if his issues keep hounding you, you're not going to let anyone get close, and you'll miss out on a lot."

"You know, I've missed you," Sharon smiled sadly.

Jean smiled and turned to Mike. "A woman knows when a man's making love to her and when she's being screwed." He laughed, and she told Sharon, "Women do it too. If you're bringing your baggage into bed and putting on your pants even before he's finished, he'll know. It won't matter that you're keeping yourself from being hurt. He'll be as angry as you've been with Kevin, even though we both know it's other things, right? If that happens, you're not being fair to the guy, or yourself. So find a way to let it go. You get older, you learn to appreciate what a good night sleep is worth."

"I had to fly three thousand miles to get a lecture from my second Jewish mother," Sharon told Mike and Barbara. As they laughed, Mike's cell phone rang. He excused himself and left the room.

Jean kissed Sharon on her forehead. "My second child this week," she said, breaking up. "I'll be a mother just a little longer. A lot happened with Kevin. When he said goodbye, he left two parents for the first time…" She wavered, but held up, shaking her head. "So much we don't deal with. Max was so, so stubborn. But by the time Kevin left he knew the mistake he had made. I don't know, maybe God kept him going until now so he could finally learn what he needed. I know when Kevin left there was a peace about him I hadn't seen in I don't know how long. It was a wonderful gift. It completed something in him that he was working on a long time. My heart goes out to you too; no one deserves this load. So much of it is unfair. You've never had closure on so many things, and with everything going on I'm sure it's even more painful."

Jean went on determinedly. "But even though we hoped to see you together, we wouldn't want to see either of you unhappy. Something had to be missing, for both of you. Like Max, Kevin may not have done what was needed and that left scars, but it wouldn't have been any good if his feelings weren't there, or yours. And realize that would have been true for your father. If that's how he was going to be, he wouldn't have done you any good by being around either. Children want their parents but you didn't need him hanging around just to do you a favor. He didn't have it in him to give you what you needed. I know it left scars. The same was true with Kevin. So try to let it go. Find it in yourself to forgive him, even if it's under your breath or just in your heart. Perhaps in years to come you'll be happy you did."

Sharon by now was crying. Jean brushed back her hair. "There's one more reason I'm telling you this. There's plenty else to be angry about."

"Oh, I know it." Sharon tried to compose herself.

"What we heard has us very worried. Kevin needs help, even if he won't admit it. There's no one who knows better how to stick it to someone," she said as Sharon gave a knowing laugh. "And heaven knows, those jerks deserve it. Focus on where your anger needs to be."

Just then, Mike walked in. "We need to head off," he said.

Jean nodded, and held Sharon's hands. "Don't let this stand. You know what to do."

"Jean, I really love you. Thanks." Sharon gave her a hug.

"Just be good to yourself," Jean smiled. "And listen, Kevin is stopping here on his way home. I don't think it would be a bad thing if you joined him. I don't mean to make trouble for the two of you, but you're always welcome here, okay? I think he'll be all right with that."

Sharon nodded, and as they rose, the two women held each other and softly cried.

Seventy-four

As Mike pulled away Sharon floated a kiss to Barbara and a teary-eyed Jean, standing in the driveway. The Explorer took the curve in the street, and the two were quickly out of sight.

Sharon sat rubbing her moistened eyes. In the twenty minutes they had been at Mike and Barbara's house, the fog had deepened, reflecting the headlights as a ghostly glow. It echoed a listless unrest that got her fidgeting. Unable to fight it, she tensed into a yawn that seemed to go on.

Mike focused on the twisty, narrow roads. He now asked, "Are you hanging in?"

"It's what I do." She sniffed the damp air, which emptied into a sigh. "Mike, thanks. I appreciate your kindness; Barbara's too. She's so nice. And Jean—"

"No thanks necessary. Life's funny, the way the Big Guy upstairs evens things out. We hit it off with Max and Jean right from the start. The four of us grew very attached. It didn't take long to see why they moved out here. Jean's right, Max wouldn't deal with it. I tried to get him to open up. He wouldn't go there. So, we decided we'd just enjoy the moment. It was always close by that he was on borrowed time, but there was a sadness about them that went beyond his illness. Seeing you and Kevin with them, I finally get it."

"I can't get over it. But too much happens in life for me to buy into that evening-out shit."

"Well, I don't know. I'm not any kind of big believer, but I sometimes see a sense to things."

"Oh, I'm no atheist, like a lot of artists I know. I believe in God. He just pisses me off."

He gave her a wry smile. "A little cynical in our old age?"

"I earned it," she glared. "Life's plenty hard. And God doesn't make it any easier."

"How so?" He didn't answer her stare.

"Because He can never relate to us. Life is full of doubt, but not to

Him. He doesn't know what it's like not to know, so He can never empathize. He's God. Knows everything. Always has an answer. Always works out. I get very pissed when people tell me to trust in Him. My life's full of not knowing things, and no one who hasn't lived it can understand what I go through. Yeah, He made me. But until He can walk a mile in my shoes, fuck Him."

Mike puffed out his cheeks and was about to respond when Sharon added, "Sounds like you have some faith. Supposedly, faith is believing in things you can't prove. Well, God can prove anything, so I guess He doesn't need faith either. So again, fu—" She grimaced. "I should listen to Jean and switch to decaf. See what happens when you get me started?"

Mike smiled to himself. He eyed the rear-view mirror, but didn't see the gray car.

"I don't want to hit another sore spot," he said, changing subjects, "but your ex is an interesting guy."

She sighed. "That he is."

"I didn't spend much time with him, but I have to say I like him."

"So do I, when I'm not looking to wring his neck." As Mike laughed, she felt a chill. "I forgot how raw it can be here," she shivered, zipping up her sweatshirt.

"That's why I grabbed my jacket." As he spoke he pressed at the bulge tucked into the left side of his waist. His black windbreaker had done as intended, concealed it.

A little ways up they turned left. Sharon was curious as to where they were headed, but for the moment was content to take in the ride.

"I always thought it was pretty here," she noted, "in a rugged kind of way. It does have that Northern California feel. I take my work with me. On a morning like this, you see the houses surrounded by those big conifers and bay trees; you see the hills disappearing into the fog. Makes you want to run home and paint."

"I can see that." Mike eyed his rear-view mirror. Several cars had joined the morning commute. He wasn't sure if any were interested in them, but knew to keep looking.

"So, we're headed to your friend's office?"

"I thought first we'd make a quick stop. Jack was telling me about your work, how you like to paint things from nature that you personally find. There's a state park less than ten miles from here. I was hiking last week and saw some deer antlers. We get blacktails here. I thought if you're interested you can pick them up, then we can head to the office. It's not far."

"I appreciate that," Sharon smiled. "Thanks. My kind of pit-stop. I can recharge my batteries."

The road to San Rafael by way of Sir Francis Drake Boulevard meant a right on San Geronimo Valley Road. Most morning traffic headed that way. Samuel P. Taylor State Park and its quiet 2,700 acres of grassland and redwoods lay fifteen minutes in the opposite direction. After Mike turned, he kept his eye on the rear view mirror. Sure enough, headlights cutting through the mist, one gray car turned left.

The houses began to grow sparse. Glancing behind them, Mike said, "I know you remember Jessica Enright."

"Need you *ask*?" Sharon let out a contemptuous chortle.

"Well, yeah, I need. I have a little story to tell you." He described the interview he, Barbara and Jean had run, and how it had mushroomed into a fiasco.

Sharon listened, first incredulous, then howling. "I can't believe it!" she cried. "Couldn't have happened to a nicer person!" She sat shaking her head, laughing up a storm. "Well, maybe things do have a way of evening out, sometimes. I knew I liked you guys."

"It is kind of ironic, I know, maybe more than you realize. We didn't mean it to happen, but it's had an effect on all this. Right now she's in damage control."

"Yeah, well don't expect me to feel sorry for her."

"I wouldn't. The thing is that now, she probably wouldn't expect you to either. It was a wake-up call for her. Before she left here, I had a talk with her. She's been knocked down several notches. She knows it. For various reasons I offered to help her. She's pretty chastened. I wouldn't be surprised when you're out there if she made an attempt to reach out to you."

Sharon crossed her arms. "You mean she's out there too?"

"Probably by now. She first stopped in Hawaii. I'm not telling you what to do, but you will probably see her. Now, this is where things start to get a little more serious."

Mike told Sharon about Kevin's experience, the device in his car, the motel break-in and Jim Leffert's death, finishing with Enright's close call in Honolulu. Sharon sat stunned, realizing that her situation was now on an entirely different level.

Mike eyed her. "Like your Princeton episode, a little more than we bargained for."

Up ahead was the park entrance. The air by now was leaden with fog. The road and land around them faded quickly into a sheet of gray. Mike slowed as they entered.

"I don't know what to say to all that, except holy shit." Sharon took a deep breath.

"Yeah. It's obvious all this has touched a nerve—"

"Oh, you think?"

"The point is, this episode now has a life of its own. Expect it to blow up very soon. You may find this surprising—Jessica decided to hit the books. I know what you think of her but she's paying her dues, uncovering a lot of information. A lot's going to come out. That call I got at the house? The other cameraman who was injured in that stabbing died this morning. He had been doing okay, but he was slipped something, an anti-clotting drug. He bled to death."

"What the fuck is going on here?" Sharon became agitated.

"Loose ends being tied up." Mike again pressed his waist, feeling the gun's handle.

"What the fuck does that mean?"

"Sharon, just keep cool a little longer." Behind them, the headlights were no longer visible.

Ahead, the road forked. The main road curved sharply right, while a small drive branched left. It then paralleled the main road. There were no other cars around, nor were any hikers to be seen. "All right," Mike said, taking the side road, "there's a campground ahead. We'll stop and walk a bit, then head to San Rafael. Just one more thing, you do know what's on the stick, right?"

"Oh, yeah. And you're going to piss in your pants." Drained, she rubbed her eyes.

Mike crept along the narrow road. All around, fern-laden redwoods lay deep in mist.

Sharon was by now antsy. "Mike, I don't know if I'm up for this anymore," she complained. "All this talk isn't sitting right. And I don't know how you can even see anything with this fog now." She was about to tell him to head back when a bright light inundated the car.

Mike floored the Explorer. "Get down!" he yelled as Sharon slammed back in her seat.

The driver of the car tailing them—a big gray Buick—had turned off its lights when Mike and Sharon entered the park. Masked by fog, he'd quickly closed in. When the car was almost upon them, he hit its high beams. The flood of light was just enough to cut down Mike's view.

"What the—" Sharon began to blurt out when a sharp crack sounded. The right rear window shattered, spraying the cab with glass. She screamed and instinctively raised her head.

"Dammit stay down!" Mike exhorted, pushing her into the seat and ducking while trying to steer. The SUV tore through the narrow road swerving left to right. Terrified, Sharon bounced about, clenching the shoulder strap so tight one of her nails dug into her fist and drew blood. Mike knew the road but the Explorer hit a bump and she smacked her head against the window. She grunted in pain and tried righting herself, but Mike kept pushing her down.

"Down, dammit!" he shouted. The rear window took two more bullets, one of which whizzed by his shoulder. She yelped in horror as it blew open the windshield, showering them with glass. She yelled, "What the fuck—"

"Just keep down!" Up ahead was the campground. "Hang on! I'm going to—"

The Buick rammed the Explorer's right bumper; the SUV spun left. Mike tried to compensate and almost immediately caught his left front tire in a shallow depression. They cartwheeled and overturned into a shallow ravine on the left side of the road. Sharon shrieked and Mike yelled to hang on as the air bags blasted out before the Explorer came to rest on its driver's side.

A sound of a car slamming its brakes and gravel grinding was heard, followed immediately by the slam of car doors and shouts.

Wedged up against his shattered window and air bags, Mike frantically tried to extricate himself and get to his gun. His hand was cut and his chin scraped, but he ignored it. Sharon was screaming, her exposed hands and face cut and scratched, while she still desperately clasped the shoulder restraint, which she had never released.

"We have to get out!" Mike huffed.

"Fuck you!" she snarled. "Go where?" She tried to right herself.

Mike scrambled desperately for his gun, hearing more sounds of braking followed by shouts.

Steam hissing from the hood along with a whirl of dust and the SUV's overturned angle made it impossible to see what was happening outside. Sharon managed to pop her seatbelt latch and promptly tumbled into a still-struggling Mike.

"Dammit, Sharon!" he ripped, "get off!" Gunfire erupted, followed by shouts.

"Get me the fuck out of here!" Sharon screamed. She began kicking her way out, but only managed to work herself on top of him more. He tried pushing her off to maneuver his gun but she crowded his arm, and he couldn't grasp it.

"Sharon, hold on!" he pleaded. "Keep quiet and get off me!"

"Fuck that!" Weighted down awkwardly, she tried clawing past the air bags to pull herself up by her seat belt. She had just pressed her foot up against the steering column to get leverage when more gunfire erupted, and someone yelled, "You fucking move and I'll kill you!"

"What is this shit!?" she yelled, wild eyed, as several men appeared around the Explorer. She screamed, "Who the fuck are you people!?!"

Gasping, Mike pressed against the door. He pushed his leg through the broken window onto the ground and forced himself up. He held her, saying, "Sharon, just hold it. Are you all right?"

"Are you fucking *nuts*?"

"Mike, you okay?" came from outside. Sharon immediately shot Mike a look.

"Rick?" he called back.

"We're clear," he replied. "Are you guys all right? We'll have you out in a minute."

Agent Rick Hughes appeared at Sharon's door and looked down at her and Mike, both blood-streaked and covered in bits of shattered glass.

"I'm going to prop open the door," Hughes declared, a hammer in his hand. "Cover your eyes."

Sharon lay panting, her legs twisted about. She looked incredulously at Mike.

"He'll get you out," Mike advised her. "Just sit back."

"Watch your eyes," Hughes called. As Mike and Sharon looked away, he pulverized the shattered window pane until it crazed into a faceted sheet, crunching open a hole big enough for his hand. He undid the lock then pried up the door.

Hughes motioned, but still stunned, Sharon froze.

"Come on now, young lady," the fifty-ish Hughes beckoned. Another agent appeared, and between the two they helped her out and took her to a nearby bench. She was scratched and bloodied by bits of glass, but otherwise okay. Another agent gave her a blanket and bandaged her wounds, while Hughes went back to help Mike.

Once out, Mike stood crouched over, hands grasping his knees, heaving labored breaths. "I'm too old for this shit," he grunted, as Hughes smiled. After several moments, he righted himself. Though lightheaded, he sauntered over to Sharon. "Are you okay?" he asked sincerely as she sat huffing and bewildered.

"What the hell happened?" she asked. She turned and looked about.

Three black Jeep Grand Cherokees sat parked around them, and a flat-bed was just driving up. The Buick, doors open, sat to the side, its right front end dented.

Then she saw the body.

"What the fuck is this?" she screamed and bolted up. "Who the hell are you people?"

Mike motioned to an agent, who took a sheet from one of the Grand Cherokees and covered the body, a rather nondescript middle-aged man. Sharon looked away and noticed another man sitting in the back seat of another SUV. He appeared handcuffed.

"That was supposed to be you," Mike explained, gesturing to the body. "And me."

"He's right," Hughes said. Her jaw dropped. She pulled her blanket tighter.

"Timing's everything," Mike said to Hughes as the flatbed was positioned to pull out his Explorer. One agent appeared with a body bag; another exited the Explorer and approached Hughes.

"The headrest?" Hughes asked. The agent nodded. Hughes handed Mike the small listening device. "Not the worst place," he noted, "un-less—"

"You happen to be looking for it." Mike turned to Sharon. "Come on," he said. "We have to get out of here before the local constabularies show up. I'll explain on the way."

Seventy-five

"Sorry about your car," Rick Hughes said as they pulled away from the campground. "You're right; timing was everything."

"Another thirty seconds we would have been in place." Mike eyed his wrecked Explorer. "Ah," he shrugged, "it was time for something new anyway."

Despite all the action it was only eight-thirty a.m. The Grand Cherokee cut through the still-dense fog on its way to San Rafael. The morning rush was well along, and nothing about the SUV gave any hint about what had just gone down. The incident at the park was over in less than five minutes, and seventeen minutes later nothing remained to show it had happened. Mike's Explorer had been towed, the Buick was driven off by an agent and the three Jeeps had scattered. One transported the prisoner back to base; the second, containing the body bag and other evidence, vanished to parts unknown. The third, bearing Sharon, Mike and Hughes, blended in seamlessly on Sir Francis Drake Boulevard, just another car heading to work. With Hughes driving, Mike sat in the passenger seat. He was banged up, but his immediate concern was their rear-seat passenger. He turned and asked, "How are you holding up?"

Clutching her blanket Sharon swayed with the road, nursing a container of hot coffee. The steam drifting off and her sleepy pose stood in stark contrast to her countenance, which was beyond severe. She stared, not yet up to talking.

Hughes eyed her in the rear-view mirror. "Hi, Sharon," he said. "I hope you're feeling better. We weren't formally introduced. Rick Hughes. It's nice to meet you, though under the circumstances I'm sure you don't feel the same." He had a Tommy Lee Jones quality about him, a no-nonsense roughness around the edges but a reassuring accessibility beneath. Oddly enough, despite what she had endured, neither of these guys left her feeling threatened. She said nothing, just grudgingly nodded.

"I want you to know. You're holding up exceptionally well. I've seen people in your situation that had to be hospitalized."

Mike agreed. "Sharon, he's right; you're doing great."

She frowned, and then blew on her coffee.

Hughes glanced at Mike. "So what happened? Retirement making us sloppy?"

Mike rubbed his bandaged chin. "I remember in San Lucas when—"

"Yeah, yeah. Not in mixed company."

There was a pregnant pause. Sharon asked, "What was San Lucas?"

"A little incident a few years back," Mike said, "which I won't bore you with."

Sharon took a sip of coffee. "Okay. Who's going to be the first to talk? Who are you guys?"

"I'm sorry for what happened," Mike said with a sympathetic eye. "We were half-a-minute away from it working out, but sometimes it doesn't go off as planned."

Hughes eyed Mike and nodded. Mike sniffed and cleared his throat. "There's a lot we can't tell you," he explained. "Suffice to say, you just got caught up in an NSA operation."

"Holy shit," she groaned. "What the fuck is going on?"

"My friend Mike here was a company man until he retired two years ago," Hughes said. "We miss him. His ops had good reads on people and subtle—"

"You fucking call that subtle?"

"Compared to some things, yeah. If you had made it to the campground, it would have gone down a lot different. We were in position waiting for you."

Mike showed her the bug that had been planted on his headrest. "They listened in our entire conversation, starting at the airport." As Sharon dropped her head in disbelief, he glanced at Hughes. "As did others."

"We figured once you landed they would make a move on you," Hughes added. "I think they reckoned that with a retired operative and a neophyte artist, they could slack off."

"I like being underestimated," Mike said. He looked back. "Must be some deal on that memory stick."

Sharon stared a few moments. Then she said, "You set them up."

"That's about it. Before they did it to us." He turned to Hughes. "A car the color of fog was a nice touch, and with the lights off. I think that's what threw me off that last minute."

"Yeah, even for someone still on payroll, it was hard to see. I'll give you that."

Sharon leaned forward. "So all that shit we were talking about, that was to egg them on?"

"I don't know if I'd call it 'shit'. I did need them to hear you'd seen what you had seen. We needed a secluded place. And I didn't want to tip them off. They were ... predictable. Problem was they struck half-a-minute early."

Sharon shook her head.

"Guess they didn't get the memo," Hughes quipped.

"Oh, fuck you," Sharon sneered.

Mike turned back to Hughes. "Rick. I ever introduce you to my friend Sharon?"

"And fuck you too! The shit I've been dragged into...."

"Well," Hughes said, "Mike here's been dragged out of retirement and lost his car for this." As Sharon frowned and looked away, Hughes added, "I know you didn't bank on this. You and your ex, I'm sorry to say, you're caught up in something pretty intense."

"Why? What the hell did I do? Open an email?"

"Pretty much, yeah. And you should know that these days, some-time's that's enough, like making a phone call is as well. But there's more to it than that."

"And what did Kevin do?" Sharon asked with a sneer. "Who the hell's doing this?"

Mike bit his lip and flipped the bug around in his hand a few times.

"Listen," she snapped, "I've had guys yanking my chain my whole life. I'll be damned I take it from you. You want to know what's in that file, you tell me what the hell's going on."

Mike looked at Hughes, then said, "Let's wait until we get to Roger's office. You will want to meet him. Jack should be there by now. But Sharon, you need to know, we weren't kidding; that was supposed to be you lying on the ground back there. If you were still in Princeton, your worrying would have already been over." She blanched, and he added, "Enough of that for now. A lot's happened since you got here. There are a lot of things coming together. We'll talk about it all when we get to the office."

Seventy-six

Across the ocean about an hour later, Jessica Enright stared out the window. "My God," she said to cameraman Erik Lundquist, "look at the thing." Lundquist, the plane's only other passenger responded in silent awe, and continued snapping a stream of shots.

For the second time that day, a Braddock Industries Learjet was beginning a descent within the Pacific Rim. It was 5:35 a.m. on Vaitupu, light enough to see what the previous night had spawned. Though knowing what to expect, they were stunned.

The plane had departed Maui at midnight. Like all arrivals following a detonation it cut a series of atypical maneuvers on approach. Pilots never flew through the atomic clouds. Instead, they arced around, then came in under the mushroom cap. These flights were as popular with pilots as with the passengers they carried. The clouds were at peak size, affording a spectacular view just before beginning to drift off. The largest event in resort history had resulted in a cloud spanning a hundred and forty miles. It was just beginning to break up, allowing the sunrise to poke through and bathe the plane in a backlit stream of gold.

Lundquist got off more shots. "My friend's brother flies in here," he noted, a hint of a Swedish accent the perfect compliment to his dangling locks. "Thanks for the opportunity. I always wanted to see this."

"Don't thank me just yet," Enright said, trying to be funny but thinking that it was probably just as well that her response played apprehensively. She pressed her bandaged cheek which still stung, then turned back to the window, all the while reflecting on how much had changed in so short a time.

The flight arranged by Mike Yahr had come about much as the one Jack Raden had organized for Sharon Velazquez. There was something of Kevin Herter's reality to it. She first saw it when Joshua Emerson reacted to the simple words, "It's a boy." What followed was all out of proportion to what she could have imagined. Knifings. Crime scene tape. Bullets whizzing by. Once the challenge would have been just moving on. But by sheer stint of her showing up lives had ended. Fortunes had been upended. She herself had come within inches of having her head blown open. She knew her life had changed, and she herself along with it. What a week earlier meant adjusting to a new reality now meant adjusting to a new her.

The night was like a runaway train. After bolting from Integrated Microphysics, she'd wanted to call Emerson. But while confident that her disposable phone wouldn't be traced, she wasn't sure about Emerson's line. There was a thin but clear line between prudence and paranoia and to her surprise she recognized the distinction. It struck her how she had begun considering events differently. She'd called Mike. With Michelle Sapena and Glen Daniels, they had forged a strategy from a dark alleyway on Ala Moana Boulevard.

Mike knew the beach shooting's visibility made any furtive operation a long shot. Their surest bet would be making the system work for them. He needed to call in favors. Those behind the incident would move swiftly to work a narrative in their favor, which meant Enright, Sapena and Daniels would be put into untenable positions. At best. After suffering Rivers and Sanderson, dodging gunfire and bandaging wounds, they were open to anything. Mike hung up, made some calls, and called back. They were raw enough to listen.

Mike knew the head of naval intelligence at Pearl Harbor. He called Oahu, and was soon speaking with Honolulu's chief of police. Sapena and Daniels would remain in what amounted to protective custody. It would head off those trying to get to them; any arrest warrants or hits on the two were for the time quashed. Enright needed to be spirited off to Tuvalu. With the focus on Sapena and Daniels, it would buy her some time as well.

By now, she needed no explanation for not taking a commercial flight. Mike made two additional calls. The one to MSNBC's New York studio had an intern rousing Emerson with a knock on his apartment door. When he heard what happened, Emerson used the intern's cell to call Enright. He knew she would need someone behind the lens. Abreau was convalescing in California, but Erik Lundquist, a seasoned cameraman, was on vacation in Maui and jumped at the assignment.

Mike's next call had been to Roger Braddock. Braddock's operatives spirited Enright's baggage from her hotel room and helicoptered her to Maui. By midnight, Lundquist had met her at Kahului Airport and Braddock's Learjet had taken off for Vaitupu, landing just before sunrise.

Peter Natano sat on a bench nursing a fresh cup of coffee. It was a beautiful dawn. He especially liked this time of day, before the island had stirred. The blue-green maritime dawn, the purple clouds rimmed in gold. The salt-teased ocean breeze. It was sublime. He loved his land, even with remnants of a twenty-megaton nuclear explosion to the east. The program and the changes it wrought had yet to detract from that. The nine small islands of Tuvalu may have been a blip on the screen to the rest of the world, but for thirty-nine years they had been home. He would do whatever it took to safeguard it.

This morning, that meant sitting on the tarmac at Vaitupu International Airport, a few minutes before six a.m. awaiting a reporter on the run, who might or might not be able to help, and whose presence might cause as much harm as good. Yesterday's drama had him tossing most of the night. On the plus side Mike Yahr was a breath of fresh air. It was rare to deal with someone who projected so fully a sense of competence. No wonder he was a friend of Jack's. Natano could tell a thing or two about the guy on the other end of the line, and when Mike closed by saying, "You know, I bet you're a good cop," he knew it wasn't sucking up. It was a sign of respect.

It was what Mike had said that left him unsettled. Presidential visit notwithstanding, his people were on alert. Natano had no place for intrigue. Murders didn't happen here. Phone calls weren't cut off, and not right before his eyes. He had been chief of security from the start and things had been nice and boring, just how he liked them. The past twenty-four hours cut into that.

He caught the jet's landing lights. With Raden in San Francisco, Mike had briefed him on Jessica Enright, the California incident, the events in Hawaii and what Enright had begun to uncover. Both understood the hornet's nest she'd stirred up. Though unsure as to what lay behind it, one thing was certain; she was marked, something she herself understood. MSNBC had also cut her loose; they hadn't given up on her, but events were moving so fast they knew to let her cover them as their only reporter on the front line.

Natano knew she was eager to land and inquire, and probably should. His dilemma was whether to let her—someone whose presence could generate risk yet might reveal something more dangerous. Either way the weight of intrigue was falling on him. Then there were the Americans. The pressure they would bear would be considerable. They would try to corral her, issuing subpoenas and prodding him to detain or deport her. By doing her job, she would help him do his; ironically, just like Herter. Mike said that she understood the risks. But first, Natano needed to talk with her.

The airport at sunrise was still asleep. A few jets sat parked, along with several Cloud Surfers looking like souped-up gliders. And Elliot Hanford's 747. The only people present were airport maintenance personnel and security. The Learjet taxied up to the benches where Natano sat, just before the terminal.

"Miss Enright, Mr. Lundquist," he smiled, "Captain Peter Natano. Welcome to Tuvalu."

Enright flashed a hint of her smile. "It's nice to meet you, but Mike didn't tell us we'd be greeted by police. I hope this isn't ominous; I left Hawaii to avoid you guys."

Natano smiled. "Very good, Miss Enright. No, we do things differently here."

They shook hands. A stunning woman, she seemed reticent. Her eyes betrayed wear and tear, and a sense that more was going on behind them than she was willing to let on. Dressed modestly in a T-shirt and jeans, her hair was tied in a simple ponytail that said expediency. Her bandaged cheek was conspicuous.

Natano's impression of Lundquist was that the thirty-ish cameraman was focused and forthright, and a hit with the opposite sex. Leanly built with unkempt blonde hair, jeans and a long sleeve button-down white shirt that hung loose with his strapped photo equipment, he seemed as if he had done this before.

Enright's attention was riveted on the incredible sight to east. The sunrise was revealing more of the explosion. Streams of gold poured forth along its backlit margins.

"That's amazing," she allowed to Natano. "Is that how they always look?"

"Mostly, though this one's large. I'm glad you were able to see it." As Lundquist took more photos, Natano added, "Miss Enright, Mike and I spoke at length. He seems upright. I know something about what happened to you. We've had an eventful twenty-four hours ourselves. About all the excitement we've had for two years has been those things out there. That's where I'd like to keep it. I realize you have a job to do. So do I. You're arriving at a time when a lot's going on. With what you've experienced and the incidents we've had here, you and I may have much to share. As long as we respect each others professional ethics, I think we can help each other."

"I'm okay with that."

"Good. Now, your president is leaving today, but he'll be back tomorrow. You might wish to speak with our prime minister. He has concerns you may wish to hear. I've dealt with enough media to know you won't be giving up your sources." She smiled. "But much of your research has considerable overlap with what I'm investigating."

"Miss Enright," he went on, "I'll be honest with you. If you have anything, I'm open to listening. I know you're from New York so you may appreciate this. I've lived here my whole life. A cop on the beat has a feel for his streets. I'm picking up something I haven't felt before. Flying in, you saw our island. And you see that out there. Our nation is very small. Those explosions are very large. Up to now, we've coexisted because we never lost our respect for their power, but I'm worried over what's gathering. I could use your help." He picked up her bag. "Come, we'll get you settled."

As they got into his police Honda Pilot, he said, "You'll see, we're very informal. But I'm glad you're here. I can't believe the questions you're looking into have gone unasked as long as they have." He started the vehicle, and they drove off.

Seventy-seven

Cindy curled into her pillow and smiled. "Good morning, sleepy head."

With his head buried in his own pillow, Kevin graveled, "What time is it?"

"6:20."

He let out a playful groan. She whacked him with her pillow. He grabbed it, covered her face and softly punched into it a few times. She let out a shriek and laughed, then drew him close.

Over the humming air conditioner, a hint of jasmine filtered through the open balcony doors, mixing with the track of lust from the previous night. Both lay nude in the hesitant light. "Sleep okay?" she asked, wrapping her leg around him.

He yawned. "Yeah. I think I went right out."

She smiled. "You did." She caressed his shoulder. "Last night was very nice," she purred.

"Unexpected, Russell. But yeah, it was nice. Very nice end to a very long day." He brushed back her bangs.

"I guess I had to go for it," she admitted bashfully. "I saw Robin and Gina. They would've been up here in a minute. I don't usually do that, but I don't regret it."

He smiled, and gave another try at her bangs. She kissed him and said softly, "You have a nice touch. And you snore cute. Not loud, just cute."

"Probably explains my prolonged bachelorhood."

"Among other things." She laughed and took his hand. "I know it's early but I want to show you something. Come." He slipped into his shorts. She put on her panties and one of his shirts and drew the curtains. He had yet to step out when he saw the sky.

Out toward the east the remnants of Eta Carinae were deconstructing in the jet stream, beginning to dissipate but still holding enough of a presence to offer up yet another incredible scene. Set between purple and pink towers of gas that billowed up like cotton candy at a summer

fair, the equatorial dawn blazed away in a riot of gold rays. The conclud-
ing act of the immense explosion seemed alive, unribboning like a clew
of glow worms.

"I didn't know whether anyone told you what the mornings are like
here afterwards." Cindy held his hand as they stood at the railing.

"No. I should have thought of it myself. My God, it's incredible."

"We unofficially call this the Silver Lining stage. Clever, huh?"

"Marketing must have spent weeks on that."

"Well," she grinned, "that's why it's unofficial. Others call it the
Diamond Ring effect."

Down on the mall to the ting and clang of cups and plates, the staff
was gearing up for breakfast. Guests slowly filtered down from their
rooms, coveting first pots of coffee. To either side others were on their
balconies sipping their own cups, caught up in the amazing sight.

At its maximum, the cloud had expanded so that its edge was nearly
overhead. Its mushroom shape had changed during the night, opening
holes that let sunrays through. It was like a meteorologist's dream, a glorious parade of clouds in every size, shape and texture. Kevin shook his
head. "Every stage of this is spectacular, but they're all so different from
each other."

Cindy started to smile, but Kevin had slumped into the railing.
"You're still bothered, aren't you," she asked. "Talk to me."

"You don't miss much. It's just that yesterday was such a weird day.
And look at all these people. I'm probably the only person here with all
the other stuff on my mind."

"It's personal. I understand. But if you can't get past it maybe you
shouldn't try. Maybe you just have to live with it. I gotta admit, you got
me thinking. My feelings are mixed and I've been here from the start. I
just never came down on it one way or the other. Maybe you can't. I met
Lisa; I saw what Tim Cain pulled. I saw Hanford. I didn't forget what you
said. If he wasn't the president, he'd be selling used cars somewhere. I
don't know how we're going to handle this, but if what's bothering you is
that you can't decide how you feel about it, well, you may not be able to."

He turned to her. "How *we're* going to handle this?"

"Yeah," she cast him a telling glance. "How *we're* going to handle it."

"Okay." He squeezed her hand. "So, Robin and Gina up here at the
same time. Hmm …"

"Such a dog," she sneered, squeezing his hand back hard. "Typical
guy." She gave him a crafty shrug. "Hey, that's what you want, go for it."

"I know when I've got it good," he smiled. As the words hung in the air he was surprised to hear himself say them after knowing her such a short time, but in the same instant, he already knew that the woman beside him was going to be someone he wouldn't so easily forget. He looked back at the sky. "Come to think of it, I would have thought we might have heard from Lisa by now."

"Yeah, me too." Just then, there was a knock at the door. "Room service," she said. "I took the liberty of ordering a little breakfast." He went to answer it, trailing a smile.

Seventy-eight

"Repeat that?" A plainly shocked Kevin stood in the anteroom eyeing Peter Natano and the two staid policemen accompanying him. Cindy sat with her arms folded straightjacket tight.

"We're still piecing it together," Natano said. "Miss Russell, your co-worker Janet Reynolds knocked on your door about a half-hour ago. She wanted to meet you and Dr. Herter for breakfast. She said she phoned but there was no answer. We checked; there was a call. She stopped by, knocked, and the door was open. When she saw what happened, she called us."

Cindy bit her quivering lip. Kevin asked, "How bad is it?"

"It's messy. They did a good job turning the place upside down. The patio door was open. I think that's how they left, though I don't see it as the point of entry. Maybe someone knocked or they were interrupted, and they climbed down."

"I don't believe this," Cindy intoned. "I feel so violated."

"Right now we're looking for physical evidence but my hunch is we won't find much. They likely wore gloves." One of the officers nodded in agreement. Natano then asked the two men to wait outside. Without missing a beat they excused themselves. He closed the door and sat down.

"Okay," he said. "Cindy, I'm assuming you spent the night." She blushed, and looked to Kevin. "It's okay," Natano smiled, "but we need to talk. Before he left, Jack told me he gave Kevin this room. I'm the only other person who knew."

She looked at Kevin. "Jack stopped by the station. I was still there."

"Point is," Natano went on, "no one knew either of you would be here. But it was common knowledge the two of you would be at Cindy's place. I don't know if they were targeting you or were looking for anything specific while you were gone. When I heard of the incident and neither of you were there, my first thought was you might be here. My next was to speak with Dr. Whiteman. We stopped by to see her. That room was ransacked as well."

"Oh, my God," Cindy gasped. "What is going on here?"

"That's what we have to discuss. Now—"

"Wait," Kevin interrupted. "Is she okay?"

"I don't know. We don't know where she is. Now, this isn't a big island and we will find out. But I don't like any of it. If you see her—"

"Oh, we'll definitely let you know." Cindy nodded vigorously.

"Thank you. Now, do you have any idea what they may have been looking for?" Cindy looked at Kevin, who took a deep breath. "I thought so," Natano said. "Let's hear it."

"I wouldn't have even thought about it until now," Kevin said. "Lisa Whiteman gave me a stick, you know, a flash drive last night. It's got technical data about—"

"Have you seen it yet?" Natano said, perking up.

"No. We had planned to look at it before I met Hanford." He turned to Cindy. "Maybe we'd better hurry it up. Can we use the computer at your office?"

"Come back to the station and use ours," Natano said. "I'll have an officer escort you."

"What's going on here?" Cindy asked Natano.

"All I know is that there's a pissing contest on my beat and I'll be damned I let it go on. But now I have a better idea why. I just dropped off Miss Enright. She flew in this morning. I'm sure she'll want to meet; she has a lot to tell you."

Kevin looked at him soberly. "I take it this isn't what you expected when you asked me to keep an eye on things. You really think something's going on here, don't you?"

He nodded. "And I want to know what's on that stick. And Cindy, it was fortunate you spent the night here. Had you—well, I'll leave it at that."

"Oh, my God!" She moved to Kevin's arms.

"I don't want to get you paranoid," Natano added, "but no one goes through this kind of effort unless they're hiding something. I suspect it's important. If that's the case, they're not about to let even someone notable like you get in the way. You know how small this force is, but I'll do everything I can to keep you safe."

The words had barely left him when the phone rang. Kevin turned towards it but Natano said, "Let me." He lifted the receiver. "One moment, please," he said, turning to Kevin. "It's your president."

"Dr. Herter," Elliot Hanford said, "my goodness! Have you been outside yet?" He sounded genuinely excited.

"Yes, Mr. President." Kevin hoped he wasn't sounding wary, given what he'd just been told. And despite his anxiety, he was intrigued by Hanford's tone. "Impressive, isn't it?"

"You scientists and your understatements. It's incredible! I know it's early, but it's that much more imperative we discuss this. I'd like to meet after breakfast. Does nine o'clock work for you?"

"Could we make it about nine thirty? I want to take a first crack at the data here."

"Just not much after that. I have to fly to Hawaii for the evening. Let's meet where we had dinner. I'll buy you a cup of coffee. Deal?"

"Okay, Mr. President. I'll see you then." Hanford hung up and Kevin said, "He wants to buy me a cup of coffee."

Cindy was ashen. "I thought no one knew you were here. How'd he find you?"

"By looking," said an intrigued Natano. "He's a president. I'll hold off judgment for now."

"Well, it wasn't your apartment that was broken into." She caught herself. "Pete, I'm sorry. But after the week Kevin had and now this, I don't know who to trust."

"Understandable. Someone's trying to, as they say, freak you out."

"Yeah, well, it's working. So what do we do?"

Natano sat down. "I'm sorry for you, but I've been trying to get people's attention for a while, including the prime minister. He doesn't fully trust your government but with the events having gone well it's been hard getting him to listen. We have a saying in these parts; a blind man fears no snake. And you've met him; he's an optimist. I don't have that luxury. Up to now, I haven't had much to go on. I have a chambermaid with a slashed throat and a jealous boyfriend, and two ransacked rooms and a missing scientist. And very little physical evidence. That's it. We filed charges against the boyfriend last night. I have nothing tying it together, but know they're connected. What I don't have is time. I had hoped something would turn up; you can't count on it, but extraneous elements do pop up. That's where that flash drive comes in."

Kevin said, "I hate to think all you're going on is your intuition."

Natano folded his arms. "Sometimes that's all a cop has. With this, I'm telling you there's something there. Please look it over and tell me how it affects me. You have a little time before your meeting. And Cindy, when Kevin is away, stick with it. We'll go from there."

Kevin and Cindy looked at each other, and nodded.

Natano rose. "Thank you. Let's get going; I have my work ahead of

me and I don't have a big force. After you meet your president heads
to Hawaii. The governor was supposed to be flying in, but something
happened there that changed his plans. Miss Enright will tell you about
it. The lieutenant governor and some business leaders are arriving instead. The prime minister wishes to speak with you as well. He's trying
to secure a new site for this region but Hanford's been putting him off.
Hear him out; it may be connected to what occurred this morning. Now,
I didn't tell Miss Enright, but your FBI issued arrest warrants for her and
her photographer."

"Oh, wow," Kevin said. Cindy looked shocked.

"But I'm letting you know that I do not intend to honor them. Our
extradition agreement with the United States says nothing of political issues. I plainly consider this to be one. I'm not going down that road. I do
intend to keep an eye on her, in case she attracts attention. By the way,"
he dead-panned, "it was also requested that I keep an eye on you. That's
between us. But don't tell her. Okay, can you meet me at the station in an
hour?" He said goodbye, then left.

They had yet to shake off being startled when Natano knocked again.
"Did either of you order breakfast?" he asked. Cindy replied yes. "Okay,
for the time being I'd like you to eat downstairs at the buffet, okay? No
room service." Cindy's jaw dropped, but she agreed.

As Natano left, Cindy and Kevin looked at each other. "We'll handle
it," Kevin said.

She looked at him and felt her heart beat faster, in fear but also relief.
"*We'll* handle it?"

"Yeah," Kevin tried to smile, "*we* will."

Seventy-nine

Even from a distance, it was impressive. The three-story glass and stone structure was contemporary in style, with an elegance that mollified its purpose. A large coral rock base on the right offset the sloping driveway that looped around to the back. The road was lined with palms and bushes flowering red and yellow. Everyone they passed extended smiles.

"This is some police station," was all Kevin could say.

"It's more than that," Cindy said as Simon Tong, the officer who'd been escorting them concurred.

It was still early, not yet seven thirty. They had just finished a quick breakfast on the mall, which despite the splendid weather neither could enjoy. Tong, whom Cindy knew, was pleasant enough, but she and Kevin were conflicted, wanting to speak to each other alone but as eager to see what the memory drive held as Peter Natano. None of them noticed Christian Deloy on the far side of the Mall, sipping coffee and eyeing them intently behind his sunglasses.

After eating, they followed Tong to the station. Natano was seated in a very substantial room filled with video displays, dominated by a huge flat screen displaying a live satellite feed of the island. A dozen technicians worked at monitoring stations. Kevin eyed the room's décor, noting that the coral base from outside was artfully integrated into the room's design.

"I see now where those guest fees go," he offered.

Natano smiled. "It's definitely a notch up from your typical police station. You're in the Executive Building of the Tuvalu Interior Ministry. This serves as our security center as well as police headquarters. My office is upstairs. This room is our Control Complex, where events are coordinated. This is the best-equipped facility of its kind in the South Pacific. It's also the most secure, so no one's going to bother us."

"That's good for a change," Kevin said as he handed Natano the stick.

"I take it few people have seen this," Natano said, inserting it into the computer before him. "I'm not up on the science behind these things, so just tell me what I need to know." He gave his seat to Cindy and motioned Kevin to a chair beside her, then pulled over one of his own.

Kevin smiled. "You're probably better with science than I am with computers." Seconds later, his smile vanished. The image was fuzzy. He tapped the screen, asking "Is it the file?"

"It might be corrupted. I think I can manage though." Cindy coaxed out an image. A DOE logo headed a file that began:

CLASSIFIED: DO NOT DUPLICATE

United States Department of Energy

Project DiFusion, DOE spec. 2016-2018. Whiteman/04/06

Her mouth curled in a condescending frown. "Everything from them is classified," she groaned. "If everything is classified, nothing is, especially when all you need is an FOI threat."

"Your Freedom of Information Act?" Natano asked.

She nodded and began scrolling down. Graphs, columns and figures flew by. "All right," she said, "this is event data. It goes back to the resort's opening. I remember these numbers. The important ones are the yields."

Natano watched intently. "Explain yield better, and why it's a concern."

"Yield is the energy of the explosion, like Richter Scales gauge earthquakes, though it's not logarithmic. In these explosions it's measured in megatons, millions of tons of TNT. It's easy to lose sight of numbers that big. The entire output of all sides in World War II was three megatons. Last night's was twenty-three. Kinda hard to wrap your mind around that."

Kevin scrutinized several columns. "What these show is that all the explosions have shown spikes in their projected yields, not just last night, correct?"

"That's right. We've seen it from the start. We weren't unconcerned, but the differential wasn't that much. We just don't think it should be there. No nuclear explosion has ever gone off exactly as predicted, but these have all been larger than expected, never smaller."

Natano rubbed his chin. "So what you're saying is they haven't gone as expected and you don't know why, but you weren't worried enough to halt the program."

"We discussed it," she said, nodding. "It was kicked upstairs. I'm out of the loop on those decisions. But none of us were alarmed, at least not enough to recommend a moratorium."

Kevin looked at Natano. "Have you been briefed of any of this?"

"I was told that there was a minor issue, and told not to worry. I hear don't worry, I worry. But I haven't been able to get a satisfactory answer, that is, to *my* satisfaction. Why this trouble for something they can live with? And why bring you all the way out here to fix it? I'll be honest, no one wants it solved more than me. But something smells. And know what stinks most? When I'm told to ignore what my own nose is telling me."

Kevin turned to Cindy. "I can see why this would be controversial but it seems to be common knowledge. Doesn't make sense. Lisa Whiteman was a nervous wreck."

"She begged us to look this over and talk to her. She implied it would have all the answers."

"Answers to what? She begs to meet today and now she's a no-show."

Natano scratched at the corner of his mouth. "Unless she walked in on something."

Kevin scrolled down further. He had to meet Hanford in a little over an hour, and he was getting frustrated. Even Cindy was getting impatient. Finally he said, "Maybe I'm missing something but there's nothing here."

"Keep looking. No one ransacks two rooms for nothing."

"But nothing is what's here. You see it. It's just what you already know."

As Cindy agreed, Natano grew irritated. "I'm telling you, keep looking."

"I want to find out what's going on as much as you, but ever think she may be a whacko?" Natano shot him a look. "All right all right; I've had a rough week," Kevin groaned. "I got used to Jack being around. My ex should be here too. Sharon's an artist but she's better at math and computers than anyone I know. She's got a knack for seeing things. There's a story about the Manhattan Project. Enrico Fermi was a physicist. Brilliant guy. He's in a room staring at a blackboard filled with equations when Oppenheimer walks in. He eyes the board for a second, takes a piece of chalk and changes a number. Fermi says, "I've been looking for that mistake for two days." That's Sharon."

Cindy smiled. "That's just what happened."

"Well," said Natano, "maybe you can do the same for us."

Kevin went back to the file. "It's not on the surface," he said. "Maybe it's in the numbers." He looked at his watch. "I gotta go; I'll pick it up later. I also have to give a statement about Cain. Too much, too much," he grumbled as he rose. "Are you staying?" he asked Cindy.

"Yes she is," Natano answered.

"Yes, she is," Cindy winked.

"Okay, I'll see you after. Wish me luck." Cindy gave him a quick kiss before he left.

"He's getting stressed," Natano observed. "I don't think he has any idea the leverage he's got. Hanford's rushing to plug a leak and he's put your friend's neck on the line to do it. If he was more of a politician, he'd realize that. Latasi would."

Cindy was scrolling down the file, not paying it attention. "I don't think that's him. But it's one of the things I like about him."

Natano smiled. "I like him as well. I had a nice talk with Jack about him. We want to get him through this, but I need his help. And yours."

There was a silence. "Please," she said, "watch out for him."

"That's my intention. I watch out for him, I watch out for this island." He smiled. "I'm still trying to get a sense of scientists. And Americans.

Cindy laughed. "Yeah, we can be a handful. Especially American scientists."

"I'll say. And my neck's out a mile as well. The prime minister means well, but this place is making so much money and he's so hell-bent getting the region a new site he's let security issues slip. So it's all fallen on my—hold it." He motioned to the computer. "You're at the end."

She eyed the screen. "Oh, I didn't even notice. I'll go back to the begin—"

"No, just back up a page or two." He stared. "Wait. What is that?"

The final three of eight-hundred and thirty-seven pages had a different font and header. They flipped back and forth between them, and then eyed the last page. After several moments, a confused Natano asked, "Am I reading this right? Tell me this says what I think it says."

"Oh, it says it all right," Cindy said with equal surprise. "But what does it mean?"

Eighty

Kevin had yet to make up his mind about Peter Natano but on one thing he was correct—the prime minister of Tuvalu sure was an optimist. He saw Lionel Latasi and an aide leaving the Terrace as he arrived for his meeting with the president.

"And a very good morning, Dr. Herter!" Latasi beamed, betraying no discouragement over what increasingly appeared to be a presidential runaround.

"Good morning, Mr. Prime Minister."

"That was some show we put on for you last night, wasn't it!" Kevin agreed, and Latasi added, "I understand you're meeting your president. We just left him."

"After you shook hands, did you count your fingers?"

Latasi roared. "Well my friend, I've learned to stop worrying about things like that." He looked up. "I must say. It's a fine morning. It's going to be warm." He leaned in. "My sense is quite a few here this morning feel warm. Some warmer than others."

Latasi's cryptic style took some getting used to. Kevin liked him, but his affability made it easy to forget how close to the vest he played his cards. His judgment seemed incisive and his tenacity well-honed, but most polished was political skill that did little to discourage one being taken for the other. Kevin saw how Natano could at once admire and find him frustrating. He also saw how a president accustomed to handlers and sound bites would have no use for him whatsoever. Whatever disconcertion came from suffering the patronizing Hanford, waiting him out with a smile would leave him invariably with the upper hand. Latasi was a survivor.

"Mr. Prime Minister," Kevin offered, "if you like, let's speak afterwards."

"I would appreciate that. By the way, Captain Natano needs to see you presently."

"Uh…okay. Thank you. We'll see each other later." Latasi smiled and left.

Kevin neared the security check surrounding Hanford. He was curious what Natano wanted to speak to him about, since he had just left him minutes earlier, when he saw Dillon Ridge leaving in the opposite direction. With everything that morning, he had forgotten Hanford's insolent chief of staff. While sure he hadn't been seen by Ridge, an anxious chill held him back until the man was gone. It gave him time to ponder what Hanford was after. It had to be something.

Elliot Hanford stood at the deck railing holding a coffee mug, staring out. Eta Carinae was raising the already stunning tropical morning to one approaching sublime. He wore a reflective air that hadn't been there yesterday. Knowing Ridge had just been there, Kevin awaited a full-court sales pitch but Hanford appeared distracted. He gestured toward a nearby coffee pot. Kevin poured himself a cup.

"Couldn't get to sleep last night," Hanford eventually said. "Usually I go right out." He shook his head. "Damnedest thing I ever saw." His contemplative expression turned to a sly grin. "I heard you got lucky last night."

Kevin almost spit out his coffee. "How'd you know—"

"Oh, you wouldn't believe what I know." Kevin blushed and Hanford chuckled, "Dr. Herter, if you knew one-eighth of what crosses my desk. Come on, let's talk." As they sat, he gestured to the east. "Can't get over that. If impressive is the best you can do she must have been good."

After an excruciating few moments, Kevin said, "I have to be honest, Mr. President. Putting aside the obvious, I had a rough night. That thing out there—it hasn't fully sunk in." He paused. "I guess what I heard was right. I was warned about you."

"And probably with good reason," Hanford said, laughing. "What did they tell you?"

Kevin grinned. "Mostly to watch my ass."

"Okay," Hanford kept chortling, "fair enough. I can live with that."

Kevin's grin faded. "Yeah, but can you live with that?" he asked sardonically, gesturing back to the horizon.

Hanford took a sip of coffee. "I know about the problems you've had. I won't minimize it. I want you to know how much I appreciate you being here but my hunch is you've pretty much given up on listening to what I might say. I'd like to see what I can do about that."

Kevin watched Hanford feign empathy for something he had to have caused. He felt like a lab rat being sweet-talked by a technician hiding a syringe behind his back. He wondered what Hanford was hiding, yet needed to hear him out. For now he changed the subject.

"I just saw Ridge. I apologize for taking off last night but he was too much."

"Dillon's Dillon," the president shrugged. "I know what people think of him. He'll never win any popularity contests. I wasn't going to subject you to him this morning."

"I appreciate that."

"Some mornings I'd prefer not subjecting *me* to him." As Kevin laughed he added, "Lyndon Johnson once said the only power he had was nuclear and he couldn't use it. Talk about irony. People think presidents can do anything but I often have less control over people down the hall than those half-a-world away. I'm not dense; it's just the nature of a government this size. Reality doesn't matter. It's perception." He tipped his gaze. "That thing out there? That my friend is perception."

Kevin listened guardedly. "I also ran into the prime minister."

"He's another one. I like the man, but he's got an agenda. Everyone here has an agenda. But if we don't fix things none of it will matter. When I couldn't sleep last night I did some reading. There's a whole history of nuclear tests online. There's even a crowd of bomb nuts out there, go figure. When they began testing in the '40s people had plenty of nutty ideas as well. Makes you wonder what they would have thought of this place." He rubbed his eyes. "Anyway, tell me what you found. Have you learned anything yet?"

"So far, nothing. I had thought I'd be meeting Dr. Whiteman this morning—"

"And another one," Hanford growled. "What the hell happened to her? You see now how often that crap happens. And Raden takes off last night as well. I need these people."

Kevin waited, listening. Hanford added, "Anyway, afterwards I did a little channel surfing. I found a station with movies from the '50s, all doing with the atom."

Kevin had to laugh. Hanford nodded, "I caught the end of *The Atomic Café*. That's the movie that made light of how they looked at the bomb back then. I grew up with that. Brought back memories. TV programmers here have a sense of humor."

As Kevin smiled Hanford added, "It was a different world. *Leave it to Beaver*, *Ozzie and Harriet*. Duck and cover. And yeah I laughed. But there's another part of it." He sat back and sighed. "I was born in October of '56. It was before your time but I was right in the middle of it. We did the drills in school. There were these yellow and black Civil Defense signs with the letters CD in triangles that led to the fallout shelters. I remember a lot. But know what I remember most? The Cuban Missile Crisis. It was right around my sixth birthday. I was too young to know what was going on, but I knew enough to know it was no drill. I remember my parents, how scared they were. They didn't talk shelters. Where could you go? That was my first experience with what I later realized was pure fear. I don't know if you ever felt that. It's not like watching a scary movie Saturday afternoon and running outside when you hear the Good Humor truck. It stays with you. Every kid has a first experience that becomes a signature event. If you're lucky it's good, but sometimes it isn't. So don't even think I don't take this seriously. You may think up this stuff sitting at a nice desk somewhere but I lived it. I was there."

The president stared for an uncomfortably long moment, then said, "Okay. So now, you look out there, and you tell me what should be done with those things."

Elliot Hanford zeroed in on a palpably quiet Kevin. "It wasn't a rhetorical question."

"Mr. President, I'm not sure what you want me to say."

"Doctor, that's just not good enough any more." Hanford's admonishment was disarming, but to Kevin's surprise, he became subdued. "I thought I knew what to expect last night," he mused. "Maybe everyone needs to see this at least once."

"I can't necessarily argue with that," Kevin said, instantly recognizing he had undercut his own position. Annoyed with himself, he was nonplused when Hanford didn't bite. He sweated out his stumble, not realizing that the president's softball had already hit its mark.

"You should know," Hanford smiled, "I was prepared to smack you down. Appealing to your patriotism, God and country, whole slew of things you probably think are bull. Were it anyone else this conversation wouldn't be happening. But I respect you. And, I think that thing out there equalizes a lot for you and me."

"How so?" asked an earnest-sounding Kevin, trying to recover.

"The terrorism findings that just came up. That's *my* unintended consequence. It complicates managing this prudently. Problem is everyone and his brother has had something to say about this place. And I gotta say a lot of it's come from your crowd."

"Come on now."

"The scientific community has had a lot to say," Hanford droned, "and you know it. You know the routine—everything about this place is wrong. So I expect this new data will be too. But ask for something constructive, they sit on their hands."

"Mr. President, you know it's not like that."

"It's all too like that," Hanford said brusquely, "and it's high time it changed. I'd have taken anything practical, but all I got was criticism. It's just like in the '40s. Put yourself in FDR's shoes, or Truman's. Out of a clear blue sky, a physicist you never met walks in and starts talking bombs made from exploding atoms. Imagine what that must have been like. Even to this day, the things you guys come up with. But what I don't hear is how to handle it. You dream up things no one knew existed, show us how to work it, and in the next breath beg us to keep you from doing it. Someone does, you blame us. No ownership."

Kevin shook his head. "That was a world war. This is nothing like that. And believe me, I'm in the field. None of us sit around like that."

"The process may be different but not the result. People like me are left holding the bag."

Kevin felt his defenses rise. "Mr. President, you should listen to my colleagues. They'd say you chose this. As for the bomb, they'd say get rid of 'em, period. *That* to them is practical."

The president smiled. "Ask them if they ever heard of Elmo Zumwalt."

Kevin paused. "Who was he?"

"He was an admiral and chief of naval operations in the '70s; actually progressive in ways, very well respected. Years back I read an interview he gave. Something he said struck me, even then. He talked about a conversation he had once with a Soviet counterpart, at a disarmament conference, if memory serves. Everyone was tripping over themselves about how great it would be to get rid of these weapons. During a break, Zumwalt casually asked him, 'Let's say both sides agree to get rid of all our bombs. And say a year later you stumble across a hundred old warheads you had completely forgotten about. What would you do?'"

Kevin folded his arms. "What did he say?"

"He said the Russian's reply was very honest. He said, 'Well, first we would tell you we had them. Then we would deliver our ultimatum'. So, how would your colleagues deal with that?"

Kevin shrugged.

"Again," Hanford reiterated, "not good enough. You know how many different versions of that I've heard? Back then it was the Soviets, today it's the Chinese, tomorrow, who knows. You know how many people think it's scientists that got us into this?"

"Oh, come on Mr. President. No one I know thinks that."

"Doctor. I hear from them all the time. You guys are smart. But just once I'd like one of you to put yourself in my position and offer a realistic response. Sitting on your hands wishing it away doesn't cut it. I told you—you don't see what I see and you don't hear what I hear. So you don't know what I know. There's a hell of a lot more I hear about than just a couple of scientists rolling around in the sack, and criticizing without offering solutions I can do without, especially from the guy who got it all going. You're bothered by these things? Get over it. I have to deal with this which means so do you. The discussion on whether to build them or not is over. You know when you'll get rid of the things? When you have enough leaders you can trust to scrap them and trust the other side to do the same. That's never been the case, and singing *Kumbaya* hoping the other guy turns out to be a human being won't work. So forget about going there. Do something practical." He paused. "Something you can't necessarily argue with."

"Okay," Kevin sneered, "I walked into that. So, why do you need me?"

"Simple. The public thinks you invented this." Before Kevin could respond, Hanford said, "I know that's not what happened. It's just how it is. And, you're a scientist. There'll always be folks who think you speak with the voice of enlightenment. No matter what you guys think up, if you're honest and sound like you know what you're talking about they'll cut you some slack. If people then knew what we know now FDR would have lined up meetings with Einstein."

Kevin frowned. "Okay, point taken. But what's the urgency? It can't be those new figures."

"It's that instability. Things like that have a way of getting away from you. So let's get real. Ridge is a pain in the ass, but what he said last night wasn't without merit."

Kevin grew annoyed. "What part is that? Where he was doing his 'bad cop' bit?"

"Thing about 'good cop, bad cop' is it loses punch if it isn't true."

"Okay. Mr. President, I said I'd give you a hearing. But after the week I've had, I'd just as soon get on that plane come Monday and head back."

Hanford walked to the railing and stared out. "You know what a big part of this job is? Briefings, up the wazoo. People run for president only to spend half their time once they win listening to a bunch of yahoos spout off about God-knows what, most of which you could figure out on your own using just a little common sense. When your work first came out I had the usual meetings with my science and security teams. They come in with their graphs, their reports. You get some insight but most of it's crap. I listened, asked questions. But the instant I heard what it implied I knew a place like this would be in the works. Saw it clear as day; terror stats too. I just had to wait for the data to catch up with the system. You may know science but I know people. That's why I have this job. So when I look at you, you know what I see? Someone who can't keep their eyes off what they're telling me they don't want any part of."

Kevin paused. "I wasn't aware of it." After a stretch, he asked, "Okay, what do you want?"

Hanford crossed his arms like a schoolmaster. "What I want first is for you to be honest."

"What does that mean?"

"You're doing what everyone does—stare, then kick it down the road. I get it; you're pissed we have the bomb, clean or dirty. But be honest—you're more pissed we *need* to have the bomb. They shouldn't need to be and we shouldn't need to have 'em," he said flippantly. "And people shouldn't need to get off watching them and watching them shouldn't be needed to keep others from using them. And, we shouldn't have screwed with your work. That pretty much it?"

"You've been talking to my ex," Kevin said grudgingly. "Okay, maybe you're right. I hate what you guys did with my work. I just can't brook how reasonable you make it all sound."

"Look out there and tell me what's reasonable. I've got half the leaders of every piss-ass country in the world wanting to get their hands on the things and the other half booking hotel rooms to watch them go off. Go figure that the most destructive thing we ever cooked up would turn into the world's hottest gig. And if that's not enough, look what's going on in the world. The Middle East is a disaster. The Russians are making trouble again; the Chinese, North Korea, Iran. For years I heard Iran would never get the bomb. Five years away, always five years. Then look what happened. I knew better. It took us four, and that was starting from scratch with typewriters and slide rules. So tell me what's reasonable. And tell me what to do about it."

Kevin broke out into a nervous chuckle. "I can't. But I also can't help but think that what's most reasonable is that you only want my help to get reelected."

Hanford nodded into a patronizing grin. "And it doesn't make a damn bit of difference, because no matter who wins, a year from now you'll be sitting here yet again listening to one of us telling you yet again to get your head out of your ass yet again and help us deal with it."

"Now, hold it a minute—"

"Come on, Doctor, cards on the table. There are realities you people just don't want to accept. A, there's not enough trust in the world to get rid of these things. B, the average guy really likes watching them. And C, that both A and B are in you as well. Which leads to most important, D—you guys ain't never gonna admit you're average."

Kevin tried waving him off, but the president added, "This is what I meant about honest. But there's more to it, isn't there. You might hate owning it but know what you hate more? You guys who think yourselves the most enlightened folks who ever lived are responsible for the most horrific thing ever made. You never got over what they did in '45. And more, that they knew what it would mean and did it all the same. To this day you're got guilt. Anything reminds you of it you want nothing to do with, even if it saves lives. So you glom onto idealized pipe dreams that don't stand a snowball's chance in hell in the real world."

"I don't need to listen to this."

"Really. Two idiots in an alley shoot each other and there's two dead idiots. But here come the physicists, smartest guys who ever lived, and now two idiots can knock off a billion. Tell me there isn't one of you who doesn't walk around with that hanging over your head. So whad'ya do? Rationalize it away. And you expect us to buy that all you're about are ideals. It's bull."

"Bull?"

"Yeah. A red herring. You'll never admit you're a stone's throw out of the cave like the rest of us. I've dealt with scientists for years," he sneered. "Never met a bigger bunch of envious, petty, biased, plain-ole average human beings in all my life. You think you're above it all, but you sleep, wake, eat, shit and yeah, get laid like the rest of us. I read that after Oppenheimer built the bomb he said now the physicists have known sin. Well, we have more sin now than we know what to do with, so don't think your sanctimonious holier-than-thous are going to wash your hands of it. You all still feel guilty. But this is a chance to do something about it. You don't, you'll never get that stain off your hands. And you know it."

Kevin could feel the blood pounding in his head. He didn't know whether he wanted to crawl under the table or kick it over. "Oh, you're making it so easy for me to—"

"Leave? That your answer to everything?"

Kevin bolted up, but Hanford pointed a sharp finger at him. "Sit." As Kevin glared, Hanford broke a slight grin. "I wondered how far I'd have to go to get your attention."

Eyes ablaze, Kevin sat down. Hanford said, "You need to know something. Those 'idiots' I spoke of also happen to run half the countries in the world. Under those circumstances no American president will ever get rid of these things. I'll be brutally honest with you. Over a dozen presidents before me have had to deal with this. All of us have felt the same way. But want to know the dirty little secret? None of us have had any idea what to do with them either."

Kevin stared at Elliot Hanford with a quizzical look. "What are you saying?"

"I have to spell it out for the rocket scientist? All along, no one's had any idea what to do with nuclear weapons, including my predecessors. Why do you think we're discussing it still?"

"That's incredible," Kevin said. "I mean, for you to admit that."

"Don't expect a press conference. But eventually you run out of road to kick things down." He leaned back. "You know those drills I did? They did them throughout the '50s. Know why? To make themselves feel good. They'd pretend to evacuate cities, but they knew we couldn't survive an attack. There's film of Eisenhower leaving the White House for some secret location. He's strolling to a car like he's off to play golf. The idea was to reassure people but it was just going through the motions. Everyone knew if the missiles got flying we were fried. Meanwhile, we kept building bombs. Know why again? No one knew what else to do. Before we knew it both sides had thousands of the things. Remember MAD, Mutually Assured Destruction? 'If you send yours over we'll send ours back, and both sides are toast'? That kind of thinking was policy for decades. So we sat down and you had SALT, START. It helped, but we never got rid of all of them. Now there are a dozen smaller players. At least with the Soviets you had two fairly conservative opponents staring each other down. The loons today have one-tenth the number of bombs but they're ten times more likely to use them. I have to remind you what happened in the Middle East a few years back? Pakistan won't be clean for decades. And look what just one tsunami can do to a nuclear power plant. It's going to take the Japanese just as long. Folks are more nervous now than when I was a kid. That, my friend, is just some of what I have to deal with. So when a place like this comes along, I take advantage of it. This is the first thing that can actually change attitudes." He frowned and let out a groan. "How about giving me a little credit, huh? You know, I'm really not out to blow up the world."

Kevin bit his lip. "You really think this is going to help?"

"Regardless of what I expected, the numbers still had to bear out.

Put yourself in my position. Someone comes to you with something that can help save lives. How do you not do it?" He crossed his leg and began picking at a rough spot on his shoe. "You're going to roll your eyes. My daughter had her second two years ago. She's doing the vaccine thing again. I don't have to tell you what vaccines are all about. Today we take them for granted. But imagine what it was like when the idea first came up."

"Oh, you're not going there."

"Think about it," Hanford smiled. "To keep people from getting sick we're going to give them a little of what makes them sick. Think how that sounded to the average guy. But it worked."

"Yep, you went there," Kevin laughed. "I can't believe I'm hearing this."

"Listen, I'm a practical guy. I may not be able to figure it out, but damn I ignore it. No one likes shots but if it guards against something worse, you do it. I know people have mixed feelings about this. They may hate the things but there's something about them that makes them stop in their tracks. Violence feeds on itself but so does its absence. If by watching a bomb go off, some nut postpones setting off his own for one more day, I'll take it and I won't make any apologies. What I'm asking of you is suck it in and take some ownership for what came from your work. Fair or not, the perception is that this is your baby. That gives you a responsibility for thinking up answers for how to deal with it." He groaned. "You think I want to deal with this crap? There's a lot else I'd rather be doing. Would it be a great world if we didn't need this place? I go to bed every night worrying that I'll get woken up with news somebody set off one of these things. So do I pretend this is the only answer? No. But it's the first thing to come along that even remotely has some of them. It may not be ideal, but it's a start."

Kevin puffed up his cheeks and let out a drawn-out sigh. "So, what do you want from me?"

"We're announcing an expansion of the program tomorrow night. I'd like for you to be there and maybe say a few words. Something simple, a little reflective. You've seen the thing. You know the impact they have. I sure do."

Kevin looked surprised. "I guess that isn't what I expected. All this for just a word or two."

"Hey, I'm a man of simple wants, other than to win another four years," joked the president. "So yeah, something simple. Thoughtful. I think that's what's called for."

"Well, I want to go over the data more thoroughly before I commit to anything."

"That's not unreasonable." Hanford shrugged. "Tell you what. Since you're going to be here anyway, show up, and if you choose to say anything, it's your decision."

Kevin paused for a moment. "Okay, Mr. President. I can live with that."

"Good! Then we'll see each other tomorrow night."

Eighty-one

The stairway he'd breezed up scant hours earlier loomed dense with effort as Kevin entered the Executive Building shortly after ten thirty. He trudged up the last few steps to the Control Complex. Just outside the door, he had to stop and gather himself.

It was like shaking off a sucker punch, one that landed so deftly he wasn't even sure he had been hit. While meeting Elliot Hanford all the admonitions of what the president was like had been forgotten. It was only as he left that he recognized something had happened, though what, he wasn't sure. He wouldn't realize it until later, but he had been handled.

Cindy and Natano were still at the desk. One look and Natano said, "Okay, let's hear it."

Kevin crumpled into a chair. "Ever see *The Ten Commandments?* Remember Aaron's face when he helped the Israelites build the golden calf? I walked in with a head of steam, and by the time I left, I was agreeing with just about everything he said. I don't know what happened."

Natano didn't look surprised. "That's your president. What did you promise him?"

"Well, not that much. I told him I'd be there tomorrow but I need to see more data before I committed to anything."

Cindy tried to smile. "Don't be too hard on yourself. He's good."

Natano said, "Let it go; no harm done. And you're right. You do need to see more."

"I'm just pissed at myself," Kevin groaned, missing the moment. "Jack warned me. The real pisser is that he made some very thoughtful points and I trust him now even less than before."

"Maybe there's reason. We have something to show you."

Cindy pulled up the end of the file. It didn't take Kevin long to see the issue. "Is this what Lisa was sitting on?" he asked. Instead of showing spikes, it listed predicted and actual explosion yields that were nearly identical. "If this is right, there isn't any discrepancy. What's going on?"

"I don't know," Cindy said. "I've never seen this before."

"Why would your Dr. Whiteman have different data?" Natano asked.

"Not different data," Kevin rejoined. "Different projections." He thought for a moment, then took Cindy's printouts and taped them together to make one continuous chart. A series of curves coursed along like a choppy wave, each rather different from the others. "This is the chronology of event yields, the original data. Has anyone here ever correlated this into any kind of mean?"

Cindy shook her head. "We've spent most of our time trying to explain the discrepancy."

"Who's shown the most interest in that?"

"The Pentagon. Up to now it's been treated as an anomaly, but within the past month they started pressing for more data. It's becoming an issue."

"So let me get this straight," Natano asked. "They worked the data, didn't have that much of a problem with it for two years, then recently got religion?" Cindy nodded.

Kevin scrutinized the graph. "There is something here," he finally said.

"I knew it," Natano exclaimed. "What is it?"

Cindy continued looking but couldn't see it. "It's tricky," Kevin said. "Instead of looking at it as an indiscriminate expression, look at it as an experimental one."

"You people have to talk English for me," Natano grumbled, good-naturedly.

Cindy examined the graphs again. Suddenly her expression changed. "Now I see it."

"Okay, you two," Natano barked. "Give it up."

"Something happened a year-and-a-half ago," she said, "and again about nine months ago. There is a definite order to the spikes. I can't believe no one noticed it."

"I think at least one person did," Kevin offered. "In laymen's terms—"

"Oh, bless you," Natano quipped.

Kevin smiled. "The old figures show yield spikes, from what was expected to what occurred. And, there is a pattern. But here's the thing, it's only apparent if you see it as variation produced by a system undergoing modification. You accept that, you see something. It doesn't make sense if you regard it as indiscriminate fluctuations of a system that's stable."

Natano rubbed his eyes. "Okay, I'm not getting it. Describe what I'm looking at."

"Remember. The shots range from about sixteen to twenty-one megatons. You divide up the history here into three time units, roughly eight to ten months apiece. You first look at them separately, then compare them. So take the first period. Every explosion shows a spike, but with the smaller shots the discrepancy between estimate and actual yield is small. As the size of the blast increases, so does the discrepancy. But with the larger blasts, it levels off."

Cindy said, "The next period shows a little different pattern. The disparity also begins small, but it stays small throughout, despite the size of the explosion. The proportion stayed even."

"And then it changed again. The disparity began small, but as the yield went up this time it didn't tail off. The three biggest shots show a predictable, steady increase, and the proportion increased. The biggest one, last night, shows the largest gap between estimate and actual yield, almost three-quarters of a megaton. That's significant, enough to destroy a city. I don't know what caused the differences or why they should even exist, but each time has its own pattern."

Natano stared. "Just like that you noticed? Your ex isn't the only one who can see things."

"Trust me," Kevin lamented, "it's a curse." Cindy smiled in admiration.

"Well," Natano said, "something's going on. Have there been any changes in the devices?"

"Funny you should ask," Cindy said. "Nothing big, but there have been some. We were told it was the usual new and improved that any system incurs, like different trims on cars. The DOD advisories said it involved space. The smaller the boats, the more you have available. People who donate boats know they're not getting them back."

"I've heard worse," Kevin shrugged. Cindy smiled in agreement and he said, "Anything else?"

"Well, the DOD rotates personnel—"

"Let me guess, with every design change. Which coincided with the yield changes. Right?"

Cindy nodded. "I think it has to do with the firing mechanisms. You can see them on the surface of the device. The yield differential correlates with changes in the firing assemblies."

"So, something's being done with the assemblies, and it's having an effect on the yield. At least according to the older projections. And they never mentioned any real purpose—"

"Nope, just space. The advisories came from the DOD but the specs came from the DOE."

Natano said, "The DOD runs the side of the program that deals with operations."

"Yeah, and their construction. The DOE has more to do with logistics."

"In other words," Kevin said, "the Pentagon fields the techies, and Energy the physicists. Has that changed in recent months?"

"The Pentagon's trying to move into areas that are DOE specified. Turf battles."

Natano began rubbing his face. "Let me get this straight. You're saying the history here can be read as some ongoing experiment. And it shows some sort of instability with the things that's affecting their power. And all that's from the data based on the original stats, correct? But the new predictions say everything's fine, so there isn't a problem. Is that about it?"

Kevin nodded. Natano leaned back in his chair and began rocking, perplexed.

"You almost seem disappointed," Kevin queried.

"No, it's not that." He groaned. "This whole thing is maddening. I get they would do upgrades, and I'd expect bureaucratic infighting. And I even get that you can read this as some sort of trial who-knows-what. But I was sure I'd see some kind of cover-up in there, I mean a normal one. It looks like what they're trying to hide is that the thing is stable. It would make more sense if it were reversed, if they were hiding the unstable figures and what we had all along showed it was okay. When you're a cop you learn to trust your gut. When it leads you one place it doesn't sit right if it drops you somewhere else, even if you hear everything's all right. But just cause it's frustrating doesn't mean I don't see anything. Something's there. Just not what I anticipated."

Kevin had been staring at the printout. "I see it as well. And, I didn't say everything was all right. I think I know what Lisa's been doing."

Cindy paused. "I have a hunch you two aren't talking about the same thing."

Kevin and Natano eyed each other. "What do you mean?" Natano asked.

"I think you're both very good at what you do," Cindy said with a knowing smile. "But Pete, your eyes glaze over at anything technical. And Kevin," she beamed, "you're brilliant, you're accomplished, but you're also incredibly decent. It insulates you from appreciating how vile people can be. And the circles you travel in keep you from meeting them."

As Natano laughed she added, "You two are great guys from different worlds, with little experience dealing with the other. Maybe you're seeing what you're used to seeing, what's familiar."

"And missing what's not," Kevin said with a shrug. Natano nodded.

"That's it. Listen, you're smart. Spend time in each other's world. It won't take long to see. I'm in both. I know there's more than one way to read what's going on. Maybe that's what Lisa Whiteman wanted, keep things apart so not only couldn't one person see it all, even if they did they wouldn't understand. You need to put your heads together and share what you know."

"She's a keeper," Kevin said. As Natano smiled, Cindy blushed and whacked Kevin's arm. "That's where I was going," Kevin went on. "I agree; this doesn't make sense. But that's to you and me."

"To others it may be eminently sensible," Natano said. "Like your Dr. Whiteman."

"Well, someone." Kevin shook his head. "I never get over how often so much in history that's so important involves so few people. It's interesting, the power she had. If she's responsible for this, which is likely, then she pulled off a neat trick. Think how this was set up. No one person or agency has complete say on anything. You'd think the Pentagon would be building the bombs and setting them off but no, it's the Energy Department. And common sense would be that Energy ran the infrastructure. But no, it's the Pentagon. It's like major league baseball ran the Super Bowl and the NFL ran the World Series. Each runs what it's least qualified to do."

Cindy said, "Or what someone doesn't mind they find out about."

Kevin nodded. "None of you know all that's needed to make it run. Except—"

"Dr. Whiteman." Natano folded his arms.

"And that's been kept quiet. Say someone's been hiding or fudging projections. She's the only one in a position to pull it off. And now, it's important to her that we find out. Why spill the beans, and why now?"

Natano sat back, hand crimping his mouth, nodding. "Which tells you what?"

"Well, let me ask you. You're a cop. Take Cindy's advice. Put aside the technical. Talk human nature. Why go through trouble like this to keep a lid on the fact that things are okay?"

"What are they trying to hide?" Cindy asked.

Natano stared at them. "Good questions. But you already have an idea, don't you?" He grimaced. "These questions should have been asked years ago. It shouldn't have been left to a cop and a scientist who never visited here to have brought it up, and trust me, there's a hell of a lot more with this than just her. But I need to know one thing from you, before I answer. Whatever you think is going on or what she may be hiding, do you feel you can trust her?"

Kevin and Cindy looked at each other. "We only met her for a few minutes," shrugged Kevin, "but we both felt she was sincere. Why ask, because of what I said about Hanford?"

Natano began rubbing his arm. "Ever have an itch you can't find? You try scratching it but you can't narrow down where it is." He eyed Kevin, who began to smile. "I won't pick apart what your president may or may not be telling you. I think your read on him is good, so assume the worst. But Dr. Whiteman is a different case. You can read her different ways. I'll accept what you say about her. But trust or not, whatever she's after, she seems agitated."

"Something's scaring her," Cindy said.

"Whatever scenario she constructed is elaborate," Natano said. "But it may be getting away from her. She chose now to bring it out and approach you. If you think you can trust her, the cop in me wants to know from the physicist in you, what you think she may be hiding."

"This is what I meant," Cindy said. "You two need to compare notes."

As Natano gave a reluctant okay, Kevin said, "There's one other thing. Hanford is looking to sell this now as some kind of antiterrorism program. He's got numbers that say because of this place, terror events worldwide are down."

Cindy stared at him. "You're kidding." Kevin shook his head no.

Just then, Natano received a text message. He excused himself and responded to it. "Nice timing," he said. He was about to explain when his phone rang, just as several officers rushed into the Complex.

"Excuse me, Captain," Officer Simon Tong said, "we have a situation."

Eighty-two

"Are you sure it's Dr. Whiteman?" Peter Natano asked.

"She was hiding under a stairway in the laundry," Officer Tong nodded. "We're still looking into it. She's in the infirmary. She was brought in fifteen minutes ago. She had no room key or ID—"

Kevin jumped up. "What kind of shape was she—"

"Kevin," Natano said, "we'll find out." Cindy tugged at him and he sat down. He was still unsettled though. The flurry of activity in the ordinarily staid Control Complex caught the attention of the other technicians around. Natano asked Tong about her condition.

"There was no outward sign of trauma but she was in a state of, I'd say, almost panic. They had some time calming her down. I thought she might be in shock, but the doctors don't think so. She's very lucid, very aware, but she refuses—"

"Then we need to see her," Kevin interrupted.

"Just wait," Natano said. "Officer, what else?"

"She refuses to see any male personnel. She became almost incoherent when they approached her. She only spoke to female officers. She won't allow male doctors even in the room. One of them tried taking her vitals and she lost it. Several nurses and our female officers had to restrain her."

"Oh, my God," Cindy said. "Do you think she would see me?"

"That's a good idea," Natano said. He turned to Tong. "Something happened."

"Our first thought was a sexual assault, but we don't see any evidence. We've been unable to get any information from her. I've never seen anyone that scared. If anyone that isn't a woman approaches her now, she'll just shut down. We're arranging for a counselor to see her."

Cindy rose. "I have to see her then." She looked at Natano, then Kevin. "You know I do."

"All right, we'll go. But just wait a moment." Natano took out his phone. "Change of plan," he began the call. "We're heading to our infirmary. Meet us there. It's close to you; just ask around. About twenty minutes? Okay, thank you."

He hung up, and turned to Kevin and Cindy. "That was your Miss Enright."

"Wow," Kevin said, surprised. "Forgot about her. Is that who texted earlier?"

"I was going to have her meet us for lunch. I was sure you would have a lot to talk over but now I'm going to insist you meet, though I don't think I need to twist your arm, do I?"

"Oh, there's a no-brainer. After Princeton I could have gone the rest of my life without running into her. Now I'm almost looking forward to it."

"This should be interesting," Cindy said. "Just a minute." She printed out the last three pages of the file. "If we get a chance we can look it over more," she said, giving them to Kevin.

"Good idea," Kevin and Natano answered, almost simultaneously. Natano pocketed the USB stick.

"Are you okay?" Cindy asked Kevin as they left. She was holding on to his arm.

He gave up a nervous laugh and shook his head. "That makes two of us," Natano said. "Let's go. And I still need to hear what you think is going on."

Eighty-three

Dillon Ridge gave a nod, indicating that the short ride to the airport was set. It was but one such prompt that Elliot Hanford relied on to wrap up whatever he was doing. Hanford knew he had a problem with time management, but that was because he so enjoyed the act of schmoozing. It was common knowledge that being personable was his strong suit. He never passed up an opportunity to cajole, finesse or handle a supporter or opponent. He knew that they were for the most part interchangeable, oftentimes one and the same. People, like nations, had not so much friends or enemies but interests, which turned as readily as the seasons. It was the rare politician who never forgot that, and if there was anything at which he excelled it was in being a political animal.

The president concluded goodbyes to Lionel Latasi and the Tuvaluan dignitaries with him. He warmly thanked them for their hospitality, and after expressions that he was looking forward to returning the next day, he and Ridge entered their car and left.

"Well, that was nice," Hanford said, settling into his seat.

"I get tired of listening to him," Ridge replied.

"He's harmless. I'm inclined to give him some of what he wants. Just not yet. Can't look too eager, now. Gotta keep up appearances."

"But you know you wouldn't have been caught dead coming out here for any other reason than last night."

"That was something, wasn't it?" Hanford was still ebullient and wasn't up to hearing complaints.

Ridge made an imperceptible scowl. "It was, but if that wasn't—"

"I know that. But so what? Listen, I'm in a good mood now and I don't want to spoil it." Hanford stared at the tropical scene for a moment and felt his eyes roll. "All right," he said, turning back to Ridge, "let's get this over with. What happened to Herter back in California? And what the hell was that in Honolulu?"

"What exactly do you mean?" Ridge said, shifting slightly in his seat.

Hanford instantly picked up on Ridge's unease, but didn't let on. "I want to know who tried to knock him off," the president asked, "and who went after the reporter."

"Right now, we—"

"I thought we had this covered. Herter's as much a pain in the ass as Latasi, but we still need him. Who put out the order?" He knew full well, but unlike his chief of staff, was much more adept at hiding his intent.

"Well, we—"

"I have no problem with him being a little paranoid. That's why we had him met at the airport. But he was just supposed to be on edge. That didn't mean have him hit. Who the hell took that upon themselves?"

Ridge began squirming. "I don't know, Mr. President. The print that was lifted was traced back to a special forces operative. Raden might already know but regardless, it didn't need to come out last night. That's why I cut off him off at dinner. It may come out later, but hopefully we'll learn what was behind it before it gets to that. In the meantime, it sounds like Herter's got enough to keep him busy here, and with Raden in Frisco, we just may be able to ride it out. Hopefully, Herter will come through so it doesn't even become an issue."

"Okay. Just make sure it doesn't. And explain what happened in Hawaii."

"We're not sure about that, Mr. President. The Honolulu cops are piecing it together. We're not even sure it had anything to do with—"

"Oh, cut the crap. Even a rocket scientist could connect those dots, and they can't see anything not under their microscopes."

Ridge squirmed more. "I'm just saying—"

"I know what you're saying," Hanford grunted, "but I don't need this. The Pentagon's finally making headway on what Whiteman sat on. I can't believe she was able to hide it this long. I told you shit would come out. And if it happens before tomorrow night, we're screwed." He groaned. "I don't need to deal with this." The car pulled up to the airport and an aide opened the door for the president. Hanford scurried out, feeling his eyes begin to roll once more.

Eighty-four

The Toaripi Lauti Medical Center was a smart, contemporary structure that reminded Kevin more of an urgent care clinic than a hospital.
Named for the first prime minister of independent Tuvalu, it was elegantly framed by frangipani trees in full bloom, their lavender playing off
perfectly to the brilliant yellow birds of paradise lining the road.

They made the five minute drive mostly in silence. Kevin lost himself in the tranquil flora, content to sit in the back of the SUV and hold
Cindy's hand while Natano let Tong drive. He wiped sweat off his upper
lip and remembered how much he hated hospitals.

Peter Natano was eager to hear what was on Kevin's mind but for the
moment put his concern on getting there as quick as possible. The sea
and sky and blinding sun were befitting diversions to the tension. In the
distant East, Eta Carinae had begun drifting off.

Kevin had slipped the folded pages Cindy had printed into his shirt
pocket. As they neared the building, she looked over at him.

"You figured something out." He answered only with a squeeze to
her hand, but her words were enough to get Natano's attention.

"You know what I'm going to say," he said.

They pulled up, apparently expected. An officer guarded the main
entrance. Natano spoke to him, then motioned Kevin and Cindy inside.
The smack of cold from the air conditioner was a welcome shock. A
doctor awaited them, flanked by another officer.

"Dr. Herter, it's a pleasure," the doctor said, extending his hand with
a friendly smile. "Tom Asanti. I head the trauma unit." He also greeted
Cindy. He seemed like many others there; in his thirties, professional,
polite.

"Manny, what do you have?" Natano asked the officer.

Officer Manuel Lombard said, "We think she spent the whole night
under the stairs. Sonia is outside her room." He explained to Kevin,
"Officer Sonia Talake. We promised Dr. Whiteman someone would
guard her, but she wouldn't have any of us guys there."

"Right now," Asanti said, "the patient is being attended by nurses and one of our counselors, Dr. Pam Sandovar. She was very combative and a touch dehydrated. We offered her some fruit juice and she went ballistic. I was prepared to administer a sedative, but Dr. Sandovar calmed her down."

"We don't have much to go on until we can speak with her," Officer Lombard said.

"We thought it might be a good idea if Miss Russell spoke with her," Natano said.

"I met her last night," Cindy said.

"That's interesting," Asanti said. "She mentioned you."

"Are you sure you don't want me to try?" Kevin asked.

"Just hold off for now," Natano said. He nodded to Cindy, and the two followed Asanti down the hall, where they turned left at the end.

Kevin, left with Officer Lombard looked around the facility, stocked with state-of-the-art equipment. "I'm impressed," he noted.

"We're equipped for most anything, but usually it's hangovers and sunburns." Although young, the easy-going officer had a professionalism that matched well with the others who worked there. "By the way, Dr. Herter, it's a pleasure to meet you. I want to thank you for what you have done for our people." Kevin brushed him off, but Lombard said, "You have to understand how it is here. The prime minister is like an uncle to me. My parents live next to his brother. We're such a small country, it's like he's family. I've heard him speak about you, and what your work has meant. So it's a pleasure to meet you, though I'm ashamed of what happened in your room."

"Thanks, but you didn't let it happen. Someone else did that. I hope you get to the bottom of it."

A commotion began from around the bend. Kevin recognized Lisa Whiteman's voice. She was yelling. He made his way down the hall, where he met Natano turning the bend. Natano held his hand up.

"She's in the room around the corner. I didn't go inside," he told Kevin. "You may—"

More yelling broke out. Cindy appeared and said, "Kev, it may not be a good time—"

"Tell him to get away from here!" shouted Lisa from inside. Kevin got to the corner and saw a woman he didn't recognize sticking her head out of a room.

"Dr. Herter," Dr. Sandovar said, "perhaps it's best if you waited out front."

"Please tell her I'd like to speak with her when she's ready," Kevin said, looking dejected.

Natano led him back toward the waiting area, and Cindy went back inside. Lisa was thrashing about, despite the efforts of the nurses to get her to calm down.

"I begged him last night to see me," Lisa shouted. "He couldn't be bothered!"

"Well," Cindy said, "I think he just wasn't sure—"

"It's too late," she cut in, her eyes wild with fright. "I have to get back home! I'm dead if I stay here! Don't you people understand?"

"Lisa, what happened? You can tell me—"

"I can't tell anyone! And you should know! I have to get out! I need the plane!"

"I don't understand."

Lisa tried pushing past the nurses. They blocked her and she began flailing punches, trying to get out.

"Lisa," Sandovar said, "if you don't calm down, the nurses will restrain you." Cindy grabbed hold of her, firm but gentle.

"Lisa, I have an idea but you're going to have to work with me. Can we speak alone?" She turned to Sandovar. "Can we have a few minutes?"

They looked at each other. Sandovar reluctantly said, "We'll be outside." Lisa nodded. "Okay, good then," added Sandovar. "Is there anyone you would like us to contact? Your husband, perha—"

"AHHH!" Lisa gasped. "No, no! Don't you call—get me out of here!" She began flailing her arms and the nurses moved in again, but Cindy managed to grab one of Lisa's arms.

"It's okay, it's okay," she said, trying to sound soothing.

"Lisa, please," Sandovar said.

"It's okay," Cindy said, gesturing vigorously. "I'll sit with her. Can I sit with you?" she asked. Lisa, visibly shaking, gave a drawn-out nod.

After making sure that she was calming down, Sandovar followed the nurses out, leaving Cindy sitting on the bed holding Lisa.

"I have to get out of here," Lisa murmured. "Please, get me out."

"Shh, shh," Cindy began repeating softly, while hugging Lisa. After about a minute, it began calming her down. Lisa still wore the black T-shirt and jeans from the previous night, but they hung on her now like yesterday's news. She sat, sunken with fatigue and dread. Cindy reached for a cup of water and took a drink, then passed it to Lisa, who took a halting sip, then slowly emptied it.

"I'm not going to push you," Cindy said gently. "But whatever spooked you, if you don't want to talk to me or Kevin or any of the counselors, you may want to meet a reporter who's here." Lisa said nothing, though bit her lip slowly.

Cindy picked up on it. "Jessica Enright, from MSNBC. I think she would love to meet you. You mentioned a plane. We have gliders we use for sightseeing flights around the clouds. Maybe the three of us can get above all this and talk alone. You think you might be up for it?"

Outside, Kevin wiped his sweaty brow. "I didn't think I'd feel this way," he said. "But I feel really bad about blowing her off last night."

"So," Peter Natano stared him square in the eye, "what was behind that?"

"I was pissed at what she did to my work. And I thought she had something going on. It's not like I wasn't going to see her. It just never occurred to me that she might be on the level."

"Don't you find it interesting that two people here meet up with someone who scares the life out of them, within a day of each other?" As Kevin's gaze solidified, Natano added, "I have an idea what set her off, but I need to hear it from her. Before Miss Enright gets here, I want you to think about something. Suppose the new stats are correct. Does that take care of the instability?"

"It does, but—"

"Bear with me. Everyone's trying to figure out the technical issue and why Dr. Whiteman kept it secret. I want you to think about whom else besides her knew about it."

"Oh, wow." Kevin's gaze popped wide open.

"No one operates in a vacuum. I don't care how careful she was, someone had to know. They may have worked together to keep a lid on it. But it's possible someone just let her think that. If she felt a need to let it out, it could explain what happened to her. I want to know who and why."

Cindy joined them outside.

"How is she?" Kevin asked.

She moved her hand back and forth. "She's calmer. But she's a mess."

"What did she tell you?" Natano asked.

"Nothing. But I suggested that when Jessica gets here, we can go up in one of the gliders, so we can have a place alone to talk alone. She seemed to be open to that."

"Good idea. All right, time to talk. I'll tell you what I told Kevin; someone else knows what's going on here. They let everyone think there was something wrong."

Cindy drew back. "It could explain a lot. If true, it puts this place in a new light."

"It was very important to Dr. Whiteman that you see that file. It's no coincidence that her trip coincides with your Pentagon trying to muscle into areas they've been kept out of, nor that your president has you out here as well. So," he pressed, "what can you tell me?"

Kevin removed the printouts from his pocket. "The White House made a big deal out of dragging me out here to fix something that doesn't seem to be broken. Whether they knew that or not, I don't know. But I do remember seeing some things that didn't make sense to me. I have to go a little technical on you, so just bear with me. I've been doing a little figuring. Something doesn't add up."

He began explaining the devices, and the theory behind them. To his surprise, Natano listened with interest.

"You should be one of those scientists on TV," he said as Kevin finished. "Anytime anyone else tried explaining this to me, my eyes would water. But didn't your Pentagon learn this when they tried to make a weapon system out of it?"

"They tried to make it work but they couldn't. But here's the thing— the key behind the whole deal is the equation. Well, those numbers came from Sandia—"

"Son of a gun, that's right. And that's your Dr. Whiteman."

"That's it. Based on what she tells them, they create this place. And they get spikes. Along the way they tweak the system trying to eliminate the problem, and they fail. They talk about an instability. It's why I was brought out here. Only there aren't any spikes. I think this is what she wanted us to see. And lost in it all is that it's being done under the guise of a tourist attraction."

"Under our noses," Natano frowned. "And all that tells you what?"

"I remember seeing something that read, "Deuterium Differential." Deuterium is the hydrogen isotope they use as fuel. Max Rosenkranz suggested they might be tinkering with it. See, what didn't add up is why there should even be spikes. It shouldn't be happening. I did give it some thought. And with all the great music here, tied into the explosions, I got to thinking about the detonation wave. I wondered what would happen if it were adjusted, basically, playing a different note to get it going. If that occurred, those numbers might even out."

"That's a great idea," Cindy said, perking up. "Why didn't we think of that?"

"Go easy on yourself. You never had all the data. You never even knew there was more."

"Well, we should have known. And we should have thought of it; *I* should have."

Natano was still confused. Kevin said, "In plain English, changing the note changes the wave and you get a different detonation pattern. But unless you use the right equation, you'll never get the correct note. No one knew it existed, so the projections were always off. If you have it, the instability disappears. But to get it, something else has to happen. By necessity, you have to shorten a critical length in the firing assembly."

"Of *course!*" Cindy exclaimed.

Natano stared for a few moments. "Explain the importance behind that."

"This spike issue looks like it can be solved if the distance between the materials in the firing arrays and the fuel core is reduced," Kevin said, "along with altering the equation. See, they were stuck. They kept trying to fit the design to an inefficient equation. What I did was back into it. The differentials are meaningless then. In fact, they're a red herring. In plainer English, changing the note and making the device smaller eliminates the problem."

"That's it," Cindy added. "We were too close to it." She seemed to back away, as if needing space to take in what she'd heard. Natano still hadn't realized its significance.

"They were close to the solution," Kevin added. "Ironically, if they'd kept tinkering, they might have got it. They just wouldn't have known why. I'm convinced Lisa knew that the theory allows for clean blasts with several designs, but they're not all the same. She built the program around the particular one she knew would lead to huge devices. The tradeoff is that it creates differentials, what you know as spikes. She purposely chose an inefficient design, and she got inefficiencies. She also sat on data that would have shown other ways to build them. Then she divvied up duties so no one would find out. I give her credit. You were all told they wanted to reduce the size of the things to reduce operating costs. Well, they do want them smaller, but for a whole other reason."

Natano now stared with an all-too-knowing gaze. "Say you're correct. What would it mean?"

"The things get smaller, the size of the explosions they create become predictable."

Natano folded his arms tighter, jaw clenched. "Now tell me what it really means."

"Say you head the nation's nuclear weapons lab. What would it mean to sit on this?"

"You know damn well what it would mean. And what it would mean for the rest of your Defense Department. If Dr. Whiteman kept us in the dark, she's been doing the same to them. It explains why they've been trying to go around her and muscle their way in. It also explains why everyone's been kissing our asses and trying to nail them at the same time. So come out and say it—your Pentagon gets to fit them on their planes and missiles." He paused. "Wow."

Cindy shook her head. "My God. We didn't even see it."

Kevin said, "I didn't want to say it. It explains why she made the things so big."

"She didn't want them to get the weapons. This whole place was just to keep throwing them off. I have new respect for her." She paused. "But with all this, I don't know why she just didn't approach you directly. She could have come to you anytime during the past two years."

"That's true. After finding all of this out, I would have listened to her."

"Like you listened last night?" Natano's remark deflated Kevin. "It just shows how little trust there is with this. Now maybe you'll appreciate what I'm up against. I need to share this with the prime minister. I'm sure he'll want to talk to you about it." He rubbed the back of his neck. "I told Miss Enright this morning I couldn't believe that so many of these questions had gone unexamined." He had barely finished his comment when they caught sight of Jessica Enright approaching. "I think now she has the story she came here for," he added wistfully.

Eighty-five

Roger Braddock's office was at the San Rafael Corporate Center, a block off Highway 101 on Landaro Street. Sharon, Mike and Hughes arrived a few minutes after nine. The third story suite was spacious, if austerely furnished, with a view of Mt. Tamalpais to the west. At 2,567 and 2,571 feet, the mountain's twin peaks were just breaking through the mist.

Seated at a table in a meeting room were Braddock and Jack Raden. Mike and Raden hadn't seen each other in a while and warmly traded greetings. Raden ribbed Mike on his war wounds while Hughes greeted Braddock, whom he had met before. They were all smiles for Sharon.

Wracked with ambivalence, she still clutched her blanket. The past hours were seared in her mind, and these men had arranged the branding. Surprisingly, her intuition had yet to flare. But as she entered, the four NSA men rising in welcome, she looked right through them. She also ignored the picturesque view. Instead her eye went to the far wall opposite the window.

"Holy shit," she said.

Occupying center attention was one of her paintings. A large canvas in ocher and sepia with teases of turquoise, black and metallic blue and green, it depicted a series of feathers and rocks.

Braddock approached her. "It's a pleasure to meet you," he smiled. "After the morning you had, take a load off." He was a distinguished-looking man of about sixty, a touch over six feet with salt and pepper flecked light brown hair and piercing gray eyes, dressed casually in a black sweater and Dockers. He eyed the painting. "I have a particular fondness for this one."

Sharon managed a smile. While the others got themselves coffee, Raden walked up.

"Sharon," he said, offering a hug, "I'm sorry for what you went through. How are you holding up?" He seemed genuinely concerned.

"Boy, you're just Jack Raincloud on both sides of the continent. Makes me wonder what you have planned out on that island."

"The idea behind bringing you here was to get you away from that crap. Can I get you something?"

"A cup of hot tea would be nice." Raden brought her a mug and they all took seats.

She held her tea closely, and studied them. Braddock in turn focused on her.

"I've watched your career for some time," he began. "I bought this four years ago, and when I saw your piece at the Rosenkranz's it cinched it for me. I'm not much into furniture and knick-knacks. I like art." He was right, she thought. Aside from several computers, a bookcase and a coffee station the room was bare, except for her canvas and a few others of like quality.

"I told you you'd find it interesting to meet Roger," Mike said.

"I know a good investment when I see one," Braddock smiled.

"Sharon," Raden said, "just so you know, this isn't official. Neither was what happened earlier."

"Somehow, I gathered that," she frowned.

"We wanted you out here to help us, but we also knew you'd be vulnerable in Princeton."

She bit her lip and shook her head. "For years I've been riding Kevin to stand up to those idiots. In a million years I never thought he'd be dealing with this kind of shit. Or that I'd be. What happened was fucked up, but I can see what *would* have happened. So, thanks."

"No thanks necessary. Now, we've learned a lot since you looked over the file. We also sent Roger a copy. He's the computer guy among us."

"We're analysts," Mike said. "The technology's moving so fast, old guys like us sometimes lose track of it."

"I just took a look at it," Braddock said. "It's ... interesting."

"If that's your word for it," Sharon said, sipping her tea.

He smiled. "We'll go over it, but first I want to tell you how much I like your work. You're a particularly conscientious study. I like the way you work in layers, how you build them up and tease out new meaning." He looked around the table. "She works with her hands, adding thin layers of oil one at a time. It's a very painstaking process. It's how Renaissance masters worked, underpainting and glazing layers of paint. If it's done right what's beneath shines through. The more she puts on, the more subtle what's beneath gets, but the more it gains depth and different meaning. It's there; you just have to be open to seeing it."

"That's very good." She eyed him, an inquisitorial smile on her face.

"That's why I like this piece. It glows. It's just feathers and rocks. But when you think about how it was made, you know there's more there than what's on the surface."

"I've seen your painting at Max and Jean's a hundred times," Mike said, "and I wouldn't have been able to say that."

"My wife loves this too," Braddock said, "but I want it here. We'll have to buy one for our home." As Sharon laughed, he told her, "Art gets under your skin." He then grew serious. "And so does intrigue, which brings you here with us."

"Then you can tell me who's behind this," she returned. "And why I'm mixed up in an NSA operation and what it has to do with Kevin."

Raden chuckled. "You don't know the can of worms he opened up. Defense policy, political policy, foreign policy; you name it. It's had huge repercussions; the stick too. It's a lousy file but we did see what you saw. It's going to raise some eyebrows."

Sharon said nothing, but looked around at the others. She and Braddock exchanged glances. He gave her an imperceptible smile, and she wondered what he was thinking.

"Jack," Mike said, "maybe you better fill us in on where things stand."

Raden opened the file and gave Mike and Hughes a quick briefing on what it contained. He then scrolled down to the end, and showed them the last three pages of alternate data. Both immediately saw its significance.

"So as far as you know," Mike added, "this has been kept under wraps until now?"

"It seems. Tuvalu has served a strategic purpose for the Administration," Raden explained to Sharon. "It's a distraction hiding in plain sight, shifting attention from problems they haven't wanted to deal with. Up to now, that's worked for them. But Hanford was smart enough to know it wouldn't last, and it didn't. That's why he's hot for those terror figures. It gives him a legitimate excuse to keep the thing going, and covers their rears if there are problems. People will cut him slack if they know it's for a good purpose."

Hughes agreed. "We've gotten a lot of pressure from the White House over the past few months to correlate the data. We frankly didn't think it was worth the time, but they took it seriously."

"Did you hear anything about problems with the system?" Mike asked.

"Word was there were issues, but nothing big to speak of."

"So what does all this have to do with me?" Sharon then asked.

"In looking at the file," Raden said, "the technical issue everyone was worried about isn't there, which was the excuse to bring in Kevin. The director ran two sets of data. The one everyone saw showed a systemic instability. The one she hid shows it can work well. We weren't sure why she'd want people to think that, but it led to much of what's occurred. His involvement does make sense."

"What do you mean?"

"It was important to Whiteman and Hanford that he be brought in. It seems to have been equally important to others that he stay out; now you as well. You two are caught in the middle."

"We've been in touch with Jessica," Mike added. "She's corroborated some of it."

"Like so much," Raden said, "it comes down to follow the money. We assumed contractors on the program had cost overruns. You always have that. She learned that one in particular had a big interest keeping things as they are, a Hawaii firm that builds the firing mechanism. The crap she went through looks like it's tied to them. We studied the figures and the piece that was planted in Kevin's car and we looked at the bug in Mike's car and did a work-up on the two characters we nailed at the park. They're a good match for the motel incident with Enright's crew. They tried to hide it, but it's all material and personnel tied to the contractor and to an intelligence wing of the Pentagon. It appears the program director wanted this exposed. By setting up flawed data that supposedly needed Kevin's involvement, certain interests bought there was an instability only he could fix. It got people's attention, and they eventually saw the kickbacks. A lot of people stand to lose a lot of money. In the meantime, Tuvalu generated security data. When Hanford decided to run with it as a terrorism deterrent, he inadvertently put a spotlight back on the money. It's all intertwined and it's coming to a head. I'm sorry you were dragged into it."

"I figured something like this was up," Mike added. "Max told me they were headed for trouble. The bill's coming due, and the interest is the unintended consequence. And to be glib, they're expecting you and Kevin to pay it."

Raden took a sip of coffee. "Since Kevin opened the door for the Pentagon to clean up their nuclear arsenal, it's also a way to cover their asses. You know they didn't pull it off. That's where the place out in Tuvalu comes in. It works like a huge CYA."

"You can make a plausible case for the whole place being built to keep testing bomb design right out in the open" Mike added. "The resort gives them a proving ground where they can charge admission. Our involvement is that the NSA has long had a problem with both it and with the Pentagon. And they have a bigger problem with the Administration."

"And why is that?" Sharon asked.

"It's a matter of short-term and long-term interests," Hughes said. "The country's interests. The resort is problematic. Keep testing bombs in public, sooner or later it gets away from you. Military secrets are fleeting at best. Even if they're never able to make the things work as weapons, all sorts of information is going to leak out. In no time, everyone's going to have a resort. What we're gaining in the interim will come back to haunt us."

"People getting payoffs don't want the boat rocked," Mike said. "Hanford's mostly concerned with his election and with legacy. I'm not saying he's uninterested in what's best for the country but he'd be a lot happier if those things overlapped. Most likely, you two represent threats to one or the other or maybe even to both, either by standing in the way of something or by being in a position to change something that would compromise them. It seems there's a hell of a lot more in the way of technical data in these files that would make more sense to your ex than to us, but I think this explains a lot of what's going on with this. We'll find out the rest soon enough. So will Kevin."

Raden agreed. "So, there you have it. We just have to figure out who, what and how."

Sharon remained quiet for a few moments, then caught Braddock's eye. He had been silent, but he leaned back with his arms folded and began rubbing his chin.

"Are all you guys this dense?" she asked, shaking her head. "You guys just don't see things. You don't get it. This is all bull."

Raden said, "What are you talking about?"

She motioned to the computer. "You mind?" Braddock nodded at her to proceed.

She minimized the file and began working the keyboard. Mike, Hughes and Raden watched intently while Braddock was content to observe. Soon, a page appeared with a Defense Intelligence Agency letterhead. Across the heading was written "Top Secret."

Raden and Mike looked at each other, stunned, while Hughes sat bewildered. Only Braddock sat unaffected, slowly rocking his chair.

"What the hell is this?" Hughes asked.

Mike looked around. "What is this? Rog, did you see this?"

"I first saw it about fifteen minutes ago, just before you came in."

Mike turned to Sharon. "Where'd you get this from?"

"It was in the file."

"What do you mean, an attachment?"

She shook her head. "Looks like Roger can tell you. Talk about red herrings; you hooked one without even realizing it. You need to stick to what you know."

Raden began reading. It was a short, five-page document signed by the former head of the DIA, Lieutenant General Paul Tyson, and addressed to Secretary of Defense Douglas Landon. By the time Raden was done reading, his aspect had noticeably changed. He met Braddock's eyes with a piercing gaze, then motioned to Mike and Hughes. "You better look at this," he said. They took less than five minutes to cover it, and when done, were visibly shocked.

Raden sat still for a few moments. "Where'd you get this?" he asked quietly.

"It was embedded in it," Sharon said.

"That was the corruption you were talking about," Mike said.

Braddock nodded. "You just didn't have enough time to examine it. You would have gotten it if you had the lab look at the stick. What you thought was a corruption of the file was a result of this being inserted in it. With things like this, the first reaction most people have is to wiggle the mouse or check the connection to clear it up. It's not a terribly deceptive program; you just have to know to look for it. This particular one—"

"It's an art program," Sharon interjected. "It's sort of a holographic outgrowth of Photoshop, for use in commercial art. It lets you work from several servers or sites at once, but it requires that at least one other tab or computer be open before you can use it. Most people are normal and only look at a time. They wouldn't think to fire up another one."

Braddock sat back with a smile. "But you did."

"I have three computers that I use for work. I used to run several at a time. This lets me interface images that I want to paint. When I opened the file I saw the fuzziness, and my mind went there. You guys have your Prism; we have this."

"Young lady, if you ever get tired of painting, you can always come work for me." As Sharon lightly laughed, he said to the others, "This isn't any kind of top-secret program artists are using to take over the world. And you know that Fort Meade has a lot better. But it turned out it's good when you're in the real world and you're pressed for time and want to hide something. Both of us picked it up in short order. Other people would as well, but not everyone might think to embed a classified file using an art program."

"Or," Raden said, "like a hotshot NSA analyst, open it using one. When Lisa Whiteman told me there was a file on the drive I thought she meant the one at the end of it. We were all caught up trying to resolve the conflicting data. I had no idea she meant this. Son of a bitch."

"Which was I'm certain the idea. Mike and I saw some amazing technical things during our time at the agency. In the short time since we retired, I'm sure there are new things back at the office that would blow even us away now."

"I'm sure other people missed it as well. Then this is what Whiteman was trying to hide."

"Or get out," Mike said. "Rick, how many people do you think have seen this?"

"No more than a dozen, and that's saying a lot." He grew stern. "In thirty years with the agency, I've never seen a document with as many repercussions that's been so well suppressed." He looked around. "You guys know when the buzz is on. Even a hint of something like this would have generated a firestorm. No one, and I mean no one has any idea this even exists." As the others agreed, he turned to Sharon. "Young lady, this situation is dicey. I'm sure this is only an outline of the main paper, but even this is loaded. It's obvious none of us were supposed to see it. I'm going to have to rely on your discretion to keep quiet. That's not only for our protection. You're in far too deep to pretend you know nothing, and even if you don't, others think you do. Whoever's behind this knows by now that the first attempt to get you failed. Don't think they won't try again."

Sharon's mouth fell open in incredulity.

"He's right," Mike said. "We thought they were after you and Kevin for some technical specs, or that it was about money. This raises things to a whole different level."

"Please tell me," she said, rubbing her eyes, "I don't have to worry about you guys too."

"It's not our style," Mike returned. "If it were, it would have happened by now." He reached past his jacket and retrieved the gun from his waist. "In case we ran into trouble earlier."

Her eyes widened and her jaw dropped.

"Finally got her speechless," he quipped, giving her a wink.

"We have a bigger concern now," Braddock said, picking up a phone. Raden and Hughes nodded.

"Our necks are on the chopping block now as well," Mike explained to Sharon.

"What the fuck did you guys get me into?" Sharon said, rolling her eyes.

"You were already in," Raden said. "Kevin too. You just didn't know it. All right, first things first." He turned to Braddock, who was hanging up the phone. "Rog, what have you got?"

"A chopper's landing in fifteen minutes. I have a Global Express on standby. That'll get us to Tuvalu by late afternoon."

"Sure you want to come?"

"After seeing this thing, hell yeah. I'll call Trish and tell her I'll be late for dinner. She'll love it when she hears I'm rubbing elbows with you guys again."

Raden and Mike managed laughs. "I'll call Barb and tell her the same," Mike said.

Sharon stared at them. "What's going on?"

"Rick," Braddock said, "there'll be mopping up. We need a tight a lid on this as possible." Hughes nodded. He had been sitting, listening as things unfolded.

"We will have to kick it upstairs. But I think in the interim it should stay covert, at least until you're in the air. Your movements are going to attract notice."

"That's what I think. Very few people know this was in the file, and we only have a short window. I have a hunch even those yahoos you ran into earlier didn't know. That's the only thing we have in our favor. We need to take advantage of it. Time's not on our side." Both Mike and Raden concurred.

"All right," snapped Sharon. "I need to know what the fuck's going on here, and now!"

"We may have missed this," Mike said, "but now that we see it, we know what it means."

"We'll explain it on the way," said Raden. "I told you before that Kevin opened up a can of worms. Well, you just opened up a nightmare."

As Sharon worked to regain her composure Hughes said to her, "Sharon, I'll need your copy of that drive." Something told her not to argue. She handed it over without comment. He thanked her and said, "People, I'm heading out. We'll keep in touch, okay?"

"Definitely," Braddock nodded as Hughes left.

Mike and Raden excused themselves to make a few calls. For the moment, Braddock was left with Sharon. "This will turn out all right," he said calmly, trying to sound reassuring.

She let out a nervous laugh. "I don't even know what that means anymore."

He walked over to her painting. "It isn't often I have the privilege of meeting one of the artists I collect. Oftentimes, too many—"

"Are dead?"

He laughed. "Oh, not so melodramatic."

"But give it time, huh?"

"No, no, *no!*" he smiled. "I collect a lot of contemporaries. Many work in other states or countries. As for this, you'll get through it, I promise."

She rubbed her eyes, and meandered over to him. "You know," she volunteered, "there's a little story connected to this piece."

"I want to hear it."

She stared at it. "I have a thing for personally collecting the subject matter I paint."

"I'd heard that. You don't like painting things you haven't found yourself."

"You do your homework," she smiled. "Anyway, there's a bird farm about fifteen minutes north of me in Princeton. I know the owners; they're great people. They raise pheasants, quail, game birds, for restaurants and stock."

"And that's where you got the feathers for this piece?"

"Yeah. They let me collect feathers from the pens. I don't drive them crazy; I just take what falls off the birds naturally. I don't go sneaking up on them and plucking the things." Braddock smiled, and she added, "Nature comes up with color and pattern that would take an artist a lifetime to dream up. The intricacies, the subtlety. Take time to study it and it leaves an impression. That's one of the things Kevin and I used to talk about when we weren't fighting. He'd show me pictures from the Hubble, and I'd show him feathers or things like patterns on large moth wings. Some of what I showed him, some patterns he'd show me in nebulas and galaxies, it's just incredible." She paused. "You ever meet him?"

Braddock shook his head no.

"He'd sometimes come with me when I went to the farm. It's kind of a rural area. When you're nearing it, you can see some of the pens. Sometimes you'd see several large birds walking along the roadside. I'm not sure if some of them got out or wild birds in the area are drawn there. A lot are Ring-necked Pheasants. They're beautiful game birds, introduced from Asia, very popular. You drive by often enough, you get used to them. They're very attractive. And big."

She stopped to scratch her brow. "It's funny; something Kevin noticed. When he mentioned it, I never forgot. Every time I see them now, I think of him and what he said."

"And what was that?"

"He noticed that the birds outside the pens, the ones that got out or showed up on their own, they looked like they couldn't decide whether they wanted to get back in or fly off. But they don't do either. They just kinda stand around. He always thought it was ironic. They hang around, they're history. But they don't take off. You want to think maybe there's some kind of romance attached to the place, but after a while you realize they're stuck. You feel like smacking them to snap them out of it. It struck him how they get drawn to what's going to be the end of them." She paused. "I never forgot that. Now, I guess I know why."

Just then, Raden and Mike walked in. "We have to get going," Raden said.

Mike looked at Sharon. "We have more to talk about. Kevin's in a lot more trouble than we thought."

She grew agitated. "Then call him up and warn him!"

"I did, indirectly, to Enright, but I couldn't go into detail. Our phones are compromised."

Her jaw dropped. Braddock eyed Mike. "What did you find out?"

"Plenty," he said soberly. Outside, they could hear an approaching helicopter.

Eighty-six

Kevin hadn't seen Jessica Enright since Princeton, and what a difference four days made. In her white T-shirt, cutoffs and shades she could have easily passed for a guest, but as she neared the front entrance there was a hesitance about her, as if she weighed her approach. Though still a knockout, her bandaged cheek added a vulnerability out of step with her looks but in line with the wariness beneath.

Kevin, Cindy and Natano were by the front desk. "Hi, Dr. Herter," Jessica began with a halting smile. "I hope I'm not disturbing you."

Kevin smiled. "You, Jessica? Never."

She cocked her head. "I just seem to bring out the best in you."

"Fastball over the plate." He turned expectantly to Cindy, but she centered him by saying, "Be nice."

He gave a self-conscious shrug. "Come on in," he said. "Make yourself homely."

"I'm prepared for a barrage of those," Jessica said, eyeing Cindy, who was already looking at Kevin with a touch of exasperation.

"Before I say anything," Jessica continued, "I want to apologize to you. And thank you."

"For what?" Kevin was expecting Jessica to begin sparring, but was caught off guard.

"Well, first, before this past week, I would have said, for you-know-what," she said, clasping her hands together. "And I probably would have said it with an attitude." Kevin was surprised, and Jessica added, "Mostly for doing what I used to think my job was."

Her unexpected civility gave Kevin pause. He turned to Cindy. "I was all set to introduce Jessica as a sterling representative of our fifth estate—"

"Oh, is he going to get it," Cindy responded.

Jessica offered up her best TV smile. "That's okay. We have a history." It drew a laugh out of everyone, and Jessica introduced herself to Cindy.

"Jessica, how are you feeling? And please, it's Kevin."

"You probably heard," she replied pensively, brushing a hand over the bandage on her cheek. "Kinda hit the Big Leagues this week. But one good thing; I had a very nice meeting with the Rosenkranz's. They're wonderful people, and they think the world of you."

"Before this week I would have said I wish you hadn't bothered them. And I probably would have said it with an attitude as well. But something tells me it was okay."

She nodded approvingly. "They were so nice. Please know that it was very casual and off the record. I learned a lot from them. It meant a great deal to me. I'm not going to forget them."

Cindy gave Kevin's arm a warm touch as a heavy-hearted smile came over him. He looked at Jessica, he began to see the reporter in a different light. She was less perfect now in her looks but more human—less the white teeth and blow-dried hair of cable news fame but more flawed and open. More complicated. And more unpretentious and pleasant to talk with and be around.

"You have to know," Kevin said, "I didn't like you when we met."

"I was pretty sure," she said. "I can't blame you. Goes with the territory. You don't give yourself time to be bothered. And with so much of the field online nowadays, people learn to like or dislike you in an instant. Saves time I guess, but it's all too quick."

Natano had been standing back while the two had talked, but now stepped forward.

"Jessica and I spoke about helping each other. Some of it rubbed off on me. In the short time since you've been here, I've already become an investigative reporter."

"And trust me," she returned, "I've more than cut my teeth as a detective." She bit her lip. "I don't know if you've heard, but Cliff Abreau didn't make it."

"Oh, wow," Kevin said, shocked. "Jessica's cameraman. He was knifed in that attack in San Francisco. I'm sorry; we didn't know. I thought he was doing okay."

"He was," she said gravely. "He was a nice guy as well. I spoke to Mike earlier. They still have to confirm it, but they're almost positive he was slipped a drug. Mike mentioned Heparin, Coumadin, something to keep blood from clotting. He hemorrhaged, and they couldn't stop—"

"That's murder," Natano said. "That proves it wasn't a burglary."

"That's what they think. Mike is going to call you. He couldn't tell me everything, but whatever's going on is starting to run away." She looked squarely at Kevin. "And there's more on the explosive that was in your car."

"We heard something about that last night, something about a print being found." Natano took a deep breath. "That also means it definitely was a bomb, not something to scare you off like your president's chief of staff was trying to peddle."

Jessica nodded, "Mike wanted me to pass that on. There was enough of a print to trace back to a former Defense Intelligence Agency operative. A name came up, Ian Forster. Forster's someone who's made the rounds. He was in Iraq for the invasion, then he investigated nuclear proliferation, collecting and analyzing data on Iran, North Korea and the like. But he moved on from there as well, and eventually left government. At that point it gets murky. The last he was heard from was some kind of involvement with—"

"Certain defense contractors?" Natano queried.

"That's it. He's being looked into by Mike's people. It's all being kept from the local police; the media too. No one knows where he is or who he's working for, but the name has raised chatter. Now I've already told you more than I've ever told anyone when I'm on an assignment, but I'm in uncharted territory. I also wanted you to know," she told Kevin, "because something happened back in California. Mike didn't go into detail but he's worried now that you're a direct target." Kevin, already ashen, froze.

"We're not going to let that happen," Natano said. "Okay, people, let's keep our wits." He turned to Cindy. "I want you to follow up with Dr. Whiteman. It's imperative now that you talk to her, and bring Miss Enright here along as well."

Cindy looked at Jessica. "We have a lot to brief you on. But first, we need to head to the airport. I hope you like to fly. I need to reserve a glider for this afternoon. Kev, I'll use your name; maybe Lisa will have changed her mind by then and you can come."

Natano said to Kevin, "You'll be okay. One of the advantages of being a small island; we can keep an eye on you." He looked at his watch. "It's almost noon. Now may be a good time to speak with the prime minister. The rest of us can work things on our end."

"I met Mr. Latasi," Jessica said. "He wanted me to pass on a lunch invitation for Kevin."

"That was fast," Kevin said, trying to regroup.

She smiled. "I do this for a living. He said to mention the Terrace."

"Okay, I guess we'll see each other later." Cindy gave him a hug before he left. Jessica turned to her.

"Before we go, I'd like to meet Lisa. Can you see if she's up to a little girl talk?"

"I think she just might." They went inside. Behind the frangipani trees, Air Force One could be seen ascending into a cloud bank.

Just a few minutes later, another jet began its approach. The charter flight from Honolulu carried a group from the Defense Department in Washington, several legislators from Hawaii including the lieutenant governor and the security chief of Sandia National Laboratories. Ron Sanderson and Major Tom Whiteman had spent most of the flight sniping at each other over the events in Hawaii and New Mexico. Dillon Ridge, Christian Deloy, Kevin Herter, the names flew as fast as the condescension, with most of the spewing coming from Sanderson. Some of the others on board were program contractor employees, including a few from Integrated Microphysics. One nondescript but urbane-looking man in his late forties sat silently in back, paying heed to the arguing. His ID from IM carried the title technical consultant and the name James Bremer, matching the name on his passport. It was just one of many aliases for Ian Forster.

Eighty-seven

It was very warm at one p.m. but the trade breeze beneath the shaded parasol made lunch at the Terrace quite pleasant. The prime minister and Kevin sat near where they had been the previous night, and were accorded the courtesies due the nation's leader and his honored guest. In the daylight Kevin could see the richly apportioned ambiance in which Lionel Latasi had taken so much pride. It lent a refinement to the meeting that the gravity of their discussion couldn't disrupt. For Kevin, it was proving a frustration.

"Well Mr. Prime Minister," Kevin said, wiping his mouth with his napkin, "that's pretty much it." He gently pushed back his plate, almost disappointed in the meal. The tropical salad of sliced chicken and spring greens with mango, pineapple and cilantro in a light lime-citrus glaze was the best he had tasted in years, but he had spent most of the time moving it around the plate. He had other things on his mind. It hadn't gone unnoticed.

"Is everything okay with your lunch, my friend?" Latasi asked.

Kevin managed a smiled. "It's fine, thank you. I'm just not that hungry."

Latasi offered a nod. It had been about all Kevin received from the prime minister so far. It was one of the things working against his appetite. The meeting Latasi had supposedly looked forward to and worked to secure had consisted of Kevin briefing him on everything he learned about the program and his concerns, and having the prime minister brush it aside with a smile.

The seeming indifference had Kevin beside himself. After a week of unimaginable developments, he had made his way to the Terrace with a sense of almost surreal irreproachability. The latest news from Jessica Enright had left him feeling as if having attained the status of Dead Man Walking, being barely a step ahead of a reality that would enjoin you were you to stop, catch up with yourself and be one in your moment. It was both liberating and debilitating. With every step the insight just acquired had been left in its track and a new level of realization would take over, lasting but an instant until the next one arose. As if clarity of perception had reached a zenith. Being a marked man on the way to lunch with a foreign head of state in his tropical paradise can do that to you.

It was mind-numbing, how much one person was expected to take in only a week. Every glance at a server came with a second look, every bite of food with doubt. He wasn't sure if prudence was warranted, or the better part of wisdom called for raging paranoia. And whether either would turn out like the ice melting in his glass of iced tea, as the prime minister dispensed with those concerns for issues of his own.

Kevin played it cool, masking his anxiety under a dispassionate presentation. He gave Latasi a comprehensive rundown of how his findings would affect the program. He discussed Hanford's intentions. He described the events in Princeton and California, the experiences of those he had met, and how everything had affected the occurrences on Vaitupu.

Latasi listened while methodically making small work of a curried red snapper filet on a toasted baguette, alternating with sips of coconut water. He seemed strangely composed, as if not quite grasping the impact of what he was hearing. Though he was attentive, it became apparent to Kevin that he was listening with filters of his own.

Kevin squinted in the bright sun, and took a sip of ice tea. "Mr. Prime Minis—"

"Oh, please, my friend. It is Lionel."

"Lionel," he smiled, "I'm honestly not sure why you wanted to meet. I probably know more than anyone what's behind this, and even I didn't know what they were doing. I've got my president looking to save the world by using my work to set off H-bombs. I've got people being killed in my hotel room and explosives set in my car. I've been followed and bugged, and the guy whose country is Ground Zero for all this is acting like it's another day at the ballpark. I expected a little different reaction. Doesn't any of this concern you?"

Latasi smiled, and called over a server. "My friend, do you trust me?" he asked Kevin.

"I suppose." Saying the words left a twinge in his throat.

"Bring us coffee and a dessert special please," Latasi told the server, who left promptly to fulfill the request. "You will see," he smiled, sipping his water. "You didn't seem to be especially hungry, so perhaps you'll allow me to order dessert for you." He patted his round belly. "This is my dessert," he chortled. "But you are still thin, so I want you to enjoy yourself."

As Kevin smiled, Latasi leaned back. "I am not at all unmoved by what you've said," he began. "I've long suspected things were not quite as our friends in Washington have made them out to be. So be it; we all play the hand we're dealt." He took a deep breath. "I don't know what Jack has told you about what's been done here. This is the largest of our nine islands. It was increased in size by over half. A lot of concrete, sand, coral and rock was brought in. We are all thrilled with the results, but it is only temporary."

Kevin looked confused. "What do you mean?"

"My friend, our nation is disappearing literally before our feet. We've been battling the ocean, and I'm afraid the ocean is winning. There isn't one of our people who hasn't noticed the intrusion of the seas. Our older people tell of a time when much of what is now under water was land they played on as children. Until this program came along we had nothing, nothing to look at down the road except having to abandon our islands to the seas."

Kevin listened intently. "I had heard, but I hadn't thought of the impact on you."

Latasi nodded. "The entire South Pacific is faced with this eventuality." He motioned out towards the remnants of Eta Carinae. "You see that out there, my friend? Everyone projects onto those explosions their own reality. Do you know what they are for us? They are the first, the only ray of sunshine to come our way. Until now our only hope was charity, hoping some in the industrialized world responsible for this situation would send us a few scraps so we could afford the last boat ride out when the last of our sands disappear. To this day, they still argue among themselves as to just what is causing the sea rise. Whether it is man-made or some natural process, or some combination of both, while they sit and argue the waters rise, and we have no way out. My people at least can look forward to a measure of financial security when our lands become uninhabitable. And they will. You may think an inch of sea rise here and there insignificant. But an inch on a grade of beach can mean three, four, five feet of loss. When we raise this at the United Nations, we are treated to patronization I would not wish on you on your worst day. The developed world has given us nothing but lip service. You don't know my friend what your little scribbles have meant to us. None of us wish to leave. But we will have to, because our nation will be gone. Your work has given us a way out."

Kevin was humbled by Latasi's words.

"I accept that you never intended this coming from your work,"

Latasi went on. "But so much of life my friend comes from things we never intended, both good and bad. Your country and others never intended that the carbon dioxide they produced would raise the level of the oceans. It did, and it's turned out to be bad for us. But those scribbles of yours have turned out to be good, at least for us. When we eventually evacuate we will be able to do so with dignity, with financial means to go where we choose. That is what your unintended consequences have meant to us.

"Now, you must know what you've said hasn't fallen on deaf ears. I share your concerns. We make it a point to stay well informed on the debate in your nation. Rest assured, I count my fingers when I shake your president's hand." Kevin laughed.

"My friend," Latasi added, "I may be prime minister of a nation smaller than your hometown, but it doesn't mean I don't find myself dealing with politics. This program is being debated in ways that could doom the entire venture. I am acutely aware of how contentious it is. If not handled with care—excuse the expression—it will blow up in our faces. We have a stake in the outcome so I desire you have as enjoyable a time as possible, and when you decide on a course of action that it be beneficial to our people and way of life."

Before Kevin could respond, the server came over with an amazing looking dish.

"My God," Kevin said.

"Coconut-mango crisp," Latasi said. "It is one of our specialties."

"That looks disgustingly good," Kevin said, his coffee taking a drizzle of cream.

"It's fashioned after your peach or apple crisps. We bake it with fresh mango, coconut milk, shaved coconut, meringue on top and serve it with vanilla ice cream." Kevin took a spoonful. With a custard-like richness, it tasted even better than it sounded.

"It's not like it's even very sweet," he effused. "That's incredible."

"It's definitely one of the more popular items on the menu," Latasi said proudly. "I'd go for one myself, but the doctors tell me I must lose weight."

As Kevin nodded with a mouthful, Latasi said, "I have a little story for you. I understand you come from your Midwest. I was born here, but I spent some of my youth in your country. My father died when I was young, and my mother was married for a time to an American. We lived in San Francisco. I was quite shy as a youngster. It was the beginning of the fourth grade. I hadn't made many friends and was not comfortable speaking in class. I remember dreading being called upon. When you are a child in a strange land, it can be very intimidating."

"Trust me," Kevin said between spoonfuls, "even when you're born there."

"So you know. The third week of school a new girl came to class, from Japan. She did not speak English well but she could communicate. But she was even shyer than I. She was given a desk next to mine, and the teacher handed her some textbooks. She was very good in mathematics but her English was not improving, nor her history. She got several Fs.

"Well, it turned out the teacher had mistakenly given her several wrong textbooks. She spent the entire semester trying to learn from the wrong books. She knew right away, but did not say anything. When the teacher learned of the mistake, he was beside himself, partly for giving her the wrong books but more so with her silence. When he asked her about it, she had difficulty explaining, but it came out she was afraid to point out his error because it would cause him to lose face. She feared having to do that to an authority figure. It was more important to her to follow her cultural norms and not say anything and fail. The overriding factor was her fear of having the teacher's error make its way back to her parents and cause her family shame. She could not bring herself to do that.

"And I knew it from the start, but I could not bring myself to say anything either. I was too shy, and too uncomfortable about my own position in the class and my new home. So I remained silent. The two of us sat consumed with fear, two silent, fearful children not learning, though I must tell you looking back, I learned a great deal."

"That's quite a story," Kevin said. "And I can see that happening."

"I must tell you; it stuck with me. I've never forgotten her. I think you may have heard that there's a running joke with us, about the irony here."

"I've honestly gotten a kick out of it."

"We all have fun with it. But for those of us with longer memories, there is a deeper meaning. You know this place as Club Afterglow. After last night you know why. But there's another meaning to the name. The peoples of what you call the Marshall Islands, the people displaced in the '40s and '50s when the Americans and French tested their bombs, those people carry their own meaning to the word. Seventy years ago these were a people uprooted, moved from their homes, their lives forever changed by the bombs. To them a different irony is at play, an entirely different experience. The true irony here is this program should find itself back where it began.

"Think what it must have been like; in the space of a decade to have their homelands invaded and irradiated, even vaporized. Can you imagine what that must do to a people? To this day those atolls are radioactive. We share a kinship with our neighbors. I feel very strongly that this gives us a responsibility to allow our friends a share of the good fortune we've been blessed with. We are amassing considerable wealth from this program. In some way, we can take what was done to them and create something positive and give their descendants a measure of dignity and worth. Nothing can compensate them fully but in some way we can make it easier for them.

"Now, what does this have to do with a young Japanese girl in a San Francisco classroom? In a way she was like our people back then. They went along without saying much, even though they knew it was wrong. So often we sit afraid and accept what happens in silence." Kevin smiled, as Latasi added, "I never forgot that girl. It's something I remind myself of to this day, to not be fearful about saying what needs to be said. I understand your mixed feelings. I've worked very hard to fight that myself. The frightened boy inside is an enduring presence. I still do hold back, but I couldn't be a politician if I let it get the best of me. So I tell you, I will do everything in my power to help my people and our region."

"What is it you'd like to see from me?" Kevin asked.

Latasi broke a bread stick in half. "My dessert," he sighed with a smile. "Don't think I haven't heard you or that I'm unaware of your president's patronization. But rest assured, I'm more of a survivor than he. He has his time frame. It goes to November. Mine is considerably longer. I can suffer him longer than he can me."

Kevin laughed.

"Suffer is an apt way to describe him."

"You have my permission to follow up anything you wish. And if you find something, by all means see Captain Natano. He has complete authority over security matters here. I can have a chat with him as well."

Kevin tried to restrain a frown. "Mr. Prime Minister, I have to say, I don't think that's strong enough. This whole thing is an accident waiting to happen."

Latasi smiled, shaking his head. "I can't imagine your people would have put so much on the line. I've yet to run into an endeavor that doesn't include its nefarious characters and hidden agendas. If there are these kinds of problems here, I'm confident they'll be solved." He paused. "My friend, you're been very open. After dealing with your president, that's very refreshing. I appreciate that, and that you've been so honest and concerned with our safety."

"Which means you don't completely trust what I'm saying either." As Latasi laughed, Kevin shrugged, "That's okay; I wouldn't either, completely."

Latasi laughed, "My friend, you can trust me implicitly!"

Kevin's gaze settled onto his plate. "Well, I trust you know how to make a hell of a dessert," he sighed as he finished the last of the crisp. "I guess that'll have to do for now."

Eighty-eight

Dillon Ridge was in the aft meeting room on Air Force One discussing the upcoming day with the president and his events staff when his phone beeped. He read the text and excused himself, trying to appear unconcerned as he made his way to an empty lounge.

The source was unknown, rare for people Ridge dealt with. Then there was the message, *The packages weren't delivered.* He deleted it and quickly dialed his phone.

"What the hell's it mean, 'the packages weren't delivered'?"

Mark Rivers hadn't expected the call. "I just heard myself. There was some kind of problem. They were redirected." He was in no mood to explain anything.

"You damn well better explain."

Rivers didn't like getting his hands dirty. Most things in his life had gone well. But Ron Sanderson had just called and had been his usual arrogant self, ripping into Rivers over the way his operatives had botched their mission. Just how Sanderson had found out, Rivers wasn't sure, but one thing was for certain—things were coming undone. IM's CEO could weather a typical Ridge salvo but for the moment, he would have to be handled.

"The package arrived early this morning," Rivers explained with corporate detachment. "They stopped in a secluded area. The operatives moved in. It appears they were surprised—"

"You *idiots!*" Ridge seethed, his mouth curling in contempt. It was supposed to be the other way around. "I want to know what happened."

"I don't have all the information yet," he said, even though he did. "Yahr's people moved in on them. One was shot at the site, while the other—"

"Don't tell me. Taken into custody."

"Well—taken. We don't know where he is. That's the extent of it."

Ridge was beyond angry. "I don't fucking believe this. And let me get this straight. This comes on the heels of him sniffing out that other thing, right? Maybe he should work for us."

"I don't want to hear it. The one who was shot didn't make it."

"I don't care. Just as well. And I want to know why you texted me. I should have known about this firsthand with a call. What the fuck are your idiots—"

"I didn't text you."

"What?"

"I don—"

"Then who the hell did? I don't believe thi—wait a minute. What about the file?"

"Right now, I haven't heard—"

"I do not want to hear this." The plane hit a pocket of turbulence. Ridge ignored it and began pacing. "So where are they now?" he demanded.

"I don't know. Just deal with it."

"Oh, I don't fucking believe this. I'm telling you right now. I don't want a lick of this getting back to the White House. You handle it. And what's the deal with those other idiots?"

"You tell me. Sanderson's flying in this morning with Whiteman, along with several of our people. We're hoping—"

"The only hope I want to hear about is the one that tells me you've dealt with that file. What if they start picking the thing apart? This should have been a closed issue by now. Now you're telling me you've lost containment."

"We have a team gathering that should tie up all the—"

"Oh, cut the bull. You can't tell me a damn thing! A fucking team? Yeah, Sanderson and Whiteman; Laurel and Hardy. Oh, I'll sleep a whole lot better now. A bunch of Keystone Cops running around getting a tan while Herter figures out what the hell's on the thing."

Rivers had his fill of Ridge. "Listen, whatever's on the thing you guys are acting like—"

"It has specs that shows him exactly how to design away that cushy lifestyle of yours, is the whatever that's on the thing, so you damn well better nip it in the bud. I don't need to know every bell and whistle to know that if it hurts the White House, it's going to bite you in the ass twice as hard. The president doesn't have to know what's on it either to know your idiots keep tripping over their own two feet. That kind of crap gets everyone's attention, understand?"

"Then *deal* with it!"

"*You* damn well better deal with it for what you're getting paid!" For someone not used to thinking outside the box, it gave Ridge little room for envisioning alternatives. Rivers would have to come up with ideas himself. "I don't want to *hear* from you until you do." Then he paused. "Know what? I don't want to hear from you, period. Have your cousin the other rocket scientist, that idiot Deloy, call from now on." He snapped the phone and paced faster, not knowing what he would tell the president.

Eighty-nine

Elliot Hanford dismissed his events staff from the conference room. He had watched his chief of staff make a quick exit, and knew something was up. Not much got by the president. Whatever it was, he would soon find out. For now, with three hours to go before landing, he sat before his laptop scanning his security updates for the day.

The President's Daily Brief, called the PDB, provides chief executives with information on national security and analysis of international intelligence and threat assessments. The PDB, a top-secret paper, has limited circulation.

With the strategic and political implications of the Tuvalu resort, Hanford also received a secret brief prepared by the Defense Intelligence Agency. The Tuvalu Report was something he initiated well before the resort opened, and was prepared exclusively for the president. It contained intelligence and data, and covered the strategic and political implications of the resort and the issue of thermonuclear quantum resonance. Both the PDB and the Tuvalu Report would occasionally cite the same data but thus far, neither the Director of National Intelligence nor the CIA or NSA knew of the report.

From a legal perspective the Tuvalu Report was at the very least problematic. While its focus was outside US jurisdiction, in practice, it concerned domestic entanglements. The manner in which it was shaped came close to violating federal statutes on monitoring and surveillance of American citizens. Direct domestic surveillance by the CIA was illegal. The issue was so toxic politically that to even just suggest it would have raised red flags. Using the FBI was thought untenable for the same reason. As a result, the White House never involved either agency.

The solution was to utilize the pre-existing intelligence apparatus of the Defense Department. The DIA already provided the military and policymakers intelligence in areas such as economics, the sciences, technological innovation, history, culture and foreign affairs. The potential of clean hydrogen weapons and the Tuvalu resort had broken into that. For Hanford, who had a political ear as finely-tuned as anyone in Washington, any consideration of policy in those areas was indistinguishable from those involving public opinion.

Hanford knew from the beginning that any credible evaluation of both on domestic, defense and foreign matters required a stream of reliable intelligence independent of the CIA and FBI. Both were politicized, and he trusted neither. By relying on the outwardly apolitical intelligence apparatus of the military, the president could work his political aims. Through the DIA, the White House forged an elaborate system of surveillance and eavesdropping.

It may have been coincidence that a legitimate US need for defense and foreign policy information bridged a political one, but it was a coincidence the White House was more than willing to exploit, even if it meant equivocating on Federal domestic surveillance statutes. Since 9/11, laws such as the Patriot Act and others broadened monitoring of organizations and individuals deemed threats to the US. Agencies focused on gathering intelligence such as the NSA, CIA and FBI were already keeping watch on individuals and groups in business, government, science and other areas, efforts that exploded in scope and notoriety in the second decade of the new millennium. In framing the Tuvalu Report, the DIA relied partly on the output of these entities; in effect, looking over the shoulders of those doing the spying. Coupled with the DIA's efforts, the Administration would formulate policy in more secretive fashion. Since prosecuting those exposed was never a goal, they had little concern over legalities. What very few knew was that the entire rationale for the approach was one that had been forced on the White House. Much as he had done through most of his political life, Elliot Hanford had made the best of the hand he was dealt. But reality was about to intervene.

Among the items in the Tuvalu Report that morning were two innocuous bits of information that usually would have escaped attention. One concerned the activity of the corporate jet fleet owned by financier Roger Braddock, a retired NSA analyst. For a week now, Braddock's moves had been being monitored, as well as those of his close associate, retired agent Michael Yahr. It was all part of keeping tabs on John Raden and his inner circle. The briefing provided the itineraries, departures, arrivals, destinations and time spent on the ground.

The other was a communication citing an NSA intercept on the apprehension of a suspect in the knifing of MSNBC reporter Jessica Enright's camera crew at a Mill Valley California motel. She and her associates had been given heightened scrutiny since her run-in with Kevin Herter earlier that week. The intercept had few details; merely citing that an unspecified incident had led to detention of an unidentified person connected to the case, and referenced another individual terminated in the effort.

It didn't take much to read between the lines. Braddock had slipped her past the locals in Honolulu and had flown her to Tuvalu, and had flown Herter's ex from Princeton to San Rafael. It also meant that a covert team believed to have been hired by Integrated Microphysics in Honolulu, the group believed responsible for assaulting Enright's camera crew had failed in the effort on Sharon Velazquez. The NSA wasn't accomplished in arresting suspects and Mirandizing them. If they had someone under lock and key, the IM operation must not have developed as intended. There was a better-than-even chance that a still-alive Velazquez was Tuvalu bound as well.

Hanford was just beginning to sort through the ramifications when his phone rang.

"Mr. President," began the head of the DIA, Lieutenant General Raymond Douglas, "a situation has come up. I'm forwarding you a short file. It's an evaluation of an email sent to an account in Princeton late last night. I think you need to see this sir, right away."

Hanford paused. "Is this something we need to be concerned about?"

"That's a fair appraisal, sir."

Hanford cleared his throat. "Okay, General." He hung up just as the email arrived.

The assessment was one page long. The first paragraph referenced an email received by an address in Princeton belonging to one Sharon Velazquez that had been sent from an as yet unknown email account in Tuvalu. The email contained a file, an extensive database of the resort's nuclear events and an evaluation indicating they were generating conflicting sets of data.

The second paragraph described the separate file found overlaying the first, a memo generated by the DIA some twenty-eight months earlier. Hanford knew all-too-well what it meant. As dispassionately as the information was cited, its import was scorching. It was the biggest secret of his presidency, probably the most incendiary foreign policy secret since the Cold War, and it threatened not only the White House but the stability of the entire West. He had endeavored to keep a lid on it for two-and-a-half years, and now it was a secret no more. The memo was out. He stared quietly at the screen, and then intensely rubbed his eyes.

Ninety

On the Winter Solstice following Elliot Hanford's Inauguration the world was still abuzz with talk of the first clean thermonuclear device tested only four days earlier. The explosion's impact was still being assessed when the president conducted a meeting with Secretary of Defense Douglas Landon and General Raymond Douglas, who had recently been elevated to head the DIA. Landon was a retired Ohio Republican who had served as Chairman of the House Armed Services Committee. Bespectacled, with a thinning mat of gray hair, he had broad across-the-aisle respect. The Pentagon's new intelligence chief was a trim, erect West Point graduate who towered over the slight Landon. Oddly, they played well off each other.

Golden sunlight filled the Oval Office on the crisp Saturday morning. Despite sitting through numerous meetings on Frontier during the past week, the president was in a good mood. The men were ushered in. Both held attaches.

"The Douglas twins," Hanford quipped to smiles. "How is it I get two Defense guys with the same name? Presidents are supposed to deal with generals named Creighton and Husband. No two people have those names. You expect to see me again, bring along a Tom, Dick or Harry, especially on a weekend." As they politely laughed, Hanford told them to take a seat. The president leaned back on his couch, looking relaxed in his cardigan.

"Mr. President," Secretary Landon began, "thank you for seeing us on such short notice."

"No problem." Landon's distinguished aura meant craning your ear to his silken voice rather than requesting that he speak louder. Hanford leaned in. "I venture to say the Pentagon should be pleased. That was one hell-of-a show you guys put on. Might not have been what you would have wanted, but it sure makes for hell-of-a rerun."

Landon held up a hand. "That would depend on the point of view," he admitted.

"Don't tell me your boys are still pissed you can't get the things to fit a briefcase. Hey," he shrugged, "it is what it is."

Landon took a deep breath. "Sir, that's part of what we need to discuss."

"I was under the impression you wanted to discuss how to fit this in with future DOD policy."

"Well—"

"Because we need to begin preliminaries on how to integrate it into next year's budget. You need to brief me on your plans for basic R & D. Work out the numbers and schedule a meeting. I'll let you know what my thoughts are." He paused. "I will tell you, it makes my life a lot easier knowing you can't blow things up the way some of your guys wanted."

Landon and Douglas traded grim glances. The secretary nodded, "Go ahead, Ray."

General Raymond Douglas shifted slightly in his seat. "Mr. President, something's come up. As you know, we've had meetings about this ourselves, the usual follow-up with something this complex and with this kind of visibility. I've been in meetings nonstop since Tuesday night. Among those who came in was our liaison with the Energy Department at the Sandia lab in New Mexico, Major Thomas Whiteman. The major's done a good job running security with Sandia for the Frontier explosion and coordinating general cyber and personnel security for the lab."

"Isn't it his wife that's involved on the science end?" Hanford asked.

"Dr. Lisa Whiteman. She's lab director. Good physicist, tight administrator. That's where they met. If you want to put a name to it, she's the one person more responsible than anyone for what we set off this week. She took that physicist Herter's theory and made it work."

Hanford silently nodded.

"Anyway," Douglas went on, "the major briefed us on what happened in the Pacific. We were all pleased. We were finishing up yesterday evening when he pulled me aside and asked to speak to me. I told him to go ahead but he wanted something away from the office. He asked if we could meet in civilian clothes. We met last night at a pub in Georgetown."

Hanford sat back, and brought his hand to his chin. "Continue, General."

"Well, sir, I thought the same thing you did. I assumed he wanted to go over a matter on future dealings with the DOE. You know those things can get a little testy. I figured he had some insight he wanted to discuss privately. I may be new in the job, but I'm fine with that."

The president looked at Landon. "You weren't there, correct?"

"That's right, Mr. President. Ray called me after he left. And I called your office."

"Okay, general, continue."

Douglas took a deep breath. "Mr. President, Major Whiteman told me things that have us, well, frankly sir, stunned. The device we set off on Tuesday was almost the size of a bus. From the start, we've been operating under the assumption that this was all we could expect. Sandia's furnished us just about everything we've needed, insofar as technological specs on the devices, the physics involved and how to integrate this with our present deterrent. We've been discussing the size issue from with them almost from the beginning. No matter how we looked at it, there didn't seem a way to reduce the thing to make it a practical weapon."

"That was my understanding as well," Hanford said. The president crimped his chin. "And you're here to tell me something different."

Douglas looked at Landon, then said, "I'm here to tell you Mr. President that it appears not only are they able to, but they've known it from the start."

"How's that?" Hanford was puzzled.

"There is absolute certainty in Sandia," Landon cut in, "that this technology can be adapted to fit existing delivery systems, both missiles and planes, and that the director has known this all along."

The president's confused look began to turn angry. "I don't get this. You're hearing this not from her, the scientists or the weapon's developers, but from the security chief there?"

"That's correct, sir," Douglas nodded.

"Oh, Christ," the president blanched. "How the hell does he know?"

"He just—knows. Sir, he found out. Mr. President, it's what he does."

"So why didn't the wife brief you? That's her job."

Douglas's gaze widened. "She's been sitting on it."

"Oh, for crying out loud." Hanford shook his head in disgust.

"From what I was able to get, she doesn't want it to get out. That's probably why she didn't share it with him. My impression is that as husband and wife go they're not exactly—"

"Ozzie and Harriet. So the two of them don't share the same bathroom sink, is what you're saying. And the major doesn't want this information out either."

"That's correct, sir. I was left with the impression his wife is the only one who knows. She seems to keep a tight lid on things. He indicated that she isn't sharing this with anyone."

Hanford began rubbing his face. "From what I know about husbands and wives, don't be so sure she didn't want him to find out, even if she didn't open her mouth and say it. Married couples are quirky, especially the ones who don't get along. And don't be so sure her inner circle doesn't know as well. People who run tight ships surround themselves with people like themselves." He groaned. "So how does the contraption work? What makes it smaller?"

"He didn't go into it, Mr. President. It's not his thing. He only mentioned it has something to do with the firing assembly, the mechanism that detonates the fuel."

"You're saying she knew from the start they could make the things fit your warheads." Hanford turned to Landon. "She doesn't want you to get them. Son of a bitch."

"That's our thinking. She's kept the devices purposely large so we couldn't weaponize."

The president leaned back and crossed his leg. "Clever girl. Which begs the question why the good major felt it necessary to get on a plane just now and spill the beans." He clasped his hands together over his head, and began shaking his head back and forth. "I don't know if you know what the hell this means, what it's going to be like to deal with this now."

"Mr. President, we know all-too-well. This is only the half of it." He reached into his attaché and took out a folder marked Top Secret in stark red.

"Now what's this?" asked an increasingly agitated president.

"Mr. President, this is an outline of a DIA feasibility study. It looked at integrating an actualized version of this technology into our arsenal, should these weapons become available."

"I've seen a hundred of these. What's so special about this one?"

With a grimace, Landon said, "Perhaps you'd better read it."

Inside was a five-page brief, also stamped Top Secret. It didn't take long to go through. By the time Hanford finished he was stupefied.

"Where the *fuck* did this come from?" he snapped.

"We just learned of it within the past few weeks," said an equally appalled Landon.

Hanford turned to Douglas. "General, I want you to tell me where the hell this came from. I didn't authorize this. As a matter of policy, no one I know authorized this."

"Mr. President, the best I can say is it worked its way up from the bureaucracy. I know this kind of talk has made the rounds at cocktail parties and bars—"

"General, we're not in a bar and this isn't a drunken rant." He rifled through the memo. "This is a comprehensive attack strategy. And what do you mean it worked its way up?"

Landon cut in, "Mr. President, this was set in motion by General Douglas's predecessor."

"General Tyson?"

"That's correct. Mr. President, how well did you know the General?"

"Not well enough, it seems. For crying out loud, how did he lock onto this?"

"You know we plan for all kinds of contingencies—"

"Oh, come on! This is not contingency, and it's damn well not advisory. This is a strategic policy paper. Everyone knows the Pentagon does scenarios for every piss-ass conflict you can imagine. This damn thing isn't what-if. This advocates a fundamental shift in United States foreign and defense policy. And more importantly, it lays out a political strategy to go over my head to attain it. You know how many lines this crosses? I've never seen anything like this!"

Douglas nodded. "Mr. President, when Paul Tyson was killed in that plane crash five months ago, he had already given this his blessings. I came over from the Joint Chiefs. What with nominating and confirmation, I only just learned of this. I looked into it and briefed the Secretary."

Hanford glared at Landon. "Believe it," Landon said, giving it back. "General Tyson was involved, from the start. Support for this is deep. You're right; we don't bring every offensive operational study to the attention of the commander in chief. But bear in mind—"

"What we just discussed," Hanford groaned. "Son of a bitch."

"The moment we heard of this technology, this debate took off. Even before knowing we could have the weapons, there was considerable support for them. Paul Tyson was good at keeping his ear to the ground. Clean thermonuclear devices would obviously be attractive to the services. It didn't take him long to back it." He shrugged. "He was doing his job Mr. President. Analysis and intelligence. He quietly set up a study on what could happen should they become available and their use in a variety of theaters. This particular policy proposal quickly went to the top of the list. It goes without saying that for some time it's been the most dangerous part of the world. Because of how sensitive it is, he kept those involved on a short leash. And they kept visibility to a minimum. He was successful; very few people have heard of this."

"Sure as hell was," said Hanford. "I hadn't heard a whisper about it."

"You would have soon. You know this has been contentious. There are those in the DIA and DOD who feel that developing and deploying these things is inherently destabilizing. Ray and I hold this view. General Tyson and others saw them as an opportunity. This study reflects that side. After Frontier they were set to implement it. Lobbying Congress to address the reduction issue is step one. The danger, irrespective that they don't yet know it's been solved, is the issue of policy. It touches a nerve. It's got an appeal, and it could take on a life of its own. It shouldn't come as any surprise that a sizeable portion of the services is fed up dealing with the Islamic world."

"I know that. The public as well. You don't think I'm not aware of that?"

"It's hard to blame them." Landon shrugged. "They ask us for aid, we give it, they hate us. We say no, they hate us. They kill each other like nobody's business; torture chambers, mass graves, it's our fault. We try to stop it, they blow themselves up, it's our fault. We sit back, they blow themselves up, it's our fault. We go in, they say it's about oil and hate us; we pull back, they say we're weak and hate us. They hate us, each other, everybody else; you can go on and on, but they're never happy. The way they treat each other, the way they treat women, non-believers, like Christians and Jews, Israel, well—many Americans have just about had it."

"I know all that," Hanford blurted. "I've heard it for years. This is completely different, and you know it. My God, no president could do something like this, even if he wanted to."

"I know Mr. President," Douglas agreed, "but debate wasn't only confined to the intelligence community. No one knows better that military secrets don't last than the military. Even if these weapons are developed, at best it'll give us just an edge. Sooner or later, someone else will get them."

"Fine. What does that have to do with what this study is proposing?"

"Sir, after World War II there was a period when we had a monopoly on the bomb. Before the Russians acquired it, there was considerable debate about whether we should firebomb their cities and military targets. That escalated as relations deteriorated, particularly during the Berlin Airlift. When they set off their version in '49 the issue became moot, but there were a lot of people who felt we missed an opportunity to settle things before it got to that point."

"And no one worried about how that would make us look?" Hanford frowned. "What the hell did they think would happen to the radiation?"

"I can't say. They didn't want to think about it. But now that part's no longer an issue."

"Like that makes a difference?" Hanford snapped. "You tell me planners today want to do that? Are they out of their minds? And they think they're going to ram this down my throat?"

"Well, Mr. President," Landon shrugged, "the thinking is that we spent the next forty years and five trillion dollars on a big dick-wave. Many today think the Cold War need never have been fought. Neither side was going to use the things and the money could have been better spent. Today our planners recognize that the adversaries we face are considerably different from seventy years ago and need to be approached differently. But what's the same is the opportunity we have to deal decisively with an enemy. Opinion is, history's repeating itself. That kind of thing rarely occurs. The feeling is that no American president would make the same mistake twice."

A beam of sunlight reflected off the glass of a picture hanging on the wall into Elliot Hanford's eye. He squinted and slid over on the couch.

"All right," he groaned, "what are we talking about here?"

"Sir," General Douglas said, "this study factored in the logistics of deploying these weapons, as well as political and diplomatic factors and public opinion. The conclusion was that this was a viable option should the weapons present themselves, particularly following Baja California and Pakistan. All it needs is political will."

Hanford began rubbing his neck. The Pakistan and Baja incidents were still fresh in the public's mind. Three years before his election, elements of Pakistan's Intelligence Services loyal to Islamic fundamentalist groups breached military firewalls and gained access to three low-grade warheads. One accidentally detonated in a suburb of Islamabad, killing over 350,000 people. Once it became known that the weapon had been headed for India, both countries ignited, almost leading to an Indo-Pakistani nuclear exchange and convulsing Pakistani society to a point where it would likely take decades to recover.

A year later in Baja California, an Al Qaeda group that had acquired a black market Soviet-era warhead was intercepted trying to smuggle it into the US. As Mexican federal authorities in concert with American support teams closed in on the cell, the warhead detonated as it was being off loaded from a cargo ship on the southern tip of the peninsula.

The first wartime use of an atomic device since World War II was caught on film, instantly elevating it to an icon, much like the images of the Trinity shot and the destruction of Hiroshima and Nagasaki. The 400-kiloton bomb killed dozens of highly skilled personnel and several hundred civilians on both sides of the border and radioactively-fouled hundreds of square miles of shoreline and environmentally-sensitive scrub land. Fallout reached the Caribbean and American southwest, nearly toppling a Mexican government already weakened by drug wars and steering the United States into a severe recession.

The bomb had been tracked from its point of origin in western Pakistan, allowing numerous support groups and cells to be identified and liquidated. Interrogations of captured operatives revealed that a far worse scenario had been averted as the Los Angeles-bound warhead was to have been the first element of the long-feared Al Qaeda plot to simultaneously detonate nuclear weapons in multiple American cities. As a result, most western intelligence agencies considered the operation a partial success. Nonetheless, recriminations set in, and both nations erupted. Elliot Hanford remembered it well. It helped propel him into the presidency.

The two incidents led to a profound shift in American public opinion on relations with the Muslim world. After 9/11 the country had little tolerance for Islamic fundamentalism, but also had little patience for civil rights abuses. The occurrences, especially the Baja event, changed that. Most Americans now felt that if excesses occurred in dealing with Islamic issues, they were easier to overlook. Elliot Hanford himself knew how things had changed, but what he held in his hands went far beyond what he could imagine the country accepting.

He stared at the memo for several moments. "You're asking—"

"Not us, Mr. President," Landon said. Douglas nodded in agreement.

"Regardless; whoever." He ran over the paper again. "This calls for firebombing targets in a dozen Muslim countries, over fifty targets. Are they *insane*? This is Strangelove territory."

"Mr. President, the thinking is that with these weapons, you're talking only heat and blast. There are no radiological effects like what might have happened in the Cold War. Whatever outrage we get over collateral damage, we deal with. It'll be worth it in the long run to decimate an entire generation of radicals."

"And fifty million others. What happens when those who are left decide to come after us?"

"We hit them again. And again. You know how many times I hear they deserve everything that's coming to them, that with these people enough is enough?"

"That's it. We could have a new kind of bomb that's a game changer." Douglas shrugged. "If we had these things seventy years ago there would have been a lot of pressure to use them. We do it right this time, once and for all, no more messing around."

Hanford sat up, his mettle now stiffened, and turned to Secretary Landon. "Okay, I've heard enough. I want to know; what's the Defense Department's position on this issue?"

"Our official position is we've yet to take one." Landon gave a reluctant shrug. "Mr. President, the Department is torn. There's plenty of heated opinion on both sides."

"But *you've* already made up your minds. I concur. I can't deploy these," he groaned, waving the memo, "not with this thing. Damn if I sign off on being the first person in history responsible for incinerating fifty million people. And you're telling me that there's a cabal in the Pentagon that wants to do precisely that." He shook his head into a groan, muttering, "The things that get dropped in my lap. God damn scientists."

"Mr. President," Landon said, "very few people know that it's possible to develop these weapons now. But that doesn't matter. The forces behind this study aren't going to sit back. After Frontier, they want them. Expect a concerted effort to solve the size reduction issue."

"Dammit, I know that! Once they hear they can get their bombs they're going to push for a policy change, no matter what the president may want. *That's* why your Major Whiteman let the cat out of the bag." He rubbed his eyes. "All right. We have to figure out how to handle this. Seems the only thing keeping your people from cracking it is they think it can't be cracked. You said very few people know about the size solution. What about the memo?"

"Some in the department," Landon said. "The planners who put it together."

"Does that include Major Whiteman?"

"He was briefed by my predecessor," Douglas replied. He paused. "He leaked it to his wife."

"Or left it for her to find. General Tyson may have been trying to light a fire under his rear end to push her to fix the thing. The major and the doctor may not talk things over in bed but she knows about the bombs, he knows about the policy. They each rummage through the other's wallet, and each has cause to keep their part under wraps. Does she know he briefed you?"

"I don't know," Douglas said.

"Marriage," Hanford sneered. "You don't know if they even spoke to each other. Each just happened to learn about the other's hush-hush data. Okay. They may not be working together but they still wound up in the same neighborhood. General, you're to make it known to the major in no uncertain terms he is to consider discussion of this issue off limits. That's with his wife, his staff; anyone. That's an order from the commander in chief. Now, Dr. Whiteman—she's in the employ of a federal agency. I can lean on her but something tells me the good doctor serves a more strategic purpose if she thinks she's still doing all this herself. You just keep a very big eye on her, without word getting back to her husband. He'd sniff it out in no time." He folded his arms, and rubbed his chin. "It sounds as if very few people know about both the bombs *and* the memo."

"That's about it, sir."

"That's how we're going to keep it, understand? Dr. Whiteman doesn't know she's doing us a favor, but I can't run thermonuclear weapon policy on the strength of a physicist with a case of the guilts. This memo cannot come out." As Landon and Douglas reacted to what they both knew to be an impossible order, Hanford groaned, "Who the hell needs this crap."

"Mr. President," Landon shrugged, "none of us saw this coming. But you have to know, things like this always have unintended consequences that pop up. We've managed to keep it out of the media. If we get the weapons though, all bets are off."

"One disaster at a time," Hanford frowned. "So the only thing keeping us from blowing up half the Middle East has been a physicist who knows how to keep a secret. Son of a bitch."

"Mr. President, we can still try sitting on the memo," Douglas said.

"Oh for crying out loud, these things never stay put, especially when they have this much support. They develop a life of their own. That drives policy and policy looks for credibility. That's when they surface. They feed off each other. You know it. Sooner or later it's going to come out. You just can't let it."

"Well then sir, I'm not sure what we can do about it, or how long we can keep it covered up."

"Fine." Hanford groaned, and shook his head. "They think they're going to get it to slip out in a way that doesn't give me a chance to oppose it. Then you have to figure out a way to cover it up without covering it up." He rolled his eyes in exasperation, his mind already going.

Ninety-one

The sound of shouting from the main cabin stirred Sharon from an uneasy sleep four hours after they'd left California. It was the first time she'd ever used an in-flight sleep compartment, but with all the other firsts of late, it barely registered. She slept in fits, punctuated by bouts of intensely focused awareness. Draped in a blanket, she shuffled out to see what the fuss was about.

"Hey," Jack Raden said, trying to smile. "I'm sorry we woke you up."

"I was too tired to sleep," she shrugged grudgingly.

Raden was sitting at a stylish desk, a laptop before him, preoccupied. Mike Yahr leaned over him. Mike looked at Sharon and winked, but quickly returned to the screen.

A rich brown leather couch stretched along the left side of the plane. At the end near the cockpit, Roger Braddock stood with a fist on his hip, barking into a phone.

"That's not good enough. Fine, then tell me how—then go over their heads. I don't care—you're not hearing me; we're sitting ducks out here. It doesn't do us any good to—okay, stop. Then go through them, over them, I don't *care*. What are they saying? Then let us know. Are we okay? All right, and get back to me." He hung up and groaning, collapsed into the couch, sending Sharon a silent salute before folding his arms up tight.

"What's going on?" she inquired as she settled on the couch. "Looks like I stepped in it."

"You could say that," Raden said.

Sharon's second flight in twelve hours was on a corporate jet every bit as plush as the one she'd been on earlier. The interior of taupe, gold and brown complemented the couch. Several leather recliners, a bar and an efficiency rounded out the cabin. She could get used to it.

The elegance stood in stark contrast to the unrest skittering about. While the others seemed pleased to see her, Sharon knew that she'd walked in on something significant.

She tried ignoring her worries. "This is kind of nice," she said lightly. "I may get me one."

"Feel free to borrow it sometime," Braddock replied, brandishing a hard grin. As she smiled, he gazed over at the desk. "Anything yet?"

Raden said no, and got up to get a water. Mike took his seat and began staring at the screen. A moment later he said, "Okay, I'm seeing it now. All right, there's—hold on—" His gaze tensed up. "Shit," he snapped, "a splash order. Two F-35s from the *Abraham Lincoln*."

"Son of a bitch." Braddock jumped up, grabbed the phone and began yelling again.

"What is going *on*?" Sharon pleaded with a wide-eyed look.

"Dammit," Braddock yelled, "that's not good enough! We don't have the time. Get on the horn and quash it! Are you—" He glared at the phone. "Son of a bitch! They're running interference." He bolted toward the cockpit.

Raden grabbed another phone; that too was dead. Mike ran over the screen again. "ETI six minutes! The *Lincoln* captain is raising hell!"

"Damn right!" Raden said. "Go Bill!" They could hear Braddock in the cockpit.

"Raise the *Lincoln*; we don't have time." He shouted back to Mike. "Anything yet?"

"Lot of arguing, but no countermand yet."

"Crap. All right, keep trying, but we can't wait."

The pilot made contact with the aircraft carrier. Braddock grabbed the radio. "Lieutenant, I want you to patch me in directly to the bridge. I want to speak to—"

"Intercept confirmed!" Mike yelled, staring at the screen. "The captain's trying to—"

"Dammit Lieutenant! You get word to Captain Anders right now! You tell him his splash order has targeted Josh Braddock—I don't care, he's going to want to know this—dammit Lieutenant, *do it!*"

"Washington's demanding the *Lincoln* break off contact with us— coming on five minutes!"

Sharon stared in disbelief. "What the hell's going on here? What's ETI?"

"That's right, lieutenant," Braddock went on, "there's no time—call off your fighters. Then order a flyby. This flight is carrying a representative of the president. That's right, Dr. John Raden. Then you damn well put on someone who—Is Captain Anders there? You tell him it's Josh Braddock and—Okay, put him on."

Mike yelled, "The *Lincoln's* demanding a hold on the splash and a fly-by instead." He turned to Sharon. "ETI. Estimated Time of Intercept." She backed up, gaze widening.

"Atta-boy, Bill," Braddock said into the phone. "Lieute—Bill, Bill, is that you? It's Roger. Yeah, we're in a mess. Yeah, I'm on board with Jack and Mike. I know, we're both of us dragged into this. No time to explain but quash the splash for now and—those bastards; what the hell does it take to get through to—I told them it's a civilian flight. You know he's a pinhead. I wouldn't want to talk to him either. Let them countermand it—however you want to handle it."

"Four minutes!" Mike yelled.

"Okay, Bill, thanks. Can you confirm? Okay," Braddock began nodding, "are you square with—I don't care any more either. Just let me know who authorized—I bet you do as well; I want to know who signed off on this. Thanks, just get back to me then. Are we okay? All right, I'll wait to hear from you. And thanks. Over and out."

He came back and rubbing his eyes, collapsed into the couch. After a few moments, he turned to Sharon. "You didn't think that little episode in the woods would be the end of it?"

She slowly drew back, biting her lip. "What the hell was that?"

Still working the screen, Mike said, "It's coming thr—okay, a hold's been ordered." He looked up and took a deep breath. "Three minutes. I thought I was done with shit for today."

"What is going *on* here?" Sharon implored. "What are you reading? What is that?"

"You don't want to know. How are you feeling?" he asked instead, beginning to relax.

"Are you *kidding*? How do I *feel*? What the hell did I just stumble into?"

Braddock was about to say something when the phone rang. As he rose to get it Raden said, "Stumbled into is about right." He eyed Braddock, who looked up and nodded yes.

"Okay," Sharon repeated, "I what to know what's going on, and *now!*"

Mike gestured to the screen. "It's a live feed from, shall we say, certain sources involved in particular activities associated with elements of the Executive Department. Enough said." Sharon's incredulous look prompted him to add, "A lot happened while you were asleep."

"That was too close for my blood," Braddock said as he got off the phone. He turned to Sharon. "You should have stayed asleep. If anything happened, you wouldn't know." She gave him an exasperated look.

"Your little adventure with Mike," he explained. "Whoever wanted the two of you out of commission didn't stop there."

"Someone didn't want you making it out here," Raden said. "None of us in fact."

Braddock folded his arms. "That memo—they're scrambling to cover their asses. Even way out here in the middle of nowhere we're in it."

"*Who's* covering their ass?" Sharon demanded, picking up on the urgency in his voice. "What's going on?"

"The chatter started shortly after we took off," Mike said.

Raden added, "It began as DEA talk—"

"Drug Enforcement Agency," Mike explained.

"An anonymous tip went out that a private plane taking off from Marin County Airport was carrying a shipment out to the South Pacific. Far fetched, but it lit up the screens."

"But that would have required forcing us to land. And they would have found nothing."

"It would have meant too many loose ends," Braddock added. "So it quickly changed."

"They floated it to take us out," Mike said, "but the credibility wasn't there. So they tried a different take at another agency, a threat to Air Force One. We're passing each other in an hour. The threat warned of a midair ramming. The Secret Service zeroes in on those things."

"What the fuck is this?" Sharon said, stunned.

"Just as someone didn't want you taking off," Raden said, "someone doesn't want us to land."

"We've been hitting up contacts," Braddock explained. "The problem is, the more we've learned, the more feathers we've ruffled. There was an intercept directive."

She paused, more awake now. "What do you mean 'intercept'? Those F-whatevers?"

"Fighters scrambled from the *Lincoln*, the carrier closest to us. There was no way to outrun them, so we had to do some scrambling ourselves." He eyed her. "It was a shoot down order."

Sharon shot up from the couch. Braddock held up his hands. "All right, calm down."

"*You* calm down! Can they do that?"

"Yeah, actually, they can," Raden said, shaking his head. "Out here it would be clean."

"Short-term," Mike added. "It would have repercussions."

"We've effectively quashed it," Braddock said. "If we'd gone through normal channels, we'd be in the drink by now. We lucked out; the *Lincoln's* captain, Bill Anders and I go way back, and we have Secret Service contacts as well. Too many people know who's on this plane now. But it was close." He turned sternly to the others. "And it shouldn't have gotten this far."

"Bill isn't one to be put in a position like that," Raden agreed. "He is *pissed*. You don't give him the runaround. He's not going to let it rest." He gestured to a tray that held bagels, along with a variety of fresh fruit. "You should be hungry," he said to Sharon.

"Another Jewish grandmother," she said with a hint of a smile. She slowly took her seat again, trying to relax. "I could use a cup of tea."

He rose to get her a cup. As he brought it over, she asked, partly alarmed, partly frustrated, "What else have you found out?"

"Don't forget," Braddock told Sharon, "you asked." He made himself a cup of coffee and sat beside her. "I know this isn't your world and you've been hit with a lot—"

"There's a fucking understatement." She twisted in her seat, and then wrapped the blanket tighter. "All right, bull aside. It's a stupid memo. So it gets out. What's the big deal?"

Braddock, Raden and Mike all laughed. "Oh," she dead panned, "I touched a nerve."

"We told you there's a lot more there than just what it said," Braddock replied.

"While you were asleep," Raden said, "between trying to not get shot out of the sky, we pieced some of it together. Those of us at the NSA and DOD unfamiliar with the memo had been on the part of the story involving the resort—money, weaponization. Several areas were converging—technical, terrorism, payoffs. The election. We figured it tied together, though no one expected this. I give the White House credit. Most people hadn't a clue. That's not easy."

Sharon took a sip of tea. "So, it's not the military, then."

"Well, not only," Raden said. He took a deep breath. "Kevin, bless him…"

"Kevin came up with something extraordinary," Mike agreed.

"Problem is," Braddock noted, "other people thought so as well. Just after he published, the president was briefed on his work. We're convinced that when he learned it led to weapons like this, he put in motion ways to cover it up, especially when he heard what the DOD was after. That's what the memo's all about. The resort serves to keep everyone's eye off the real issue."

"So," Sharon asked, "why hide it? You'd think he'd be in love with the things."

"Because these *things* are enormously destabilizing. Every president since Truman's had to deal with them. Hanford's just the latest. And in a way, he's had the hardest deal of all."

"How is that?"

Raden said, "In a perverse way, the only thing more unstable than a world full of dirty bombs is a world full of clean ones." Sharon frowned. He added, "Just bear with me. As part of basic research the director of the DOD's nuclear lab in New Mexico studied Kevin's work. Her name is Dr. Lisa Whiteman. She's the one who found it led to bombs that don't create fallout."

"I know that," Sharon said, testily.

"Which led to the first explosion in the Pacific. Hanford saw the buzz it generated. That got the resort going. But the Pentagon couldn't get it to work as a weapon."

"None of us were naive enough to assume they gave up," Braddock said. "Appreciate how much of a game changer that is."

"As well as a huge shift in global power," Mike noted, "you're talking hundreds of billions in contracts to retool our nuclear arsenal. Hanford knew, the minute he was briefed. He realized the popularity of watching the things offered options. That got everything else going."

"And Hanford wasn't the only one," Raden said. "Whiteman did too. The conventional wisdom that said the things wouldn't work—it all began with her."

"Listen," Sharon said, "not too much gets by me, but I don't get why that's such a big deal. So they put bombs on their bombs. I hate it all, but why should they? Isn't that what they'd want?"

Mike shook his head. "Clean nuclear bombs are a nightmare. Not that dirty ones are any less so, but while we've had some close calls since World War II, that exchange they were all afraid of never happened. Remove the possibility of radioactively poisoning the world and using them is a lot easier to justify. Knock off the enemy and still breathe the air, drink the water and have kids."

"Of course," Raden added, "if they have 'em, they can do it to you. So you whack 'em first."

"Think fallout from dirty bombs is bad?" Braddock said. "The fallout from clean ones would be political suicide. No president could live that down. And that's only the half of it. Whiteman saw all this coming. That's why she sat on it. So what did Hanford do? Played dumb, let her sit, and let her keep thinking no one else knew."

"Holy shit," Sharon said, shaking her head. "I never thought about it like that."

"She built a power base to keep the secret and he sat back and watched," Raden said. "She felt it was noble and no one was onto her, but it played right into his hands. The Pentagon had their own people on it. Hanford knew he couldn't stop it but he could slow them down. When he saw Whiteman hid data, he let her cover that up too. The resort let him avoid dealing with it until his hand was forced. Think what it does—lets people watch bombs without thinking about the crap connected to them. It's brilliant. It did create a proving ground hiding in plain sight, but since it was based on flawed data it still bought time. With the average Joe happy watching the blasts, it's a very legitimate red herring. In a way, its success forced her hand."

"She was convinced Hanford never gave up on weapons," Braddock added. "She was wrong, but believing that she tried outsmarting him. Her design specs are loaded with bells and whistles that made the things too big. She was in a position to sell it. And people bought it."

"He saw that as well," Mike said. "And I hate to say it, but then she did him a bigger favor. She had the memo, but she never really understood its political implications."

"That's what happens when you think like a scientist, and not a politician."

Sharon waved her hand. "My head hurts."

"Wait," Raden said, "it gets better. That design opened the door for contractors to pad expenses and the brass to dip their bills, which has been going on since the days of the Roman Empire. The contractor that builds the main firing assembly has been cleaning up. They know the things can be smaller, but why upset the gravy train?"

"Secret leaks or someone decides to switch to a smaller design," Braddock noted, "they're screwed. But the one they're using now has a slew of problems in its own right."

"And that's what happens when you think like a politician, and not a scientist," Raden said.

"My God," Sharon said, "I have a headache."

Braddock said, "It's called plausible deniability and obfuscation. Muddying the waters. But Washington's loaded with unintended consequences. By trying to avoid an arms race and having things destabilize, what she got is a design that's inherently inefficient. And unstable."

Sharon shook her head incredulously. "Anyway," Raden said,

"Defense intelligence explored policy potentials for these weapons; the Islamist issue in particular. The memo was the result."

"But why would it piss people off enough to want to blow us out of the sky?"

"Politics," Mike said. "And money. If it got out that the Pentagon was orchestrating a first strike against the Muslim World, wouldn't matter Hanford didn't know or the public hates the bomb or Muslims. Guaranteed to whip up impeachment proceedings. The cover-up needed buffers. It's kind of *Wag the Dog*, but what he's really afraid of is another Reichstag."

Braddock said, "In the '30s the Nazis burned down the Reichstag, the German parliament, and blamed the Communists. Back then it worked. Today it's just the opposite—cover-ups are worse than what they hide. Hanford has to conceal this, but he needs to throw smoke between him and the thing. Kevin, IM, the resort, the terror angle; the more confusing the better."

Sharon shook her head. "I would have never guessed it, but, yeah."

"And those with a financial interest in the status quo see us as a direct threat as well," Mike said. "And Kevin. Which brings us to today. On the surface, it's unraveling. But ..."

"He expected it," Braddock said. "He knew it would leak. He couldn't hide it, so he made it work for him. He knew the DOD would do an end run around Sandia to fix it themselves. He also figured on payoffs. It's a business expense—IM's making a lot more on their oversized bombs. They're the ones who went after you and Mike. And Enright. She's learned too much."

"Unbelievable," Sharon said. "Shouldn't Hanford have been worried about all this?"

"On the contrary," Raden said, "all the interests muddied the waters in case anyone got too curious. He could work a new narrative. Nobody likes corporate greed."

"All this sounds too clever by half for me," Sharon said.

"A cover-up like this demands a narrative that's convoluted," Braddock explained. "Nowadays with life so busy, people want simple. Simple is quick. Simple works. It's made for a world with no attention span. When things get complicated, eyes glaze over. People lose interest."

"He didn't waste time trying to control what others do, which never works," Raden said. "He worked what he could control, where they do it. The man knows human nature; he knew what to expect from those around him and he's an astute observer. They didn't disappoint. See, a good magician keeps your eyes focused on one hand while he does his trick with the other. We all thought it was some kind of policy dispute. Rick Hughes was right, no one had a whiff of it."

Sharon wrapped the blanket tighter around herself. "Why are you telling me all this?"

Raden looked at the computer screen. "Now's when the trouble starts."

Sharon's eyes began darting about. In the narrow cabin, a feeling of claustrophobia took over. "All right," she snapped, "enough. Turn this thing around and take me back home." There was a constrained silence, and then she added, "I'm serious."

Braddock eyed both Raden and Mike, then turned to her. "We've already passed Hawaii."

"Oh, enough with the 'point of no return' bull! Just get me the fuck out of here!"

"Sharon," Raden said, trying to sound supportive, "we've been over this. What do you think would happen if you went back?"

"I don't care! I just don't want to deal with this any more!"

"We understand," Mike said, "but you're in this. Let's make the best of it."

"You know, I'm getting really sick of you guys. What the hell you want from me?"

"Sharon, if you're going to ask us what we learned, you have to accept what we tell you."

A look of disgust flashed across her face. She was set to jump down his throat when Raden's tone changed. "Okay," he said sharply, "tell you what. Time for you to earn your keep."

"Excuse me?" she said, curtly.

"Just listen," he snapped. "You don't want to deal with this; too damn bad."

"What? Fuck yo—"

"Shut up and listen. This isn't only about you. We almost got our asses shot off as well."

"Not my fault!" she sneered.

"Nor ours!"

Braddock hesitantly said, "Jack—"

"No," Raden glared, "I've been on the receiving end of this from one end of the globe to the other. Enough with the complaints! And quit blaming the messenger. For once just do something about it. You don't want to, we'll take you back, but I don't ever want to hear about any of this from you again, assuming we ever do hear from you again."

Sharon sat fuming, the crease between her eyes searing itself in place.

"Kevin gave it to me as well in Princeton," Raden went on. "You want to go back, fine. But I have just one question for you. Why do you think that of all people, it was you who first noticed what was on that file?"

She folded up her arms as her lips contorted into a curled silence. "That's a good question."

"Damn right it's a good question. Want the short answer? Someone wanted you to. First they made sure it wouldn't be noticed right away. Then they made sure that when it was, it would be by the right person. Someone went to a lot of effort to learn that the person closest to Kevin would know an obscure program that would slip under most other people's radar and that it might motivate them to bring it to his attention, the person they absolutely needed to get it to. Maybe they didn't know you two split up, but since that just happened I'd say they did their homework. Now, just so happens that someone heads the main nuclear weapons laboratory of the United States Department of Defense. She felt it important enough you be involved. Sooo ..." he grit his teeth, "*be* involved. I didn't think I needed to explain this to you."

"Okay, okay," she huffed. "With you guys you gotta catch your breath." She frowned, and then turned to stare out the window. "How is it you missed that memo?"

"We're analysts," Mike said, "not hackers. We would have gotten it."

"When you see Kevin ask him what it meant to have Mike notice something he wouldn't have noticed if his life depended on it," Raden said. "You don't know what got you into this, you're not going to know how to get out. I'll tell you the same thing I told Kevin—whoever's behind this is relying on people to be exactly who they are. I think you can say it's worked for them."

Sharon stared. "What are you saying?"

"This. You have a choice. Are you who they think you are, something common, a foregone conclusion? Or is there another part of you that you just might want to surprise them with? Because I'll tell you without any doubt, some people are surprised you made it this far."

She stared for an uncomfortable moment. "I don't know what you're looking for."

"I think you do."

"What does that mean?" she said, recoiling.

"You're creative, intelligent, you're," he smiled, "a pain in the ass."

She snickered, and he said, "You think outside the box. I just wonder how far. You want to stick it to them or be a stick in the mud? Because if you want, I'm sure Rog could have you back home tomorrow."

Braddock nodded silently. Mike said, "Listen, we get it. There are few things worse than being stuck on a plane with three analysts. Just ask our wives."

"Turns out we need your help now even more than we thought," Braddock said.

An awkward silence settled into the cabin. The only sound was the drone of the engines. She gazed out the window again. "I never saw a sky such a dark blue," she noted.

"This plane flies higher than you're used to," Braddock said. "We're at 43,000 feet."

She paused for a few moments. "I still don't know what you guys want."

"We have to make sure Kevin isn't anywhere near Hanford when he makes that announcement of his tomorrow," Raden said. "And we need your help."

"And we're running out of time," Mike said, pointing to the computer. "The White House just released a statement. The president will be making a major policy announcement tomorrow in Tuvalu. They're posting that among the guests attending will be Dr. Kevin Herter."

"Crap," Braddock said.

Sharon shook her head. "What?"

"He got to him," he frowned. "You don't know how serious this is."

"I don't get it. Listen, I can't stand the SOB either, and anything I can do to spite him works for me. But what's the big deal? And Kevin's not going to listen to me."

"You're just going to have to make him," Raden said.

"But why? And why me?"

"Because the more reasonable we've sounded, the crazier things have gotten for him. And I can tell you without even having been there that's exactly how Hanford is pitching him as well. We can appeal to his head, but he's not going to believe us anymore. You're the one person who can hit him in his gut. And it might already be too late."

"Oh ..." Sharon flailed her hand in a throe of frustration, "... enough! You want my help? Then let's go after the piece of shit, once and for all!"

"Is that what you think we want?" Raden asked.

"Damn right! I'm tired of this crap!"

"Explain how three analysts and an artist are supposed to get to a president," Braddock asked.

Sharon rubbed her eyes as if trying to get a stain out. "Straight answer!" she snarled, chopping the air with her hands. "I hear you. But I still don't know what the fuck you want me to do. Buy Kevin a cup of coffee while Hanford's talking?"

"Hold it," Raden cut in. "Sharon, I get the same from you; you heard us. But you're not really buying it. I have to know—just what do you think is going on here?"

"What do I think? I think Hanford's some kind of megalomaniac and he's out to get us!"

"No he's not. He's been trying to keep you guys alive."

Sharon rolled her head in disgust. "Oh, enough with the bull!" she winced, imploring Mike and Braddock to throw her a scrap of sanity. Instead, both nodded in accord with Raden.

"I don't believe this," she snarled. "We come a minute from being blown to bits by his air force and you tell me he's not the guy giving the orders. Don't insult my intelligence."

Raden's gaze pierced the tension. "Just listen to me," he said. "That wasn't—"

"Then you tell me what happened," Sharon snapped. "What the hell's he want?"

"You and Kevin don't want to believe it, but it's simple. A second term and a legacy."

She broke out in a half smile. "Well, that's the first thing you guys said that's right. I don't believe a word you're saying."

"Well then," Braddock said, leaning back and crossing his arms, "I'd say the White House is well on its way to having this all work out for them."

As Mike and Raden nodded again, Sharon stopped and stared. "All right," she finally said. "I need to know what the hell's going on. What is it that Kevin won't believe?"

"That all along it has been the White House looking to set him up," Raden said.

Sharon chortled in exasperation.

"Just hear me out," he said. "You're right. The White House is behind this. But they're not the ones after you. Up till now they've been trying their best to keep you alive. And that's why all of you have that much more to be afraid of from them."

Sharon huffed in feigned astonishment. "I'm gonna open the door and jump out—"

"Listen," Raden snapped, "and learn. The Administration is not after you. They're after the contractor, Integrated Microphysics. The way they're going to get them is to let them get you."

Sharon began waving him off. Braddock turned to her and said, "Just hear us out."

"IM's done very well," Raden added, "but the money's gotten to them. They think he wants to chart a new course for the technology. The money train will come to an end. They're trying to force his hand. So he's decided to get them first. Hanford's betting they haven't caught wind of the memo. We agree. He knows he doesn't need Kevin to fix anything but he's let him think so. If Kevin signs off on it and gets a look at the data, he becomes an existential threat to IM. It's why they tried to take him out, and anyone near him. Hanford knows it, so he's maneuvered Kevin into a position where they have no choice but to strike. Once they move on you, he moves on them and rides good intentions to a second term. He's smart enough not to coordinate things with them, but he's does keep track. Timing's key. You know they've already made attempts. The White House has to keep you around until the announcement. After that, well …"

"I don't believe what I'm hearing. This is crazy." she stammered, shaking her head.

"No, it's not crazy," Braddock said. "It's stone-cold rational, and all the more dangerous. He feels every bit as justified about what he's doing as you do opposing it, and nobody's better playing one off against the other. He's furious with people he feels put him in this position and heading that list is Kevin. Doesn't matter he didn't see it coming. He feels he should have. There's no love lost between science and lots more people than you know. They think that scientists dream up one thing after another then do nothing to solve the crap their ideas create. That to them is crazy."

"Which is why not only does he think what he's doing is expedient," Raden said, "he has no problem with either of you being expendable. If he was able to bend Kevin's ear to get him to show up tomorrow, the two of you have a hell-of-a-problem ahead of you. And so do we."

"Sharon," Braddock added, "everyone's got a dog in this fight. IM wants to keep the cash going. The DOD wants the bombs and wants to hide the fact they used the resort to test them. Whiteman doesn't want them to get it. Hawaii wants the new site. Tuvalu wants it as well. And in addition to keeping all those balls in the air and reining in the most dangerous weapon ever created, Hanford wants a new term and place in the history books. So what dogs do you two have? Run a coffee shop, do a little finger painting and stare at the stars. You have no idea what you're up against. You're in a completely different league."

"Any of them would throw you under a bus in an instant, or get someone to do it," Mike said.

"The White House knows full well what's up," Raden said. "The president is livid that IM has targeted Kevin. But he can't tip his hand. He's trying to run out the clock. After tomorrow, the situation changes. After that's over, it helps Hanford if your ex becomes an ex."

"Why is that?" Sharon asked.

"They're selling the program as a correlate to their terror policy," Braddock explained. "Once it's out there Kevin's usefulness changes, from alive to … well, not alive. Hanford knows IM set Kevin up. If it goes down, it shows he had powerful enemies. When the memo surfaces, he'll say he anticipated it, proof that all this had merit. Either way if Kevin's liquidated, it bolsters his argument."

"Why do they need him there tomorrow?"

"Ever notice when Congress holds hearings, instead of hauling in experts to testify they get the actors who play them? The instant the cameras show Hanford next to the scientist whose work began it all, it legitimizes his entire approach. Perception. And if anything goes wrong—"

"It gives him a buffer," Mike said. "Doesn't matter if Kevin stands there with his hands in his pockets. If there's an accident or God-forbid something worse, Hanford can always say, "Hey, it was his idea." Enough people will buy it. More perception."

Sharon shook her head. "Shit."

"Hanford pinned his entire strategy on the terror stats," Raden said. "Go figure; his hunch was correct. There's been a reduction. It's perverse, but it blows off steam for the masses."

"He may be a cynical sleeze," Mike added, "but he's a hell of a politician. Everything he's worked towards revolved around those stats. And topping that list, make sure the eminent Dr. Herter endorses the policy before the memo goes public. That's the key. Kevin shows up, he raises the stakes not only for himself but the White House as well. It's all the more compelling if he's then eliminated, and that only matters if he was there to support it in the first place."

Sharon grew quiet. "So," Braddock asked her after a moment, "any thoughts?"

"How'd you find out all this stuff?"

"Phone calls, contacts. A little deductive reasoning."

"A healthy dose of BS," Mike added.

She smirked, and looked away. "I don't know what to think. I have to let it sink in."

"Fine," Raden challenged her, "you do that. And by the time you're finished, it'll all be over and there won't be anything left to discuss."

"Just chill out," she frowned in disgust. "You know. I didn't expect this."

"Neither did we," Mike said. "But it is what it is."

"You want something to expect?" Raden added. He held a thumb and forefinger a hair apart. "They're this close to pulling it off. All the pieces are in place; they're just running out the clock. And you know the biggest thing going for them? You and Kevin."

"Oh, that is so unfair," Sharon sneered. "You're just pissed none of you knew about it."

Mike smiled at her. "We meant it as a compliment."

"Sharon," Braddock said, "even now you and Kevin have enough decency to doubt that anyone could be cynical enough to do anything like this. It's commendable, but trust me, it's also one of your biggest liabilities."

"Oh, come on—"

"Someone bright as you," Raden cut in, "and you don't get it. People count on that. The people behind this did. Know what else they counted on? That you'd then do exactly what you're doing now, look for a whole dissertation to understand it then muddle around once you heard it. I had the same thing with Kevin. Why do you think they have so much riding on the place we're going? Going "Ooh and Ah" keeps you from seeing what's really going on."

"And what's that?"

"That they're invested in keeping you stuck." Braddock smiled. "Most people when they're ambivalent try to resolve it. Ironically, that keeps you ambivalent. And nothing leaves you more ambivalent than the bomb. Ask Kevin. So at this late date? They're happy with things just iffy enough to run them out for you just a *liiiiiittle* more."

"It's one thing for us as analysts to try to convince you," Mike said. "It's quite another when that itself is part of the other guy's scheme. We get it— you're pissed, and no one's fingerprints are coming up, least of all Hanford's."

"What, are you kidding?" Sharon burst out.

"All you can definitively prove is that he's taken advantage of folks being themselves. What do you charge him with, being an opportunist? Some conspiracy. And if people coincidentally bring about what he wants, he'll say he's dealing with a problem that wasn't his doing. Then he'll say he's more of a realist than any of you. I can't say I completely blame him."

"I can't believe you're saying that," Sharon winced.

"I said I appreciate his problem, not how he's solving it."

"That's it," Raden echoed. "Keep the pot simmering so when it boils over you can take credit for mopping up the spill? Not my idea of Top Chef. The problem with setting the bar on leadership that low is after a while doing nothing looks so much like doing well that people can't tell the difference. Give 'em a little while longer, they don't even care. Sound familiar?"

"So that's where it stands," Braddock said. "You know as much as we do. I just wonder what's worse for you, not knowing or knowing too much."

"What do you mean?" Sharon asked.

"We can talk till we're blue in the face explaining this," Raden said, "and trust me, at the White House, they couldn't be happier. I just want to know what you personally intend to do."

"Listen, I hate this just as much as you guys, even more. I just don't know what I *can* do."

"Well, you've got less than a day to think of something."

"We don't know what'll happen if Kevin backs out," Mike said. "But we do know what happens if he goes ahead. Sit down with that box and start thinking outside of it. Just know, neither business nor bureaucracy is inclined to do anything to upset the applecart, and aside from Enright and a few people at her studio this part of the story hasn't grabbed attention. However you approach him it'll pretty much be just the two of you and a few others who'll be interested."

She groaned. "You have no idea how much bullshit I think this is."

"That's why most people steer clear of it. But you see how hard it is to avoid."

"You're so hot to get back at Hanford," Raden said. "This is your chance to do it smart."

"And you know Kevin better than anyone," Mike said. "You'll think of something. Be creative."

"Thanks. Like it's a painting I can work." She leaned back and then asked, "Why Josh?"

Braddock laughed. "Back in our heyday," Raden said, "Rog was quite the practical joker."

"Okay, so I have to ask. You say everyone's got a dog in this fight.

What's yours?"

The men eyed each other. Mike then said, "You want the company line? Or just the truth?"

Sharon laughed. "The NSA's had a problem with this concept from the start," Raden said. "There's no argument it would be destabilizing. And the other thing?" He turned to Mike.

"I like to think we have a little more regard for certain things than our president," he said.

"Like science. And scientists," Braddock said. He smiled. "And artists."

"Hanford gives people what they want," Mike said. "But our country invests too much in stupidity. Sitting around a keg watching those things go off is stupid on steroids. Yeah, they're a hell of a thing to see. We just expect a little more from ourselves."

"The White House has had that issue with Kevin from the start. We don't think he's responsible for what was done with his work. But for Hanford, it's different. Even though Tuvalu was his idea and his own DOD undercut him, he blames Kevin for dropping it in his lap. It's why he has no problem with him as fall guy. Scientists were never his favorites to begin with. This whole thing shifts blame on them and shows how it's left to enlightened leaders like him to clean up the mess. The arc of the resort is to take that mess and make the best of it."

Raden agreed. "Understand something. Politicians, scientists, bigwigs; to this day there isn't one of them who really knows what to do with these things. They think they do but then they trip over themselves when reality knocks. Know what they do then? Like everyone else, they sit and watch. Or they work up the rest of the world in pissing contests like the ones we've had since World War II. I don't know if you appreciate how it affects a Hanford. People like him are pissed that they even have to deal with that. They're pissed at experts who are supposed to deal with them and don't. And they're especially pissed at scientists who come up with the things in the first place. So just know, a lot of this is payback. He found the perfect way to get back at them—beat 'em at their own game. Get back at them the same way they do to everyone else; get them to sit and watch. And the biggest irony? They're not even aware they're being taken, which I bet he gets more a kick out of than anything." Everyone grew quiet.

"Serves you right for taking a flight with three analysts," Mike said, breaking the tension. Both Raden and Braddock quietly laughed.

"Well," Sharon said, "I guess it was worth it, to hear Jack use expedient and expendable in the same sentence." As they laughed, she added, "It occurs to me, someone threatened to leak the memo. It forced his hand."

Raden's eyes widened. "Know what? That's right. If it comes out early it cuts the legs out from the White House's argument. The problem wasn't that it wouldn't work, but that it would. And it explains the pressure on Kevin." As the others nodded, he added, "Very good."

"It was my tip of the hat to your bad cop," she smiled. "I guess a little of you rubbed off."

As Braddock laughed, Mike told Raden, "You'll have to work on it."

Sharon sighed. "One of those stupid movies Kevin used to watch was *Patton*—"

"*Patton*? Stupid?"

"After a while, they all were stupid. Anyway, in one scene, George C. Scott goes off on some soldiers, and they don't know if he's kidding or not. And he doesn't care if they know, he only cares if he knows."

Braddock turned to Raden. "So Jack, were you kidding?"

"I'll never tell," he said with a glint in his eye.

Sharon smiled for a moment, and then grew more serious. "What is it you want me to do?"

"When we land, get Kevin's ear and convince him to hold off on his endorsement."

"Why can't I tell him now?"

Raden turned to Braddock, who said, "We can't raise the island."

"We're being blocked," Mike said. "We can't get through the normal security channels, and our phone calls aren't getting through either."

Sharon began twisting in her seat. "I don't believe this."

"It's why we have to land as soon as possible. It's also why we're damn lucky Bill Anders was captain of that carrier. Had it been anyone else, this conversation wouldn't be happening."

"What happened earlier caused a commotion," Raden said. "They won't take another shot at us. People know we're up here now. Hanford's headed to Hawaii for a day, so we have time to bend Kevin's ear. He just has to buy it."

"He damn well's going to," Sharon snapped. "For once I'm going to sit his ass down and make him listen to me and I won't take no for an answer. After all the shit we went through." For a moment, she flashed anger, then began to calm down. She decided she had enough of her blanket and put it aside. "I wonder," she mused, "just what it would take to embarrass that SOB."

"Who do you mean, the president?" asked Braddock.

She said nothing, but folded her blanket before sitting back down and smiling. The three men looked at each other. "Okayyyyy," Mike smiled.

A moment later he glanced down at the computer and his smile vanished. "Something's going on with Air Force One."

Ninety-two

An incredulous Dillon Ridge sat alone in the lounge. A squall had forced an alteration in Air Force One's flight path toward Honolulu. A thunderhead churned on the left side of the plane but he disregarded it, focusing instead on the phone he held.

"How's that again?" he snarled, trying not to let his voice carry.

"What, I gotta repeat it?" Christian Deloy said. "I'm done."

"What the fuck do you mean you're *done?*"

"Hey, pal. I told you I wasn't sticking my neck out any farther than I had to."

"What the hell does that mean?"

Deloy sipped his piña colada, squinted in the sunlight and propped up his feet on the balcony railing. "It means your pinhead friends in California and Hawaii made my decision for me. I told you, stop drawing attention to yourselves. So what do you do? After heaping on extra-curricular activities in Waikiki you had to go traipsing through the woods in Marin County."

"That had nothing to do with—"

"I don't care. I told you your dicking around would compromise my ability to perform my task. I conducted a risk assessment with myself. The perils now outweigh the benefits. My work ethic—"

"Work ethic?" Ridge erupted.

"Yeah," Deloy laughed, "the one where I refuse to jeopardize my future mobility or health? You could have stepped in and hit the brakes but you couldn't be bothered. Now it's blowing up. Sheriff Andy here just issued some kind of fire drill and there's a plane-load of Barney Fifes on the way out, not to mention what your boss's navy just tried to do. This place looks like a PBA convention. I'm done. I did my part; I stuck to my end of the bargain. I got my money, and I'm out of here."

"You son of a bitch! We just wired you a half a million bucks! You damn well better—"

"Temper, temper—"

"I swear to God! You will never work—"

"I'm not interested. Talk to your boss. You're the one who fucked this up from the minute—"

"If this compromises the integrity of the White House, I'll—"

"You're doing that all on your own. It's gonna be a pleasure to sit back and watch."

"You piece of shit! What the hell am I supposed to tell—"

"Colonel, you really need to calm your nerves. Take a few days off. Maybe you should come back here. And oh, by the way, next time you expect people to do important things for you it might not be such a good idea to call them idiots behind their back."

"And what happened to the drive?"

Deloy laughed. "Hey, *iz nah my yob. No my pwoblum.*"

"You son of a bitch! What am I supposed to—" He heard a clicking noise and the call ended.

Ridge began furiously pacing. Instantly, the lounge became too small. Containment of the file was now completely lost.

Twenty minutes had passed since he had hung up on Mark Rivers. Since then he had been frantically plowing through emails and texting messages while blaring into his phone, desperate to get answers before the president could pepper him with questions. Every new detail presented a new wrinkle. He knew he had to keep with it, but he also knew that his time had run out. The call from Deloy cut like a death row prisoner choking on his last meal.

The NSA operation with Mike Yahr hadn't been picked up by the media. The lead agent on the ground had kept a tight lid on the incident. But the loss of the data from Sandia was already generating blowback. Factions opposed to the White House at the NSA and elsewhere that had bided their time now saw blood in the water, and prepared to seize any opportunity that appeared. And to Ridge's astonishment and alarm, they were aided mightily by IM.

When the company's operatives learned about the file's loss and the incidents on the beach in Honolulu and at the park north of San Francisco, they immediately acted, almost without thinking. At first they tried intercepting the intelligence. When that failed, they got more reckless, maneuvering to interdict the chain of evidence.

No more effective than their previous moves on Yahr, Velazquez or Herter, these efforts proved disastrous. Steeped in overreach, they drew unwelcome attention to the operatives themselves and to an operation that might otherwise have gone unnoticed. Sloppy, clumsy, fraught with impatience, they were products of a corporate structure that for the better part of two years had been used to events going its way. They had grown rusty dealing with adversity.

When the NSA learned that an anonymous tip had been placed with the DEA on the flight plan of a certain private jet departing Novato, California and the contraband it supposedly carried, it was quickly able to locate the source. When the rationale for the tip swiftly fell apart and the Secret Service was almost immediately alerted to a threat to the president from the same jet, it set in motion events which just days before would have been considered unimaginable.

The splash order to the *Abraham Lincoln* had come perilously close to being executed. Even before it was countermanded, the carrier's captain was in an uproar. Roger Braddock had been right. In no time, what the Secret Service had considered a credible threat, warranting investigation, had become something more grave for the White House, a threat of investigation. IM's histrionics at the potential loss of their contracts was enough of a miscalculation that within three hours of departing Tuvalu, the upshot was knocking on the cabin doors of Air Force One. And now with Deloy bailing, the bottom was falling out.

Ridge was feverishly trying to process this new disaster when the phone rang. Though he was the only person in the lounge, he hesitated before picking it up. He knew what awaited him.

"Dammit!" the president barked over the phone to Ridge, "Where the hell are you?"

Ridge mumbled something about tying up loose ends and told him he would be right in.

In the three years and two plus months since taking office, Elliot Hanford had thought about other presidents and how they handled their difficult days. It was a matter of perspective, keeping one's eye on the bigger picture while suffering the idiotic and obnoxious, and weathering the momentous and grave. Roosevelt, Truman, to Kennedy; Nixon, Reagan to Clinton; all endured events they wished had never happened. Whether problems were imposed or were of their own making, much came down to the man himself. Hanford was certain he would get beyond this.

Hanford was seated in a black swivel chair in the plane's aft meeting room. The long table was empty except for a few papers and a water bottle. His laptop lay open, its screen facing away from the door. He held a ball point pen, clicking it on and off.

It had been a half an hour since he'd heard from General Douglas.

The director's message about losing containment of the memo was the first in a cascade of bad news. Hanford had long anticipated this day, thinking it less catastrophe than complication. Supremely confident in his ability to draw success from any situation, he looked at its potential for political gain. Had it not been the volley of other factors, he could have ridden out the loss. But they were piling up.

Hanford had also spent most of the time on the phone, and was now convinced that his chief of staff still hadn't heard of the DIA memo. Just how he wanted it. Ridge was still obsessing over the Sandia file. Also, just what he wanted.

He sat consumed with how much was riding on tomorrow night. Everything from the election to setting a legacy depended on the pieces lining up, and all of them hung on a quirky scientist showing up without an attitude. Hanford had never thought himself a cynic but it was hard not to feel frustration toward the enigmatic physicist, so clueless over the impact of his own work. Never suffering fools well, the president wished tomorrow was already over.

One issue overrode everything that had occurred since he took office—he had presided over the creation of clean thermonuclear weapons. He was fortunate that the public had taken to the things, enough to cut him some slack. But he knew his luck could just as easily run out if some solution to the issue wasn't forthcoming. Something serious he could sell.

The president knew that as the announcement neared, tensions were building. He knew because he had worked to make it so. Stirring up complications reduced the likelihood of any connection being made to him and any problems that emerged. There may have been instabilities in the system, but they were at most an inconvenience. He knew it was a ruse. Political instability was something he cultivated. Keeping everyone on edge and stuck was just what the situation called for. He was acutely aware of the irony involved. For decades global stability was maintained through instability, and the absurdity of MAD. Hanford knew that cleaning up the weapons would be considered stabilizing, but would be inherently destabilizing. A resolution to the issue would be the most destabilizing solution of all. Every party involved had its own agenda. By playing one off against the other on an issue thought equally absurd, the factions were so busy doing the same to each other that they wouldn't notice that he was doing it to them all. He would remain above the fray and appear to be the only adult left on the playing field.

He could see that those around him were already feeling the strain.

Lisa Whiteman, for instance, who had been running her own version of a shell game. She had been on edge from the start, and her stress had shown signs of increasing now for months. And Kevin Herter himself, who was stressed out to begin with and could scarcely have known what he was up against.

And Dillon Ridge, now visibly agitated. Hanford was more than willing to let his regimented chief of staff squirm. For years now Ridge, who ran a tight ship and was an able enforcer had envisioned himself *consigliere*, almost deputy president in his own right. What Hanford never admitted was that while he let him think what he may and was fine with political adversaries regarding him as a capo to be feared, he had never looked upon the retired colonel as anything more than a soldier with an attitude. In return for Oval Office muscle, Ridge's fringe benefit was to let him think he was part of its brain trust, although he was not now and never had been. With Ridge now caught up in the file controversy and doing his best to insulate the White House from its unpleasantries, Hanford would let him wallow in anxiety and do his worrying for him. Despite issues compounding themselves, in his parochial chief of staff he had a true useful idiot. If there was an investigation of the White House to prepare for, Hanford knew who to put front and center. Ridge would take the slings and arrows. By the time he had summoned him, Hanford already knew what the colonel was all-too reluctant to share. He would use it all.

Ninety-three

Ridge knocked hesitantly. He had barely rapped twice when Hanford yelled, "Get in here!" He slowly entered.

"Shut the door!" Hanford barked.

Ridge stepped slowly over to the table. Usually he would just take a seat, but he knew to stand.

For the first time in several years the idiosyncratic Ridge, who had evoked fear in so many was himself riddled with trepidation. Hanford went off on him so rarely that it would gain notice. Ridge had taken the lack of ire to mean the president and he were of the same mind on things, but to Hanford the churlish Ridge never rose to the level of someone worth the bother. Fury was to be wielded sparingly, and devastatingly.

"You know the calls I've been getting?" Hanford bellowed. "What the hell's going on?"

"Mr. President, I—"

"I just got off the phone with the director of the Secret Service and the secretary of the navy. You know what those idiots in Hawaii did? A carrier group came a minute away from shooting that piece of shit Raden and his friend Braddock out of the sky!" Hanford's pen clicked furiously.

"I know sir. I ... I—"

"You know who those IM geniuses got to shoot them down?" He rapped the pen on the table. "The one ship whose captain goes back thirty years with Braddock! Son of a *BITCH!*"

"I just heard—"

"I just spoke with Pat Warren. Our secretary of the navy tells me the esteemed Captain Anders is hot under the collar for an investigation! You know who the secretary tells me is the one fleet captain to get an inquest if he calls for it, no questions asked? What the hell happened?"

As Hanford began furiously tapping his pen, Ridge rubbed his hand over his face. "Sir—"

"You know Raden's on his way out there with Braddock?" He stopped again. "And that other agent, what's his name. They're hauling Herter's old squeeze out there with them."

"I know. We—"

Hanford went back to clicking the pen. "You know what those idiots did in California? I have a briefing scheduled in an hour. Our National Security advisor is set to update me on an incident in some damn woods north of San Francisco. Seems your Honolulu friends couldn't leave well enough alone. Had to go after them! They're tripping over themselves to take out a gnat with a howitzer. I'll be damned they take me down with them!"

"I know Mr. President," Ridge said as Hanford shifted to tapping. "I can't believe it myself—"

Hanford slammed the pen into the table. "You think Raden and Braddock will let that sit? You think they're not going to raise hell over almost being shot out of the air?"

"Mr. President. I don't know—"

"Well you damn well better do something about it!"

Ridge tried to look shocked. "Mr. Presi—"

"And to top it all off, I got another call from Washington." Hanford held the pen quiet, a whisper of a sneer appearing. "Seems word got out from Captain Anders to Homeland Security. The head of the Secret Service doesn't take kindly to false reports being filed about threats to this plane. He's mighty concerned that it involved dispatching two hundred million dollar jets from a two billion dollar aircraft carrier." He fired the pen across the table. It slid off and hit the far wall. "He's what you might call *PISSED*! You get my *DRIFT*?"

Ridge looked away in agony.

Hanford wasn't done. He wound into a tight scowl, tapping his fists into one another. "All that other crap is *BULLSHIT* if proceedings are undertaken by the Justice Department! Up until now *NONE* of this had even a hint of impropriety. Sending out false leads to the DEA? Filing false threats with the Secret Service? You think I need this?"

Ridge began biting his lip and careening his gaze about the cabin.

"And don't even think of tying this office to that crap with the carrier. Now, what the hell are we going to do? What's it mean if we lose the file and this other crap gets out?"

Ridge took a deep breath, the weight of his predicament pressing on him. "Mr. President, it's serious. If the media get hold of the Sandia data, it won't take long to piece together the shenanigans with the warheads. It could jeopardize everything we've worked tow—"

"Dammit! I know that! I don't need *you* to tell me what I already know! If that's the best you can do—" He threw a briefing paper across the table. It followed the pen onto the floor.

Ridge shuddered. For the first time, he felt the very real possibility of losing his position.

Hanford saw it plainly, precisely the reaction he'd wanted. "Our asses are on the line," he hissed. "And they're going to be out there another twenty-four until that news conference tomorrow night. That's an awful lot of time for an awful lot to go wrong. Now what the hell are we going to do about it?"

Ridge rubbed his eyes. "Mr. President, we can ... intercede with the NSA and find out—"

"Oh, for crying out loud," Hanford sneered, "that's what your morons in Hawaii tried doing. See where it got them? I cannot put my hand on any kind of official obstruction of justice!" he snapped, stabbing the air with a bony finger, drawing out every last syllable. He rolled his eyes, which sent a tremble through Ridge, then waved his thought off. "All right," he shifted. "We need a plan of action; I mean now! I can't wait twenty-four hours to see if we dodged a bullet. You still want to be in the game this time tomorrow, you think fast. We're out of time!" Hanford had just about had enough of Ridge's inability to connect the dots, but knew he had to wait him out a little more.

Ridge froze in indecision. He scratched his head, then buried his face in his hand. "Why the hell can't it already be tomorrow," he mumbled under his breath.

Hanford's gaze widened, and he leaned back in his seat. He drew his hand back, then shot an index finger straight at Ridge. "What would that mean?" he demanded.

"Well, Mr. President," Ridge lit up, "if we held the conference tonight—Jesus, it would be a logistical nightmare. We'd have to turn around. Well, it would serve the purpose of—"

"It would save our ass, is the purpose it would serve."

Ridge nodded. "Even if the file leaked out now, I doubt any news organization could put the story together in enough time to spoil what we'd be announcing."

"Then make it work. Our friends on the island need to come through. Square things with Hawaii; they're expecting us. I like this. It doesn't give Herter time to think about thinking. It'll be over before he knows what happened. Work out the details with Latasi and his people. And come up with a good excuse as to why we turned this bird around. I don't know if any president has ever turned around in mid-air. But this is your idea, so you make it work."

"Yes, Mr. President." Ridge turned and left the meeting room, invigorated in his reprieve. He headed for the lounge he had left twenty minutes earlier. Before beginning to put together the rushed new itinerary he took out his phone and texted a message, a directive to Mark Rivers to terminate the contract of Christian Deloy.

Back in the meeting room, Hanford called for his press secretary. He then pulled up a pre-written statement on his computer, announcing that Air Force One would be heading back to Tuvalu and that the president would be making a major policy statement from Vaitupu that evening.

Ninety-four

The normally placid Control Center was crammed, buzzing with activity. The huge video displays on the long wall were ablaze with images while the chatter of technicians and security agents crackled through the air. The riot of noise and color was too much for Peter Natano, pacing at the far end near a monitoring station. He could barely hear above the din.

"I don't care Mr. Prime Minister," he kept repeating. "I don't like this."

Lionel Latasi was trying to placate his agitated security chief. "Pete my friend, we must have faith. I know this means last-minute maneuvering, but we must seize this opportunity."

Natano wasn't biting. "Mr. Prime Minister," he responded, "last-minute maneuvering is the least of my worries. I don't think you appreciate how serious this is."

Latasi rolled his tongue up against his cheek as if to dislodge a sesame seed from his teeth. Kevin, Cindy Russell and Jessica Enright listened, sharing skeptical looks. He turned to Cindy. "What do you think?" he asked, trolling for support.

"I don't think we can pull it off," she said earnestly.

Latasi's lips disappeared into a deepening sigh.

He had summoned them just after the call from Air Force One. The conversation with Elliot Hanford's aide and then the president himself had lasted less than ten minutes. The president's visit, his news conference and even a detonation were now all hastily rescheduled for that evening. Work crews mobilized as arrangements were altered and agendas were reset.

The result was barely contained chaos, scrambling to make a deadline everyone knew was nearly impossible to honor. In addition, the flight from Honolulu had just landed. Latasi would be briefing them on what Natano was as yet unwilling to accept.

"I'm sure the president had good reason to advance this," Latasi said to the chief of security. "You must understand—we have a powerful friend. When they request a favor, we need to give it serious consideration. For whatever reason, the Americans wish to take this course. This secures us a second site for our region, which was our goal all along. And when the Hawaiian group arrives, I'll explain to them they'll be getting a site eighteen months—"

"Mr. Prime Minister, frankly, I'm not concerned with them. What we're getting doesn't concern me as much as what we could lose. This is moving too fast. The president took off barely two hours ago. A cagey old fox like him doesn't change his mind or give up anything without good reason. Something is going on." The others agreed.

"Pete, we're not giving up anything other than pushing an event up a day," Latasi said.

"We've already pushed it up a day. Now it's another one."

Latasi began patting his hands reassuringly. "Everything's okay. It is tight, but we can stage again tonight. We adjust our schedule, put everyone on time-and-a-half and we get what we've been lobbying for the past year." He smiled. "Did you see the president last night? How do they say, a child in a candy shop? He was completely taken. We can accommodate him." He took a deep breath. "The councils have authorized the decision. Please do what you must."

"If that's the case, I'm not signing on without issuing an additional state of alert."

With a shrug Latasi agreed, then noticed that the group from Hawaii had just entered. "I must explain to our friends," he said. With that, he smiled and headed over to them.

"When he's done he can explain it again to me," Natano groaned as he took a seat. "And of course I'd expect the governing councils on our islands to go along with him. He's the kind of guy that gets people to agree with him. But he just doesn't see what he doesn't want to see."

Kevin sighed. "That's how he was when we met for lunch. I just don't think he gets it."

"He doesn't want to get it. I can't talk to him when he's like this. You think with everything this week this will get anyone to back off? Two years ago, this country didn't have an army. I could barely patrol Princeton today with the force I have. He forgets that."

As he frowned and picked up a phone to issue the Alert, Cindy said, "I don't have a good feeling about this." Just then Jessica excused herself to answer her ringing phone.

Kevin suddenly winced.

"Are you okay?" Cindy asked.

"I'm listening to this and I'm getting frustrated with how he's avoiding things. And it hit me. I realize I've been doing the same thing. Max and Sharon both told me so. I must come across obnoxious to more people than I know." Cindy smiled.

"I held my tongue, you being an honored guest and such," Natano said.

Not far from where they sat was a prominent station manned by two technicians, sitting on either side of a panel featuring a lever with a handle. Past the station, sliding glass doors twenty feet away led to an observation deck, offering an unobstructed view to the sea.

"So," Kevin asked Cindy, "what's all this we're in the middle of?"

"This is the Detonation Relay. It's the heart of the complex. It's where the final detonation sequence to the boat is keyed in. The explosive yield is set there," she said, pointing to the lever. "And outside's where the president's going to speak," she added, motioning toward the deck.

Kevin studied the assembly. The lever was set in a curved base marked with numbers starting at ten and running to twenty-five. From thirteen to twenty-two they were subdivided into eighths.

"I take it," he asked, "these numbers correspond to yield in megatons?"

"That's right. We detonate mainly between the two ends, which explains the extra divisions. Come to think of it, the lever's never moved to the bottom or top."

"This one small handle runs the whole show? I'd have thought it would be—fancier."

"Yeah, it's quaint, but it's actually the least complicated part of the process. There's a new digital panel on order. It's due next month." She paused. "I know what you're thinking."

Natano had just gotten off the phone and heard her comment. He asked, "What is that?"

"Remember the file? Those spikes? The lever calibrations don't match up with the yield."

"It's not only that," Kevin added, sweeping his arm in a wide circle to show how open and accessible it was.

"Those guys are extremely careful," she nodded, gesturing to the two men sitting there. As one sent back a thumbs up, she added, "The system is patterned after nuclear missile silos. It takes two people to arm the device. One can't do it alone. They key it in simultaneously, and then the yield is set with the lever. It's the last number set before we detonate.

That's one thing the new panel will do—streamline the process."

"But one person adjusts the yield, correct?" As Cindy nodded, Kevin turned to Natano.

"What we found on that file is that the design they're currently using only works between certain yields. It doesn't allow detonation below ten megatons. You get a dud. That sound right?"

Cindy nodded. Kevin added, "And beyond a certain setting the yields accelerate. The higher the setting, that differential escalates proportionally. What's significant is that the way the design is currently configured represents the upper limit of where they can safely detonate."

"It means," Cindy said, "when the settings are right, the yields can be almost limitless."

"It also means," Kevin said, "that they need to be very careful when they set the things. Last night is close to the limit of where they can go. Anything higher represents a threat."

"So much of this I never knew," said a grim Natano. Kevin stood eyeing the lever. The flaw in the system, earlier just an abstract conception, now loomed as a stark reality.

A moment later their attention was diverted to the other end of the hall, where a tall, thin man seemed to be arguing with Lionel Latasi, his sharp voice heard above the bustle without his words being clear.

Just then an ashen Jessica came back. Before Natano could ask her if she was okay, she motioned towards the arguing man.

"That's Hawaii's lieutenant governor."

"Yes," Natano replied. "Mr. Sanderson. The governor was going to be here but after your incident last night and the president's visit, he sent him instead. I wonder what that's about," he mused while watching the angry Sanderson, then turning to Jessica, asking, "Are you okay?"

She paused to sit before answering. "I got a call from my editor in New York. He has a contact in the Pentagon. Something happened a little while ago over the Pacific. There's a plane flying out here from California—"

"Jack," Kevin snapped. "I bet he's coming back early too." Natano nodded.

"Yeah," she went on. "And some people are coming in with him, like Mike Yahr."

"Mike too?" Kevin said. "That means something. So, what happened?"

Her eyes darted around the room. "This stays between us." She paused, looking about again. "They were almost shot down by one of our aircraft carriers—"

"Holy *crap!*" Kevin hissed, trying to keep his voice low in spite of the shock he felt. His feelings were reflected in the other's faces.

"It hasn't gone public, but it's blowing up into a big incident. And there's something else I have to tell you." She eyed Sanderson, her voice lowering. "That incident on the beach at Waikiki ... there was more to it than what you heard."

Jessica then told them about her visit to IM in Hawaii, meeting Michelle Sapena and Glen Daniels and sneaking into IM's office to use the computer. Natano reacted sharply to hearing that Mark Rivers had met with Ron Sanderson and that the lieutenant governor had left with a briefcase, looking over at Sanderson with new interest as Jessica described the shooting on the beach.

Natano eyed Kevin, the twin bombs that Jessica just dropped lingering in the air. "People who know me," Natano offered, "they'd never call me an alarmist. But I hope you realize your president didn't decide to turn around and come back here for our desserts."

Jessica agreed. "From what I'm hearing, the incident with Jack and Mike isn't the reason. But they're connected. Joshua told me there's a lot running away from them. I think Hanford feels he needs to stop the bleeding."

"I keep thinking of Max," Kevin said. "You know what he would say."

As she smiled, Natano folded his arms. "Had enough?" he said.

"That's about what I'd be hearing. Enough is enough."

"I have a feeling he and I would get along. I wondered what it would take."

Kevin smiled sadly. He missed Max and his reassuring carping.

Natano looked grim. "The worst?" he said. "None of this will have the slightest effect on the prime minister. Bless him, he's gone over to what do you call it, the dark side. He's going to play ball. He's in complete denial, which means it falls on me. So," he groaned, "what am I up against? Your president has his Pentagon, his CIA, the NSA plus the best technology in the world behind him. I have a skeleton crew and the three of you. I need your help people. I'm putting you on the hot seat with me. First things first. This Sanderson business—you're absolutely sure it was him?"

"Pete, I can't believe this," Cindy remonstrated. "You don't believe her?"

He held up his hand. "I have to ask. I've had it with trying to convince people. That's how it's been for me here. I'm running out of time. If I had my way, I'd cancel the entire event and put the island on martial law, but the government's not going to back me up."

"That's what happened," Jessica replied gravely. "They tell you you're not supposed to become part of what you're reporting. But with this, I don't know how not to." Although she was sure Sanderson hadn't seen her at IM, she positioned herself to keep him from getting a glimpse at her. It made little difference; he was still too busy ripping Lionel Latasi.

Cindy turned to Kevin. "Whatever you decide, I hope you realize it all comes back to you."

Natano said, "That's what I need to hear. What do you have in mind?"

"I've had a target on my back from the start," Kevin conceded. "Maybe it's time to reverse that. If I put myself out there, can you grab who shows up?"

Natano nodded. "It's a risk, but it makes sense. You're already getting attention." He paused. "I notice Hanford didn't ask if you were okay with his schedule change."

"Yeah," Kevin mused. "And I wonder what would happen if I told him I wasn't."

"So do I. I don't know how it'll play back in your country, but seeing what he gave up and how quick it happened he's after something a lot more important. You've got more leverage than you know. But whatever the reason, his enemies will be raising their stakes as well."

"That explains what happened to Jack's plane," Cindy said. "And Jessica."

"Yeah. The prime minister doesn't want to hear it, but this island is now a battlefield."

Kevin said, "Well, I'm not going to sit around waiting to see what else they have."

"There's a thought," Natano said. He swiveled to the computer behind him and began typing. "Okaaaayyyy," he said, studying the screen.

"What's that?" Kevin asked.

"It's the manifest of the flight that just arrived. The usual charter; business, military people, legislators, your lieutenant governor—" He moved aside so Kevin could see. "Anything catch your eye?"

Kevin looked it over. Several seconds later, he pointed to a name. "This guy here."

Natano looked at Jessica. "Mr. James Bremer. A representative of—"

"Let me guess," she said. "Integrated Microphysics."

"Yup. Did he just decide to fly in? I think not. Time we introduce ourselves to Mr. Bremer."

Kevin said, "And the lieutenant governor as well."

Natano agreed. "I want to know why they're here. And even if it's just to get a tan, I want them to know they're attracting notice. Let's see what we come up with. Jessica, you and Cindy have a date with an airplane. With the event this evening we'll be clearing air traffic by four o'clock. Go up, see what Dr. Whiteman has to say and get back. According to the manifest her husband came in too. Somehow, I'm not sure she's up for seeing him. Cindy, you and Dr. Whiteman can share some of your technical expertise with Jessica."

"I wonder what they'd say if they knew we're taking a flight later?" she said.

"Call in the reservations now, but confirm them in person. Let them see you."

"Use my name," Kevin said. Natano turned to him and he added, "Let's see what happens."

"Yeah, good idea," Natano replied. As Cindy picked up the phone he added, "Meanwhile, Kevin and I will ... startle the snakes?" He rose. "Okay. Time we met the prime minister's guests."

Ninety-five

Ron Sanderson was stewing. He had been unceremoniously shuffled off of a flight he hadn't wanted to take, during which he sat like a sardine arguing about something that had been dumped in his lap. Now he stood reading the riot act to a smiling figurehead whose idiocy was matched by his cluelessness. For the ambitious and impertinent lieutenant governor of Hawaii, nothing was going right.

He had left Honolulu after a night spent fending off blowback from the Waikiki Beach sniper incident. The shooting was escalating into a major event, involving law enforcement, the media and even the US Department of Homeland Security. Governor Steve Hinson had sent him as a reluctant stand-in, opting to stay behind to host a last-minute visit by Elliot Hanford, who then abruptly cancelled. Since word had come only after his flight departed, the already indignant Sanderson was fuming. And upon landing he learned the agenda was being pushed up.

The latest in a string of bad news had him seething, and couldn't have come at a worse time. Where once he could count on Mark Rivers as a solid source of intelligence, now he couldn't get a straight answer out of the fool. And inexplicably, he couldn't reach any of the others on the take. The White House had just announced Air Force One would be turning around since an unacceptable security risk had been created for the president because of the beach shooting. The Secret Service had pressed to cancel the trip and Hanford agreed. With Hinson tasking Sanderson to take his place, everything he'd labored to hide was now threatened. And if that wasn't enough, that unpredictable weasel Christian Deloy was giving every indication of going off the deep end.

Meanwhile, the White House seemed to be completely enamored with their mushroom clouds. Hanford's clueless wonderment threatened to blow the lid off everything Sanderson had worked for over the past two years. Most galling of all, in a hall crammed with pushing and shoving that he had already had his fill of, there was Kevin Herter, the idiot who started it all. The physicist who wasn't even supposed to be there was approaching, following some damn cop.

The past ten minutes spent reaming the prime minister had fallen on deaf ears, but at least the fool had pretended to listen. It was more than he had gotten earlier that day. When he'd heard about Hanford's cancellation, Sanderson had spent the last two hours of the flight going off on Tom Whiteman, who unlike Latasi didn't take to being a punching bag. They had nearly came to blows, and needed to be separated. Sanderson was torn between wanting to get to the bottom of an incident he was certain was connected to the IM payoffs and dealing with the pressure from Hinson to investigate the shooting officially, something he was just as eager to avoid. He was fit to be tied.

The governor stayed behind to put a public face on the shooting, an event the media was calling a possible terrorist attack. As his stand-in, Sanderson was expected to lobby for a coveted expansion site. He resented the drop-off from statesman to salesman. Hinson, out of the IM loop, was both pushing and pulling Sanderson, who was immersed in it more than anyone. Sanderson was so caught up with losing containment on the payoff cover-up that he lost sight of the selling job expected of him. Though the payoffs had been kept quiet, the pretense behind them had been fraying at the edges. It was now falling in on itself, and he felt himself stretched to the limit.

The cancellation of the president's trip reeked of expediency. It wasn't difficult to imagine his preoccupation with using the program to fight terrorism wouldn't jibe with visiting a place that just suffered an attack. Who knew what other problems the incident would cause?

The president's return meant Sanderson would have to deal with Hanford and his newfound fixation one on one. Word of his exuberance over last night's event had gone viral. With so much imploding the irony was that Herter's arrival, which had once seemed the most pressing of things to prevent, now barely registered. Keeping IM in the game, working a new site for Hawaii, keeping the payoffs going, fending off Hanford and a dozen other things that now seemed a blur; everything had changed. It was too much.

The other passengers were huddled near the doorway. Several were sniping at Sanderson to cool off and head to the hotel but he continued holding court, chewing out Lionel Latasi and the Tuvaluan officials with him. Tom Whiteman stood ready to pick up with Sanderson where they'd left off. As Kevin and Natano approached followed by Cindy and Jessica, Sanderson didn't give them much heed. Several others, including Whiteman, noticed Kevin. Whiteman also recognized Jessica, but said nothing to either of them.

"Is there a problem here?" Natano asked cautiously, trying to sound helpful.

Latasi looked browbeaten. "This is the lieutenant governor," he said, sounding chastened. "Mr. Sanderson is upset with our scheduling change."

"You're damn right," Sanderson barked. He had over a half a foot on the 5'9" Latasi and almost as much on Natano, and glared down on both. "Who the hell are you?" he snapped.

"This is Captain Natano," Latasi said. He is our chief security offi—"

"I don't really give a damn," Sanderson said, in his best bluster. "We land expecting to relax and meet people we've been scheduled to see for months and then we get told everything's off. Then we get hustled off like some tour group whose credit got declined and before we know it, you're telling us you're bumping everything up a day? That's bullshit!"

"Mr. Sanderson," Natano said, undeterred, "this was a decision your presi—"

"Like hell!" Sanderson snapped. "I don't need to hear this from some mall cop! This screws up all our plans! I want to talk to the American in charge!"

Natano stiffened, not intimidated in the least. "Mr. Sanderson, trying to be nice won't get you any special favors here. Just know that I'm the final authority on this island when it comes to matters of security, not any of your countrymen."

Kevin stepped forward. The one person more than any that Sanderson had worked to keep away from Tuvalu now stood front and center.

Sanderson, his condescension evident, blurted out, "You're the kid, right?"

"Yeah, Dad." Kevin instantly disliked him.

Sanderson flashed a sneer. "You got some weight here. Tell your boss here what they cooked up ain't going to cut it. What are you going to do for us?"

Kevin glanced at Natano before replying, "I can't help you. I wasn't consulted about what they're doing and they don't let me have the car keys here, so I'm pretty much just along for the ride. Besides, my afternoon's socked—a reporter wants to interview me and the project director from New Mexico about the program. We're taking a sightseeing flight within the hour—we figured we'd take in a little cloud watching at the same time. So, I'm sorry." He wasn't.

Sanderson's interest perked up before the anger hit. "That's very nice," he sneered. "Then you tell your boss here we're—oh hell, you people aren't going to do a damn thing! I'll have to handle this my own way!" With a grunt, he made for the exit, followed by most of the others from the flight, though Tom Whiteman seemed to lag.

With newfound awareness, Natano and Kevin looked at each other, then at Latasi.

"Why was he so mad?" Natano asked the prime minister.

"He didn't say, just that the change wasn't what he agreed to or was promised. I told him I was sorry but there wasn't much we could do about it. No one else objected; only him."

"Interesting." Natano turned to Kevin. "Well, it's not because his luggage was lost. I like what you said. We'll see what happens."

"I thought it might be worth a shot." Cindy and Jessica nodded in agreement.

Just then the lone man left from the flight approached. He had been quietly listening quietly to the dust-up with Sanderson, but hadn't followed the others out.

"Oh, my apologies; I just met this gentleman. Mr—" Latasi paused, abashedly having forgotten the man's name.

"Jim Bremer," he said, stepping up with a smile and extending his hand.

Kevin and Natano locked glances, holding back surprise.

"Oh, yes," Latasi said to Kevin, wholly missing the moment. "Mr. Bremer. He asked to meet you." He turned to Bremer, "I'm sure Captain Natano can also help. Please forgive me; the schedule change has us in a rush. I have much to do before this evening." He said goodbye and hurried out.

Natano gave Bremer a cautionary handshake, as did Kevin. "I recognized you," Bremer said to Kevin. The trim, toned six-footer in his late forties looked casual in his beige slacks and olive shirt. A brown leather overnight bag slung over his shoulder.

Natano's thoughts were in a whirl, aware that Kevin was thinking the same thing. They had wanted to check out Bremer, but he had beaten them to the punch.

"You've caught us at a bad time," Natano began, playing along.

"My apologies, captain. The prime minister filled us in."

"Mr. Bremer—"

"Please, call me Jim."

Natano paused. "Mr. Bremer, I'll be honest with you. Had you not come forward, we were going to look you up ourselves. Issues have arisen with your company that deeply concern us. And here you show up. We wonder if you wouldn't mind speaking with us."

Bremer's gaze stiffened. "Sure, sir. What can I help you with?"

"I want to know what you're doing here. I also want to know your company's plans."

"I wonder about that myself," he said offhandedly, to Natano's surprise. "Not to beat around the bush, but my duties with Integrated have recently changed. I'm currently assigned to the Hawaiian Department of Science, Technology and Innovation. The state's been trying to acquire a site. The Department's trying to square technical and environmental concerns with the program's contractors. Because of our contribution, we've been involved from the start."

Natano nodded. "We're aware of the design issues."

"The company's looking to integrate your experience here with state guidelines. But after listening to the prime minister, I guess it's all moot. It looks as if it's already been agreed to." He rubbed his face. "I'm not sure who to talk with at this point."

"Why do you say that?"

"I got the impression a decision's been made. I hope they know what they're doing."

Natano eyed him sternly. "Exactly, what do you mean?"

Bremer shook his head. "I see your reaction. Yours isn't the first. You know we build the bomb trigger. I was assigned to the latest design upgrade. But with the recent events I also have some damage control to do. IM has a big presence in the state but the company's at a crossroad. There are certain ... considerations we've had to accommodate. Part of why I'm here is to address that. I have issues as well."

Kevin chortled incredulously, "Boy, are you an expert in understatement."

Bremer nodded. "Some on the board feel that it's better to work with people here and DC up front than behind everyone's back. It's no surprise that the state agrees."

Kevin and Natano tried to hide their surprise. Bremer added, "Dr. Herter, the state's been working on the premise it would get a site. But issues have come up; physics, engineering. We feel you're better prepared to address them than most people. We know the White House is working with you. We'd like to as well. We've explored alternatives but they've turned out to be dicey. I'm here to listen and to ask for help. I'm concerned."

Kevin eyed Natano who said, "I appreciate your frankness."

As Bremer thanked him Natano found himself paying particular attention to his guest. As ex-military, Natano recognized one of his own, but wasn't sure what to make of him. Bremer sounded like more than just a bureaucrat and a technocrat as well. He was frank; in fact, too sincere. The cop in Natano was telling him that below the affability was something he was less inclined to share. His thoughts ran from Bremer being a plant to a techie out of the loop, though he didn't think that likely. With wavy gray-flecked brown hair and casual beige slacks and olive shirt, Bremer's features, while distinct, were unremarkable, and as Natano listened he had a curious thought. Bremer was one of those people who could stand in a room without being noticed. He knew what that meant. And he knew Bremer was aware of it himself.

Bremer said to Kevin, "After I check in Dr. Herter, I'd appreciate it if we could meet."

"I have a plane to catch. I have to head to my room to change. But we'll make the time."

"Thank you. I'll leave it there for now." He looked around at the packed center. "You people sure look like you've got your work cut out for you."

Natano said, "There's as much of an on-target statement as I've heard in a while." He sniffed the busy air. "After you check in, we can meet. You just picked one hell of a day."

"Excellent, sir. I understand. I would appreciate that." Bremer smiled then left.

Cindy and Jessica walked over, as Kevin and Natano looked at each other. Kevin grumbled, "All these people I meet; they all want to talk to me."

Natano said, "Talks a lot of sense, but maybe it's what he thinks that we want to hear."

"I had the same thought. What do you make of it?"

"I know what the prime minister makes of it. I'm not even done saying we have to keep an eye on who shows up when this guy drops in sounding like the most reasonable person in the world and he gets his ear. He's giving me gray hair. Don't think for a moment that with everything that company has pulled, that they're not trying to slip one by again. And don't think he isn't aware and that he thinks we don't know as well. This guy isn't here by accident, just like your president isn't coming back by accident. They're related. I just don't know how."

Kevin agreed. "At one point, I would have wanted to talk to someone like him. Not now."

Jessica said, "But in my world, that's the kind of person who has something to say."

Natano said, "No doubt, but I wouldn't be surprised he had his hand in most of it himself. This guy has seen his share. Okay," he thought out loud, "he wants to be friends? Be his friend. I'm glad you said you'd meet and you're headed to your room. Keep telegraphing your moves; we'll see who bites. Stick to him like glue. Whatever he suggests, say yes. That won't be hard—whatever you say, he'll want to do. Expect him to be your shadow. We'll be his. This is where getting the bum's rush hits reality. I don't have time or resources to do background checks this late on people who show up unannounced. Nothing's easy with this thing." He gave Kevin an earnest stare. "Are you still okay with your commitment to your president?"

"Give me more credit than that. By tonight a lot of things are going to be different."

"Good," Natano smiled. He looked at his watch and the smile vanished. "It's two o'clock. We have barely four hours."

"Pete, we'll head to the airport," Cindy said. "Just watch out for this guy," she winked at Kevin.

"You hear that? Just watch out for yourself," Natano said to Kevin, who gave Cindy a hug before she and Jessica left.

"All right," Natano said, "let's go see what we can learn." They made for the door. Kevin left the building while Natano turned for his office.

Ten minutes later, Ian Forster's James Bremer reached the hotel. After checking in at the front desk, he walked around a corner and slipped into a men's room. Entering a stall, he texted a message, receiving a reply a few moments later, a simple three-digit number. He left the restroom and took an elevator to the third floor.

As the door opened, he turned left down the corridor. A couple was walking toward him and he proceeded nonchalantly, smiling as they passed. When they got on the elevator, he sped up to room 347, where a Do Not Disturb sign hung from the door handle. He knocked three times fast, then paused and rapped twice, then once. From inside, the knocks were repeated. Bremer slipped a manila envelope under the door then continued down the hall until he reached the stairs, where he walked down a flight to his room. Everything was going as planned.

The operative in 347 took the envelope and the Do Not Disturb sign and left, leaving the room as it was for the people who had unwittingly let him use it for ten minutes. He walked gingerly down the stairs to the second floor, politely greeting people he passed on the way. When he reached Kevin Herter's room he checked to see no one was around, then slipped the envelope under the door and hung the sign on the handle, before disappearing into the sun-drenched afternoon.

Ninety-six

"Ba-*boom*, ba-*boom* ... ba *bomb*, ba *bomb*...."

Christian Deloy leaned back in his chair, feet propped up on the balcony railing, tapping his foot to the tune wafting up from the mall below. The early afternoon sun burned high, and he paused to wipe the sweat from his lip and take a swig of his margarita. An empty pitcher beside him, he was feeling no pain.

"*Tey tieutenant gubenor*," he ribbed Ron Sanderson, "feeling hot?"

"Will you fucking keep your mind on things?" Sanderson barked down on him.

"Hey, man, chill. Buster gets into you—"

"Get serious! I didn't track you down to fucking play games!" He wiped off his own sweat.

"Chill! I'm the one who said you guys were fucking up and now that it happened, you're the one bitchin'." In his shorts and Club Afterglow T Shirt, he looked like a guest. "So chill."

"I don't have time for your bullshit! You better start taking things seriously."

Deloy methodically slid his shades down his nose and peered up. "You know," he droned, "you are becoming a *real* pain in the ass. Just enjoy the sight." He motioned out to the remnants of Eta Carinae. "Look at that," he slurred. "Can't stop staring."

"I don't have time to stare at shit when it's about to blow up in my face!"

"Hey, that's the American way." Deloy took a gulp of margarita, and then raised the glass to the cloud. "Here's to the pinhead scientist," he toasted. "Give the piece of shit credit. When you get your own Tiki Bar up and running, you guys are going to clean up."

"You let me worry about that. Keep your mind on what you have to."

"That's the problem; you worry too much."

"Cut the crap! You know what the hell's been going on the past twenty-four hours? You're in it up to your ears! Now what are we going to do?"

Deloy slid his shades back up. "You know Ridge's problem? I figured it out. He needs to get laid more. Spent a whole night here with all these great lookin´ babes running around, and didn't even have a drink. Man's a repressed sack of shit."

"Fucking get serious! You have to deal with that sack of shit! He's on his way back here with his boss. And speaking of bosses, I just ran into yours, the other piece of shit. Had to listen to him making excuses for two hours."

Deloy straightened his legs out and sat up. "Yeah, well him I can handle."

"What the fuck's your problem? He's looking for you. Wants to know what you've been doing. And it's already going around that Ridge wants you out."

"Him I can handle as well. He may be a hot piece of shit in the Oval Office but rile him up, he's the easiest pigeon I ever plucked. I told him I was done with my job here—"

"Yeah, we heard all about it. You damn well better—"

"Man, I told you; chill." Deloy gave up a wicked giggle. "Shoulda heard him. I love yanking his chain; watching him freak out. Such a pin-head. Gotta get my kicks somehow."

As Sanderson glared, Deloy stretched out his legs again. "Okay," he said, "update. Hanford's on his way back to make his precious little an-nouncement with Herter next to him on a leash—"

"I know, damn it! Which we tried desperately not to let happen, you twit!"

"Temper, temper. Then you should have listened to me from the start. But, just wait. The cops and the reporter are falling down over themselves trying to unravel the—drum roll—" he rattled out a thrum-ming, "scoop of the century! They don't know what the fuck's going on."

"Instead of sitting here like a fucking prima donna," Sanderson groaned in exasperation, "you could be checking out Herter. You know what he's doing? I just heard he taking a plane—"

"*MEEEEP!* News flash! Already on it. One of my projects here is a pinhead who has the hots for this broad who just happened to take a shine to Herter. He reacted in, shall we say, less than works and plays well with others fashion. Went off on Herter and got himself demoted. They're shipping him out next week but didn't know what to do with him until then, so they stuck him at the airport as a baggage handler. Our physicist has a reservation for one of those glider flights. And he's also going up with—"

"I heard—what's her face from MSNBC."

"And the bimbo. They're going up for some sightseeing before Fearless Leader makes his big announcement, which means they want to talk all by their lonesome. So I told my pigeon to take another shot at making a good impression with his lady friend. I took the liberty of ordering them a nice lunch spread in his name." He laughed. "I'm his best friend now."

"That's your big fucking news?"

"So, I get an ear. Herter, the reporter; the bimbo. My pigeon gets the scoop from the pilot. All the bull you're worried about, we get to hear everything being discussed." He took another sip of margarita and sat back with a supremely contented smirk. "This thing's a cinch."

"And what are you going to do about your piece of shit boss's wife?" Sanderson frowned.

Deloy's smirk vanished. "Whadda ya mean? Whiteman?"

"Yeah. She's going too." Sanderson saw Deloy's expression and said, "You didn't know. Too busy getting ripped. You haven't done shit keeping her quiet. She made it all the way out here just like Herter and what'd you do? Nothin´! What happens if she starts spilling her guts?"

Deloy paused, then licked some salt off his lip. Damn if he would show any concern.

"Like maybe it occurred to you to do something more than just rely on a pilot catching half a conversation he won't understand?" Sanderson sneered, "I can't believe these fuck-ups!"

Deloy polished off his margarita and rose. "Already got it all set up," he replied, though he hadn't. Thinking fast on his feet came easy to him, margaritas notwithstanding. "Just chill. Bug's all set to go in the picnic basket. Equipment's standard issue, courtesy of Ridge's DOD friends. Anyone sees it, they draw a line back to that twerp."

"I don't want to hear about it. Just do it!"

"Lighten up! Ridge is a moron. Sometimes you want to bitch slap 'em. You get pissed when they make it so easy. It would be more fun if he wasn't so damn predictable. And just watch how they throw him under the bus."

Sanderson looked at his watch. "I gotta get out of here. I have work to do. You just damn well better make sure this goes down, with what you're getting paid for it."

"Just chill out. I'll keep you posted." Deloy motioned Sanderson toward the door.

"Just do it. And I don't want any fuck-ups. Where are you headed?"

"The airport. Gotta check up on the pigeon and set my little surprise. Just chill," Deloy said as he let Sanderson out. He changed into the shorts and patterned shirt of a resort worker, all the while wondering whether Lisa Whiteman might talk and what she would say or if the time had come to finally deal with Kevin Herter, whether he opened his mouth or not.

Ninety-seven

"I need to see you." Even over the phone, Kevin's voice rippled with urgency, raising Peter Natano's interest.

"What's the matter?" Natano asked.

"I'm leaving my room," Kevin said, missing the constrained note in Natano's response. "I'll be right there. We have to talk."

"All right. I'll see you in a few." Natano hung up, and turned back to his laptop.

Kevin hesitantly eased the door open. The lock assembly clanked into place, sounding like a prison gate. Heart rushing, he peered out but no one was there. The only sound was his breathing, loud and forced. Clutching the envelope he'd just found, he stepped down the hall, warily at first but before he knew it, in full sprint.

He got to the elevator, pushed the button then decided he couldn't wait and made for the stairs, catapulting down three steps at a time until he got to the main floor. He peeked out the stairwell. Not recognizing anyone, unsure whether anyone was watching, he blended in on the way to the mall, winded.

He turned from the portico and immediately ran into Cindy and Jessica. One look at him and they knew something was up. He motioned them back to a wall near a large palm.

"I found this in my room," he announced, catching his breath. He opened the envelope and pulled out a series of letter-sized photos. They were dark, but the detail was plain.

Cindy looked them over. "Is this you?"

"Yeah. I've had it with shit slipped under my door," he groused.

"I don't get it," she added. "It looks like you're in a car. And who's this guy? A cop?"

"Oh, my God," Jessica said, backing up as she realized what she was looking at.

"I don't get—oh, my God!" Cindy echoed as Kevin nodded.

"Yeah," he said. "Someone bugged my car. These must have been taken this past Sunday in New Jersey. I was pulled over by state troopers; twice that night, actually. This was the first stop. I later found out that he wasn't a real cop."

"Holy shit!" Cindy said.

"This is more serious than you realize," Jessica offered. "It happened back there but this was slipped to you here."

Cindy's expression began to change. "Uh … this guy looks familiar." She nodded, tapping the photo. "Yeah, I've seen him before."

Kevin and Jessica locked stares. "Okay," Kevin said, "I gotta find Pete. You guys headed to the airport?"

"Yeah," Cindy said. "Not sure if we should go now."

"No. You go. We play this out."

As Jessica agreed, Cindy added, "What is going on here?"

Kevin shook his head in bewilderment, as Jessica glanced at a text message she'd just received. "Cindy, can I meet you there? I have to make a call." She headed back to the mall.

"Come on, walk with me. We're going the same way," Kevin said. Cindy took his arm, trying to smile.

All around an iridescent blue reigned in the warm air. A lively trade wind whipped them along and ruffled their hair, picking up leaves and proving a challenge for the butterflies flitting about. The walkway was lined with bushes displaying brilliant yellow and red blooms, amid flower pots dripping with jasmine scenting the air.

"You don't know what this does for me," Kevin said, shaking his head. "If it wasn't for the bull." He felt a growing frustration. The people around them couldn't have known what he knew but part of him felt they should, as if they were sleepwalking and needed to snap out of their dreamworld of tropical denial. "You want to smack them in the head and yell, 'Don't you people *get it?*'"

She patted his arm. "I know just what you mean."

A large jet could be seen rising above the palms.

"There are a lot of those leaving today," Kevin said.

"The schedule change forced a lot of people to make different plans. The Secret Service wants to clear the place out. There's been a load of complaining."

"Can't blame 'em." They walked a bit further and Kevin added, "I have to be honest. Even though I love it here, I can't wait to get out myself." Cindy's face took on a melancholy look and he added, "Present company excepted."

"I know," she said sadly. "I don't think any of us expected this."

He gave her a hug and a peck on the forehead. "Do you see yourself staying here?"

"Continuing to work here?" She shrugged. "I suppose."

He took her hand. "I was wondering, do you have any time saved up?"

"I don't know, Herter," she smiled, coyly. "What are you suggesting?"

"Well, I wondered if you want to fly back with me and check out Princeton."

She smacked her hand on his chest. "What a coincidence," she declared. "That was the first place on my vacation list. I'd love to!" she beamed. "You know any good hotels?"

"One. It's not a bed and breakfast, but it's got a bed, and you can get breakfast. I know the owner, so I can get you a good rate."

She drew him close. "As long as I don't get any better offers," she said. "I saw a few cute guys today."

"Up yours Russell." She laughed, and he said, "Thanks, I needed this now. And honestly, I think your time here is winding down." She squeezed his hand. They soon reached the end of the walk. The airport was ahead while the Center lay to the right. "Okay," he said, "we'll meet up."

"You just be very careful." She drew him close and gave him a kiss. He smiled, and then looked around at the crystal blue day. "I can't wait to get out of here," he said as they parted.

Forty feet behind them, blending in the crowd, Christian Deloy casually turned to follow Cindy.

Ninety-eight

Peter Natano looked up from his computer. It was 2:37 p.m. Kevin had just run up to his office, a Spartan windowless workplace featuring a potted cycad, an adjacent door, a map of Tuvalu and photos of the country's prime ministers, including Lionel Latasi.

Natano was pressing a forefinger against his lips when Kevin entered. As they looked at each other, they knew instinctively that as bad as what each had to share with the other might be, it could very well be topped by what they would hear in return.

Natano noted the large manila envelope Kevin clutched. "I take it that's not an autographed picture for my wall." He waved a hand at a chair. "Let's hear it."

"Someone's been watching me," Kevin said anxiously. He launched into a description of what happened on the highway in New Jersey, as Natano examined the photos.

"Actually, watching both you and Jack," Natano replied. "And following you both here. And wants you to know."

"I've had it with this crap," Kevin said, his hands clenching the chair's arm rests. "So what do you think?"

Natano turned his laptop around. On the screen was Captain Christian Deloy's service photo.

"Damn!" shouted Kevin, "that's him! Son of a bitch!"

"Jack asked me to look into this guy. He hadn't broken any of our laws and there was nothing outstanding on him, but I started paying attention. It's been, well, interesting."

"Who the hell is he? Cindy said she's seen him. Why's he interested in me?"

"And who's so interested in him? Before we get to that, there's a lot going on you should know. Jack *is* on that plane flying in. Mike's with him. And I just got notice that their plane's being diverted."

"Where? And why?"

"Your White House pressured our government not to let them land here. They raised security issues over the shoot-down incident. They're landing in our capital Funafuti within the hour."

Kevin swiveled his chair apprehensively. "They got to him! I—"

"Calm down. They may be able to keep the plane away but there are ways around it. Meantime, Jessica's in the conference room next door."

"She got a text and said she had to make a call. What happened?"

"It was from her editor in New York. I got the information the same time. Since then it's been nonstop." He looked at the screen. "This Captain Deloy, he works for Tom Whiteman."

"Is that the same—"

"Her husband. This is his aide. The major flew in on the same plane as the one that brought in that charming Mr. Sanderson. I have my men looking for him—he's been asking about his wife."

The phone rang. "Send them up," Natano said, and hung up. "Whiteman," he said. Kevin rose to leave but Natano said, "I want you here." He closed the laptop as the door opened.

A Tuvalu police officer walked in, followed by Tom Whiteman and another officer.

Natano rose. "Major Whiteman, Peter Natano. Tom, isn't it?" Whiteman nodded tightly, and Natano added, "Perhaps you know Dr. Herter? Major Whiteman here is in charge of security for your country's program in New Mexico," Natano explained to Kevin.

Whiteman and Kevin shook hands. Natano offered Whiteman a seat before sitting down himself. Whiteman looked over to the two officers and noticed they were still at the door.

"Major," Natano began, "I understand you've been inquiring about your wife. We were going to contact you, so I'm glad to see you."

"Captain, I've been asking around since I landed. No one can give me a straight answer. I want to know what's going on. Where is she?" He motioned to the officers. "Do they know?"

"Dr. Herter met your wife briefly last night," Natano said.

"We were supposed to meet again this morning," Kevin said, "but she never showed."

"Why?" Whiteman asked. "What happened? And why did she want to meet with you?"

"I don't know."

"Then who does? And what's with them?" he asked Natano, gesturing to the officers.

"Major, something happened last night. We don't know what but your wife's in the hospital."

"What do you mean something happened? Why the hell didn't any-one tell me! Is that how you people—"

"Major, we're still investigating. Your wife seems to have had some kind of traumatic experience. There's no evidence of any outward in-juries, but she refused to meet me or Dr. Herter afterwards. The only people she agreed to speak with were some of our female staff."

Whiteman's gaze burned. "Are you saying—"

"No. There wasn't any sexual assault."

"Then I want to see her."

"Major, we'll get word to her that you're here, and if she's up for it—"

"What the hell you mean *if she's up for it?* She's my wife, dammit! I want to see her now, and if that means dragging the prime minister in here, you do it!" He looked ready to bolt, and the two officers moved as if to restrain him. Whiteman caught himself and backed off.

Natano looked at Kevin, then lifted his phone. "This is Captain Natano. Please let Dr. Whiteman know that her husband arrived this morning." He hung up then said, "Your wife had also agreed to meet several other people this afternoon; some of our staff here and a jour-nalist."

Whiteman's expression tightened, and he pulled back slightly into his seat.

"Major," Natano said, "something else has come up. We need to speak." He opened his laptop and turned the screen towards Whiteman.

Whiteman's eyes widened slightly, though he said nothing.

"So," Natano said. "What can you tell me about this gentleman?"

Whiteman frowned slightly, and remained silent.

"Major," Natano said, scratching his brow, "I'll tell you a little about things here. This place has been operating smooth as silk since it opened two years ago. But recently we've had all kind of incidents. We've had people killed, questions have come up about the system's safety and there's been enough intrigue to last a lifetime. And with every incident, your Captain Deloy here was nearby. Now I'm a funny guy; I don't be-lieve in coincidence. I like things nice and boring. I intend to get them back to nice and boring. So why don't we save each other any unneces-sary aggravation and you can tell me about your aide because frankly, I've had a lousy couple of days."

"What the hell do you want me to tell you?" Whiteman growled, sitting back.

"We can start with the truth. The captain is your aide, correct?"

Whiteman cocked his head to the side. "Yeah, I suppose."

"You need to qualify that?"

"I haven't seen much of him lately. He's been on special assignment, or so they tell me."

Kevin leaned forward. "What does that mean?" Natano said.

"Well—"

"Because it seems to have included an inordinate amount of frequent flyer miles, both to here and to the US. Your aide has visited us five times the past four months. I'd like to say he's taken with our ambiance but every one of his visits coincides with some kind of drama. How 'bout it?"

"I don't know much of what he does." He groaned and added, "The man's a psychopath. You know what we call him behind his back? Ted. As in Ted Bundy."

"A charming psycho who killed about three dozen women back in the US," Kevin explained. "He went to the chair. That's a nice aide you've got," he explained to Whiteman.

"I put up with his crap in New Mexico because I had to. He's got friends in higher places. But I kept him at arms' length. I don't know what he's done, but not much would surprise me. Now, I want to see my wife."

Natano eyed Kevin then took the envelope and pulled out the photos.

Whiteman looked them over then rubbed his face and laughed. "Someone bugged your car." Kevin huffed as Whiteman kept viewing the photos, eyes widening. "Dr. Herter," he said shaking his head, "I don't know anything about that."

"It's interesting that you don't know anything about the surveillance on Dr. Herter," Natano said, "but not that you don't know about your Captain Deloy's involvement with it. It occurs to me that if someone were watching Captain Deloy, they would know who he was speaking with as well."

Kevin crossed his arms. "That's right."

"I have nothing to say about it," Whiteman snapped, his face tightening up again.

"Okay." Natano took the photos and leaned back in his chair. "You know one of the things I enjoy most about my job?" he said to Whiteman. "You get to meet interesting people. Kevin here, for one. Presidents; prime ministers." He smiled. "You. I don't know if you know, but you're an interesting guy. This job lets you study people. You can learn a lot about a person if you take the time to observe and listen. For instance, there's a lot of drama swirling around you, yet the only thing you're concerned about is your wife. I admire that."

As Whiteman stared, Natano added, "I've met other people recently; fascinating folks. For instance, there's a guy coming in today, Mike Yahr. I just spoke with him. Mike's an interesting chap. He's retired from your NSA. He knows some interesting folks too. Coincidentally, he has a friend in Honolulu, which is where you and your wife live. Guess who his friend is? John Bennitt, the police chief. Mike also keeps in touch with others from his agency. A lot of them are coming in today, that's if your government doesn't raise too much of a stink. One is a guy named Roger Braddock, who also was with your NSA. He also lives in Hawaii. Sure a lot of coincidences with this."

"Is there a point to all of this?" Whiteman frowned.

"We all heard about the shooting back there. Terrible for those people. It's had huge repercussions, even here. I just had a talk with the chief. He sent me the ballistic report. He hasn't been able to match the gun yet, but he assured me they're working hard on it."

Whiteman shifted slightly in his seat, his mouth tensing up.

"Thing about being retired or being somewhere like the NSA," Natano said to Kevin, "it lets you get away with things that we in regular law enforcement might not be able to. I just had a little chat with Jack, Roger and Mike. Your government's making it very difficult to communicate, but we found a way. We discussed the ballistic report and it's pointing to an unexpected conclusion." He eyed Whiteman. "You wouldn't be willing to discuss any of this, would you?"

Whiteman cleared his throat and sniffed. "I don't have time for this," he said, rising.

"Actually, you do," said Natano, as the two officers moved into position behind Whiteman.

Natano stared down at his phone. "Do you want to come in now?" he asked. Before anyone could react to the realization that the speaker had been on, the conference room door opened and Jessica Enright walked in. Whiteman was shocked, even more so when Lisa Whiteman followed her in.

"Are you okay?" Whiteman jumped up and asked his wife. "Where were you?" He made a halting move toward her, but she cringed and pulled back. The two officers closed in, causing Whiteman to pause.

Lisa glanced at Kevin before giving her husband an icy stare, which swiftly turned to scorn.

"You know what he did?" she sneered through clenched teeth. Jessica gently touched her shoulder. She flinched but announced, "I'm okay."

"Lisa—" Whiteman began.

"I don't want to hear it! I heard everything you said!"

"Heard *what?*"

"I told you what he was! You didn't want to listen! And to hear you say that you *knew?*" Whatever fear she had was gone, replaced by fire.

"What are you *talking* about?" Whiteman stammered. "I want to know what happened!"

Lisa stood shaking. Jessica offered her a chair. She slowly sat, crossing her arms in a straitjacketed grip. Kevin sat silently watching, thoroughly confused.

"It seems we have some matters to discuss," Natano said. He turned to Lisa, "I'm sorry for what happened to you here. I give you a lot of credit for gathering yourself up to come in."

She nodded haltingly as Whiteman demanded, "I want to know what the hell happened!"

"Your wife had a run-in with your aide last night," Natano said.

"Oh, Christ," Whiteman growled. "What happened? Why didn't anyone tell me?"

"Because there are doubts as to just where your loyalties lie."

"What the hell does that mean?"

"I warned you about him for a *year!*" Lisa said. "You weren't *interested! Nobody* was!"

Whiteman looked ready to argue but Natano said, "Whatever happened then won't be solved now. Captain Deloy's conduct has spilled into my jurisdiction. He's made it my business." He turned to Jessica. "As are other matters connected to this issue. By the way, how is your cheek?"

"It's okay," she said. "Stings a little." Her brow furrowed up in confusion.

"You may wish to take a seat." Unsure where he was headed, she pulled up the last chair and sat next to Lisa. He pointed to Whiteman and to the chair, and Whiteman sat without argument.

"This is the ballistic report Chief Bennitt sent me from Hawaii," Natano began, picking up a paper. He looked at Whiteman. "Again, Major, feel free to jump in."

"Screw you."

As he looked away Lisa glared at him and asked, "What's this about?"

"Jack may still be a consultant for your NSA," Natano said, "but

Mr. Braddock and Mr. Yahr are retired. None of them have the legal constraints Chief Bennitt has. After the major left to follow his wife out here, Mr. Braddock had his operatives enter the Whiteman's—"

"You broke into our *place*?" Whiteman snapped.

"Personally, I did nothing. The NSA was interested in your Captain Deloy, and since he's your subordinate, it's something they took upon themselves."

Whiteman began shaking in anger. Lisa said, "I can't believe this! What were they looking for?"

"Dr. Whiteman, I have no idea what they were looking for. It's what they found—"

"You've got no right!" blurted out Whiteman.

"Again, major, it wasn't my doing. And again, feel free to add to this."

Enright turned slowly to Whiteman, stunned. "Oh, my God ..."

"What do you mean?" Lisa said.

Whiteman stiffened before falling back into his chair, his face contorted.

Natano eyed him. "Your mistake was not disposing of the rifle—"

"*What?*" Lisa shrieked.

Jessica drew back in revulsion. Natano added, "A preliminary examination of the firearm shows it's a match for the rounds that were recovered from the beach incident."

"Oh my God!" Lisa moaned, burying her head into her hand.

Whiteman crossed his arms and turned away from his wife. Kevin sat dumbfounded.

"You wanted to kill me?" Jessica glared at Whiteman as she pressed a fist up against her bandage.

Natano held up his hand. "There's more that—"

"Hold it!" Jessica asserted. "I want to know *why!*"

"And so do I!" Lisa said. "You did this?" She sat on the edge of her seat, ready to bolt.

"I have nothing to say." Whiteman sat stoic.

Natano took another paper from his desk. "There's more. Jack sent me another report. This is from the major's service record, from when you were in basic training; your marksmanship record to be exact." Whiteman met his gaze then looked off.

"What does that have to do with anything?" Kevin asked.

"Turns out the major was quite proficient with a rifle. Actually, more than proficient. It says here you attained the rank of expert. You won numerous badges."

"I know about that," Lisa said. She paused. "What are you saying?"

"Hearing this," Natano said to Jessica, "what do your instincts as a reporter tell you?"

She eyed Whiteman for several moments. "He missed." Whiteman looked away.

"Why?" Lisa said. "I want to know why." She began shaking her head in disbelief. "I don't understand any of this."

"I take it you've learned a lot about this program's seamier side," Natano said to Enright.

"Oh, yeah," she chortled sarcastically.

"Jessica's been busy," he nodded. "There's a lot she's uncovered; political underhandedness, the money trail. Much that the parties involved would prefer not come out. An incident like the beach shooting would go a long way to deflect that. And it worked. It's now a terror incident. You can give Roger's people credit for finding the gun but they'd be the first to admit that they were as surprised as anyone. The question remains why; what lies behind it."

"You can talk all you want," Whiteman announced. "I'm not saying a damn thing."

"Then I will," Natano said, eyeing him. "We had a long talk about you. Though I would never agree with your actions, part of me can understand."

"Then maybe you can explain it to me," Lisa said, appalled. She cupped her face, caught between disbelief at her husband's brazen act and her newfound realization that there was more to him than he had let on. "I don't believe this," she kept repeating.

Jessica sat, caught between her instincts as a journalist, which compelled her to sit and wait out the once-in-a-lifetime story and her instincts as a human being which were compelling her to take the chair upon which she sat and smash it into the man who'd fired at her. Kevin remained stunned by the turn of events, more acutely aware than ever before that it had begun in his kitchen as a series of scribbles on the back of a Val Pak envelope set for recycling.

"Okay, people," Natano said, "this is how we're going to proceed. I find myself in unfamiliar territory here. The search was carried out by private operatives, not by police or in accordance with what your courts would consider legal." He smiled. "We get your *Law and Order* here too. Even if I weren't a cop, I'd know what would hold up and what would be thrown out. None of what was found would stand the kind of scrutiny that a legally-obtained chain of evidence would allow." Whiteman's jaw dropped in incredulity.

"As well," Natano went on, "all I have is a ballistic report forwarded to me by a police chief. As it turns out he and I spoke before I talked to Jack. I bet Chief Bennitt has yet to hear from your NSA, but he knows as much as anyone that he won't be able to do much with the rifle. I rather doubt he'll hear from them. And," he said eyeing Whiteman, "I've yet to hear anything along the lines of a confession. Right now all I have is a lot of conjecture and circumstance. So as I've said, I find myself in unfamiliar territory, which means—"

"It might not be enough for you," Lisa cut in, "but it sure is for me." As Jessica nodded in agreement she began to rise but Natano held up his hands.

"I can appreciate how you feel," he said, "but we still need to talk."

"There's nothing to talk about. I don't get any of this and frankly, I don't want to. I'm done."

Whiteman said, "Well maybe if you had—"

"Tom, I don't want to hear it. We've been butting heads with this for over a year and now you pull this kind of stunt? There's nothing left to get. We're done. I just want to know why."

"Dr. Whiteman," Natano said, "I know what you need to hear. I'd like to hear a 'why' as well, but the one I'm looking for is different. After speaking with Jack, what I got is that what you learned as director of your lab put you in an untenable situation. I'm in no position to pass judgment on that but I do have an idea about what motivated the major." He paused, and gave her a reflective stare. "I have a sense here of a husband who loves his wife more than he knows to admit. I think that in his own way he was trying to protect you."

"I have to get out of here!" Lisa cried, jumping up. Jessica put a hand out to restrain her. Whiteman tried to move to her but Natano's officers held him down.

"All right," Natano admonished, "let's calm down."

"*You* calm down!" Lisa cried. "I can't take much more of this!"

"Dr. Whiteman, please. You've been doing fine. Please keep it together."

"Oh, you don't even know! I can't deal with this anymore. I have to get out of here!"

"Please," Jessica implored. A moment later, she smiled and added, "I'm telling you how to act and I don't even know the rules for myself. I missed the journalism class in Columbia on what you're supposed to do when you get shot on the job."

Lisa took a deep breath and sighed. "I feel guilty, too," she confessed. "It's my husband, and it's you." She gathered herself and looked down on Whiteman. "I don't even know what to say to you anymore. I can't believe this."

Whiteman sat with arms folded tight, biting the inside of his cheek. Natano and Kevin traded looks then Natano said, "Major, I'll need you to surrender your passport."

"You're not arresting him?" Lisa asked.

"Your husband hasn't broken our laws. In addition, I have no formal request to detain him. And I don't anticipate any. But I still have my job to do. That means major, for now you're not going anywhere. And this may sound cold but it's just reality—I hate what happened on that beach, but it was much farther away than the device we're setting off tonight. I'm not unmoved, but you need to deal with it. I have to deal with the part that affects me. So, what so motivates a husband that he would take it upon himself to do something like this to protect his wife?"

"That's what I want to know," Lisa said, glaring at her husband. "Because if it's the—"

"Lisa," Whiteman snapped, "be quiet."

Kevin had reserved comment so far. As Tom Whiteman fumed, he said, "Lisa, I'm sorry. If I hadn't blown you off, none of this would have happened."

"Thank you," she said, biting her lip, "but things would have happened regardless."

He eyed her with a new awareness. "Is it the same thing you wanted to talk to me about?"

"Lisa," Whiteman jumped in.

"No! You don't tell me what to do," she snapped at him.

"Well someone has to! You keep your mouth shut or someone's going to shut it for you!"

"Major," Natano said, "you're on thin ice here. When I spoke to the men on the plane, they hinted at something they needed to brief me on when they landed. They wouldn't tell me over the phone."

"I don't like where this is going," Whiteman said.

"I don't really care," Lisa said. "It's too late for that."

Natano eyed Whiteman. "Lisa, the thinking is that your husband found himself stuck between a version of the rock and hard place that you found yourself in—"

"I don't have to listen to this!" Whiteman snarled.

"Tom," Lisa snapped, "for once just shut up!"

"Major, I appreciate your position," Natano said. "But this has moved beyond your—"

"Captain," Whiteman cut in, "you have no idea what you're opening up."

"Well, I do," Lisa snapped.

"Lisa, shut the hell up! You knew what I was up against!"

"And you knew how I felt! And after what you did, you don't talk to me like that and you don't tell me what to do! So you better say something, because if you don't I sure will!"

As Whiteman sneered, Kevin leaned forward. "Uh," he began, "does this have anything to do with it?" He reached into his pocket and took out the USB drive Lisa had given him.

"I don't believe it!" Whiteman shouted. "I do everything I can to keep you from getting caught up in this and you leak it? Are you out of your mind? None of you have any idea what you're messing with! We're dead!"

"I don't want anything to do with it anymore," Lisa glared at him. "You hear? I'm tired of it!"

"All right," Natano said. "I need to know just what's going on."

"Well, you saw what Cindy found," Kevin said. He turned to Lisa. "When we looked it over, we saw the numbers, how they could be a problem." He paused. "Unless …"

Lisa motioned for the drive. As Kevin handed it to her, Whiteman yelled, "Lisa, don't—"

"No more! The hell with consequences! I've been living them for two years! Your psycho was the last straw! That's what dealing with it your way got! I'm done!"

She asked to use Natano's computer. Whiteman bolted up to stop her but the officers pushed him down. "Major," Natano threatened, "don't make me cuff you."

"Fine. Fuck it. We're all done." Whiteman threw his hands up, exasperated.

Lisa inserted the disk and pulled up the memo. Kevin, Natano and Enright huddled around the screen, reading. With her husband stewing she waited patiently for them to finish. It took a little more than ten minutes. They were subdued and confused when they were done.

Jessica saw through the fog first, a profound look of shock coming over her.

Lisa focused in on her. "You get it," she said. Jessica slowly nodded as Natano and Kevin's confusion cleared.

"So," Natano observed, "this is what they were trying to hide."

"It was staring us in the face the whole time," Kevin said.

"I wanted to get this to you since I first saw it but I didn't know how," Lisa told Kevin.

Natano turned to Jessica, "I have an idea what this means, but I want to hear your read."

"My read is this: trillions in defense spending, a huge shift in global power, human rights issues, political instability and a PR nightmare." She eyed Whiteman. "You're right," she allowed. "People would kill to keep this secret. And I don't mean just you," she added bitingly.

Whiteman looked away.

"This explains why the president's rushing back here," Natano said.

"I can't even begin to imagine what would happen if this got out," Jessica said.

Natano added, "But Mr. Hanford can. He's racing to finish up here before it does." He gave a polite cackle. "Look at the date on it—you can draw a line right back to this place. It predates everything here. He would need something to distract people from that document."

"He's been trying to keep it under wraps for at least two years," Lisa said.

"It's plain as day that his new policy ties in with this," Jessica said. "If he can make the argument that he's got a way to reduce terrorism, the country will ignore it. They'll even ignore a plane being shot down by accident."

"Accident, huh?" Kevin was about to add something else when he drew his hands together and pressed them against his face. "Oh, jeez," he exclaimed.

"What?" Jessica asked.

"You know what I hate about all this crap? I'm thinking differently now." He turned to Lisa. "Hanford knew. He knew you were trying to hide this. And he used it."

"Oh my God," Jessica said, nodding vigorously. "You're right."

Natano agreed. "Anything went wrong, he had someone to pin it on. The same would hold true for Kevin here. The one person to blame everything on." Lisa sat stunned.

Jessica turned to Tom Whiteman. "And you knew."

"What?" Lisa yelled. She jumped up, churning with incredulity. "You *knew?*"

"Don't even go there," Whiteman barked, unconvincingly, from his chair.

Jessica wasn't buying it. "It gave you a new narrative, just like taking shots at me and at Lisa's friends. Hey," she said, savoring the moment, "it's going to come out."

"Well," Natano said, "that's what motivates a husband to protect his wife."

Lisa buried her head into her hands, trembling, and Jessica patted her shoulder, trying to comfort her. Whiteman folded his arms tighter.

"There'll be time for the geopolitical subplots," Natano said, "but I have to get back to the main issue." He eyed Whiteman, who wouldn't meet his gaze. "Major. This is what we're gonna do."

"What do you mean," Whiteman said, locking eyes with him, "what *we're* going to do?"

"I'm going to offer you a deal, but this isn't a negotiation. It's clear that your president is rushing to get back here and conclude his business before this goes public. Your country's politics will sort themselves out, but it's coming together in my backyard. I don't know what it means for the future of this program, and I don't really care. Everyone has their own agenda, and no one has thought out the consequences. I need to know what this means, whether corners were cut that would jeopardize my people. No one can give me the answers I need. I'm trying to avoid a potential disaster and no one takes it seriously. Well, that's going to end."

Whiteman frowned. "What the hell you want from me?"

"Major," Natano said, clearly annoyed, "it's your aide on the loose. On my turf."

"I have no control over him."

"But you are going to help me. I have a murder I'm certain I can trace back to him along with a lot of other incidents. I need to know what he's up to and how it affects me. I want him out of here. I can arrest him right now, but I wouldn't learn anything. You're going to find out for me."

For a moment, Whiteman was silent. Then he said, "And what do I get out of it?"

"Oh, you selfish prick," Lisa snapped. "You're just going to do it, that's all!"

"No," Natano said, "I'm willing to offer you something." As Whiteman shrank in surprise, Natano added, "Come tomorrow, you can just go. I don't expect any legal queries from your government in your regard. Find something I can use against Deloy, I'll ignore anything about you that crosses my desk. Where you go after that, that's your business."

As Whiteman silently stared, Natano turned to Jessica. "Are you okay with this?"

She winced and paused, before replying, "Yeah, I guess."

"I guess this kind of cancels that glider you were looking to take," Kevin said to her.

Natano raised his index finger. "No, you make your reservations."

"Since we're staying put," Jessica said to Lisa, "I can tell you what I was going to share this afternoon. You may find this interesting. There's a lot I'm learning about the financing behind this. A lot of it's gone on right in your backyard."

"Integrated?"

"And not only that. A lot's going to be coming out about your lieutenant governor."

Lisa began to laugh. "And how come I'm not surprised." Whiteman rubbed his nose.

"You have something to add, major?" Natano asked.

Whiteman clasped his hands together and stared at them. "Let's just say the lieutenant governor's not my favorite person," he said. "You know, they're joined at the hip."

"Sanderson and IM?"

"No, Sanderson and Deloy." He cleared his throat before turning to Lisa. "I guess I owe my wife something. And Jessica too." He turned to Natano. "You want two for the price of one?"

Natano studied him. "Keep talking."

"I'll give you Deloy. I'd just as soon be rid of him. But Sanderson— he'll be a gift. My Justice Department, you guys, I don't care who gets him; I can't stand the son of a bitch." He turned to Jessica. "Get your paper and pencil ready."

Jessica weighed his offer and guardedly said, "Okay, I'll listen."

"See what you come up with," Natano said, "but do it fast. I have a feeling once your president leaves his people will tie up all the loose ends. All these things, the people involved, will fall between the cracks and you'll never see them again. And you people are loose ends."

"Looks like I'm heading to the airport then," Kevin said.

Natano nodded, glancing at the clock. "It's three o'clock. Let's get going. Maybe we can wrap this up." He turned to Whiteman. "Major, can I trust you to take care of your end?"

Whiteman nodded.

"For this, I'm going to turn away," Natano added. "Just bring me something." He turned to Lisa and Jessica. "Perhaps it's best if you two stay here, out of sight. And Jessica—what will the reporter do with this?"

"I'm washing my hands of it," Whiteman said. "You just better know what you're up against."

"Oh, I know," Jessica said, rubbing her bandaged cheek. Whiteman made a face and she added to Natano, "I'll get it out. How, I don't know yet. I need to see what plays out."

Whiteman shrugged, then motioned to Kevin. They rose, said good-bye and left.

Ninety-nine

Kevin followed Whiteman to the stairs, on their way to the ground floor. An awkward silence followed, which Whiteman made up for in haste. Kevin was pressed to keep up and was mulling over what he could say when Whiteman announced, "You were a topic of conversation between my wife and her staff for two years." Kevin laughed, but it came out as a confused guffaw. Whiteman stopped at the main entrance.

"Doctor," he said, "we don't have to like each other. I know what you think of me but I want you to know I never had it out for any of those people. Natano was right; I was looking out for Lisa, whatever good that did me."

Kevin paused, and then nodded. "Okay, it'll have to do for now."

"Good. Just be aware that there's more going on here than you or Natano know. So just watch your ass." He reached into his pocket and took out a small card. "Here, take this."

"What's this?" Kevin asked.

"Deloy's room key."

"What? Where'd you get it?"

"Don't ask so many questions."

"Listen, I want to nail the SOB as much as anyone, but I'm a physicist. I don't know from cloak and dagger."

"Then learn, fast. I told you there's more going on than you know. I'll go to the airport. He's on his way over there. I'll deal with him. You have a little window; go look around."

"For what? What am I supposed to be looking for?"

"Come on, Doctor, use your head. Anything that doesn't belong. A weasel like Deloy has to be hiding something. Maybe a physicist will see something a cop would have missed. It will be a shock though." At Kevin's confused look, Whiteman added, "Just trust me."

Kevin shrugged. "All right. After the crap that idiot pulled on me…"

"Good. Give me your phone."

"Huh?"

"Stop giving me a hard time. Just give me your phone."

Kevin handed it over. Whiteman quickly punched in some numbers and hit a few keys. "My number," he said. "And, it's on silent. It doesn't need to be ringing in there. Text me when you get there and I'll walk you through. Get in, and get out."

Kevin gave up a nervous laugh. "The things I do for my country ..." For the first time that afternoon, Whiteman smiled. Kevin eyed him. "I have to ask; that paper—"

"Do yourself a favor and forget you saw it."

"Major, I've got no patience for behind-the-scenes crap—"

"Good, because I'm in no position to fill you in."

"That's not what I'm asking. I just want to know—are those pages at the heart of this?"

Whiteman wet his lips, took a deep breath and looked around. "What I'm going to say is off the record; not only that, we never had this conversation. That was probably the most important position paper put out by a branch of the federal government in the past fifty years."

"Oh, jeez."

"You can't begin to imagine, so don't even try. Enright and Lisa both think they know, but neither of them have a clue. That enough for you?" Whiteman looked around. "Enough said. All right Doctor, get out of here. And just watch yourself. I'll see you soon." With that he turned and the two men parted.

One hundred

Vaitupu International Airport jutted out from the western side of the island like a poke in the eye to the ocean whose encroachment threatened the nation. Built on land reclaimed from the shallow waters offshore, it was designed to be unobtrusive for the hotel and staff living quarters. It increased the total area of Vaitupu by almost fifty percent. Two main runways joined up at the terminal, an L-shaped edifice modest in size but thoroughly contemporary and efficient. Two years into operation it was considered one of the premier airfields in the South Pacific.

Cindy had flown in and out of the airport many times. The roadway to the airport was lined with palm trees and lush with red, yellow and orange blossoms and a generous carpeting of the jasmine so popular as ground cover. Like many at the resort the walk was a botanical feast for the eye. Designed to entice visitors with a welcome mat of colors and scents it worked magnificently, not only for guests but the staff as well. Cindy often took walks to indulge in the floral paradise. It was easy to lose yourself.

This afternoon though, her mind was laden with thought. She knew many of the staff and considered most of them friends, but as they greeted her affably, she returned the pleasantries without paying much attention. The afternoon sun beat true and the breeze blew just as invitingly but she moved with a sense that Kevin was right. Her time in Vaitupu was drawing to a close. And there was Kevin himself. She wondered if the two realities weren't one and the same.

She thought back to the previous night. The sex had been great; he was a gentle and attentive lover, but what followed left a more lasting impression. He wasn't perfect, no guy was, but there was something about the way they got along that told her that even if he left for good that afternoon, it would be some time before she forgot him.

As they lay tangled in the sheets, she took his arm, wrapping it across her. In the darkened room Eta Carinae blazed its kaleidoscope through the rafters. Kevin remarked how even inside he could tell how much the cloud had changed.

She ran her foot up his leg. "You like to have fun in bed," she said with a touch of sadness. "That's special."

"You're not used to that, huh?"

She lay back on the pillow, and softly shook her head no. "All guys think sex is fun. Not many have fun with sex." She looked back at him. "It's been awhile."

He softly brushed back her hair, and she playfully reminded him that he could have been with Gina. He smiled and said, "Gina's nice, but ... well ... Gina's someone I can talk *to*. You're someone I can talk *with*. Does that make sense?"

She nodded, knowing all too well. Outside, the extravaganza in the heavens beckoned as a once-in-a-lifetime event, but instead of looking to rush out the door they desired nothing more than to hold each other and talk. It was a pleasant surprise, one they seemed to draw energy from. She regaled him with stories of her experience at the resort. They talked about their field, how physics revealed truth through the simplicity of theory and equations. They spoke of how difficult that was to share with others. And even then she knew that the longer they spoke and shared, the more difficult it would be to let go. It revealed an emptiness she hadn't been aware of; she had no one in her life to talk with, really talk with, and soon her defenses flared. Maybe she was a rebound, a security blanket. Maybe he was there just because she was interested. Too much was going on too quickly to be fair, and he would soon forget. He would soon be gone, leaving her there.

The pretexts came and went like so many wisps of a dandelion wish a child might lift to the wind. And after they had been scrutinized and disposed, she was left with whom he was from the start, a guy of intelligence and depth with whom she could sit and talk, who would challenge and explore whatever she could deliver or imagine. He was sensitive and warm, and so easy on the eye. He possessed a genuinely good soul. And he could give and take with the best. He was funny. And fun. He had her number, and it was okay. She could be herself.

And he could watch those things on TV that others would tease her about. She reached over and turned on the set. *It Came From Beneath the Sea* was on The Atomic Channel. They fell back and watched the movie.

After a while she broke into a vulnerable smile. "I have to be careful with you," she admitted. "You're very easy for me to fall for." She paused. "Maybe I shouldn't have said that. You haven't promised me anything, and I wouldn't expect you to."

"I know, but—"

"No," she offered in an accepting vein, "you don't owe me anything."

He brought her face to his. "I do. I owe you enough to tell you I'd like to get to know you better," he said with complete sincerity. She gave him a loving kiss, and soon they were asleep.

The memory was fresh when he asked her to come back to Princeton. She didn't allow herself to think it would come to anything but she couldn't help notice how the place she had called home for the past two years felt different. Against her inclinations and to her surprise she was beginning to imagine a life apart, though she couldn't as yet imagine a new one together.

She entered the terminal just after three p.m., past numerous travelers, and almost at the same moment Kevin and Whiteman were leaving Peter Natano's office. She turned to the rear, towards the reservation desk off to the side of the check-in and security sector, just ahead of the baggage area. Still engrossed in her thoughts, she didn't at first notice the military personnel. While there was always a security presence to the resort, this seemed more overt. She thought it curious.

She walked up to the desk where reservations manager Patricia Solomon was working.

"Hey, girl," Solomon said. Also in her thirties, alluring with a nice figure and like temperament, she and Cindy met when they first began working there and had become good friends, often spending time together after hours. Men working at the resort and guests would often hit on them but most of the time they politely deflected the attention. Solomon was of Polynesian ancestry and she and Cindy would share stories of their backgrounds. In the end, they came to realize that while cultures differed, people were by and large the same.

Cindy leaned over the desk. "What's with the GI Joes?" she whispered.

"They're beefing up security with the president coming back."

"Oh, yeah. I forgot. My mind's kind of a blur. Pat, could you just confirm a reservation for me please? It's for one of the—"

"It's all set," Solomon smiled. "I saw it in the system, and made sure to double check it." She leaned in and got serious. "We heard about last night. I never liked that asshole." She pulled up the reservation on her screen and began reading. "It's here; you, a Dr. Lisa Whiteman, Jessica Enright and ooh, that hot doc. It's under his name." She smiled. "He looks interesting."

She grinned. "He is."

Solomon broke out in a laugh. "Go for it! Tell me how it goes. Oh, and—"

The phone rang and Solomon excused herself. Cindy looked around. A large food basket from the hotel sat to the side of the desk, leading her thoughts back to the previous night and the incident with Tim Cain. It was one of the many things she and Kevin had discussed in bed. She had massaged his sore shoulder, and he asked her about Cain.

"I can't believe he did that," she said to Kevin of the attack. "Damn, I already thought he was a creep."

"He's more than a creep. If you don't mind me asking, what happened with you guys?"

"Absolutely nothing! I can't believe I even gave him the courtesy of having a cup of coffee."

"Did you know he was interested like that?"

"I don't know. I guess in a way, but it never registered. Guys like that, they're so far off your radar you don't waste any thoughts on them, not even the bad ones. You don't want to think about it, so you don't. Maybe I should start."

"Well, at least you won't have to put up with him anymore."

"I know people had problems with him," she shuddered. "I think of him, and my skin crawls."

Kevin teased his fingers up her arm and she smacked them. "Watch it buster," she laughed. "I know the cops here!" He gave her a kiss, she wrapped his arm over her and they settled back into the movie.

"Okay, the plane's set." Solomon's words brought Cindy back from her thoughts. "They want to shut down operations by four thirty, so you have a little time. Have fun!"

"Pat, could you also make a reservation for me for Monday."

"Sure, where to?"

"I'm flying back to Princeton with Kevin," Cindy said with a grin.

"Look at you girl! You leave it to me! Oh," she said, pointing at the basket, "and—"

She had barely begun her comment when Tim Cain appeared from around a corner.

"You're not supposed to be here," Solomon warned.

"Tim," Cindy said sharply, waving her hands, "I've got nothing to say to you."

"I'm sorry about last night," Cain said haltingly. "I just want to talk to you for a minute."

"Well that's appreciated," Cindy said coldly, "but it's not me you need to apologize to." Cain frowned over the thought of groveling to Kevin Herter.

"You need to get back to work and leave her alone," Solomon cut in. Cain ignored her.

"Cindy, I just want to talk. I'm leaving tomorrow and I want to explain."

"Tim, there's nothing to explain. I hope things work out for you, but after last night—"

"Well I'm just trying to explain!"

"Hey," Solomon snarled, "she doesn't want to talk to you! You're supposed to be in back and you know it!" A no-nonsense type, even more so than Cindy, she had never liked Cain and had told Cindy several times to keep an eye on him. She didn't like that he had been literally dumped in the baggage department so close to her station, and was eagerly awaiting his departure. "Now leave!" she yelled, hoping to get the attention of the police fifty feet away.

"I don't have to fucking listen to you," he snapped.

"Then fucking listen to me!" Cindy yelled. "I don't know what it takes to get through to you! Now leave me alone and Patty as well! I don't want to have anything to do with you, understand! You're just going to have to accept that Tim!"

"Well I don't!" he snarled. "I don't believe it! After all the things I did for you—"

"What you did for *me?*" Cindy recoiled in disgust. "You did nothing for me! I tried to be nice to you, and you never took the hint! You don't know how to take no for an answer!"

"Then why can't you just talk to me? I did more things for you than you ever knew—"

"I don't want you doing anything for me! And you have the balls to attack someone I like very much! Don't ever try to talk to me again, you hear?" She was shaking.

Cain's eyes erupted in fury. "You *bitch!*" he yelled, jumping over the counter. Cindy screamed and stumbled back, falling to the floor. Solomon threw a notebook at Cain, enraging him further. She ran for her desk a few feet away, fumbling for the can of pepper spray she kept in her handbag.

An instant later three officers ran over, who had been attracted by the scene. One drew his weapon, while the others wrestled Cain onto the floor. Cindy recognized the officer with the weapon as Kenney Talake, one of the three who had tackled Cain the previous night.

"Hold it!" Talake ordered. "Freeze!"

"I just want to talk to her!" Cain yelled, struggling to get up.

"I said freeze!" Talake repeated.

"You never gave it a chance!" Cain yelled as he scuffled, trying to wrestle free. They managed to cuff him. Solomon hovered with her can of spray until one of the other officers told her to drop it. She backed off, and the officers yanked him to his feet and sat him in a chair.

Cindy was still on the floor. Solomon rushed over and helped her to her feet. She was panting in terror, but it quickly was supplanted by anger.

"You piece of *shit!*" she screamed at Cain, who wouldn't meet her gaze. Solomon held her back, while Officer Talake called in the incident.

"Calm down, now," Solomon appealed, holding Cindy as she shook with anger. "He's not worth it." She roared defiantly to Cain. "Hear that, you piece of shit! You're not *worth* it!"

Cain groaned out and tried scrambling to his feet. Both officers pushed him down hard, and he almost went over onto the floor.

"Sit and don't move!" Tanaka yelled, as more officers moved over to hold back the gathering crowd. Solomon led a still shaking Cindy to a chair.

"Are you all right?" Solomon asked her.

"I'll be okay," Cindy panted, watching as several of the police escorted Cain away.

Solomon brought over a cup of water and sat down with her. Cindy shook her head.

"Kevin invited me back with him to Princeton. I was looking forward to spending some time with him, you know, see if anything was there. I wasn't sure if it was the right time. But now ... I need to get away from here, for a while at least." She took Solomon's hand. "Pat, there's a lot going on here, a lot that isn't good. You just watch yourself when I'm gone."

Solomon tried smiling. "Thanks," she said. "I'll miss you. You have fun. You deserve it."

Cindy turned her gaze to the large basket. "What's that?" she asked as Talake and another officer walked over to get her statement.

"I was just going to tell you about it when the piece of shit showed up. Someone from the hotel delivered it about five minutes before you got here. It's for you."

She pulled back. "For me?"

"Well, for you and the people you're going up with."

"Who dropped it off?" she asked, the officers listening to the exchange.

"I didn't recognize him."

Talake looked at the other officer, then walked over to the basket and looked at the attached card. Talake read it, then showed it to Cindy.

"My God, it's from him!" she yelped, handing it back like it was infectious.

"Cindy," Talake asked, "did Cain know you were taking a flight this afternoon?"

"No, how could he?"

"We're going to take this with us. I can get your statement later."

"Take it, take it! I don't want to touch it." They took the basket and left.

Solomon looked at her. "Are you going to be all right?"

"Yeah …" She looked at her watch. It was now three twenty. "I need to go tell them what happened." Teary-eyed, she gave Solomon a hug. "I love you, you know?" she said.

"Yeah, sis," Solomon laughed. "Me too!"

At the far end of the terminal Christian Deloy stood in his hotel staff garb, pretending to read a paper and look unobtrusive while seething. The police had the basket, and with it the small bug he had planted. He took the receiver from his ear, wrapped it in the paper and tossed it in a nearby trash can before exiting the terminal, muttering "Stupid fuck" under his breath.

One hundred one

Room 106 was at the far end of the left wing, at the most isolated corner of the hotel. Kevin didn't know that Christian Deloy chose his room locations that way deliberately. Being off the beaten path wasn't where he would have stayed, but maybe the quiet would give him cover for what he was about to do.

He was starkly aware that he wasn't cut out for this. He wanted to help Natano flush Deloy out but cloak and dagger wasn't what he had in mind. Breaking and entering? Ransacking? Larceny? Even if it was sanctioned by the authorities themselves, he didn't care—he had no stomach for this. Deloy may have been the biggest SOB he had come across in years but the sooner he was out of there the better, no matter what he found to nail the bastard.

As Kevin passed a housekeeping cart parked by Room 104, the chambermaid walked out. She smiled and he nodded hello, but as he got to Deloy's door he got the feeling that maybe she knew who was currently occupying the room and thought the wrong person was entering. Heart pounding he flashed a smile, put out the Do Not Disturb sign and went in, another worry to add to his burgeoning sense of dread. No way could anyone do this for a living.

He flipped the light switch. Deloy's room was a small single unit. Aware that housekeeping had yet to stop by, he thought at first that he had made a mistake. The room was immaculate and smelled of pine. He walked around, peered in the bathroom and checked the closet. The bed was made, there was no clutter and the bathroom was spotless. Even the soap dishes were clean.

Unsure, he eased the door back open, and saw that housekeeping had already passed. Kevin closed the door and shook his head. He couldn't believe this guy.

He took out his phone and texted Tom Whiteman. *I'm in.*

A moment later a message came back. *So what do you think of Adrian Monk?*

Never seen anything like it. Anal.

So were the Nazis.

Kevin got it. Psychopath Deloy. Meticulous and wholly evil. Instantly, Kevin felt naked and vulnerable. He began looking around fast.

Check out the luggage; look under the bed and under the cushions.

U sure he's not coming back?

Get going.

Kevin opened the closet again. Inside were two carry-on bags, neatly lined up. He took the larger one out, opened it and saw perfectly folded clothes; shirts, shorts, pants and socks. He then went through the pockets and the sides of the bag and found nothing.

The smaller bag held a notepad in a leather case, and a smart black leather valise. Inside he found several USB drives and a spiral-bound notebook filled with cramped writing.

He texted Whiteman. *Take them* was the answer.

The smaller bag had several side compartments. Kevin opened the first. Inside was another notebook, with a slot that held a red marker. The paper looked very familiar. The discovery took the edge off his nervousness as a stab of anger toward the twisted army captain replaced it.

A moment later the air conditioner kicked in, startling him before he eased up as he recognized the noise. The unit clanked with disrepair and he almost wanted to give it a whack to quiet it down.

The other compartment held a small piece of technical equipment. He wasn't sure what it was, but something told him to pocket the thing, along with the notepad and red pen.

He searched the drawers and tables and looked under the bed, but found nothing. It was looking like a wasted trip. He texted Whiteman and let him know he would be leaving.

He had just hit send when the air conditioner began rattling. It was annoying, but he found himself eyeing the unit. A gap between two panels covering the device drew his attention. He texted again, saying he wanted to check something out.

Don't take too much time.

What's wrong?

Just do what you have to and get out.

Kevin felt around the panel and pried it off. Taped neatly inside was a series of USB drives, labeled in the same writing as in the spiral notebook. In small print on the sides of the sticks were names, dates, and numbers. Grayson, LoBiondo, Rivers and several others meant nothing, but when he saw Sanderson on one and Hanford on another, he realized that the significance was considerable. He took them, and replaced the panel.

Got something he messaged.

Okay, we'll take a look. Now get out. From his table in the welcome shade under a stand of palms at the mall, Whiteman snapped shut his phone.

Five feet in front of him, Captain Christian Deloy stood erect. He had been standing at attention in the hot sun during the entire time his commanding officer had been texting.

"Permission to be at ease, sir," Deloy said as Whiteman finished.

"No, you stand there," Whiteman replied, taking a slow refreshing drink of iced tea as his steely gaze fell on a sweating Deloy. Arrogant, conceited, yet nothing more than a twisted deviant. "They tell me you been a one-man wreckin' crew here, boy," Whiteman added, falling into the Georgia twang he'd learned to hide in Washington. "Lucky ah saw you walkin' fore you got yourself inta any more trouble. And, you out of uniform, soldier."

"Yes sir," Deloy answered, sharply.

Whiteman continued staring at Deloy with a level of contempt he could scarcely have imagined just a week earlier. That was saying a lot, as he had never liked the aide who had been dumped on him back in New Mexico almost at the start of the program. In spite of Deloy's underhanded behind-the-scenes intrigue and his sense of invulnerability borne of supposedly having the right friends, one-on-one he always came across as timid. Whiteman could smell the fear in his subordinate; one reason why he never took him as a serious threat. For now he held back his knowledge of Deloy's actions against Lisa, letting Deloy think that his composed pretense was a departmental rebuke.

"So," Whiteman said, "you gonna explain the get-up?"

"Sir, it was a surveillance operation. This is the uniform of the—"

"That's bull," Whiteman laughed. "You bin runnin' round doing who knows what for God knows who and gettin' away with it. Well, that's over. You got yourself a peck of trouble, an' ah won't even begin to tell you how to handle it 'cause it ain't my problem, it's yours."

Deloy didn't move.

Whiteman savored his ice tea in front of the parched Deloy. "Know what else?" he added. "Ah never liked you. You got a mean streak a mile long, so ah'm enjoyin' this now. Lucky for me, ah don't have to deal with it any more. Son, people here's just itchin' to talk to you. Ah do believe you're gonna be movin' on. But ah'll tell you one thing ah'll do for you, just 'cause ah like ta think ah'm not too much a son of a bitch." He held up his phone. "Ah'll pass on a little info ah just got. Seems that scientist of yours made himself some friends here. Someone just saw him goin´ inta your room."

Deloy stiffened, and in the bright sunlight seemed to blanch. Whiteman had never seen him react so strongly. "Kinda funny, you think of it," he said, "the hunted huntin´ the hunter. Ah don't know what you got, boy, but someone's int´rested." He laughed. "Ah sure as hell wouldn't like anyone rummagin´ through my shit. So you just go and take care of it. Ah'm not sure where he's headed, but you figure it out. Then boy, you on your own. Might wanna think of hightailin´ it out of here then, ´cause ah get the impression you've pissed off the wrong people, ah mean besides me. Now, get the fuck outta here."

Deloy saluted sharply and bolted into the sun. Back in Room 106 Kevin drew the door open, and seeing no one, darted out, heading to his room for a few minutes before going back to Natano's office.

One hundred two

It was an increasingly hot afternoon and Kevin was dragging as he went up to his room. The long day was taking its toll and it wasn't over. He called Peter Natano from the elevator and told him he'd be stopping by with a bag of items taken from Deloy's room. The six minutes he'd spent in there had sapped him and he was looking forward to closing his eyes for a few minutes.

He got off the elevator and smiled at a young couple waiting to get on. As he walked down the hall, he didn't notice the tall staff worker behind him wearing sunglasses and carrying towels.

Kevin got to his door. He inserted his key and had yet to walk through the door when a massive shove sent him hurling onto the ante-room floor. A torrent of pain ripped his shoulder, the same one he had fallen on the previous night. He didn't know what hit him and could barely right himself before the door was kicked closed. From under the towels the man produced a knife.

"You fucking piece of shit!" Deloy screamed, whipping off his shades to reveal wild eyes. "You fucking go through my room? I should have taken care of you back in Jersey!"

He lunged and Kevin yelped and scrambled back on the floor. He was next to a lamp table, and kicked it out. It was enough to trip up Deloy.

Kevin jumped up, frantically looking around for a weapon. The closest thing was a chair by the desk. He grabbed it and as Deloy charged he slammed it into his side, causing Deloy to stumble with a roar as the knife he held went flying. Stunned, Kevin hesitated for a moment, long enough for Deloy to clamber back up.

With a grunt Kevin swung the chair again. It clipped Deloy and he tumbled over again, landing near the knife. He grabbed it and got up. "Think you can take me, science boy?" he sang, grinning sickly.

"You're the sickest piece of shit I ever saw!" Kevin yelled, clutching the chair as Deloy's taunting sneer flashed to pure rage as he lunged.

The knife went into the base of the chair but sliced through enough to run across Kevin's arm. He shrieked as blood shot out. He pivoted to his left, and swung his leg so that his foot connected with Deloy's leg. Deloy managed to stay upright but buckled, enough for Kevin to heave the chair the other way. It got Deloy's side and he fell over, enraged further by the fall but not knocked out.

That instant the door kicked in, splintering the frame and swinging hard enough to slam back into the wall. A picture shattered as police barreled in, guns drawn, shouting.

"Freeze asshole!" one yelled to Deloy.

"Go fuck yourself!" he yelled back. "This dick broke into my room!"

"I said *freeze!*" the officer repeated. Several police surrounded Deloy. "Drop the knife! Drop it!" Deloy stared for a moment, then let it slip from his hand.

The officers swarmed around and got him on the floor.

"You *shits!*" he yelled. "What are you doing to me? That fuck broke into my room!"

"Captain Deloy," said the first officer, "you're under arrest."

Deloy heaved in frustration, trying to shake off the officers and get away. Two of the officers grabbed him, one on each arm, hauled him up and hustled him out.

Officer Steve Luka helped Kevin up and led him to a chair.

"We're sorry, Dr. Herter," he began, taking a towel from the pile Deloy had dropped and wrapping it around Kevin's left arm to stop the blood dripping.

Officer Kenney Talake added more as he came in. "Dr. Herter, we apologize."

"What happened?" Kevin gasped, more for reassurance than in surprise.

"We were following Deloy. Can I get you some water?" Kevin nodded and Officer Luka brought him a glass.

"Dr. Herter," Talake continued, "we're going to take you to the infirmary. That arm's going to need stitches. After that, Captain Natano wants to see you. He said it was important."

Officer Luka took the bag of items Kevin had taken from Deloy's room, and at Talake's nod, left. Kevin watched the simple package that caused so much trouble disappear from sight.

"If I hear one more person say that they need to talk to me today," he said wearily.

"I didn't think we'd see you again so soon," Dr. Tom Asanti said, more in regret than jest as he came in to the emergency room. "This may sting," he added, as he lifted a needle. Kevin winced as the local anesthesia was injected in his left shoulder.

The towel wrapping his arm was wet with blood when he'd walked in just after four, escorted by three police officers. He plopped down on the gurney as much from fatigue as shock. Dr. Asanti examined the wound.

"We're looking at about twenty stitches," he told Kevin as the nurses prepped the ER for its only patient and laid out a surgical tray. "A few internals as well. He gave you a nice cut."

"Well," Kevin cringed, "do what you have to. Just don't expect me to watch."

"At least you haven't lost your sense of humor." Kevin looked up to see Peter Natano at the door.

"If you want me to pull combat duty," Kevin said, trying to grin, "I expect to go on payroll."

"Don't take this wrong," Natano smiled, "but I can't wait for you to go back home."

"And don't you take this wrong," Kevin said with a weak laugh, "I can't wait to leave."

"I do want to thank you," Natano said, entering the room. "I'm sorry this happened. The prime minister sends his regrets. But I think the heavy lifting is over now."

Kevin nodded his appreciation. A nurse began swabbing his arm and he winced.

"I think we can begin to wrap this thing up," Natano said. "You should know that you came up with some interesting information in your few minutes there. And a lot's turning up on Deloy."

"The man is sick."

"I know but he's got friends in high places. I think his luck might have run out though."

"I don't get it," Kevin said, confused. "What happened back there?"

"Tom Whiteman baited him. The idiot fell for it. My men were following him. We were less than a minute behind. You're lucky, actually. Deloy was so worked up, he lashed out in anger, not with his training. If he'd been smarter, we wouldn't be talking like this."

"Well, thanks." Kevin tensed up as Dr. Asanti began stitching his arm. "Where is the good major?" he asked. "Gotta have a talk with him."

"We'll see him soon; he's tying up some loose ends. Meantime, we have much to discuss." He waved a couple of officers in from the door, one carrying a laptop.

"We're pressed for time," Natano said to Asanti and the nurses. "I'm deputizing you. Whatever you hear is strictly confidential." They looked at each other, and then nodded their agreement.

Natano continued, "Jack landed on Funafuti a half hour ago. Your president thinks he got the upper hand by keeping them away from here, but it may turn out to be an advantage for us."

"Kevin, I'm so sorry," Jessica Enright said as she rushed in, avoiding looking at his arm. "And Lisa feels horrible."

"I wish she didn't. That asshole got both of us, in different ways. How is she?"

"Overwhelmed. She feels responsible." She gave him a kiss and asked, "You okay?"

He shrugged. "Another chapter for my memoirs. Now we can compare war wounds."

She laughed and turned to Natano, "Did you tell him?"

"Tell me what?" Kevin asked.

Natano looked over at Officer Tommy Metia, who was setting up the computer. "I was just going to, when you came in. We're hooking up a Skype call with Jack, Mike and Roger Braddock."

"I just spoke with them," Jessica said. "You need to hear what they have to say. Now, Cindy—"

"What happened?" Kevin asked.

Metia looked up from the computer. "Miss Russell had a run-in with Mr. Cain at the airport."

"What happened? Is she okay?" Kevin groaned, shaking his head in exasperation. "Another piece of—I thought we were done with him."

"The prime minister can be too forgiving," Natano said. "He didn't want to just fire him so he thought letting him sort baggage would do until we shipped him out. When Cindy stopped by, he tried to get something going with her. She blew him off and he went ballistic."

Jessica's phone beeped and she excused herself just as Officer Metia added, "She's okay; a little shaken up, but fine. Cain seems to have dug a much bigger hole for himself though."

"What do you mean?"

"Just hold that thought," Natano said. "When we leave here, we're going to make a stop. Cain's in a lot more trouble than he realizes. So's Captain Deloy."

Kevin held off pushing for information when the images of Jack Raden, Mike Yahr and a man he didn't recognize came up on the screen.

Raden could only shake his head. The sight of a roughed-up Kevin being stitched up in an ER wasn't what he would have envisioned just a day earlier.

"Jesus," he said. "I leave you for a day and look at you."

Kevin tried to smile. "It's good to see you too, Jack."

"How are you feeling?"

"A pint low but hanging in," Kevin sighed. "I'm beat. How are you guys? We've been keeping up with you as well. At least with your deal, the three of you look the better for it."

Raden, Yahr and Braddock nodded.

"Yeah," Raden said, "we didn't expect it either."

"Kevin," Mike asked, "how are you holding up?"

Kevin turned to Dr. Asanti. "How am I holding up?"

Asanti was snipping off a stitch. "He'll be fine. He's a great patient."

Kevin shrugged and Mike introduced Roger Braddock. "It's a pleasure to meet you," Braddock said. "I wish we could meet in person but a certain party had other ideas."

"We heard. I agree."

"The least we could do was to send you something," Raden said. "It should be there soon."

"Guys," Kevin groaned, "I think I've had enough surprises."

Raden looked at Mike, who shrugged, "Tell him."

"Okay," Raden said. "We brought a—"

Just then, Jessica walked back in from the hallway outside. "Gentlemen," she greeted the onscreen trio.

"Jessica," Mike replied. "We didn't know you were there."

"I wanted to brief everyone here before I called you back," she said, not smiling. "I was able to corroborate what we heard."

"We're hearing the same thing," Braddock said.

"What are you guys talking about?" Kevin asked.

"Some news from the states," she said. "Something we just learned from—" She was interrupted as Cindy hurried in.

"Are you okay?" she blurted, moving quickly to Kevin and embracing him on his good side. "I just heard. I couldn't believe it." She didn't notice the open laptop.

Kevin smiled. "I'm all right. They fixed me up nice. But my God, how are you?"

"I'm okay." She bit her lip, tears coming to her eyes. "I was very scared. For a moment, I thought he ..." She shook her head. "He freaked out."

"Cindy," Peter Natano said, "we have Cain locked up. He's facing a lot of charges. Stupid, stupid man. If he had just behaved himself he would be heading out next week. Now he's going to be with us for a long time to come."

Jessica was distracted, engrossed in sending a text as Dr. Asanti continued with the stitches. Cindy pulled up a chair and took Kevin's right hand. "I'm really looking forward to going back to Princeton with you," she said to Kevin. "I wasn't sure if getting away from here right now was the right thing to do. But after today, I can't wait."

"Don't worry," Natano said, "your job will be here when you get back."

Cindy smiled, while Kevin said, "Princeton's a lot different from the South Pacific."

"I know," she laughed. "I've been there." She looked down for a moment. "Are there going to be any problems with your ex-girlfriend?"

Kevin looked at their joined hands. "I don't think so, but it was on its last legs and we did end on a rough note. So I hope not. I don't want that to be the way it is—we're still going to be running into each other, I'm sure." He shook their hands. "We'll see."

Cindy nodded as Jessica, done with her texting, added, "I have a lot to say to her myself."

On the screen, Raden and Mike looked at each other like two boys who forgot they left the family dog in the hot car. Raden cleared his throat, causing Cindy to notice them.

"Kevin," he said, "there's a few things we need to go over." Before Kevin could respond, an officer entered and told Kevin that someone was there to see him.

"Jessica," Kevin said, "could you please go see who that is? I'm not up for company right now."

Back on Funafuti, Raden whispered to Mike, "Next time, I mind my own business."

One hundred three

Jessica Enright stepped out of the ER holding her cell phone, ready to make another call. She turned a corner and let out a gasp.

Sharon Velazquez was sitting in the waiting area.

"Oh, my God!" Jessica yelped, covering her mouth with her hand.

"I was going to tell Kevin that I happened to be in the neighborhood. I should have given someone a heads up, but that look on your face was worth it." Sharon laughed.

Jessica lowered her hand. "I can't believe you're here. Please! Please sit. I literally was just talking about you. I had all this stuff I was going to say to you at the right time, but in a million years I never would've thought it'd be here and now."

"I can understand that," Sharon said as Jessica took a seat beside her. "I didn't expect it to be like this either. But first of all, how are you feeling? I heard what happened."

Jessica grew misty eyed. "I'm sorry," she whispered, "it's been tough."

Sharon looked at the up-and-coming journalist who had been the source of so much grief just days ago and surprisingly felt sorry for her. There were hints of her on-air radiance but Sharon sensed that here was a person in many ways changed. She was scraped and bruised, and her once enviable hair was tied up in a demure ponytail. The bandage on her face captured as much attention as the person beneath, but more evident was the difference in her spirit. It seemed shorn of some of its confidence. Oddly, she looked more likeable; human.

"I'm sorry," Jessica repeated. "After everything, it's a bit much to hear you ask how I'm feeling. I've felt very ashamed of how I behaved in Princeton and what happened after that." She wiped her eyes. "I'm not very good at this. In a way, I think I feel the way you must have, backed up with nowhere to go."

Sharon grinned lightly. "I hadn't thought of that. I left my cameramen home though."

"Please, let me say I'm truly sorry for the situation I put you in and what happened on-air." She looked down and began smoothing out a crease in the chair's fabric. "I know all about staying objective and how the public has a right to know anything we think is important. You get so caught up trying to get the biggest, the hottest." Her eyes met Sharon's. "It never hit home how it must be on the other end, I mean for someone who hadn't done anything and just wanted to be left alone. I'm very sorry. I hope you can forgive me."

"Thanks," Sharon smiled through her tension. "It hurt a lot but I do appreciate the apology. I should say you're lucky you didn't get me earlier in the week. I'd be apologizing to you right now."

Jessica smiled sadly. "I can understand. I planned on stopping in to see you as soon as I got back. I was hoping you'd see me, though I was prepared for you not wanting to. And believe me, I wasn't going to drop in the way I did before. I just hoped we could talk. "

"I believe that." She added, "I heard about what happened in California."

"Thanks. That means a lot. You may not accept this but I'm so glad to see you. I just—what are you doing here? They said someone was here to see Kevin, but I didn't expect you."

"When I decided to fly out, I didn't know you were here. I came out to help him."

"Really? That is so nice. That says a lot about you; especially where you two are now."

"I'm having trouble with it myself," she said. Jessica smiled and Sharon added, "It's been some trip. He owes me big."

Jessica laughed, then leaned forward. "Sharon, we all heard. I know Kevin's been worried as well. I know you guys have moved on but he has a lot of love left for you."

Sharon turned away. "Same with me."

Jessica's hand went to her mouth. "I hope I wasn't the one who broke you guys up."

"Oh, no. That one you can't blame on yourself. We were drifting apart long before you came along. Just lousy timing." She looked around. "But what am I doing here? I land ten minutes ago and all they said was to meet him here. What's going on? I hope he's visiting someone."

"Sharon, there's a lot you need to know." Jessica told her about the knifing.

Sharon shot up. "I knew something like this would happen! I told him, but did he listen?" She slowly sat back down. "I have to stop doing this."

"You wouldn't believe what I've seen in just the past few days. But you're right; he does need help. I think you can do something for him."

Sharon looked confused. "Like what?"

Jessica shook her head. "This situation is very fluid. It's changing literally hour to hour. Now before we go inside there's something else you need to hear." She told her about Cindy.

Sharon leaned back and a smile broke over her face. "So, what's she like?"

Jessica looked surprised, but quickly went with it. "Oh, very attractive, intelligent. Sharp. Quick sense of humor. In a way, kind of like you."

"She probably doesn't have my sarcasm though."

Jessica laughed. "Not quite. But maybe you have more cause than she does."

"Know what? I'm glad for him." She paused. "I wasn't going to say this and I'm surprised to hear myself even mouth the words. I'm sitting here and I'm not hating you."

Jessica laughed. "Thanks, really. You'd be perfectly entitled to but I'm glad you're not. I mean, I know you were part of a story for me but I was actually very impressed by you; what you did, your work, everything. I'm glad you don't hate me."

"This is another surprise for me. The first was coming here. I never thought I'd fly halfway around the world to help out an ex. The second is that earlier this week I would have been perfectly happy to see you tarred and feathered." As Jessica glanced down she added, "But I was feeling that about Kevin too." She laughed lightly. "I must be mellowing in my old age."

Jessica looked graciously at her. "Sharon, I'm glad. I don't know if you want to hear this or not but I hope someday we could be friends."

Sharon shrugged. "Who knows? Stranger things ..."

"... have happened." They smiled at each other.

"And Kevin too," Sharon added. "Jack Raden had asked me before I agreed to come out here if I had wanted to get back together with him. And I told Jack no, that I wanted to be friends with him as well, but you know how it is—you always say that to save some face. I wasn't completely sure. But it didn't really hit me until just now, that's what I want. We just don't work well being involved. Jeez, I'm just making all new kind of friends this week."

Jessica smiled, and then took a deep breath. "Sharon, Cindy's inside with him."

Sharon smiled. "You know, that's cool. I want to meet this girl. I just hope she's okay with me, if I have to take his head out of his ass. That's the main reason why I came out here."

Jessica sighed. "Somehow, I don't think that's going to be a problem anymore."

One hundred four

Kevin was sitting up in bed with his arm propped up on a pillow when Jessica returned to his room. "What happened," he asked, "you get lost?"

"I ran into a friend of yours," Jessica smiled. She stepped aside. A moment later, Sharon poked her head into the room.

"Hi, Kevin," Sharon said.

"Oh my God!" he blurted. Sharon walked in and gave him a kiss, then smiled at Cindy, who was handling her own state of shock.

"I am so glad to see you!" Kevin said, "but what on earth are you doing here?"

"That was my doing." Jack Raden's voice diverted their attention back to the laptop.

"Yeah," Sharon said, "blame it on the big troublemaker. When he's done here, he has a great future selling freezers to the Eskimos."

"At the time," Raden shrugged, "it seemed the thing to do."

"You came in with Jack?" Kevin asked. Sharon nodded.

Cindy managed to regain her composure, though she was noticeably red-cheeked. She let go of Kevin's hand.

Sharon walked up to her and reached out to shake Cindy's hand. "Hi," she smiled, "I'm Sharon." They shook then Sharon took Kevin's hand and joined it back with Cindy's. With a wink she said, "When we get some time, I'll tell you all about your friend here."

Still blushing, Cindy smiled as Kevin said, "I'm doomed." They all began to laugh.

Kevin stared at Sharon. A day on a plane had done her no injustice. Wearing a light sweatshirt and jeans with her hair swept back gave her a casual flair that spoke of indifference. Despite what she had been through, she looked serene.

He called her over for a hug. She bent down and began slowly rocking in his arms.

"Oh, you piece of work," she smiled. "Let me look at you." She backed up, took a tissue and wiped her damp eyes. "You know something," she beamed, "I really didn't know until just now whether I'd made the right decision in coming. I'm so glad to see you. A lot has happened."

He bit his lip. "Yeah, we heard about California. And, you hear about Max?"

"I couldn't believe it," she answered, taking a chair.

"And we heard about your flight, but I didn't know you were on it. Are you all right?"

"I'm okay now, but earlier, not so much. The guys were busy."

"The White House tried its damnedest to keep us from landing in Vaitupu," Raden said. "It worked."

"But no one said a thing about a police flight taking off from Funafuti and landing here," Natano added.

"We sent Sharon but we stayed to do research, the kind we might not be able to do there."

"What does that mean?" Kevin asked.

Mike smiled. "None of your business. In the meantime, you have your own work cut out for you." He turned to Natano. "Pete, you want to brief them?"

"Very soon. Meantime, I'm signing off. We'll talk, okay?"

Mike nodded. Raden then said, "Kevin, we'll talk to you later this afternoon."

"Yeah, Jack, thanks. I owe you one."

"Not at all. We thought we'd stepped in it but I think it worked out." They said goodbye.

"I'll be outside," Natano said. "You people finish up here, then I need you to come with me." He and Jessica walked out. Kevin was left with Sharon and Cindy.

"I'm going to leave you guys to talk," Cindy said, smiling.

"Thanks Cin," Kevin said.

Sharon thanked her, and then asked, "You're coming back to Princeton?"

Cindy nodded and Sharon added, "I'll take you around. There's a lot to see, and I know the town better than anyone. We'll ditch this guy a bit and have some fun."

Cindy broke out in a big smile and gave her a hug. "It is so good to meet you," she said. She then bent over to Kevin and gave him a kiss, then left the ER.

Sharon looked at him. "I like her already."

"I can't believe you're here," he said warmly. "I spent a lot of time thinking about you."

"Me too."

"Forgetting all this, I think we needed some time away from each other."

"Oh, don't I know it," Sharon smiled. "Kevin, we were at each other's throats."

"I know! Don't you think I know? It was no good."

"For either of us." She paused. "It gave me time to think without the drama. I know you had enough to last a year but other than the bull with Jessica and coming out here, for me it was quiet. I needed that, so much you have no idea. And I realized something. I love you, I love you with all my heart and I always will, but ..."

"You're not in love with me."

"That's right!"

"Know what? Me neither." Sharon began laughing as Kevin said, "Isn't that amazing?"

"I know! We're like the most evenly-matched couple."

"People tell me that all the time."

Sharon leaned back. "I thought a lot about us. I know I was a pain in the ass." She took his hand. "And you were so damn close to what I was looking for! I was so hell bent on making you into what I needed, I didn't take time to enjoy who you were. You can't do that. I was so caught up with the drama that I never stopped to notice my heart wasn't going thump-thump. I mean it was but for all the wrong reasons, getting mad and getting laid instead of getting closer. Since you left that part just kinda vanished. It wasn't an issue anymore. It's as if when I didn't have to worry about you leaving any more, it was okay that you did. I wasn't angry any more."

"Wow. I guess I was doing the same thing in my own way. I know I'm difficult. You were very close to what I wanted, and my reaction—"

"You mean your push pull."

"That was always easier. And face it, Velazquez, we always pushed each other's buttons."

"Yeah, good and bad." She laughed. "Yup, never had problems in that area."

"I know. I'm just amazed we spent so much time working at something that wasn't working."

She sadly smiled, then said, "Kevin, Cindy—"

"Sharon, I didn't plan on anything happening."

"Oh, I *know!* No, that's not what I meant. Kev, I'm not mad. It's funny—I would have been even recently but it just didn't hit me that way.

It's a surprise—not you meeting someone but my reaction to it. I know I made things difficult by flying off the handle so much but since you left, a lot has changed. Dealing with you, with Jessica … I'm surprised, but I can't deny it."

"Thanks." He grew wistful. "This week has been too much."

"I know. I saw Jean. I knew how you must have felt. You know how much they meant to me, but I know what he means to you. I would have been infuriated."

"Oh believe me I was but what was I going to do, bop him? Not talk to him for a month?"

"I know," she sighed. "Anger is great for keeping you angry."

"That's it. And then they sent me off like typical Jewish parents; 'Go, *enjoy*, we'll be *okay*, call us when you get back'. All these things coming together. Too much."

"Yeah, like Mike and Max knowing each other. And Jack. He's a piece of work, getting me to come out here." She laughed. "One minute I'm ripping you and God and everyone a new one, the next I'm packing. Like I got nothing better to do."

"So why did you?"

"I asked myself that. He asked me whether I'd want to be friends with you or get back together. It got me thinking. There was just a symmetry about it. You and I; we're like oil and water. The only thing that keeps us together is agitation. But Kev, I do love you and I realized I want you in my life. It may not be as a life partner but you're very important to me; enough to fly out here and help you. And you need it. I thought you needed it back home, but you were too much of a fathead to admit it."

He laughed. "You know," he said nodding, "I really love you too."

"I know," she grinned. "You just can't help yourself."

"I think that myself. Put aside the fighting. We always had a great friendship. I don't want to lose that. I told Cindy about you. I actually thought you two would hit it off."

"I can already see it." Sharon smiled. "Maybe even Jessica as well."

"She's not the same person. You hear what happened in California?" Sharon nodded, and he added, "She got knocked down pretty good, but she's tried to learn from it."

"Jean said she was very contrite when she stopped by."

Kevin agreed. "I give her credit. Not many people would have dealt with it. In a strange way, we've actually become friends. She's been a big help to us."

"I can see that." She then grew serious. "Kevin, what's going on here?"

"You see that memo? None of us really understand what it means. But this place isn't the same. When I first got here, there was a sense of stability. Now it's falling apart, fast. Things are changing by the hour and not in a good way." He paused. "Sharon, I saw it last night. Most amazing thing I've ever seen. As an artist, it would have knocked your socks off."

"I wouldn't even want to see it."

"That's how I felt. You know that. But there's just something about seeing it. You know what I learned? You can't figure how you're going to feel about things till they happen. I knew exactly what to expect and it still floored me. That's the shame here. If done properly, it could really be something. And there is a way that can be done. But not the way they've done it."

"And let me guess. They don't want to."

"Whoever started this decided early on to be too clever by half, and if nothing's done to fix it, it's going to catch up with them. Cindy's got as good a working knowledge of this place as anyone and even she was floored by what we learned. She can't put on a happy face anymore. And I'm not even talking about the memo. You were right all along."

"I was right, but I think for the wrong reasons. So what do you want to do?"

"With everything that's happened to us both, I won't be so arrogant to think I can stop it. Even you have to admit, there's only so much you can control. And the memo's going to have consequences. But I'll tell you what I can do. They're expecting me to show up with a happy face, even if I say nothing. After what I've seen, I'll be damned if I get involved. I've had it."

Sharon smiled. "I'd love to see you tell Hanford where to stick it."

"Looks like you'll get your chance. He's on his way back here. And lucky you, you get to see an explosion too. They're setting off another one tonight to usher in his big announcement."

"Oh, great." She paused. "You do understand that this is coming down to you and him?"

"I know. I already had a long talk with him today and now there's going to be another. My mind's a blur. They wear you down. I think this time will be different." He smiled. "Still can't believe you came all the way out here. You don't know what that means to me."

She smiled back. "I think I do. But honestly, I'm selfish. It's as much for me. Sometimes I think it's okay to be a right fighter. Let's stick it to those assholes."

A moment later Dr. Asanti walked in. "We have a little business to take care of," he told Kevin. "Tetanus and an antibiotic. The wound was deep." Dr. Asanti gave Kevin a shot in his arm, and then gave him a pill.

Just then, Natano returned. "Your president just landed. He's already looking for you."

Kevin frowned. "He's not wasting any time."

"No he's not. I hope you realize things are coming to a head with you and him."

Kevin and Sharon eyed each other. Kevin replied, "Sharon just said that."

"Then you need to listen to her. If I had to guess though, I don't think it will go down quite the same. And there's something you both need to see. Let's go."

One hundred five

"This looks as clean as the hospital," Kevin said to Natano as they stood in the Tauri Complex. He eyed the light turquoise walls and coral trim. "You can still smell the fresh paint."

"This building cost two hundred eighty million dollars but we've never used this floor until this week. That's how boring it's been here. After two years, the only person we questioned down here was the boy-friend of the girl we found in your old room."

They stood with Sharon and Jessica outside the interrogation room. The rooms set aside for police matters included a holding room and several jail cells, all located on the bottom floor, and were as well-furnished as those in the states.

The scene through the one-way glass reminded Kevin of any of a dozen TV crime shows. Christian Deloy sat at a large gray table, intent on lining it up with the walls so it was even. Officer Talake stood off to the side, expressionless as he watched Deloy.

"So," Deloy said smugly, "who's out there?" Talake ignored him.

Outside, Sharon stared with her arms folded. "So that's the shit," she said.

"He looks like a weasel," Jessica added.

"That he is," Natano echoed.

From a room down the hall, Officer Tong appeared, followed by Cindy. She rushed up to Kevin, smiling at Jessica and Sharon.

"Any problems?" Natano asked Tong, who shook his head no.

"Did it go all right?" Natano asked Cindy.

She nodded. Natano explained to the others, "Procedural, identification of Tim Cain."

"He still tried to convince me we could be an item," Cindy said. "The piece of garbage." Kevin gave her a hug and she leaned in to rest her head on his chest.

"How does he tie in with this fool?" Sharon asked.

"Like this," Natano said. He signaled Tong, who lifted a wall phone and said, "Okay."

A moment later, another door opened. Major Tom Whiteman walked out with an officer, carrying the basket left for Cindy at the airport. They approached the group.

Whiteman was obviously contrite. He nodded to everyone, then hesitantly approached Jessica. "I hope you're feeling better," he said to her. She bit the inside of her cheek, staring back silently with a narrowing gaze. He quickly looked away.

The officer gave the basket to Whiteman, handed a bag to Natano, and left.

"What did you learn?" Natano asked Whiteman.

"A lot." He turned to Jessica. "This'll fill in some of your blanks." She nodded stiffly. Natano then asked Whiteman, "Major, how is your wife?"

"Still shaken up. I'm taking her home, right after I finish up here."

"Please send her our best." Kevin and the others echoed his sentiments.

Whiteman thanked them, adding, "Just watch it. He's a manipulative shit."

Natano winked, took the file folder in the rack on the door and went inside.

"I want a lawyer!" Deloy immediately demanded. "I know my rights!"

"Well," Natano said casually, opening the folder and flipping through the file while avoiding eye contact, "we do things a little differently here. In time." He held up a paper with extensive notations, eyeing it intently. "Captain," he said, "you're quite the world traveler. Seems you've visited us several times over the past few months."

"Yeah, well, I like the show you guys put on."

"Uh huh." Natano sat down across from Deloy. "We have a serious situation here," he said. "You've been charged with a number of felonies. Conspiracy, breaking and entering, assault with a deadly weapon—"

"That's bull! I went after someone who broke into my room!"

"... attempted murder—"

"What? *Bullshit!* I'm an American military officer. I want to see the American Defense Department liaison! You get your ass out there and tell him to get his in here! Now!"

Natano ignored the bluster. "I don't think they're interested in seeing you, Captain. My sense is, from now on you're going to find your friends few and far between."

"What the fuck does that mean?" Deloy's sneered.

"We had the misfortune of experiencing our first homicide this week. Poor girl was assaulted by a jealous boyfriend. He sat in the very chair where you're sitting now. During the course of our conversation, we showed him several photos. Most didn't mean anything to him. But he did react quite strongly to one." He took out Deloy's service picture.

"I know didley squat bout that," Deloy said, his gaze narrowing.

Natano scratched his ear. "Okay." He motioned to the mirror.

A moment later, Tom Whiteman entered, causing Deloy to snap up and salute. When he noticed the basket that Whiteman carried, he turned ashen.

Whiteman eyed him with a hard resolve. "Son, this talk's a long time comin´."

"This is the basket your Mr. Cain had made for Miss Russell," Natano added. "Now don't insult our intelligence and tell us you and he don't know each other. Mr. Cain's dug a big enough hole for himself that he's willing to serve you up. He's down the hall. He confirms that."

Outside, Cindy's expression tightened and she pulled closer to Kevin.

"So I met the dickweed," Deloy said. "So what?"

Whiteman took out a yellow and pink floral arrangement from the basket. Deloy's bug was still attached. "This was easy to spot," he said, "along with your fingerprints inside."

Deloy made a face, but quickly swallowed hard.

"I don't believe it!" Cindy gasped, her jaw dropping.

"He wanted to eavesdrop on you guys in the air," Officer Tong said. "But keep listening."

Natano took the package the officer had given him. Inside was the newspaper containing the monitoring equipment Deloy had thrown in the garbage can at the airport

"We took the liberty of recycling your trash," Natano added.

Deloy turned white. "I was involved in surveillance against individuals identified as threats to the United States Government," he declared, trying to recover. "This was done with full knowledge of my government. I have nothing more to say. This line of questioning is going to result in serious breaches of classified information, and all of you—"

"Son," Whiteman directed, "cut the shit." He turned to Natano. "I want to apologize for my government for letting this imbecile loose on you."

"Now hold it, sir," Deloy said. "Don't you—"

"Boy, shut up. You're going down and I'm gonna enjoy watchin´. Sit your ass down, right now."

Deloy quietly sat down. Whiteman began removing items from the basket—several wrapped sandwiches, bags of snacks, drinks, napkins.

"That idiot you were working was completely out of his league with you," Whiteman said. He looked at Natano, then removed the bottom of the basket. Beneath was a compartment, which opened to reveal a small device.

"That ain't mine!" Deloy cried, jumping up.

Officer Talake pushed Deloy back down in his chair. Outside, the observers reacted sharply.

"Holy *shit!*" Sharon said.

"Oh, my *God!*" Cindy cried. Kevin held her tighter.

"Sophisticated," Officer Tong said. "It would have gone off when you were in the air."

"We have several witnesses who identify you as the person delivering this," Natano said.

"No way, man! No way you stick that on me!" Deloy jumped up, but before he could move away, Officer Talake restrained him once more.

"Sit your fucking ass down, boy," Whiteman said. He walked over and glared down. "You fuckin´ attack my wife?"

Deloy pulled back, his lip beginning to quiver.

"Out of respect for her and the people here I kept my cool around you this fine day more than I ever did in my life," Whiteman said. "They'd be scraping you off the sidewalk otherwise."

He backed off slightly as if in thought, then suddenly lunged. He grabbed Deloy, lifted him and slammed him into the wall.

"That's enough!" Natano yelled as Talake dove for Whiteman. Deloy tried pushing his superior off but Whiteman got off a clean punch to the gut. Deloy crumpled, less in pain than in submission.

Before Talake got to Whiteman, he broke off his assault, seemingly satisfied with his work as Talake reluctantly helped Deloy to his feet and back to his chair. Whiteman's attack shifted to a gaze so piercing that Deoy didn't dare meet it. Whiteman nodded deliberately to Natano, reassuring him, "Ah'm okay." Then grinning, he informed Deloy, "Boy, when you're done doin´ your time here you and ah gonna have ourselves a nice talk. Ah can wait."

"All right, major, that's going to be a long ways off," Natano said as Whiteman withdrew to the side of the room. Deloy was obviously angry that the police hadn't tried harder to stop Whiteman.

Natano went back to flipping through the file. "We sent photos of this device to some of our contacts," he said. "This little contraption of yours bears a striking resemblance to a device that was rigged to a car rented by Dr. Herter in California earlier this week—"

"Major," Deloy pleaded, trying to recover, "I swear, I had nothing to do with this!"

"Prints, delivery, motive, opportunity." He began to laugh. "And shit for brains arrogance. You're done, boy."

"You gotta believe me! Why would I want to whack someone I bugged? I—"

"I don't want to hear it!" He turned to Natano. "You ready?" Natano turned to the mirror and nodded. "You wanted to know who was outside. All the people you fucked with. They're going to love watching you go down."

"We can go in now," Tong said to the group outside.

"I'm not going in there with him!" Cindy protested.

"It's okay," Tong said. "You'll be all right. And the gadget is deactivated."

"And then," Jessica said, "there's something else you all need to hear."

"I swear to God you gotta believe me!" Deloy rose, zeroing in on Cindy as the group entered the room. "I had nothin´ to do with it!"

She held on tight to Kevin's good arm while he coldly eyed the man who had knifed him.

"Hey," Deloy pleaded to Kevin, "I'm sorry I jumped you. I was just doing my job. I thought you were—"

"I really don't care," Kevin said. "You've been a thorn in my side since Sunday night."

"Sit your ass down, boy," Whiteman ordered.

Deloy sat down, beseeching Cindy, "You gotta believe me! I'm being set up!"

"We're keeping the captain here tonight," Natano said, "then flying him to Funafuti in the morning for more extensive interrogation." He turned to Deloy. "I'm glad you enjoyed your visits here. Looks like you're going to be with us for a while."

Deloy bolted up but Talake pushed him down again. Natano said, "We've begun analyzing what we found in your room. See, Dr. Herter here was acting as our agent, so he wasn't breaking and entering. You on the other hand seem to have come into possession of some rather—"

"I swear, I can explain!" Deloy implored.

"—classified and sensitive materials."

"Is that all you know how to do," Kevin said with disgust, "plant bombs and bugs?"

Deloy glared back but Kevin was looking over the small device that would have taken down the plane. "Is this really like what Mike found in my car?" he asked Natano.

"Similar. We sent him a scan. He's sure the same hand—"

"I swear to God!" Deloy yelled, "I had nothing—"

"Shut the fuck up!" Whiteman snapped.

"All right, people," Natano said, "let's calm down." He turned to Deloy. "Son, this is the least of your worries." He turned back to Kevin. "There's something else we need to address. We discussed it with Funafuti while you were at the hospital."

Jessica nodded stiffly. "We spoke with Mike and Jack. I also spoke with Joshua in New York. The reports are sketchy but he was able to confirm two of them. And there are unconfirmed reports of four others."

"What's going on?" Kevin asked.

"Two deaths back in the states that we learned about this morning, and they're both suspicious. One was James Grayson, a brigadier general who was stationed in the Pentagon at the DIA. His car ran off a road last night in Virginia. The other's a retired colonel who was with the Department of Energy. They found him slumped over his desk. A guy named Anthony LoBiondo."

"Those are names on the drives I came across in Deloy's room." Kevin was shocked.

"Yeah," Natano said. "Both were associated with the program."

"I worked with them in Washington two years ago," Tom Whiteman added. "Damn."

"From what I learned," Jessica said, "both were getting payoffs from IM from the start."

"Is there anything you want to add to this, captain?" Natano asked a resigned and apparently disinterested Deloy.

"Fuck you. You got nothin´. You don't know who you're fucking with. I'll be out of here before you know it."

"Well, captain. These men are dead, on the same day your president announces a new policy that would squeeze out the contractor paying them off. Someone's decided to cut their losses." Natano put the papers back in the folder and said, "I feel sorry for you son. I get the sense you think whoever you're working for is going to step in and whisk you away from all this. But you should know that we've received several calls about you within the last half-hour. Whoever's cutting those losses now considers you to be one."

"What?"

"Your people are disavowing any and all knowledge of your actions. I've been instructed to prosecute you however I see fit, which to me means to the fullest extent for whatever violations you may have undertaken against our people and laws. It would seem," Natano added, savoring the moment, "you're being, how do you say, thrown under the bus."

Kevin and Whiteman smiled as Deloy's jaw dropped.

"Cuff him and get him the hell out of here," Natano said to Officers Talake and Tong.

"Mother *fucker!*" Deloy yelled. "I can't believe it!" He jumped up but both officers grabbed him immediately and had him handcuffed in seconds. He yelled, "I can give you Sanderson! I can give you—"

"I don't really care," Natano said. The officers shuffled Deloy out and down the hall.

"Couldn't have happened to a nicer guy," Kevin said to a dumbfounded Cindy.

"In the end," Whiteman said, "he turned out to be exactly what I thought he was, a psychotic twerp."

"There's more," Jessica said, still looking concerned.

"Yeah," Sharon said, "like whom he's working for. My God."

Natano agreed. He turned to Kevin. "And those loose ends. There's more."

Whiteman added, "I had a feeling this would wind up going down like this."

"What does that mean?" Kevin asked.

"Finding out who cut his check. But there are more names, right?"

"There was a lot of money going around," Jessica nodded.

"What's going on?" Sharon asked.

Natano took a deep breath. "If you know money's changing hands and you propose something that's going to cut it off—and piss those people off—how would you handle it?"

"Well, you either hope they don't mind ..." Sharon said, and they all smiled in response.

"Or," Whiteman added, "you make a deal."

"Question is, with whom?" Kevin asked.

"You're starting to get the hang of this," Natano said, looking at Kevin.

"I'm hearing that's what might have happened," Jessica said.

"That was our view," Whiteman added. "Someone in the White House got themselves a new partner. Until now, they turned a blind eye to it. Now, instead of paying them off or having it go public it just got simpler to—"

"The expression is kill fee," Kevin said.

"That's pretty much it."

"Hanford's determined to push through his idea and tidy up the memo mess," Jessica explained.

"Or someone near him. It was a nice operation. Whether it went through or not wasn't the point. The point was to discredit everyone involved, send them off on a wild goose chase, or have them found in a ditch on the side of a road. One way or another, you guys were all distracted just long enough. Man's trying to run out the clock. He just may succeed."

"And that's why you went so far out of your way to protect your wife," Jessica said.

Whiteman took a deep breath. "That's one thing people close to him don't understand about him. They think it breeds loyalty. They don't get that he'll throw *anyone* under the bus in order to get what he wants. I wasn't going to let that happen."

"So you see," Kevin said, "even if you walk away, it'll catch up with you."

"More than you know," Natano said.

"What does that mean?"

"Those USB sticks you found," Jessica said. "Your name was on one of those lists."

One hundred six

Kevin sat in Natano's office, staring with a blank expression at the computer screen. They had gathered there to make another Skype call to Funafuti.

Knowing that Kevin was a marked man had led to a flurry of activity among those around him, as they scrambled to get on top of the situation. For himself, he couldn't decide whether the news was liberating or exhausting. Natano suggested they call the analysts again. As the call went through, Kevin sat rubbing his bandaged arm, staring off at a far wall.

Tom Whiteman had left to go meet Lisa. She had already met Jack Raden, and she and Tom had offered to fill in some blanks for Natano. They were preparing to fly to Funafuti.

In a moment of honesty, Whiteman had made a comment about his relationship with his wife needing work. After he left, Cindy said, "It took me a little time to get those two. They're so different. You wonder how they ever got together but then it hits you. He's like the dog that finally catches the car and doesn't know what to do with it." They laughed, and then Natano escorted them upstairs.

"Well, that's it," Natano said after the briefing.

Raden said, "I'm not surprised; there was always that possibility."

Sharon jumped up from her chair. "Possibility? That's what you hauled my ass out here to do? Discuss *possibilities?*" She shot a look to Kevin. "We go after these shits!"

Kevin said, "I'm not saying no. I just don't know how. Believe me, I've had it. I told Pete I was ready to leave, and I'm sure he'll be more than happy to see me go. But, I go after them or I back off, either way it seems the White House comes out on top."

"Don't make me say it," Sharon glared.

"I know. I just don't want to cause trouble for anyone here."

"In the short time you've been here," Natano smiled, "you've already caused enough trouble."

"I know," Kevin replied with a grin. "Even when I sat and did nothing."

"True," Cindy said, "but you know this is coming to a head." She eyed Raden. "You're not telling him to back off, are you?"

"No. I can understand and you're right. But there's more to it than that."

"They're right," Jessica said. "We can't walk away; none of us can."

"Oh I know that," Kevin said. "And you; you're in an unusual position yourself. You're part of your story now. You should know, physicists love that. In physics, there's no such thing as a casual observer. By just being there you become part of what you observe. Someone douses themselves with gasoline and you have a camera. Do you stop them or film it? You've already crossed that line. Like it or not, you're an active participant now. It just has to play itself out. Either way, there's a book in this." Jessica gave him a knowing smile.

Natano turned to Kevin. "Know you'll be okay here. Just no more freelancing, agreed?"

"We concur," Mike said. "It's true that loose ends are being tied up—"

"You don't think it's the White House?" Kevin asked.

"Can't say for sure. Presidents don't usually get involved putting out hits—"

"I don't believe I'm hearing this," Sharon said with a groan.

"Sharon, we agree," Raden said with a smile. "There just aren't any direct fingerprints. He was behind the people who left them though, and they're the ones cutting the checks. Either way, all this comes back to Kevin. That's why whatever he decides has to be done smart."

"We detonate in an hour," Natano said, rubbing his eyes. "The president is buzzing around looking for Kevin. I suggest we tie up our own loose ends before then."

The three analysts agreed. "Hanford thinks he cut us off at the knees by making us land here," Braddock said, "but it lets us work without them looking over our shoulders. Kevin, see what you can come up with there. I'm sure Captain Natano will give you cover."

Natano agreed, but Sharon snapped, "That's not enough."

"What are you suggesting?" Cindy asked.

Sharon turned to Kevin with a piercing resolve. "I didn't fly all the way out here to kiss your ass. Someone's going down for this and I don't want it to be you. Whatever you decide, if you think this is between you and them you're going to lose. It never was and never will be, especially if it's that fool in the White House. This has always been between you and yourself. Once you get on top of that, the rest will fall into place. You just have to do it."

They were interrupted by shouting outside the office, followed by a knock on the door. One of Lionel Latasi's aides walked in.

"Pete," he said to Natano, "we've been looking for Dr. Her—"

He turned and saw Kevin sitting across from the desk. "Dr. Herter. We've been—"

Just then the door swung open again. Dillon Ridge barged in. He took one look at Kevin and snapped, "Where the hell have you been? The president is looking all over for you!"

"Uh," Kevin said, purposely understated and holding up his bandaged arm, "ran into a little trouble—"

"I don't give a damn! The president is trying to make a deadline and you're—"

"You know, I'm sick and tired of you. Go tell your boss I'll be there when I'm ready!"

Ridge backed up with a sneer. "I've been instructed—"

"I don't give a damn what you've been instructed! Get the hell out of here before you have to tell him *you're* the one who blew this!"

"Colonel, I have to debrief Dr. Herter here," Natano said, annoyed, "after he was stabbed by one of *your* people. You go tell the president Dr. Herter will be along presently. Those are *my* instructions."

He motioned to the officer, who approached Ridge sternly. Ridge raised both his hands, made a face and turned. "Fine, fine," he muttered as he went out, slamming the door. The aide shrugged, and left right after.

Sharon frowned. "Who the hell was that?"

"*That*," Kevin groaned, "was the White House chief of staff."

"You're kidding. What an asshole!"

"I'd love to see *him* go down."

"Well, maybe you will," Jessica said. "People are dropping left and right. And don't forget, Sanderson's out there causing trouble as well. *Someone's* going down."

Kevin nodded, then leaned his head back and closed his eyes. "Guys," he yawned, "I'm exhausted. I need a few minutes to splash some water on my face."

Sharon began nodding. "He's tired. You're entitled," she smiled.

"We moved your bags," Natano said. "You're setting a record here with the amount of rooms one person can have over one stay." He went to his desk and took out the key. "I want to thank you. This is falling into place and I appreciate your help. But however you decide to answer your president I'd like to hear how that memo would affect me." He turned to the screen. "I take it, it's changed things a lot."

"You have no idea," Braddock said as Raden and Mike broke out in tepid smiles.

"I need to know how to proceed. What should I expect if it goes through?"

"There are technical issues you'll come across," Raden said. "We'll brief you as it goes along. Right now, the political ones are the most pressing."

"Oh, that much I know."

"There's one I can already think of that needs to be addressed," Kevin said. "That bomb."

Natano agreed. "There wasn't enough time for Deloy to have planted it. I have plenty to charge him with and I had to flush him out so I went along with it, but I still have a problem."

As the three analysts nodded in accord, a wide-eyed Cindy huffed, "Oh, wow!"

"That's right," Jessica added as Sharon shook her head.

"I'm not cut out for cloak and dagger," Kevin said with a tired laugh. "He rubbed his wound in frustration, and a little blood began seeping through the gauze.

"Leave it alone," an annoyed Sharon said as she reworked the dressing.

He looked at the number on his key, groaning, "One more thing to deal with. And, that thing I've been throwing around inside my head; I'll bring it up when I get back. I'll see you back here in twenty."

One hundred seven

Kevin made it to the hotel in five minutes. It was by now a brilliant late afternoon, the sky shimmering blue. While the eighty-six degree warmth could have worn him down further, the spirited trade wind had the effect of clearing his head. The remnants of Eta Carinae had pretty much drifted off, in time for the new detonation within the hour.

Room 278 was near the end of the hall on the right wing of the hotel. Sure enough his bags were on his bed. He took out a light blue shirt for the event, and went into the bathroom.

It was amazing what a little fresh water on the face could do. Clouds lifted. The entire week came full circle. From the incident on the highway in Princeton to meeting Jack Raden and losing Sharon, the run-in with Jessica, the flight to San Francisco, Max's illness, Mike and the car bomb, the flight to Vaitupu, meeting Cindy, watching the explosion, meeting Pete Natano, getting a dressing down from Elliot Hanford and dealing with all of the associated bull that came along with it, it was a Life Review in miniature.

Another confrontation with the president loomed but now things were different. Sharon was more than right. All along it had been a struggle within himself. In times past he would have done a number on himself, torn over which side would win out. But the trap was that there would always be a losing side, and it was he himself who lost either way. A perfect formula for tying oneself up in knots, one he knew he would have fallen victim to at one point. A no-win situation that would leave him where he began, wallowing in his own ambivalence. And a reality ripe for the picking of an Elliot Hanford, who was all too willing to seize opportunity wherever he saw it. For the first time he saw plainly how the president and those around him had counted on that.

By now, he had enough of dealing with Hanford. Maybe it was the ache of the stitches or just fatigue. Or perhaps the clarity that arises when one reaches a threshold. Regardless, a cascade of insight broke through, and Kevin knew precisely what he wanted to do. The question was whether he had the confidence to do it. His anxiety was rooted less in fear than in impatience. Streams of conversation ran by; he had it all mapped out. There would be no endorsement; he didn't care what Hanford thought; he appreciated the president's position with the memo but frankly, it wasn't his problem. He was done, all presidential protests notwithstanding. Time to go home.

He stood over the sink letting the water course down his face. An irony surfaced; a week in the South Pacific and with all the pools he had walked past and the ocean he had sailed, he had yet to take a dip. It had been that kind of trip. Standing over a hotel sink was small consolation, but he'd get his money's worth. He splashed his face a few more times.

It served to recharge his batteries. He took a fresh towel and buried his face in it, slowly walking out of the bathroom. As he opened his eyes, he jumped.

Sitting on a chair near the balcony door was Jim Bremer.

"Shit!" Kevin snapped, trying to temper his shock. "What are you doing here?"

"You weren't coming to see me, sooooo …"

Kevin took a halting step, slowly wiping his face. "Things got a little out of hand."

"I heard. Take a seat. I won't stay long."

"You know the kind of week I've had? People break into my room and I don't even ask how any more." Bremer laughed as Kevin got a chair from the anteroom and sat down near the desk. "I take it all that talk earlier didn't mean anything," he added. "Who are you? Who do you work for?"

"It doesn't really matter. I … represent people. What did you think of Deloy?"

"You know him? Figures. I thought he was a sick son of a bitch."

"That's the prevailing notion. Leave it to Ridge to put stock in a psychopath. He's a lost cause now, but he served his purpose. We wouldn't have let him get much further with you."

"Well," he said, rubbing his arm, "he went far enough. Just what precisely was his purpose?"

"To keep you busy. You and the others were right. There are people to be dealt with."

Kevin narrowed his gaze. "Why are you telling me this?" he asked, as much in bewilderment as in anxiety. "Are you here to finish up his dirty work?"

"If I wanted you dead, you'd already be. It'd look like you slipped in the shower."

Kevin felt an icy tremor but managed to hide it.

"He did what he was sent to do," Bremer added. "But he got cocky. He forgot while he was watching you that others were watching him. He wasn't supposed to get out of hand with you."

Kevin stared, unsure whether to keep listening or run. "So why are you telling me this?"

Bremer looked around the room and nodding, mused, "They do a nice job here." He then said, "It was a good idea to bait me back there in the hall. I would have done the same thing."

Kevin lightly laughed.

"I had to play along," Bremer added, "but you should know, you give someone an opportunity like that they'll take it. It bought me time to finish what I had to."

"What's that?"

"I love analysts. They're right; you get worked up about the minutia you lose sight of the bigger picture. So, they got all caught up with the minutia and forgot the bigger picture. Most people don't get enough explanations, so they stumble around for answers. You guys did the opposite; spent so much time explaining things, you gave them time to work their deals. People in my line? Most of the time, we explain nothing."

He leaned back. "Doctor, you deserve to know a few things. You have no idea the forces arrayed against you; the money, the power. Smart people pick their battles. If you're smart and I hope you are, you won't even try to fight it. It all seems small, this piss-ass rock and the Club Med bull here but think of it as the apex of a pyramid. You don't see what's below. Natano's a good man for a small town cop. I give him credit, but he's hopelessly out of his league with what he's been dealt. You can't stop this, so do yourself a favor, don't even try."

Kevin took a deep breath. "So, why are you letting the cat out of the bag?"

"I've been following your career some time now. You don't do what you do without attracting attention. I respect what you do." He scratched his ear. "Next time you hit the road at two in the morning though, be more careful. You almost hit that guardrail."

Kevin's jaw dropped. "Holy shit."

"Normally," Bremer smiled, "someone in my position would let the chips fall where they may. But I wanted to give you a head's up. Deloy was an idiot. He made a mess that needs to be cleaned up. Being a mechanic went to his head. It made it easy for him to do himself in. You set up the situation and let people be who they are. You probably know something about that."

"Well, I'm learning."

Bremer laughed. "People who need dealing with usually aren't the most solid of citizens. You don't mind taking care of them. It just got cheaper to knock off those SOBs. Your reporter babe nailed it; IM teamed up with the White House to handle them."

"We had come to that conclusion ourselves," Kevin nodded.

"It was out there if you didn't take your eyes off the ball. But, that's what you do. It's who you are. See, dealing with someone like you is different. You are disgustingly boring."

Kevin began laughing. "I don't know what to say. Thanks."

"Don't thank me. You should know, there were people looking to whack you just because you annoyed them by being such a Boy Scout. Deloy was part of that crowd. But cooler heads prevailed."

"I don't even know how to begin to respond to that."

"At this point there's not much that's going to change things. The program will go through its modification and the White House will get its redesignation. You just do your part."

"What do you mean?"

Bremer rose and approached Kevin. His calm air was effectively intimidating. "Deloy bollixed things up," he said. "Don't use that as an excuse to back out. You're smarter than that." He began fidgeting with a pen on the desk. "It's a shame about your mentor."

"You know about Max?" Kevin felt his jaw tighten.

"Shitty disease. I know he was involved with the collider down in Texas years ago. Shame. Waste all that money and nothing to show for it. They got a billion dollar hole in the ground. You heard they want to bring it back. You may even find after all's said and done that they wind up naming it after him. His wife would probably like that." Bremer clicked the pen on the desk a few times. "You get my drift?" he added.

"That would be something to see. You know, I was going back and forth about what to do, but I know what I have to do now. I appreciate you telling me this."

Bremer put the pen down. "I'm glad we understand each other. You might hear about some people, trouble they may get into. You might even see some of it go down. You're smart enough not to let that happen to you." He extended his hand and Kevin took it. It had been some time since he felt a handshake so solid. Bremer gave a nod and left.

Kevin paused, then looked at his watch. It was 5:28. He quickly changed his shirt and left the room. Although he had his cell phone with him, he no longer trusted it, any more than he trusted the room phone.

He bolted down the nearest staircase to the main floor. He looked around, then went to a secluded spot where there was a row of courtesy phones and called Peter Natano.

"Is Jessica still with you?" he asked Natano.

A moment later, she was on the phone. "Round up your cameraman with his equipment," Kevin told her, "and be in Pete's office in ten minutes. Have Pete run him down if you have to. And hurry; we don't have much time."

"Why? What's the ma—"

"No time to explain. I'll be there in five minutes."

One hundred eight

Ten minutes later, Erik Lundquist was escorted to Peter Natano's office. Natano didn't know what Kevin was planning but he had immediately put in a call to the hotel security. They found Lundquist in his room.

Kevin hustled to the Complex and arrived at Natano's office immediately after Jessica. Cindy was already there, nursing an iced tea. He burst in with a strange head of steam. Sharon took one look at him and said, "Okay, let's have it."

He looked at her, then Jessica. "For a long time now Sharon's been on me to go after them. I was ready, and then I wasn't sure what to do. But I just had a visitor."

"Who was that?" Natano asked.

"Our friend Bremer. And just so you know, your door lock system needs an upgrade."

"That's what I've been telling them," Natano said with a frown. "What did he say?"

"It was partly what he said, partly the way he said it. Basically, I'd be smart to tow the company line." At the chorus of groans, he added, "It's not even worth discussing. I've had it." He nodded to himself, as if reinforcing something he had already decided. "There's something I've thought about doing."

"It's about time," Sharon said.

"You may not like my solution. But I think it's best for all concerned."

"Kevin," said Cindy, "anything's gotta be better than what's been going on."

"As long as it's not too messy," Natano said, "I'll support you."

"I'm going to be proposing something," Kevin added, choosing his words with care. "It may surprise you and you might not completely agree but when you see it, I think you'll see what I mean, especially after the week you've all had. That fool in my room just confirmed my decision for me. It's a risk, but I hope I can count on your support and your help."

"So," Sharon asked, "what do we do? You want us to leave?"

"No, just the opposite." He turned to Jessica. "I want to record a statement." Jessica's eyes widened. Kevin motioned towards the meeting room. Within a minute Lundquist was setting up his equipment while Natano dialed Funafuti for another Skype call.

They began taping at 5:42. It was over in seven minutes. The hookup let Braddock, Raden and Mike watch. Kevin had Natano email the video to five addresses as well as to Funafuti, with a message containing instructions on how to handle the narrative. Five copies were burned onto USB drives and given to Enright, Sharon, Cindy and Natano, while Kevin kept one himself. At 5:50, less than a minute after they finished, Lionel Latasi's aide was calling to prod them again. It wasn't nearly enough time for the astonishment to have left their faces.

Kevin swiveled back in his chair and looked to Sharon. "So?"

She skipped over with a big hug and laid a wet kiss on his cheek. "If we hadn't split up I'd throw you down and fuck the shit out of you."

As they convulsed in laughter, Cindy included, Kevin said, "That's why I had Jack bring you out here—the chance for make-up sex." Everyone laughed again.

"I never thought you'd do it," Sharon added.

"I know." He turned to the others. "You guys okay?"

Jessica fiddled with the USB stick. She was still laughing, but added, "It's gotta sink in. I've heard you don't recognize the most important moments of your life when they happen. Well, I think we'll remember this one." She turned to the laptop screen. "How are you guys?"

Raden and Mike were subdued. "Wow," Raden said. Braddock folded his arms, brandishing a contented smile.

"I know I asked an enormous amount of you," Kevin told Jessica. "Thank you."

"It's funny," she said. "I thought it would be the whole journalistic ethics thing that would make me hesitate, but it wasn't. I just don't know if it'll work."

"I thought that myself. It's a gamble, I know. But I had to stir things up, and had to do it now. And this is the only thing those fools understand."

"I just got here," Sharon said, "and you can't help but feel the tension. And playing defense catches up with you."

Kevin agreed. He then reached for a bottle of white glue near some office supplies.

"Don't you dare," Sharon said.

"Up yours, Velazquez," he sneered back.

"What's the matter?" Cindy asked Sharon.

"He rubs it on his hand and peels it off. I hate when he does that! Maybe you can break him."

"I haven't done that in years, since I was young," she said. Jessica said the same thing.

"Well," Sharon huffed, grabbing the bottle, "nobody's doing it." Kevin frowned at her.

"Your president is expecting you upstairs," Natano said to Kevin. "How do you want to handle this?"

"What are you going to tell him?" Raden asked.

"Simple," Kevin shrugged. "The truth. What we just did."

"This should be interesting," Cindy said.

"Yeah," Sharon said. "It's a novel concept for him. This one I want to see as well."

"You ever meet a president before?"

"Nope, and I couldn't care less about this one." The others broke up.

A moment later Jessica viewed a text on her phone. She said, "There might be more fireworks than the ones you're setting off." She turned to Natano. "Are you guys set?"

"It's going down right now. Did you confirm it?"

"Yeah. Dates, amounts, locations; a lot of other stuff. I have a whole history."

"We corroborated it ourselves," Mike said. "Just before you called."

Kevin looked confused. "What's going on?"

"Mr. Sanderson," Natano replied. "All this is about to come crashing down on him."

One hundred nine

The Taupi Complex was jammed with activity with less than twelve minutes remaining before the event and the statement by Elliot Hanford that would follow.

Peter Natano led the group upstairs to the Central Control hall. The security was even tighter than the previous evening. While support personnel rushed to make the compressed schedule, a stream of journalists, dignitaries and invited guests bustled through to their seats on the deck.

On the far end near the detonation relay, Lionel Latasi was walking away from Dillon Ridge. The prime minister looked rattled. Ridge saw Kevin and hustled over, surlier than ever.

"The president is waiting for you," he shouted over the buzz.

"I'll bet. Where is he?"

"Outside. He's going to be speaking with the cloud as the backdrop. We're starting right after the all clear sounds, which means you'd better get your ass out there."

"Boy, you are a piece of work," Sharon said, turning her nose up at him.

Ridge gave her a dismissive stare. "Who is this *person*?"

"She's my guest," Kevin said. "But that doesn't matter. You need to give a message—"

"There's no time! Get the hell out there! No guests!" He glared at Jessica. "And no press!"

"You have no say on what I cover," she laughed, watching the stream of media go by. Kevin caught the look she'd thrown at Lundquist, and glanced at her cameraman. Lundquist was filming surreptitiously. She hadn't noticed that Kevin had picked up on it.

"Let's get one thing straight," Ridge snarled. "I have complete say as to—"

At that moment, several Secret Service agents came in from the deck followed by Elliot Hanford, shining like a demigod on a spiritual retreat. He saw Kevin and smiling, walked over.

"We were beginning to get worried," Hanford said, sounding sincere. "Come on, our seats are all ready." He turned to the others. "We have seats for your friends. And Ms. Enright, I'm sure we have room for one more member of the press."

Cindy and Sharon eyed each other while Natano stepped over with several of his officers.

Hanford looked over, and asked, "What's the problem?"

"I'll make this short, Mr. President," Kevin said. "We have a change in plan."

Hanford tensed. He knew exactly what he meant. "Kevin," he said trying to regroup, "whatever your concerns, they'll take more time to address than this explosion. I'm sure I can allay them, but if we don't get out there we're going to miss a hell of a spectacle! Remember last night? One of the reasons I rescheduled my statement was because I wanted to see one of these again. Come on, let's watch and when it's over we'll talk."

"Ten minutes, Mr. President," an agent advised.

"I can't solve anything in ten minutes," Hanford said. "We'll sit and go over—"

"Just hold it," Kevin said, waved his hand. Hanford grew still. Technicians scurrying about cast looks as they went by, picking up on the tension while media were beginning to poke their heads in, though Lionel Latasi was trying to get them seated.

"Mr. President," Kevin began, "in the short time since we spoke in Princeton I've been followed, bugged, decked, stabbed and almost blown up, just for starters. Just so you guys could feel better about having pissed on my work. You know what? I'm not doing it anymore."

"You can at least give me the courtesy of an explanation as to why."

"I have a million reasons, but there's only one that matters, and I don't even mean that memo. This has disaster written all over it and you're just not interested. I'm done trying to convince people of the obvious. I'm just not playing into it anymore."

"Oh, come on," Hanford said with disgust. "If you know what I'm dealing with then you can put your concerns aside and work with me. You damn well know my position and what I'm trying to manage. You can't spring this on me at the last minute."

"Damn right!" Ridge snapped. He turned to Kevin. "Where the hell do you come off telling—"

"Don't talk to him like that!" Sharon yelled. "All I've heard from you is bitching!"

"Sharon," Kevin said, "it's okay—"

"No it's not!" Ridge yelled. "It's about time you stopped being a selfish prick and began thinking about what's best for your country!"

Kevin coughed up a condescending laugh. "You tell yourself that the next time someone tries to whack you in the name of your country. Does doing what's best for my country mean I do your dirty work for you? Does it mean people have to live with a red herring to keep their eyes off something a hell of a lot more serious? Maybe what's best is they learn that everyone who came out here was a guinea pig in a Pentagon fireworks display. Maybe they need to know the more stable you made it, the more dangerous it got."

"What does that mean?" said a grim president.

"It means we've learned that there's a flaw in the system. There's no limit to the size of the blasts. The spike you're so worried about isn't a spike at all. It's an inherent property of the system. It's predictable. Based on the computer models and the analysis of the explosions, this technology doesn't work below ten megatons. If the device is set below that, the nuclear reaction fizzles. You get a dud. But once you go beyond twenty-two, twenty-three, it runs away. As the yields go up, the potential energy in the system goes up exponentially. We honestly don't know how big the explosions will get. Once you go beyond that it goes off the chart."

"But so what?" said a clearly exasperated Hanford. "So you don't explode beyond twenty-three. I don't see what the problem is."

"The problem," Cindy said, "is you can't control something like that. Just last night we had the biggest explosion we ever had, over twenty three-megatons. We set it at a little over twenty-two. That's nearly a million tons of TNT higher."

"The point is, had it been set for twenty-three," Kevin added, "set it for exactly what we got, it would have been a lot higher. It's a quirky system. They were lucky." Peter Natano stood triumphantly nodding his head.

Ridge snapped, "I don't even know what the hell you're talking about. Just deal with it."

An instant later one of Latasi's aides came over and said, "Eight minutes, Mr. President."

Kevin ignored Ridge and stared at Hanford. "Understand. These things have been set for a maximum degree of entertainment effect. But they've made a deal with the devil and they don't even know it. The system is set at the upper level of its safety margin. No one here knew that. They've been playing with fire and didn't even know it. The way the technology works, there's no way to control it other than the honor system. It's an accident waiting to happen."

"Kevin said something I found very chilling," Cindy said. "Up to now, everyone's been willing to live with the instability in the system. Only it turns out what they thought was an instability really isn't. It's predictable. This thing is a lot more dangerous stable than unstable."

Kevin said, "It's like the situation you find yourself in with that memo. You can control the system but not the people working it. You control what you can, and what you can't, you can't. And what you can't has catastrophic potential. That's just what's going to happen here. The yield isn't programmed at the factory, but at the control panel when you fire it off. It's a different kind of technology. And that's the part you can't control. Suppose some techie got plastered the night before and misplaces a decimal point. Suppose he has a seizure an instant before it goes off and his hand shifts the lever. Suppose he didn't clean his contact lenses and he types in a six instead of a two. This is a lot more dangerous than any of you realize."

Ridge waved him off. "There isn't a damn thing that's happened with this," he remonstrated, "and I trust they'll keep working to improve it. It's about time you stepped up to the plate, or you're going to find yourself in a position you don't want to be in."

"What the hell does that mean?" Sharon said.

"Ridge, just shut up!" Hanford hissed, trying to keep from attracting attention from the media out on the deck.

Kevin was by now getting angry. "You can make all the noise you want. My response to this has been a matter of public record. This entire thing began without my support. Maybe I could have been more forthright in speaking up against it, but if people want to connect me to anything seedy with this well, good luck, it won't stick. They tried dangling the Texas supercollider in front of my face as a bribe. I didn't bite on that either. I've kept my mouth shut too long. Those days are over. You're a politician. What do you think people will say if they find out you knew about this all along but just went ahead with it? If you're so worried about doing what's best for the people, just see what happens when they learn what you guys have been doing behind their backs. And you know it. Now, there's something I need to tell you."

"People will learn what I let them learn," Hanford snapped. "And listen to what I tell them. Now *you* listen. You think people want change? They don't want change. They say they do but only on their own terms. What they really want is to be spoon fed. I can go out there and tell them exactly what they say they want to hear and the next day they'll rip me for being too honest. It's not a matter of giving them what they want, it's giving them what they can handle."

A technician called out, "Six minutes!"

Hanford waved his hand dismissively. "I'm not arguing with you. I'm going to ask you as a presidential favor to put whatever considerations you have aside for now and get out there."

The technical teams distracted by the tense discussion in the midst of trying to bring off the event on time were further aggravated by yelling out in the hall. Several Tuvalu police officers came in with a shouting Ron Sanderson.

"What the hell's going on here?" he yelled, intent on shaking off the officers detaining him. "You people *invited* me out here, dammit!" He saw Elliot Hanford and barked, "Is this your doing?"

"Don't talk to the president like that!" Ridge shouted.

Hanford barked, "Ron, I don't know what you've done but I don't have time for it."

"It's not going to work, *Mister* President. I'll be damned I take the hit for you!"

"What's that supposed to mean?" Hanford said with a disinterested face.

Jessica Enright stepped forward. "Mr. President, I'm not sure you want to go there." She turned to Sanderson. "It all fell into place over the past few days. The payoffs from Integrated Microsystems, amounts, when they were delivered, who got them—"

"You little bitch!" he snapped. "Who the hell—"

"Now just hold it!" Ridge bellowed, glaring at Jessica. "There isn't any evidence leading back to—"

"You don't want to go there either," she said as Peter Natano stood by, listening intently.

"What the hell is going on with you people?" Hanford asked.

"Oh," Sanderson sneered, "you think you're going to play innocent?"

"Get him out of here!" Ridge yelled, trying to salvage the situation as the technicians kept looking over at the commotion.

"People," Natano said, "I'm not playing host to a sparring match. But Mr. President, this is going to have to be resolved. It's having a material affect on the operation of this facility."

"And what does that mean?" Hanford said.

"We're putting together a report on how all this began," Jessica replied, "beginning with the DOD memo and what it influenced along the way. It revolves around what's gone on here, with the lieutenant governor, people around him and frankly Mr. President, you too."

Hanford was defiant. "And you think you've got goods on me? Think again."

Sanderson turned to Ridge. "I'll be damned I go down for this, you twerp! Shut her up!"

"Mr. Sanderson, you keep your place," Natano ordered. "You're also being detained because the State of Hawaii is handing down an indictment on you for a host of charges; bribery, misappropriation of—"

"That is *bullshit!*"

An agitated Lionel Latasi walked in from the deck. "My friends, it's less than five minutes now."

Hanford lifted his hands. "Yeah yeah yeah yeah!" he rattled. "We'll be right there!"

Latasi was taken aback. Clearly offended, he walked back outside as Lundquist continued secretly filming, keeping the camera low and the recording light covered.

Kevin watched the mounting uproar with a curious detachment. Maybe it was knowing everything was being recorded or maybe events were reaching a threshold of tension. He caught sight of Jim Bremer in the hall. The doors had swung open for an instant, long enough for them to lock eyes, then closed. When it opened again, Bremer was gone.

Kevin wasn't surprised to see him. He didn't know what to expect from the furtive operative but he wasn't being held back by fear. A week swimming with sharks had left him battle-hardened. With all the interests elbowing each other out of the way to become the last one standing, it was less like being circled by adversaries who smelled blood in the water and more like being in a shark cage with a harpoon, cautiously observing but aware that if one got too close, you could dispatch it if needed. He would keep his powder dry and let the drama play out.

An incredulous Sanderson was having none of it. "I don't believe this," he snapped. "No way you're making me fall guy for this. I demand to see a lawyer!"

"Ron, you're on your own!" Ridge declared. "The White House disavows—"

"You fucking piece of shit! I don't want to *hear* disavows!"

"Enough!" Hanford yelled. He turned to Kevin. "Now you see why I needed your help!"

Before Kevin could respond, Sanderson snapped, "This is all bullshit!"

"On the contrary," Jessica said. "You're more right than you realize.

You are all pawns, just like everyone else connected with this. If one of you has to be sacrificed here and there—"

"And what's that supposed to mean?" Hanford asked, flushed with anger.

Sanderson turned to Hanford, fury in his eyes and seethed, "You son of a bitch!"

"Four minutes," said a technician, coming up quickly and then leaving just as fast, clearly uncomfortable with the tension surrounding the group.

"The hell with that!" Hanford snapped. "I will not allow this to go on."

Sanderson grabbed Ridge. "I don't believe you're letting *this* go on! You've been brown-nosing so long, you don't know when you're being fucked yourself! You think he's going to let you walk? We're screwed if you don't stop it!"

"Unbelievable," Cindy muttered to Sharon as they looked on.

"Dammit!" Hanford roared, "I said that's enough!"

"Damn if I let you throw me under the bus!" Sanderson shouted. "I'm ready to make a statement."

Hanford motioned to the Secret Service men hovering behind him, "Get him out of here!"

Three agents moved closer but Natano stopped them, saying, "Hold it. You have no jurisdiction here, so stop."

"Yeah, all that shit went down," Sanderson said to Kevin. "He dicked you around, then hung you out to dry. They needed a cover-up. This place works perfectly to hide it and yeah, the terror figures sealed the deal. I got it all." Everyone froze in shock.

"Enough!" Hanford cut in. "I'm not going to stand here and listen to this bull!"

Jessica turned to Kevin and said, "The talk was to get you to give them cover until November, and then keep you on the fence until the rest fell into place. That climate bred the payoffs. It gained a life of its own."

"She's full of shit," Sanderson sniped, seemingly having a change of heart. "You going to believe a raving bimbo who doesn't even know who the hell she's interviewing?"

"Say what you want, but the facts speak for themselves," Jessica said, cutting him a steely look but holding firm. "You want to challenge them as a matter of contempt for me, go ahead. But if you challenge them as a matter of policy, you're going to lose. We're citing numerous DOE and DOD sources attesting to the veracity of the Pentagon's effort to hone its nuclear arsenal by using the recreational program here as a testing ground. It provided ideal cover for perfecting deliverable fallout-free nuclear weapons. The data shows the program has operated with a much narrower safety margin than promised. And the warhead contractor kept several individuals on the take, including you, individuals who are now being eliminated."

"You can't prove that," Hanford dismissively said, shaking his head in disgust.

"Actually, I can. And it all began with a DOD memo calling for a coordinated nuclear strike using those clean weapons against multiple targets in the Middle East."

"I don't believe this," Sharon said. "It's like *Wag the Dog* meets *Dr. Strangelove.*"

Off to the side, Lundquist had never stopped filming, with no one noticing as they focused on the unfolding drama.

"You had to dip your bill, huh?" Hanford barked to Sanderson.

Sanderson visibly flushed. "I didn't do a damn thing and you can't prove it, no matter what she says! Others did!"

"And there's nothing that can be traced back to the White House," Ridge yelled.

"Still kissing ass, huh? You deserve what you get."

"On that subject," Jessica said to Ridge, "we've got evidence for the payoffs you took as well."

Sanderson and Ridge glared at her. "I don't believe it!" Hanford hissed. "You stupid idiot!"

A flustered Don Frazier came in from the deck. The commotion inside was attracting attention outside as time grew short. "People, three minutes!" he said and ducked out.

"We also have Deloy's statement. Do you want to make one?" Natano asked Sanderson.

"You go fuck yourself too," Sanderson barked. "I didn't do a damn thing wrong."

"Well, we'll let your superiors sort it out. In the meantime, we'll conclude our business here and our officers will avail you of our jurisprudential accommodations."

Kevin stood with a satisfied grin. "I just love the way he talks," he quipped as Sanderson moved away from the officers and backed into the detonation relay, almost tripping over a technician sitting there.

"Damn it!" Natano yelled, "Watch it! That's sensitive equipment!"

He shook his head.

Hanford turned to glare at Ridge. "You stupid ..." he sneered, "what the hell were you trying to prove? I didn't know!" He turned to the others. "I didn't know!"

"You didn't want to," Sharon said.

"Oh, and you might want to ask Sanderson who made the payoffs," Jessica said.

"Enough of this!" yelled the president. "I don't have time for this! How much time—"

The sliding glass doors of the observation deck began to close automatically.

"Oh no," Cindy said. "We lost track."

"Then let's get out there, dammit!"

"We can't now," Natano said. "We'll have to wait here until the flash goes down."

"Son of a bitch!" Hanford yelled. "Everything I planned!"

"Serves you right," Sanderson barked.

"Get him out of here!" the president signaled at the officers.

As they began leading Sanderson out, Natano noticed a characteristic bulge in his back pocket. "Did this man go through security?" he asked. "Did anybody bother to frisk him?"

"He went through the detectors like everyone else," Agent Gerald Knight said. Natano motioned his gaze towards Sanderson. Knight patted Sanderson down and quickly found a small pistol in his back pants pocket.

"That's not mine!" Sanderson yelled.

Natano took the weapon. "It's plastic. It wouldn't have been picked up."

"You fucking people! You damn well know that's not mine! You planted that!"

"My people would never do such a thing. I doubt the president's would either."

Kevin glanced back towards the door leading to the hall, remembering Bremer, but he was long gone.

Hanford glared at Sanderson. "I don't believe it! Going to take care of me?"

Jessica recovered enough to say, "Actually, Mr. President, it might not have been meant for you." She turned to Sanderson. "Get used to it—you *are* being set up."

"Get her out of here!" Ridge roared.

Natano cut in, "You be quiet. I want to hear this." Sanderson echoed her.

"Back in the states, they've been whittling down that list of people," Jessica said. She turned to Kevin. "We know you were on it. When they are this close to the president, it's cleaner to just set them up as opposed to knocking them off."

"Damn right!" Sanderson barked.

"You people are going to have to answer for this!" Ridge said, still invested in denial.

Hanford rolled his eyes and turned to Kevin. "Now you see what I've dealt with. See how far you get when you need one of your projects financed."

"I'll deal with it," Kevin smiled, waving Hanford off. "Just as well, dealing with the bull to learn what was going on. You unravel this knot. Ain't mine. It's yours."

A technician called out, "One minute."

"What's this shot called?" Kevin asked him coolly.

"Deneb," he said, trying to look as if he hadn't heard anything else that had been said.

"Interesting star. It's like a hundred and fifty thousand times brighter than the sun. Probably the brightest in the galaxy. I can't even imagine that. What's the yield?"

"A little over twenty megatons. One of our bigger events."

Natano motioned to the solid coral wall adjacent to the observation deck. "We'll have to wait here until the all-clear sounds," he said.

"There's one more thing left to say," Kevin said, turning to Sanderson. "I came an inch from being blown up because of your people. Jessica's right. The story's out. You're history."

"You can go kiss my ass! When I get out of here all of you just better look out." He backed up and again bumped into the relay station, causing Natano to yell again his warning about sensitive equipment.

"Ron," Hanford said, "I swear if one iota of what you're accused of turns out to be true you'll be lucky to get a job in the prison hospital cleaning bedpans!"

"And you can go fuck yourself and your saintly routine as well, Mr. President! I didn't do anything more than your cronies kissing *your* ass the past two years. So you can go kiss mine!"

As a warning bell sounded signaling thirty seconds, the Secret Service men moved to block Sanderson. "When this is over," one agent told him, "you'll have to come with us."

"You'll have to wait in line," Natano said. "And I'm sure your Justice Department will begin a formal investigation as well. The rest of you, just hunch down next to the wall." The clock showed fifteen seconds to detonation.

"Son of a bitch!" Hanford snarled to Ridge. "This is your damn fault!" He backed up, moving toward the wall near Kevin.

Ridge grimaced and looked away as a technician counted down, "Ten, nine, eight ..."

Sharon and Jessica leaned up against the wall and looked at each other. "Whooo," Sharon said. "What the hell did I get myself in for?"

"Yeah, me too," Jessica replied, her eyes widening.

Cindy nestled up against Kevin while Lundquist squatted. He had yet to stop filming.

"All right, everyone," Natano said, "close your eyes. Don't open them until the all clear sounds." Everyone looked away from the deck.

"Seven, six, five ..."

"Captain," Hanford said to Natano, "I don't feel like waiting. Cuff the lieutenant governor." He glared at Sanderson. "You blew it, ass wipe." He bent down and covered his eyes.

"Four, three, two ..."

"Fine!" Sanderson yelled as the officer approached, "You can all go fuck yourselves!" With less than two seconds left to go Kevin watched in horror as he grabbed the officer and tried to throw him aside. The officer held on and both went tumbling into the relay, knocking over the technician. The officer hit the panel and the yield lever, sending it all the way to the top.

"Oh, my God!" Kevin yelled, lunging at Hanford, throwing him to the floor, screaming, "*EVERYBODY, GET DOWN!*"

One hundred ten

Deneb detonated exactly on schedule at 6:10 p.m. A blinding pulse of light and unimaginable heat filled the Control Center in a millisecond, before anyone hit the floor.

To those there who would later remember, they knew right away that something was wrong. The luminous violet-whiteness flooding the room was infinitely brighter than any seen before. It was accompanied by an unearthly silence that hovered with a haunting presence. It had no time to register for almost immediately there came a searing orange bloom that burst forth from the deck like a thousand sunrises. The glow was the instantaneous combustion of the building's facade.

At once the room grew as hot as a runaway furnace. Kevin threw the president down before the Secret Service could react. Everyone screamed, overcome before they were even aware of what happened. No one knew what hit them except Kevin, and he knew all too well. He saw a tongue of flame burst out around the doorframe leading to the deck. The glass doors instantly melted and blew in, and pillows of heavy black smoke poured forth. The fire rolled along the ceiling, igniting walls, desks and consoles. Anything in direct line of sight of the fireball burst immediately into flames, including horrifically, people.

From the corner of his eye Kevin saw Ron Sanderson erupt in a mass of orange and searing fire and knew that he was gone in less time than it takes to strike a match. So were Dillon Ridge, the officer wrestling with Sanderson, a Secret Service agent and the relay technicians, all gone in a flash, too fast for their screams to register as they were instantly snuffed out in a whoosh of fire.

Forty-two miles away, Deneb's fireball had expanded almost eight miles in diameter, the largest thermonuclear explosion in history. Out on the deck Lionel Latasi, Don Frazier and a whole host of politicians, dignitaries, journalists and staff all died without ever knowing what hit them, instantly incinerated, as were untold numbers on the island, in the hotel, on the ships and boats and those floating on the water awaiting the waves, as well as everyone on the beach.

The flames sent everyone still standing scurrying to clear the room, but anyone too close to the deck was burned, some just singed, others scorched, before they had a chance to get away. Although Kevin had knocked Elliot Hanford to the floor, the president's arm had been in the path of the fierce heat and had been singed. A Secret Service agent who'd been standing near the doorway lay screaming from massive second and third degree burns.

Next to Peter Natano, the door frame exploded into flames, near enough to lick the side of his face and his arm with burns. He wheeled around and shrieked, trying to put out the cuff of his shirt. Kevin tripped into broken light fixtures and digital displays that had fallen, and dodging flames and cinders he grabbed the nearest fire extinguisher and snuffed out the fire. A police officer doused Natano with a bottle of water, herself brushing off fiery splinters as Natano looked at her in stunned horror.

Kevin tried dousing the agent near the doorframe but the heat held him back. He aimed the extinguisher as best as he could, and from a distance managed to get a handle on the flame. The fog momentarily masked orange and black-specked flesh of the agent as he screamed in agony, the others powerless to help. Sanderson and Ridge were burned beyond recognition.

The flames were beginning to spread out from the deck entrance. On the other side of the room smoke was working its way in from under the door to the hallway.

"Quick!" Kevin yelled to those who were still standing, cut by flying debris but otherwise unharmed, "get more extinguishers!" Two more were found and were used on the fires. The room's sprinkler system had activated but was quickly overwhelmed, and soon shut off. The heat outside had yet to diminish.

"Stay away from the doorway!" Kevin yelled. In some parts of the room, the heat from the fireball was hotter than the fires in the hall. Smoke was massing near the ceiling.

Elliot Hanford had crumpled into stunned silence, covered in a wet black goo of debris and dirty water. Small cuts covered his exposed skin. Sharon kept to the floor as she frantically collecting plastic water bottles that hadn't melted in the fireball. She found several more and some towels in a closet and brought them to the stunned and injured survivors.

The heat was keeping her from moving anywhere near the doorframe.

"Wet towels and start covering your faces!" Kevin ordered. "The smoke is going to get you before you know it!" Those who could began wrapping them around their heads.

Jessica lay on the floor bruised but not burned, covered by wet soot and abrasions. Erik Lundquist had been thrown back by the heat, but was otherwise okay. His camera forgotten, he began scurrying about for towels and water.

Cindy was stunned but she worked to right herself and get her wits back. Sharon gave her water and wiped her face with a wet towel. Kevin crawled over to them, trying to avoid cutting his hands on glass and shards on the floor.

"What in God's name happened?" Jessica screamed.

"Sanderson," Kevin said. "He grabbed that cop and when they fell over, they hit the lever. It went to the top."

"Oh my God," Cindy said, locking eyes with him.

"I don't understand," Sharon said incredulously. "What does that mean?"

Kevin shook his head, not ready to go into it. But he knew all-too-well. The design flaw on the relay station, the one scheduled to be fixed whenever the powers-that-be got around to it after dealing with sup-posedly more important things, the one no one was worried about had crossed paths with a one-in-a-million intangible—a fool's split-second outburst. The bomb had gone off many times over its projected yield. How much, Kevin didn't know.

"Everyone, listen up!" Kevin yelled. "We have to work fast! Anyone who can move has to come over to the wall here. We don't have much time, only another minute or so."

"Why?" Hanford shouted, beginning to come out of his stupor. The only Secret Service agent still alive, Gerald Knight, helped him to his feet and towards a chair by the wall. The other agent had stopped moving.

"Just move!" Kevin snapped.

Kevin tied a wet towel across his face as smoke continued filling the room. The orange glow from outside still lit the space and the smell of burning shingles and sheet rock mixed with the sickly scent of singed skin. He yelled, "Stay low! Make your way over to Cindy and Jessica!"

Shouts and screams could be heard from elsewhere in the building. "We have to try to get to them," Natano said, emerging from his shock.

"There's no time! Just get everyone over here. Do it!" The heat was almost unbearable. Every breath felt like a searing bellows inside the chest. "Come on!" Kevin implored.

Off to the side, Simon Tong had passed out. It was hard getting leverage on him but Kevin reached under his arms and Natano grabbed his legs and they dragged him over to the wall. Sharon wet a towel and wiped soot and debris off Tong's face, reviving him. He began coughing.

Several minutes had passed since the detonation. Cindy was gasping but was otherwise okay, while Jessica sat on the floor slumped against the wall. Sharon had been the farthest away from the door and was the least affected of the three. She wet a towel and offered it silently to the president, who was coughing heavily. He nodded his thanks and took the towel.

Kevin, still trying to catch his breath, yelled again, "Okay, listen up! The shock wave is about to hit us. It'll probably put out the fires but I don't know if the building is going to hold up. We're going to have to crowd around the wall. It's the only thing that may keep us alive."

"What about people outside?" Natano panted, wiping his face. "We have to get them!"

"They're dead," Kevin said.

"We can't give up on them," Hanford added, coughing. "Maybe someone alive—"

"All dead. And so are most of the people on the island."

"Oh my God!" Laina shrieked, the only technician still alive. She'd been at the far end of the hall and had crawled over to the wall. She began to wail and Sharon said, "Hold it together."

Outside, the island was on fire. The sides of the buildings facing the fireball burned out of control. Trees and plants had burst into flames. Half the people in the open had been killed instantly. Thousands more who had survived, protected in one way or another, were severely burned, in shock or injury.

Out on the water, *Star Princess* and a new Carnival Line ship *Celestial Voyager*, along with every small craft were aflame.

The fireball had slowly begun to ascend, much larger than the previous night's. The sky glowed yellow-orange, completely overwhelming the setting sun, which had retreated to a near afterthought. Inside the fires were growing, but the outside heat was beginning to subside.

"Kev!" Sharon said, pointing to the flames, "we're going to cook if we stay here!"

"God!" Laina yelled, adding a stream of Polynesian words.

"Kevin," Jessica said, "maybe they're ..." She was about to add something when they all began to feel a vibration.

"HOLD ON!" Kevin yelled. They scrambled to huddle against the wall.

"My God we're going to die!" Laina wailed, joined by others as the vibrations quickly grew stronger.

A sudden and cataclysmic pressure wave blasted into the building. It burst over the deck and through the Control Room, its concussion extinguishing the fires but filling the room with smoke, blowing debris everywhere. It blew out part of the wall adjoining the deck and caused a section of the roof to collapse. On the other side of the room, it tore up part of the ceiling and blasted out a section of the back wall, opening a view to the ocean.

Everyone screamed as glass and shrapnel lacerated exposed skin. Elliot Hanford was thrown from his chair and scrap of metal tore into the back of one of the policemen, who screeched in agony. Kevin felt a sudden pain in his left ear as his eardrum ruptured.

The worst hit was Erik Lundquist. A piece of wood shot out of the broken door frame and impaled him in the chest. He let loose a blood-curdling shriek as he collapsed.

Almost as quickly as it hit the wave was gone, settling down to a listless breeze that wafted eddies of smoke and floating paper and debris.

Sharon and Jessica ran to Lundquist. Natano retrieved a First Aid pack from the debris. The wood had gone deeply into Lundquist's chest. As he writhed in pain, Laina pressed down to stem the bleeding, and they dressed the wound. Laina kept applying pressure but it did little to arrest the blood flow.

Sharon and Jessica were forced to attend to the others. Kevin, knowing the worst of the explosion's effects had passed, went up to Hanford. Agent Knight was helping him to his feet.

"Mr. President," Kevin asked, "are you okay?"

For a moment, he stared. "I don't know," he finally replied. Panting, scuffed up and cut he looked around. "My God," he added. "What the hell happened?"

"Just stay put for a minute." He waited. The vibrations were gone and most of the fires were out. The heat from the detonation had also begun to lessen. An eerie quiet had descended.

He went over to what had been the entrance to the deck. The corner of the building had blown away. An ugly gash cut through the structure and into the floor, which had collapsed in places. He had to step around burnt wood and smoldering debris, bypassing charred masses he knew to be body parts. His ear still hurt. He rubbed it, trying to relieve the pain. His wrenched shoulder throbbed. He had completely forgotten about his bandaged arm, which was bleeding again.

He managed to get to a spot where he could keep his footing. Most of the deck was gone but a small section with a support beam anchored in the ground remained. An incinerated body was plastered onto a remnant of the railing which had blown into the wall. He had to look away.

Off to the east, the immense mushroom cloud of Deneb had begun to unfold. Much bigger than Eta Carinae, it took up most of the eastern sky and was growing larger still. The sun had just set and the sky surrounding the cloud had darkened to a royal blue.

But the island itself was the embodiment of hell. The explosion had stripped away nearly everything above the sands, leaving wrecked vehicles and pieces of structures strewn about like so many children's toys forgotten on a beach. Buildings lay flattened, unrecognizable.

Though the shock wave had put out the major fires pockets of red still smoldered, releasing streams of gray smoke that cast a low-lying shroud on the land. A few lost souls wandered about unscathed or mildly hurt, more in shock than affected by their physical injuries. Bodies lay indiscriminately about, some discernable, others scorched beyond recognition.

"My God," he moaned.

Inside, a dazed Hanford sat. Natano, Cindy and some of the police officers were moving about, checking on the others. Simon Tong was conscious though not moving. Cindy gave him water. Laina continued to apply pressure to Erik Lundquist's chest as he lay unconscious.

Sharon made her way around the debris and walked out to Kevin.

"My God, Kev," she said, surveying the landscape.

"Are you okay?" he asked.

Tears formed in her eyes. "I'm never going to be okay." He embraced her, brushing off flakes of debris from her shirt and hair.

Jessica came to join them, but there was little deck left to stand on. "Are you guys all right?" she asked. Kevin turned and just looked at her as Sharon nodded.

"I am too but Erik's not. We can't stop the bleeding."

Sharon shook her head and turned to Kevin. "I had to get away from him," she spoke angrily. "I don't care that he's a president."

"Don't go there now," he implored through clenched teeth. "There'll be a time. And a place. Trust me." She quieted, and began looking around.

Reflected gold from the thermonuclear cloud shone off their faces with a warm glow that seemed just flat-out wrong for the devastation surrounding them. Dusk had begun to settle and the growing haze cut down on visibility. They heard a sound and then saw a plainly dazed man in his late twenties stumbling along. Kevin braced himself on a sturdy part of the railing and called out to him. The man slowly looked up but said nothing.

A moment later Sharon asked, "Kevin, what's that?"

He looked at her, then turned to where she was staring. A white line parallel to the horizon was visible on the water out toward the expanding cloud.

"Oh my God!" he yelled. He turned back to the man below. "Get up here now! You have to move! Get up here!" The man just stood in silence, his mouth agape.

"Kev, what is it?"

"The waves! I can't believe I forgot. I was so stupid." He yelled again, "Get up here!"

Sharon looked again. The line had gotten closer. "Oh my God!" she screamed. She ran back into the room. "We gotta get out of here! There's a wave coming!"

The others were slow to respond, although some began screaming.

"Where the hell are we supposed to go?" Hanford yelled.

"I have to get the president out of here!" yelled an agitated Knight. "What do we do?"

"Is there a way to get to the roof?" Jessica said.

"Yeah!" Cindy said. "Come on! There's an access ladder just outside in the hall."

"That's right," Natano said. "Come on!" Cindy scurried after him towards the door to the hall, dodging debris and overhanging support structures. She tried opening it but it was stuck.

From the deck, Sharon could see the line on the horizon looming closer. "Hurry!" she screamed. "We have to move! Come on!"

Kevin rushed back in with her and up to Hanford. "Mr. President, you gotta get up!" He and Knight helped him to his feet. He was alert but dragging.

"Mr. President," Knight said, "we have to move!" Hanford was having difficulty navigating the debris.

"Come on, man! Move your ass!" Sharon prodded. Knight glared at her insolence towards the president, but she snarled, "You move his fucking ass or you're both going to die!" Laina abandoned Lundquist and trailed behind them as they helped Hanford along to the door.

Natano was kicking at the door and after several strong blows managed to knock it partway open. A slab of concrete that had wedged itself against the jamb blocked the way.

Out in the hall, it was obvious that half the building beyond had blown away.

Natano ran to the access ladder and flipped the lever. The metal stairs clanked down into place. He scooted up. The ceiling space was dark but he felt around for the hinge securing the metal door leading to the roof. He jerked open the latch and pushed the door up but it wouldn't open. "It's stuck!"

"It has to open!" Sharon yelled.

"I'll get it," he cried. "Just get everyone over here!"

She ran back to the room. "We have to move!" she yelled. "Hurry! Let's go!"

Lundquist and Tong were both still on the floor. Lundquist was unresponsive, his shirt covered in blood. Tong was dazed but conscious, and Kevin and a police officer helped him sit up, then they lifted him and carried him to the door.

"We'll have to come back for Erik," Kevin said.

They carried Tong to the door, then into the hall and to the stairs where Hanford was waiting with Knight.

"Move it everyone!" Cindy yelled. She looked up at Natano. "Pete, gotta go faster!"

"I can't budge it!" he yelled. "Get me a length of wood or something!"

"You guys go for it," Kevin ordered the two officers. "Let's get Erik," he said to the third, and followed him back to Lundquist. The policeman bent over to grab hold, then paused as he looked at Lundquist. He checked for a pulse, then looked up at Kevin and shook his head no.

"We'd better go," Kevin sighed.

The officer headed out to help the two other policemen, who were heaving at a broken support beam. As Kevin turned to follow, he saw Lundquist's camera half buried in debris. Without pausing to think, he reached down, pulled it out, and then opened the slot for the memory card. He popped it out, pocketed it and snapped the slot shut.

In the hallway, the three police officers managed to lift up the wood beam. They were positioning it to thrust it up into the crawlspace when Jessica looked out through a crack in the wall, across the lagoon.

"Oh my God!" she yelled. "It's almost here! And what is that?"

The wave had lifted *Star Princess*, pushing it along towards the island, sending spouts of water into the air. As the huge ship crossed the beach, it raised a hellish roar of crunching steel and cinder, snapping palm trees like toothpicks. Jessica screamed, "Hurry!"

The men managed to position the beam up the ladder. Natano guided it, yelling, "Okay! Push!" They heaved and the door popped open with a clang, ripping the hinges off and shifting the piece of roofing that had jammed it.

"Come on!" Natano yelled. "Everybody up!"

Kevin slung Tong over his shoulders and with the policemen's help was able to push him up. Tong was alert enough to help himself.

Kevin then turned to Hanford. "Mr. President, we have to move!"

Hanford slipped on the rails several times but Knight helped him. As they squeezed through the narrow opening, Kevin felt his aching shoulder hurt. His hand was covered in blood. He paused, then looked at Natano, "Pete," he asked, "where's Deloy?"

"My God, he's in the holding cell in the basement! And so is Tim Cain."

"We have to—"

Just then a whoosh began, a nightmarish groan that grew in intensity like a freight train approaching, heralding the arrival of the massive wave as it crashed over the beach. It towered over twenty-five feet high, smashing dozens of small craft and pleasure boats into each other and propelling the 951 foot long *Star Princess* into the building, destroying the entire north wing of the hotel. The south wing remained intact, though water splashed up to the third floor. Still smoldering, all 106,000 tons of the cruise ship came to rest on the wing as the waves rolled on.

Natano scampered up the stairway and Kevin reached the foot of the stairs just as the waves hit the building, shooting water across the floor where Kevin stood.

On the roof Sharon and Cindy screamed for them to hurry. "Hold on!" Sharon yelled.

"It's going to get us!" Laina screamed as the water hit the floor below.

The president's eyes were wild with fear. He steadied himself against a palm trunk that had been hurled atop the building. Agent Knight braced him.

Natano pushed through the narrow crawl way and immediately reached down for Kevin.

The waters swirled around the hall and up the ladder. Kevin had reached the top rungs when a vortex overtook him, pulling him down and knocking him about. Natano went back down, felt around in the dark and touched a hand clinging onto a single rung. He grabbed it hard. Another hand reached up and Kevin's face popped out of the water.

"Come on," Natano pleaded, "stay with us!"

Kevin coughed up spasms of sea and tried to catch his breath in the pummeling torrent. His ear hurt and he had taken a lungful of water. He thrashed his legs and got one of his feet on another rung. The waters still swirled about but he was able to get his other foot on and pulled himself up.

Sharon stood over the opening on the roof and positioned herself to help. She frantically tried to maneuver down but Natano pushed her back, yelling, "Grab my arm!" With one arm hooked under Kevin's armpit, he pulled at him while Sharon reached down and began tugging on Natano's other arm. With one last grunt she fell back. Natano dragged himself through the opening, and Kevin was able to reach the top. Once on the roof, Kevin saw what was happening.

For miles on either side walls of water could be seen spreading out from the cloud like immense ripples. Several more waves surged by, spraying the roof as they slammed the building, not toppling it but rolling on toward the open water in a thundering rush. Everyone got soaked as they huddled in a small spot in the center of the roof that miraculously had not washed away.

Over the din, Kevin collapsed. "Thanks," he heaved between breaths to Natano.

"Oh, no," Natano gasped. "Thank you. If it wasn't for you we wouldn't have known to get our asses moving."

Jessica was panting as she asked, "What about Erik?"

He shook his head no. She bit her lip and looked away.

"Cin, thank you too," Kevin said, giving her a hug. "Getting to the roof saved our asses."

She sat on her knees on a palm frond trying to catch her breath, unable to muster a comment. Finally she waved thanks as the surrounding catastrophe continued to unfold.

One hundred eleven

Kevin sat, coughing. Soaked and exhausted, he was unable to catch a full breath. He was having trouble hearing with his left ear, which still hurt.

The others huddled in the evening chill, soaked and exhausted as well. In a height of irony, the only comfort came from the thermonuclear cloud. Though no longer scorching hot, it still radiated enough infrared energy to keep them warm.

Kevin looked around. "I don't know how the building stayed up," he said, astounded.

"Probably the coral rock face," Natano said. "It's quite solid. If we had been standing anywhere else when the bomb went off, we wouldn't be here right now."

"If we hadn't been dicking around," Sharon said, "we wouldn't have *needed* to be standing there and that piece of shit wouldn't have slammed into that thing."

Kevin and Natano nodded in agreement.

A few feet away, a stunned Elliot Hanford sat. Any visible skin was bruised and scraped, and his once-immaculate clothes clung tattered and damp. A lifetime of wheeling and dealing that had him ascend to the most powerful office on Earth had scarcely prepared him for what he had just endured. He leaned against the palm trunk, grasping for some measure of insight.

"People," he finally managed, "I just want to give you a heartfelt thank you." He turned to Kevin. "And I want to thank you especially."

Sharon guffawed, but a look from Kevin had her turning away. Hanford ignored her.

"Are they going to come for us?" Cindy asked no one in particular.

"They know on Funafuti that something went very wrong," Natano replied. Hanford nodded slowly in agreement.

"They'll be here," he said with an air that let everyone know that a threat to an American president would be enough to summon forth the full resources of the United States government. He paused to catch his breath, then his bearing grew determined. "Dr. Herter," he demanded, "what the *hell* happened?"

"The technical answer? There was a design flaw in the panel that set the yield. It probably never would have shown up, but with that idiot Sanderson around, it hit that one-in-a-million chance that something catastrophic would happen." Kevin turned to Natano. "It's what you were afraid of. Just not where you were afraid of it."

"No one wanted to listen. And now there aren't even enough left to hear me say I told you so."

"If the changes we discussed had been made this would never have happened," Cindy added. She turned to Kevin. "That's the technical explanation. Tell him the real one."

"Kids shooting off M-80s, and one blew up in their hand," he replied, staring off into the distance.

"Oh, come on," Hanford said caustically, drawing a look of disgust from Kevin.

"Pete and Cindy are right," Kevin added. "No one wanted to deal with it."

"Dr. Herter, now's not the time," Knight cut in, asserting his Secret Service authority.

"Oh, I think now's the perfect time," Sharon replied. She turned to Hanford. "Hey, it's just us. All that drivel about being the most powerful guy in the world don't mean much out here. We're just a bunch of people sitting on a rooftop hoping to get rescued. So you might as well 'fess up."

"Young lady—"

"I don't know how you can sit there. You want to know what happened? What Kevin warned you about not much more than a half an hour ago is what happened!"

"Ma'am," Knight cut in, "you just—"

"No, it's okay." Hanford turned to her. "Sharon, isn't it? I don't know why you'd think that, but no one would have wanted something like this to happen less than me."

"Yeah, I can see you're really broken up. I just had to scrape your chief of staff off my shoe. Twenty thousand people just died, and you're sitting there like—"

"Are you *kidding*? I came five feet from being incinerated myself! You think I'd put myself or anyone else in this situation knowing something this catastrophic could happen?"

"No, not you. But you set the whole thing in motion so—"

Kevin said, "All right everyone—*enough!* This will get sorted out."

Sharon glared at Kevin. "After all this, if you damn-well don't say anything—"

"Twenty thousand people?" Hanford barked, cutting her off. "Then we damn-well owe it to them to make sure nothing like this ever happens again!" Sharon rolled her eyes.

"Happen again?" Jessica chimed in.

The president frowned. "You don't think I feel for them? Dr. Herter's right. We'll have to sort this out. But don't think for a moment I'm not feeling any sympathy for those people." He looked at Natano. "And we'll do everything we can to help you."

Natano just stared back.

"We have to get off this roof and out of here first," Kevin pointed out.

Hanford turned to Natano. "What are the emergency plans? When do they come for us?"

Natano shook his head and sighed. "We have rescue choppers on Funafuti. It'll probably be an hour or so before they're able to get here."

"How many do you have?" Sharon asked.

"Six."

"Oh, Christ," Hanford snapped, "that's not going to be enough."

"They're not going to need much more than that," Kevin reservedly pointed out.

They grew quiet. The sound of water sloshing against the roof was all that could be heard. Finally, Sharon looked at Kevin and asked, "What did you mean by a design flaw?"

"There was a quirk in the system. The way it was configured the explosive potential of the device was unlimited. The control panel that set the yield didn't allow for that. A technician would set the yield using a lever right before the blast. Problem was it wasn't idiot-proof." He eyed Hanford. "That was the minor technical problem you wanted looked at, the one that covered up what you were really doing. Lisa Whiteman chose an impractical design to keep the DOD from getting their hands on the things. That fool Sanderson didn't know about it. When he went off on the policeman, they hit the lever and pushed it all the way up. Because of the quirk, the bomb went off a lot higher than it was set. I was too far away and it happened so fast the techs never had a chance to stop it. Everyone was so concerned with the spikes that made the blasts bigger that they ignored the simple flaw staring you right in the face, the one that so easily set the yield bigger."

"Unbelievable," Sharon groaned.

Cindy agreed. "This whole place was based on a design that tried to avoid problems and in the process it turned out to have bigger problems. All those safeguards, you can't control stupid."

"I'd just said the whole thing was an accident waiting to happen," Kevin added.

Natano let out an anguished sigh. Cindy reached over and gave him a hug. They sat quietly then, looking at the cloud, now a brilliant gold.

"How big?" Natano asked.

"Not sure. If I had to guess I'd say fifty or sixty megatons."

"My God," Cindy said.

"You'd think pushing the lever to twenty-five, that's what you get but it didn't work like that. Going from twenty to twenty-five didn't add five megatons but something much higher. Usually one and one make two but in this case it was more like eleven. The only bit of luck we had is that when an explosion's that big, most of it goes straight up instead of out."

"Oh, joy," Sharon said.

"And," Cindy added, "the hotel was right between us and the shore. I think it might have taken some of the energy out of the waves. Otherwise, I don't think we would have made it."

"Yeah," Kevin replied. "Small comfort, huh?"

"So why the hell *wasn't* anything done to fix it?" Hanford asked testily. "It didn't have to come to this!"

Natano gave out a palpable groan.

"I don't believe this!" Jessica cried.

"It's your fault this thing happened in the first place!" Sharon yelled at Hanford.

"I don't want to hear it!" Hanford snapped in response. "I did my damnedest to *keep* this from happening!"

"Mr. President, I've got paper trails that lead right up to your office!" Jessica replied.

"Mr. President, I'm having a hard time listening to this," Natano challenged. "Everyone knows what I did to keep this from happening. I don't even want to hear about how this could have been prevented." It was the first time the always proper Natano spoke aggressively towards Hanford. It was unlike him to challenge anyone in authority, and his blunt remark jolted them.

The president wasn't budging. "Captain," he declared, "when this story comes out it's going to show one thing—how much I tried to corral an absurd reality and keep it from getting out of hand. Everything leading up to that fool Sanderson hitting that panel has been one cluster fuck after another. I tried to deal sanely with an insane situation, and people are going to know."

"Oh, and you think you can make that argument?" Jessica was only asking what they were all thinking.

"You're damn right I can! How long will it be before the water levels go down?"

Confused, Natano looked at Kevin who shrugged and said, "By tomorrow. Why?"

"All right, then. I want to see how much data can be salvaged. All these discussions aren't going to do anything to help."

"I don't believe it!" Sharon cried, clearly offended. "You're still looking to dick around with this thing!"

"Young lady, there are more important things than your indignation or even mine. I don't need lectures. This thing can't be allowed to happen again."

"Yeah, especially during an election year."

Hanford looked like he wanted to smack Sharon when Natano held up his hand.

"Mr. President, you're right. It will be sorted out. When the water drains off, we'll go through what's left. But you're going to have to understand that whatever *is* left, we still have jurisdiction over."

"Captain, I respect your sovereignty but other issues will need to be discussed. There are national security concerns with the data contained in our equipment if it can be retrieved. I'm sorry, but this area is going to have to be secured."

Sharon shook her head incredulously. "I don't believe this! Pete and Kevin save your ass and you're back with the pissing contest!" She eyed Kevin. "If you don't say something—"

"Sharon—"

"*No!*" she snapped, staring at Hanford. "I can smell when someone's covering their ass."

"Chill!" Kevin cut in. "It'll be all right."

"Well," Jessica said, "then I'll say something. Mr. President, from the time we came into Central Control to the moment the lieutenant governor hit that lever, we got it all. My cameraman Erik was recording the whole time, including everything you said."

Hanford stared. "How's that again?" he demanded to know.

Jessica hesitated, uncertain whether in her eagerness to show up Hanford she had tripped over her own position. "Mr. President," she began, drawing out her words in hope her confidence would match her impulsiveness, "Erik recorded the entire episode downstairs. Maybe he shouldn't have but if he were alive now I'd give him a kiss and nominate him for a Pulitzer." Her voice broke and tears flooded her eyes as she stared determinedly at the president.

Hanford looked up, locking eyes with his Secret Service agent. Knight was the one remaining sympathetic person left to him. Kevin quietly watched as they awaited the president's response. As much as being in the driver's seat was uncharted territory for him he was genuinely curious as to how everyone would play out their hands.

Hanford sat as if in thought, then began nodding in self-righteous determination.

"Okay, young lady," he announced. "We're going to have to secure that as well."

"Excuse me?"

"If footage exists showing what happened, then it'll show just what I spoke of, the idiocy that led up to this. I have no problem owning my words. That represents a historical record of this tragedy every bit as tied up in the outcome of its resolution as the data in those stations, and it's going to have to be secured. People are going to want to see it."

Jessica grew just as determined. "Oh, they will. Mr. President, that footage is protected property. There are First Amendment issues connected to it. *We'll* decide what's done with it."

"Now I'll tell both of you," Natano cut in. "This is still my country and we still have sovereignty over it. Your constitutional concerns don't carry the weight of law here. If there is footage that shows Mr. Sanderson tripping that lever, I intend to assert jurisdiction over it. There are enormous legal implications with what happened here, not to mention insurance questions."

"I don't fucking believe this," Sharon began laughing. "It's whip it out and piss time."

The president huffed. "Young lady—"

"Don't fucking call me 'young lady!'"

"Hey!" Agent Knight yelled.

"That's enough!" Natano said. "Both of you!"

"Damn right it's enough!" snapped a now indignant president. "My God, look at this place! Forget the security concerns. I'll be damned if something can be done so this doesn't happen again!"

"Kevin just *TOLD* you what happened!" Sharon yelled back. "You don't wanna listen!"

"I have more to listen to than you know!" Hanford said angrily. "I'll tell you the same thing I told your friend here this morning. Look at that thing out there! You think I woke up one morning and said, '*Oh*, I got a *great* idea! Let's set off *H-bombs* for kicks!' This thing was dropped in my lap! I got the scientists on one end, the military on the other—one's ideas are crazier than the other's! And I'm stuck in the middle trying to deal with it!"

"It's your damn *job* to deal with it!"

"Well, *fine!*" Hanford barked. "We *DID*! *You* have a damn DOD memo drop in *your* lap telling you *your* armed forces are pushing to nuke a dozen countries in the Middle East! Idiocy! We did the best we could! And when people see that video, they'll see for themselves just how much craziness we had to deal with."

"Yeah, well they're also going to know just what you think of them."

Hanford was by now consumed with anger, an ire boiling up from three years of work and planning that had come to naught.

Sharon glared at Kevin. "I'll be damned if I flew ten thousand miles to watch you bend over again! How the hell do you sit with this guy when you know he tried to have you killed?"

"That's a damn lie!" Hanford yelled.

"Yeah. I'm sorry. You didn't try to do it. You just weren't going to do anything to stop the people who *did*! God forbid you get *your* hands dirty!"

"Sharon, dammit!" Kevin yelled. "Enough!"

"Damn right it's enough!" Hanford shouted. "You think this was a disaster? Watch what happens when that memo gets out. See that thing out there? Watch when everyone gets one and what happened here happens everywhere! Watch when every little piss-ass dictator decides he can have one of these things too. Then you can blame that on me as well! Oh, the hell with this!"

The president appeared to have reached his limit. He staggered up and flagged Knight, who got up and followed Hanford over to the furthest end of the roof remaining.

One hundred twelve

Sharon chafed while the others tried calming her down.

"He's going to fucking get away with it!" she complained bitterly, glaring at Kevin. "I can't believe you sat there and said nothing! That thing we taped doesn't mean a thing, does it? Why the hell did we even make the thing if we weren't going to use it?"

"Will you for once learn to sit there and keep your mouth shut! He's not going to get away with anything! For God sakes, just have a little faith in me."

She folded her arms tight. "You damn well better not be dicking me around, Herter."

"Just trust me, all of you."

"I shouldn't have said anything," Jessica conceded. "My anger got the best of me. I should've just tried to get the memory card. Now he's going to get it." She eyed Natano plaintively. "He doesn't give a damn about you."

"Getting him to own anything is like trying to nail Jello to a wall," Cindy agreed.

"I'm not conceding anything yet," Natano said with a forced smile.

Kevin rubbed his ear absent-mindedly. He still couldn't hear from it, and his arm was still oozing blood. He gazed out at the cloud, seeming to lose himself. He could see Natano's despondency. The man was crushed by the realization that the prime minister, his friends, co-workers and so many others were gone, and all the work and effort to build up the island had been consumed by the disaster.

Cindy rubbed Natano's back. "I know how hard you tried to keep this from happening," she said sadly. "It'll be all right." The others nodded in agreement.

"We'll get through this, Pete. Just trust me." Kevin said, his heart heavy for the bear of a policeman with the heart of gold that he had come to regard so fondly. He paused, before turning to Sharon.

"Remember what happened when I bought my house?"

She smiled. "This is a good story," she told everyone.

"Sharon can tell you," he began. "I'm on a small street in Princeton. You know those neighborhoods where the houses are like a hundred years old, but they're kept up well. When I was first invited to the Institute for Advanced Study, I needed a place to live. Now I'd never bought a house before. No idea what I was doing. So I get hooked up with this real estate agent, Beverly. I'll never forget her. I get to the house and this woman gets out of her car. I knew it was her because when I was a half-a-block away, I'd seen her put a for sale sign out. It had her picture on it, one of those smiley pictures that show how nice the person is even when they're trying to wring every last bit of commission out of you."

Smiles appeared on the other's faces.

"So," Kevin went on, "she walks up. She's about fifty-five, kinda chunky, with this blonde hair and this voice. I figured she smoked even though I couldn't smell it, but she must have with the raspy voice she had, like a cheese grater rubbing against sandpaper."

"Ooowww," Cindy shuddered. "I felt that."

"And raspy hair. Ever meet someone with raspy hair?" They all softly laughed and he added, "A blonde bush like a platinum scouring brush. Really patrician; huge handbag, bright red lipstick, the whole stereotype. Anyway I give her credit; she's trying to be nice. She asks me if there's anything I had in mind. I'm honest; I tell her I don't know cause it's the first time I ever bought a house. And the condescension just pours out. She starts, 'Oh *my*, buying a house in Princeton is *quite* a first step for someone who's never bought a house before'. So we go inside."

"What was it like?" Jessica asked.

"Not bad. You know how old houses are. It was when they built them one at a time. No two look alike but none of them are out of place. Lot of history; charm. Crown molding, a quarter-inch of lacquer on the floors. None of the floors even but that didn't bother me. And you know how it is with old windows; they shimmy. It's a quiet street; small plots of grass in front with flowers and hedges. Nice in the springtime. So she goes into this big spiel how Princeton's full of history, how it's got good schools, one of the world's foremost centers of higher learning. And I'm just nodding."

Natano was trying not to enjoy the story, but asked, "So what happened?"

"We go through the house and she says, 'So, what do you think?' Like I know the first thing about houses. And like I know Princeton real estate, where houses get gobbled up in a minute and when you're from out of the area you're supposed to grab it. So I said, 'I don't know. I guess I'll know what I'm looking for when I see it.'"

"I probably would have said the same thing," Cindy remarked.

"Well—*wrong*. She's all annoyed because she's used to houses selling themselves. Right away I see she's tired of dealing with a scatter-brained scientist with his head in the clouds. I've gotten it before. But it's a nice April day, the sun is shining, the birds are singing, the flowers are blooming, I'm in the same place Albert Einstein was, so I don't let it bother me. By now it's about eleven and I could use a cup of coffee. So I ask her if there's anywhere I could get one. And she starts the sales talk. "Oh, of *course!* As you know this is a college town. One thing Princeton's got is a lot of coffeehouses. And you don't have to drive; a nice thing about this house is that several are in walking distance. It's just a couple of blocks away." So off we go." He paused, and everyone waited expectantly.

"Well we're walking, and—like I said, I give her credit; she's trying with the small talk but you could tell it's an effort. She's telling me how she's worked with the Institute before, the last time about six months earlier. I'm just listening."

"Not being too friendly, huh?" Cindy said.

"It's not that. It's just that, well, ever talk to people who think because they're aware of history or science it makes them versed in history or science? Like when someone hears I'm a *nook*uler physicist." He smiled. "I guess you guys heard that one."

"Oh, yeah. We get them all the time here." Natano bit his lip and nodded.

"Well," Kevin smiled, "that's what I'm hearing. So I'm keeping it short and sweet. Anyway, she asks what goes on there. So I said I was just starting so I didn't know the routine yet. I gotta be honest; I wasn't up for her. But anyway, she asked me what I do. So I told her." He paused again.

"Okaaaay," Jessica said, "let's hear it."

"It's simple. I just told her the truth. I told her I was a physicist and my field of study was gravitational interaction on the Planck scale in a posited multi-dimensional fabric and that being the case, I'd be mostly taking up empty space there."

As Cindy shook her head and laughed, Jessica remarked, "Oh, that poor woman. So what happened next?"

"Nothing. That pretty much put an end to our meaningful conversation."

"Well, *duh*," Cindy said. "So how did you wind up with the house?"

"Well, two blocks later we get to Nassau Street, the main road in town. We walk into the Princeton Tea Room. Kind of artsy. The furniture reminded me of the houses on Park Place, no two pieces matched but none were out of place. Sharon owns it, though I didn't know it then."

Sharon smiled. "That's right. We didn't meet until months later. Turns out he'd been coming in for months and I didn't know it. We had missed each other all that time."

"You're kidding." Cindy said. "That's unbelievable."

"Yeah," Kevin said. "So anyway I get a cup of coffee and tell her to make them an offer."

Cindy stared. "Just like that? Let's hear it. Why did you change your mind?"

"Well, I noticed it was right next door to PJ's Pancake House." She gave him a quizzical look. "It was Albert Einstein's favorite pancake place."

"You bought a house because it's a block away from Einstein's favorite IHOP?" Jessica said in disbelief.

"That he did," Sharon replied. "True story."

As the others broke into smiles, Kevin said to Natano with a bit of melancholy, "It's funny, what makes for affections. And what you remember. I knew it would never be the way it was when he was alive and lived there. But you have your memories. And something will come back. Nothing ever is as it was, but just let it become what it will be."

Natano quietly looked out toward the water, then back to Kevin. "Thanks," he said softly.

"We'll see what we can do." Kevin slowly got to his feet and steadied himself. His shoulder hurt and his arm ached but wasn't as much of a bother as was his ear. "I'll be back," he added. Cindy began to shiver. Sharon moved up next to her, and the two women huddled together and settled in to wait.

One hundred thirteen

Fifty feet away, Hanford stood with Knight staring at the enormous cloud. It was still expanding, filling the entire eastern sky. With the breeze and water sloshing about, they hadn't heard the chatter at the other end of the roof. The president was brushing debris off his pants. The warmth of the thermonuclear cloud was proving a relief for the nuisance of his wet clothes.

"Jurisdiction hell," he murmured. "I want this site secured. We need to make doubly sure we get our people in here but pronto."

"Yes, Mr. President," Knight answered, keeping his voice low as well.

"And I want inquires made. I want the data retrieved. I want to know what the hell happened. I'll be damned if I listen to those idiots."

"Mr. President," Knight said, "I'm just part of your security contingent."

"Consider it a battlefield promotion. My chief of staff is lying downstairs like a charcoal briquette. I don't know who on my staff is even left. For the time being, you run shotgun for me." He paused. "And I want that camera secured."

"Yes, sir."

Hanford shook his head, barely containing his anger. "You work your butt off, you deal with one pain in the ass after another, you put *your* ass on the line trying to deal with *their* bullshit and look what happens! I'll be damned I let them stick this on me!"

Hanford heard someone approaching, and turned as Kevin walked up.

"The inestimable Dr. Herter," said the president. "Whose work is responsible for this."

Kevin gave a half-hearted laugh. "There's a quote I heard once," he said with a shrug, "that people in conflict come to resemble each other. I don't know who said it. But I'm starting to get an appreciation of what that's about."

"Heh ... yeah."

"How are you feeling, Mr. President?"

"I'm all right. Not like all these other people, God rest their souls. Look at this!" He shook his head and his expression changed to anger. "That ex of yours is a piece of work."

"That she is, at times." Kevin rubbed his ear. It felt like it was full of water. He noticed Hanford and Knight were looking at the cloud. "Still looking, huh?" he added dryly.

"Don't even go there. You know, being president entitles you to a never-ending parade of people who think it's their job to tell you how to do yours. They all know exactly how things should be done. All along, I've been trying to get you to see my position; put yourself in my shoes and think of what it was like to deal with the shit I've had to deal with. Maybe now you have an idea."

Kevin was in no mood to spar with Hanford. He put his hand on his bandaged arm and noted it was still oozing blood, which he wiped off on his shirt. It seeped into the wet fabric.

"Mr. President, I can't answer for them," he said. "But me? It was less me telling you how to do your job than telling you what would happen if you didn't listen when I told you about mine."

"Well, that's nice," Hanford frowned, "but I still have to worry about those things. Whether you like it or not, something has to be salvaged from this. I'll be damned all this work goes down the drain. You think I'm making speeches? There're still threats out there. What happened here is going to happen somewhere else on a whole different scale unless something's done to stop it. Which means what I was trying to do before is even more important now. This is going to be a lesson learned. When we get back, I'm expecting certain things from you and I don't want to hear any problems. Consider yourself drafted."

"Well if you don't mind, until then, I have to go sit down," Kevin said with a fleeting smile. He walked back to the others and collapsed onto the tree trunk.

"What did he have to say?" Natano asked.

Kevin just shook his head. "Not even worth going into."

"Well, he's right about one thing. This place needs to be secured. It's not only the lawyers and the insurance companies. I consider this a crime scene. Regardless what he thinks, my government still has jurisdiction. He's so worried about blowing this up to an international incident, he's not seeing that it's already one. That little mishap of his represents the most monstrous occurrence ever to have happened in this region. My God, twenty thousand people!"

Sharon turned to Cindy. "Princeton's looking better and better, huh?"

"I have nothing left here," she sighed. She turned to Kevin and noticed his bloody arm.

"Kev," she said, "you're going to have to get this looked at. You can't let it get infected."

"I know." He tried adjusting the bandage, but soon gave up. It would have to wait.

Sharon picked up a palm frond. "I would have wanted to paint this at one time," she sighed before laying it back down.

Kevin shook his head in a sad comprehension, and then looked around.

Though it was still light enough to see, the sky had darkened. The waves had completely covered the island, washing away most of the buildings left standing after the shock wave. The airport, normally visible from the roof, had disappeared. The only evidence it had once been there were three jet vertical stabilizers protruding from the water, one from Air Force One.

Off to the east *Celestial Voyager* had foundered. It lay capsized, smoke rising from its hull. *Star Princess* lay on its side as well, next to the south wall of the hotel, its one-time magnificence awash in a dark silty bilge.

Kevin looked at the others. The enormity of what had happened was obviously weighing on them. They stared silently at each other, jolted every now and then out of their bewilderment by a piece of debris, a small boat or a tree crashing up against the building. Everyone studiously ignored the bodies that floated by.

The waves were beginning to subside. The water didn't drain off, but it looked as if the worst had past. At its height it had reached more than thirty-five feet.

Natano wiped away a few tears, and Cindy wrapped her arms about his shoulders and tried to comfort him.

Jessica stared blankly toward the cloud then looked silently to Sharon, acknowledging their burgeoning friendship. Although Tong had briefly come to when he was lifted onto the roof, he now lay unconscious near the palm trunk, watched over by his surviving colleagues. The officers huddled together, scanning the horizon for lights that would point to a rescue and taking turns cleaning debris off the rooftop.

Elliot Hanford and Gerald Knight still stood at the rim of the roof. They appeared to be talking, but no one could hear what they were saying.

Sharon turned to Kevin. "I wonder what Max will say about this."

He nodded his head in agreement.

No one spoke much after that.

The evening was getting darker, making the cloud that much more imposing. It had grown to immense size, dozens of miles wide and high. As it had the previous night, it was reflecting the gold and yellow and orange and ruddiness of the setting sun, blazing away against the deep blue of the sky. With every light on the island destroyed, the reflected light and heat cast a warm afterglow on the faces of the survivors, now huddled together trying to keep warm.

As he sat on the palm trunk, Kevin was loathe to admit it, but he found himself thinking that the enormous cloud was even more sublime than the one the previous night. Try as he might he couldn't look away. In the quiet that followed the catastrophe, he noticed the others watching as well. Despite the horror of the past few hours, the sight of the cloud spawned that evening was awe-inspiring. He was sure they were all thinking the same thing. And he was also sure that it was a sentiment they would zealously guard, something they would never bring themselves to share.

Saturday, April 9

One hundred fourteen

Funafuti, the capital of Tuvalu was an atoll of perhaps five thousand people on an area of a square mile, stretched out in long narrow sand bars and coral outcrops. The TV in the lobby of Princess Margaret Hospital was set to CNN International. Early Saturday morning in the island's main medical facility usually meant a light work load, and the staff would steal a few moments between sips of coffee to catch a glimpse at the goings-on in the rest of the world. This morning, for the first time anyone could remember, the lead story was about a local event, but no one at the hospital was watching.

As news of the disaster on Vaitupu unfolded, the hospital became a scene of frenzied activity, made even more heated by the presence of an American president at the center of the calamity. The full magnitude of the disaster became apparent as the first survivors were brought in. The hospital had an excellent trauma center that was more than adequate for a patient load that covered the island's residents and the occasional emergency from Vaitupu, but the number of casualties and their horrific condition quickly overwhelmed the staff. Calls went out across the region for doctors and volunteers while it was still dark. They had yet to arrive before more frantic calls followed, pleading for burn units across the entire Pacific Rim.

That something had gone seriously wrong was apparent almost immediately on Funafuti and Nukufetau, the two nearest islands. By themselves the detonations had never caused alarm. The explosions were set off at a spot about seventy-five miles from each island and residents had grown accustomed to the burst of light and unfolding cloud. But Deneb's enormous fireball was instantly recognized as different, as the heat started fires and the shock wave broke windows and blew down trees, fences and structures, effects that never before happened.

Communications and uplink with Vaitupu were lost the moment the device went off. Waves twenty feet high left no doubt that this event was horrendous and within minutes, when contact could not be reestablished and the growing cloud dwarfed any they had seen before, rescue operations sprang into action. Funafuti's rescue helicopters were dispatched. More were soon pledged from governments across the region. The choppers had to contend with a witch's brew of precipitates made up of the vast amount of water and seabed vaporized and carried aloft by the tremendous explosion. It began covering the surrounding region in a dirty drizzle, barely twenty minutes after detonation.

Every available rescue ship, including the aircraft carrier *Abraham Lincoln* so recently central to the developments with Roger Braddock's plane, sped towards the island.

The first helicopters arrived an hour after the explosion to an island wiped clean. What little was left of Vaitupu was unrecognizable and what had been the resort of Tuvalu Alofa was no more. The hotel, the largest building in Tuvalu was two-thirds gone and one of the most elegant cruise ships afloat was a fixture on its grounds. Numerous fires still smoldered, though the blast and the waves had destroyed so much there was little left to burn. Full dark had arrived, making search and rescue difficult.

Survivors huddled in parts of the buildings still standing. A few dazed souls wandered out in the open where they could. Rescuers began combing through the ships in the dark, searching for the many remained trapped in air pockets within the hulls.

Star Princess lay on its side. The first choppers on the scene found survivors clustering about the higher sections of the ship. *Celestial Voyager* had capsized a half-mile offshore, where it lay in shallow water, and survivors clung onto the parts of the ship there as well.

Everywhere, survivors and rescuers encountered charred bodies. As the injured were ferried to Funafuti, it soon became evident that most survivors were resort staff who'd been working inside when the bomb detonated, or who had not been in direct line of sight of the fireball. The worst casualties were the guests, those who had paid to fly out and see the spectacle from ringside seats in the open.

It was well into the night when a ragged band of survivors on the rooftop remains of the resort's Central Control complex was sighted. Although the group had seen the lights of numerous helicopters while the choppers were well out to sea, they weren't noticed until the fourth flyover by one of the craft. Once it was realized that Elliot Hanford was one of the survivors, two choppers were dispatched, one to take the president, his Secret Service agent, the seriously wounded Simon Tong and the remaining police and resort staff. Kevin, Sharon, Cindy, Jessica and Peter Natano were on the other. On both of the half-hour flights to Funafuti, the passengers were mostly silent and nodding off due to exhaustion.

Kevin struggled to open his eyes shortly after nine a.m. The blinds were drawn and the curtains half closed in the hospital office where he'd fallen asleep. Although he had slept through the clatter of gurneys and the shouts of doctors and orderlies, the soft swish of the door opening and closing stirred him. As his eyes focused, he saw Cindy on a nearby chair, and Sharon on the other couch. Both were still asleep.

Jack Raden stood just inside the door. Kevin sat up. Still in his torn and dirty but nearly dry clothes, he felt his pants pocket and was relieved to feel the memory card he had taken from Lundquist's camera.

"Hey," he said. "Long time no see." He motioned Raden to a seat next to him on the couch.

Cindy slowly opened her eyes, and got to her feet. She walked over to Kevin.

"Come on," he said softly as he stood to embrace her. "Sit. Sharon's still sleeping."

"I'm up," came a low voice from the other couch.

"It was nearly midnight when they brought us in here," Kevin told Raden.

"I know. I poked my head in right after they stitched you back up. The three of you were completely out." He shook his head. "How are you guys feeling?"

Cindy looked over at Sharon, who looked back dazedly and asked, "How are *you* feeling?"

"Considering—" her voice broke.

"I'm a little banged up," Kevin said. "And my eardrum's punctured, but ..." he tailed off and rubbed his eyes, settling into the chair. "I can't complain. Do you believe this?" he asked.

"Unbelievable," Raden said. "I'm glad you guys made it. A lot of people didn't."

"How did you find out?"

"I saw it. I was in a meeting and we saw the flash. We all looked at each other. The people here had never seen it so bright. We went outside and we knew right away. You can still see it."

He got up and went to the blinds, letting in some gray light and a view of the outside. Thick clouds covered the entire sky. A flurry of stretchers and whirling red lights filled the hospital's entrance ramp. The media had descended, and were cordoned off with the curious residents but were pushing out of the area set aside for them.

"It's the lead story all over the world," Raden added.

Kevin shook his head in disbelief. "Any number yet on the size of the thing?"

"We think it was about eighty-five—"

"Oh, my God!"

"Yeah. Eighty-five to eighty-eight megatons, nearer the higher end. There are satellite images already. The thing looks like a hurricane. Black rain's been falling. And your Herterite is all over the place. You go outside, you'll see the cloud. It's going to spread out two hundred fifty miles or so. It went up at least thirty miles, maybe more."

"That's literally in outer space," Kevin said as Cindy squeezed his hand and Raden nodded yes.

A knock at the door announced Mike Yahr, followed by Roger Braddock carrying a tray of coffees and a plate of muffins and bagels.

"Oh, thank you!" Sharon said as she helped herself to a coffee and bagel.

"This should tide you guys over for a while," Braddock said. He extended his hand to Kevin. "We didn't get the chance to meet right," he smiled. Kevin introduced Cindy to Mike and Roger.

"Thank you for everything you've done," Kevin said, "and for bringing Sharon here."

"No thanks necessary. I had wanted to meet you for some time now, just not like this."

"He flew me here," Sharon said, "so maybe I should really be looking to let him have it." As she and Braddock traded smiles, she said, "Trust me, you wouldn't have wanted to be there."

"I think I'm going to like getting to know you," Cindy said as she sipped her coffee.

Sharon smiled, scratched her head and yawned.

"Jack," Kevin asked as he took a bagel, "thanks for this, but what's going on?"

"A lot. We're going to have to talk but I just wanted to see how you guys were. I also wanted to give you a head's up on a few things. Just prepare yourselves. It's a madhouse. There's a lot of cameras, so you might want to avoid them. Your call."

"They don't scare me anymore," Kevin said.

Raden smiled. "No, at this point I don't imagine they would. Just be aware."

Kevin shrugged, then asked, "How is Jessica? Have you seen her?"

"She got up about a half-hour ago. She was banged up really good, so they gave her a bed. She's being debriefed by the Tuvalu authorities and our own people. But she's itching to get back to work. She wants to see you when you're up for it."

"Her, I'll talk to," he said. "She's the only person in the media I'd talk to at this point."

"Me too," Sharon said with a shrug. "Kind of a switch, huh?"

"Yeah," Raden laughed lightly. "And the officer you helped is holding his own."

As Cindy sighed in relief, Mike asked, "Kevin, how did they find you?"

"We started seeing helicopters about eight. We were waving palm leaves to get their attention. After the initial blast of heat, the cloud began to cool down. We were all soaked, and it helped us keep warm. Go figure. But after it cooled down more, we mostly just tried to keep warm. We figured a lot of people had it worse than us."

"Not if you listen to our Fearless Leader," Sharon said.

"Well," Mike said, "that's part of what we need to talk about."

Raden nodded, adding, "First, they have preliminary estimates on the casualties. We're looking at fifty-eight hundred dead right now—"

"Oh, my God!" Sharon moaned.

"Yeah. But it's going up. The injured number close to a thousand, and there's more of them too. There had to be close to twenty-five thousand people between the two ships, the resort and residents. Some of them they'll never find."

"Oh, no," Cindy said.

"Yeah," Braddock said. "Far too many to be treated here. The Australians have volunteered to take many, the Japanese, and hospitals in the region are fitting in as many as they can as well."

"What about us?" Kevin said. "The good-ole U S of A?"

"The governor of Hawaii's arranged to take as many as they can. And hospitals all along the west coast from San Diego up to Juneau are opening their burn units as well. No one's ever dealt with this before, needing this many burn and trauma centers. And of course, the president has pledged the full resources of the United States government."

"How is the president?" Kevin asked.

"A little burned. Bruised, but alive. He's hanging in. He wants to see you this morning."

"Well," Kevin dead-panned, "I want to see him. I think we'll all meet. What about Pete Natano?"

"Physically, he's okay," Raden said. "But he's a mess. I think it's finally catching up with him. I don't think he'll ever be the same."

Kevin shook his head in sadness. Raden traded gazes with Mike and Braddock, then said, "I'm not sure what happened with you out there, but there's some things you should know. The White House spin machine is in full gear. It started the minute word got out on what happened."

"Oh, you're kidding," Sharon said, rolling her eyes.

"Nope," Mike said. "They released a statement even before the president was picked up saying that he had come back to Tuvalu to unveil a new counter-terrorism program; basically, the statement he was set to make before the accident. They're spinning it as him being some kind of heroic visionary in the trenches and getting caught up in the very thing he was trying to fight. The media's picking up on it. It's well on its way to working for him."

"I don't fucking believe it!" Sharon ripped out.

"Word's out that Kevin pushed him out of harm's way the instant before the bomb went off. They're playing you up as well, which is why he wants to be seen with you."

Kevin turned to Sharon and Cindy, stunned. "I don't believe it."

"You better," Braddock said.

"So think about how you want to handle this," Mike said.

Kevin sat back and took a deep breath. "I have a few ideas." Jack Raden, Roger Braddock and Mike Yahr pulled up chairs.

"This looks official," Cindy said as she looked at Kevin.

"Actually," Raden said, "it is."

"There's a few things we need to go over," Mike said. "The White House issued a statement offering condolences to the people of Tuvalu and pledging the full weight of the United States government to help with the wounded and find out what happened."

"Which they already know," Sharon said.

"Everyone's in CYA mode," Raden said. "The government here is going ape-shit, threatening to sic every lawyer in the states against Washington. They're lining up. They know they have a good case. Washington and Honolulu are painting Sanderson as a rogue who got what he deserved but had no right to take twenty thousand people with him. The governor and the state are distancing themselves from him so fast they could start posthumous impeachment proceedings. Tuvalu's blaming Washington for setting them up with a design they knew was faulty and Washington's blaming Tuvalu for repeatedly putting up someone they knew was psychotic, that idiot Deloy."

Sharon looked at Kevin. "I have a headache."

"Oh, by the way, they found him this morning; Tim Cain too. The water drained off." Raden paused. "It wasn't pretty."

"Oh, wow," Cindy said, shaking her head. "They were creeps, but—"

"Anyway," Braddock said, "the DOD blames the DOE for withholding data that would have fixed the problem and the DOE claims that they kept it to themselves for security reasons. And, the memo just leaked. The White House is spinning that too, saying the president put himself in harm's way to forestall a greater disaster."

"That weasel," Sharon said.

"Well," Mike said, "no one's blaming him. They're saying no one would put themselves so close to a problem if they knew how risky it was. It seems to be taking hold."

"Which means he's going to get away with it. The shit."

Raden raised his hand. "It's trickling out that there's video of Sanderson flipping the lever. If Jessica hadn't said anything no one would have known. But no one knows what's on it."

"Just what would it mean if that thing came out?" Kevin asked.

"Well," Braddock said, "from the sound of it, it would seal the deal as far as liability for the accident. That's from the standpoint of the government here."

"And for Jessica," Mike said, "it would get her career back on track. I'd like to see that."

"But the president?" Raden said. "Depends what it shows."

"Well, I was there," Sharon said. "You should have heard him. If it got out, he'd be toast. Cynical doesn't even begin to describe it. Undermines everything he's done here. If people ever heard what he had to say, he'd be lucky to get twenty percent of the vote in November."

"Then forget legacy. Might even bring him down." Mike and Braddock nodded in agreement.

"I'm sure that's why he's so interested in finding the thing," Braddock added.

Kevin wasn't ready to say anything about the contents of his pocket yet. "You should have seen him and Pete and Jessica go at it," he remarked.

"So what happened out there?" Raden asked earnestly. "Jessica corroborates Pete's account." He paused, then said, "I don't know what you have in mind but we may need to move on. At this point, the White House appears to have the upper hand. From a practical outlook you may just want to call it a day, even with that statement you recorded."

"You don't think it's worth putting out there?"

"Before the accident it might have carried some weight. Now it may not get noticed."

Kevin shrugged. "I guess that plus the memory card would be—"

"That would be different. That would be a bigger disaster for him than the explosion. But in lieu of that, you gotta go with what you've got."

Sharon agreed. "What happens if they do find it?" she asked.

"Depends *who* finds it," Mike said. "And no one knows what shape it's in. It's not like it's a black box from a plane. But odds are it can be salvaged. This is becoming a real mess."

"Not that it wasn't one before," Sharon added.

"Tuvalu set up a restricted zone around what's left of the complex," Braddock said, "and Hanford's got the navy out. They're already butting heads. Both sides know that without the video, there are enough witnesses to corroborate that Sanderson flipped the thing but it would be icing on the cake in court to be able to show it. The lawyers are going to have a field day with this. It's a shame, but the Tuvaluans might wind up making more from lawsuits than they were making from the program itself. Mess is right."

"Jessica's got a lot to report now," Raden said. "It's all out, the whole DOD-DOE turf war, the payoffs and especially that the Pentagon used the program as a way to test warheads in front of paying customers. Anything the White House can use to scrape together a best-case narrative for the president, he's going to latch on to. So I think it mostly has to do with Hanford keeping what he said from coming out. People will support him if they think he's looking out for them, but not if he's knocking them. That's why he wants to see Kevin again."

"You had to save the SOB," Sharon said. As Kevin shrugged, she added, "But they'll never find that camera." She sat back and rubbed her eyes as if they were about to fall out. "I thought I was going to come out here and help this genius with a few problems and go home with a tan."

Kevin folded his arms. "Well, you can still help me with a problem." He turned to Braddock. "I know you guys have been busy since you got here. Are the tech facilities here well equipped?"

"They're fine." He paused, eyeing Kevin. "I've seen that look before."

Kevin reached into his pants pocket, pulled out the memory card and held it out.

"Holy *shit!*" Sharon said.

Cindy's jaw dropped. "Kevin!"

"I saw Erik filming," he said, in a matter-of-fact tone. "I didn't say anything."

Braddock leaned back in his chair and took a deep breath, letting it out in an audible huff. He turned to Mike and Raden. "I think you guys are rubbing off on him."

Mike shook his head and laughed, while Raden began scratching the back of his neck.

"This is what I want to do," Kevin announced. "I need to make copies of this, right now." He turned to Raden. "Don't tell Pete anything yet, nor Jessica. I want to go talk to her first. And definitely don't tell Hanford; in fact, it doesn't go beyond this room. What I do want is for you to go tell him that it's time we all met, all of us. It's nine thirty now. Let's shoot for an hour, okay?"

One hundred fifteen

The office in Funafuti where Mike Yahr, Jack Raden and Roger Braddock had been working was along the lines of an Internet café, sufficiently equipped for them to do their research and fortunately, just a couple of blocks away from the hospital. Sharon began making copies of the card, and Kevin emailed copies to several accounts, as he'd done with his earlier taped statement. It took no more than fifteen minutes. Kevin then went to meet Jessica and Natano, while the others worked on arrangements for the meeting with the president.

Kevin had to make his way through a phalanx of frenetic medical personnel still dealing with survivors, some literally at the limits of pain. He passed halls filled with singed flesh and screams, with staff calling out stat!, and realized that some measure of deep-seated responsibility for what had happened would linger, despite knowing that he had nothing to do with the accident. It already gnawed at him.

He was recognized by several doctors and nurses who had momentarily stopped in their tracks to catch their breath and who insisted on thanking him profusely for his efforts to help the island and for trying his best to rein in what many had come to understand was an accident waiting to happen. Above, the skies were filled with the sound of jet engines as supplies and medical teams arrived and the empty planes then took off.

Jessica had been given a bed at the far end of a ward. She had numerous cuts and bruises, but was otherwise all right. She was sitting up writing notes on a small pad, trying not to be overwhelmed by what surrounded her. Kevin walked over with a smile, and sat down beside her.

"Oh, I'm so happy to see you," she said, tears filling her eyes.

"How are you doing?" he asked.

She shook her head. "Kev, I just want to thank you for everything."

He waved his hands around. "For this?"

"No," she said, trying to smile, "you know what I mean. I just can't believe how things happen in this life. I know I wouldn't have been able to handle all this a week ago. Was it only last Monday that I was hounding you guys back in Princeton?"

"Yeah," he said. "I think there's a book in it. Jess, I'm so sorry. This one is just beyond me. How are you holding up?"

"I'm okay. I mean, my God, I count my blessings. It all happened so fast. But I'm going to have to call my office and renegotiate my contract. I didn't figure in combat pay. And thank you, for trying to save us. You're on my Christmas list from now on."

"Thanks," he said wryly, "but I already have enough fruitcakes in my life."

She laughed and gave him a playful smack.

Kevin couldn't believe how differently he felt toward the upstart journalist. A week earlier, he would have been perfectly willing to step over her had she been lying on the walk. She was now a friend.

"Do you believe this?" she asked.

"No. I can't make sense of it. But I think sense *can* be made of it. Does that make sense?"

"Yeah," she smiled. "In a weird way, it's the only thing around here that does. I talked with my editor earlier. When I get out, looks like I've got a lot of work to do. A story like this comes along once in a lifetime, so I have to cover it. It's funny though. I don't feel the fire in the belly to be first, even though I already am. It's just not all that important anymore. It's more like I know it's something I have to do. And I think I just might want to write instead."

"And you and Sharon look like you hit it off in a way. Go figure. Wouldn't have had a number on that one a week ago either."

"I know. But yeah, we'll probably keep in touch. I'd like to be able to with you as well."

"Yeah, that'd be nice. And if you want an exclusive, feel free."

"Thanks," she smiled. "I appreciate that."

"You know why I offered?"

"Because I didn't ask." He smiled, and she admitted, "I just didn't think about it right away. But I do appreciate it."

"Jess, listen. I'm meeting Hanford at ten thirty. I want you to be there. It concerns you."

"Okay. Is there something I need to know or worry about?"

"No, but you do need to be there. I'm asking you to trust me, okay?"

"Okay. You've been fair with me, and I appreciate that as well. Just let me know where."

"All right, good." He got up, hesitated, then gave her a kiss on her cheek.

Jessica beamed. "I think you lucked out with Cindy," she added. "Is she coming back to Princeton with you?"

"I think so, if she wants. She has nothing here. Lot's of changes in my life; all of ours."

She took his hand and warmly said, "Kevin, all the best then."

"Thanks; I appreciate it, really. You make sure you're there at ten thirty, okay?"

He kissed her again and left the ward.

Kevin made his way past the crush of patients and gurneys to the hall where he had spent the night and saw Jack and Mike.

"All set?" he asked.

"Yeah," Raden said. "We confirmed with the president. He wanted to see you himself, but was curious as to why you wanted to meet with him."

"Yeah, well let him stew." A moment later, he saw Peter Natano exiting a room. They locked eyes, and Kevin held up his finger to tell him to wait. "Let me go talk to Pete. I'll see you in a few." He looked around. "I hate hospitals," he sighed.

Kevin skirted the doctors and nurses rushing about, not wanting to get in the way, thinking that if he never saw another hospital the rest of his life it would suit him just fine. He thought of Max and how he'd already had his fill of IVs and white linen earlier in the week.

As he reached Natano he could see how shattered the man was. The self-assured security chief he had met just days ago now seemed shrunken, a wreck. He still wore yesterday's uniform. Finally dry, it hung tired. Although obviously fatigued, Natano still held a curious and determined air that reminded Kevin of an expectant father.

"I guess we're meeting your president in a few," Natano told Kevin. "What do you have to say to him?"

Kevin eyed him, trying to summon up a response. But as he stared, he saw something.

"Come on." He pressed Natano back into the office, then turned and locked the door.

"What's that about?" Natano asked.

Kevin continued to lock eyes with him. "Okay," he said resolutely, "let's have it."

"What?"

"Pete, I'm going to ask you nice. I want it. And don't make me take it."

Natano pulled back. "Just who are you to come to my country and—"

"Pete, we don't have time for this. I know how you feel—"

"No you *don't!*"

"I know you think he's responsible for vaporizing one ninth of your country—"

"Well if you understand that—"

"But this isn't the way to handle it. I'm asking you to trust me. Let me work it out."

"Kevin, my reservoir of trust is empty. Gone, dried up."

"Then you have to trust yourself. You have to hang in and keep it together for your people, now more than ever, because they need you and this isn't the way to take care of them. Now give it to me and it'll go no further."

"I did not want this!" Natano's eyes watered as he spoke through clenched teeth. "I did everything I could to stop it! Twenty thousand souls on me! Know what that's like?"

"I know. It's not your fault. But you can't lose it now, understand? Now give it to me."

Natano took several deep breaths, then reached into his pants pocket and took out the plastic gun confiscated from Ron Sanderson just a day earlier. The thoroughly clean surface of the weapon stood in stark contrast to the disheveled law enforcement officer carrying it. Natano stared at it as he slowly handed it to Kevin.

Kevin took out the ammunition, then walked over to the small bathroom connected to the office and smashed the weapon into the sink several times until it broke. He took the pieces, wrapped them in paper towels and dropped them into the garbage can.

"Now let's go meet Hanford," Kevin said. Natano stared at his friend, then closed his eyes as his anger faded. He took another deep breath, nodded okay, and they left the room.

One hundred sixteen

Not having been built for the calamity in which it found itself, Princess Margaret Hospital had only one conference room suitable for the meeting Kevin wanted. Elliot Hanford had monopolized it from the time he arrived. He'd spent the night there, and had been on the phone from the moment he awoke at six. Scraped up and sporting a patchwork of bandages, he'd been released that morning, partly due to his satisfactory condition but mostly as a result of the tremendous need for rooms and beds for patients in much worse shape. The clothes he wore were the result of an American consulate worker's predawn scamper through the streets of Funafuti. Working with a skeleton crew he'd managed to set up communications to Washington.

The accident had completely undone the Administration's political narrative. Taking its place was damage control but true to form Hanford had shaped it to his favor. By the time word of the disaster crossed the globe and the media began descending a working story had emerged. The White House spin machine was now in full effect.

The White House couldn't ignore the catastrophe caused by Deneb. The idea was to turn it around. The president who'd lobbied the world to place its nuclear fears on pause now exhorted it to presume something different. The new narrative was that the goal had all along been noble: a world free from fear of a nuclear holocaust. The White House likened his initiative to the oft-quoted commencement address given by President John Kennedy in June 1963 at American University. Kennedy had laid out a vision of peace that humanized an enemy, saying, "In the final analysis, our most basic common link is that we all inhabit this small planet. We all breathe the same air. We all cherish our children's futures. And we are all mortal."

The accident became validation of the approach and made it no less moral. In a world where scientists threw out insane ideas without an ounce of ownership for what others did with them and the Pentagon took those spinoffs to ever more absurd heights, accidents were bound to happen. Science and the military had lied to him, and to the world. The president had barely escaped with his life. It was a testament to his leadership that he had shepherded the absurdity along without something even worse having happened.

Hanford was completely comfortable with the strategy. It met his political needs by changing the subject and focus of the disaster and plausibly shifting the blame. More than that, it fed his personal outrage. It wasn't his fault. It was no more complicated than that.

The developments took on a life of their own. In Honolulu, the late lieutenant governor of Hawaii was being cast in a sinister light. His recklessness and bribe-taking had led to a horrific disaster, aided by a faulty design furthered by a group of ambitious and amoral scientists. For his heroism, Dr. Kevin Herter was spared some of the retribution directed toward the scientific community, but stateside, the weekend talk shows were already lining up with Administration spokespersons primed to lace into a group whose arrogance and elitism had created yet another technological debacle, and who seemed cut off from any kind of ownership for their part in it.

In Washington, the DIA memo was being cast in light of a rogue element of the Pentagon. The late General Tyson had run away with his paranoia. Administration spokespersons were racing to denounce the former DIA head, a task made much easier since he was no longer around to defend himself.

It was almost ten thirty as Kevin and Peter Natano made their way through the frenzy of activity in the hospital, unaware of the developing story. Natano was quiet but just before turning into the hallway, he stopped Kevin.

"I want to thank you," he said.

"Don't mention it. I don't know how I managed to keep it together myself this week."

"No, I need to. That's not me." He paused. "How did you know?"

Kevin managed a weak smile, and lifted his hands in a silent, "I don't know."

"Well, I'm glad you snapped me out of it. It's what I needed. Thanks again. You'll always be welcome here. I live five blocks from here, and my wife is the best cook on the island."

"Thanks," Kevin laughed, "but why haven't you gone home to change?"

"I haven't even thought about it," Natano said, shaking his head. "I usually get back weekends, so she's seen enough of me stopping by with laundry."

Kevin smiled again, and then moved on towards the conference room.

The Secret Service contingent so visible on Vaitupu was nowhere to be seen. A plane-load of agents was set to arrive, but for now, the president was being guarded by a lone Tuvaluan policeman who was not particularly happy to be protecting the person widely believed responsible for the accident. He greeted Natano and Kevin with a lot more enthusiasm than he'd greeted Hanford. Jack Raden, Mike Yahr and Roger Braddock were standing in the hall.

"I'm not sure how happy he's going to be to see you," Raden told Kevin.

"Why? I thought he wanted to meet."

"On his terms; if he summons you. When the shoe's on the other foot, all bets are off."

"Too damn bad."

"Have you thought about what you're going to say to him?" Mike asked.

"I've been wondering the same thing," Raden and Braddock said, almost simultaneously.

Kevin shook his head no. Just then, Sharon and Cindy appeared from around a bend. "You ready?" he asked.

"Oh yeah," Sharon said.

She grabbed him by the arm and pulled him close. "What are you going to say?"

"Just enjoy the moment," he said with a tired smile. "Enjoy the moment."

Elliot Hanford was alone at the large conference room table, which was already set up with several computer terminals and a coffee maker. The large windows let in gray light from the thermonuclear cloud. The policeman ushered them in. Hanford was just hanging up the phone.

The president stood slowly and extended his hand. "Whatever our differences," he said, "I want to thank you again." Kevin smiled.

As everyone took a seat, Kevin went over to the coffee maker. "I really need this," he admitted. He gingerly poured himself a coffee. The Styrofoam cup was thin, a bit too pliable, calling for a delicate touch lest it collapse on itself.

"Doctor," Hanford began, warily eyeing the others, "I don't mind speaking with you but all due respect, I'm not discussing anything with an audience."

"Mr. President, consider them my cabinet. Jack, Mike and Roger are my intelligence team while Cindy is my science advisor. No one here knew the program better." He turned to Sharon. "And Sharon's my chief counsel." They all smiled as he took a seat.

"All right," Hanford grumbled. "I trust you to be on your best behavior," he said to Sharon.

"Me? Always." Cindy, sitting next to her, suppressed a grin.

"Fine," Hanford said curtly.

A knock at the door heralded Jessica Enright's entrance.

"I'm sorry," she said, moving carefully as she sat herself next to Raden. "I got held up."

"Okay, Doctor," Hanford began, "there are a number of things to go over." He turned to Natano. "First, I want to say to you as the unofficial representative of your country that we're going to do everything in our power to get to the bottom of what happened, and make sure your nation is as well-taken care of as possible."

Natano responded with silence, and slowly turned to Kevin.

"That all right?" Kevin asked.

"Doctor," Hanford said, seemingly taken back, "I told you last night and it bears repeating now—this cannot be allowed to happen again. A lot's going to change when we get back. I'm expecting things from you, and I don't want any problems. When I told you to consider yourself drafted, it might have sounded amusing but I'm very serious. This was a wake-up call. I take my responsibilities even more seriously now than before."

"Mr. President, you may consider me drafted but I think of myself as a conscientious objector. I've had enough."

Just then, the door burst open. Five Secret Service agents, including Gerald Knight rushed in. Hanford stood to greet them as the others tensed, especially Mike Yahr, who recognized better than any a show of force when he saw one.

Hanford turned to Kevin. "Doctor," he said sternly, "I appreciate your position, but the thing you need to understand about being drafted is that you have no choice."

Kevin looked around the table. The others all had the look of passengers on a train not wanting to be first to point out an unattended bag.

"Mr. President, will you please ask your agents to wait outside?" he said after a pause.

"Excuse me?" asked Hanford, impertinently.

"Mr. President, we were stuck on a roof with you half the night after surviving a hydrogen bomb. And this is the island's chief of security. We weren't a threat to you then, and we're not one now. Agent Knight is fine, but frankly we can do without the bravado."

Hanford frowned before nodding at the security contingent to indicate that he was okay with them leaving. Knight conferred quickly with them, then took a position behind the president as the other agents walked out.

"Okay," Kevin said, "thank you."

"All right, Doctor," Hanford said. "What do you want to see me about?"

"You know, I really hate meetings," Kevin said, taking a sip of coffee. "I have to wonder just what they accomplish. I've had a barrage of them this week, and with everyone I've had there was an attempt on my life." He shrugged, "I wonder if they're related."

"Doctor," Hanford responded, ignoring Kevin's comment, "we have a lot of important things to discuss. And I believe you had something you wanted to tell me yesterday, right before all this happened."

"I'll get to it. It occurred to me on my way here that every time I went to meet with you this week, I was thinking about what I would say when I got there. It seemed important at the time. But it's funny; this morning, I didn't give it much thought. *That* I find interesting."

Hanford stared, and then shuffled some papers on the table. "And your point?"

"There's a little story that bears mention. In physics, we have our own afterglow, what we call cosmic background radiation. It's the energy left over after the universe was created by the Big Bang thirteen and a half billion years ago. It's spread out so much and become so diffused, it's barely detectable."

"I've heard of that," Jessica said.

"You're not going to give us one of your lectures, are you?" Hanford complained.

"Nope." Kevin caught Sharon rolling her eyes. "But, there's a lesson to it. See, you can't even imagine an event that powerful. No one can. People today don't think about it. We just live with the residuals, what it left. Out of sight, out of mind."

"And your point?"

"Point is, when things get that diffused people forget what got it started, even when it's something incredibly powerful. Just yesterday morning you pointed to that cloud and asked what to do about it. How it got started wasn't even on your radar."

"Okay, but that's ancient history now."

"Just let him talk," Sharon sniped.

"You did a good job cleaning these things up," Kevin went on. "So much that you polished your heavy metal into Muzak. In the process, you lost sight of what started it all. You lost respect for it. Well, it reminded you."

"That's too abstract for me," Hanford responded. "Something went horribly wrong somewhere."

"I don't think that's what happened. I think there's something else at work."

"And what's that?"

"Back in the '50s, people watched these things with the same oohs and aahs they made here. A few times, they ran into problems as well; the bombs went off bigger than expected. People then were terrified too. But that's because they didn't know what to expect. That's why they tested. That's why they *called* them tests. But this is supposed to be an established technology. These things aren't called tests. They're called events. They're staged. They have audiences and admission charges. The fear is gone, at least it was until last night. But not for us. All of us here, Pete, Cindy, the rest of us, we were all still afraid about what could happen. And what we were afraid could happen is what did happen. But it occurred to me, that's not what was going on with you."

Hanford's disgust was thinly-veiled. "And what the hell was that?"

"I realized this morning—we've had different goals. All of us had one goal—make sure the things were safe and nothing happened. But your goal was different. Your goal was make sure no one found out not just what you were trying to hide but that you were *trying* to hide it."

"Doctor," Hanford sneered, "I have no time for this."

"Well, make the time. The point is that it all came down to fear. See, I made a mistake. I thought that for you the fear was gone, that you weren't afraid of these things. But we're all afraid of something. It's not that you weren't afraid of *anything*, it's that you were afraid of *different* things. Fear is a very powerful motivator. Trust me; it's something I've learned a lot about the past few days. You fear different things, you set different goals. I thought we were all working toward the same goal. But we weren't. Because all along, we had different fears."

"And what the hell was that?"

"Simple. We were afraid of the thing itself. But you were afraid people might learn you were afraid. What's the old adage—it's not the crime that gets you, it's the cover-up."

"Oh, *bull!*"

"No," Sharon said resolutely, "that's it."

"That memo you were so hot and bothered over," Kevin continued, "a person might be a little afraid about blowing up the whole Middle East. I would. But not you. You guys were less afraid it might happen than people finding out that you thought about it. This whole place came about because someone was afraid somebody else would find something out."

"You pretty much just described the whole Cold War," Roger Braddock said.

"Oh, another fucking historian," Hanford groaned.

Braddock snorted out a laugh, and Kevin added, "Everything connected to this came down to someone being scared and putting up some kind of red herring to keep from dealing with it. And after time, even the red herrings had red herrings. Amazing." He turned to Raden, who nodded.

"Doctor, all of you, just grow up," Hanford said, exasperated. "Or if you don't want to, leave these decisions to people who already are."

"You know, you've got some balls," Sharon began.

"Just hold it," Kevin said. "We're not going there."

"I would like to know what the president has to offer in the way of an explanation if this doesn't cut it for him," Natano said, leaning forward. "Because my people are already demanding answers, sir, and so far, I've heard nothing from you but platitudes."

"Pete, hold that thought," Kevin said, rubbing his ear again. It still bothered him. "Jack can tell everyone how I promised myself a week ago I wouldn't get caught up in the bull. But I still did. It's hard to avoid. Mr. President, I give you a lot of credit. I guess that's why this place was so successful. The other night before the blast, Jack made a comment to us. I don't know if he knew I noticed, but I did. He said we should get ready for a whole different scale of what we took as entertainment. Well, I sure as hell have. This is an entertainment experience on a scale never imagined. And like everything like that, people thought they knew what they were in for, but they didn't. They thought they could handle it, at least until it blew up in their faces."

Raden smiled and nodded yes.

"Well, congratulations Doctor," Hanford said. "I'm glad you think you've become enlightened. You don't know the kind of trouble you set the world up for." He pointed to Jessica. "You ask the reporter here the things people will do to get ahead. You don't know what I've seen, the things people do. She'll tell you. Not like in your ivory towers back in

Princeton. They'll step on you, trip you, stab you in the back, screw you, anything you can imagine and all the while smile to your face and tell you you're their best friend. I see it every day. Now add these monstrosities to the mix. I shudder to think where we're headed. So, congratulations. Thanks to you, now the skids are greased for what happened here to happen everywhere."

"I'm not taking ownership for that anymore. Whatever you may think of me, my bottom line is that I'm a scientist. I'm not a politician. I'm not a Democrat or a Republican. I'm not liberal or conservative; I'm not a communist, a socialist, nor am I whatever the opposite of those things are. And, I'm not a hawk and I'm not a dove. I'm not even a pacifist. I don't think about those things. I'm just a scientist, which means I'm a realist. All I can do is deal with things the way they are. I'm not used to this crap. My mind doesn't work this way—this spook trying to outspook that spook, all the spooks outspooking each other. All these people congratulating themselves on their ingenuity in having gotten themselves out of messes I wouldn't have even thought to get into in the first place. Keeping secrets from other people who are going to find them out on their own, regardless. It's not secrets, it's physics. But you guys don't want to deal with that. I try thinking like that and my head hurts. I don't get it but you know what? I don't want to. I'm tired. When I think about what happened here, I have to cry. Tomorrow I'm heading back to California. I've got personal business there, and then I'm just going back to Princeton to work, and that's it."

"And what the hell's that supposed to mean? I thought we already covered that."

"We haven't even begun. I feel like I've aged a year this past week. I'm done. I'm not mad, not like some people here are going to be, believe me. I'm not the one who has explaining to do. I'm just tired. And hey, I can't prove any of this. It's just my conjecture. But it did occur to me just how much time I've spent over the past week dealing with people who didn't want to deal with reality. So on that subject, there's a few things I need to finish up with before I go."

One hundred seventeen

Kevin eyed Hanford, and knew without doubt that he was stripped bare of any pretense. Without the buffer of staff or protocol, he had the same look he'd had when Sanderson railed against him in the moments before the bomb went off. He felt no pity for the president, as he felt that here was someone who was at long last getting a full measure of comeuppance.

"Mr. President," he went on, "there was something I was set to tell you last night, before the you-know-what hit the fan. He breathed in deeply, and shifted in his seat. "Yesterday afternoon, Miss Enright and her crew taped a statement I made. It's already been sent to several individuals around the world, with instructions as to its dispensation. In it, I laid out the events leading to my declaration and the reasons for making it."

"And what was that?"

"I gave a detailed history of the program here, and my experience with it."

"*What?*" Hanford lurched forward. "You did *what?*"

"I described the program here. I explained how it was based on my work, and how that work has led to a concerted and covert effort to create a new class of thermonuclear weapons that detonate without residual radiation. I announced that the United States Defense Department has been perfecting this weapon system by using the recreational component here as a cover, in effect a testing program for hydrogen bombs hiding in plain sight of the world. I laid out a detailed history of the kickbacks, and the mopping up exercises that have been going on trying to keep the secret. I also announced the existence of the memo from General Tyson—"

"Are you out of your fucking mind?"

"—and how that memo morphed into the recreational program here. I also announced that as discoverer of the theory underlying the technology it is my intention it never be weaponized."

"Doctor," Hanford blasted, glaring at everyone in the room, "forget opening Pandora's Box, you just opened the door to a lifetime of Federal charges. You think what happened to that fool Edward Snowden is anything? I swear, by the time the FBI is done with you, you'll be facing espionage charges! You don't know what's about to hit you!"

Sharon snapped, "Oh, for fucking out loud—"

"I've heard about enough from you!" Hanford hissed at Sharon.

"Well," Kevin went on, "after the disaster last night, it turns out it's less dramatic than I was hoping for. Partly, I had talked about how it's my desire that the program continue without interruption, provided the necessary modifications were made to stabilize the technology. I also stated that it was my wish none of this information as laid out in my statement or the statement itself ever be made public, provided my suggested course of action proceed."

As Hanford continued to sputter in exasperation, Kevin added, "I also stated that should there be any deviation in this, as measured or indicated by a subsequent developmental program by the DOD, or more ominously, should *anything* happen of a nefarious nature to me or more importantly to any of the principals involved in the making or distribution of the statement it was my wish that my statement and the information it contains be made fully available by the remaining principals to the media for worldwide dissemination. Now, at the time, it seemed like a worthwhile course of action. But considering what happened last night, I'm not sure it'll carry any real weight."

"Doctor, I don't care! That is completely unacceptable."

"Mr. President, that is reality. I basically just told the truth. It's done."

Hanford stared off, and then looked back. "How dare you even *think* about doing something like that, let alone going ahead and doing it? Where do you come off even—"

"Just hold it, Mr. President. Time we were straight with each other. I wasn't sent out here to consult or run this thing, and I damn well didn't set out to be a whistleblower. I was sent out as a fall guy. The thing works, you claim victory by shepherding a potential disaster into a roaring success and for the good sense to send out the guy who invented it and knows how it works. If it blows up in your face, you have *my* face to hang it on. I invented it; it's my fault. It's a win/win for you. This is April in an election year. I wouldn't have been out here last year, or next year. I should be pissed. You sent me out here to solve a problem you never wanted fixed, and then put all kinds of stumbling blocks in my way to trip me up when I tried to do it, including sitting on your hands when you knew some of the people involved were looking to knock me off.

I should be taking it personally. That I'm not is something you should consider an asset. But hey, go figure, it *did* blow up in your face."

"You know, we could hunt down what you sent out and destroy it and liquidate everyone involved before they even knew what hit them." Hanford began shaking his head.

"I know that. But there's the chance you wouldn't get them all. Someone's going to download it on a memory card and bury it in a flowerpot somewhere, and you'll never find it. And, I have some good friends in the NSA now who know all about how to hide things."

"By the way," Raden cut in. "FYI. One of your statements has been released."

"What?" Hanford nearly screamed as the others sat back astonished.

"Oh, you're kidding!" Kevin said. "Who let it out?"

"I don't know. After last night, someone—I don't know who yet—wanted the word to get out that you had serious misgivings about the program before the accident."

"Son of a bitch!" Hanford smacked the table. "I swear Doctor, you don't know the can of worms you opened! And you don't know the trouble you've made for yourself!"

"It hit the news within the past hour," Raden said. He added to Kevin, "Word is that every reporter in the states is angling to get on the air with you. Mr. President, you should know that before you set out to do anything, Dr. Herter's reputation is about as high as a person's can get right now. So just keep that in mind."

"Well Jess," Kevin shrugged, shaking his head in an awkward laugh, "there's your exclusive." She smiled as she'd heard the news just before she came in.

"People are seeing that he warned against it," Raden said. "Back in the states, it's as much of a story as the accident. He's probably the only person connected to this now that doesn't have an ulterior motive, and people realize that. The thing about Edward Snowden that people got pissed off at is that he let on to secrets that weren't his. All this comes from Kevin's work. He didn't talk about anything other than what was done with his own sweat and blood. And on top of that, he didn't spill any beans about the technology; telling our adversaries how to build the things." He turned to Kevin. "If you poke your head out of here now you're going to get swamped, so just prepare yourself."

"Oh, crap," Kevin said. "I hate that."

"I don't give a fuck about that!" yelled a livid Hanford as he rose to go. "You're done!"

"Uh, Mr. President," Kevin added, "sit down. There's more." He reached into his pocket and took out three small memory cards. He went around the table, placing one in front of Peter Natano and Jessica Enright, and paused as he stopped in front of Elliot Hanford, putting one down on the table beside him before returning to his seat.

"I apologize, but I felt this was the best way to handle this," he told Natano and Jessica.

"What is this?" Hanford said, knowing full well what he held.

"These are copies of the footage Erik Lundquist took last night. Jess, I'm sorry—yours is the original, but I had to make copies. I hope you'll understand."

"This is it? The footage before the explosion?" Natano's expression changed abruptly as Kevin nodded, and he smiled broadly before glaring at Hanford.

The president sat shocked. He looked about before turning to Gerald Knight. "I don't fucking believe it," he said.

"Believe it," Kevin said. "And so you know, this also was emailed out. So even if Agent Knight here lets loose on all of us and takes the copies, it's out there."

Hanford began visibly shaking. "Doctor, what the fuck do you want? Why do this?"

"Mr. President, you may not believe me, but I don't hold any animosity toward you." He looked at the others, before taking a deep breath and continuing.

"I've seen things this week that I never in a million years would have expected to see. I have no room in my heart for revenge, or getting even with you or anybody else. I've made my peace. When I go home, it's with a clear head and conscience. I don't know why this happened; no, let me rephrase that. I know exactly *why* it happened. I just don't know what kind of meaning we're all going to take from it. Yesterday was a very long day. I don't ever wish to have another one like it as long as I live. But all of you have a choice now. Pete, this will help you gain some measure of justice for your people. You shouldn't have to go through any legal or bureaucratic red tape to move ahead. I've seen the footage; it's as plain as day what Sanderson did."

"And Jess, I'm sorry I didn't tip you off, but for once, I was taking care of things for myself. One thing I've learned this week has been that if I don't watch my back, no one will. So, you have one hell of an exclusive. It's yours. I recognize that there are First Amendment issues, but I don't think they carry much weight out here. So while it's technically your network's card, others need it to cover themselves. I took it upon myself to make that decision. My apologies."

She studied the card, then looked up. "You're forgiven," she said with a wink. "I can stand being knocked down a notch." Sharon reached over and patted her hand and she blushed.

Kevin then took a deep breath and turned to Hanford. "And, Mr. President." He shook his head. "What can I say? I learned from the best—"

"Don't even bother," Hanford said.

"I don't know how to say this any other way, but for crying out loud, this is all you understand. Funny thing about reality; sooner or later, you gotta deal with it. It's real. Problem with avoiding it is that it magnifies proportionally to the degree it's being evaded. Sooner or later, we all have to deal with the reality we create. Might as well start now."

"Oh, and how is that? By blackmailing me? By blackmailing the office of the president and the entire government? "

"I'm not blackmailing anybody. I expect nothing in return. All I'm doing is putting reality out there and telling people to deal with it. I could say you guys got yourselves into this, and I'm just trying to clean it up. And you did. But I really don't care." He sighed. "You know, you spend so much time getting used to things being stuck and not resolving themselves, it becomes a lifestyle. Maybe clearing the air and introducing a little resolution to the situation is what you need. I know it scares the Dickens out of you but that just shows how out of whack things have gotten. Instability is stability; MAD is security. People might be ready for a little honesty. I've seen the footage. I don't envy you, but you don't come across the same way Sanderson did, for instance. And I know the problems you face aren't easy but frankly I'm tired of getting blamed for them. You have to figure out a better way to deal with it. You might want to try just being honest with people. Act like an adult. Take it out and test drive it a little. Might be surprised." He rubbed his eyes. "I don't know what to say anymore. I tried to make some sense of this, but I give up. You can't. And I realize that was the point. I think you got out of it what you put into it. A lot of confusion, wasted time and resources, and things guaranteed to blow up in your face. I just want to head back home and go back to work."

"You may think you're sinking me, but you may be surprised. Suppose people see this and decide it was an honest effort? What if they think we had their best intentions at heart? You're going to look like some kind of Cassandra. I don't envy you."

"So be it," Kevin shrugged. "People will figure it out."

"Great. Doctor, you're a fucking nightmare."

"Hey, again, so be it. It's simple. You do what's right, and let things take their own course. You just do what you know should be done. I mean, for crying out loud, what's the alternative? What are you defending? You think everyone is going to want these things? They'll only want them if they think the guy down the block builds them as well. And fifty years from now and twenty trillion dollars later, people will be sitting around having blown up fifty cities and a hundred million people and saying, 'Oh, if we only could do it over again'. The only ones who don't ever seem to get it is you guys. You do what you should and people will see. And they'll cut you some slack."

"Actually Mr. President, that *is* just what happened during the Cold War," Braddock said.

"And you think doing what the Doctor here did is the way to do it?"

"Actually, yes. The people who get the message are people who think the same way I do. They have as much incentive to follow through as anyone. You try to outwit the Law of Unintended Consequences and it can catch up with you in ways you never figured, which is precisely the meaning of the law and why you can't outrun it."

"I guess that remains to be seen," Kevin added with a smile. "But I thought you would say something like that. I remember an old saying, Mr. President, about diplomats. Someone once said that when a diplomat says yes, he means maybe. And when he says maybe, he means no. And when he says no, he's no diplomat. Anyway, I came here as a scientist. But in the little time I've spent here, I've come to learn we're all diplomats. We all have eggshells we tiptoe over. I really don't know what's going to come from this.

"In all honesty it doesn't matter. Do you think I really want to be here telling you this? Until now, I've avoided this like the plague. You know that. I hadn't thought about it, but Roger is right. If you build these things, you defeat your purpose, which is to keep the secret you could do it. Hell of a paradox, huh? The only way for it to work is if it doesn't get built. That's what happened at the end of World War II. It wasn't that they built the bomb. It's that they used it. The secret was out, and they couldn't unring the bell.

"What did it take for them to finally realize they couldn't use the things? It's a ridiculous question. They always knew it. They just had to be dragged kicking and screaming to doing something about it, to cut back on the things. Well, whatever it cost back then, today, just increase it by a factor of a hundred. Some people still haven't got it. They still want to use them. You know that. All that money, all those missiles and bombs, and all of them knew they could never use the things. I know the politics behind it and that in a way it made sense. I'm just saying they knew it as well, but they couldn't get out of it. Forget what else could have been done with that money, but you get the point. I guess that's something about human nature. We all loved watching the things. People just don't know when to quit."

Hanford frowned and Kevin added, "I'd make a lousy politician. I think of things like this and my head pounds. I don't know geopolitical garbage. I don't have time for it. I do know what I saw last night. I couldn't live with myself knowing I had a chance to stop it from happening again and didn't try. I don't know if any of what I've done will work. I do know doing things the other way led to this. I only have one goal; that's to be able to sleep at night. Unfortunately, I've had to accept that half of the world, no matter what they do, sleeps a hell of a lot better than I do. I know that once these things get used, every little piss-ass conflict is going to end with this country or that dropping them like confetti. At least with Mutually Assured Destruction you knew your opponent wouldn't launch a first strike because he'd wind up killing himself as well. You don't have that with these things. They're clean. I wonder if they had to do a forty-year Cold War over again, knowing what followed, whether they would have gone the same route after all. I guess we'll never know. That's for people smarter than me to figure out." He paused and sighed. "I know this sounds like a lecture, but to tell you the truth, I hate this moralizing crap. I'd rather just be left alone to work. I just hope you see it for that."

"Fine," snapped the president. "Then you tell me just what the hell I'm supposed to do?"

"I really don't know. I don't even think it's idealism. It's just practical. I hate pissing contests, and I'm learning that the best way to deal with them is not to unzip your fly."

"Well, Herter, seems you've tied our hands. You'll forgive me if I don't thank you now."

"I can understand that, Mr. President."

"Oh, cut the patronizing crap. You understand shit. Use your brains. One thing people understand is the atom. You know what's going to happen. And I'll tell you something else. People complain about politicians not being up front with them, but do the honesty thing, and they label you as being weak and naïve. You just watch and see what happens." He snorted in resentment. "I just hope you think this was worth it, and it works out the way you want. Unfortunately, I've learned nothing in life does." He rose. "You'll forgive me if I don't shake hands with anyone. I have a hell of a lot of work to do to dig out of the mess you people left me with." With that, Hanford took the memory card and some of his notes and headed for the door, followed by Knight.

One hundred eighteen

"So," Kevin asked Sharon, "what did you think of your experience talking to the president of the United States?" She stuck her finger in her mouth and let out a gag. As they laughed, he added, "I don't know if it was the right thing to do. But right now, I feel okay."

"I have a feeling people are going to be talking about this for a long time to come," Cindy said with a sigh.

"It's not denial," Raden said. "He'll never give an inch by admitting he blew it. He's lived the lie so long, I'm not sure even he knows where it ends and the truth begins."

"I know what you're saying," Kevin agreed.

"And don't worry about the Snowden episode. You didn't steal anything classified. All you did was to basically share your diary. He can't go after you for that."

"I have to admit, there aren't any clean choices, any good roads to take. They all come with a price."

"I never knew how much you had to weigh," Sharon said with a sigh. "I mean, being in your position. I guess it's easy for someone on the outside to get into a long philosophical jag about how you should do this or that, but I have to admit living it was different. Maybe I needed to see that instead of being so critical for so long."

"Shar," Kevin smiled, "thanks. I appreciate that."

Sharon gazed around the table. "I do think he's a piece of work. He just doesn't get it."

Natano stood, and walked over to Kevin. "I want to thank you in more ways than one, my friend. And in ways that I'll never be able to repay." As Kevin smiled, his eyes barely hiding the tears he felt, Natano stood almost embarrassed, rubbing the little card in his hand.

"I need to go," he said softly. "I have a lot of work ahead of me, including checking in with my wife. I would like to have you over for dinner this evening, all of you in fact. I don't think we're going to be doing anything formal here for some time to come, but I would consider it an honor. Is that okay?"

Kevin smiled, and the two men embraced. Natano said goodbye to everyone, and left.

"I feel for him," Cindy said. "I've worked with him for two years. He's a great guy."

"I know," Kevin said. "I just know him a week, and my heart goes out to him."

"I don't know if he knows what he's in for," Braddock said. "He's going to have to try and reform some semblance of government here. So many of the leaders here were killed that they'll have to make it up as they go along, and he's right in the middle of it. He's going to go from being a chief of police to being something like acting prime minister, overnight."

"And dealing with the shock of having been there when it happened," Mike said. "He's got to be shouldering a lot of guilt."

"Why should he feel guilty?" Sharon asked. "I'd be pissed more than anything."

"Because he lived," Raden said. "And so many others died." They all shook their heads in silence, not knowing what else to add.

Jessica stood, and walked up to Kevin. "I need to go myself," she said quietly. "I have just as much work ahead of me as Pete does." She warmly embraced him. "I want to thank you as well," she added, "in fact, all of you."

"Been quite a week," he smiled. "Quite a story."

"That it has." She gave him another hug, and then went around saying goodbye to the others. When she got to Mike, she said, "I want to thank you especially. You tell your wife for me—"

"Tell her yourself. She promised me to tell you that you have a standing invite to come back for coffee and muffins anytime you want."

"That I'll definitely do!" she laughed.

Jessica saved her last embrace for Sharon. "Earlier this week, if you told me that I would be doing this—"

"No girl, if you told *me*." Sharon gave her a hug, and said, "You keep in touch, okay?"

Jessica smiled warmly. "I would like that a great deal," she said. She wiped a tear from her eye, and added, "I guess I'll see everyone a little later, huh?"

Kevin said, "Jess, thanks. To a reporter, parsing is such sweet sorrow."

"I bet you've been saving that one up all week," she laughed and walked out.

Kevin rubbed his ear, and sat back down. Raden sat down beside him, and everyone took a seat again.

"So tell me," Kevin asked, looking at Raden. "You think he survives this?"

"Can't say." His voice was hesitant, though no one noticed.

"He's finished," Braddock said. "I'd lay odds of no more than forty percent."

"It might be enough," Mike said. "He made his mark by distracting people. Depends how much they still *want* to be distracted. It's just gotta play itself out." The other two agreed.

"I can't believe you're such a cynic too," Sharon said.

"A cynic is just a realist earlier in the morning," he smiled. "Before the coffee kicks in."

"Yeah, I forgot," she quipped, "I've driven with you." He laughed.

"And what about you?" Braddock asked Kevin.

"What," Sharon asked, "you think they'll still try and take Kevin out?"

"Well," Raden said, "sixty years ago they went after Oppenheimer for not supporting the hydrogen bomb. They crucified him, and it was all a sham. He had no idea what hit him, because he had no idea how they worked. If there's one thing you've learned the past week, it's that. I have a feeling you're going to come out of this a lot better than he did."

"I hope so," Cindy said.

Kevin smiled at her. "You gonna do me the honor of being my date tonight?"

"Yeah, but don't get any ideas, buster. Remember, I'm not some cheap arm candy."

"Toldja," Sharon added.

"Oh, don't you start," Kevin said.

Sharon grinned and was about to say something when Raden said, "Actually, Kevin here may be the only one who comes out of this in a stronger position than when he went in."

"That's a good point," Braddock said. "There are people on our end who are going to sit back and congratulate you, who'll think it was masterful." Mike nodded in agreement.

"Are you for real?" Sharon asked.

"I need to hear this one myself," Cindy said.

"It's simple," Raden said. "Who do you think tried to set you up?"

Kevin looked at him like he was crazy. "What, are you kidding? The

White House, the Pentagon, you name it."

"Okay. And where's Hanford today? A wounded president who's lucky if he survives the weekend. The Pentagon? With more trouble than they'll be able to sort out in the next ten years. The Hawaiian Statehouse? More egg on their face than they know what to do with. And you? A week ago, you were a brilliant scientist with a reputation as a reserved pain in the rear. Today, you're a brilliant scientist with a reputation as one of the world's most enlightened humanitarian, scientific, and social thinkers who saved the president who would have been happy to see him whacked. Now, I know it wasn't intentional on your part but believe me, there are plenty of people in our field right now thinking you couldn't have designed it any better."

"Oh, for crying out loud," Sharon exclaimed.

"No," Cindy said, "he's right."

"You know it wasn't intentional," Kevin said, "but I know what you're saying."

"What if he hadn't hit back?" Sharon asked. "Would they have tried again?"

"They would have, but not in the way you mean."

"What does that mean? Suppose Kevin still didn't want anything to do with it?"

"That wasn't an option," Braddock said.

"What?" Sharon bolted forward. "What does that mean?"

"Too many forces lined up to not allow him not to sign on," Mike said.

"So then you're saying if he said no, they were going to have him hit?"

"No, but almost as bad. He would have been discredited."

"If he hadn't gotten on board," Braddock added, "it might not have gotten done, and if that was the case they'd find a way to blame him."

"How so?"

"Oh, denying grants, creating negative press, marginalizing him to where he looks like a nut, pressuring peers, and that's not even outright making things up. A whole slew of things. No one thing is fatal but it can often turn out to be death by a thousand paper cuts. No cash, no institute, no home turf, no audience, no career. So, lesson learned. You did what you had to do."

Kevin was at a loss for words. He turned to Sharon. "Remember when we'd visit Max and Jean? There was a coffee shop in the center of town down the road from Woodacre. The first time I went in there,

I waited in line for a cup of coffee. When I got up to the counter and I ordered, a girl there pointed to a table on the side with coffee pots and a tray of money. She told me next time I could just pour it myself and leave the money. The honor system."

"I know the place," Mike said. "I've done that myself a lot of times."

"I never forgot that," Sharon said wistfully. "They'd just trust you. People they don't know. They would just trust you to do the right thing. I always thought it was interesting. There aren't too many other places where you would see that. I know back east, people would either be bumming cups of coffee without paying or just emptying the till and taking off."

"Who knows," Kevin said. "Maybe this'll strike the fear of God in him. Or something." He rubbed his ear, then said, "You know what guys, maybe I'll go talk to Jessica now."

"Okay," Sharon said. "So we'll meet up when you're done, all right?"

He nodded yes, then went out the door.

Raden looked at Sharon and Cindy. "And what about you two?" he asked.

"I think it's one day at a time," Cindy said. She looked at Sharon. "Are you okay with—"

"Absolutely."

"I don't know what's going to happen with me and him."

"You'll be great. We'll have fun too." She sighed. "This isn't what I expected. After the past few days, I know without a doubt that Kev and I were just meant to be friends, but—"

"Now don't you start, woman," Raden said.

"Oh, Jack. I'm not going mushy. It's just that …" She seemed to stare into nowhere, and then looked at him. He thought he could see a tear. "I'm thirty-one," she went on. "I know I'm not old, but I'd like to settle down some time, not be chasing ex's across the world trying to get them to take their heads out of their rear ends. I just like to think this isn't all there is."

"It's not." He looked at Cindy, and then smiled at Sharon. "I just hope though that since you extricated his head from his rear end, you don't wind up putting your own into yours."

"Now what does that mean?" Sharon said defiantly.

"There aren't a dozen women in the country who have the talent you do who own a successful business, with your looks that are able to make a decent cup of coffee." She laughed and wiped her eyes. "You're an exceptionally good catch. You sometimes need to remind yourself.

I'm tempted to fix you up with my son. He's a hell of a catch himself."

"Okay," she laughed, wiping her eyes again. "Thanks, Jack."

"I'll second that," Mike said. "Count me in too," added Braddock.

"Thanks guys," she beamed as Cindy smiled.

Outside, the breeze picked up and rattled the screen on the window, while a stream of sunlight broke through the cloud for a moment, then disappeared again. It had the effect of drawing the meeting to a close. They began to gather themselves up to leave.

"Okay," Raden said. He turned to Mike, and the two of them nodded to each other. "I guess we'll see each other later. But before we leave, there's something we need to tell you. Kevin doesn't know yet." He took a deep breath. "Max Rosenkranz passed away this morning."

"Oh, no," Cindy said, covering her mouth in surprise.

Mike grew heavy-hearted. "I really had a soft spot for that SOB," he lamented.

"That's going to rip Kevin apart," Sharon added, her voice breaking as the tears came.

Raden looked at Sharon with a sad turn. "Do you want me to tell him? Or do you?"

She turned to Cindy, and they exchanged a silent nod. "We will."

Epilogue

The news of Max Rosenkranz's death cast a pall on the room. Raden sighed and looked out on the gray morning.

"It's funny," he said softly. "This light. It's the same that was in the Oval Office when I was in Washington earlier this week. It's remarkable how things come full circle."

"I was with Max when Kevin stopped by a few days ago," Mike nodded. "After he left, Max dozed off. Jean said to me that she thought there had been a sense of unfinished business about Max, something that had been resolved by Kevin's visit. I get the same sense here. This is going to change Kevin, but I think he'll be all right."

"He was looking forward to heading back there tomorrow," Sharon sighed.

"Well," Raden said, "I think he'll still want to go."

"Oh yeah. And," Mike said to Sharon and Cindy, "you two are more than welcome."

As they thanked him, Raden said, "There's more to tell Kevin. You might want to know too. Lisa and Tom were landing here when the bomb went off. The shock wave almost blew them off the runway, but they're okay. And those two girls Kevin met on the plane, Gina and Robin; they're okay as well. We saw them earlier. They would have been outside for the detonation but one of them broke a nail right before it happened."

Cindy and Sharon began laughing. "I don't believe it," Sharon said.

"Yeah," Braddock said, "they were still in their room, handling the emergency. It saved them. You can't make this stuff up. I'm sure they'll be talking about it the rest of their lives."

"Also, Cindy, your friend Patty Solomon is okay," Raden smiled.

"Oh, thank God. I'll find her. And thanks for telling me."

"And the operative Kevin met," Mike said, "that guy Bremer—no one's found him yet."

"I guess we'll find out one way or another as time goes on," Cindy said.

"Pretty much." They all grew quiet again.

"So I guess we'll meet at Pete's place for dinner, huh?" Raden said.

"Yeah," Cindy said. "In the meantime, we can see what we can do to help out here."

Sharon agreed. She turned to the men. "When are you guys going back?"

"Probably tomorrow," Braddock said. "Mike and I have some mopping up to do. We'll be in the room here if you need us. And Jack, well—"

"I have a little stop to make," Raden said.

"Okay," Cindy said. "We'll see you later."

Raden left with Sharon and Cindy. He made his way through the rush, past the screams and moaning. Outside he could see Jessica Enright in the press pool that had formed on the hospital grounds. Her singular position of being the only media person on the island when the disaster occurred put her front and center, before she had even gone in front of the cameras.

Elliot Hanford had taken over the second floor doctor's lounge, where he was trying to manage the disaster from a telephone and a computer monitor. With Air Force One destroyed on Vaitupu, another plane wouldn't be ready to take him back to Hawaii for at least another day.

Raden found himself weighing the course of the past week. How fitting, he thought, that the arc of the story should begin and end with the same man. There was a certain symmetry to it, one that Kevin Herter would surely appreciate, were he ever to find out. Which he wouldn't.

He stopped by and asked if he could meet with the president privately. The dreariness outside had yet to break. The office was filled with a somber light, lit only by a desk lamp and the glare of a computer screen. Hanford shooed away his security contingent and collapsed into a sofa. He glared up at Raden, who stood rather casually and asked, "So what the hell you want?"

Raden broke into a slight smile. "Well, I—"

"I pretty much had my fill of that collection of whackos you put together downstairs."

"Well actually, they're not my—"

"All right, what's up?" Hanford cut in sharply, seemingly unwilling to give Raden a chance to begin.

"I thought we should talk."

"I just want to tell you," Hanford stated, "that people will see what our intentions were. They'll be able to see what we were working toward. They'll cut us some slack."

"I—"

"You know, Herter and his cronies, they don't understand. They shovel out shit that the rest of us have to deal with, then sit back and think they can wash their hands of it. I think they're in for a rude awakening when they get back. It's already beginning to break our way." He paused, then almost as an afterthought said, "All right, what's up?"

"Mr. President, a bit of information came in this morning from Hawaii. It hasn't gone public yet. A business executive was killed in a freak accident at his house in Honolulu this morning."

"Who was it?" Hanford stared. "And why are you telling me this?"

"He was the CEO of Integrated Microphysics, a firm that did extensive work for the Defense Department. The exec's name was Mark Rivers."

"And?"

"His firm was responsible for the assembly that allowed the reactions in the nuclear devices they used here to detonate."

The president sat stoically, but Raden could see that beneath the measured exterior there were primal forces churning. Hanford was as good as anyone at hiding his innermost thoughts and intentions. And he still couldn't help asking questions to which he already knew the answers. Raden knew the president knew exactly who Rivers was.

"Oh yeah," Hanford said, "I've heard of him. All right. So what happened to this guy?"

"The preliminary report is that he was electrocuted."

"Electrocuted? What, in his bath?"

"No, it doesn't seem so. Some kind of faulty wire connected to an electric shaver."

"Was it an accident?"

"That's how it appears, for now."

"So, why are you telling me this?"

Raden rubbed his nose. "There was a preliminary investigation of some of his papers and hard drives—"

"By who? The police?"

"Actually, the police haven't been notified yet."

"And why not?" Hanford's face tensed.

"Well it seems there were certain, shall we say, matters of a security nature that necessitated the case being handled by authorities of other jurisdictions."

"What matters?" The president's countenance tightened. "And just who handled it?"

"Well sir, it's less an issue of who handled it and more one of what came to light in the investigation. There's certain information of a sensitive nature."

Raden watched Hanford. It had been a long time since he could remember seeing the color drain from someone's face, but there was no escaping the president's reaction. Raden added, "I thought you might want to hear about it."

"What are the chances of local authorities becoming involved?"

"Right now, it seems minimal."

"Well, then how did *other* authorities learn about this? Are they investigating this as an accident? That's what it sounds like."

"I can't answer that at this time. I just thought you should know."

Hanford shifted restlessly on the couch. "Jack, thank you for bringing this to my attention. I would be interested in hearing about the progression of the case, and knowing who is in charge. It's never good when the head of one of our premier contracting firms dies tragically."

"That I can do, Mr. President." With that, Raden gave Hanford a quick nod, then turned around. He was nearly at the door when he did an about face.

"At this point, Mr. President," he said, "it may be that some clarity is in order. Rivers did a good job encrypting his information, but a lousy job of hiding it. Maybe he thought he was immune from concerns like having to keep things under lock and key. And I'm sure, like most of us, he hadn't planned on dying when he did. There are a lot of questions that I'm sure will be coming up. Anyway, how he was able to come up with the court records that were found I'd only be guessing, but he managed to get his hands on them, despite how well they were sealed five years ago. And even though it had been suppressed, he was also able to get hold of the evidence collected in the case. The order calling for the records to be closed was adjudicated on behalf of what the court was told was a seventeen-year-old. How Rivers learned the boy being prosecuted was really twenty-four I can only guess, but he had enough of a pipeline in place to find the name Clark Hanford on the complaint. I've been told the photos are of good enough quality that you can readily see the child's face. And you can also plainly see that the person with him is your son."

The End

Acknowledgments

As a writer, you never know the ups and downs you'll endure until you experience them. Will I find my voice, will the story hold, will the effort resonate; a multitude of conceptions that arise and contend with each other and can leave even the most dedicated and passionate individual adrift in a sea of doubt. And with all the profundities, there's an unexpected one that rears its head upon the completion of a work, one that you never see coming and that rivals any apprehension with the work itself – damn, did I remember everyone in the acknowledgments?

This book was years in the making, and there were many times it seemed as if it would never see the light of day. Life has a way of intruding, especially for those of us in the arts. It's oftentimes so much easier to just put aside a work that's in its infancy, especially when it gives off the unmistakable feel of being a dead end, as works are wont to do. During those times, very few of us would continue were it not for the support system we have. Those selfless people are truly unsung heroes, as indispensible as they can appear unseen. The little word of encouragement, the periodic "How's the book doing?", even if it at times lands a bit annoying because it holds a mirror up to our current creative impasse, are sometimes enough to get a writer back to hitting the books, so to speak. They're as much responsible for our efforts as we are, and we owe those who suffer our eccentricities a measure of gratitude that we can never repay.

Susan Rabinowitz was my first friend to give my nascent manuscript a go-over, and her encouragement helped me prod on. Susan left this world far too soon, and I wish she could have been here to see what she helped nurture. Grace Hancock and Jessica Ernst read an earlier version of the story, and their astute feedback helped in the rewrite. Marty Dowd was a diligent reader, and I could always rely on his pointed critique. Marie Julian is a wonderful person and great sounding board. Her thoughtful comments and support proved invaluable. Thanks to Meli Coulson Lussier for her help, and Heidi Binz, who waited patiently. Ryka George and Crystal Whiting's critique helped immensely. And thanks to Anna Burgard, Dan LoRusso, Nancy Stupay, Rabbi Ron Issacs, Lisa

Ferrante Bassillo, and Susan Tumblety for their support and counsel.

Stacy Zeller had some wonderful suggestions, and her encouragement was infectious. Pam Barett, my sista from another mista, is a great reader and friend. And Kenney Sills, my brodda from anotha motha, is an inspiration. I'm glad we crossed paths. Tracie Bennitt helped not only with her critique, but also for introducing me to Gayle George and 10 Day Book Club, which proved an indispensible resource, as was Gayle's counsel. Gayle in turn connected me to Micheline Brodeur, whose copy edit added immeasurably to the work without interfering with my voice. For all novelists, first-timers and veterans, I can't say it enough — have a set of trained eyes look over your efforts. Even Michael Jordan had a coach.

While this is a work of fiction, I drew upon two sources that proved invaluable. *Dark Sun, The Making of the Hydrogen Bomb*, by Richard Rhodes, © 1995, Simon & Schuster, was not only of immense help for reference, but is a fascinating and enjoyable read. And the 1999 film *Race For The Superbomb*, produced, written and directed by Thomas Ott for the PBS series *The American Experience*, and narrated by David Ogden Stiers, is a wonderful piece of filmmaking. *Trinity and Beyond*, a 1995 film by Peter Kuran and narrated by William Shatner, is referenced in this book as well, as is *The Atomic Café*, the iconic 1982 film by Jayne Loader, Kevin Rafferty and Pierce Rafferty.

Many thanks to my cousin Dave Felder, a talented novelist and filmmaker, who was kind enough to let me pick his brain. Thanks go as well to Neil Clarke, who did the formatting for the Kindle version, and let me pick his considerable brain.

Meryl Yourish is a wonderful friend and an equally wonderful storyteller. Her series, The Catmage Chronicles, is a must read. Meryl was kind enough to format the CreateSpace version of this book, and in putting up with my constant revisions and incredible naivete with respect to indie publishing, she set new standards for patience and tolerance. She was of extraordinary help, and bears very special mention and thanks.

Dr. Mark Hubble has been a constant source of much-needed support and insight, and most important, friendship. I couldn't have finished this book without his support. Whenever there were moments when doubt or fog crept into my world, I could always count on him for a kind word, a measure of wisdom, and a laugh. It truly is a blessing when you learn that in Life, family need not be confined to relatives.

And special thanks go to Samantha Goldberg, for her support, enduring friendship and insightful advice.

I hope I have remembered to include everyone who contributed their time and considerations, without whose kind word, critical eye and helping hand this book would not have been possible. If I've left anyone out, please forgive me my addled brain, no doubt atrophied by countless late nights spent hovering over my laptop.

Edwina Wong Felder was a special help, and her support and encouragement will always be appreciated. And to Meg and Zoey, my wonderful daughters to whom this book is dedicated, thank you so much for letting your Daddy work, even when you wanted him to play with you. I hope the extra hugs and kisses in a way helped make up for it. You will be inheriting this world. I hope it proves to be one with a little less of the craziness that served as the basis for this story.

About the Author

Larry Felder is an artist and writer. A 1980 graduate of Montclair State College, where he received a BA in Fine Art and Political Science, he has become well known for his work in the field of Dinosaur and Prehistoric Wildlife restoration. His work has been featured in numerous books, magazines, national parks, television and on-line sites, and can be found in many museums and private collections. His 2000 book *In the Presence of Dinosaurs*, co-authored with John Colagrande, was the only TIME/LIFE book ever to have received a Starred Review in *Publisher's Weekly*. He is also an accomplished landscape and figure painter, and is currently working on a traveling exhibit for museums and science centers called *Bringing Dinosaurs to Life*. He currently lives in Bridgewater, New Jersey. *Afterglow* is his first novel